TWISTED FAE
THE COMPLETE TRILOGY

LUCINDA DARK
HELEN SCOTT

CONTENTS

COURT OF CRIMSON

COURT OF FROST

COURT OF MIDNIGHT

COURT OF CRIMSON

Three Fae Princes and a Death sentence...

They are nothing but monsters—bloodstained by battle and
addicted to their own magic.

I am nothing but a burden—troublesome and worthless to
those around me.

But it doesn't have to stay that way.
On the verge of being cast from the only place I'd ever
known, _it_ appeared. Or rather, _they_ appeared.

The answer.
My way out.

A magical castle full of the one thing all humans should have
feared … Fae. Not just any Fae–the most powerful of all:
Royal Fae

To trust a Fae is to risk dying at their cruel hands.
To follow them into their castle means something far worse:
Finding out the truth

CHAPTER 1

CRESS

A yawn stretched my mouth as I lounged back on the sun warmed stone rooftop. Even at the depths of twilight, when the air was growing colder, the feel of the dying sunshine on my face lulled me into a listless half-asleep state. Sleeping, after all, was the best past time to have. Not that the nuns of the Abbey of Amnestia would necessarily agree with me, but they didn't know where I was, so I didn't have to listen to their scolding and I could nap in peace. It was only the ricocheting clanking sounds of someone climbing up the creaky old half-rusted ladder I'd stashed on the side of the storehouse that drew me out of my dreamy state. I peeked one eyelid open as a petite form appeared over the side of the stone roof—wispy strawberry blonde hair flitting in the semi-cool breeze. I sighed.

"Sister Lena is going to be so mad at me if she finds out the reason you're missing is because you came looking for me again," I commented lightly as Nellie finished clambering onto the slanted rooftop.

"Sister—*ugh!*" Nellie grunted as she gripped the edge of the

3

roof and shimmied up and over the last rung of the ladder where there was still a two foot difference from that to the roof. "Lena," she continued once she was stable, "wouldn't have anything to worry about if you'd stop coming up here."

Nellie crawled across the space left until she made it to my side. I let my eye slide shut again now that I knew she was safe. She may only be a year or two younger than me but there was something fragile about her, something that was far too delicate to be climbing up onto rooftops—not that I was much taller—but let's be honest, I was far more adept at not killing myself. Most of the time, anyway. Minor bruises, some fractured bones, and lacerations were not cause for concern when it came to me. Just the norm. The sisters liked to say that I was prone to accidents. I liked to say that accidents were prone to me. "Where else am I going to find a place to nap? If I try to stay in my bed, Sister Madeline finds me and makes me work in the stables."

"You're just lazy," Nellie snapped. "Maybe if you did your work, Sister Madeline wouldn't have to chastise you so much." I didn't have to see it to know that Nellie had both of her fists planted on her hips as she sat on her knees and glared down at me. Sister Lena did that same thing when she was pushed past her breaking point, and Nellie followed that woman around like she was her little duckling.

I grinned without opening my eyes, the feel of it stretching my cheeks. "She can chastise all she wants," I replied. "It won't suddenly turn me into her favorite person." I re-cracked the same eye. "Or make me not want to nap. Napping is the best." I closed my eye again.

Nellie huffed out a breath and a moment later, I felt her petite form thump beside me as her arm brushed my side. "Heard you refused to eat again today," she said quietly, making me stiffen.

"I didn't refuse," I said, pouting petulantly. "I just ... told them I wasn't hungry."

"Did you tell them you weren't hungry after calling them murderers and dumping a plate of ham on someone's head?"

I grimaced and then snorted. I *had* done that, but only after the sisters in charge of feeding us orphans had called me an ungrateful leech who was too lazy and stupid to survive if it weren't for their goodwill. I wasn't ungrateful for everything they did, but I couldn't stomach some of the things that made their way across the table—specifically if said things had previously had a face. And since we were surrounded by farmland, a lot of faces made it across our table—pigs, cows, chickens, and even wild boar. But the meat, for some reason, always made me sick.

"You can't call what they were trying to serve ham," I replied tartly, opening my eyes. "It was burnt to a crisp and smelled of oil. I was pretty sure they just stuck some mold and meat together and tried to burn it so no one would notice."

"And if it hadn't been burnt?" Nellie pressed. "If it was just ham, would you have eaten it?" When I didn't answer, she sighed. "I don't know what to do with you, Cress." She shook her head forlornly. "You have to eat."

"I *do* eat," I reminded her, staring up as a cloud drifted in front of the sun.

"Usually when kids refuse to eat, it's their vegetables they're not interested in. That's *all* you eat. It's probably why you're so short."

I sat up and turned, casting her a dark glare. "I am *not* short," I snapped. I was a perfectly acceptable height for my age. I was taller than Nellie, for sure ... sometimes ... when she didn't stand up straight or get on her tip toes. I scowled. "You're not one to talk. You're a whole two inches shorter. I'm still the taller one of us both."

"I'm seventeen," she deadpanned. "I'm still growing. You're twenty—almost twenty-one."

I groaned and flopped back against the roof. She had a point. "I don't know why I can't eat it," I admitted quietly. "I've tried before—it just made my stomach hurt really bad for days. Sister Lena thought I was gonna die."

"Pretty sure Sister Madeline would've liked that," Nellie muttered.

I laughed. "Yeah, you're probably right. She hates me."

Nellie looked at me, her soft brown eyes beseeching. "Just come down and do your chores and eat, won't you? Be nice to the sisters and when the Abbess gets back from her trip, maybe they won't mention everything."

I snorted at that. "They always mention it, doesn't matter what I do."

I turned my head and looked out over the vast countryside. Sheep and cows munched on dry grass in the near distance. Little hut houses dotted the land, most of them in a collection not far from our little convent. I glanced down and picked at a piece of fringe from the frayed hem on my uniform shirt—it was just like the one Nellie wore. The nuns had taken us in—some as babies like I'd been and some as older children, like Nellie—but none of us were unique in their eyes. We were just mouths to feed. Every year, more and more arrived after losing their parents in the southern wars with the Fae.

Across the small courtyard of the abbey's land, church bells for evening service rang. Nellie sat up abruptly. "Oh shoot," she said. "We're late."

"You can make it if you shimmy down and cut through the kitchens," I said absently as I settled back against the stones.

"Aren't you coming?" she asked as she crawled back across the roof towards where the ladder was.

I shook my head and let my eyes slide shut as the sun began

to set over the horizon. "Nah, I don't think so," I said. "I'd rather take another nap."

She scoffed. "If they catch you sneaking in after missing evening services, they're going to thrash you."

"That's *if* they catch me," I replied, opening my eyes and shooting her a grin as she slipped over the side of the roof.

When just the top half of her face was visible, she narrowed her gaze on me and huffed. "Fine," she snapped. "Suit yourself. It's *your* hide that's gonna be reddened before the day is through."

I shrugged, which only served to irritate her more and true to her age, she rolled her eyes at me before disappearing altogether, leaving me to relish in the last remaining rays of sunlight as the big glowing red ball of heat slipped behind the mountain range. I didn't understand it, but feeling the sun on my skin—even as far from it as it felt like our little backwoods rural community was—made me feel energized. I'd lied when I said I was going to take a nap. The truth was that I'd been waiting for the evening service all day. Every day, like clockwork, the nuns—or brides of Coreliath as some referred to them—would gather the rest of the orphans and preach about the feats of the God King they spent their lives worshipping, forgoing all physical pleasures and remaining chaste in the hopes that he would pluck the most virtuous of them to live with him in the afterlife.

While they were absorbed in their prayers, however, I had to think about the real world. Sure, Gods might've been real once—long ago—but now we had more tangible monsters to concern ourselves with. Like starvation and homelessness. In two days' time, it would be my twenty-first birthday and that meant that in less than forty-eight hours, I'd be exiled from the Abbey of Amnestia unless I took the vows of chastity required of the Brides of Coreliath. I laughed internally at that thought.

Yeah, fat chance of that happening. I didn't want to remain

a virgin for the rest of my life. I *wanted* them to exile me. I needed to leave these walls. The sooner I did, the better. Who wanted to be stuck on the same little patch of land for their entire lives? Certainly not me. I was getting out even if it killed me. Which it might. Hopefully not. But I mean ... there was always a chance. What with dangerous Faeries and all sorts of other creatures crawling over the countryside, and I'd been known to trip over nothing but air a time or two.

It was a blessing that our little rural community was as far from the war as possible. When I was kicked out, at least I wouldn't have to worry about running headfirst into a battlefield. Knowing my luck, I'd somehow find a way. I swore, if I didn't know any better, I'd think I was cursed by Coreliath— but why would he give a shit about a nobody like me? Answer: he didn't. Thank the Gods. But that left me with one understanding—I was the one responsible for all of my mishaps and accidents. Clumsy, thy name is Cressida.

Still, my impending expatriation from the abbey brought with it other ... issues. If I was gonna be homeless for the foreseeable future, I'd need far more than the scraps they were likely to give me—barely enough for a three day journey. I'd need money to get, well, basically anywhere.

I sat up as the church bells rang into silence and the sound of the church's large door echoed up the stone building's exterior walls as it was slammed shut. It was time to execute plan A.

I slipped down the ladder and headed for the convent's main building. It housed the nuns' sleeping quarters, but more than that, it housed the Abbess' office—the head honcho, the big cheese, the end all be all of the sister's lives—other than their imagined God husband. The Abbess was rarely ever there —since she chose to traverse the countryside for some ridiculous reason or another—spreading charity or love or whatever Abbesses did. A horse whinnied at me as I passed through the stables and I lifted a palm with a smile, pressing a finger to my lips with a wink.

"Shhh, Isabelle," I whispered. "You don't want to get me caught, do you?"

I shook my head with a small smile as if the horse could understand me, but she quieted nonetheless, stomping her feet in her hay before she turned her head and whipped a bit of her mane into my face. Rude horse. I chuckled anyway, flicking her dark horsehair out of my face. "Sassy girl," I chastised, reaching through her stall to give her a gentle pat before I continued on my way.

I peeked into the empty courtyard, darting my gaze left and then right before I left the safety of the stables and raced up the front steps and into the building. I had to go faster, move quicker—before anyone thought to leave the church. Before the chance was gone. The Abbess' office was in the back—next to the kitchens and the nuns' sleeping quarters. I hurried for it, pausing when I thought I heard someone beyond the kitchen doorway.

Sweat coated the back of my neck, making the white-blonde strands of my hair stick to me. I gulped back a breath, reaching for the doorknob, turning it, and moving at the same time as a footstep creaked on the wood flooring several paces down the hallway. I eased the door shut behind me and pressed my back to the door, panting with relief when a woman's voice —Sister Madeline's, I realized—sounded from beyond the door. A few seconds more and the mean, old coot would've caught me.

"Stupid girl, of course she's not here. Where the hell could she be? Missing evening service after all that she's been given. Ungrateful little—" I breathed a sigh of relief when her voice faded off down the hall. She'd been in the building looking for me. That wasn't surprising. Her vitriol didn't surprise me either. From Sister Madeline, it'd always been 'you're such a lazabout' this or 'can't you do anything right?' that. I could certainly do things right. I could hold my breath underwater for two and a half minutes. According to Nellie, that was an accomplishment and I'd take those when I could get them.

I let my head sink back on my shoulders as I stared up at the ceiling. My heart thundered in my ears, and it took several moments of even breaths to calm it. Once I had it under control, I looked back to the rest of the room. A large oak wood desk with a plush cushioned chair behind it. Velvet drapes lined the window even further back and twin floor-to-ceiling wooden shelves lined the walls. I whistled quietly as I tiptoed further into the space. I'd never been called to the Abbess' office before, and to my knowledge, none of the other orphans had either. I wondered what Nellie would do if she knew that the Abbess was living large while we were all scraping to survive.

Ducking behind the desk, I rummaged through the drawers. Papers. Ink quills. More papers. Seals. But no purse. No money. No coins. No nothing! I grew frustrated the longer I searched, clenching my hands into fists as I huffed and snarled, digging through what was left in the drawers. But of course, I still found nothing more than dust and more parchment. My stomach rumbled, reminding me that I'd refused to eat the stuff they'd called food earlier. Hunger made me that much crankier.

Slamming the last drawer shut with a curse, I gave up on searching the Abbess' office. *I should've known better*, I thought as I headed back into the hallway. What with the wars down south and the famine from last year's harvest, the nuns weren't likely to have just any extra coins lying about. It was a ridiculous notion to begin with, one born of panic at my nearing homelessness. My strings would be cut, and I'd be left with nothing but the clothes on my back—going back into the world practically as I'd come into it. I mean there were worse things, right? I had my looks, but I'd heard about what happened to pretty young girls who didn't have anywhere to go, and I had absolutely no intention of being a kept woman. Maybe. Probably not. But then, what did being a kept woman even mean?

As I thought about it, I did hear that they, at least, got to sleep in. Maybe that wouldn't be so bad. I'd always preferred to sleep in than get up at the asscrack of dawn like the nuns required us to.

CHAPTER 2
CRESS

My stomach rumbled again as I quietly shut the door to the Abbess' office. That was a big fat waste of my time. I took a quick peek behind me and once I was secure that the coast was clear that way, I turned and headed for the kitchen. Maybe I'd be able to hoard a few extra days of rationings for the journey I'd have before me at the very least. Mmmmm … I loved bread.

Upon my first step down into the room that smells of the fresh baked slices of God heaven, I knew that plan was going to be dashed all to hell. "Aha! I knew you were bound to come searching for food after this morning." Sister Madeline's proud scoffing sounded far more like an enraged baker's wife than a kind nun. I froze with my foot on the stone floor and blinked like a deer caught at the wrong end of someone's bow and arrow just before the arrow was released. Sister Madeline came huffing and puffing around the corner and snatched up my wrist before I had a chance to escape. "I'm taking you to Mother Collette as soon as service ends," she hissed, tightening her grip as her dull brown eyes narrowed on my face. "You'll get what's coming to you—first for your insolence this morning then for sneaking in here and trying to steal food."

"I—I—" There was no use in trying to deny it. Her wickedly sharp nails bit into the flesh of my wrist, tightening until I was sure she would break the skin.

"I caught you, little thief," she hissed into my face, spittle flying from her dry, cracked lips and hitting me in the face as she towered over me in her dark nun garb, "and I'll make sure you're punished this time."

My lips turned down as she hauled me out of the kitchen, dragging me behind her. There was no doubt in my mind she would. Sister Madeline was perhaps the most violent nun I'd ever met, and I couldn't count the number of times she'd been all too happy to wallop me on my ass or across my knuckles for even the smallest transgression. Though there was nothing in my hands to proclaim me caught red-handed, missing evening service was good enough for a serious ass whipping.

Letting out a breath, I cursed myself for not being more observant. I must have missed her returning to the kitchen while I was in the Abbess' office. At the very least, though, she hadn't caught me there. I didn't want to think what would've happened had I been caught trying to pilfer money rather than an extra loaf of bread.

HOURS AND ONE BURNING BACKSIDE LATER, I CRAWLED ONTO MY cot next to Nellie's well after evening service had ended and released a deep groan. My belly continued to cramp with its emptiness, but that was the least of my concerns. I laid out on my stomach to avoid any more touching of my back and ass. Mother Catherine hadn't gone easy. She never did. I buried my face into the stiff, straw pillow in front of me and forced back the scream of frustration.

"Hey," Nellie's soft voice reached my ears, "are you awake?"

I lifted my head and blew a strand of white-blonde hair out of my eyes. "What do you think?" I grumbled.

After a beat, she replied, "You're right, that was a dumb question."

When she didn't say anything more and the silence began to beat at me harder than Mother Catherine's thrashing, I groaned again and looked her way. Nellie had her thin sheet pulled up over her tiny frame. Her small fingers tightened around the edge of the blanket, her knuckles white with strain. "What?" I asked.

"I know you don't like it here," she whispered, "but do you think you could try to get along with everything. I don't want … I don't want them to throw you out."

"Throw me out?" I scoffed. "Nel, my birthday's in two days. As soon as I hit the big two-one, I'm out of here."

"What?" Nellie sat up abruptly, squeaking out the word, and somewhere in the room, one of the other girls grumbled in their sleep.

I blew out a breath. "What did you think would happen?" I asked. "Twenty-one is when you leave. Doesn't matter what I do."

"But I-I thought you were gonna take the vows," she said. "I'm going to take them."

I snorted. "Why the hell would I do that?" I asked. That was the most ridiculous thing I'd ever heard. "Listen, Nel," I slowly pushed myself up from the bed and edged over onto my side so I could see her better, "I was dropped here at three months old. I've lived in Amnestia all my life, and for me, this place is a prison. I don't fit in and I never have. Like Sister Madeline always says, I'm too wild a creature to ever belong with civilized people." And if wild was code for fun, then I didn't mind being wild. Sister Madeline was as staid as an old cow.

"She was upset when she said that," Nellie defended.

I chuckled as I raised one brow. "She's upset with me a lot then. She hates me."

"Only because you provoke her," Nellie snapped, squeezing her blanket in her fists. One of the girls, who wasn't yet asleep, shushed us from several rows down. Nellie winced and laid back down, pulling her sheet up to her chin. "If you didn't provoke the sisters so much, everything would be fine."

"Whether I provoke them or not, Nel, I just don't belong here. Besides … there's something I have to find."

"What is it?" she asked, turning her head curiously.

I pressed my lips together and rolled back onto my front, folding my arms under my head. "Just … something," I hedged. I didn't want to tell her that just like the rest of the orphans here, I wanted to find out where I came from. Deep down, it was more than a desire—it was a need. I had to find out why I'd been left here twenty-one years ago.

Nellie watched me for a moment more before shaking her head. "It's dangerous out there. You don't know it because you've never left the abbey before—or well, not past the village —but there are things out in the wild—creatures of magic and lore. I've seen them with my own eyes."

My eyes snapped to the side. "What? Really? Why haven't you ever said anything? What were they like?" I asked, edging closer to her excitedly. I'd only heard brief mentions of the creatures the King and his knights fought with on the southern battlefields. Never before had I heard of anyone who'd actually seen them. "What did you see?"

Nellie's eyes found the ceiling overhead and she stared at it unblinkingly. "My parents were doctors," she whispered. "Did I ever tell you that?"

I shook my head, frowning. *What did that have to do with Fae? I thought.* "Uh … no?"

"They were," she nodded as if affirming that fact. "They were doctors on one of the battlefields in the southern quarter.

And because we didn't have any other family, they took me with them. I helped bring bandages and take care of the men who..." She drifted off, her breath catching as her fingers tightened even further on the sheets tugged up to her chest. "We weren't in the middle of the action—that's why they thought it would be okay—but we were on the edge. The soldiers should've known better. The creatures they were fighting—I saw one. It was big, as big as a dragon but without the scales. It had wings of the finest feathers like a shower of autumn leaves. And riding upon it was something far more magnificent."

I sat up and scooted as close to the corner of my bed as I could. "What was it?"

"It was a Faerie," she whispered, her voice catching and lowering as if just the word itself might make one appear out of thin air.

"A Faerie," I repeated the word, letting the syllables dangle on my tongue. It felt like such a strange word on my lips, and yet at the same time, it felt familiar.

"They're otherworldly," she confessed. "Beautiful and savage. It was that Faerie and whatever the creature it rode upon that destroyed the entire human base my parents lived in. It only took one. The magic he possessed—it was so strong and it rained down in a wave of fire. I'd been running a message to someone else," she said. "I was spared. But sometimes I wonder what would have happened had I been in the camp with everyone else. Would I have felt pain? Did my parents...?"

Her eyes were foggy, clouded over by the images of her past and guilt ate away at my insides, curdling like spoiled milk in my stomach. I shouldn't have pushed her to relay the memories. They were obviously painful and terrifying for her.

"It's okay. You don't have to tell me anything else," I promised. "That's enough."

Nellie sucked in a shaky breath and turned to look at me. "When you leave, no matter what you do," she said, "don't go south. They're dangerous. Faeries may look like fallen Gods, but they're much worse. They're death incarnate and they destroy everything they touch."

I nodded and despite the pain in my back and ass, I reached over and patted her hand. "Okay," I said. "It'll be okay. You're safe here."

She closed her eyes and turned away, but not before I saw the single crystalline tear that slid from her closed eye down her cheek. To Nellie—and others like her—Faeries meant danger. It was what we humans feared. It was what our King and his knights battled against. But me ... I felt something else —something that had gotten me into trouble far more often than not.

Curiosity.

CHAPTER 3
CRESS

I slept fitfully that night. My ass and back were covered in red welts, but that wasn't the reason. My dreams, or rather my nightmares, kept me tossing and turning. I never had nightmares like this. But even in my half-awake state, I could sense that something was different. My insides churned with agony and a violent pitchy noise scratched at the back of my head. I didn't know when it had started, only that it wasn't gone by the time the sun was beginning to lighten the sky outside of our windows. At first, I thought it was a clanging—like someone was banging pots and pans nearby—but then by the time the bells rang in the morning to rouse the others, it was more of a whistling or whooshing sound as though something was moving faster and faster every second that ticked by.

I groaned as I forced myself to get up, pressing a hand to my temple. With the state my back and ass were in, I couldn't afford to get another whipping today, not unless I wanted to be scarred for life. Sister Madeline had made sure no one went easy on me. I was sore from my top to my bottom—quite literally.

Everyone else was already gone from their bunks, doing

their chores no doubt, like good little girls and boys. I, on the other hand, was not going to do that. I had other plans for the day and none of them involved doing my chores. Not that any of the sisters expected me to do my chores anymore—they'd gotten used to my "laziness" as they called it. Whereas I preferred to call it conserving my energy.

Less than two days until I would be booted from the convent and the time seemed to be streaking by. That was fine by me, there was a big world out there to see and I wanted to see it all, especially if I managed to find what I was looking for. The only problem that still presented itself to me was that if I was going to see it all then I needed money to do so—money to travel, to pay for room and board, or just food. If I didn't have something figured out before they kicked me out then I'd be homeless and penniless and whatever scraps they fed me before effectively closing the gates on my ass weren't going to last me very long.

The loud noise I'd been hearing screeched throughout the room. I had to cover my ears to try and protect them from the awful noise as it reverberated off the stone walls. I hurried to wash and dress so I could get downstairs and find out what the hell was going on. Had the war made its way north? Was a battle coming to the grounds of Amnestia? We hadn't heard anything from the local village.

Thoughts and questions bounced around my mind as I hurried to get ready. My feet slapped the stone steps, my shoes barely hanging onto them as I rushed downstairs, only to find everyone acting as though nothing was happening—as if that whistling, rushing noise wasn't ringing through the air.

"Don't you fucking hear that?" I practically yelled to one of the cooks as I barreled through the kitchen. I was almost completely out of the kitchen and into the gravel area between the main building and the barns when Sister Ermine's quiet response registered in my frazzled brain.

"Watch your mouth!" she snapped before frowning at me and moving my way. "And what the blazes are you talking about? Hear what?"

I clamped my hands over my ears once more and turned to find everyone that was working in the kitchen staring through the open door, gaping at me like I was going mad. Maybe I was. Only one way to find out.

"Can you really not hear it?" I yelled over the sound. "That infernal noise!"

A few of the kitchen staff jumped at my words before rushing back to what they were doing, as though whatever was going on with me was catching. They had to be playing a joke on me, surely? The sisters weren't known for their sense of humor but there was a first time for everything.

I turned, looking for the source of the sound, but there were no clues as to what it was or where it was coming from. My inability to find the source of the noise made it almost more painful. It was like I was standing inside one of the large bells at the top of the church while someone repeatedly hit it with a giant stick. The force of it was enough to vibrate through my whole body and left me on my knees in the dirt as I panted and tried, unsuccessfully, to block it from my mind.

Sister Madeline was there the next instant, the sneer on her lips enough to tell me I'd find no sympathy from her, not that I'd expected any. I avoided her, unable to hear her when she started talking. The noise grew louder, banging around inside my skull. I squinted and felt tears start to leak down my cheeks. Gods, it hurt so fucking badly. *Would it ever stop?* I wondered. *Would I have to live the rest of my life, shouting over the sound in my head, crying at the pain?* I collapsed against a wall with a horrible sob.

It was when Nellie's worried face appeared in front of mine, her mouth creased into a frown as she squinted at me, that I actually started to panic. Her lips moved, but I couldn't hear her voice anymore, all I could hear was the high-pitched spin-ning racket as it spiraled through my head.

I couldn't feel the hands moving over me, but soon enough someone must have called for the nurse's stretcher. The noise was so debilitating that it was all I could do to force more tears back as I was rolled onto it. Even my groan didn't make it to my ears, I only knew I'd made the noise from the rise of my chest and the reverberation as I parted my dry lips. Nothing good ever came from being on the stretcher. It meant a visit to see Sister Christine, and she didn't tolerate fools or pranks. The bed in her office was about as old as the rickety stretcher I curled up on. I squeezed my eyes shut as whoever it was that had been called to carry me—likely a couple of the older orphan boys—hefted me up from the ground. The stretcher's middle sagged under my weight, and I was nearly dropped back onto the cold hard gravel. I was worried the old fabric and wood wouldn't be able to hold me, but I couldn't even speak to tell them to stop trying.

Sharp spikes of pain lanced through me. Something cool and wet leaked from my ears. My eyes popped open and I reached up to touch the liquid. When I pulled my hands away, a red sheen of blood covered my fingertips nearly making my heart stop. I looked up. They had to see this. I wasn't making it up. Sister Madeline was standing alongside the stretcher and there was no doubt in my mind that she saw. Her eyes were focused on my fingers, her expression morphing from a sneer of contempt to actual concern. She lifted her head to the ones holding me.

"Hurry," she snapped—her voice coming through muffled and warped around the noise still screeching through my eardrums. "Get her to Sister Christine." To have this woman—the one who'd hated me for years—act out of genuine worry only made me panic even more.

If she was being nice to me, then I was almost certainly dying.

By the time we got to Sister Christine's office, the noise had grown so impossible, I was clenching my teeth and forcing back screams. I parted my lips as breathy pants escaped. I wanted to slam my head into the stone floor—anything that would end this torture. No matter how I tried to plug my ears, I couldn't stop the shrill loudness of it as it drilled into my head one pound of my heart at a time. Sister Christine rushed to direct the boys who carried me to the single bed she kept in the nurse's quarters. Her cool hands were on me then, trying to hold me down even while she looked me over. I couldn't stand it. I threw her off, rolling over and nearly sliding off the bed as I tried to get away. Her touch was too much. The volume of sound in my head was enough. I couldn't stand more of it as she began talking, trying to calm me.

"Stop it," I rasped out through gritted teeth. "Please, fucking stop it!" Someone said something but it was lost to the noise.

My arms were yanked away from my body as I was promptly repositioned on the bed and then my head was tilted back and cool liquid filled my mouth. I coughed, wheezing when someone held my head still as the fluid slid to the back of my throat and down into my belly. I struggled, but there were multiple hands on me—holding me steady, massaging my neck to make the liquid go down faster. No sooner had I been released than I began to feel the liquid's effects. I wavered and slumped back into the bed as sleep—no, not sleep, unconsciousness filled my mind.

They'd drugged me. Without my consent. Irritation flared bright and I clenched my nails against my palms, wishing I could get up and punch the daylights out of someone, but my limbs were lax. I was lethargic. Perhaps they'd drugged me so that they could try to figure out what was going on, but they still hadn't fucking asked. I tried to fight against the oblivion as it overtook me. I wanted to keep fighting them, but whatever herbs the nurse had mixed into the liquid were potent. They clouded my thoughts and soon enough, I didn't feel or hear anything at all.

Oh, well, this wasn't as bad as I thought, I conceded murkily just as my mind winked out like a dying star disappearing from the sky.

CHAPTER 4

CRESS

W hen I awoke, it was like the whole world had gone silent. I lay there for several moments, wondering if it was a trick. Or Gods—what if I was deaf? All that noise and now, nothing? It was eerie, to say the least. My head was pounding and my mouth felt like it was made of the same material as the nuns' habits, but dirtier—not the pristine black that they normally wore. I smacked my lips a few times, swiping my tongue over my teeth feeling a gritty film over them as I turned my head and took in my surroundings. As soon as my eyes lit on the glass of water sitting by the bed, I forgot my earlier fear of being deaf and lunged for it—downing it like a dehydrated man dragged out of the desert as I tried to wash the grimy sensations away.

The cool water slipped over my lips and tongue, bringing relief with it. Once the glass was emptied and my mouth didn't feel fuzzy or gritty anymore, I pushed myself up and looked around. It was night outside, that much was clear. Not even a single candle had been left lit. Darkness blanketed the room, and for some reason, it soothed my raw nerves.

On a table in the corner of the nurse's office, there was a

small clock. I squinted at it, barely able to make out the time using the moon's rays as they shone in through the single window. Midnight. I sighed. It was officially my birthday, or at least what the nun's thought was my birthday.

Sliding the sheets that covered me to the side, I hopped off the bed. The cool night air flowed in through the window like a stream. I paused and lifted my head a bit, sniffing lightly. A scent hovered on the wind. It was like none I'd ever smelled. *Huh,* I wondered. *If I was deaf now, did that mean my other senses would get stronger to compensate? Wouldn't I have heard it when I set the glass back down?* I turned my head, looking at it on the bedside table. I hadn't even been paying attention. *What if I really was deaf?!* When I heard the first of the insect noises, however, as I leaned forward, that idea was thrown out the window. *Guess not,* I decided.

My heart lurched in my chest and my stomach growled with hunger. I shouldn't have been surprised by the rumbling. If it was nighttime and only a day had passed then that meant I hadn't eaten in over a day. But this hunger was different than any I'd felt before. It slithered bone deep—no, deeper. It went to the very core of my being, calling to me and forcing me to follow it. That scent leading the way as I got out of bed and headed for the door.

At first, I wasn't even paying attention to where the smell was coming from, I just followed it. Rocks and dirt and leaves crunched under my feet and I paused, the sound carrying with it a memory. I wasn't supposed to leave the grounds of the abbey without permission. My legs paused even as my body vibrated with the need to keep going. I weighed what I was supposed to do against my curiosity. It was only a moment, but at least I did it. I patted my mental self on the back even as I grinned, knowing full well what the outcome would be. I lifted my foot and kept going until my legs carried me onto the grass beyond the edge of the convent and further.

Invisible limbs grasped me as wind blew past my face, lifting the light strands of my hair and slapping my cheeks. It almost knocked me back, or it would have had those invisible grips not held me steady and firm against it. That scent refilled my nostrils. It was so strange—first the noise and now this scent. My fingers trembled as I lifted them to my face, touching my nose.

The forest beyond the convent was dark. The dark stretches of branches created a veritable ceiling of leaves that hid almost all of the moon's light from me. I felt my way blindly through the greenery, pulled by some invisible force. Those limbs that had once held me now pushed me forward. Faster and faster my legs pumped. I followed the trail I couldn't see until I came out on the other side of the treeline, stopping cold.

My lips parted, my mouth gaping as I looked up and up some more. Stone. Stacked as high as my eyes could see, nearly blocking out the mountain range behind it. I glanced back over my shoulder, through the dark forest. I'd never gone this far from the convent—at least not on this side since the local village was in the other direction, but I was sure I would've heard of this ... castle.

Castles didn't just appear out of thin air ... did they? Why had the nuns never said anything? Never mentioned it? It was crazy, absolutely insane, to say the least. I had no idea what had happened. What could make something that looked like a castle big enough to house an entire Court of people suddenly appear? Was I hallucinating? Was it some trick of the light, or lack thereof? I turned in a circle. Nope. I was still on the hillside of Amnestia. I hadn't been magically transported in my sleep. But the same couldn't be said for this monstrosity.

I froze as a thought suddenly occurred. Even when standing still, the body still moves somewhat. The chest pumps up and down as you breathe. You sway—even unintentionally—as the wind brushes against you or as you try to keep your footing.

But I just ... stopped. Breathing. Moving. Swaying. Anything. Everything. As one looming question forced its way to the forefront of my mind.

Was I dead? If so, that would really suck.

I stood there, staring up at the castle for a moment more before I decided to keep going. I wasn't going to find the answers to my questions if I just stood there frozen like that. Sliding closer to the line of trees, I felt along in the semi-darkness as I began to circle the tall structure. The castle was huge —taller than the trees—with a giant wall surrounding it.

How a structure of that size and approximate age, going by the wear on the stones, as well as the complexity of its build could suddenly appear was beyond me, but it was here and it was where the smell seemed to originate from. I lifted my head and sniffed again. Sure enough, that delicious scent was emanating from somewhere beyond the wall—slightly sweet and titillating. It was almost hypnotic in its all consuming power to make me trail after it.

Even as my body leaned forward, enticed by the smell, my eyes gobbled up the sight of the castle. For the last twenty years, all I'd ever laid eyes on was the bland countryside of the convent, some cows, and chickens. Maybe some travelers, if I was lucky, not that they ever came close enough to talk to. Even the convent itself was plain. The pale cream walls covered the two levels of the building which was topped with terracotta tiles, save for the flat stone area of the roof over the storage house where I liked to bathe in the sun. The only other buildings were the barns and chicken coops. All of which I'd been through more than a dozen times.

This building, though, was different in so many ways. Spires shot so high into the sky that it looked as if they were touching the clouds. Thin bridges that looked like they could collapse with a strong breeze went between the spires and others seemed to roll down to the ground like great staircases.

There were so many points going up into the sky that it was easy to miss the biggest one at first. It sat in the middle of the others, pointing heavenward, patiently waiting for the viewer to notice its majesty. Some kind of metal reflected the moonlight off the ridges of the spires and seemed to wink at me, daring me to come closer still.

Something shuddered through the air, filling my chest. The vibrations didn't just ripple through my skin, but deeper— somewhere in my heart—as though I was being pulled towards several directions at once. It forced me to slow my pace, but I couldn't quite bring myself to turn back to the safety of the convent. What lay in front of me felt too important, too ... magical.

Nellie's story came to mind, nearly stopping me completely in my tracks. Danger lay ahead. The unknown. But hadn't that been what I'd said I wanted just yesterday? I wanted to escape, to go somewhere else. Well, here was my desire come true. Be careful what you wish for and all that. Whatever it was beyond this wall was far too interesting for me to pass up. I'd never seen real magic. This might be my only chance. *Was this mysterious castle the work of the Fae?* I wondered even as I moved towards it. *Were they here to scout or slaughter? Had the war reached our small backwoods piece of the kingdom?*

I bit down on my lip hard as my legs kept going. Maybe it was the fact that this was the first fascinating thing to happen in ... well ... *ever*, but I couldn't help myself. I had to know. I couldn't *not* find out what was in there. Maybe this was all some insanely vivid dream thanks to the herbal tonic the nuns had forced down my throat, but I didn't feel drugged or impaired. I grimaced and reached up to scratch my jaw. That wasn't to say that I was in my right mind—who ever was, really? Everyone back at the convent had always thought I was a bit odd. Truth be told, if they could see me now, wandering around the hillside in whatever nightdress they had put me in, looking for the entrance to a strange castle? Well, I'm sure the sisters would have plenty to say about that.

I pushed those old and tired thoughts away when I stumbled over something on the ground. A thick black vine protruded up through the dark soil; thorns as big as my hand littered its trunk like a warning label. *Beware*, it said. *Go any farther and risk your life.* I pursed my lips even as my eyes tracked it across the ground, searching for what it could be growing from, only to find that it was coming from the wall that wrapped around the strange castle that was, quite possibly, a hallucination. Maybe. Probably not. Hopefully? No, definitely, not hopefully. I wanted this thing to be real, not a dream. Real equaled adventure. Then again ... real could also mean death. Only one way to find out.

I shrugged and decided to risk it as I tried to step over the vines. I lifted my foot and moved forward only to have something prick me. I yelped and scrambled back, stopping and glaring down at the appendage. I lifted my foot again, higher this time—staring at the vine all the while. I didn't see it shift or move to block my path, but once again, I felt a prick. No matter how high I lifted my foot, it seemed like it wasn't enough. I sighed and dropped my foot. If I kept this up, I'd run the risk of flashing anyone that might be watching. Not the greatest first impression. *Hi, I've come to poke around your crazy, magical castle, here are my lady bits.* Yeah, not so much.

If I couldn't go over, then I'd go through. It was as simple as that, at least in my head. One hundred percent, a great plan. You know, in theory. In practice, it was just a smidge more complicated. The vines and thorns dragged at my legs and against the nightdress I was wearing, slicing through the thin cotton until anything past my knees was in tatters. A thorn caught my newly exposed leg and ripped into the skin. It wasn't a prick this time, but a slice. Like a knife blade being dragged down my flesh, not a protrusion on a plant.

I gasped as pain lanced through me. Biting down hard on my lower lip, I struggled not to cry out as I watched blood flow freely down my leg and puddle on the ground next to my foot. It didn't stop flowing either, continuing down like a river over the paleness of my leg. I needed to make a tourniquet out of something or at least bind it so that it would stem the flow. I tore two pieces off my already shredded nightdress and wrapped the cloth around my calf above the wound, tying it tight enough that the blood slowed. The second piece I used to cover the wound. It soaked through rather quickly, but at least I wasn't feeling the steady stream of liquid down my calf.

When I glanced at the ground to try and see how much blood I'd left behind, there was nothing there. I frowned, narrowing my eyes and dipping my head down. But there was nothing—it was like it had never happened at all. If it wasn't for the still fresh blood on my leg, I might have started to question my sanity even more.

The vines, however, did appear to back away from me as I began to move forward once more. The more my blood dripped against the ground, the farther back they shrank. *What was that about?* I wondered as I kept going. I stared at them, wanting answers but coming up with nothing. Nada. Zip. Zilch. Pain radiated down my legs as fresh blood continued to well and slip down my skin onto the ground. Maybe I had stumbled onto a path through the brambles, or maybe the plants really were moving out of my way. Maybe I had the power to control plants now! I reached my hand out and concentrated on the nearest bramble, trying to make it grow straight instead of curling in on itself, but nothing happened. Guess that was out. I pouted as I lifted my foot and stomped forward. If I was going to go crazy, the least my mind could do was give me magic powers.

When I came to the stone wall I felt alongside it. I paused as the stones heated under my palms. My eyes widened and I quickly snatched them back as they shifted all on their own—moving to form an entrance of sorts. More like a short dark hallway. I poked my head inside, but it didn't give me much other than more of that enticing scent—like berries and sugar. Tapping my fingers against my side, I huffed out a breath. I'd come this far. Might as well keep going. I shifted through the entryway and popped out on the opposite side, coming into an empty courtyard.

And the castle was right in front of me. It was even taller up close. I swallowed. Maybe this hadn't been such a good idea. I lifted my hand and chewed my thumbnail thoughtfully. If the sisters woke and found me missing, what would they think? Would they send someone after me? Probably not. They had been planning to kick me out anyway. They'd probably be grateful. And if I died before I could get back ... what would poor Nellie think? The sisters couldn't have cared less about me if they tried, but Nellie? She'd been determined to be my friend. Lonely as that position was.

Yeah, maybe it was better that I go back. I could at least just say goodbye and inform everyone about the strange magical fortress that had suddenly appeared. I nodded to myself. That was a great idea. The best one I'd had all night. I turned, intending to do just that when I realized the entryway I'd come in through was gone.

"No, no, no, no, no," I hissed through my teeth as I spread my palms along the stones, searching for the exit, but the damn thing was gone. Vanished. Into thin air. I banged my fist against the wall in irritation, wincing when I slammed it down too hard and my fingers pressed down against my thumb. I pulled back and looked down at my thumb before glaring at the wall. "Stupid magic wall."

I kicked it, nearly falling as my foot slid out from under me. I reached out and slapped my hand against the offensive structure. When I was sure I had my footing, I turned away from it and focused my attention forward. After all, apparently the wall—or perhaps the castle?—didn't want me leaving.

It was dark, but as I moved closer to the castle, I realized that the stones that made up the fortress weren't the color of normal stones. They were encased in a layer of frost—ice creeping up and down and through the edges. The reflective twinkling on the sides that I had seen from further away was the ice glinting in the moonlight. I shivered, reaching up and rubbing my palms down my bare arms. My breath appeared in front of my face as tiny white clouds puffing from my lips. The closer I got to it, the colder I became.

I forced myself to take a deep breath of the cold air, letting it fill my lungs. My nose twitched and I leaned forward, nearly pressing my face into the stones before me. I found that the scent I'd been chasing this whole time was there, it was just dampened slightly by the cold. The intensity of it in the breath I'd taken, though, was enough to rouse my hunger once more, pushing me ever onward.

The phrase 'so close, yet so far' came to mind as I searched for a way into the castle. I just needed to get to the other side of the wall and I'd find what I was looking for—I could feel it in my bones. A door, however, eluded me. There wasn't any way inside. The ice was a barrier, coating the stone walls and even what looked like the windows higher up.

It was the most beautiful thing I'd ever seen. It took my breath away as I watched the silvery moonlight glint off all the different facets of the frost. Yet, at the same time, it was quite bothersome. I craned my head back, staring up at the top of the spires. I hadn't realized just how far back I'd leaned when I slipped, my foot shooting out from beneath me as I fell backwards, landing on my still very sensitive behind.

A shriek of frustration escaped me, and part of me expected someone from the building to come out and tell me off for trespassing. But the castle, and the ice, remained solid and impenetrable. I pushed myself back up onto my feet and took a deep breath, letting the scent that had drawn me to the building in the first place wash over me and fill my lungs before I began searching for an entrance once more.

Finally, after it felt like I'd been hobbling around the outside for ages, I saw what had to be an opening. A huge arch opened up over the ground, making it look like the building had a gaping maw ready to devour whatever came close enough. Fear skated up and down my spine making me feel the cold of the ice even more in my thin nightdress.

I took a breath to steady myself and edged under the archway. Part of me expected a portcullis to slam down on me, but nothing did. Instead, the cold faded and the ice seemed to thaw. A large black wood door hung in the center of the wall facing the entrance as I entered the area. The planks that made up the door were broad—easily two men wide. When I tried to open it, I had to brace one foot against the wall next to it and heave with all my might.

When the blasted thing finally gave and swung open, it slapped me in the side, shoving me to the ground like a sack of potatoes. Cursing the sisters as my butt hit the rocky floor once more, I reached back and rubbed against my sore flesh. Getting to my feet for what felt like the umpteenth time, I hurried inside before the door swung shut. I just had to hope I'd be able to open it and get back out again. The thought sent a tendril of fear winding through me, but I ignored it. It was too late to turn back now.

The hallway was dark once the door clicked shut behind me, and I wasn't sure which way to go, especially because I couldn't see what lay in either direction. Sconces on the walls burst into flame, making me yelp in surprise as light bloomed down the hallway on each side.

I chuckled uncomfortably to myself. "Well, that's convenient..." *Too convenient, perhaps?*

The scent I'd been following wound its way into my nose and down to my belly, making my mouth water. It was definitely stronger on one side than the other so I followed my nose, like I had been doing all night. The further I traveled, the more sconces lit up. It was as though they could sense my presence and were responding to an unspoken request to light my way.

Eventually, after countless twists and turns, I found myself standing at a side entrance to a giant ballroom or possibly a throne room. I wasn't sure which without venturing further inside. Tables lined each side, piled high with food, all of which smelled delicious.

Hesitantly, I stepped forward, edging into the room a fraction at a time until I reached a pillar that seemed to be one of many that lined the outskirts of the massive area. Definitely a ballroom, I decided. Perhaps one that could be transformed into a throne room. The table closest to me was overflowing with rolls. Steam rose from them, like they were fresh out of the oven. It wafted my way. There was absolutely no way I could resist.

I reached out and swiped two, before disappearing back into the hallway where I greedily took a giant bite of one. The doughy mixture melted in my mouth and tasted divine. It put anything the nuns had ever made to shame and made me wonder what I'd been missing out on all my life if this was what a simple roll tasted like.

When I had finished the rolls I'd pilfered, I debated for only a split second before creeping back into the room and making my way to the table again. I grabbed another roll, but this time I also grabbed what looked like a pastry of some kind. I didn't care what it was, so long as it tasted as good as the rolls.

"Well, well, what do we have here?" A voice sounded behind me, making me freeze and drop the food I'd collected to the floor.

CHAPTER 5

ROAN

The three of us stood in a circle over the yawning opening of the Lanuaet—the giant sphere of magical energy that allowed the three of us to control the entirety of our castle, moving the monstrosity at will. Unlike most other Fae forts, however, powered by at least four Court royals, ours was only powered by three.

Across from me, Orion and Sorrell's faces were masked with pain as they held their arms up, pouring their energy into the sphere. I winced and nearly stumbled under the backlash of the weight of the magic.

"Don't you fucking dare," Orion cursed, sweat pouring down his face. "We're almost there."

"Go fuck a Gryphon," I snarled, righting my footing and shoving the magical pulsing back into the ball of energy. "I've got this."

Sorrell snorted quietly, the white-blue strands of his hair blowing against his lips as he made the sound, but he said nothing more. Not that the bastard would. No, he was as cold as the ice magic he was currently forcing into the coalition of magics that was necessary to move the fortress. My stomach churned as I forced more of my crimson power alongside his and Orion's.

We weren't going to make it, I realized soon thereafter. It was sucking too much magic from us. We were losing control. I cursed as more sweat poured down my temples and the churning pain in my gut moved up to my chest, tightening around my Fae heart. "We have to land it," I hissed.

Orion threw me a look of surprise. "We're not there yet," he said.

I shook my head. "If we don't land it, we're not going to fucking make it."

"He's right," Sorrell said. "We land it or it'll kill us."

Orion refocused on his task, the muscles of his face pulled taut as he fought against the dark hold of his power. "Where?" he barked a moment later.

It didn't matter where, I thought. But I supposed landing smack dab in the middle of a human army camp wouldn't do. I closed my eyes and opened them once more, looking into the Lanuaet and searching for a place to land this Gods forsaken castle. I felt blood slide out of my nose. "There!" I nodded to a section of land not far off from a human village, but just secluded enough for us to remain off their radar. Orion and Sorrell nodded and together, we steered our portalled Court in the direction we wanted.

After several more gut wrenching minutes of energy, we managed to land the fortress in a remote location. As soon as the Lanuaet released us, the three of us collapsed against the floor. I lay on my back, my torso aching with each breath I dragged into my lungs.

"Gods," I swore. "Is it just me or does it get harder every time we move this blasted thing?"

Orion grunted his agreement as he got to his feet, weaving like a drunkard as he left the oratory that housed our fort's Lanuaet. I laid there for a moment more, needing the extra time to catch my breath. As soon as I had, I leveraged up and gripped the railing that overlooked the Lanuaet, glancing up at the glowing orb with a scowl. Though we were of the strongest of the Courts, controlling such a powerful spell was still an exhausting maneuver.

"I'm hungry," I grunted as I headed for the door, not looking back as Sorrell, too, got up and moved to follow me. "The pixies better have left us a feast in the throne room. I need it."

"They always do," Sorrell said simply. I turned and watched as he faded into the dark hallway of the castle, heading back to his quarters to likely rest and recuperate.

I pivoted and went the opposite way. Bath first. Then food and maybe a fuck. I scratched my jawline, going through the list of my normal bedmates. Most of them would be asleep by now—we'd taken much longer to move the fortress than usual. I scowled as I got to the bathing room. Stripping my tunic over my head and jerking the flap of my trousers open as I divested myself of the rest of my clothes, I waded into the pool of cool waters and dunked my head beneath the surface.

It took longer and longer to move this monstrosity the more we did it—sapping our strength and leaving us practically helpless for several hours afterwards. I lifted one arm from the waters and stared at my skin—practically translucent. My blood was weak now and would be until I ate and fucked.

Slumping back against the pool's underwater settee, I grumbled. My usual bedmate, Ariana, would be furious if I woke her now. I'd make it good for her, as I always did, but the whining and complaining I'd have to deal with later would be such a fucking hassle.

I finished washing up and left the pool, finding new clothes left for me by the resident cleaning pixies on a long bench just outside of the bathing chambers. Drying off and redressing, I headed for the throne room. Food first, I decided.

No sooner had I taken a step into the throne room and I

saw a small little creature—a girl—dart out from one of the pillars aligning the grand hall to snatch a roll from the feast table. I paused and frowned. I didn't recognize the girl. She was thin and wispy, big eyes, and a small mouth. She looked to be hardly more than a child until she turned and I caught a full glimpse of her from the front. *No, definitely not a child*, I thought with a grin. This was a woman. Her shape was tapered, her breasts full, and though she moved like a little mouse—biting into the food meant for my stomach like it was manna from the realm of the Gods—I did find her to be quite attractive. Perhaps I wouldn't have to forgo my post-energy sapping fuck.

"Well, well," I said. "What do we have here?"

The girl froze, the pastry and roll in her hand falling to the floor. She turned in slow, tiny increments—like a puppet being pulled on a string—until she faced me, her eyes even wider now than before. That's when her scent hit me.

Human.

Just as abruptly as I'd been startled by her presence, I was more than floored by it now. How the hell had she gotten into the castle? I strode forward, inhaling a deep breath and letting it fill me up—stretching my chest.

The girl squeaked and backed up as I towered over her.

"I don't know how a *human*," I spat the name of what she was with disgust, "got into my castle, but..." I stopped when I had her up against a pillar and punched the stone above her head, making her eyes widen as she blinked up at me. "I'm going to make sure you regret coming here."

CHAPTER 6
CRESS

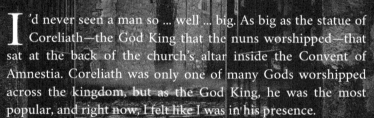

I'd never seen a man so ... well ... big. As big as the statue of Coreliath—the God King that the nuns worshipped—that sat at the back of the church's altar inside the Convent of Amnestia. Coreliath was only one of many Gods worshipped across the kingdom, but as the God King, he was the most popular, and right now, I felt like I was in his presence.

The man—God?—stalked forward after startling me, his face a mask of darkness—eyes boiling with anger and something more, something I wasn't quite sure how to describe. His lips—full and beautiful—curled down into a scowl as he backed me into a pillar and pinned me there with his glare.

"Human," he snapped and it took me a moment to realize he meant me. Me. *I* was the human. And if he was referring to me as human then that must have meant that he ... wasn't? "Speak."

I frowned up at him. "I'm not a dog," I replied. "You can't just order me to speak like a well-trained mongrel."

The anger in his face didn't disappear, but it did shift, parting to allow confused shock through as his brows rose ever so slightly and his scowl slackened. I crossed my arms over my chest, noticing that the movement drew his gaze downward.

Which reminded me that I was still dressed in the nightdress I'd woken up in and the lower half of it was ripped to shreds. I swallowed roughly as my skin heated under his gaze, pressing my lips together as I tried to ignore my embarrassment. I had no reason to feel embarrassed. If anyone should feel embarrassed, it was this asshole. I mean, who came upon an innocent maiden—meaning me—while she was procuring food and scared the daylights out of her. Sure, I was stealing it and probably from him, but disrupting a lady while she was eating was just plain rude.

When his eyes rose and met mine once more there was a fire glowing in their depths and a wicked grin that spread over his face. "And yet you did."

It took me a second to realize he was referring to the command to speak that he had given me. He was right. He'd demanded I speak and I did, even if it was to throw his words back in his face. I opened my mouth to respond and watched as he quirked one of the thick slashes of his eyebrows at me in challenge. My mouth snapped shut before I could get into an argument with this ... *man*. I scowled.

"Oh, come now, human, where did all that fire go so quickly?" he asked with a dark chuckle. A shiver chased up my spine at the low tone of his voice. Goosebumps rose down the lengths of my arms as images of scandalous things infiltrated my mind at the sound. When I stubbornly refused to respond, the chuckle deepened. "You're going to regret breaking into my castle. I assure you. I want to know how you came to find this place, how you managed to sneak inside without tripping any of our alarms, and I want to know if there are more of you."

Before I could react or open my mouth to ask what he was talking about, he turned and strode across the room, back to the entrance.

"Get her cleaned up," he called out to the seemingly empty air before turning an eye back on me. "She reeks of humans," he finished with an indelicate curl of his upper lip. My lips popped open. I did not reek! ... Did I? As discreetly as possible, I tilted my head down and to the side trying to smell myself. Okay, I didn't smell like roses, that was for sure, but I'd smelled far worse than me.

With a shake of my head, I peered around, looking for who he was talking to when little figures began emerging, coming out of the walls themselves. No, not the walls. They dropped out from the shadows, their little dragonfly wings fluttering. My eyes widened as I took them in. Their skin shimmered. It was the same hue of the walls themselves as if they'd camouflaged themselves to blend in with the stone.

Their little bodies, as they drew near, were human in shape, though they had large black eyes that dominated their face as well as tiny, sharp fangs that peeked out from their mouths as they flew towards me. Any more than the eyes and fangs would have been too much, but it also appeared that they didn't even have noses. The section between their eyes and mouth was not only small but flat and smooth. Each creature was no bigger than the palm of my hand, but they zipped and swooped around me until I began to stumble in the only direction that they had left open to me.

Even as I tried to avoid them, they followed, directing me with their incessant buzzing and fluttering. I turned towards the tunnel I came through when I first found the ballroom, but apparently, they didn't like that because as soon as I took a step in that direction, they swarmed. Small teeth sank into the skin visible on my arms and legs, some latching on as they tried to redirect me, each tooth like sharp tiny needles.

"Ouch!" I cried, glaring at the ones stuck to my skin while trying to remove them without hurting their fragile, little bodies. I pulled and tugged, ripping a few off and letting them go. For every one I pulled off, though, another three latched themselves to my skin until I was more covered in these odd little creatures than not and I had no choice but to admit defeat and let them, quite literally, pull me in the direction they wanted me to go.

They led me through hallways and doors until I was so turned around there wasn't a chance of me ever escaping the castle without help, and I didn't think that the man—God being—whatever, that I had met before was about to give me that help. I'd only just met him, but he struck me as an asshole already. Just my luck, he'd be the first person I ran into in this castle. Oh no, I couldn't run into someone friendly like a little old lady who would pull out a chair and offer me a seat before she piled a plate high with delicious foods for me. Nope. Instead, I got a crusty and mean-faced man—okay, he was handsome, but his personality was seriously lacking.

Finally, the little creatures stopped pulling and released me. Their teeth were even more painful coming out than they had been going in, which just seemed wrong on so many levels. I gasped as each of them withdrew at the same time, my skin stinging sharply from the removal of their little fangs.

When the pain subsided, I was finally able to focus on where I was. With a look, I saw that the room I'd been brought to was as large as a barn, and it was full of giant pools of water. Walls seemed to rise out of the back somewhere and were covered in blues and greens. They were much brighter than the gray stones of the hallway and reminded me of paintings I'd seen of the forest.

The back two pools had steam rising from the surface in billowing clouds and my body ached to sink into that warmth. I hadn't realized how cold I was until that moment. The pool closest to me was my intended location, at least according to the strange little creatures who kept flying from me to the pool and back again.

"Okay, I get it! You want me to get in the water," I muttered more to myself than to actually talk to them, but apparently they didn't see it that way. One of the small creatures came and hovered in front of my face and for the first time, I noticed that it wasn't skin I was seeing as I'd thought before but fine hair all over their bodies. Hair that, if my eyes weren't playing tricks on me, was changing color to blend with this room better. "What are you?" I mused out loud.

"Pixie," one of the creatures growled. The word was barely comprehensible but it was enough. At least, I knew what these little flying demons were now.

"You can talk?" I asked, though the answer was obvious.

The pixie that had spoken just growled and I got the sense that they could understand better than they could speak. We stared at each other for a moment before the creature hissed. It seemed to be a signal for the others because they began swooping down and pulling at my nightdress, tearing the material away from my body with a viciousness that surprised me even after they had been biting me and pulling me to get me into the room.

I had no choice but to stand and let them do whatever it was they were doing. After a few moments they stopped and I felt the remaining few slivers of fabric that had been left slip down my body and pool on the floor.

I was stark naked.

In a strange castle.

What in the name of Coreliath was going on? It was my birthday for the sake of the Gods! Why did it have to be the strangest day of the year? I tried to cover myself with my hands as best as I could but I couldn't seem to cover everything all at once. There was always something left exposed.

The solution, of course, was to get into the water; at least then I'd have some semblance of privacy, even if it wasn't perfect. I dipped my toe into the pool the pixies had been pushing me towards. The icy cold water seemed to suck the remaining heat from my body, leaving my teeth chattering.

There was no freaking way I was getting in that pool.

I padded around the outside, stepping carefully across the rocks that formed the edge of the pools and made my way around to the back. The billows of steam made it almost impossible to see the surface of the water, but I was so cold I didn't care if there was something or someone in there already. I dipped my toe in once again and felt a delicious warmth climb up my skin, one that made me want to climb in and not get out until that warmth had reached the depths of my soul.

Inch by slow inch I descended into the pool, knowing that if I went too fast it would hurt because it was so hot. When it was up to my shoulders I settled back on the underwater bench that seemed to be in place and let myself relax. How could I relax in a strange castle? Well, it wasn't easy. That was for sure. But the heat of the water did steal the tension from my muscles. I moaned and sank down even further. I lifted my arm from the surface of the milky water and let the liquid sluice down my limb. Odd. So very odd. I didn't feel any different than I had the day before. Except that horrible shrieking sound had disappeared. And what a blessing that was.

A moment later, the pixies were putting down bottles on the side of the pool, pushing them towards me. I had no idea what was what so I didn't dare touch them, instead, choosing to eye the little beings with suspicion. The pixies, however, had no such qualms. Two of them picked a bottle, flying over my head—their wings buzzing—and dumped it onto my hair. I gasped reaching up to swat them away, but the damage was done. A third landed on my head and began scrubbing, its pointy, clawed fingers, scraping against my scalp. That ... actually didn't feel that bad. In fact, it was kind of nice.

It continued this way for some time until I felt like a bowl of super warm jelly. When they began to push my head underwater, I knew I was supposed to rinse. What I didn't expect was the sound of voices when I emerged. I froze as two women entered, chatting with one another. Silently praying that they would pass by the bathing room, I held my breath. My luck wasn't that good, it appeared. The door swung open. I could just see the edge of it through the steam so I was able to duck down into the water before anyone could see me.

I was nervous when I had stolen the rolls and the pastry, but now I was terrified. The food had been too much of a treasure to resist. But this was ... I was ... man, I really needed to think my actions through before I did things. Perhaps for the first time in my life, I agreed with the nuns. Had I not followed my instincts here, I would have been ... well, probably about to be kicked out of the convent as soon as everyone realized I was awake.

I shook my head and refocused. I was naked and probably at my most vulnerable with strange women walking towards me. A shriek sounded and I had to fight not to jump out of the water and make a run for it, but the women weren't looking at me, they were too busy sneering in disgust at the pixies.

"Ugh. You know you're not allowed in the baths. Get out! Now, or I'll have your wings torn off!" The woman that screamed had hair the color of starlight and an angular face that looked almost painful with her ivory skin stretched to perfection over the bones of her face. Her naked form strode into one of the pools and I couldn't seem to take my eyes off her. Those were some big ... what had Marcus—the farmer who often frequented the convent called a woman's breasts? —bazoongas?

"What do you think they were doing in here?" the other woman asked, her tone more confused and curious than offended. Peeking up just a little bit more over the edge of the pool I was in, I examined the second woman. Her hair was white at the top, slowly descending into a deep blue at the ends, like frost creeping over the ground. Just like the first woman, she too, was naked. A buzzing noise drew my attention and I turned my head just in time to notice a pixie struggling under the weight of heavy material as it made its way out of the doorway. It wasn't part of my nightdress, so it had to have been whatever clothing these women had shed.

The blue haired woman strode forward into the pool of ice cold water as though it was the perfect temperature. When they were both submerged up to their shoulders they each let out a sigh of what I imagined was relaxation, although they hadn't looked particularly tense when they came in.

"Nasty little creatures were probably using our bathing water," the silver-haired woman said with a shudder. As I watched I realized that it wasn't silver or grey like she was getting old, but more metallic as though she had strands of actual silver spun through her hair.

They were both silent for a moment, soaking in the water, like I had been until they interrupted. I wanted to get out, to move at least, but there was no way to do that without drawing their attention, and something told me I didn't want the type of attention they would give me.

"Did Roan come to you?" the blue-haired woman asked.

"No," the silver-haired woman replied with a frustrated pout before asking, "Did Sorrell come to you?"

"Did he ever. The things that male can do with his cock and his tongue should be illegal," the blue-haired woman said with a dreamy sigh.

I'd never heard anyone talk about sex before and the casualness of their conversation surprised me. I bit my lip. The nuns always made it sound like the moment I saw a cock I'd be condemned to burn for eternity at Coreliath's pleasure. I'd never understood why Coreliath would condemn pleasure like that. It didn't make any sense to me; Gods were known specifically for their own seeking of it. The tales I'd read of the sky God—Zander's—exploits would make anyone blush.

"He wasn't too much this time?" Silver asked, genuine

concern filling her voice. I'd decided to think of them as their hair colors since anything else seemed too judgmental on my part.

Blue turned serious for a moment and said, "His cock is massive, of course it's too much, but we work it out. Or more like he works it out on me. He might not be able to fuck me the way he wants, but he sure does make it good. By the Gods, I love screaming his name." Blue giggled and a pang of jealousy ran through me.

Neither of these women looked much older than me and yet they seemed to know so much more about life. I wanted that. I wanted to be worldly and grown-up, not some convent-raised bumpkin that had never even seen a ... what had they called it? A cock? Yeah, I wanted to see that. I smirked to myself. Once I had, maybe I'd go back and tell the nuns all about it. I slid deeper into the water, just picturing the looks of horror on their faces when I did. I wondered if Sister Madeline would even faint.

CHAPTER 7

CRESS

After listening to the two women talk for what felt like hours about their sex lives I was left not only feeling jealous of their romantic relationships but their friendship as well. None of the nuns were my friends, I was too wild for them. The only person who had made an effort over the last few years was Nellie. The other girls, and most of the boys for that matter, at the convent didn't like the negative attention I had received so they'd all given me a wide berth. As if merely being caught by association with me would result in some sort of punishment.

The women continued chatting as they exited the pools and rubbed their bodies with scented oils, which I hadn't even noticed sitting off to the side. They twisted their hair up, creating intricate designs and decorating it with jewels that appeared to be sitting around for anyone to use. Elegance for these two creatures appeared effortless, and my own body felt clunky in comparison. I looked down at my slight frame, palming my breasts. They filled my hands, but not much more. Not compared to theirs. I shot the women a look and sighed.

The kind of friendship these two women had was beyond

my understanding. It had always just been me against the world, or the nuns, as it were. I was deep in thought when they left and was startled when a pixie landed on the edge of the pool next to me.

"I don't think you're supposed to be in here," I replied quietly in case the two women were still outside the door.

The pixie simply stuck its little purple tongue out at me and waved at me to follow it. With a grumble, I did as it asked, rising from the warm water and shivering under the coolness of the air. The pixie stopped by the oils and mimed rubbing them on myself. I smiled and nodded to show that I understood and perched on the edge of the bench before opening and smelling each bottle. Floral scents and wood scents, even animal-like scents came from bottle after bottle.

When I saw a dust covered bottle at the back that was almost full I picked it up and gently uncorked it. My nose was greeted by a scent unlike any other I'd tried. It was soft and homey, making me think of being wrapped in safety and light. I began to rub it over my skin, letting the oil sink into my pores and soften my hard edges, if only it would work on my personality as well.

The pixie waved me over to the door when I was done but I didn't follow, instead, I hissed, "I can't go out there naked!"

It flew away and out of the cracked door before returning with several other pixies that were carrying material. White and gold fabric was hanging between them and I could see various strips and shapes but I had no idea what the piece of clothing was supposed to look like. That didn't matter to the pixies as they swarmed me and pulled the material this way and that, getting way too close to some very personal areas.

By the time they were done, I was in something similar to a dress. The bodice had a wide strip at the front and the back, but the sides were cut out, so my pale flesh was on display from the curve of my breasts to the swell of my hips. Each side had straps attaching to a bra-like piece that cupped my breasts and pushed them up and out in a way that would have made the nun's eyes bug out of their heads. The base of the bra was made of gold fabric and a stripe of it ran over the edges of the V shape in the middle, barely covering my nipples. Straps went up over my shoulders to hold the bra bit in place, but then another set formed something akin to loose sleeves that hung down my upper arms.

The gold returned on my hips outlining the cutout section and forming the trim around the sections of white fabric that hung down in front of me and at the sides. I pulled the fabric and saw that it came apart all the way up to the edge of the cut out, meaning at any point I could be completely exposed since the pixies hadn't bothered to provide underwear. They slid gold slipper like shoes onto my feet, which had a slight rise to them, making me walk on the balls of my feet more than anything else.

Before I knew what they were doing my hair was being styled up and back, so it cascaded down the back of my head like a waterfall. A necklace was looped around my throat and other jewelry was hung from my wrists and ankles. Thick leather straps were wrapped around my thighs, but even those had delicate beads and jewels that hung from them, winking in the light as I moved. It all seemed designed to catch the light, to draw attention to me, which was the last thing I wanted, but since I didn't have any other clothing to wear I was stuck. Maybe I could take the jewelry off later and use it as a distraction while I escaped.

The pixies began to hustle me out of the room through the door, but I paused and they looked at me expectantly as though they didn't want to bite me again but would if I made them. When I remembered the bites I looked down at my arms. There was no trace of any wounds, no signs that anything had happened at all, which just confused me. How had the bites healed so quickly? Maybe it was something in the bathing water? That would explain why Blue was bathing after spending time with some guy with a massive cock.

"Are they out there?" I asked, trying to avoid being bitten but wanting to make sure I wasn't going to be discovered either.

Two of the pixies flew to the door and peeked through the crack between the wood and the stone. They flew back a moment later shaking their heads.

"Okay, fine. Lead the way, but I don't want to get caught. Do you understand?"

The one that seemed to be the leader of their little group nodded.

"Maybe I can sneak you a roll or something later," I said as a thank you.

A wide, fanged smile that looked more vicious than grateful spread over the pixie's face. I decided I'd take that as an agreement and began to follow them back through the winding corridors, hurrying through different rooms and doorways, pausing when they did, just in time to hear the swell of voices coming and going as people seemed to move past me completely unaware of my presence. I couldn't help but wonder if the pixies were literally hiding me. They seemed to have some kind of camouflage ability that they could use, but they wouldn't use that on me, would they? I wasn't sure, and I didn't want to risk our good luck by questioning it if they weren't.

Before I knew it, we were back in the throne room. I could see the man that had commanded the pixies earlier, his dark hair shone with red undertones in the light as he talked with two other men. I froze and gaped. Standing next to the first man were two men of equal stature. Both as tall as the first, but different in color. The second man had a face that had to have been sculpted by the Gods. His features were sharp, angular but in no way unpleasant. He was beauty incarnate. Skin paler than ice with equally pale hair that flowed over his shoulders. Directly in contrast, however, was the third and final man. His face made me want to back up and make a run for it. Hair the color of shadows, strewn with gray and black, with small pale scars littering his olive skin made my heartbeat pick up speed.

Between them—the light and the dark—the man with the red hair appeared to be a shining light, his hair deeper—like freshly spilled wine. He drew my attention just as much as the other two. I couldn't stop flicking my gaze between the three of them as I stood there like a statue. My eyes feasted on the sight of the three of them. Each so different, but so attractive, at least from this distance. Their shirts hung open as though they were comparing who had the best muscles, and their dark pants were tight around their hips and ... my eyebrows rose as I tilted my head. Those butts ... if the Gods knew about these speci-mens, they'd surely be pissed. The Gods were known for their pride in being the most beautiful of all creatures. But I would be hard pressed to name anything Godly or ungodly that could compare.

Spotting the table of food I'd left behind still piled high, I scurried behind the pillars moving as quickly as I could. As soon as I was close enough, I snatched a couple rolls and tossed them to the pixies before anyone could tell me otherwise. They fell on the food before it even hit the ground in a cloud of fury, all teeth and claws, making me smile as I snatched one for myself and shoved it into my mouth.

"Here's the human. See? Not dead after all," the red-haired man from before spoke. I turned my head slowly—cheeks ballooned by the food in my mouth. He sounded much more jovial than before. I narrowed my eyes on him in suspicion as I chewed and swallowed.

The red haired man strode down the steps of what looked to be a platform at the back of the room complete with not one, not two, but three lavish thrones. He moved with a grace I'd never possessed in my life. Though he was a veritable giant, he moved across the room with a speed and agility that spoke of confidence. At his back, the others followed.

Perhaps a smarter person would have realized the danger I was in and would have been ready to run. I had, after all, broken into a strange castle that had shown up out of nowhere. I had left my entire life behind with little regard for where it would leave me. I should have been scared; however, in direct contrast with what I knew I should've been feeling, my mouth watered.

"You said she was hideous," the white-haired man muttered. "And that she stank of the human realm." Eyes the color of crystallized frost raked over my form. "I don't detect that odor, though." I stared at him just as much as he stared at me, curiosity warring with intrigue.

"She did," the red-haired man agreed. "I had her cleaned." His nose wrinkled as he examined me from head to toe. "She was absolutely filthy before. This is a considerable improvement." The red-haired man's eyes slid to the side where I'd tossed a few of the rolls to the pixies. I followed his gaze. There was nothing left now, but I wondered if he'd caught me. I stiffened as he moved closer, leaning down into my personal space. When he smiled, it was decidedly threatening, but instead of speaking to me, he threw a question over his shoulder. "What do you think, Orion?"

The shadowed man answered. "I still smell human on her skin," he said, his tone a low growl, like boulders crashing together. "But there's something else. It's not unpleasant." Eyes the color of burned stone met mine. "In fact, I'd say she smells good enough to eat."

"Eat?" I squeaked. Were they going to eat me? I glanced nervously between the three of them. "I-I thought you wanted answers from me," I said quickly, hoping they'd vie against wanting to eat me in favor of getting the red-haired man's questions answered.

"True." The red-haired man lifted a strand of my pale hair and sniffed at it delicately. "It should have been impossible for a human to not only find our castle, but to enter it without any warning." His fingers slid the rest of the way into my hair, locking onto my scalp and drawing it back as a fire burned brighter in his eyes. He stared down at me, his smile twisting into something cruel.

My body reacted to the tone of his voice, but not in the way I'd expected. Instead of struggling to get away, I leaned forward. What would it feel like to have those teeth against my skin? Those lips moving over my own?

Orion, the dark man, stepped up alongside his red friend. "She must be some human," he said, tilting his head to the side as he gazed down at me. Never before had I held such attention. It was both terrifying and thrilling. My body practically vibrated with it, as if screaming *oh my Gods, someone's looking at me! What do I do?*

The red-haired man's smile widened and Nellie's warning chose that moment to come barreling through my mind full throttle. *They're otherworldly,* she'd said. *Beautiful and savage.* Just like these men who were, perhaps, not men at all.

I stared at the man before me, directly at his full lips. They were a deep ruby color and looked softer than anything I'd ever felt before. My desire to find out brought me even closer to him. I lifted on my tiptoes as I reached up. I wanted to feel, to find out if they were as soft as I thought they were. He frowned down at me, those very lips curling down as he watched my movements. The fire that had been ignited in the depth of his eyes burned ever brighter, drawing me like a moth to a flame. No good could come from messing with it, and yet I was willing to burn my wings anyway just to find out.

CHAPTER 8
CRESS

"*S top.*" I jerked back just before my fingers brushed his lips. The man before me turned his cheek, towards the one who'd spoken. White hair flashed at my side, cold fingers gripping my arm as the third man—the one with hair as white as snow—pulled me away. "She's human or did you forget, Roan?"

Roan? I looked back at the red-haired man. His name was Roan? The same Roan the two women had been talking about. I looked to the shadowed man. If black was Orion, red was Roan, then ... my unspoken thoughts were answered a moment later as Roan replied.

"I haven't forgotten, Sorrell," he growled.

"Then what do you think you're doing?" His fingers tightened against my upper arm, squeezing roughly. I winced. *Damn that hurt.* I waited a moment, letting the two of them do their whole-eye-stare-glare nonsense before I got tired of it.

"Um, excuse me?" I politely tapped the man holding me— Sorrell. He glanced down, white eyebrows shooting up as if he was just now realizing that I could speak. That's right, buddy, I talk. "You're hurting me," I told him. "Do you think you could..."

I lifted my arm, the very one that he still held, and looked at it pointedly.

He released me almost immediately. So abruptly that I stumbled and nearly fell over. I shook my head and sent him a dirty look. *Was that really necessary?* But he didn't even notice. Sorrell whirled on his friend, a frown marring his otherwise perfect features. "What are you going to do about this disaster?" he demanded, gesturing back at me. I looked down. I'd taken a bath. I looked a lot nicer than I had before. I wasn't a disaster, at least, not by appearances anymore. How rude.

"He does have a small point," the dark one—Orion—said. "What if others found out that our Court was breached? There would be a riot."

"No one will find out," Roan said. "We'll question her and have her executed with no one the wiser."

"Executed!" I squeaked. "Don't I get a say?" Three very different colored gazes settled on me.

"A say?" the dark one repeated.

"Yeah," I said. "I don't think I've done anything to warrant death. So, I should get a say."

"You broke into our Court," Roan said with a scowl. "That is a treasonous offense."

"But I didn't know I was breaking in," I defended. "The doorway just opened on its own! When I went to turn back, it was gone." I huffed and puffed, my face heating as the three of them exchanged a look before fixating back on me. The weight of their stares made my whole body tense. I didn't know what to expect from them next.

"That ... you're sure that's what happened?" the white one asked. Man, I really needed to get a bead on them. White. Black. Red. Sorrell. Orion. Roan. I knew their names, but for some reason, I kept fixating on their colors. Maybe I'd just call them by their color. That would make things easier. At least, it would for me.

I nodded. "Of course, why would I lie?"

Orion came towards me, curling his lip back intimidatingly. "There are many reasons why one would lie. To harm. To deceive. To escape their fate."

I gulped before I crossed my arms over my chest in what was hopefully a tough gesture. "Well, I'm not," I stated, hoping my voice sounded strong and defiant and not breathy.

He flipped his head towards Roan. "You're sure she's human?"

"Smell her yourself, she smells completely human to me," he said sliding a hand my way.

"Whoa!" I put my hands out. "You already sniffed my hair. No one else is *smelling* me! That's weird. You can't just smell someone; it's rude." I looked pointedly at Roan.

"It's either that or you die," Sorrell said carefully, arching a brow my way.

I shoved my arm out. On second thought ... "Well, if you're going to be that way..." I said. "Sniff away. While you're doing that, my name is Cress, by the way. I feel like you should know my name if you're going to be sniffing me and all that."

The dark Fae didn't say anything as his fingers gripped my wrist, his massive hands engulfing my much smaller limb as he dipped his head. His eyes remained on mine. I sucked in a breath as he pressed the tip of his nose to the inner crook of my arm and ran it slowly upward as he inhaled. Tingles raced through my flesh where we were connected—and startlingly, the space between my legs tightened and grew wet. I clenched my thighs. *Dangerous*, I thought. *These men were very, very dangerous.*

Orion hummed in his throat. "Her scent is weak," he said, the words vibrating against my flesh. "The human smell is there, but there's something beneath it." He lifted his head and stared at me. "What region are your parents from?" he demanded.

"I—um ... don't..." I swallowed roughly before continuing. "I'm an orphan," I admitted. "I don't know who my parents are or where they're from."

"What if she's a Changeling?" Sorrell said suddenly, looking to Roan.

Roan shook his head, red locks sliding over his temple as he moved. "There hasn't been a Changeling in years," he said. "The last Court that participated in that ridiculous ritual was..." He stopped, frowning as he lifted his head and stared straight at me. With so much attention on me—far more than I was used to—I was starting to develop a complex. I kept feeling like there was something on my face.

"What?" I asked as Orion's fingers released me enough so that I could take a step back from all three of them. My flight reflex was screaming inside of me. But along with it, there was another instinct telling me to move closer to these three. There was something magnetic about them.

"How old are you?" Roan asked, striding through the others until he reached me, hovering dangerously close, smelling like fire and cinder.

My head tilted back. "I'm ... uh ... my birthday is today. I-I'm twenty-one." The words stuttered out as my eyebrows inched slowly upward.

"It's impossible," Sorrell said. "The Brightling Court was exterminated. All of them. There were no survivors."

"Orion has the best nose out of all of us; if he agrees with your Changeling idea then she could be," Roan replied.

Orion nodded slowly, seeming to turn the idea over in his mind.

"What's a Changeling?" I asked before I let myself get too distracted by Orion's dark intelligence.

Instead of answering, however, the three turned towards each other and began to speak in low tones. I gaped at them for a moment as they talked fast and quiet. Every once in a while, one of them would lift their head and look at me before returning to the others.

"Then it's decided," Roan said, standing up fully once more as they all pivoted back to me.

"What's decided?" I asked. I really hoped they weren't going to kill me. Or eat me. Neither of those things would work for my future plans—which all depended on me remaining alive. "I haven't decided anything," I said quickly. "So, nothing's been decided. Do you hear me? Nothing!"

"You'll join our Court," he said. "We'll have to completely eradicate your scent, imprint one of ours on you, and then we'll put you through a series of tests to determine if you are, in fact, a Changeling."

"And how exactly are you going to do that?" I asked. "Eradicate my scent that is?"

Roan stepped forward and gripped my wrist when I would have stumbled away. "The fastest way would be for me to lay with you. Come, we'll take care of that right now."

"Wait, what!" I shrieked as he dragged me towards the exit. I grabbed onto his arm and tried to pry my wrist from his grip even as I kicked at his legs. "You can't just—urg! Why don't you —for the love of the Gods, *what* are you made of?" He was pure freaking mountain beneath my struggles, pausing only when he realized I wasn't falling all over myself and jumping to get him in bed. "Listen, buddy," I snapped, "we can't have sex. I mean, don't get me wrong, I want to have sex. I'd like to know what it's like because the nuns said it was a sin and I've come to learn that anything the nuns deem as sinful is actually pretty fun. They said it was sinful to eat too much, but eating is awesome, especially if the food tastes good…" Three sets of eyes stared at me unblinkingly. "Anyway…" I waved my hand in front of my face, "you're right, that's not the point. The point *is* —you can't just decide something like that on your own."

"Would you prefer Orion or Sorrell?" he asked.

"What?" I looked over my shoulder at them. "Maybe..." I said, eyeing Sorrell's form and then Orion's before shaking my head. "I mean no!" *What was I doing?* "That's not—I wasn't trying to choose someone else."

"Then you will lay with me," he stated as if it was a given conclusion.

I eyed him. "You're really full of yourself, aren't you?"

He shrugged, but his hand never released me. "I am quite accomplished in the task of bedding and pleasuring women. You will enjoy yourself."

"I'm a virgin!" No sooner had I shrieked that very embarrassing truth than a woman came through the entrance of the throne room—one of the women from earlier, the one with the silver hair and perfect face. She stopped dead, her mouth dropping as she took in the scene before her.

"M-my Lord?" she stammered.

I groaned and slapped my face. This day really wasn't working out. I needed to find a bed, crawl in it, and hope that when I woke up, this whole thing would blow over and be nothing but a terrible dream.

CHAPTER 9

ROAN

Of course. Of. Fucking. Course. Ariana had to walk in right then, didn't she? Because why would the Goddess ever do anything to assist me?

"Lady Ariana, how are you this morning?" Sorrell asked, dipping his head in greeting.

"Is that a human?" she demanded pointing at the woman in my arms.

"If you want to live, don't leave this spot and don't say a word," I whispered as I set the female down, though I could feel her quaking in my arms. For a moment, I thought the human might fall over, so I kept a hand on her waist to keep that from happening. The action did not go unnoticed as it drew a glare from Ariana as her eyes focused directly on where my palm rested on the human's side. I could tell from the way she had dressed—as if she were about to attend one of my mother's signature balls rather than simply walk through the Court— that she was upset I hadn't come to her after we had moved the castle. Expending so much stamina required a boost of magic and Fae were known for their voracious sexual appetites, specifically to lift our magical energy.

"Darling Ariana, I didn't expect you to be up this early," I crooned at her as I released the other female.

"Clearly." She crossed her arms over her more than ample chest, and I wondered what had kept me from burying my cock in her when I'd had the chance. At the very least, it would have avoided this whole mess with the … Changeling. I let my eyes slide down over her luscious curves, noting the way her gaze slid to the front of my trousers and the growing bulge there. She was a scrumptious little piece ... when she kept her mouth shut that is. Ariana smirked just enough to let me know I was off the hook for not coming to her chambers. "Is that a human?" she asked again, but this time she sounded far more scandalized than furious as she leaned around trying to get a peek at the creature. I shoved the girl behind me.

"Changeling. We suspected a few in the area, which is why we stopped the castle here," I lied through my teeth, gritting them in a facsimile of an actual smile. "An investigation needs to be made before we continue on." No reason to tell her that we had all but spent our magical reserves, and if we hadn't stopped here then the castle certainly would have crash landed somewhere completely off the grid of our maps. And I saw no reason to tell her how the possible Changeling had infiltrated our castle either. Ariana was born of the High Court for sure, but she was no princess.

"But ... that's practically unheard of!" Her eyes had gone wide and she stepped closer, craning her elegant neck even more.

I lowered my voice conspiratorially as I took a step forward—towards Ariana and away from the Changeling. "We aren't sure how much a threat they are so I wouldn't get too close. Don't want you getting hurt by some filth." I hooked my hand around her waist before she could pass me and brought my lips to her cheek in a delicate kiss, while my hand slid down the front of her dress to cup her through the front of her gown.

"You're much too precious to risk. Now, why don't you wait for me in your chambers and as soon as I get this creature secured, I'll come and pay tribute." I nipped her ear and moved down her neck, my lips and teeth working her skin between words as I spoke, while my fingers danced against the space between her legs through the fabric of her dress.

Her silver eyes caught mine as I began to pull away. "Don't let me down, Roan, I need you to finish what you started here," she said, her voice husky with need. She licked her lips.

"As my lady commands." I brushed my lips against hers before I turned and headed back towards the Changeling. The clicking of Ariana's heeled shoes sounded in my ear as she left the room.

I was surprised to find the girl's face paler than it had been when I first saw her and anger dancing in her gaze. Before I spoke, I glanced over my shoulder just to be sure the other woman had gone. Now that she was taken care of, I could return to the matter at hand, at least momentarily, until I needed to go and bed the needy Faerie.

"Masterfully done," Sorrell complimented with a cool raised brow. Orion hummed his agreement.

I nodded my thanks. My ability to bend Ariana to my will was probably one of my most treasured talents. She could be a thorn in the side if I wasn't careful, but as long as I kept her compliant she was more like a flower. Pretty and amenable when all of her thorns had been trimmed.

My gaze traveled over the Changeling once more, and I took in every detail. She was quite different from Ariana in many ways. Where Ariana was buxom and curvaceous, this girl was lithely muscular, with a tautness to her skin that spoke of youth and physical activity that was certainly closer to work than anything Ariana would ever do in her lifetime. I knew from experience, Ariana's nipples were quite round, a dark rose. Staring down at the possible Changeling woman, noting the way her nipples poked at the fabric of her dress, I wondered what color hers would be. Perhaps a light pink. A cherry red? She might prove to be quite interesting if she was, in fact, a Changeling. If she was human, then she would be executed without question. As was custom.

"Come, let's get the remaining human scent off you," I said as I went to scoop her back up.

"You—you can't seriously expect me to give you my virginity when we just met!" she said suddenly. "And you were just seducing another woman. I'm not stupid, even if you did fuck me—you'd surely go right to her. How do I know you don't have some kind of disease?"

I looked at her, clearly the idea of being bedmates offended her, but to accuse me of disease ... I growled low in my throat. "Fae do not contract human disease," I snapped. Humans were strange creatures. Maybe she had been taught humankind's tight-laced sense of propriety. I sighed, done playing games with the Changeling until she could answer some basic questions. "If you refuse me, then pick either Orion or Sorrell and be done with it. Virginity is not the end all, be all in the Fae Courts; in fact, you are more likely to be looked down on for being so prudish. The society you were born to be a part of—"

"If she is actually a Changeling," Sorrell reminded me.

"The society you may have been born to be a part of is one that runs on pleasure," I continued without comment. "Pleasure of food, drink, flesh, you name it, we know how to find pleasure in it. The only thing we don't find pleasure in is humans. Now, make your choice." I gestured to the two men standing off to my right.

She just gaped at me and I had to wonder if her time spent with the humans had impacted her development, because she seemed awfully slow to pick up on ideas or take action.

"Orion," she said eventually.

I had expected fear or trepidation in her voice, but none

came. It was calm and steady, just like her form. Her Changeling nature was already asserting itself, I knew it. The fact that I was right, not that my friends would admit it yet, was like a balm to my frazzled nerves. Now I just had to go and make Ariana forget that she had ever seen the Changeling and everything would be fine. With a nod to my friend, I turned and walked away.

CHAPTER 10

CRESS

What trouble had I found myself in this time? The nuns were always telling me I was dangerous, that I'd put the others in jeopardy with my actions, but I'd never expected anything like this to happen the first time I ventured away from the convent. The two remaining Fae were staring down at me like I was a bug trapped under a glass. I had opted for Orion since I hadn't heard any horror stories about him yet or watched him practically shove his hand up another woman's skirts right in front of me. But even as I looked over at him—I was doubting my choice. Of all three of them, he was the scariest. Shadows seemed to cling to his very skin, highlighting the darkness in his gaze as well as the numerous scars that peeked out from beneath his shirtsleeves and collar. I knew better than to think any of them were safe.

Besides, if I was what they claimed—a Changeling—then would I be allowed to leave when we were done? If I did, where would I go? It wasn't like the nuns were going to welcome me back with open arms, not unless I gave my vows and joined them, which was never going to happen. *I mean, seriously, a life of chastity? For someone like me? Not happening.*

"Shall we?" Orion said as he offered me his arm like he was a knight in shining armor and I was a princess from a fairytale. I blinked dumbly at it before reaching forward, hesitantly and letting my hand wrap around his bicep. *Oh Gods, he had some muscles.* I squeezed lightly, admiring the thickness of his arm. Orion smirked down at me and I paused, having been caught. I pursed my lips and turned my head away as heat warmed my cheeks.

With little other to look at, my gaze landed on Sorrell. The heat from Sorrell's stare as he looked at our joined arms speared me. The expression accompanying that heat was ... enigmatic. I couldn't tell if he was happy, angry, sad, or ... I couldn't tell anything from the way he was looking at us. His face was just a blank mask, reminding me of the perfect sheet of ice that used to form on the water bucket for the pigs at the convent. His pale blue eyes met mine briefly before he turned and stormed away, his steps echoing loudly up the throne room walls. I guess that meant he was angry. *Had I insulted him by choosing Orion? How was I supposed to know?*

Orion had started walking though, and if I didn't want to fall flat on my face, I needed to move or he might just drag me along behind him. I had been hauled plenty of places in my life by the nuns, and sliding along the ground with your face in the dirt wasn't a good look for anyone. I started walking, taking a couple longer strides to catch up until we fell into an easy rhythm that wasn't too slow for him or too fast for me. Why was I focusing on walking so much? Oh, yeah, because this guy was supposed to take my virginity, something which the nuns had drilled into me was sacred. *I wondered how one took someone's virginity and why was it called taking and giving? Was it such a big deal?* Roan hadn't seemed to think it was.

It had never made sense to me—the invisible status of someone's *innocence* that supposedly made the nuns better than everyone else, more devoted to their faith, when yet their other behaviors were often so different. While some of the nuns had been kind, there were those like Sister Madeline who were harsh and often cruel, violent, and quick to punish. But the fact that they had saved themselves from temptations of the flesh somehow absolved all of that? That was a big steaming pile of horse manure if I ever heard one. And if that was the case—if having this unsatisfied need inside you made the nuns twisted and mean—then I would gladly give up my virginity and keep my sanity.

"What are you thinking about?" The question came from the man holding me and when I looked up into his obsidian eyes, I panicked.

"Horse manure," I blurted.

He nearly tripped over his own two feet and took me down with him. Barely managing to catch himself in time, he slid his arm away from mine and caught me by the waist to keep from tumbling to the floor. I blinked. So did he. His lids slowly lowered and then lifted. I focused on his lashes—why the hell were they so long and beautiful? In fact, all of him was beautiful—even with the lines of white scars marring his skin. He just had this otherworldliness to him—probably a Fae aspect.

"I am about to bed you and you're thinking of ... horse shit?"

"Well, to be fair, I wasn't thinking about the fact that you're going to have—I mean you're gonna do ... you know, *that*," I emphasized without using the actual term. "I mean, I was, but I wasn't thinking that you were going to be horse shit at it, I was just—"

He placed a palm over my mouth, his brows lowered together—nearly touching as he frowned. "Do you ever stop talking?"

"Yes," I replied, the sound muffled behind his massive paw. I turned my cheek and slid my face out from beneath his hand. "I have to sleep sometime, don't I?"

He just continued to stare at me. I wondered if he didn't

realize that humans actually had to sleep. "You do know that humans sleep, right?" I asked. "I mean, if I am human that is. Fae sleep too, right? Or do you guys just like..." I trailed off, reaching up with both hands and placed my fingers above my eyes, stretching the skin slightly so it'd look like I was peeling my eyeballs open.

The frown didn't leave his face. "You are a strange creature," he finally said with a shake of his head. We continued down the hallway, but his hand never left my hip—anchoring me to the side of his body beneath his arm. Gods, he was like a fire— burning hot. I was already sweating. I could feel little sweat beads popping up along my temple and my upper lip. They slid down the small of my back even through the little skimpy dress as it fluttered around me leaving me feeling like I didn't have enough air.

Our feet tapped against the flagstone tiles of the floor while I tried to wrap my head around the events that had just tran- spired—both the stuff that had already happened and what was about to happen. I wondered what time it was. We hadn't passed a single window since we'd set off from the throne room. The walls that surrounded us now were dark, almost as dark as Orion's hair, which I swear looked more like it was absorbing light than reflecting it like mine usually did. Cool blonde strands fluttered in front of my face and I blew them out of the way. Flames flickered on torches that were dotted along the hallway, but the light never seemed to reach far beyond the torch itself.

Occasionally, I caught a glimpse of a door, the thick wood looking bright in comparison to the dark, deep gray of every- thing else. Sometimes the light was reflected enough that I was fairly sure the walls were made of a dark marble or something similar. They weren't regular brick or stone, of that much I was sure. As we moved through the dark halls in silence, my mind began to focus on my other senses and I caught a whiff of something dark and exotic. Bergamot and jasmine mixed with something woodsy that made me think of the forest that was just at the edge of the convent grounds.

I took a deep breath, soaking in the delicious fragrance. If I could bottle the way he smelled, I'd make a fortune in a fortnight.

"Did you just smell me?" Orion asked, his voice a low rumble that was barely audible even though I was standing right next to him.

Heat flared back to life in my face. "You did it to me first," I said defensively. It hadn't been intentional, but damn I couldn't help doing it again, inhaling the scent wafting from his skin.

Once again, he shook his head. "Here." He stopped before an alcove, reaching forward and finding the door's handle beyond in the shadows. His hand turned and the door opened, creaking softly as it swung inward. I gulped, wanting to back away, but he was already ushering me inside, the door closing behind us and sealing us into a room full of shadows and darkness.

The room we entered was even darker than the hallway. So pitch black that I put my hands out, afraid that I would run into a wall or something. There was a shifting sound at my back and then I felt Orion move around me, and as he did, lights began to flicker to life, illuminating the room. Flames danced behind glass vases anchored to the walls, casting around as if each light spurred the next one on until the whole room was bathed in the warm glow.

Even though I saw the lights flare and come to life, I had no idea how they were doing so. There was no switch, no flame in Orion's hand. It was ... pure magic. Fae magic, I realized. "Holy horse shit," I whispered. Orion paused, his back to me before casting a look back. "What?" I asked.

He didn't say anything, though, and I returned to gazing at the wonder of the flames.

They reflected off the walls, but instead of the charcoal gray I'd expected, a deep indigo color with a hint of violet was reflected back. Gold filigree decorated the edges and corners of the walls, drawing my eyes up to the most impressive ceiling I'd ever seen. Something twinkled, embedded in the rafters above me. The longer I stared at it the more I realized it was constellations. Somehow the stars seemed to shine through the castle and into Orion's bedroom. My eyes caught on a large, yet delicate, painting of the moon on the ceiling and I became even more fascinated.

"How..." I whispered, but didn't know what to ask so my voice trailed off into nothingness.

"Glass, embedded in the ceiling, but if you come over here you can see the real thing," Orion said from the base of a spiral staircase I hadn't even noticed yet. My feet carried me towards him without me even thinking about it. On the way, I passed a massive bed, one that could easily sleep all of the children at the convent with room to spare. A large cornice stuck out in the shape of a crown, hanging over half the bed with long velvety curtains slipping from the top to the edge of the bed.

Next to the bed was a small library of books and cushioned chairs. A large structure sat in the center of the space. It was made up of multiple rings, all attached to one another in the shape of a globe, with a small sphere at the center. It was fascinating to look at, especially as the gold of the structure glinted in the light showing that there were markings and words on it that I was too far away to read.

A soft clearing of a masculine throat drew my attention away from the many books and the structure I had started towards without even realizing it. I froze mid-step and pouted as I considered whether or not to ignore the Fae at my back and continue towards my objective or answer the obvious call he'd administered. It took several heartbeats for me to come to a decision, and with a sigh, I put my foot down and turned back to Orion. He arched one brow before gesturing to the staircase. My eyes rounded. Abandoning all caution, I made a straight line for the bottom of it and began to climb. I marveled as it twisted around over itself until it came out to the most breathtaking sight.

My jaw dropped as that familiar scent that I'd caught on Orion's body met me. Flowers. Dozens of them lined up in rows. He had a garden above his bedroom. It was surrounded by glass walls and topped with a domed glass ceiling that had the most intricate lead work I had ever seen. Nothing like anything the convent possessed. The room made it look like it was still nightfall, but was it? Hadn't the sun been coming up as I'd come into the castle? Looking beyond the lead that made captivating patterns in the glass I was able to see the stars for real this time.

"Beautiful, is it not?" Orion asked, leading me along a path that ran between tall plants, the likes of which I had never seen before.

"I ... don't know what to say. It's stunning," I breathed, still staring up at the dome while simultaneously trying not to miss any of the gorgeous flowers we were passing and stay on the path so I didn't crush any of his plants.

"Here, have a seat," he said as he gestured to where a large blanket and pillows were laid out on the ground. The patch had evidently been kept clear for a time and I got the feeling that this was a more personal space than he might admit. I slid a glance his way. If it was, why would he be showing me this when we'd only just met? Before I could think about it too hard, though, I moved to where he'd waved me. I didn't just sit; I laid back on the blanket and stared up, watching the stars and trying to orient myself. A difficult task to be sure, but one that was all encompassing. I couldn't tear my eyes away.

"It's a different sky than the one you're used to seeing," he said quietly.

I glanced up and caught him watching me, a small smile tugging at his lips. "It is?" I asked.

"This room channels night. No matter where we are or what time it is, the windows only show night whether it's from where the castle is at that moment or somewhere it has been that is currently experiencing night." He paused for a second as I just stared at him with my mouth agape. "All the flowers and plants in this room flourish during the night time, so you can experience them whenever you want."

I started to speak, a million questions fluttered in my head all at once, but none of them came out. Instead, I squeaked. A friggin' squeak. Like a mouse. I covered my face with my hands and moaned in awkward embarrassment.

"You said you're a virgin, and I want to respect that, but if you wish to survive this place, then we can't risk anyone mistaking you for a human," he said as he sat on the blanket next to me, his long limbs stretching out next to mine as he leaned close to me. Orion was massive, far bigger than the few men I'd seen regularly in my life. Larger than the butcher that delivered food to the convent. Larger than the blacksmith that I'd seen in the local village. Each of his features—from his hands to his whole body radiated heat and strength. He was big enough to break me, I knew, and it should have scared me. In a way, it did. But not to the extent I expected, that it was supposed to. His dark eyes seemed to glow in the moonlight and from this proximity I could see flecks of gray and white, as though I was looking into the night sky itself in his eyes. The effect was only enhanced by the long strands of hair that hung down over his shoulder, creating an ebony backdrop for his sparkling eyes.

The weight of reality crashed down around me once more when his words finally registered. My eyes snapped away from his but caught on his open shirt. Stretched out next to me like this I could see all the tiny scars that covered his body along with the depth of color in his skin. It wasn't just olive as I had thought earlier; there was a different kind of darkness there as well, whether it was the color of smoke or slightly more purple, it seemed to swirl over his skin like the ocean, constantly changing course and shifting. I couldn't help but notice his muscular frame as well, lean and strong, I wanted to bite my lip as I took it in, especially as my eyes lingered over the way his pants fit around his ass and thighs. *Was this what lust felt like?*

His dark eyes watched me as I checked him out; I could feel them on me as surely as a caress, and it made my body hum with need. My mind threw the memory of his smelling me earlier back at me, the soft feeling of his skin against my own and I wondered what it would feel like to kiss his full lips, to feel his touch on other parts of my body. Just the thought of it set my heart galloping in my chest as we stared at each other.

CHAPTER 11
ORION

Females were such intriguing creatures and this one was no different. Though, perhaps, she was a bit more interesting than most. Her small pert little nose tilted up as she stared at the ceiling of my secret garden. Her eyes glittered, reflecting the millions of fragments of pseudo-moonlight—a spell of my own making.

She was so small, soft—fragile. Her scent as a human was weak after Roan had ordered her cleaned but still there. Likely, it had seeped into her skin after all the years she'd spent in their realm. I leaned closer to her and when she didn't pull away, I knew she would accept this. I pressed small, chaste kisses to her temple. Something, I'd never done for any female. This one wasn't just any female though. She was special. She'd chosen me—over Sorrell, over Roan. Something the other women of the Court hadn't done.

My fingers trailed down her arm, circling her wrist and bringing it up so that she wound the limb around my neck as I moved my face lower. "It may hurt at first," I whispered into the quiet of the room. "But after the initial pain, I will ensure you feel only pleasure."

"Does it have to hurt?" she asked. "I mean, can't you just like ... make me think it doesn't? You're a Fae. Fae have magical powers."

I smirked as I pressed another one of those close-mouthed kisses to the underside of her jaw. Her heart picked up pace as it beat a consistent rhythm. I could feel it pounding, hear it in my ears as well as I could scent the telltale sign of her arousal. Her legs shifted and when I pulled her onto my lap, wrapping those legs around my waist, that scent blossomed and became heavier—overwhelming the scent of the flowers surrounding us.

"Different types of Fae have different types of powers, and that is not one I possess," I confessed as I parted my lips and licked a path up her throat. Her spine bowed as if she wanted to arch away, but as soon as I pulled away, she pressed closer—her breasts crushed against my chest. I chuckled, and the sound reverberated through both of our bodies. "If I could take your pain away, little one, I would."

Her breath hitched as I cupped her backside, pulled her so that the center of her was pressed to my groin. I knew she would feel how hard I already was—it'd been quite a while since I'd bedded a female like this. Amber eyes flickered at me, her lashes throwing shadows across her cheeks. Shadows I called to me, stealing from her and leaving her in nothing but illuminating moonlight. Her skin glowed, iridescent and beautiful. Cool and smooth like ivory, soft like nothing I'd ever known. I would enjoy taking this creature to my bed, I knew. I would ensure she enjoyed it too.

I turned, placing her back against the cushions and blankets as I came down on top of her. We were like light and dark, and I wondered briefly if that faint hint of otherness I'd caught a whiff of—the very thing that made me stop Roan from immediately demanding her execution—really was of the Brightling Court. A Court that had perished in the war nearly the same time as she would've been born. She had no clue—that much was obvious. But then the Brightling Court had been far more tolerant of humans than any other Court—to their demise.

I shook my head and pressed a kiss to her lips, parting my mine and letting my tongue dip between hers. She tasted of a freshness that was uniquely her. I rolled my hips as I dug my fingers into her sides. She was such a slight little thing. If I wasn't careful I'd snap her in half. She, on the other hand, didn't seem at all worried about it.

A low moan rumbled out of her throat as she pressed her hips up into mine and when her eyes crossed my face, they were clouded with surprise and lust. I had to remind myself that she was untouched, she would not appreciate being thrust into like a fast adolescent. It would not just hurt, but likely make her unwilling to do it again and I wanted to sample this beauty many more times after tonight if she was, in fact, a Changeling.

The female was a quick study. In no time at all, she was arching her hips into mine, rubbing herself wantonly—moaning as she, too, thrust her tongue into my mouth. She was mimicking me, I realized. Taking everything I gave her and giving it back. Tenfold. I pulled back and gritted my teeth as she nearly came off the floor as she pressed into me. My cock was stiff beneath my trousers and I knew I needed to slow things down if I was to make this as good for the little virgin as I wanted to.

Reaching back, I removed her legs from around my waist and set her feet down flat on the floor. Her eyes, which had been lowered halfway, popped open. She blinked at me, frowning in confusion. "What is it?" she asked. "Did I mess up? Did I do something wrong?"

I shook my head, lifting my tunic up and over my head. I tossed the fabric to the side, moving back to her as my hands went to the strips of fabric covering her small breasts. I froze at the look of utter astonishment on her face. I looked down. *Was it the scars?* I wondered. She'd seen them through the opening, surely she wouldn't be shocked.

But no, she wasn't shocked. She was curious, I realized a moment later as she sat up, her hands moving to my skin. Her fingers ran through the matt of hair that covered my chest. She followed it down to the line that trailed into the waistband of my pants. I inhaled sharply, capturing her wandering hand in one of mine before she could go too far. Dangerous. This little Changeling was dangerous.

I took the hand she'd been exploring with and placed it down on the pillows, holding it there with one of my own as I reached for her other arm. I couldn't take any chances with this girl. Capturing and keeping both of her hands above her head, I used my free hand to untie the strips of fabric covering her breasts. Slipping one away and pulling it free from her body, I used it to tie her hands together.

"Keep those there for me," I commanded. Big, wondrous eyes stared at me. "Do you understand, little one?" I asked when she didn't reply. "Keep your hands above your head and I'll give you a gift," I said, pinching her chin between my thumb and forefinger as I stared down into her gaze.

"What will you give me?" she countered.

I laughed. "The stars," I said. A promise.

She looked up at the ceiling. "You kind of already did that."

Another laugh. "Different stars," I assured her. "Ones you can't see any other way."

She stared at me, narrowing her gaze slightly as if in suspicion. I waited, nonetheless, for the small but perceptive nod of acquiescence. Once I had that, I left her chin, pressing a kiss to the center of her chest. She inhaled as if just realizing that her breasts were bared to my gaze. Her nipples peaked beneath my palms as I skated both of my hands over the small but plump mounds. I squeezed each before circling with my fingers, first pinching one pretty pink bud before doing the same to the other. Her breath came in ragged pants. Her stomach sucked in and out. Her legs shifted beneath me.

I moved further down, removing the rest of her dress as I went until she was wholly and completely naked before me. "W-what are you doing?" She gasped as I pressed an open mouthed kiss to the inside of one thigh, lifting it until I could see the spot between her legs that called to me. Oh it was pretty. A nice pink just like her nipples.

"Taking you to paradise, little one," I whispered back just as I leaned forward and gave her my mouth. I sucked the needy little bud that poked out between her lower lips and relished in her cry of pleasure. She arched up, her hands coming down immediately—fingers spearing into the hair at the back of my head. That was alright. I'd been doubtful of her ability to hold back with my mouth on her. I liked it, in fact. Loved the feeling of a woman losing control beneath me.

I licked and sucked at her like I was eating the juiciest of fruits. My tongue swiped a path up the center of her before delving deeper. She shivered, panted, and moaned. Wetness oozed down my chin as I licked some more, fighting to catch as much of the delicious juice as I could. When her thighs tightened around my head, I reached up and shoved her wide open —eliciting a cry of surprise.

She shivered beneath me, the whole of her body fighting upward every time I pulled away to catch a breath. It was as if she couldn't stand for me to be away. I grinned, sliding up so that my shoulders blocked her from tightening her thighs once more. With my fingers, I spread her pretty lower lips and then gently touched the small opening that would soon take my cock. She was so small there. Tiny. Vulnerable.

I licked her essence from my lips as I slipped first one finger inside and then a second. She clamped down around the digits, squirming as her eyes looked up at me in awe. I loved that look on a woman's face just before I showed her the other side of paradise.

Holding her gaze, I let my head descend once more. I pumped my fingers in and out as I licked that needy bud once more. A moment—two—passed. I couldn't tell if she was even breathing. She could feel it, though. That much I did know. She could sense what was about to happen.

Slowly. Ever so slowly, I pulled my fingers clear from her passage, added a third and held them positioned just inside the opening. I didn't wait or give her any warning. I sucked her bud into my mouth at the same time that I shoved them forward, curling them towards me in a fast, hard motion. And the expression that came over her face ... it was glorious.

Her lips parted on a silent scream. Her eyes widened and then squeezed shut just before she threw her head back and I felt the gush of her reaching peak over my hand and lips. I sucked it all down, closing my own eyes and relishing in her first orgasm. When I was done and she was trembling with exhaustion beneath me—and only then—did I finally remove my fingers from her pussy and rear back to undo the front placket of my trousers.

Reaching up, I undid the strip of fabric binding her hands. Her limbs were lax and slender in my grip. I chuckled as she moaned lightly while I positioned her over my lap, lifting her slightly so that I could fit her opening at the tip of my cock.

"Ready?" I asked.

She didn't answer—at least, not in words. Instead, she lifted her head, cupped the back of my neck and pressed her mouth over mine. I took that to mean she was and I let her sink slowly upon my rod. More of her squirming made me nearly shoot my load in her, I clenched my teeth as I pulled away from her kiss. Pressing my face into her throat, I found the barrier of her virginity and sank further inside. There was no hiccup, no quick inhale of pain. Her insides squeezed me impossibly tight.

A few quick pumps and I knew I'd be gone. Yet, I couldn't seem to help myself.

I'd sank fully into her and then, using my grip on her waist, I lifted her and thrust inside again and again and again, until I felt a tingle at the base of my spine rip through me. Pleasure raced into my mind and a split second later, I came, unleashing a torrent of my cum inside her. I pulled back a moment later, looking down at her half hooded eyes.

"I thought you said you couldn't take someone's pain away..." she muttered absently.

"I can't," I said.

She smiled. "Funny ... it didn't hurt at all."

Oh yes, this little Changeling was very dangerous indeed.

CHAPTER 12
CRESS

There was a certain languidness that I had only ever felt a few times before, usually after sunning myself until I almost burnt to a crisp on top of the convent storehouse. I'd never felt this way in the dark before, but it was luxurious. It made me realize that the nuns were probably so uptight because they'd never had an orgasm as good as the two Orion just gave me. I mean, seriously, the world could always benefit from more orgasms. They should be the currency of life. You want to buy some food? Get an orgasm. You want to solve an argument? Orgasm. Are you angry? Orgasm. Sad? Orgasm. It literally fixed every known problem.

Part of me was still freaking out that I'd just slept with, and thereby given my virginity to, someone who was essentially a stranger, but most of me just felt relieved that I didn't have that imaginary sign pointing at me anymore saying 'Here stands a Virgin.' I had always been more interested in sex than any of the other orphans at the convent—far too much for the nuns' self-preservation, but this ... if I had the energy to whistle, I would've. I mean *dear Gods*, Orion knew how to work that thing between his legs ... and his fingers ... and his mouth.

If I had been allowed to go to town more than once a year, I may have even experimented before now, but it was like the nuns had wanted to keep me prisoner, were scared of what would happen if they let me loose on an unsuspecting world. *Why?* I wondered absently. Because sex, I'd suddenly discovered, was the absolute best thing in the world.

Ha! If only they could see me now, naked in a conservatory with a strange Fae who looked more dangerous than anyone I'd met my whole life—he certainly had enough scars to deter the average person. I rolled to face him and lifted my head to settle it into my palm as I braced my elbow on the cushioned floor. "So," I started, "do I still smell human?"

Orion shook his head. "Your scent has been overwhelmed."

"Yeah, it has," I snorted. "But just to be sure..." I batted my eyelashes and reached for his arm. "I think I might need to get some more Fae scent on me—just in case. You know, for safety's sake."

Orion chuckled, deep and throaty, sending a shiver down my spine, before rolling on top of me. He pushed me onto my back and leaned over me to run his nose along one of my outstretched arms until he switched direction and headed for my upper chest, stopping just over my heart and breast. By the time he was done with the feather light touches, I was panting and arching my back, pressing myself against him once more. By Coreliath's beard, I wanted to feel him inside me again.

"Have an appetite for it now, do you?" Orion asked with a knowing smile.

"I mean, I could go for round two, if you're interested," I said with a nonchalant shrug. "I mean, if it's necessary—we should, definitely." I kept my face straight—or as straight as possible. All business. *One thousand percent ... just ... business,* I thought as my hands wandered down over his skin. We both knew that he had awoken a hunger in me that would not be easily sated.

"I would if I could, sweet Changeling, but if I do not return you to Court soon, then Roan and Sorrell will come and find us." He paused, lifting a brow as he looked down at me. "Unless you'd like that?" he inquired, keeping his expression even. At first, I thought he was joking, but the longer he stared at me the more I realized that he was serious.

"Stop messing around," I replied, my voice coming out more breathy than I had intended. The idea of the three of them doing the same things that Orion had done ... together ... at the same time. Them. And me. Me. And them. Them worshipping at the altar of my body. It was absurd, but it wasn't *un*appealing —I mean, if a girl liked that kind of thing. Which I might. Wouldn't know unless I tried.

"I'm not." Orion pushed to a sitting position and even half tousled, he looked gorgeous. His muscles bunched beneath his skin were displayed beautifully. Was there even a smidge of fat on him? If so, I hadn't been able to find it in all the time we'd been intertwined. "If you would like to explore your sexuality, then we'd be more than happy to help you. Fae are sexual creatures by nature; you saw from that small display between Roan and Ariana. Most of our celebrations involve a coalition of appetites or at least a party where everyone leaves with at least one partner. The fact that you remained untouched in the human world shows a strength of will I doubt many in our Court possess. I know some of it may not have been your choice since you were sequestered, but most Fae require physicality to access their abilities. It's a wonder you lived for as long as you did without acting on your sexual needs."

"It wasn't like I didn't think about it," I said defensively. "I was just never given the opportunity." Unless you counted the old men who'd come by the convent. "And the nuns weren't exactly forthcoming with information about it."

"There is nothing to be ashamed of in enjoying sex. I gave

you pleasure, you gave me pleasure. We enjoyed ourselves, or at least I hope you did?"

I nodded vigorously. "Oh yes," I said quickly. "Definitely enjoyable. The most enjoyable experience of my life—so far."

He grinned, the stretch of his lips lighting up his face in a way that made him ten times as handsome. "Then there's nothing to worry about."

I couldn't help but return his smile. It felt like a weight had been lifted from my shoulders. My chest seemed to expand with breath more easily than it had done for most of my adult life.

"Come on," Orion said as he stood and offered me his hand, his gloriously naked form completely on display.

I bit my lip as I let him help me stand before swiping my dress up from the ground. "Can you help me put this back on? I've never worn anything like it before. The nuns would be scandalized," I said with a chuckle.

Orion's deft fingers had the straps in place with only a minimum of teasing before he dressed himself. Honestly, I was a little sad when he tucked his cock away. I hadn't had a chance to study one before and now that this whole new world had opened up to me, I couldn't deny that I was curious and excited. I wanted more of whatever he'd just given me. I wanted to know what I could do that would make him lose control just as much as I had. But right now, unfortunately, we had other things to focus on.

"Why is it so important that I'm a Changeling?" I asked as we worked our way back down the stairs to the main section of Orion's bedroom.

He paused at the bottom, turning as I stopped as well. His shoulders ratcheted up with tension and I watched the play of confused emotions cross his expression as he tried to come up with a response. After several moments of awkward silence and uncomfortable waiting, I sighed.

"Please don't lie to me," I said. "If you don't want to tell me, that's fine, I'll figure it out eventually—but just don't lie." There was nothing I hated more than I liar, which was probably why I butted heads with some of the nuns so much. It was ironic considering I was in the middle of lying my ass off, but that was to save my life. The nuns though ... they may not outright lie, but they deceived and lied by omission which to me was the same thing.

Orion faced me completely as I stood on the bottom step. We were almost eye level with one another. His scars and beautiful raven's black hair combined with his night sky eyes had me captured and in his control once more, even though I knew that wasn't really the case. Still, if he had asked me to jump in that moment, I would have ... onto him. "I think it's better if one of the others tells you; they know the history better than I do. I just have a good sense of smell, and you, pretty little Changeling, smell like you belong here," he said, lifting my hand and kissing the back of my knuckles.

"I do?" I whispered, my breath catching in my throat.

He nodded. "You smell like an old faction of the Fae Courts that hasn't been seen in years, but again, I don't know the history very well. I was a mere babe when it all happened."

I nodded and let him lead me out of the room. I followed him through the hallways, my footsteps grazing lightly over the stones as I fixated on Orion, letting myself fall into a rhythm that matched his. I hadn't even realized where he'd been leading me until we were back in the banquet area—the throne room.

While I might have expected that the other Fae—Sorrell and Roan—to be waiting to hear about how it'd all gone down—the loss of my virginity—that wasn't the case. Instead, it appeared as if all the other Fae living within the castle walls had suddenly been called to the room. The noise reached me first, and as we turned and entered the room, Orion's hand drifted to the small of my back to guide me through as I glanced around.

More tables had been added in the time we'd been away. Several long, elegant benches hosting creatures that were far more beautiful and elegant than any figure I'd ever seen before. Orion steered me to a table furthest from the doorway, where Roan and Sorrell were sitting along with a few others.

Roan caught my eye, a knowing smirk curving one side of his delectable lips. Sorrell's icy gaze met mine and his head tipped ever so slightly in what I was going to take as a nod of greeting. I could feel unfamiliar eyes land on me as we made our way around the table and took our seats. Ice skated down my spine and my skin lit with a burning feeling of discomfort. Sensations of all different kinds bombarded me. Was I losing my mind? Or was someone doing this to me?

The table we sat at was a large wooden circle with plates piled high with food in the middle. I watched as several of the others gathered at the table took a few of the pastries from the larger plates and felt my stomach rumble to life. I snatched a roll and stuffed it in my mouth as soon as I was situated. It ballooned my cheeks at the same time as the delicious taste of buttery freshness hit my tongue. I chewed and swallowed, already reaching for another, when a little buzzing figure entered my vision. A pixie, loaded down with a tray filled with empty and dirty plates flitted from the room. A kernel of guilt rose forth and I resolved to tuck something away to give to them later.

"Changeling," Roan said in greeting, drawing everyone's attention as Orion sat next to me.

The other Fae sitting at the table looked up with big curious eyes. A few leaned over and whispered to their neighbors in a tone so low I couldn't hear. It made me feel like a very small bug. The woman from earlier, Ariana, pursed her lips and shot a glare my way as her friend from the baths earlier, just stared longingly at Sorrell. If I was recalling correctly, she'd been complaining about their earlier ... session together and now she looked ready to do it all over again and right here, if he so much as looked her way. He didn't, though. Sorrell didn't let his gaze stray from me. Not even once.

"Roan," I replied, causing a gasp to go up from the others at our table and the tables around us.

"You may address me as Lord Carmine," Roan said coolly.

Yeah, fat chance, I thought. People had names for a reason and even with the sisters, I hadn't been much for using fancy titles. "Whatever you say, Roan," I replied, popping a chunk of those delicious rolls into my mouth.

A splotch of red formed over Roan's neck and spread upward and outward. It looked like that one time Nellie had walked into a patch of poisoned leaves that grew near the storage house. It had made her skin a fiery red for a fortnight and had itched like nothing she'd ever felt before, she'd said.

"That's a pretty color you're turning, *Lord Carmine*," I said, emphasizing his ridiculous title.

"Lord Chalcedony, would you mind introducing our guest this evening?" Roan said, nodding to Sorrell. They sounded so fancy now. I preferred them as just Roan, Sorrell, and Orion—though I couldn't help but wonder what Orion's last name was and if it was as fancy as the others.

"Are you sure that Orion doesn't want that pleasure? After all, he has tasted the Changeling," Sorrell said, his eyes on me as if he sought some sort of outward sign of my embarrassment. I didn't even blink. I'd taken the conversation I had with Orion to heart and if they really were as sexually open as he claimed, which—judging from some of the sounds coming from the corners of the room—didn't seem to be an exaggeration, then why should I feel shame just because I'd been raised differently.

I took the slight embarrassment I was feeling and shoved it into a mental box where Sorrell and Roan couldn't get to it and then shoved another roll in my mouth. I waited until I'd quietly chewed and swallowed the delicious offering before replying. "He does do wonderful things with his tongue," I commented lightly. "Things I didn't think possible." My voice sounded husky and filled with need, as though I couldn't wait to experience it again, which was true. I honestly couldn't wait to do all of that again. Soon. Preferably with him lying on his back and me sitting on his handsome face. I felt my groin tighten with the mental image that'd drawn.

Sorrell's face went carefully blank as his eyes traveled down the front of my body. Roan's expression darkened as the red splotches worked their way up his jawline. Orion choked, nearly spitting out the mouthful of whatever it was he'd been drinking. The orangish-gold liquid looked like nothing I'd ever seen before, but then that seemed to be the way of the Fae. Everything that they had was new to my eyes.

"May I ask what this drink is?" I asked, raising the glass in front of me with the orange-gold liquid.

"Fae wine. It packs a punch if you're not used to it so be careful," Orion said quietly as Sorrell got up and the temperature in the room dropped significantly until I could see my breath —and everyone else's—like clouds of fog. Quickly enough the room became quiet and as I looked around from my seat I saw that most of the Fae in attendance were turning to watch Sorrell.

"Friends, we have a guest in our midst tonight, someone who arrived unexpectedly, but the surprise was worth it. Cress, please stand," Sorrell said, raising his hand in my direction. I complied but shot him a glare as I did so, and I could swear I saw his mouth twitch with a grin before his face smoothed out once again. As I stood he twirled his finger in a circle and I followed his directions, spinning so I faced the majority of the Fae in attendance. "Cress is a Changeling that found her way to the castle when we landed. Of course, we couldn't turn her away, so she is staying with our Court until we can conduct the appropriate tests to discover her parentage, and where she belongs. I hope you all will be welcoming to our new arrival and be aware that she is unfamiliar with Fae customs."

As Sorrell spoke, the temperature surrounding me began to drop. All of the warmth was leached away from me until I felt the need to cross my arms over my chest, feeling how my nipples had grown so painfully hard that I felt as if they could practically tear a hole through the strips of fabric covering me. I shivered on the spot and when he finished speaking, I sank back into my chair, surprised to find it warm and the air temperature around it vastly different than where I had been standing a moment ago. *What in Coreliath's beard was that about?*

"Looks like someone likes being the center of attention," Ariana said from across the table. Several Fae around the table that had yet to be introduced to me snickered.

"And I'm sure you wore a sheer dress because you're such a wallflower," I replied testily before I could stop myself. The thing she wore could hardly pass for a dress. It was practically see through, her tits on full display for the whole world to see.

She gasped and turned to Roan. "Are you going to let a Changeling talk to me like that, my Lord?"

"Lady Ariana, if you can't handle it then you shouldn't start it. If it helps, I do find your dress this evening quite ravishing." He paused, lifting his brow as he smirked and looked downward—or more specifically, at her abundant bosom. She smiled back for a brief moment, arching her spine so that the curves of her breasts were thrust out and even more eye-catching. He continued a second later. "It probably seems strange to our guest."

Irritation spiked through me. I glanced down at my own breasts. Sure they weren't the size of melons, but they were alright. They were noticeable, at least. I frowned, glancing up at Orion from beneath my lashes. He'd seemed to like them just fine. Why did Ariana seem so intent on getting Roan's praise? Were all female Fae like that with these three? Would that be expected of me? I reached forward and snagged another pastry, this one filled with some sort of cream. Maybe that's what women did in the Fae Courts, but I certainly wasn't about to fall all over myself just to get their undivided attention, and if any of them expected me to be then they would be sorely disappointed.

As soon as I'd finished my pastry, pixies appeared out of the corners of the room—flocking together as they began carting away dishes before I'd even had a chance to try anything more. I pouted, but a moment later, new dishes were brought out. As they set down the new plates, I watched with fascination as the three lords served themselves, setting aside the choicest bits. I stared hard when Orion picked up a very interesting looking fruit. I noticed, too, that none of the other Fae even approached the new plates of food until the three princes had selected their bits. Pixies darted out in front of each of them and I watched as each prince held up a bite of food and let the little creatures nibble at whatever they held in their hands.

I expected them to be smacked away or yelled at but none of the lords responded at all, simply watching the pixie until it nodded, at which point they began eating their food.

"Why did you let them bite your food?" I asked quietly, leaning closer to Orion.

"They are poison testers," he replied, keeping his voice low so the conversation remained between the two of us.

"People try to poison you?" I gasped.

Orion nodded. "In this Court, we are royalty. The three of us are the pillars of the castle's magic. There are those who would try and steal our power and positions simply for the status it would offer them, although most would be incapable of controlling it. We have had many attempts on our lives over the years, some obvious, some not so much. Our parents instituted a rule that there are always at least a dozen pixies trained for tasting poison at any one time. Poison meant for Fae does not affect them as prevalently."

"I'm glad you survived," I replied, my voice barely above a whisper.

"Awww, is the Changeling sweet on you since you took her virginity?" Ariana asked loudly from across the table. Oppressive silence followed. She succeeded where others had failed. Embarrassment lit my face, heating my skin until I felt emblazoned.

Instead of letting that embarrassment keep me silent, however, it came out in fiery anger. My lips parted as murmurs began to fly through the hall. Orion's expression shut down—as did Sorrell's and Roan's. The three of them grew quiet in a way that reminded me of the absence of sound right before a giant thunderstorm.

"Perhaps I am," I snapped, sitting up straighter. I met Ariana's gaze and held it. "I understand being a virgin is practically unheard of in Fae Courts—but I wasn't raised with the Fae. Less than a day ago, I had never even met one."

"Well, I'm sure you weren't hard to please then," Ariana replied with a lifted brow.

A low growl emitted from Orion, but before he could say anything, I spoke again. "You seem to be really interested in what I do with Orion," I said. "I wonder why that is."

"Lord Evenfall," Orion muttered.

"I mean, what I do with *Lord Evenfall*," I said loudly before anyone could be offended on his behalf.

Ariana glared at me, but her silence spoke volumes. Ergo—she didn't have a response. The rest of the table soon lost interest as more and more people dug into their food. Orion became quiet at my side. He didn't even comment when I snagged the fruit from his plate that I'd had my eye on. I bit into it, the whole thing bursting with flavor on my tongue that left me moaning and consuming the rest of it in wet, sticky bites. Several eyes lifted and watched as I did so, but no one said a word.

As I continued to snag food from the available plates as well as from Orion's platter, I watched as several different Fae in various colors of gowns—from deep forest green to bright sparkling blue—approached the table to speak with Roan and Sorrell. Interestingly enough, no one spoke with Orion, though they nodded his way in polite acknowledgment, and I wondered why that was. No matter who was talking, though, their gazes would inevitably travel over to me, skirting down in a sometimes curious glance or hostile glare until they'd satisfied their curiosity before leaving the hall to go and do whatever it was Fae did when not stuffing their faces.

Ariana stood, floated around the table and stopped to run her fingers over Roan's shoulders in a slow, seductive glide. Her head lifted and her eyes zeroed in on me as she leaned down and pressed her breasts against him, marking her territory with a kiss to his cheek and a whisper against his ear before standing straight and moving back. As she passed me, she murmured, "Keep eating like that and no one will want to explore your desires with you, Switch."

"Switch?" I asked, but she was already gone.

The storm clouds were back on Orion's face and pity swam in the depths of his night sky eyes as he glared after her while absently answering me. "It's an insult for Changelings. Along the lines of your parents didn't even want you so they switched you for a human, which to us is about as low as it can get." His voice sounded like thunder in the distance and while part of me was screaming that I should be scared of him, all I wanted to do was climb him like a damn tree.

"I see," I replied, letting him know that I understood. I couldn't deny that the comment stung, but I'd been called worse by the nuns, so it wasn't anything new.

"Come," Orion said, standing and offering me his hand as he finally pulled his gaze away from where Ariana had exited and looked at me. "I'll give you a tour of the castle and we'll meet up with the others later to discuss your tests." I nodded, taking his hand and rising from my seat, snagging two rolls and squishing them in my free palm so the others wouldn't see. Hopefully, I'd be able to drop them for the pixies later. "Roan. Sorrell," Orion called as he stepped back, pulling me with him. The other two lifted their heads, nodding our way before returning to whatever conversations they'd been having among themselves.

I followed Orion out of the room, happy to be away from the peering eyes and muttered remarks of the other Fae. *Who knew that ignoring petty commentary from uptight Fae for the duration of a meal would be so tiring?* It was even a little more concerning, though, that these people really thought I was some sort of Changeling.

To be fair, I'd never really thought I'd belonged in the convent and I'd certainly been told how odd I'd been by everyone, but a Changeling? A lost Fae? Me? I snorted silently to myself. But if these guys thought I was a Fae, who was I to say they were wrong? Especially if telling them they were wrong would most assuredly land me on an executioner's block. I was willing to do whatever it took to avoid that. So, all that was left was for me to pass these tests and show them that I belonged here.

That didn't sound too hard ... right?

CHAPTER 13
SORRELL

Anger coated my vision, layering the room in a cool hue of blue frost. I could feel my skin grow cold and my breath puff out in a little white cloud in front of my face. The woman to my right shivered as my power stretched outward, reaching—seeking the warmth of others to suck it inside and freeze it over.

"L-Lord Ch-Chalcedony?" The woman spoke when I suddenly stood up as soon as Orion had taken the Changeling from the room. With her bright golden eyes and her even paler hair, she was a beauty. But the real irritation lay in her mouth. Every time, it seemed, she parted those pink lips of hers something rebellious was said.

"I'm going to the library," I said to Roan, ignoring the woman's faint call.

Victoria—one of my many bed partners—stood from across the table. "I'll attend to you, my Lord," she offered.

I held up a hand, staying her. "No," I said. "I wish to be alone." I didn't leave her much room for argument. Roan gave a nod of his understanding and I turned, striding from the room with quick, sure steps.

The library was my sanctuary. When I came to the double doors, I pushed through, turning and slamming them closed at my back, startling Groffet into dumping a stack of books he'd been putting back after my morning study session. "Lord Chalcedony!" he piped up, shock evident in both his tone and on his face as his big, bushy gray brows shot up, nearly disappearing beneath the green cap he wore.

The old dwarf ambled down the small ladder he had propped against the bookcase he'd been reshelving books on. I strode by, barely sparing him a glance as I headed to my desk where it was situated on the second platform in the center of the octagonal room.

"You're back early," Groffet commented.

I shot him a look of irritation that made it plain that I didn't want to talk about why that was, but as Groffet was as old as the Fae Courts themselves—he wasn't particularly put off by my glare or by the way the room dropped in temperature. Dwarves were few and far between and almost always immune to powerful Fae. They were like nature's neutral creatures. They were neither as powerful as Fae nor as weak as humans. They lived for hundreds of years, rarely contracting disease but held little magic. The one great thing they were known for was their stoutness and knowledge.

Giving up on ignoring the library's caretaker, I decided to question him for information. Perhaps he would know something about how to test a Changeling. "Groffet," I started as I stopped in front of my desk, turning and crossing my arms over my chest. "What can you tell me about Changelings?"

Groffet grunted as he shoved a stack of books onto a nearby table, the stack nearly higher than his head. "Well," he said, "I can tell you that there hasn't been one in several decades. The practice of switching Fae children for defective human ones has not been well received for centuries. The last Court to participate in such a practice was—"

"The Brightling Court, I know," I said. "What else can you tell me aside from the fact that they were the last Court to practice it?"

He nodded, his fat, grubby fingers coming up to stroke his full beard. The hair stretched from his face to halfway down his barrel chest. "Are you aware of the purpose of Changelings?" he asked.

I shook my head. "I didn't realize there was a point to it," I said. "I thought the whole issue with it was that it had no true purpose."

"There is always a purpose to old customs, my boy." Groffet waddled around the side of the table and across the floor, making his way to a section of books piled so high that even as tall as I was and standing on the platform, he disappeared from my view. "Old customs," he grunted from beyond the stacks, "are often set to maintain magical connection. Humans— although weak and without magic—come from nature. Their connection is to the land, itself, whereas Fae's connection comes from the Gods."

The tip of his pointed green cap appeared and I stared at it, watching it bob up and down as he did whatever he did out of my sight. "So, what was the purpose of trading Fae children for humans and subjecting Fae to spend years with the beasts?" I asked sharply.

Groffet chuckled, the sound dry and rather grating. I gritted my teeth to keep from using my usual commands on him. Unlike the others of our Court, Groffet wasn't just another subject. He was a pillar of our Court and the old creature knew it. He knew that I had no true power over him. Not unless I wished to speak with one of the head Courts. I pinched the bridge of my nose as I blew out a breath. Doing that would cause far more headache than I was willing to experience.

"Humans have their strengths," Groffet finally said, his voice slightly muffled. "The Brightling Court had their reasons for practicing in the Changeling switch. As you're aware, they were far more sympathetic to humankind's plight than any other Court."

"Yes, and look where that got them," I said, turning and uncrossing my arms as I circled my desk to take a seat. I pulled a book out of a pile to my right and flipped it open. On a single yellowed page was the list of all known Fae Courts and the one black mark, the one in which someone who'd had the volume before me had burned a line through that of the Brightling Court's name. "Humans are nothing if not treacherous."

"Humans are complex." I jumped and scowled when Groffet appeared in front of me, his fat, red nose peeking over the lip of my desk. He lifted up on his toes, placing a book on the edge of the workspace and shoving it until it rested flat. "This is an account of all things to do with Changelings," he said. "It should have some ideas as to tests you can perform on an individual to assess whether or not they are Fae."

"Can we determine which Court they would be from if they are a Changeling?" I asked.

Groffet backed away with a shrug. "You'll know when the Changeling's powers begin to show—as you know, each Court has a specific signature so to speak. For Prince Roan, it's fire and blood. For you, ice. And for Prince Orion—"

I waved my hand. "I'm aware," I snapped.

Groffet continued. "Among humans, without proper training and encouragement, their powers would've been weak. Around their own kind, they may experience some extreme shifts."

"Extreme shifts how?" I asked with narrowed eyes.

"Won't know until it happens," he said. "It changes per person. You have to understand that Changelings are creatures that are neither human nor Fae, yet they are both. Raised in one world, born from another. Being switched so suddenly will make them experience a lot of changes in a very short span of time. They might experience rapid mood swings. It's recommended that Changelings bond to a person of one Court when in their training period. Unlike you and the rest of your Court, who have all had years to understand your magic and who you are, they've had absolutely no time."

I grabbed the book he'd placed on my desk and flipped it open, scanning the pages. My eyes widened. "These are tests?" I asked.

He nodded. "Says it right there on the book, doesn't it?"

Cocky little bastard, I thought, returning my attention to the book. "She's already engaged in sexual activity with a Court member," I said, the words scraping from my throat as I'd recalled the way Orion had taken her from the banquet. It was clear she'd enjoyed her time with him. I was not usually one to limit someone's sexual appetites, and I had no doubt he would have her again before the day was through, but she had come from the human realm. Orion was so rarely with female company, sometimes by his own choice—but more often than not by the ostracism of his beliefs and kindness towards the humans as well as the scars that littered his body. I wondered, briefly, if the Changeling had sensed that about him. Whereas Roan and I understood that humans could not be trusted as they were all deceptive and disloyal, time on the battlefields south of the human kingdom had made Orion particularly sympathetic towards them.

I shook my head. I would not let another brother in arms in this war against humanity fall victim to one of their plots, I decided. I would find out if the female was a Changeling and if she wasn't, I'd kill her myself if that's what it took. I slammed the book closed and stood abruptly.

"Find what you're looking for, Prince Sorrell?" Groffet asked with an arched brow.

I scowled, picking up the tome and tucking it under my

arm. "I will be in my chambers," I said. "Make sure I'm not disturbed."

"Of course." He bowed as I passed, but I was not fooled. He did so only out of marginal respect—not for me, but for my home Court. The Court of Frost was one of the most powerful in the land and I was the second heir.

CHAPTER 14
ROAN

I groaned as I rolled off the willing body beneath me. My chest pumped up and down. Sweat coated every inch of my skin. Ariana turned and cuddled up against me and I allowed it for a moment. Then, as always, it grew annoying. I withdrew my arm from under her back and waved to the sheer robe waiting for her on the back of my desk chair. With a sigh and an eye roll, she crawled out of my bed and reached for the robe.

"I would have thought you'd be used to sleeping with another body near by now," she said tightly.

I sat up, stretching my arms as I pushed them behind my head, propping my neck at an angle as I watched her stride through the room and find the remainder of the dress I'd ripped from her as soon as I'd gotten her alone in my chambers. "Maybe another time," I offered with a playful smirk.

She shot me a look. We both knew the truth. There would never be a time that I'd allow a woman to sleep alongside me. Not since my ex-fiancée had nearly carved my heart from my chest in a bid to claim my position of power over my own Court.

"Have you given much thought to my proposal from last

time?" she asked, lifting the long silky strands of her hair out of the back of her robe and quickly braiding it down the side of her breast. I watched the mundane task, wondering if I continued to return to Ariana out of true pleasure or out of a sense of routine.

"I have," I said blandly.

Her head jerked up and her eyes blazed with excitement. "And?" she prompted.

I stretched again, turning and swinging my legs over the side of the bed before standing up. "The Court of Crimson does not need another member."

As expected, Ariana's exuberant expression soured. Her arms clamped beneath her buxom chest, lifting the soft mounds I'd just granted more than an hour of attention—*each*. "You will have to announce a new fiancée soon, Roan—" I cut her a look so dark that she snapped her mouth shut and her eyes moved to the ground as she corrected herself. "Lord Carmine."

Strangely enough, I hadn't done the same to the little Changeling now attached to Orion's side. Hearing my given name from her lips had been ... almost refreshing. From Ariana, however, it was an insult to refer to me with such informality. She might have been my regular bed partner but she was nothing but a warm body to help restore my magic, someone to pass the time with. I would not marry her.

"The answer is no," I said. "I have been granted all the time I would desire in choosing a new fiancée." Within reason, my mother had stated, but there was no need to specify that part to Ariana.

Ariana stiffened her spine. "Of course, my Lord." She bowed briefly. "May I be excused?"

I waved her away as I found my trousers and pulled them up my legs. A moment later, I was alone. I found myself moving to the window and staring out over the vast space we now inhabited. Before, we'd been stationed in the Eastern quadrant—just outside of the human kingdom's border. Now, we were inside, to the north. We were not at all where we were supposed to be.

I looked down and clenched my fist. I called my magic to me, felt sweat bead on my brow and the air around me crackle with energy as I conjured a ball of flame in my palm. It flared to life and dispersed, causing me to turn away from the window with a curse. What a disappointment we were as a Court.

Oh yes, the others and I held sway—we held our power and position—but we were only three. It took, on average, *four* royals to power a monstrosity such as a Fae castle. Perhaps the elders had thought that with our lineages—Sorrell, Orion, and I could handle it, and for a time, we had. But after Franchesca's betrayal and Orion's continued wounds in battle, we were running dry. Add a Changeling into the mix and we were well and truly fucked.

I moved to my desk and lifted a letter that had appeared, tucked just inside of the portal alongside my bed where it always did. I hoped when I read it that it'd be good news. I tore the crimson seal and flattened the parchment, leaning over the desk as my eyes read over the black script in my mother's handwriting. I breathed a sigh of relief as I scanned the words.

She was giving us time. A reprieve that we all sorely needed. Dealing with Fae Court politics, the war with the humans, and a Changeling? We were already stretched too thin as it was. All the elders had managed to do in placing the three of us in charge of this Court had been to sow the seeds of our inevitable failure. We now had a fortnight before Sorrell, Orion, and I needed to have the castle moved into position. It wasn't much, but it was something.

Once I was done reading the letter, I lifted it up and conjured another ball of fire. The parchment lit up in my palm and was burned away until only ash remained. Two weeks to deal with the Changeling. Two weeks to restore our magical reserves. Hopefully, by then we'd be prepared enough for the impending siege we were tasked with.

By the Gods, we had better be ready.

CHAPTER 15

CRESS

Apparently, when Orion had offered to take me on a tour of the castle, what he really meant was a tour of his bedroom ... again. I'm sure he meant to take me on a tour, but there was something electric moving between us. As we left the banquet hall, a few heated glances and the brush of his fingertips against my arm was all it had taken. We'd barely made it in the door of his tower room before his lips were crashing against mine. We'd replayed and expanded on the events from earlier.

My body collapsed against his several hours later and as a yawn stretched my jaw, I finally let myself cave in to the exhaustion the last day had left in me. Almost as soon as I surrendered to sleep, however, a new anxiety sprang forth.

My dreams weren't usually anything exciting or terribly surprising. They were the same kinds of dreams that I'd heard several of the orphans at the convent talk about. I was often falling down long dark tunnels or searching for something that I could never find in dense forests that were too smoky to navigate.

Shocking, I know, someone who was abandoned searching for something in their dreams. Like perhaps ... birth parents?

But this dream was different. In this dream, I was flying—soaring through the air. I dipped and weaved, using great golden wings that looked as if they belonged on a dragonfly to sail through the clouds. I lowered them, falling down several hundreds of feet until I found the tops of the trees. As I moved between the trees, the minds of the animals further below reached out and touched my own, greeting me as they might a familiar friend. Each time I climbed higher than the treetops I felt the frigid air slap against my cheeks, growing colder each time I tried to ascend again into the clouds, and ducked back down, taking shelter between the branches once more.

The farther I flew, the darker it seemed to get. The trees grew closer together, making it increasingly difficult to maneuver through them, their branches blocking out the light. Yet at the same time, the darker it grew amidst the branches, the clearer the ground below became. Just once, right before I dipped down below for the last time, I looked over my shoulder and saw the fire of a burning sun following me. It scared me, that sun.

My wings beat faster and what had originally been friendly greetings from the animals were now pleas for help, screaming in my ears. They grew louder and louder, echoing in my mind. I couldn't stop, though; if I stopped, I knew the sun would catch up to me. I ignored the cries from the animals as I darted above the treetops, turning in a circle. An icy wind blew against me, shoving me back, forcing me down into the branches. It lashed against me, painful and sharp. I gasped for breath as a branch slapped me in the face. I turned again, panting, searching. I needed a way out. I couldn't stay down here. The darkness was preferable to the chasing sun, but something told me that I wasn't just being chased—I was being herded into the waiting darkness. The darkness wasn't scary, it was comforting.

I sucked in a breath and made my choice. I dove straight down, caving into the feelings and sliding as far into the darkness waiting below as I could. As soon as the treetops closed in, removing all of the sun's rays and the ice from above, a light burst forth from my body, breaking through the darkness. I gaped as my skin glowed to life, a golden hue emanating from me, chasing away the shadows even as I followed after them—trying to catch them before they could disappear entirely. Small dark smoky trails disappeared in my hands as I reached for them, capturing them just as they slipped through my fingers. I didn't want it to leave. I didn't want to be alone again, but it was already gone. The darkness having been chased away by something inside of me.

A scream of frustration erupted out of me, both in my dream and in real life, startling me awake as I bolted upright in bed. My heart was pounding and sweat dripped down my neck as my breath heaved in and out of my chest.

For a moment, I just blinked and tried to breathe. It took me several more moments before I remembered why I wasn't back in the bunk room at the Convent of Amnestia. I wasn't there because I'd left, I'd been led away—again, by something inside of me just like my dream—to this place. A Fae castle on the edge of the human kingdom of Amnestia. My whole life had changed.

I wiped sweat from the back of my neck and turned to the side, wondering if my scream had woken Orion, but he was gone. I frowned. The rumpled sheets were the only sign he had ever been there at all. Stretching and pushing out of the bed, I got up and paused when I glanced over a slip of parchment that had been left, neatly folded on an assortment of clothes waiting for me on a chair next to my side of the bed. I picked up the creamy, thick paper and opened it.

A dress for you for today. We will be in the library. Come and meet us when you're ready. Feel free to use the facilities and eat first. - O

Well, that answered one question at least, I thought. I considered going to the bathing chamber and washing before getting dressed but decided against it. I didn't want to run into any of the other Fae if I could help it. As dinner last night had proven, I wasn't exactly a favorite of theirs.

I groaned when I finished dressing and turned to survey myself in the tall, oval mirror in the corner of Orion's bedroom. I should have known ... even though the material was thicker, it was still scandalous by human standards. The dress didn't so much have a slit up the side, as a side completely cut out of it up to the top of my hip, so that one need only push the material slightly, or possibly even walking too fast, and the wearer—which would be me—would be exposed. There was also a section cut from the opposite shoulder down to the hip where the slit came up. The material, itself, looked as if it were held together by little more than a tiny section of metal no larger than a fat coin. Some beading and a flower covered the area where the fabric connected and I couldn't help but wonder if it had been torn many times with the Fae's proclivity for sexual activities or if this was just how it was originally designed to be worn. It also made me wonder who these clothes belonged to.

With the dress on and my hair finger combed, I set off to the throne room since that seemed to double as a banquet room. *If that was where they kept the food then that was where I was going*, I decided as my stomach grumbled to life. I headed out, but after the third hallway I'd turned down, I stopped and looked around. I could've sworn this was the way to the banquet hall, but I should have already arrived. All of the hallways looked the same to me; there were only so many perfectly carved rock walls and fiery sconces I could look at before they all seemed to repeat themselves. Wait, *were* they repeating themselves? Had I been going in circles?

I had no clue what to do. Without any pixies or Fae in sight, I grimaced and turned, heading back the way I came. I'd just start from where I'd come from and hope I managed to figure it out from there. I followed my feet, as odd as that sounded, letting them lead me back through the odd twists and turns. My mind wandered and I let myself meander through the hallways until finally, as my stomach grumbled for the hundredth time, I stopped and stomped my foot in outrage. If they were going to have such a confusing castle, the least they could do was provide some sort of map.

Shoving my fingers through my short blonde hair and pulling in irritation as I let out another grunt of frustration, I looked to the empty walls and narrowed my eyes. "Hello?" I called. Nothing. "Pixies?" Surely the pixies wouldn't abandon me here. I fed those little bastards more than once. "If you help me out, I'll get you more Fae food," I offered aloud. I wasn't sure why they didn't eat the leftover food that the Fae didn't touch, but they constantly seemed to be starving and the few times I'd tossed them rolls or pastries they had been devoured in a matter of seconds.

A long corridor stretched in front of me and I was about to turn around when I felt this hum in my bones that made me want to move towards it. As I moved down the hallway, the hum only grew in its intensity until I stepped through an arch and the room opened up before me. A railing curled around a walkway that jutted out from the edges of the room, all of which hung above a giant spinning ball of strands of light. One was blue, one red, and one purple. As I continued to stare at it, the glass orb shuddered, vibrating with energy.

Inside the strands of light, there was something else. Another, smaller, orb. The second one looked as though it was made of all the elements and none, light and dark, fire and ice, lightning, but not the natural kind of lightning I'd seen strike the mountain during horrible thunderstorms that tore through the countryside in the summertime. I couldn't help but lean forward as I tried to get a closer look. As I did, the colors changed, distorted into one another so the flames that flickered across the surface occasionally morphed from the natural yellow and red to purples, blues, and greens.

It was like looking at all of creation and destruction. If I were to go back thousands of years and watch as the whole of our world was born, I might have seen something like this as it exploded—forming vast mountain ranges and valleys and plains and ... life. Life and death. Because there was no such thing as life without death. It was breathtaking. I might have stared at it forever if it wasn't for the footsteps that sounded down the hallway at my back.

I panicked. I didn't know if I was supposed to be here or not. Without a second thought, I backed up and pressed myself against the wall just by the door, hiding in the corner shadows as male voices flowed down the corridor. Hopefully, no one would be able to see me here.

"She needs to be tested. We can't just have a human milling around our Court harassing other Fae." Roan's voice was the first I could distinguish.

"She's a Changeling." That was Orion. "Not a human."

"We've established that with the fucking," Sorrell spoke— the third and final voice as they stopped just beyond the room, not yet entering but right there. So close. "Did you feel your magic replenish?" he asked.

Orion was quiet for a moment before speaking. "The Changeling was very responsive," he said. I waited for more, but after a moment when he hadn't spoken again, Sorrell responded.

"That doesn't answer my question," he said.

Someone sighed heavily. "I wasn't really paying attention," Orion answered. "During. I do feel stronger, though."

I cringed. *Wow*, I thought, *what a glowing review.* Then again, Orion wasn't the talker of the bunch.

"But do you feel stronger because of the girl or because you had sex?" Sorrell pressed.

"I don't know!" Orion snapped.

"Great," Roan said. "Shadow boy is too pussy sick to think straight."

"You're just mad that she didn't want to fuck you," Orion replied sharply.

"Enough!" Sorrell cut in. "There are other tests we can perform, but it will be tricky to get her to agree to it." He paused and I assumed there was some sort of silent exchange between the three of them. Maybe some eyebrow raising or swaggering. *Ugh, men.* These three gossiped and kept secrets worse than the women from the local villages. "We need to bombard her with enough magic to challenge her."

"But if she's not truly a Changeling, that might kill her," Orion said.

My eyes widened. *What was it with these Fae and trying to kill me? I mean, seriously, what did I ever do but break into their castle, eat their food, learn their secrets, sleep in their beds ...* I stopped and shook my head. Thinking about it really wasn't helping my case.

"If she's human," Sorrell repeated. "If you're so sure that she's a Changeling, then she should be fine. According to the book Groffet gave me, introducing her to high levels of powerful magic will trigger *her* magic. Fae who have not been taught or raised in the Courts often can't reach their magic for long stretches. If Fae children are not raised around magic, then they don't know how to actively recognize it. An adult Fae without magic is a liability. She needs magic if she's to survive the Courts. If she's human then, obviously, she will die, but she would be put to death anyway so it won't matter."

A cold lump formed in my stomach at Sorrell's words. What if this was all just a mistake? What if I really was human and Orion had just smelled something else on me? They were going to kill me. Maybe not intentionally, but they were going to do it. A shudder worked its way down my spine. Okay, I decided internally. It was time to cut and run. I needed to get out of here. How? I didn't know, but it needed to happen. Maybe I could talk the pixies into helping me, but first I needed to figure out what else they might be planning and then figure out a way to get out of this room without them knowing that I'd been listening.

"You want to risk killing a Changeling because a book that is centuries old says it works as a test to bring out her Fae powers?" Orion scoffed. At least he sounded offended by my potential death. Good to know that I'd chosen the one with a conscience to fuck me.

"Listen, just because you've got your cock wet for once doesn't mean I don't know what I'm talking about. Groffet and I did plenty of research and this is the fastest, most reliable test we could find."

"What harm could it do?" Roan asked.

"It could kill her, you idiots," Orion said, a growl in his tone.

"Then there's one less Changeling," Sorrell said dryly. "The last member of the Brightling Court is snuffed out like the rest of her Court. She's not supposed to exist anyway," he hissed, his voice cold and hard.

I swallowed and tried to steady my breathing, but I was getting dangerously close to full on panicking. I could feel sweat forming against my brow and sliding down the small of my back. My hands were damp.

"I'm not agreeing to anything until I see this book for myself," Orion said, his voice low and rough.

"Fine, come to my section of the library," Sorrell said, his words clipped and tight with irritation.

As their footsteps faded back down the hall, I allowed myself a few shaky breaths before I got myself back under control. I stepped into the corridor, moving quickly as I retraced my steps. When I was back in the main hallway, I called out again, "Pixies? Could someone lead me to the throne room? I'll give you some food when we get there if it's out."

This time a gaggle of pixies descended from the ceiling all seeming to jockey for position in front of me as they waved me forward to follow them. If I had any amusement left in my body to laugh, I might've, but I was far too concerned with the fact that the three Fae in charge of this Court were trying to kill me. I smiled at the buzzing pixies and let them lead me, pushing and shoving each other as they tried to get my attention—and the food I was offering at the end of our journey. I forced myself to relax, breathing in through my nose and releasing the air through my lips as we strode down the corridor.

I nodded to the pixies and whispered a promise to come back soon with food, as they led me straight to the entrance of the throne and banquet room. They nodded and disappeared back into the walls and ceilings as I leaned around the corner, peering into the large room as quietly as possible. As far as I could see, though, there was no one waiting for me. I ventured towards the closest table with food on it and grabbed a handful of rolls before tossing a few—snickering lightly as pixies shot back out of the walls and ceiling to snatch the food and buzz away as their tiny little sharp teeth ripped into the succulent pastries.

As I wandered around the different food laden tables I realized I'd never consistently liked the food the nuns made, although no one else seemed to have any issues with it, but I loved the food here. Was Fae food addicting for humans? If I escaped would I be able to find food this good again? The questions plagued me as I began to stuff my face with fruit, what I assumed were vegetable dishes, pastries, and anything else I could get my hands on. I even tried some of the Fae wine that Orion had warned me about. It was all delicious. And okay, maybe I was stuffing my face to comfort myself. Food made me feel better.

If I was going to escape and be on the run from potentially murderous Fae, then I needed to fuel up and that was something I'd never had the opportunity to do before. The pixies came and went, clearing plate after plate as I worked my way through all the different dishes, trying everything and having seconds of what I liked the most. By the time I was done, I was ready for a nap, my belly pleasantly full and my mind completely relaxed despite the thoughts of my imminent death. The food had done its job.

"By the Gods look at this one, gorged herself stupid, she has," a rough feminine voice came from behind me, but I couldn't see who was speaking.

"She'll need it for what's coming, though. Dark times ahead, indeed," another, more masculine voice replied.

I wanted to turn and give whoever was speaking a piece of my mind, but I couldn't get my eyes to open, sleep had taken me too far down. It was only when someone shook my shoulder that I startled back to reality to find Orion's night sky eyes staring down at me.

"Feeling okay, Changeling?" he asked.

Back to Changeling, was it? Their conversation in the hallway replayed at hyper speed in my head. My mouth dried up, no words willing to make it past my lips, so instead, I just made a croaking sound.

"Here, have some water," he said as he handed me the glass that had been sitting to my right while I ate.

I gratefully accepted it and guzzled the contents, wetting

my chapped lips and dry throat as though I hadn't had a drink in days.

"Better?" he asked.

"Much. Thank you," I said, feeling suddenly wary.

"Are you feeling okay? I left the note for you to meet us in the library, but when you didn't show up I came looking for you," he said, concern pinching his brows, but there was something off about his face, as though he was reading from a script.

"Fine, just ate too much and fell asleep."

"Would you like to see what we've found?" he asked, holding his hand out to me.

I stood and noticed his eyes rake over me even though he seemed to try and resist it at first. We walked out into the hall and towards what I assumed was the library where the others were waiting to kill me. Death by magic. At least it would be a fancy exit, not many people in this region could say they went out that way. I looked up at Orion, which was silly because I almost stumbled as we were walking, which made him stop and look at me. I felt something pushing inside me and then words came spilling out.

"Please don't kill me," I blurted, startling him. "Don't let them kill me. You have such good food, and I just started having sex, and that's fun, and it would be really awful if I couldn't do that again. And you have really pretty eyes and a nice chest, and an even better cock." My Gods, I couldn't seem to stop talking. "I really don't understand why people don't talk to you more when you're the nicest Fae I've ever met and really good in bed. I mean seriously the best—not that I've had a whole lot of experience, but do you really need experience to know what makes you feel good?" I couldn't stop. It just kept coming out. Word vomit. I clamped a hand over my mouth to stop myself from talking.

Orion's eyes went wide and his jaw dropped open for a

moment before he visibly seemed to regain his composure and asked, "Why do you think we're going to kill you?"

I pressed my lips together and held my hand over them so I couldn't answer, but when Orion pried my fingers away my lips popped open and I said, "Because I found this big spiny orb thing that is all magic-y and makes me want to touch it, then I heard you talking about testing me with magic and if I'm human it will just kill me and I'm pretty sure I'm human. At least, I think I am. I've never had Fae powers—even when I was a kid. Seriously, why am I saying all this out loud? I can't stop!"

"Someone must have put a charm in your drink," he began and when I narrowed my eyes he quickly raised his hands defensively and added, "It wasn't me! It's a loose lips charm. It lowers the barrier between what the person is thinking and what they say, it also makes them more suggestible to ideas."

"Can we skip the library and have sex again?" The question popped out before I could even register that I was thinking it. I clamped my hand over my mouth again, pinning my lips in place.

Orion stared at me, his wide eyes watching me with concern and confusion. Then he laughed. Not just any laugh, but an uncontrollable one. He covered his mouth, but I heard the laughs as they escaped. He shook his head, turning away as he tried to get himself under control. It was so startling that it made me laugh too. I dropped my hand slowly and when he looked back at me, still stifling laughter, I couldn't help it anymore. A small chuckle turned into a laugh and then another and another, until the both of us were wiping tears from our eyes.

I paused when I looked back at his face and saw black streaks cascading down his cheeks. I dropped my hands and reached out towards him. He stilled, his laughter cutting off abruptly, as I brushed my thumb against his skin, swiping the tear from its path. I pulled my hand back and looked at the black liquid on my skin for a moment before it was oddly absorbed into me.

"What is this?" I asked.

"It's part of being a prince of the Night Court," he said quietly. "It's one of the reasons people stay away from me."

"Why?" I asked.

"The Night Court is..." He grimaced, cutting himself off. "It's difficult to explain and I'm not sure now is the right time for that."

"Well," I started, "I think you're sexy, and if they are turning away from you because of the color of your tears then that's their loss. I want you, Orion. I want to get to know you, learn about you and your past and what you want for the future if you'll let me and don't end up killing me when you bombard me with magic. Are you sure you don't want to have sex one last time?" I slapped my hand over my mouth again as my, apparently filthy, mind took a left turn from complimenting the man to trying to get him into bed. Again.

He chuckled softly, before he said, "I wouldn't let them do this if I didn't believe you were a Changeling. You trusted me to make your first time good, trust me with this?"

I wanted to tell him there was a huge difference between making sex good and possibly dying, but I did trust him, all the way down to my toes, and that was what mattered, so I nodded. He took my hand once more and led me onward.

CHAPTER 16
CRESS

Orion led me to a great big room that looked as if it'd been taken straight from a storybook. The nuns at the convent had kept a few books here and there, but nothing so grand as this. I released him as I stumbled forward, standing in the middle of the room with my head craned back as I just turned and turned.

"These are all yours?" I asked, mouth agape.

He chuckled, but before he could respond, the doors opened and Sorrell and Roan appeared. They'd been talking quietly, their heads tilted down towards each other as if they were sharing secrets, but as soon as they looked up and saw me, their words cut off. *Wow,* I thought, *way to not hide the fact that they were talking about me. Who knew I could be so popular?*

"You found her," Sorrell said with a nod Orion's way.

"Was I lost?" I asked. Other than the look of irritation he shot me, he didn't respond to my question. Asshole.

"Where's Groffet?" Orion asked.

"He's doing his duties," Roan said.

I pursed my lips, but despite the fact that Orion nodded in understanding, neither of them gave me anything—not a look, not an explanation of who this Groffet was or what duties he was doing. It was like I was invisible. Lovely.

I headed for the desk towards the back and center of the library, clambering up onto the platform, my skirts tangling around my legs as I hefted my much smaller frame onto the small stage. "Hasn't anyone here heard of stairs?" I grumbled as I rolled and popped up to my feet.

Roan smirked as he strode forward without saying anything. He moved around the side of the platform. He waved his hand over a section of the floor and a set of small stairs leading up to the desk appeared—rising from the floor.

"Oh." I blinked down at it dumbly. Well then ...

I scooted several stacks of books to the side and perched on the corner of the desk, folding my hands in my lap and adjusting myself so that all of my bits were covered before finally looking up and meeting their gazes. Sorrell looked as if he'd swallowed a particularly sour fruit. "Well," I started, "let's do this. Test me. Hit me with the magic. Wham. Bam. Magic me, man."

Sorrell walked past Roan and with a twist of his hand in the air, he made a spiral of blue sparks appear. "Wait—" Orion held his hand out but it was too late. The blue sparks slammed into my chest, nearly knocking me off the desk.

I let out an *oomph* and sent a stack of books to the floor when I reached out and grabbed onto the edge of the desk, clutching it for all that I was worth as frost crept through my veins. A shiver skirted down my spine and when I breathed, cold clouds of air escaped from between my lips.

"I thought I said to wait!" Orion snapped as I managed to get myself under control. Other than a sharp and barely bearable cold wave that hit my system, it honestly wasn't that bad.

"We don't have time to wait, Orion," Sorrell replied coolly. "We need to ascertain if this girl is, in fact, a Changeling and if she is, if she's from the Brightling Court."

I huffed out a breath, inhaling and exhaling quickly as if doing so would make the cold go away faster. Gods, it was freezing. I put my hands to my arms and rubbed up and down rapidly, trying to get some warmth back into my limbs. When I looked up, Orion was standing in front of Sorrell, clutching his shirt in his hands that swirled with darkness. I shook my head, sure I was seeing things—but I wasn't. Dark tendrils seeped out of his skin, between his knuckles. Sorrell didn't even flinch as the curls reached up and stroked him with their magic.

"It's your turn," Sorrell said calmly.

"Orion," I called, sliding off of the desk onto shaky legs. "I-it's fine."

Orion's gaze snapped to mine and he cursed. "Your lips are turning blue," he growled.

I shrugged. "Ice man has that effect on people, I guess."

"Ice man?" Sorrell's white-blue eyes narrowed on me at the insult.

I arched a brow his way. "Problem?" I countered. I really wanted to punch him in his smug handsome face. Yeah, okay, I could admit he was handsome, but he was also an asshole. And if I knew how to punch then I totally would've done it. Punched him right in his nose.

"This is a fucking disaster," Orion said.

"If you won't do it, then I guess I'll have to take my turn," Roan announced. All heads turned his way and this time, I didn't even see it coming before a wave of fire stole through me, red coils of magic—crimson smoke—wrapped around me. It sucked all of the coldness away until nothing was left but a burning heat. Sweat poured down my spine. I fanned my face and stumbled away from the desk as I tried to get my dress off.

"What are you doing?" Orion rushed towards me.

"It's hot," I complained. It was more than hot, it was impossibly humid. Sweltering.

"Stop." He stayed my hands, holding my wrists. I squirmed,

wrestling to get free of him. I needed my clothes off. I needed something to relieve the feel of fire boiling in my veins. Man, they hadn't been kidding about this magic nearly killing me. I felt like I was already dying from heatstroke or something. My lips and tongue were dry. My throat parched. I needed something to drink.

"Water," I croaked. "I need water."

Orion shook his head, his lips moving as he spoke, but whatever he said was lost to me. I couldn't hear anything but the rushing of blood in my veins—powering through my ears. The rush of it was like a mighty storm.

One more ... I just had one more magic to deal with. His. One more and this would all be over. I could feel his darkness reaching for me. When I looked down at where he clasped my wrists, I saw the tendrils curling around my fingers—brushing against my skin. It didn't hurt.

My skin looked strangely golden, as if it were glowing under all that darkness. Orion's eyes met mine. His lips parted. I didn't know what he was saying, but I nodded my head anyway—hoping he was asking for permission. Man, I really wanted to get this test over with. I was getting tired. My lids drooped as I slumped forward.

Orion caught me and cradled me against his chest. Over his shoulder, I saw Roan move closer—his red hair like a flame under the light of the room. His lips were turned down in a frown. I knew Sorrell was behind him, but I couldn't see that far back. Roan was enough. His eyes as they lifted and met mine were confused and ... almost apologetic. He hadn't seemed apologetic a moment ago when he'd shot me with his magic. I knew I'd asked for it and all that, but man, he could've at least warned me.

I stared at him, keeping my eyes on his as Orion's black magic swirled around me—around us. It rose up from his skin and burst outward until all that I saw was black. A dark oblivion. I was almost completely shrouded by darkness when something else crept forward—that fire from before. It wrapped around me, coiling tightly and shielded me from the dark gloom of Orion's magic. It clung to me, but this time, it wasn't burning. It was ... nice, actually. Really nice. I snuggled into it and felt my body being lifted and passed to someone else.

New arms closed around me, warm and safe. Strange. I'd never felt safe with anyone before. Not until Orion, but as these new limbs curled beneath my back and thighs, hoisting me against an equally warm chest, I realized I felt that now. I felt protected. Maybe I was crazy—it wouldn't have been the first time I thought that. Fae were supposed to be enemies of the human race—my own best friend had been terrified of them—but ever since arriving at this magical castle, I'd felt everything but afraid. I'd felt confused, angry, excited, irritated, and hungry, but never terrified. Not true fear. They didn't scare me, but if I was honest with myself, what they made me feel was far more dangerous. They made me feel almost ... secure.

CHAPTER 17
CRESS

I woke up with a headache. I tried to open my eyes and was met with a burning light. With a groan, I slammed them shut again and rolled over onto my side. My hands spread out. Without my sight, I had to feel out where I was. Covers—sheets softer than anything I'd ever felt—moved against my skin, sliding down to my waist as I hesitantly sat up.

It took several more minutes for me to even crack my eyelids open without feeling like a shard of pure sunlight was being stabbed through my skull. When I did, I surveyed my surroundings. It wasn't Orion's room, but it was a bedroom. I sat up and moved to the side, frowning down at my body. My clothes had been removed and I'd been changed. I should've felt violated, perhaps even angry, but honestly—whoever had dressed me had far better sense than the guys because no longer was I wearing a skimpy dress made of nothing. Instead, I was dressed in a man's shirt that hung down to my thighs and tight trousers that were obviously made for someone much taller. At least, it had to have been made for someone taller considering that the ends of each leg were bunched up several inches at my ankles and the waistband was above my belly button. At least they were comfortable, I decided as I stretched out a leg and then my other and hopped off the bed.

I looked back as I stood up and noticed that the bed, itself, was much larger than anything I'd ever seen. It was larger, even, than Orion's had been with dark red sheets tucked around the edges. The rest of the room was set to match as well. With deep burgundy curtains covering the windows and similarly colored drapes hanging from the ceiling. Paintings marred the surface of the stone walls. Depictions of beasts I'd never before seen—soaring through the skies, hunting through forests, swimming in deep oceans. Each was more detailed than the last. One beast was so lifelike that I could've sworn its fur was glistening and shifting with an invisible breeze blowing across it.

I reached out to see if it was when a voice stopped me. "I see you're awake."

I paused, my hand half raised—the itch to stroke the fur warring with my need to look over my shoulder. The second urge won out over the first as I sighed and turned around.

Roan stood in the doorway, his arms crossed over his massive chest as he eyed me. "Did you paint this?" I asked, pointing to the image.

"I did." He dropped his arms and strode further into the room. I didn't flinch away as he walked right up to me, towering over me with his much larger frame. I just tilted my head back and looked up at him, waiting. "You're not afraid of me?" he asked.

"Should I be?"

He frowned, but instead of answering he asked another question. "Do you remember what happened?"

"I remember you hitting me with magic—all three of you— and then I remember passing out," I answered. "That's about it. What happened? I'm not dead, so I assume I passed the test."

His lips pressed together before he parted them again on a

sigh. "You passed," he said, but it didn't sound like he was happy about that. "The results, however, were inconclusive."

"What does that mean?"

"It means that while you survived being bombarded with three different types of magic, we still weren't able to say if you're from the Brightling Court. You showed an affinity for a different type of magic."

"Which magic?" I asked. He leaned forward as if he wanted to touch me, his eyes scanning down my form. I shifted, frowning as my curiosity rose. "Roan?"

His lips twitched. "Why aren't you afraid?" I wasn't sure if he was asking me or if the question just slipped out. His eyes appeared unfocused. Even though he was looking straight at me, it felt like he was looking *through* me.

"I don't know," I answered anyway. "I guess you just don't seem that scary to me."

He hummed beneath his breath. The scent of spices and burning wood filled my nostrils. It was actually quite pleasant. It made me want to push my face forward and bury it in his chest—the source of the scent—and breathe it in as deeply as I could.

"You showed an affinity for the Court of Crimson's magic," he finally said after a beat of silence.

"Okay..." I didn't know what that meant.

"It's magic from *my* Court," he continued.

"What does that mean?" I pressed. I felt my body incline forward, slanting towards his. I couldn't seem to help it.

"It means, little Changeling," he started, reaching up and pinching my chin between his thumb and forefinger, "that you might actually be from my Court."

"Is that bad?" I asked.

He shook his head. "It's not bad so much as it's ... unexpected."

"Why unexpected?" I pulled myself back, removing my chin

from his grasp as my brows lowered. "Do you think I'm not good enough for the Court of fire?"

"Court of Crimson," he corrected.

"Whatever." I waved my hands before propping them on my hips. "Do you think I'm not good enough?"

"It's not about being good enough," Roan said with a grin. "It's just that Fae from the Court of Crimson are ... well, they're not like you."

The more my eyes narrowed, the wider his lips stretched. His smile irritated me—like he was laughing at my expense. "And what's that supposed to mean?" I grumbled irritably.

He chuckled, the sound low and vibrating. I felt like it reached deep within my body and lit a flame. My palms began to sweat. I wiped them down my sides. "No need to get defensive, little Changeling," he said. "I'm merely saying that you're not what I'd expect of a crimson Fae."

"What's a crimson Fae like then?" I asked.

Roan moved until he was pressed against me. Then he leaned down and a shiver stole through me as his lips brushed my ear as he spoke. "Crimson Fae are dangerous creatures. Full of blood and fire and sex," he whispered.

My thoughts poofed. They were there one second and gone the next. When Roan pulled away again, all I could do was blink up at him. Stunned. My jaw dropped as he gave me another smile, wicked and charming all at once. He nudged my face up.

"I'm here to find out why a creature such as yourself—like an innocent baby bird—would have an affinity for magic such as mine," he said.

Gods help me, but that sounded far more dangerous than nearly dying, and I wasn't at all sure I was ready to find out what he meant this time.

CHAPTER 18
CRESS

His words beat at my skin like my very pulse. *Full of blood and fire and sex. Blood and fire and sex. Fire and sex. Sex with Roan.* I had to bite my lip to stop the moan that was building within me from escaping. A shudder rippled through my body and I knew he felt it considering how he was pressed against me.

"Are you having naughty thoughts about me?" he asked, his voice a low growl next to me as his lips brushed against the delicate skin of the shell of my ear while his breath warmed my neck.

When a strangled sound of embarrassment escaped my throat, he chuckled. The dark sound sank into me and became one with my very bones. I knew in that moment as I stared up at eyes the color of glowing embers and hair I couldn't wait to run my fingers through that I wanted to hear that sound again. I'd do whatever I could to make that happen. Here in his room, alone with me, Roan was different. Gone was the cocky asshole, the brutish leader I'd first met; instead, there was a softer man, one who actually seemed to give a shit, and that was almost more than I could handle in my current state.

"What do you want, Roan?" I asked, my voice breathier than I would have liked.

"I told you, I want to find out why your body likes my magic so much," he replied with a grin.

"And we have to do this in your bedroom?"

"If we want privacy, yes. If you'd prefer the rest of the castle to watch then we can return to the throne room if you'd like?" He raised both his eyebrows in question, the dark red slashes mocking me, knowing that the last thing I would want was an audience.

"Here's fine," I said before sliding out from where he had pinned me to the wall.

Amusement danced in his eyes as he turned and watch me search for somewhere to sit that wasn't the bed. He had a writing desk that looked so fancy I was scared to touch it for fear that my very presence might destroy it somehow. Then there was an armchair that looked so overly stuffed that if I sat on it, it might explode. All of his room was done in dark tones of red, with bright areas coming from the sconces on the wall and the windows that opened up to the rays of daylight currently streaming through. It suddenly reminded me of a question I'd never had the chance to even ask let alone see if they would answer. They may not have before when they were suspicious of me being human but now that I was officially a Changeling—*don't freak out, don't freak out, don't freak out*—I was hoping they'd be more honest with me, or at least give me a chance to process it before throwing the next test at me. That might be too much to ask of three Fae princes though.

"Why did you land the castle here? There's nothing around, it would take ages to get anywhere, and it's certainly not close to the battlefields. Why choose this valley?" I asked, crossing my arms over my chest as I stopped on the other side of his bed.

Roan's eyes tightened at the edges. Clearly, he hadn't

expected my question and it made him tense. Why, I wasn't sure, but there was something behind it that bothered him, something he didn't want to tell me. "We just needed a break, little bird. It was either here or keep going to our final destination. As you said, this isn't near the battlefields, so we thought it would be a good place to stop."

He never looked away when he spoke to me and yet during that entire speech, he'd barely made eye contact with me. It was a lie. That much was as plain as the sun in the sky. Ever since he had almost scared me to death in the throne room, I had known that he'd been a very direct person, charismatic, but direct, in an almost off putting way; the way only a prince could be in my limited experience.

I wouldn't let that dissuade me though, so I asked, "Why did you just lie to me?"

His eyes shot to mine, a little wider than they had been a moment ago. "You accuse me of lying to you?" He sounded astonished that someone would dare say such a thing. I was beginning to think that these princes had everyone in this castle licking their boots and thanking them for the opportunity to be helpful.

"I do. You just lied. I want to know why and I want to know what the truth is or I'll leave the room and won't let you test your precious Court of Crimson magic on me," I said.

I wasn't sure when I had become so brave with these men, but I was tired of being yanked around. I'd done what they asked, submitted to their tests, now all I wanted was some answers. That, surely, was not too much to ask.

"Fine, go, but if you do, you will be burning with your desire for me from the moment you set foot through those doors," he growled, heat washing into his gaze, and I knew he was pulling on his magic. He meant his threat literally. I thought of the warm heat that made me want to strip down in the library, that had me begging Orion for a glass of water, and had me tuning out everything anyone was saying because all I could focus on was the need to find some relief from it. That was not something I wanted to experience again, and yet I couldn't help but goad him slightly.

"Trying to get me to wander around the castle naked?" I teased. When he responded with a silent sneer I huffed out a sigh and finally sat down on the armchair, no longer caring if it exploded around me. Roan would deserve it if it did. It didn't though, and I sank into it as I imagined one would sink into a cloud. When I tried to readjust to find a better position that didn't have the cushions trying to swallow me whole I realized I couldn't move. I was stuck exactly where I was, the cushions of the chair holding me tightly in their fluffy grip. "Um, Roan? Why is your chair trying to eat me?"

A wicked smile curved the edge of his lips. "It's a safety precaution," he replied quietly as he rounded the bed and sat down opposite me.

"How is a chair a safety precaution?" I demanded.

"You can't get up, can you?" he asked, cocking an eyebrow at me.

I shook my head.

"So, if someone were to say, break into my room and wait for me so they could attack me, most likely they would take a seat, then when they try to get up... As a bonus, I get to see who wants to do me harm and interrogate them," he said, his voice turning cold at the end.

"People try to attack you?" I asked, suddenly wondering why he was even trusting me to be there if that was the case.

"Sorrell, Orion, and I are frequently at risk of assassination. I know Orion told you about the pixie taste testers. Well, we each have something in our rooms that keeps it secure from anyone it's not aligned to as well. It helps prevent some nasty surprises. Not all by any means, but some."

"So, this chair is rigged to trap anyone who sits in it that's not you?" I asked to make sure I understood what he was saying.

He nodded and said, "Or Sorrell and Orion. The three of us never trap each other. It would leave us too vulnerable."

The seriousness with which he spoke sent a shiver down my spine. Their lives were constantly in danger. No wonder they'd reacted to me the way they had. Hell, that made Orion a little crazy if he was willing to go to bed with me and risk me trying to kill him. "Will you release me?" I asked, feeling vulnerable myself.

The wicked smile returned and made my insides melt and heat pool in my core. I'd just been with Orion and here I was lusting after Roan, but I didn't care. To me, it felt as natural as breathing, and I wasn't going to apologize for who I was, not anymore. That behavior could stay with the nuns and their shame ridden lives.

"Maybe. If you promise to let me experiment on you with my magic," he said finally, as he let his eyes roam over my body. I felt sexier in the shirt and pants than I had in the scraps of material they had called a dress the day before.

"Will you answer my question truthfully?" I asked.

Disappointment flashed across his features, and if I hadn't been staring at him I would have missed it. He'd been hoping that I had forgotten about his lie, about the question I'd asked, but I hadn't. I was more curious than a cat and it would prob-ably get me killed one day but I was willing to risk it at least in that moment. "I will, if you'll answer one of mine truthfully," he countered.

"Deal," I replied, extending the one arm that wasn't suctioned to the armchair.

We shook like civilized beings. Tingles ran over my skin everywhere he touched me as we both grinned at each other as if we both knew it was a facade and neither of us was very good at being civilized. He was obviously more talented at faking it than I was, but there was a wildness hiding just underneath that I wanted to rile up and see explode out of this Fae until all the shreds of civility were gone. It didn't help that every time he smiled I could see it just a little more in the set of his jaw. Something about Roan drove me wild in a different way than Orion.

Roan muttered something and made a gesture with his hand and the armchair relaxed, the cushions deflating and turning to normal. I remained seated, I wasn't going to let some fabric and stuffing almost eating me scare me out of my comfy seat. I straightened my shirt and looked at Roan once more, staring him dead in the eye as I said, "So, why land the castle here?"

"It wasn't by choice," he said quietly, pausing for a moment as if to take in my reaction. When I didn't give one, simply sat there and blinked at him—waiting for the rest of it—he continued. "In each Fae Court, there is a Lanuaet. This is a magical device that we use to move the castles and Courts to ensure that we cannot be pinned down by the enemy. The device was designed to use the magic of four powerful Fae in combination to control the movements of the Court. We've found, over the years, that royals seem to be the only Fae capable of powering the Lanuaet. Unfortunately, however, as the years have progressed—with the war with humankind—bloodlines have grown thin. Where once there had been a multitude of royals to choose from, there are now very few."

"Four powerful Fae?" I repeated. "But there's only three of you."

He nodded. "Exactly. For our Court, we only have Orion, Sorrell, and me. Usually, we manage to handle it, but if we're not all in top form, completely charged with magic, then it becomes more challenging. We landed here because we had to. It was either land somewhere we knew was safe or risk landing in a dangerous zone or on top of a human settlement when we ran out of power." He pulled a hand through the dark red locks of his hair and I watched as I processed the words he'd just said.

"And, just for clarification purposes, you charge your magic with sex?"

He nodded, a wicked grin curving his lips. "Want to try?"

I ignored his suggestion and said, "So, it had nothing to do with the area or with me? It was just because one of you didn't get laid enough?" I asked, a small smile curving my lips in return even though I didn't mean for it to happen.

He shook his head with a chuckle. "Sorry to disappoint, little bird, but we didn't know you were here," he replied.

Somehow, I thought the three of them were drowning in willing partners, but whether they actually took them to bed or not I couldn't say, and I tried not to care either. I wanted to know more, so much more, about how this castle worked and what it meant to be a Changeling that the feeling was almost overwhelming. Everything in my life had changed so quickly and so completely that I felt like a totally different person than the girl who had stumbled into the castle in her nightdress.

"I wonder if that had anything to do with the noise I heard," I mused aloud, intending for the words to only be for myself.

Roan's eyes sought my gaze. "What noise?"

"The night I stumbled into the castle, well, earlier that day, I'd woken up to this awful screeching noise that was so bad my ears were bleeding and the nuns had to sedate me to get me to stop screaming. Once the sedation wore off it was night and the castle was here. It's why I was just in a nightdress when I was wandering around," I replied, feeling unsure about sharing something so private with him.

"The Lanuaet was fighting us that day, resisting the directions we were giving it, which is why it was taking so much magic to make it move the castle."

"And it wasn't working?" I asked.

"No, it was working, but it was fighting us, like it had a mind of its own or something. It's always loud to us when we use it, but I've never heard of it being loud to someone else, and to hear it across a distance like that... I'll have to get Sorrell to do some research on it, or maybe even Groffet. That dwarf is a wizard at finding out obscure pieces of information, not literally though. I just wish I knew why it was fighting us." His voice had gone distant as though he was remembering how it had felt to work with the magic while it was fighting him, and I could see lines of strain pop up on his face.

"Has it ever done that before?" I asked, hopefully breaking the replay of the memory, I knew from experience that those could be painful to be stuck in.

He shook his head. We both sat in silence mulling over the information we had shared. After a moment Roan looked up at me, his eyes sparkling once again and he said, "Want to see what kind of Crimson magic you've got?"

I nodded, at least that would be something that could be useful in the future. I might have real, live magic and not know it, and if Roan could help me find it then I was all for it, even if he was a dick sometimes.

CHAPTER 19
ROAN

S he was a curious little thing, Cress. Unique in a way that I'd never seen before. Then again, I shouldn't have been surprised since she was the first Changeling I'd ever met. Changelings in lore were known to be powerful and I assumed she would be, but Changelings were also often ostracized for their upbringing. With how things were between mankind and Fae, it wouldn't surprise me if she would be as well. So far, she'd only had to deal with me, Orion, and Sorrell, but soon the time would come that she'd have to be released on the rest of the Court.

My thoughts permeated my actions as I led her to an open section of the room. A place where the stone floor had been charred and left black by many a spell I'd cast there. She let me lead her and position her as I would without a fight, and as I circled her, stepping close to her back, I leaned down and inhaled her unique scent.

"Lift your arms," I commanded gruffly. She did as I ordered, her arms rising up, pale and slender as I watched. In this, I was the composer and she was my instrument. "Repeat after me." I waited for her to nod before I recited an old incantation—one of the first I'd learned in my lessons of magic—as I touched her and pushed some of my magic into her skin. She repeated my words in a soft whisper and within moments, a glow began to form along her flesh. I moved away from her back and returned to her front once more, noting how her eyes had widened as she stared at her hands and arms—glowing and getting brighter as time went on.

"What did I do?" she asked.

"It's a light spell," I answered. "Nothing too dangerous."

She waved her arms up and down, flapping them like a bird might flap its wings and I found myself chuckling at the movement. "No, stop that." I reached forward and caught her hands in mine. She froze, her small face tipped back as she stared up at me. I felt the magic leave her skin and sink into me. Her arms and hands lost their glow.

"What else can I do?" She whispered the question.

I blinked, realizing how close I'd gotten to her. So close that we were nearly chest to chest. I could feel her breath on me. I released her and backed up. "We don't know yet, but we do know that you have a capacity for magic, so you're definitely a Changeling."

"Does that mean no more tests?" she asked, louder than before.

I nodded. "I don't see why it'd be necessary."

She tilted her head to the side, white-blonde hair sliding over her shoulders. "What's the Court of Crimson like?" she asked suddenly.

An automatic stiffness stole over my shoulders, atrophying my muscles. The feeling spread, moving into my chest and down my arms and legs making it difficult for me to turn away and stride back across the room. "It's a Fae Court like any other," I said without looking up.

"Then why won't you look at me when you say that?" she asked, the sound of her footsteps following me as I moved to a table with a pitcher on it. I stopped at the table and retrieved a glass, pouring some of the fresh water into it before lifting the cup to my lips and downing it. "Roan?"

I shook my head. It didn't matter how many times I reminded her, she continued with that damn name. No prince or my Lord for her. No, she went straight for the name. "The Court of Crimson is a dangerous Court," I finally admitted, keeping my gaze on the surface of the table, tracing the marks and scars that had been left from many years of use.

"Why?" she pressed, curiosity coloring her tone.

Memories surfaced—of blood sacrifices, of cold faces, of Franchesca's betrayal. My hand clamped around the glass in my fist until it shattered. I turned abruptly and glared at the source of my irritation.

"It just is," I gritted out. "Leave it alone."

With that, I shook out my hand, letting the glass shards rain down on the tabletop. "Call the pixies to clean this up," I ordered before turning and striding from the room.

CHAPTER 20

CRESS

R oan left the room angry. I didn't understand it, but even
after I called the pixies to help clean up the broken cup
he'd left behind, I couldn't find the patience to wait for him to
come back. I left Roan's bedroom and began searching the
castle. Instead of finding him, however, I found myself back in
the library where I'd passed out from magic overload. As I
strode into the room, curving around a stack of books taller
than myself, I heard a grumble followed by a grunt and then
watched as a landslide of books fell off of a nearby table onto a
small creature.

"Hello?" I called out as several books were swatted away
and the small creature squirmed and wiggled out of the pile all
the while cursing quietly.

The whispers cut off. "Yes?" the creature called back.

"Do you need some help?"

"I wouldn't be averse to it," the creature replied. The prim
way he said it made me grin as I got on my knees and began
lifting books away from his small body until I uncovered a
rather hairy little man with a long scraggly gray beard and a
crooked nose. I blinked at him and he blinked back.

"What are you?" I blurted.

"I am not a what," he huffed, getting to his feet and dusting himself off. "I am a who. I'm Groffet, my lady." He held out his hand. "Prince Sorrell's personal steward, at your service."

"Steward?" I took his hand anyway even as I frowned in confusion.

"Yes. You must be the Changeling."

"That's me—how'd you know?"

"Young lady,"—Groffet found a pair of spectacles on the ground and lifted them up, holding them in front of his face and grimacing at the single crack that ran down the center of one lens—"I have been around for quite some time and I have been Master Sorrell's steward for the last twenty years or so. You are not the first Changeling I've ever met. There's a tell."

"There is?" My eyes widened and I nearly choked as I watched Groffet point one fat, grubby finger at the crack of his lens and run the tip of his finger down the fissure, and as he did so, the broken pieces sealed themselves together, leaving behind nothing but a perfect pair of spectacles. "How did you do that?" I demanded.

Groffet placed his glasses on his nose, pushing them up until they settled against his face perfectly before he looked at me. "Magic," he answered. "And there is—your wonderment is tell enough."

I scooted back as the small man got up and waddled around me, waving his finger again. My mouth popped open as books began to ascend from where they'd fallen and restack themselves on the nearest surface. Some remained on the floor, some lifted and settled on the table and some flew about the room until they found places on the shelves and squeezed themselves in.

"Mother of the Gods..." I breathed in startled bewilderment, "that's amazing."

"It's nothing," Groffet commented as he moved towards the

platform in the center of the room and continued up the stair-case in the back until he reached the desk. "Now," he clambered up into the seat, pressed a lever and was lifted until the top of his hat was visible over the top, "what can I do for you, young Changeling?"

"Um..." I glanced around. "You can tell me where the guys are?"

"Guys?" he repeated, lifting up further in his seat until he stood and leaned over the top of the desk. "You wouldn't, perhaps, be referring to the princes, would you?"

I nodded. "Yeah, them."

"*Guys*," he muttered, shaking his head. Had I said something wrong? "Prince Sorrell is reading in his personal study; I would highly recommend not interrupting him, and Prince Orion is—"

"What about Roan?" I interrupted.

"Prince Roan is unavailable," Groffet said.

I frowned. "Why?"

Groffet lifted one bushy eyebrow. "Why is he unavailable?"

"Yes," I said. "Why is he unavailable? Where is he? What is he doing? He was supposed to teach me Crimson magic." Groffet chuckled lowly. "Is that funny?" I asked.

Instead of answering, he clambered back down from his chair and continued to chuckle as he descended the stairs and began waddling around the room, flicking his finger in the air —pointing to various shelves as books came flying out. I ducked when one almost collided with my head. Another sailed over my shoulder, nearly clipping me in the side. I backed away from the flying books as Groffet collected another moun-tainous stack of them at his side.

Finally, when it appeared that he was done, he turned to me and gestured me forward. Slowly—hesitantly—I stepped away from my safe place against the wall and moved towards him. "Take these," he said, nodding to the stack of books. "Read them. Study them and you just might be able to learn something."

"What are they?" I asked.

Groffet's spectacles gleamed in the light as he tipped his head back and looked at me through the lenses perched on the end of his bulbous nose. "They're the complete history of Fae Courts. Start at the top, you'll learn everything you need to about Prince Roan's Court of Crimson before you start anything else."

I stopped beside the stack and lifted the first book, reading the title: "The Complete Works of Magnus Crimson." I arched a brow at Groffet. "Who's Magnus Crimson?"

Groffet shook his head and flipped his finger at me. A force unlike any other overcame me and my whole body was spun back towards the library's doors. My feet lifted and marched me—against my will—not stopping until I landed in the corridor outside the library.

"Magnus Crimson was the first King of Crimson," Groffet said.

I turned around, wiggling my fingers and toes and frowning down at my body as I made sure I had full control once more. "Why do I—"

Groffet shook his head as he appeared on the other side of the library's entryway, both hands latched on the doors. "Read the book, child," he ordered. "Then direct your questions to Prince Roan, himself."

"But—"

The doors slammed shut, echoing throughout the empty hallway and leaving me even more baffled than before. I simply stood there for a moment, staring at the closed doors of the library before I glanced back down at the book in my hand. *Well, it was a starting point,* I supposed. I turned and headed off again. *A starting point was better than nothing.*

CHAPTER 21

CRESS

I hadn't planned on falling asleep in the throne room, it just kind of happened. The books that Groffet gave me weren't exactly exciting reading material. Falling asleep wasn't quite the shock, but waking up left me groggy. Something had woken me, but I wasn't sure what. I pulled myself together, straightening my clothes, and wiping the drool away from my mouth and the book I'd fallen asleep on. I hoped Groffet didn't mind too much. I cringed at the dried saliva that was still stuck to the page. Hopefully, he wouldn't notice.

My hands were midway through finger combing my hair when I heard Ariana's laugh. It was distinctive in a way that only a laugh that belongs to someone you loathe could be. The hair on the nape of my neck stood on end and my teeth clenched so hard that the back of my jaw twinged slightly. I took a deep breath in through my nose and slowly let it out through my mouth as I tried to center myself before she and her cronies arrived. Maybe they wouldn't see me. I was tucked back in the corner, after all. I hadn't intended on hiding—I'd just found a comfortable space to read the book Groffet had given me—but now it worked in my favor.

I ducked my head and opened the book once more, turning to the last page I remembered before I'd fallen asleep. I'd keep reading about Magnus Crimson, and hope that at some point, I would get to where he stopped regaling the reader with his sexual conquests and started talking about actual magic. So far, all I'd learned was that the Crimson Court, founded in his name, was one of the most sexually active and adventurous Courts and all of it was because of him. I wondered how many children he must have had. Other than some explicit sexual conquests on ladies from various Courts, the only thing of true value I'd learned so far was that there used to be a whole lot more Fae Courts than there were currently. I mean, hundreds of Fae Courts—all spaced out across the land—and yet, from the small footnotes at the bottom of various pages, I learned that there were maybe a couple dozen left. *What had caused that?* I wondered.

"Ugh. I don't want to eat in here if *it's* in here," Ariana's voice sounded, echoing all around the room. There was no doubt that she wanted me to hear. I didn't react, though, didn't allow myself a flinch or even a blink as I continued scanning the page in front of me. "Ladies, let's get a plate and leave. Apparently, it's not even smart enough to know when it's being spoken to."

This time, I did raise my eyes, and I shot her a glare that I hoped was pure fire, something to burn her from the inside out. My glares must have been defective or something, though, because it had no effect. Go figure, I'd be just the girl to try and glare her way out of a problem and instead of looking deadly or dangerous, I probably looked like my eyes were broken. Could someone even glare their way out of trouble? I'd have to try it next time—not that I was thinking there definitely *would* be a next time, but for research purposes, if there *was*, in fact, a next time, I'd try it out.

Ariana, bitch of all bitches, approached me and pulled me from my thoughts. I met her gaze with one of my glares—*come on glare powers,* I thought. *Intensify or something.* Her silvery eyes remained cool and distant. "So, you do understand me."

"Of course, I understand you," I replied, even though I knew I shouldn't engage her in conversation, especially when it seemed the power of my glare wasn't doing anything.

"Lady Ariana. That's what you should say. 'Of course, I understand you, Lady Ariana.' I am a Lady of the Courts, most likely to be Roan's next fiancée. You will address me with respect or I will have you thrown in the dungeon."

They had a dungeon? Honestly, I wouldn't be surprised if she wasn't bluffing. This was a castle after all. *Didn't all castles come with dungeons?* And if anyone was going to throw me in one, it would be Ariana.

"Yes, *Lady Ariana,*" I replied, trying to sound as snooty as she had as I spoke. Even as I did, my brain finally caught up to what she'd said. Next fiancée? Roan? That couldn't be accurate. Roan didn't seem to particularly care for Ariana—okay, he might have felt her up a bit when I'd first come around but did that mean he really liked her?—and if he didn't, why would she think he'd want to marry her? Maybe it was just a political thing? He was a prince after all. Whatever the case was, I didn't like it. It made my chest feel tight and my stomach twist into knots. Then again, that could've been because I hadn't eaten since I woke up.

"Leave," Ariana snapped. "My ladies and I wish to eat in peace, not being hovered over by some mongrel half-breed."

I rolled my eyes. A part of me wanted to fight her, to tell her to go to the deepest circle of hell, but the truth was, I just didn't have the energy for dealing with her. Not when I was trying to figure my own stuff out. She wasn't worth it.

Though it was a struggle, I gathered the books Groffet had given me and left, wandering out of the throne room as Ariana and her company of girls laughed at my back and started up with the insults once more. If there was a spell in Groffet's books that would sew their fucking mouths shut, I intended to find it. I meandered through the castle until I found myself outside of Roan's room once more. Hefting the books against my chest, I reached up and knocked as hard as I could while holding the pile. When no answer greeted me, I debated what to do next. I could go and find Roan or I could try and find Orion, since his room was the only other place I knew of in this section of the castle.

At the thought of walking back through the corridors and trying to find my way to his room, though, the books in my grip suddenly felt like they gained weight. I didn't want to amble around with these books anymore. I was tired, cranky, kinda hungry, and these books were freaking heavy. I knocked on the door again, more firmly this time.

After a moment, the telltale sounds of footsteps approached from the other side, the knob turned, and the door creaked open to reveal a half naked Roan with a towel wrapped around his waist and water droplets clinging to his skin. My eyes widened as I watched as whatever magical heat emitting from his body made the droplets evaporate from his skin and turn to steam. I swallowed against a dry throat. Holy Gods, he was ... divination in Fae form. He had to be a demi god or something because I'd never seen a man who looked like *that*. His muscles could've been carved from stone. Orion, I'd thought, was ripped, but Roan was chiseled. Pure fucking ropes of muscle and sinew and skin—and was I drooling? I reached up and wiped at the corner of my mouth as I juggled the books. Yup. There was a little bit of drool. Had he noticed?

As soon as his eyes settled on mine, Roan nodded and turned from the door, allowing me to come in and nudge it shut with my foot before looking for somewhere to set the pile in my arms down.

"I see Groffet loaded you up on history books, hmmm?" Roan asked.

"He did?" I couldn't stop staring. When he glanced back at me with a frown, I straightened abruptly. "I mean, he did. Yes. Books—history. I read them sometimes. I can read." I jerked my gaze down to the pile still in my arms and then back up to see him turn back to his wardrobe.

He chuckled as he dropped the towel and by Coreliath's fucking beard, I thought I might perish. Right there and then. In fact, I was a little shocked I hadn't already gone up in smoke. His butt—mother of Gods—I was drooling again. I really needed to stop that. I lifted my books back up my chest as I struggled to wipe the drool from my chin. "H-he told me to start there instead of with you. I was reading them in the throne room since I don't have a place to stay, but Ariana found me in there and kicked me out so I just ... I didn't know where else to go," I ended lamely.

"Out of the frying pan, into the fire," Roan said, pulling on a pair of loose trousers. When he turned to face me it was like the world slowed down for just a moment as my eyes greedily devoured every inch of exposed skin, every curve of muscle. He hadn't even done up the laces. All the water was gone and his hair was dry. I tried to picture him strutting around the castle in just a towel and couldn't, at least not without causing the females to faint at just the sight of him.

By the Gods, it should've been impossible to be so attractive.

I must have loosened my grip on the books because the next thing I knew they were falling from my grasp onto the floor and my toes. I cursed before dropping to the floor to pick them up. Surprisingly, Roan's hands were there a moment later.

"Groffet will be most unhappy if you damage one of his books," the Fae prince cautioned.

I looked up at him, at the fire dancing in the depths of his eyes, at the flame red hair that I wanted to run my hands through, at the lush lips I wanted to bite and suck and slide my tongue over. Roan was temperamental, just like fire itself. He needed to be encouraged, fed the right thoughts to see him flourish, but he could turn on you in a snap if you betrayed him. I could sense it from the way he was hesitant with me, the way he was different when we were alone versus when we were with the others.

"Are you engaged to Ariana?" The question blurted from my mouth before I could stop it. The fire I'd seen glowing in his eyes seemed to stutter out and they turned cold and dark.

"No, why would you think that?" His voice was a low, vicious growl.

"She was bragging about possibly getting engaged to you when she kicked me out of the throne room—she said she was going to be your next fiancée," I replied, noting his flinch at the word *next*.

"Yes, she's been hinting at it for a while now," he said with a low, irritated snarl.

"You don't seem all that happy about it," I commented.

Roan was quiet for a moment, his head lowering as he continued to gather books in his arms. "She's not the only one who has been hinting at it," he admitted.

"Who else?" I asked.

He froze. Then, in a nearly indiscernible whisper, he hissed. "My mother wants the union as well." He lifted his head, his gaze meeting mine. Roan's eyes darkened and the fire I'd seen there earlier was back. This time, however, it was a raging inferno of powerlessness.

I may not have ever had a parent, but I had the nuns, and I knew what being powerless against those who held sway over your life felt like. I'd been ridiculed, called lazy, a burden, and difficult among other things. I hadn't been able to stomach meat or a lot of the food the nuns had served and since coming to the Fae Court, that hadn't been a problem. Their food didn't taste like rocks on my tongue or churn in my gut and make my stomach coil and knot up. There, I hadn't possessed any agency over my own life. Here—I was still somewhat out of my depth, but I didn't feel completely powerless.

Even if I couldn't be in charge of myself yet, one day I hoped to be free to do whatever the hell I wanted. When that happened, I'd finally be able to do all of the things I'd wanted to. I'd travel, visit new and interesting places, meet people, and just live to be free. But big changes didn't happen overnight. It was one day at a time, one small step after another. All I knew now was that I was on my path towards freedom, inching ever closer, and no one was going to stop me.

Roan handed over the books he'd picked up and stood, taking a step away from me. We locked eyes, but neither of us said a word. Instead, silence descended over the room. I sat, surrounded by books on the floor, while Roan paced around the room, burning off his anger. I blinked when a few times, his hands went up in flames only to disperse a second later, his skin perfectly fine. When his pacing slowed and he hadn't set anything ablaze for a while I tempted fate by asking, "What did she mean when she said she'd be your *next* fiancée?"

Roan was pacing away from me when I spoke but when the question left my lips, he stopped. He didn't look back but remained right where he was. He didn't move, didn't even look like he was breathing for so long that I was beginning to worry. I adjusted the books on my lap and stacked them to the side as I got up off the floor. Not a twitch, not even a blink—nothing that I could see that would give me any indication that he had heard me and hadn't just frozen on the spot.

As I debated what to do, Roan finally looked back over his shoulder. His face was etched in agony. "Her name was Franchesca," he said, his voice barely above a whisper. "We met when we were children."

I took a step towards him and he turned, facing me completely. "Roan?"

He shook his head and continued. "We grew up together in my mother's Court. The Court of Crimson."

"Was she a Crimson Fae too?" I asked.

He nodded. "But she wasn't..." He stopped, swallowing as he closed his eyes and reached up with both hands to scrub his palms against his face. When his arms dropped back down to his sides, he reopened his eyes. "Chesca was my best friend," he said, and as he stared at me, his eyes shone with some sort of fiery light, and I felt like he was trying to tell me something. As if he were begging me not to judge him for the emotion currently covering his face.

I strode towards him, not stopping until I was right in front of him. "It's okay," I said, reaching out and taking one of his hands.

His eyes never left my face. "She wasn't royal," he said as if imparting some secret. "Her family was lower in the Court. They had migrated from an older Court that no longer had a royal line. We were young when I asked her to marry me. My mother didn't approve. She was my world, though. My father is gone now, but even before he died, my parents didn't have the type of union I'd always wanted for myself."

"What kind of union?" I asked.

He inhaled, his eyelids lowering once more as he breathed out through his mouth. "Crimson Fae are sexual," he said.

"Really?" I chuckled lightly. "You could've fooled me."

His eyes opened and he shot me a look. I shrugged, but he shook his head. By the curl at the corner of his mouth, I'd accomplished what I'd set out to do. Break some of the tension. His hand squeezed mine. "My parents' union was cold. They came together to procreate, but not much else. Of my five brothers and sisters, I am the only surviving heir."

I gaped. "They're all dead?"

Roan tilted his head to the side. "This war with the humans has taken many lives," was all he said in response to that question.

I didn't know what else to say to that, so I simply nodded and he continued. "Chesca and I were engaged for several months, at which point I was being groomed to take the throne. Several weeks before what would have been our wedding, she came to me and offered herself. We'd already come together so many times, but love is strange—I trusted her completely. I thought she was my life mate. After we had joined and I'd fallen asleep, though, I woke to find her lifting a dagger over my chest. Had I not woken when I did, she would have killed me. As it turns out, her family had been plotting to overthrow the Court of Crimson for some time. Without an heir, the Court of Crimson would have fallen."

My breath caught in my chest as his voice grew tighter with each spoken word. He sounded hollow, as though he was talking about someone else's past and not his own. It reminded me somewhat of how Nellie had spoken when she talked about losing her parents. I couldn't even imagine trusting someone so much and wanting to spend my life with them only to be betrayed by them.

"I'm so sorry, Roan," I whispered, my voice quiet as I reached for his other hand. I looked up into his face, keeping his eyes with mine. "No one should have to go through something like that."

"If I was a stronger man I would have asked her why," he said. "I still wonder if any of it was real or if she thinks about me, if she regrets it."

I frowned. "She's still alive?"

"In the dungeon of my mother's Court," he said with a nod. "Surrounded and imprisoned by iron—completely devoid of her magic. It's the absolute worst punishment for a Fae other than death." He pulled his hands from mine and took a step back, moving to the bed.

I tried to keep myself from going to him, but I couldn't, not when the pain that was radiating out of him was so brutal and sharp. He'd given his heart to this woman and she'd tried to murder him. My feet carried me towards the bed, and as I approached, I reached for him, unable to stop myself from doing anything else.

As soon as my skin connected with his, it felt like a match had been struck. All the air seemed to be sucked out of the room as I crawled onto the bed and reached around, awkwardly hugging his back to my chest. I felt it when he inhaled sharply, his chest shooting up and holding when he didn't release the breath right away.

I don't know what told me to say what I did, but without thinking, I let the words spill from me. "I'm not her," I said. "I'm me. I do my own thing, react my own way, screw things up, react badly to Fae Court politics that are normal for you. I want to learn about magic and Court life and customs, but I don't want you to think I'm her, trying to weasel my way in for some ulterior motive. Before I even came here, I had one friend in the whole world. She'd probably hate me now if she knew what I was. The only people I have now are you, Orion, and Sorrell—well, if Sorrell can stop being such a butthead to me, but you get my meaning."

Roan burst out laughing and pulled from my arms before turning to face me. "Ahhh, Cress. Sorrell is the best of us all. He's as loyal as they come. He saved me from myself and my grief and anger after Chesca. He saved Orion when he was fighting on the frontlines. We each have our stories to tell, but I assure you, Ariana is not going to be my next fiancée—even if my mother approves of it. I'll have to correct her. This has been enlightening, little bird. Thank you."

He moved to stand from the bed, but before he could, I took the opportunity to ask, "Can I read in here since I don't have anywhere else?"

"For now. I'll get the pixies to make you up a room, clothes and all, then you'll have your own space, but for now, I need to go and have a chat with Ariana."

It wasn't until after Roan had left and I was halfway down another page of sexual exploits in the book about Magnus Crimson that I realized my mistake. Roan was going to talk with Ariana and there was no doubt—she'd know it was me that turned her in. *What if she retaliated even further?*

After a moment of contemplation, I cursed and put the book down. I needed to find out exactly what Roan was going to say to her, perhaps stop him if it was too horrible. I hurried from the room, hoping I wasn't too late.

CHAPTER 22
ROAN

Ariana was still in the throne room when I arrived. She cackled with several other women at one of the high tables, but I knew when she sensed my approach. Her head lifted and a seductive grin curled her lips. I frowned as I stomped down the aisles of banquet tables while the pixies flitted back and forth cleaning up messes and bringing in more food.

"Darling," she called, standing from her seat as I stopped before her.

"We need to talk," I said.

She smiled brightly. "Goodness," she said, putting a hand to her chest, "I didn't believe you'd want to do this here."

My brows pinched together as my frown deepened until I realized what she meant. I shook my head. "Ariana, I have neither the intention nor the desire to ask you to be my fiancée," I said.

Her smile fell away as her mouth gaped open. Every single Fae in the vicinity went silent. Eyes were rooted on the two of us, but she had brought this upon herself. I was not a cruel man, but neither was I a patient one, and I was quite finished with her assumptions and petty manipulation. I moved closer, dropping my voice. "You warmed my bed," I said. "That was all. We were playmates, nothing more."

"Were?" It seemed she was in shock. She lifted her chin and stared at me, confusion etched into her features as she began to shake her head back and forth. "I don't understand what you're saying." Her palm lifted. She reached for me. I took a step back.

"Yes," I stated flatly. "Whatever we were is no longer possible. I cannot and will not lay with you if you believe that you have a chance at marriage."

Ariana breathed in and out through her nose so sharply that she resembled an angry bull. When her eyes lifted and zeroed in over my shoulder, I turned my head back. "*You.*" The vehemence that spat from Ariana's lips was only a precursor to her wrath.

No sooner had I seen Cress stop just inside the room and Ariana was circling me and heading straight for her. "You did this!" she shrieked. "You turned him against me!"

Before I could predict what she might do, Ariana released a bolt of fire magic from her fingertips. I watched in horror as the flames arched out and slammed into the Changeling's chest, sending her flying out of the room and into the corridor. Her back slammed into the stone wall with an audible noise.

"Enough!" My voice boomed across the room, making tables and plates alike tremble. Ariana whipped around as if just realizing her error. My anger snapped through me and I felt flames dance against the nape of my neck as I descended the high table and headed for her.

"My Lord," she said quickly, "I'm so sorry, I didn't realize what I was doing. I—"

Her words were cut off when my hand closed around her throat. "You disrespect me," I growled lowly.

"No!" She shook her head back and forth, eyes widening in true fear. "I swear, I—"

"*Silence!*"

She clamped her mouth shut, trembling in my grip. Two figures appeared in the doorway to the throne room. Orion and Sorrell. Orion went to the Changeling while Sorrell approached me.

"Roan." His voice was quiet, reserved. Gentle even. I did not want to be gentle. I wanted to unleash my anger. It was held barely in check, just beneath the surface of my flesh, writhing with the desire to be let out. "Release her."

"No." My voice was flat. I didn't even look at Orion as he lifted the Changeling into his arms. She was unconscious, that much I knew. "Take her to my chambers, Orion," I bit out. In my periphery, I noticed that my words gave him pause. He glanced to Sorrell and only when Sorrell nodded did he continue off down the hallway. That, too, angered me. How dare he not follow my orders immediately! In my irritation, I didn't realize that my grasp on Ariana's throat had tightened.

Sorrell put a hand on my arm. "You're strangling her, Roan."

"Good," I snapped. "This is what happens when an unranked Fae attempts to manipulate a royal, when an unranked Fae disrespects a royal."

"Roan, release her to me," Sorrell tried again. "I will ensure that she spends some time in the iron dungeons, reflecting on her actions."

I shivered with the need to contract my grip even harder. I watched Ariana's squirms as, for the first time ever, she was completely meek and submissive. Her eyes pleaded with me even as she struggled to breathe. Before I could change my mind, I released her throat.

"To your chambers," I ordered.

"Yes, my Lord," she croaked, getting up and practically running from the room.

When no one else spoke or made a move to leave, I turned to the rest of them. "All of you," I ordered. "Get out. This space is off limits for the foreseeable future. You may take your meals in your chambers or anywhere else. For now, get the fuck out of my throne room."

There was a flurry of activity as the rest of the Fae moved to follow my orders. Several ran from the room, many followed at a much slower pace—watching as Sorrell guided me to the side. The pixies had disappeared almost as soon as magic had been unleashed. I felt heat building beneath my skin. When still there remained a few slower Fae, I grew impatient. "*Get out!*" I roared, sending them scrambling as they bolted to the exit. As soon as the last Fae was gone, I waved a hand and the doors to the throne room slammed shut. I turned and a pixie flitted down from the ceiling. I curled a finger at the creature and it hesitantly followed my silent command. "Get rid of the food," I snapped. "I want the tables gone. Everything." It nodded its little head and then pixies poured from the ceiling and walls— rushing to do as I'd ordered.

"Roan, what is this about?" Sorrell asked, calling my attention back to him.

"This is about me reminding our subjects who is royal here and who is not," I growled.

Sorrell sighed. "It's not just about that," he said. "It's the Changeling, isn't it?" He shook his head and turned away. "She's not staying, Roan. Don't get attached."

"Since when did we decide that?" I snapped. It took me two steps to reach him. I grabbed his shoulder and pulled him around to meet my gaze. "The Changeling's fate hasn't yet been decided."

Sorrell gaped at me. "We don't even know for sure if she is a Changeling!"

"She handled the magic test *you* wanted to put her through."

"She passed out," he replied.

"But she didn't die," I said. "She would have if she were human. Her survival proves that she's a Changeling!"

"What is this really about?" Sorrell demanded, pulling back from me as he cut me a glare with those cold eyes of his like fucking shards of ice.

"Ariana is out of control," I stated. "She was laboring under the impression that I was going to make her my next fiancée and as you well fucking know that won't be happening."

Sorrell grimaced. "Your mother expects you to choose someone, Roan."

"I know," I replied through gritted teeth even as I shoved a hand through my hair, pausing just long enough to grab a hunk of the stuff and yank at it in frustration. "But not her. I will not marry her."

"Okay." Sorrell's voice lost its edge as he moved slowly towards me again. "It's okay, Roan. You don't have to decide now."

"She'll expect it at some point, but I don't—I can't—it's not the right time. We're in the middle of a war."

"I know." A knock sounded on the door, loud and disruptive. There were only a few people left in this castle that would knock like that after the scene that had just been observed by half of the Court.

Sorrell backed away and I dropped my hand as he called for the person on the other side to come in. The door opened and Groffet waddled into the throne room, eyeing me. "My Lords," he said, nodding in respectful acknowledgment.

"Did you check on the girl?" I asked.

He nodded. "She is still asleep, but I have given her an elixir that should have her injuries healed soon."

"How bad were they?"

"Her injuries?" he inquired, tilting his head.

"No, her fucking breasts—yes, her injuries," I snapped.

Groffet blinked. "Her injuries from the magic are minor, sir. She merely hit her head against the stone. Her breasts are average."

I slapped a palm over my face. The old bastard knew I couldn't kill him. He was far too valuable. "Thank you, Groffet," Sorrell said before I could say or do anything else. "You may go."

Groffet nodded, turning around and waddling back towards the throne room doors. As soon as the old man was out of the room, I flipped back to Sorrell. "I'm going to her," I said.

"Are you sure that's a good idea?" he asked, grabbing my arm as I took a step towards the doors. "In your condition, you could hurt her. And you do seem rather concerned with the girl's well being."

I paused and arched a brow at him. "What condition is that?"

"You're riled, Roan, and we both know what happens when you're like that. Look at your hair." I hadn't even noticed, but he was right. Flames danced through the strands of my hair, circling my head in a halo of fire. He released me as I reached up and patted them out, sucking in a deep breath and letting it out as I forced the tension in my shoulders to ease.

"I'll be fine," I said after a moment.

"Roan!" Sorrell called after me as I stomped away.

"Later," I called back.

Right now, I needed to ensure that the Changeling was alright. Even Fae could be hurt by fire magic. I couldn't explain it, but there was a strange desire taking root inside of me to make sure that the girl—Cress—was okay, and this time, I wouldn't deny it.

CHAPTER 23
CRESS

I woke up feeling like I was burning in hellfire. Sweat rolled down my temples and around to my neck where my head rested on a pillow. Gods, it was hot. Hotter than hot. Was I boiling alive? It felt like it. I cracked my eyes open but the room was so dark I couldn't see anything. All I knew was that I had two heavy bands across me, one that went from my shoulders and curved over my breasts, tucking behind my waist, and another that I soon realized wasn't a band at all but a leg that was thrown across my right leg, the knee of the person's leg dangerously close to areas only Orion had touched.

My hands tentatively reached up awkwardly and confirmed that the band around my chest was, in fact, an arm. It didn't feel like Orion's though. No scars. So, who was holding me? I tried to ease away from the mystery person but didn't get very far before they tightened their grip and pulled me even closer than before. Close enough to feel everything about their body, and how naked they were, which made me realize how naked *I* was, which was when I started to get concerned.

If it wasn't Orion who the hell was touching me? Roan? I didn't seem likely since he had told me himself he didn't literally sleep with others after everything with Franchesca, so why would he with me now? It made no sense. I nudged whoever was cuddling me into an early grave and hoped I could wake them before I lost all the fluid in my body. I tried to track back in my mind, to remember how I got wherever I was, but the last thing I remembered was a furious Ariana and fire.

I nudged the person next to me harder until I heard a grumpy mumble from somewhere around my shoulder. Finally, I gave up trying to be gentle and rolled towards them, pushing them. "Hey," I hissed as loud as I dared. "Wake up."

Three things happened all at once. The lights in the room turned on, blinding me, I was rolled onto my back and pinned down, and not in a particularly sexy way. Finally, when I could see again I realized I was being pinned down by someone that, in that moment, looked more like an avenging angel than a Fae. A ring of fire circled Roan's head. It resembled a crown and lit up the area around us, illuminating his face. Flames licked down his hair to his shoulders as his normally red hair bled to white. His amber eyes seemed to glow as bright as embers of a fire as they looked through me. To top that off, his skin was practically luminescent. He looked like he could set this whole place on fire if he wanted to with just a thought.

Given the vicious snarl on his face and the way he was baring his teeth at me I knew he wasn't in his right mind. Whatever was happening right now, he was reliving his memories with Franchesca and not seeing me. One of the hands that was pinning my wrists down came around to my throat, resting on it and slowly squeezing as he snarled at me. I got the feeling he thought he was saying words but I couldn't understand them in his current state.

"Roan," I said softly. "I'm not her. I'm Cress, the Changeling. Cressida. Please, you're starting to hurt me." As I spoke his grip tightened. My free hand came up and began clawing at his hand that was around my throat. I realized that was pointless, he was stronger than me and had magic; he could kill me in a second if he wanted to. I took a deep calming breath—well, as much as I could with his hand around my throat, and instead lifted my hand up even further to cup his face. "Roan, look at me." He flinched but his gaze was still distant. "Hey, remember when you accused me of breaking into the castle, then demanded I have sex with you to get the human smell off me? Or when you threw magic at me to see if I was a Changeling? Then decided I was part of the Court of Crimson? Remember all that? That happened with me, with Cress, not with her."

As I spoke I saw the recognition flicker back to his eyes, but when he made contact with mine, panic filled his as he took in the scene around him. Instead of calming down like I'd hoped it made him even worse. The flames in his hair that had been orange and yellow in color turned a bluish white and his eyes went wide a moment before he dropped down on me. I felt heat like nothing I'd ever felt before; I wanted to say I was burning up, but I wasn't. Somehow, Roan was protecting me, or maybe it was because I was part of the Court of Crimson?

It could have lasted seconds or hours—it certainly felt like hours. When it was over and Roan pushed up, we were both able to look around and see that his room was ruined. Everything had been reduced to ash and charred chunks of furniture. "What happened?" I murmured.

Roan pushed back onto his knees so he was sitting between my legs and the rest of my ash and soot covered body. The human upbringing in me demanded I be embarrassed, but if he wasn't then I wasn't going to be either. "Cress, I—I'm so sorry," he said quietly.

"It's okay, I know that wasn't you," I assured him. I watched as he scrubbed a hand down his face. "What happened?" I asked again quietly a moment later when he didn't say anything more.

"Ariana attacked you," he said. I narrowed my eyes at him,

but he didn't seem to realize that hadn't been what I was referring to.

I nodded nonetheless, the memory of a giant ball of flame aimed directly at me resurfacing. I grimaced and reached up to rub my chest absently. It hadn't felt like actual fire, but it'd been hot and heavy—like a giant steel ball had smacked me in the chest. It'd sent me flying, I knew that much. Damn. It'd hurt.

Roan blew out a long breath and ran a hand through his once again red hair before speaking. "When you hit the wall, you hit your head," he explained. "Orion brought you back to my quarters so Groffet could check you over and let you rest. When I returned to check on you, I sent Orion back to his room. I didn't intend to..." He gestured to the bed beneath us. "I never meant to fall asleep." His eyes slid downward and in a movement that was kind of awkward for a Fae prince, he frowned and tilted his head down. "I shouldn't have fallen asleep next to you," he continued.

"Roan, it's fine." I put my hands up but he wasn't done.

"No it's not." He shook his head fervently. "I—I still have nightmares—after what happened with Chesca." I swallowed. "I thought you were her. I thought you were trying to kill—or rather I thought she was."

"Well, I'm fine." I lifted one arm and slapped the nonexistent muscle. "It'll take a little more than that to kill me, believe me—people have tried." I'd intended for it to be a joke, but Roan's head whipped towards me and in a flash, his hair turned white once more.

"Who?" he demanded.

"Who—no!" I yelled when he moved to stand. "No, I was joking. It was a joke. Calm down there, boar-man."

"I will rip their—boar-man?" The white of his hair slowly receded and he regarded me with confusion.

"Yeah," I said with a shrug. "You're acting like a wild boar—all grrrr and charging right at something."

"A wild boar?" He gaped at me as though I'd grown an extra head. "Did you just growl at me?"

"Don't tell me you don't know what a wild boar is." Roan simply continued to stare at me. Lord. Did he know nothing of the world outside of his castle? "It's an animal," I explained. *A nasty one*, I thought, recalling once when a man had brought one to donate to the abbey and the thing had gotten out. Even years later, I felt like I could still feel the boar's tusks as he'd charged straight at my backside. I'd gotten off with no more than a few scratches. Never before had I been so thankful to be such a good climber. "And it's pretty dangerous for hunters—they're impossible to tame, but lots of people kill them to eat."

"Fae do not hunt animals," he said. "We cannot eat the meat."

"You—wait, what?" I blinked up at him as he hovered a bit before slowly sitting back down.

"We can't eat animal meat," he repeated.

Huh, I thought. *Neither could I.* I'd never been able to stomach the stuff. It always made me impossibly sick. "Oh," was all I managed to say and we slipped into a quiet and somewhat tense silence after that. Neither of us seemed to have any idea what to say next.

Then, "I'm sure you'd rather ... erm ... be alone," Roan said, his shoulders stiffening as he rubbed the back of his neck and moved to stand again.

"Wait!" I reached out and grabbed ahold of his arm before he could go anywhere. "I promise you, I'm fine." He closed his eyes and inhaled, but I noticed he didn't pull his arm from my grip even though I knew he very well could with only a bit of effort. I worked at a smile, my lips twitching up. "I'm actually kinda flattered," I admitted. "I mean, you fell asleep with me. You said you don't sleep with anyone. That must mean I'm awesome, right? I'm the favorite. You fell asleep with me," I blathered on, blurting out the first thing that came to mind and somehow, it just. Kept. Going. Gods. He must have thought there was something wrong with me.

"Don't get too full of yourself, Changeling. It was bound to happen with someone eventually. I'm just glad it wasn't with a high-ranking Fae or something," Roan said, brushing me off. He hid it well, but I could tell—even my chatter was growing on him. I watched his lips twitch as he turned away. I was totally the favorite.

"And um..." I glanced down at my lap. "What about the ... erm ... naked bits?"

"I sleep naked," he said.

"Yeah, but you didn't mean to fall asleep, remember?" I pointed out.

"My pixies are under orders to undress me when I fall asleep, since I prefer to sleep naked, I assume they decided to apply that to you as well," he said. "I assure you, you were still clothed when I came back last night."

"Riiighhhhht." I pushed myself to up and rolled away to stand on my own two feet as I took in the ashes that surrounded us. At least he hadn't burned away our clothes because I was pretty sure this nakedness had happened before the whole fire and brimstone temper tantrum he'd thrown—accidentally, of course.

"It's the truth," he said.

"Uh huh. Sure it is."

"It is," he insisted, his voice dropping low as a growl filled his tone.

"Alright."

"Changeling."

"What?" I put my hands up in a movement of surrender before I realized that I was literally flashing *everything* at him—I mean, no big deal. It wasn't like he hadn't seen a woman's body before, but still ... I put my hands back down, covering my body as much as I could as I searched the room for something to put on. "I didn't say anything."

His eyes narrowed. "You are challenging my authority."

"Nope." I popped the *p* in the word as I spoke. "Not at all."

He folded his arms across his chest. "Your tone suggests otherwise."

"Hey, if you want to live in denial, that's on you," I said with a shake of my head.

"Denial?"

"Yup." Another popped *p*.

"Stop that," he hissed.

"Stop what?"

"That thing you're doing with your mouth." Roan's gaze slid down to my lips and heat began to rise to the surface of my skin.

"Okay, I'm done." I slapped a soot and ash covered hand over my mouth immediately disrupting his view. Roan blinked and then lifted his eyes back to mine. Something flashed in the depths of his gaze, something heated. Shaking his head, he turned away and after a moment, I lowered my arm.

After carefully maneuvering through various piles of debris and ash to make my way out of the destroyed bed frame, I found a shirt crumpled in the corner of the room, beneath several pieces of a destroyed trunk. The only reason it had probably survived Roan's little accident had probably been due to the fact that it was so far away and beneath something so big that had taken the brunt of the magical fire. I snatched it up and slid it on immediately. Unfortunately, however, underwear and trousers that would fit me were a little harder to come by. I headed for the bedroom door, but just before I opened it, I paused and glanced back. "I know the whole falling asleep with me thing wasn't what you planned, but it was kind of nice."

"Nice?" Roan's brows rose up in shock before quickly

lowering as his expression morphed into one of suspicion. "What do you mean?"

I shrugged. "Sleeping alone can suck," I said. "I'm used to sleeping in a room with multiple people, but it's nice to sleep next to someone too." I hadn't done it since I was really little and despite the heat I'd felt when I'd woken and the fact that I hadn't known who it was holding me, I'd liked feeling close to someone again. Sleeping with Orion had definitely ruined me. Waking up with a big muscled man all plastered against me was ... well, it was nice. "Even if you didn't mean to do it, you trusted me enough to fall asleep next to me," I said.

"And look where it got you," he snapped, gesturing to the red marks still visible on my skin.

I lifted my shoulders again. "So?"

Roan's mouth dropped open and he shook his head. "You are one strange human."

"Not a human," I said with a wink. "Changeling, remember."

After a moment, he grumbled a response. "Perhaps."

I laughed as I walked out and shut the door behind me. He might not have realized it yet, but the fact that he was able to fall asleep with me there showed that he trusted me already. *Definitely the favorite,* I thought with a smile.

CHAPTER 24
CRESS

The tap-tap of shoes on stone caught my ear and before I could get away, a familiar face rounded the corner and stopped a few feet away. Without even thinking about it, I turned suspicious eyes skyward. Okay, now the Gods were just fucking with me and it wasn't funny. This was not exactly how I'd hoped to see Ariana again—not that'd I'd really been planning to see her again, but this castle felt very small when there was definitely someone you didn't want to be around living in it. That someone being her. I'd also specifically would have preferred to not run into her again wearing nothing but a man's shirt and covered in soot and ash. Maybe it was just too much to ask of the Gods, but I'd really been hoping to wear something with a little more coverage. Like maybe metal plated armor.

Her eyes moved from me to the door I'd just exited and back again. She looked just as shocked as I was, but unlike me, she managed to recover a bit faster. "Just who I wanted to speak with," she said.

My eyebrows shot up to my hairline. "Oh?" I asked.

"Yes." She nodded. "I wanted to talk with you about my outburst earlier."

Outburst? That's what she was calling it. I resisted the urge to remind her that her little *emotional outburst* had resulted in me being knocked unconscious by a flying magic fireball. I mean, no problem—I was alive and all, but at the same time, I felt like she definitely meant to do a bit more damage than that. Emotional outburst, attempted murder—it was all the same thing, really.

Left without a response to her gross underestimation of my brush with fire magic, I managed to cough out a, "you did?"

"I did," she confirmed. "I—" She cut herself off, her face scrunching up as she tried to force the words out. I stared at her, waiting. "I apologize," she said through gritted teeth, "for my behavior. It was unacceptable."

Hell yeah, it was. Totally unacceptable. You didn't just decide you hated someone because they were different from you. You decided to hate someone because they threw a fireball at your head.

"Okay," I said anyway. "Thanks for the apology."

She tipped her head in acknowledgment of my words before she moved to the side and gestured. "I was hoping you'd walk with me," she said.

"You were?" Why did I not believe her?

"I'd like to explain my actions," she said.

Did I want to go for a walk with her? No. But what would refusing get me? Maybe letting her speak her mind would get her to back off for a while. I glanced down at my attire—or rather my lack thereof. I couldn't go traipsing around the castle looking like I'd just had a fight with a fireball, not even if I had. "Let me get washed up and changed," I said with a sigh.

She nodded. "Of course. Would you meet me at the southern wall? I think a walk outside would be lovely."

"Um ... sure. I don't know how to get there, though."

She shook her head and snapped her fingers. Almost immediately, a pixie appeared. "Not to worry," she said. "The pixies will show you the way."

And they did. I followed the pixie as it led me to the bathing chamber from before. I washed up in record time, dipping myself into the water and diving out as soon as I was clean. The pixies brought me a new change of clothes as well, and in a whisper, I promised that I'd repay them with more food later.

I stepped out of the bathing chamber with a pair of trousers and a shirt tucked into the front waistband and she was waiting. The smile on her face was forced, but at least she was trying, I guess? We didn't need to see eye-to-eye, just not snipe and try to kill each other anymore.

"Ready to go?" she chirped.

I gave her a nod and a tight smile before the two of us set off down the halls; she led the way since I had no idea how to get around the castle yet. Everything was still so new and confusing but to her, it was normal. She wove through the hallways and up and down stairs clearly with a specific destination in mind.

"So," I said eventually, "what's on the southern wall?"

"It's an incredible view," she said, "but just beneath it is this adorable little garden I thought I could show you. It's just through here."

She pushed a door open and the wind slapped me in the face. I winced but trailed behind her as we left the inside of the castle. Once we were out in it, it wasn't so bad, but the difference between inside and outside the castle was stark. When was the last time I'd been outside? My eyes widened when I realized just how high up the castle wall was. We walked along the parapet and when we rounded a corner I was struck by the sudden explosion of different shades of green and the variety of vibrant colors that seemed to come from nowhere.

"I wanted the chance to explain my position and yours,"

Ariana said suddenly. I frowned, turning towards her as she spoke. "You see, the problem I'm having is that Roan was promised to me by his mother. After the whole fiasco with his last fiancée, the Crimson Queen wanted to ensure that her son wouldn't choose an unsuitable partner again. Franchesca, the little fool, thought she could be the next Crimson Queen, not that Roan's mother would have ever given her seat up. She'd keep the damn thing for herself before giving it up to a child like Frannie." Ariana sighed. *Interesting,* I thought. So, Ariana had known his last fiancée personally. "And everything was going swimmingly. Roan and I enjoyed each other physically quite frequently and with the pressure I know he's getting from his mother and the Court of Crimson, I was expecting a proposal any day."

We came to a slow stop at the top of the wall and I looked down into the castle's garden. It was beautiful, but her words were ruining the magical feeling of being in a Fae castle.

"Then, you came into the picture," she continued, her smile tightening until it looked like someone had taken a hammer and nails to her face to keep the corners of her lips tilted up. "Roan has lost sight of his potential—*again.*" She paused and gave me the look. The one that was a precursor to something insulting. Why did everyone want to insult me so badly? What had I ever done? I mean, sure, I'd accidentally broken into a magical Fae castle. There was that. And okay, maybe Roan was a little bit interested in me. I was his favorite after all. And I could see how I'd be perceived as a homewrecker if he was actually interested in marrying Ariana, but from what I'd seen thus far, he wasn't. So, really, all of this insulting was just uncalled for.

As I rambled on in my head, trying to work out the logistics of insulting, Ariana had kept talking. "He's completely fascinated by you, doesn't even want me in his bed anymore, when

I'm the only one that can put up with his particular ... interests."
My ears perked up at that.

"Interests?" I repeated. What kind of interests was she talking about?

She nodded. "Most women prefer lovers who are more giving —less selfish and demanding." *Oh?* I thought, not sure exactly how that explained his interests. Sexual, I got that, but I'd assumed she'd meant something darker like ... well, honestly, I couldn't think of anything. "I don't care about the sex," she said suddenly, drawing my attention back to her. "I've had my sights set on him for ages, now. Roan was almost mine, too. Until you. You just waltzed in and blew up my carefully orchestrated plans. Now, we've been informed that we aren't allowed out of our rooms, the throne room is off limits to anyone who isn't a royal, and anyone who looks at Roan wrong is threatened with the iron dungeon— oh the others might've been the ones to inform the rest of the court, but I know it's from Roan. And it's all because of you."

She came to a stop at the end of her tirade and I stood there, shifting from one foot to the other. I wished I could say I was surprised by her speech, but it had been along the lines of what I had expected. Essentially, it was the 'keep your hands off my toy because it's mine and I don't share' speech. I couldn't deny that there was something between Roan and me, some kind of attraction, a pull, that seemed to make us fight our more rational sides and follow our baser instincts. When Ariana stepped closer to the edge of the wall and looked out beyond on the other side, I automatically followed. I lifted my head and turned my cheek as I gazed out over the land.

If I squinted hard enough, I could make out the top of the church at the abbey over the treetops. The twilight sun reflected off of the roof for a split second before dipping down over the mountains and sending the rest of the area into shadows. A part of me missed it. It was unexpected, but with everything that had happened to me in the past several days, I craved a piece of normalcy. And that was what the abbey represented to me. A mundane life. Normal. Boring.

"Now," Ariana said, turning to look at me as she leaned over the edge of the parapet, "I would ask you to stay away from him, but after that oh so touching 'thank you for trusting me' speech you gave him, I'm sure you won't. I understand what happens when a female spends the night in Roan's room. I'm sure he showed you a good time and made that little virgin pussy of yours ache in just the right way. He can be spectacular in bed, with the right coaching, of course, and he will make a powerful husband and ruler, but I'll be the one pulling the strings from behind the throne, just like his mother did with his father. That, my dear, is the power of being a female Fae. One you will never fully get to understand, I'm afraid."

"What?" I blinked as I turned away from the trees and mountains and faced her, but it was too late. Ariana lifted her hand, palm outward and my eyes widened as a fireball erupted from her fingertips and slammed into me in much the same way it had before. Unlike last time, however, there was no wall at my back.

Instead, I was sent flying outward and right over the parapet. The wind that surrounded the fire was what hit me first, right in the face, knocking my head back just as the back of my knees hit the lower wall. I grabbed and clawed with my hands as I went over and tried to find something to grab onto, sure that if I let myself fall, it would be to my death. From this height, there was no doubt that's what it would be, but I found nothing except smooth stone. As I fell, a shrill scream was ripped from my throat.

Ariana's face was the last thing I saw, peeking out over the edge of the wall as I fell down, down, down into nothing but darkness.

CHAPTER 25

CRESS

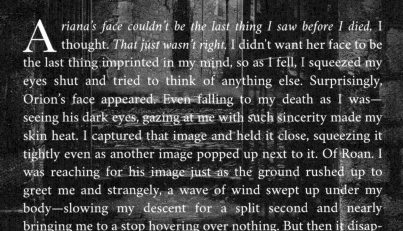

Ariana's face couldn't be the last thing I saw before I died, I thought. *That just wasn't right.* I didn't want her face to be the last thing imprinted in my mind, so as I fell, I squeezed my eyes shut and tried to think of anything else. Surprisingly, Orion's face appeared. Even falling to my death as I was— seeing his dark eyes, gazing at me with such sincerity made my skin heat. I captured that image and held it close, squeezing it tightly even as another image popped up next to it. Of Roan. I was reaching for his image just as the ground rushed up to greet me and strangely, a wave of wind swept up under my body—slowing my descent for a split second and nearly bringing me to a stop hovering over nothing. But then it disappeared, and I landed.

When my back slammed into the ground, it felt like every bone in my body broke, organs were shredded. It hurt. Gods, it fucking hurt. This was it. This was the end. The agony. The pain. Oh, the humanity! The sheer torture whipped through me and ... *actually,* I pulled up short a moment later. I'd really expected that falling from the top of a castle would hurt a bit more than this. I cracked open one eye and peered around.

There was no mistaking it, I'd definitely landed from a great height, the tall mountain of a castle towered over me. Ariana had disappeared too. So, why the fuck wasn't I a broken, bleeding mess? Oh, scratch that, I was bleeding—but my legs and arms weren't broken. Nothing was shattered. It was ... odd.

I hesitated to get up, sure that my mind just hadn't caught up with what happened to me. After several moments of just lying there, my back against the cold ground, I decided to just chance it. I leveraged up and found a nearby trunk to help me stand. My legs were shaky and there were going to be bruises, but I was alive. More than alive, my skull wasn't cracked open like a chicken egg. It was a Gods damned miracle.

I blinked as I looked over at the castle wall and shoved away from the trunk of the tree I'd used to stand. My hands were on the cold stone of the castle's outside wall, but unlike the first time, it didn't budge. I swept my fingers up and down, side to side—still nothing. A wave of panic filled me. What would Roan and Orion think when I just didn't show up again? Would they think I'd run away? What could I do? How could I get back in?

Try as I might, I couldn't find the entrance. A branch broke in the near distance, sending me on high alert. I whirled around and backed up against the castle wall, my eyes darting left and right. As I'd been searching for a way back into the castle, the darkness had stretched further and the last sun rays from over the mountain tops faded. Left with little recourse, I hesitantly edged away from the stone wall and headed into the forest. If I couldn't get back into the castle, then I'd just have to head back to the village and think of another way.

Despite my earlier reminiscent thoughts of the abbey and normal, the farther and farther I walked from the Fae castle at my back, the heavier my body became. Exhaustion pulled at my mind, and I began to feel the little aches and pains—far below what I should've been feeling after that fall—of what I'd endured.

Halfway through the woods, my foot slipped and I went down—careening into a dark and dank hole. I twisted and reached back, scrambling to find anything. Unlike my last fall, however, there was no wind to stop me. My ankle twisted, screaming in sharp discomfort as I fought for purchase, finding nothing but roots and dirt. It was only a moment before what little hold I'd managed to obtain was ripped from my grasp. Something swung out, appearing in my peripheral just a moment before my temple collided with a hardened root— more like a branch—sticking straight out of the hole's inner wall. Lights exploded behind my eyes and as I slid further into the ground, darkness swallowed me whole.

THERE WAS NOTHING BUT DARKNESS FOR A LONG TIME, SO LONG that I thought I might be going insane. It felt like some part of me had just reached up and pulled me back into the darkness with it, and now I was stuck, hiding—from myself—which was the strangest part. I needed to wake up, so when I heard voices I followed the sound joyfully.

The joy was short lived.

The voice was one I recognized, one I had never wanted to hear again.

Sister Madeline.

The next voice gave me a modicum of relief though. Nellie was clearly worried about me. As she spoke, I felt like I was swimming to the surface and gathered from their conversation that I'd been found by some sheep, no joke, and their shepherds. One of them recognized me as belonging to the convent so they returned me there. Fan-freaking-tastic.

I supposed it was better than being unconscious on a hillside, but this was about as far away from the castle as I could get and still be within walking distance. I needed to get back and hope that I could find a way back in before Ariana convinced the guys that I had run away or something.

"I'll sit with her, Sister Madeline, and make sure she doesn't roam the grounds. She'll listen to me, you know that," Nellie said.

"Fine, but I don't want her corrupting any of the new boys. Understood?" The sister's voice was sharp enough that it almost pulled me from my strange restful sleep just so I could defend Nellie and lay into Sister Madeline now that she didn't control me anymore.

"Understood, Sister," Nellie said, her voice the perfect blend of respectful and subservient.

I wasn't sure how much time had passed since I heard them talking that my eyes flickered open but I could tell it was late in the day. The sun was starting to sink below the skyline, creating great golden swaths of light that I used to chase and play in when I was a child. Much to Sister Madeline's distress.

"Nellie?" I croaked when I saw her sitting towards the end of the bed.

"Cress! Thank the Gods you're okay. I've been so worried about you," Nellie whisper-shouted.

"Don't let the sisters hear you saying that," I replied, referring to the Gods comment. They didn't like it when their charges talked about any of the Gods other than Coreliath, at least outside of educational purposes.

Nellie flashed me a smile, but before she could butt in with the thousands of questions I was sure were dancing on her tongue, I tried to push up into a sitting position, hesitated and nearly laid back down.

Her smile dropped and she rushed to my side. "Don't try and move too quickly; the shepherds said there was a lot of blood where they found you, and we don't know how long you were there, or how long you'd been unconscious. You could have some serious injuries."

"I'm sure that would make Sister Madeline jump with glee," I grumbled as I rubbed the back of my head. I could feel the crusted dry blood in my hair and was sure it made my blonde locks look just lovely. Absolutely fantastic. The desire to get clean was strong, but I wanted to use one of the bathing chambers at the castle, not one of the freezing cold buckets of water that the sisters called a shower as they poured it over you. I refused. I would rather remain disgustingly covered in old blood and dirt. I was surprised no one had tried to clean me, but as I looked down it looked like someone had at least taken a washcloth to my hands, arms, and when I reached up, my face too. Whatever remained behind would just have to be proof enough of what had happened, of what Ariana had tried to do —kill me.

"Enough of that," Nellie hissed, pulling my thoughts back to her and away from the treacherous Fae. "Where have you been? The sisters were debating on letting you stay a few days more when you got so sick, but when we woke up, you were just gone! No goodbye or anything." The hurt in her voice was there even though she was trying to hide it.

"It's a long story, Nel. One I'm not sure I have time to tell," I said quietly as I pushed to my feet and wobbled, unable to find my stability, and plunked back down on the sickbed. Nellie had risen at the same time as I did, but instead of wobbling and sitting back down she just went and stood in front of the door, the *only* door, in and out of the infirmary. When I raised my eyebrows at her she simply cocked one at me in return. I pursed my lips. Had she always been this feisty? I kind of liked it. "What's gotten into you, Nel?"

"Oh, I don't know," she replied. "My best friend up and disappeared on me. You left a gap, and I just filled it." Then her voice dropped and in a quieter tone, she said, "Just like someone will fill mine once I take my vows."

"Still think that's a bad idea," I grumbled. I looked up at her and could see the doubt written all over her face. "Tell you what, you pinky promise me you'll seriously reconsider taking your vows and I'll tell you what I've been up to."

Nellie narrowed her eyes on me. I waited. She took her pinky promises very seriously. It was not a promise she'd make lightly. So, when she stuck her pinky finger out after only a moment, I was more than a little surprised. Nellie had been more serious about taking her vows than anything else since we first met. The simple fact that she was willing to even remotely reconsider them was a huge victory for me. She didn't deserve to be locked away on a hillside with nothing and no one except the other nuns for company. She was too sweet and too kind for that, and I knew, I just knew, that they would twist her into something bitter and cruel like they were.

I watched her carefully as I extended my own pinky, waiting for her to snatch hers back when she had second thoughts, but she didn't. It seemed my being gone for as long as I had might have changed her more than I thought possible. We wrapped our pinkies around one another and shook solemnly. "Now," she said, blowing out a breath I hadn't realized she was holding, "tell me everything."

"Okay." I nodded and then swallowed roughly. "Just ... try not to freak out too much, okay?" She eyed me suspiciously, but I waited until she nodded in assurance before I continued.

Starting from the time I'd gotten so confusingly sick—the noise in my ears that had nearly left me deafened—I relayed everything that had happened and watched as her eyes got progressively wider. So wide that I was starting to worry that I was overloading her, but when I paused unsure if I should continue, she slapped my arm and ordered me to keep going. Damn. I rubbed the spot she'd hit. For a small thing, she hit surprisingly hard. I took a breath and launched back into it, telling her about the castle and the princes and the tests and the possibility that I might not be human at all. Her look of amazement morphed into one of horror and I watched, trying to hide my hurt as she leaned away from me ever so slightly. I forced myself not to reach for her even though I frowned. "I'm still me, Nellie. I'm the same person I've always been. I just ... might be a little more. Maybe. Possibly—considering I survived that fall, probably."

"Fae..." She choked out the word, fear making her voice quiet. After a moment, as the shock seemed to settle in, she inhaled and looked straight at me. "So, you're a Fae?" she asked.

"I don't know yet," I hedged. "But there's definitely a possibility."

"And you're friends with these princes?"

I winced. "To call them my friends would be ... I mean, it's not that—let's just say things are complicated between us."

She shook her head, her mouth hanging open slightly. "I can't believe this."

I blinked and shrugged. "I mean, yeah, honestly, neither can I—"

"No, I mean, I cannot believe you've never known. Fae have —Fae are magic," Nellie hissed, though not unkindly. She couldn't seem to understand how I didn't know, and I had no way of explaining it to her because I didn't understand it either. "How have you never shown any signs before now?"

I raised my hands in a defensive gesture. "I don't know," I said. "Something about going into the castle might have ... activated it? I guess?" She put a hand to her forehead, still shaking her head back and forth as if she couldn't believe what she was hearing. Were I in her shoes, I would probably react the same, but we didn't have time to debate over the possibility of me being Fae or not right now. "Listen, Nel," I said, leaning forward and capturing her hand, thankful when she didn't immediately tug away, "I need to get back. I need to tell them what happened and prove to them that I'm still alive before they leave without me. If I actually am Fae, then I can't stay here. I need your help. Will you let me go?" I knew if it was just up to Nellie she would, but she was thinking about the whole convent, all of the sisters, Mother Collette, even the Abbess if she ever returned.

After several tense moments, she released a breath. "Is it bad that I want to say no?" she replied.

"Wh—"

Before I could finish my question, she turned her hand over and squeezed mine back, startling me. "I missed you, Cress," she whispered, her voice choked. "I was worried and I don't want to lose you again."

I didn't know what to say. I'd missed her too—in the back of my mind, I'd wondered if she was missing me or if she was better off here. She'd always managed the sisters far better than I had and just because I didn't think she'd be happy living here for the rest of her life, didn't mean that she didn't think she could be happy here.

When I didn't respond immediately, she sighed. "I can just say I fell asleep or something, and when I woke you were gone. Not much different to the first time you disappeared," Nellie said as she smiled sadly at me. "You're right, if you actually are Fae, you can't stay here. If anyone were to find out—what with the war..."

"Will you come with me?" I asked, the question popping out before I could stop it.

"I—" Whatever Nellie's response was going to be it was interrupted by the sound of footsteps at the end of the hallway, ones that could only belong to one of the sisters. Nellie released my hand. "Lay down, pretend to be out again," Nellie whispered as she hurriedly pushed me back down onto the bed and took her seat by the door once more, pretending to read whatever book she had brought with her.

There were a few tense moments of silence where I tried to get my breathing under control so it still looked like I was asleep or unconscious. The footsteps stopped just inside the door. "Is she still unconscious?" a somewhat familiar voice inquired.

Mother Collette? She never came down to the infirmary.

"Yes, Mother," Nellie replied, her voice trembling as though she was terrified of the woman.

"Do you remember what the punishment is for lying to one of the sisters, Eleanor?" Mother Collette's voice was icy cold and I had a seriously bad feeling in my gut about what was about to happen. Nellie must have nodded because the room remained silent for a moment before the Mother continued. "Do you think the punishment is worse for lying to me?"

"Probably, Mother Collette," Nellie whispered.

"And what is the punishment for lying to one of the sisters? Do you remember?" Mother Collette asked.

"Lashes across the bottom of the feet, Mother, the quantity depending on the severity of the lie," Nellie replied dutifully.

Mother Collette's heels clicked on the stone floor of the infirmary as she stepped closer to the sickbed. "So, if I told you that I knew Cressida is awake right now and has been filling your head with nonsense and young James was just down here and overheard the two of you speaking about a nearby Fae stronghold, you would say he was lying?" My heart nearly stopped in my chest. "A Changeling," she said, and I could sense more than see the shake of her head. Her voice dropped as she continued. "Sheltering a Fae, child? Like the ones that killed young James' parents, like the ones that killed *your* parents? I'm disappointed in you."

Nellie spluttered but didn't manage to get any kind of a response out.

"Eleanor, do you think me an imbecile?" There was an odd calmness to the Mother's voice that made me want to shiver but I shoved the feeling down, remaining still under the blanket.

"N-n-no, Mother Collette," Nellie stuttered. The sound of someone moving closer registered in my ears. It wasn't Nel, though, that much I knew.

Something sharp pricked my finger. A needle? Dagger? I wasn't sure. Mother Collette always was creative. When I didn't react, holding my breath and hoping she was just testing Nellie, the pinching sensation moved along my hand, slicing through the pad of my finger, scoring over the bones of my knuckles, and into the flesh of my palm. When she dug in deeper I couldn't stop the cry of pain that escaped me. I jerked up and yanked my arm back.

"Welcome back, Cressida," Mother Collette said with a glare at me before turning to Nellie. "You are going to have quite the punishment, young lady."

"Mother Collette," I growled as I felt my skin heat up. Beyond Mother Collette's back, Nellie's eyes grew wide and she backed up several steps. I looked down at my hand as I stood up from the bed. The red liquid dripped along the tile as a burning sensation began to rise within me. From the wound she'd carved into my hand, a glow began to spread. My breath came in heavier pants. She whipped around and held out the dagger she'd used to cut me.

"I'm warning you, Fae. This is an iron dagger and I'm not afraid to use it," she snapped.

"You don't get to threaten my friend," I said, feeling the burn reach my eyes. I had no clue what I must've looked like, but for the first time, I felt actual power slide through my veins.

Her eyes were glued to whatever was happening just below my skin. The light from my wound was spreading up my arm. I slowly edged around the other side of the bed, feeling along the floor with my bare feet. I glanced back to Nel to see her staring wide eyed at me still. Her eyes were filled with fascination, whereas Mother Collette's were filled with horror.

Mother Collette kept the dagger out, pointed at me. I circled her, backing up and moving as subtly as I could towards the door. I met Nellie's gaze before holding out my uninjured hand. "Come with me, Nel," I said.

Nellie's lips pinched down and though there was a moment's hesitation, where her eyes flicked to Mother Collette and back to me. "You go with her, child, and you'll be signing your death certificate," Mother Collette warned. "I've already called the local soldiers stationed in the village."

Nel didn't even blink at that statement. If anything, it made her move faster as she reached back for my hand and took it. I squeezed her and yanked her close to me as we turned and fled the room. The two of us took off, flying like birds through the familiar hallways of the convent. Unlike the castle, these twists and turns I knew like the back of my hand.

We reached the outdoors and I kept my hand on hers as I rushed towards the woods, dodging around buildings that once had felt like all I'd ever known and now felt like obstacles in our path. Once we reached the edge of the convent's land, just before we would reach the forest beyond, Nel slowed and hesitated.

I turned back to her and when I saw the look on her face— full of fear and uncertainty—I grabbed her other hand and held them both in mine, even as the wound in my palm seemed to be trying to heal itself. The power I'd released still flowed from me, my hair lifting against my shoulders despite there being no breeze. I could feel a certain call behind me, like the trees at my back were reaching for me. "Help me get to the castle," I said. "You can always turn around if you want—though I really think you should come with me." When still she hesitated, I squeezed her reassuringly. I hoped the expression on my face wasn't as panicked as I felt as warning bells began to go off in the back of my mind. Mother Collette said she'd already called the soldiers from the local village. We were out of time.

"I need someone to make sure I don't fall on my ass and crack my head open again," I said, trying for a smile and hoping I didn't fail.

Nellie snickered and then sighed. "I'm surprised you made it to the castle the first time," she muttered before pushing me towards the tree line. Relief filled me but just as we turned to go, a voice called out from behind us.

"So it's true then, a female Fae was here all along."

We froze.

I glanced over my shoulder and saw them—soldiers from the village. *They've never seen the battlefields*, I tried to remind myself. *They've probably never fought a day in their lives. After all, they've spent their time here, in the rural countryside, as far from the war zones as possible.* Still, the halberds they held made me gulp. "We can outrun them," I said quietly to Nellie. She nodded and before the soldiers could say anything more, the two of us put on a boost of speed.

Even still, the man who'd spoken before called out after us. "Don't think you can get away, pretty little Fae. It's already too late for your castle. Reinforcements have been called. It's only a matter of time before they breach the gates."

No! Horror and fear pounded through me at the same time that my bare feet slapped the cold ground. Nellie looked up at me, but we couldn't stop. I pushed her forward, faster and faster. We couldn't stop. We had to get back to the castle.

In the distance, I could see lights moving, men with torches marching through the fields that ran alongside the forest, heading in the direction of the castle. I had to get there first, and I couldn't get caught by these men or any others. That'd be easy enough ... right? Gods, I fucking hoped so.

CHAPTER 26

SORRELL

"What the fuck is going on?" Roan's voice arched over the air as he came to a standstill at my side.

"The humans have found our castle," I snapped. "Where is the Changeling?" I turned on him as Orion came to stand at his back.

"She left my room this morning, but I haven't seen her since," he admitted as he gazed out over the sea of torches that were marching towards us. With our magic, we could take them no problem, but the issue was that we hadn't been given permission to kill. I gritted my teeth in irritation. We couldn't do shit unless we'd been given our orders. There was no telling what the Crimson Queen would do to us—or even my own mother. I shuddered to think of the possibilities.

A scent of floral perfume wafted our way as Ariana appeared on the wall overlooking the front gates. "Your Changeling is gone," she said. "She ran away, I saw her leave the castle myself."

Roan whipped around and would've taken her throat in his fist had I not stepped forward to stop him. Orion grabbed onto one arm while I, the other. "Stop," Orion said. "Not now. We have more important things to worry about."

"We should've killed her when we had the chance," I said. No doubt she'd been the one to lead the humans to our front door. This was turning out to be quite the fine mess.

Roan yanked himself away and turned, throwing the first punch. I grunted as his knuckles slammed into my cheekbone. "You bastard!"

"You're under her Gods damned spell," I growled, narrowly avoiding his next jab.

Orion's dark eyes met mine as he stepped back, and from the way he shook his head at me, I could tell that he too was as absorbed in the little Changeling as Roan was. He, at least, had an excuse. He'd fucked the girl. I knew for a fact that Roan hadn't. Otherwise, he wouldn't have been this worked up.

"Stop!" I grabbed his arm the next time he dove for me and pushed my power into his skin. Ice met fire with a hiss, and he yanked himself away from me to rub at the spot as his chest pumped up and down. He glared daggers my way.

Orion turned to Roan. "She wouldn't leave," he said.

"How can you know that?" I scoffed.

"She did," Ariana piped up again. "I saw it myself. She left this morning." Her face turned towards Roan and she sidled closer. "I've been trying to find you all day. When I went to your room earlier, you weren't there." I narrowed my gaze on her. From anyone else, I might believe it—in fact, a part of me already did. I hadn't trusted the girl from the very start and I still didn't, but Ariana was as serpentine as they came. She was even less trustworthy than the Changeling.

"Hmmmm." I turned back to the lights as they grew closer. Fuck, we really didn't have time to deal with this. "We need to move the castle," I announced a moment later.

Roan pulled himself away from Ariana as she attempted to

plaster herself against his side. Before he could say anything, however, Orion spoke up. "It's only been days since we last moved the castle," he said. "Do you think that's wise?"

"Why wouldn't it be?" Ariana asked, once again pushing herself against Roan.

With a growl, he turned and shoved her away. "Go back to your chambers," he snapped. "I still haven't forgotten what you did."

I watched her carefully as her face went red with anger. "Why do you continue to push me away, Roan?" she snapped. "Your Changeling has left you. She ran away. She led the humans straight to our castle." She stopped and gestured. "And yet, still, you defend her."

Roan's eyes lit with fire. The kind that would burn a man to ash if he lost control of it. This time it was I—and not Roan—who made the command. "Ariana," I called, waiting until she turned her head my way, almost hopefully. She knew—as everyone did, since I hadn't made it much of a secret—that I was no fonder of the Changeling than she was. But here and now, she would not disrupt us as we were to make our next move. "If you do not heed Roan's orders, then I'll have no other recourse but to have you shackled in iron and thrown in the dungeon."

Her eyes widened and she backed up a step. She knew I would. I had no compunction about punishing those who disobeyed. Despite Orion's looks and Roan's hotheadedness, they were far more lenient than I in such matters. When one was raised as I was, they learned to command far more than respect—they learned to command the fear in others. I had no doubt as Ariana gave a shaky nod and turned, fleeing my presence, that I had such control over hers.

"Now," I said once she'd gone. "What are we to do about this?"

"We could fight," Orion said.

"That would certainly please the Queen Mothers," I said lightly. Both he and Roan flinched.

"Do we have the reserves of magic to move the castle again?" he asked.

"After your night with the Changeling, you should."

"And you?" he replied.

"I will be just fine." I always replenished my reserves immediately.

"We have to find the Changeling," Roan said.

I turned to him with a sigh. "And if what Ariana says is true? If the girl left?" I inquired. "What then?"

"Then we capture her and make her pay for her treachery," Roan replied immediately, his face darkened.

Orion reached forward and clapped him on the shoulder, leaning close as he said in a low tone, "Not everyone is Franchesca, Roan."

Roan didn't think. He jerked his shoulder out from under Orion's grasp. "I'm aware," he said through gritted teeth. I looked down over the human kingdom's countryside as the soldiers arrived. Flaming arrows were launched, swords unsheathed. To be honest, I was quite surprised by the group of militia the humans had managed to gather. Though, upon closer inspection, I realized that the majority of these soldiers weren't soldiers at all, but young men—farmers most likely—in soldier-like uniforms and chainmail. As if that would protect them from Fae magic. Insects, the lot of humans. So angry and they didn't even know why.

"If we can't kill them," I said. "Then we must move the castle."

Roan's face darkened and Orion turned to look out beyond the castle walls, ignoring the cries and jeers from below. Inside the castle, the other Court members must have realized that something wasn't right because as the humans below grew louder, I could feel the shiver of Fae power ripple through my mind and body—the ties I had, the same ties Orion and Roan had to the members of our Court.

"I agree with Roan," Orion said suddenly. "We need to find the Changeling. We cannot leave her—regardless of whether or not she's responsible for this." *By the Gods, these two—* "But," he continued, stopping me before I could say anything, "I also agree with you. We can't just let the humans overrun us and we can't kill them—not without permission."

"Then what are you suggesting?" I demanded. "We cannot sit and wait."

"Roan will go look for her," Orion replied, shocking the man in question if the way he jerked his head up and snapped it to the side to stare at Orion was anything to go by. "You and I will begin the process of infusing the Lanuaet. We'll give him as much time as possible, but—" Orion turned to Roan for the last bit, "if you can't find her, you must give it up and come help us. We can't move the castle alone."

Roan bared his teeth, obviously finding flaw with this plan, and as much as I didn't like it either—the fact that neither of us seemed pleased with it made it a decent compromise. "One hour," I said, holding up a finger. "The gates will hold for that long—"

"They can hold for longer," Roan snapped, interrupting me.

"But we can't," I said. "Orion and I will need you at the Lanuaet. An hour is pushing it. Be back before then."

Roan looked from me to Orion, and when Orion nodded to him, he cursed—whirling about and dashing off. I watched him leave and once he was out of my sight, I closed my eyes and released a growl of frustration before shoving my fingers up through my hair. I wanted to yank the damn locks out.

"That girl is going to be the death of us," I snapped at Orion as I swung around and started off, heading straight for the Lanuaet room. If Roan was even a second later than the hour he'd been granted, I'd kill the bastard myself—after we moved this Gods forsaken castle.

CHAPTER 27
CRESS

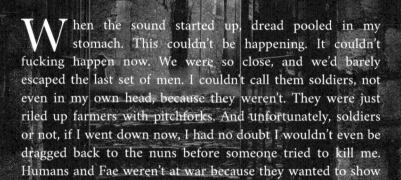

When the sound started up, dread pooled in my stomach. This couldn't be happening. It couldn't fucking happen now. We were so close, and we'd barely escaped the last set of men. I couldn't call them soldiers, not even in my own head, because they weren't. They were just riled up farmers with pitchforks. And unfortunately, soldiers or not, if I went down now, I had no doubt I wouldn't even be dragged back to the nuns before someone tried to kill me. Humans and Fae weren't at war because they wanted to show off their battle skills. Humans and Fae *hated* each other, and I was no longer on the human side. If I died right now it would put Nellie at risk which was something I couldn't do.

I tried to block it out, focusing on the shouting of the angry mob that was closing in on the castle just as quickly as we were. While they had a nice road to travel down we were fighting brambles and prickly grasses that grew wild in the area. It reminded me of the first night when I found the castle. *What a wild way to come full circle*, I thought.

The sound in my head was increasing in intensity the closer we got to the castle. *What the fuck was it?* I winced as it pierced through my skull and nearly brought me to my knees. I stopped, my hand finding a nearby tree trunk as I panted and waited for the noise to die down. It never did, I just had to suck it up like a big girl and keep going. I forced one foot in front of the other even as I felt my mind splinter at the horrid sound. Why did it seem so much worse now—yet, I could still stand? Maybe because my Changeling side had been revealed? Or because my powers were starting to activate? Something was different and I wanted to know what.

Nellie stumbled along beside me, hissing in pain. I turned her way, prepared to haul her after me if she so much as thought about stopping and found one of the black vines from the castle's outer walls wrapped around her leg. They extended a lot further this time.

I wondered ...

Before—the first time I came across these things—they hadn't moved away until I'd bled on them, leading me to stumble into the castle and into this whole mess. As I moved my injured hand, cracking the blood that had started to dry on the skin there and opening the wound, fresh blood began to flow, and I really hoped they'd do the same thing now. I wasn't ready to leave the mess—or the princes. I was just finding out who I was and I also really didn't want to get caught by a bunch of country folk with too many sharp things at their disposal. I sucked in a breath and let my blood fall, hoping and praying ... but a girl couldn't exist on prayers to the Gods alone. She had to bleed a little first.

I held my hand over the vine and big, fat drops of blood fell onto its black surface. For a moment, I thought I was, yet again, wrong—that the vines weren't designed to detect Fae presence and stand down, but after a few tense minutes where my ears started to feel more and more like they were going to burst, the vine loosened its grip and released Nellie.

It wasn't much, but it was enough for us to keep moving

and get a little closer to the castle. When another vine caught her leg I wanted to scream. Apparently, this section hadn't got the information yet. I dripped some more blood onto it and when it released her I turned to Nellie and said, "Let's go." I turned and dropped down, holding my arms out on either side.

"W-what?" she stuttered.

"We don't have time for me to keep stopping to bleed on everything," I said. "Piggyback ride time. Hop on."

"Can you even hold me?" she asked.

"Just do it," I huffed.

This time, she didn't object, which was just as well, because I would have hauled her over my shoulder like a sack of potatoes if she kept fighting me. I wasn't strong, but I was determined and stubborn. The two of us made it through what was now a field of the black vines and to the edge of the castle without stopping again. The closer we got, surprisingly, the less painful the noise became—though it remained in my head throughout. Unfortunately, my exhaustion only mounted. When I set Nellie down, I wanted to crumple to the ground and sleep for years. We didn't have time for that though. There was an alarm ringing in me, maybe it was this sound that I could still hear, I wasn't sure, but every fiber of my being was telling me I needed to be inside that castle before the sound stopped or something very bad was going to happen.

Nellie leaned against the wall and stared back the way we'd come, her eyes growing wide and full of fear. I glanced back, following the direction of her gaze. I could see them as well, but just as my eyes lit on the makeshift soldier's powering through the forest now, while their counterparts marched over the nearby fields—I saw the vines spreading out in a fan. The men began to trip, going down amidst the brush and tall grasses. They were getting stuck in the vines. Men who were trying to capture us, to harm us, possibly even kill us were being attacked by vines. Never thought I'd be so grateful for some nature. Even as the men used their torches to try and burn the vines away, it only seemed to add to the strength and size of the long animated plants. I turned back and focused on the task at hand.

I placed my hands on the wall, not knowing what else to do and took a deep breath. *Okay, time to convince a big ol' magic castle to let me in.* "Hi there," I started, earning a look of 'what the fuck' from Nellie. "Give me a break," I whispered her way before she could say anything. "I've only done this once before and it was an accident."

"Dear Gods," she whispered, smacking herself in the face, "you're going to get us both killed."

I ignored that and turned my gaze back to the big stone wall in front of me. "If you could just let us in, that would really be great." I waited a beat. When nothing happened, my breath hitched and Nel released a terrified groan. I looked back over my shoulder. A few of the men had managed to bypass the vines, hacking them away with their halberds. They were getting far too close for my peace of mind. "Alright," I said, standing up straighter as I pressed both of my palms forward against the wall. "Come on, magic wall," I entreated. "You let me in before, you can do it again. I'm a Fae. I promise I belong! Your vines know it too, that's why they let me through, isn't it?" I paused and took a breath. No one in their right mind talked to inanimate objects—but I wasn't giving up. If it made me crazy, then it made me crazy—Gods knew I hadn't exactly been sane before meeting the princes.

The ground rumbled beneath my feet and I panicked, slipping and leaving a smear of blood on the stone. I could hear cries over the top of the Castle wall. Men and horses. *There'd been horses in the castle?* I thought before shaking my head. It was a castle, of course there were horses. Probably stables too. I'd just never been given the chance to explore.

"Please," I said. "If you don't let us in then we'll die, and I'm too young to die—and Nel's too pretty to die. We'd really like to avoid that if at all possible."

Nel groaned again. "I can't believe this," she hissed.

Again, I ignored her. Her new name was now going to be Negative Nellie—I snickered internally. At the moment, it was very apt. "They're looking for me, aren't they?" I asked the castle. "I know they are, right? The longer they delay, the more damage you take from the attackers. If you won't do it for me, then do it for yourself. Besides, it wasn't even my choice to leave you, I was pushed." Still, nothing happened and I was starting to lose hope. I didn't know what the price was to get the door to open, but I hadn't hit on it yet.

My shoulders slumped and I leaned forward, pressing my forehead against the wall. "I want to be who I was born to be," I said quietly. "I want to learn what it means to be Fae, to be a member of the Court of Crimson—to be well and truly fucked by Prince Orion, to eat food I actually enjoy, and to devour all the knowledge I can in that library that Groffet cares for. Please, don't let me miss out on that. I don't want to be left behind again."

The ground beneath our feet rumbled for a second time, this time much harder. It shook as though a great wheel was turning. When a door appeared in the brick I wanted to weep with joy, but we weren't safe yet. Without even stopping to think, I turned, snatched Nellie's hand and yanked her behind me until the both of us went tumbling through the door, and into the main courtyard, which shouldn't have been possible since the courtyard would have been on the opposite side of the castle by my estimations. I looked up and eyed the castle and its walls now surrounding us. Magic castles, so temperamental.

CHAPTER 28

CRESS

I pushed to my feet and brushed some of the dirt from my clothing before noticing a streak of black and red as a certain prince sped towards the castle's front gates on a tall, ebony stallion. "Roan!" I cried as I sprinted towards him, the horse not giving a damn that I was trying to get its rider's attention. Finally, my mad dash and frantic waving must have succeeded because his eyes went as big as saucers and he jerked on the reins of the stallion, bringing the giant creature to a halt before directing it my way.

Nel coughed behind me and slowly began to get off the ground as Roan rode up, releasing the reins long enough to leverage one thick, masculine leg over his saddle and hop down. His long legs ate up the remainder of the distance between us as he stormed my way. He didn't stop when he reached me either. His arms came down on either side of me, fingers digging into my sides as he wrapped me up and lifted me until I had to wrap my legs around his waist to keep from sliding back down. His hold tightened as he threatened to squeeze the life out of me. I couldn't help myself, I relished in the embrace. I leaned forward and stuffed my face against his throat as I inhaled his scent and tightened my arms around his shoulders. Abruptly, his arms loosened, and he pulled his head away as though he just remembered who I was and where we were. My heart deflated more than I wanted to admit when he set me back on the ground and his eyes took on a dangerous glint.

"Where were you?" he growled. "Do you have any fucking clue the mess we're in? And who is this?" He pointed at Nellie, wrinkling his nose as her scent caught on the wind. He growled again, stepping back. "A human? You brought a human here? Were you the one responsible for this?"

As Nellie reached my side, I scooted her behind me just a little so she wasn't facing the brunt of his ire. "I can explain," I said quickly. "Ariana pushed me over the castle wall. I tried to get back in, but the castle wouldn't let me. I was going to the village, but I got hurt—I think a hunter's trap. I passed out and some sheep found me. I was taken back to the convent that I came from before. This is Nellie, she's my best friend. She helped me when no one else would and I couldn't leave her behind to be punished. She knows that I'm Fae, she didn't hurt me—I had to help her. We escaped and came back here," I said, watching the expression on his face morph from anger to confusion to more anger and then to frustration.

Roan lifted a palm and ran it through his hair, some of which was literally flaming. "We don't have time to deal with this now," he snapped. His eyes moved down to my attire and he cursed. His lips parted but before he could say anything, a loud clang erupted at the front gates. Several male Fae crossed the courtyard, racing up the steps to the top of the castle walls. "The humans have made it to the gate," he said with a hiss.

"They're just farmers," Nellie piped up.

Roan's eyes darted over my shoulder. "Farmers or no, they

would have killed you for helping a Fae, wouldn't they?" he growled.

She grew quiet and I frowned at him. "She helped me," I snapped, moving forward to poke him in the chest with a finger. "Be nice."

"She's human."

"I thought I was too," I replied.

Roan's eyes grew heated as I continued to glare up at him. Without any warning, his hands came up and grasped my upper arms, holding me still as his mouth came down hard on mine. I yelped even as his tongue pushed past my lips and he stole all of my anger and rational thoughts away with his mouth. His kiss swept me up and consumed me, growing more and more heated—both in temperature and in passion as his tongue twined with mine. The kiss released within me a myriad of emotions. I latched onto him just as he had me and I kissed him back.

He was demanding in his kiss, so demanding that it's all I could do not to melt into a puddle at his feet as he continued his assault on my senses. Something soft moved against my skin, the half-shredded, dirtied clothes that hung on me moving in what felt like a force of wind. Soon enough, however, everything else disappeared and all that was left was me and him.

When we finally broke away and both of us were breathing hard, Roan's eyes closed for a moment and he rested his forehead against mine as I glanced down. "Um ... Roan?" I coughed to clear my throat. "What happened to my clothes?" The torn shirt and ragged trousers that I'd put on before I'd been pushed over the castle wall—the same torn shirt and ragged trousers that had traipsed with me through the woods twice, gotten me in a hunters trap and out of the convent for a second time—had disappeared. In their place were a pair of skin tight black pants with a swish of floor length fabric around the majority of my legs even shielding the new trousers. Across my chest, a thin metal plating of armor covered my breasts over an equally tight, sleeveless shirt the same material as my new pants.

"You can't walk around the castle half naked," he replied. "I can't handle it. I wouldn't be able to keep my hands off of you and we really need to go."

"You could change my clothes like this the entire time?" I clarified.

He sighed. "It's useless energy if you can change them yourself," he responded with a shrug as he pulled away from me almost regretfully.

"Why would you use energy to change my clothes?" I asked, surprised.

His head turned as another clanging sound ricocheted through the nearly empty courtyard. Male Fae at the tops of the castle walls were doing something—throwing fireballs with their bare hands and shouting as they tried to hold off the human horde on the other side. It almost seemed funny that so few Fae could hold off so many—albeit untrained—humans.

"Because I don't know if we'll be able to move the castle," Roan answered on a whisper. One of his hands tightened on my arm while the other released me. "Come on, we have to get to the Lanuaet. Orion will want to know you're safe—but more than that, we have to transport the castle or we're going to be overrun."

We set off at a quick pace, with Nellie running to keep up on her shorter legs. I was no giant, but I was taller than her so it was easier for me to follow after Roan. As soon as we made our way back into the castle proper, I felt like I could actually breathe again. Roan's stride didn't slow as he led us around curves and corners, twisting this way and that, only pausing once to have Nellie peel off. "Go through that door on the right just there and you'll meet Groffet. Tell him Prince Carmine sent you. You're to stay there until the castle is moved."

Without thinking, I reached out and grabbed Nellie's arm, pulling her in for a quick hug. She hugged me back before doing as Roan commanded. Before I could truly fret about being separated from her, Roan took my hand and we were running again. The further in we went, the more I began to recognize the hallways. Within moments, we were sprinting down the long hallway that I knew led to the big ball of magic I'd seen before.

When we burst into the room my eyes darted first to Orion, who broke into a wide grin, and then to Sorrell, who looked, well, like Sorrell. Pissed, grumpy, and ice cold. He didn't exactly wear his emotions on his sleeve like the others. The dark scowl on his face only lightened slightly when Roan stepped into what I assumed was his spot and the three of them began wordlessly working their magic to get the orb to start spinning.

Strain was evident on all three of their faces, even Mr. Stoic himself. Sorrell grimaced with the effort they were putting in. A feeling, a crackle of energy as large as a storm swept through the air for a moment, but it dissipated almost as soon as it appeared. The noise I'd heard before—the horrible screeching sound that had plagued me—was now a humming. I looked around realizing that every beat of the hum matched the same moment when one of the guys pushed another wave of magic into the orb floating between them. The noise, I realized, had been coming from this room the entire time. The hum grew and faded in my mind—sometimes growing so loud that it was a scream and sometimes quieting until it was nothing more than a whisper. It remained constant even as I waited, and waited, and waited.

"We haven't recovered enough," Orion said through

clenched teeth, releasing his hold on the giant ball of magical energy.

"We have no choice," Sorrell practically growled at him as he redoubled his own efforts.

"Orion's right. The castle can take a beating. We can get some of the lower ranking Fae to reinforce the ward and protections and—"

"And what do you think your mother would say about that? Not to mention mine." Sorrell released his hold on the magic with a blackened curse slipping from his lips as he wavered on his feet. The three of them stared at each other, their eyes darting to one another as sweat poured down their faces. They continued to snipe and growl at each other like caged predators awaiting their chains to be unlocked and once they did? It would all be over for the fool that got in their way.

Turns out ... I was that fool.

"What if I helped?" I asked. My question was greeted by immediate silence as the three of them turned my way. Even the cold one looked shocked. I sighed and gestured to the opening between Roan and Sorrell. "It's clear there is supposed to be a fourth person, but it's just you three. I have magic—if I didn't then I would've died when I was pushed over the side of the castle wall. Something stopped me. And my blood stopped the castle vines from hurting me. What if adding another person—another Fae—made you stronger?"

"You would do well to keep quiet and let the grownups handle this, little Changeling," Sorrell bit out. "Only royal Fae can interact with the Lanuaet's magic. A lesser Fae, as you likely are if you're even a Fae—"

"I am," I interrupted with an angry snarl.

"Regardless," he continued without blinking, "a lesser Fae would offset the balance of power and not in a good way. Now, stand back and let us do this."

I frowned at him as Orion and Roan offered me apologetic looks while they stepped back into their spots and refocused themselves and their magic onto the orb floating between them. Once again, they were back where they started—their faces strained and even pinching in pain as they poured magical energy into the ball. All around me, I felt a whistling as the castle shook and trembled. Obviously, whatever they were doing was affecting it. I inched closer to where I would need to be if I wanted to help, not that I was planning on jumping in or anything. It was just in case they asked. I snapped a look at Sorrell. He wouldn't, I knew. But if Roan or Orion even gave me half of a look of desperation, I'd jump right in. Sorrell could fuck all the way off, but those two cared and I wasn't going to let them down if I could help it.

I watched their movements carefully, seeing exactly what their hands were doing and mimicking it in my mind so I could remember it, in case I needed it in the near future. The three of them only worked for a few minutes before their handsome faces grew pale as their features contorted with strain and what could only be described as suffering. I knew I should follow their request and stay where I was unless they asked, but I couldn't shake the feeling in my heart telling me if I just took another step forward, I could do something.

My bottom lip was raw from my nervous chewing by the time I made the decision. When I stepped forward, none of them even blinked. They were all concentrating so hard on what was right in front of them that they didn't see me slip into place. I lifted my hands, stretching my fingers out as I moved in the same way they were. Whatever they were doing with their hands, I began to copy and almost immediately, I felt the orb's magic like a tidal wave sweeping through me.

Magic slammed into my chest, and it was all I could do to keep standing and moving as a gasp slipped out of my lips. The three of them jolted, their heads coming up when they finally realize what I'd done. I could ... feel the echo of the orbs magic within myself. I slowly breathed out as the weight of the magic eased a bit and instead of feeling like a pile of rocks on my chest, it began to trickle down into my limbs like water running over my body. I felt their magic, too. Ice frosting over my skin from Sorrell. Fire that sizzled in my blood from Roan. And something else, something darker creeping into my mind from Orion. It was like the four of us were all part of the same being, all thinking and feeling, but within the same body.

"We need to stop," Orion ground out. "She'll burn out all her magic."

"She wants to help so badly, then let her help," Sorrell snarled. "It's her death."

"Cress," Roan said, "stop."

"Wait..." This came from Sorrell. I darted a glance at him as his eyes widened. "It's ... working?"

"Dear Gods," Orion cursed as the magic whipped through me—through all of us, stronger than before and the castle's shaking evened out.

"Follow our movements and focus on the fields of Arenthry, that's our next destination," Roan barked.

I nodded and tried my best to follow along, but the hand gestures were more than a little complicated, and I felt sure I was messing some of them up, but the Gods awful noise had quieted and the magic ball was spinning faster with parts of it expanding outward before it changed directions and different parts extended, like it was trying to lock in some kind of coordinates. Through it all, I could feel Sorrell boring holes into me with his glare. I turned my gaze onto him instead of the spinning ball that was so captivating and met his glare with one of my own. I wished I understood why he disliked me so, but I doubted I ever would.

The magic began to burn across my palm where Mother Collette had wounded me and I hissed in pain. The blood there was flowing freely again and not just a little either; more than had been flowing before was streaming from my palm and into the swirling vortex of the ball of magic and its coordinate setting spinning and twisting, like a red stripe across iridescent silver. My head felt light and I felt sick, but the only thing I could see was Sorrell staring at me with a sneer marring his perfect face as he seemed to get even taller.

CHAPTER 29

CRESS

My sickness only seemed to grow the more magic I used. The Lanuaet's power slid through me just as Orion's, Roan's, and Sorrell's. The ice man had been right. It was far too much for me to handle. Not that I was going to let him know that, even if my insides felt like they were heating up and my skin stretched tight across my bones, I was stubborn enough to keep going.

The castle rumbled and swayed. I kept my gaze focused on the magical orb. At least now I realized what this thing did. So much was starting to make sense that hadn't before. The noise in my head. The castle's magic. This orb—the Lanuaet thingy—was a transporter of sorts. And as I looked around the room, the Fae princes—and now I, too—were the conduits.

Across from me, Orion grunted and went down on one knee. I almost stopped the movements to go to him, but Roan barked at me to stay where I was. Sweat collected at the back of my neck and slid down my spine. I felt something wet ooze out of my left nostril. I paused just long enough to wipe it away, and my hand came away red.

"Almost there," Roan panted through tightly clenched teeth.

Orion staggered back to his feet and kept going.

Sorrell said nothing.

My head began to ache and more wetness leaked out of my nose. No one said anything, but something was very wrong. A wall of resistance met the four of us and pushed back. My eyes widened when I felt it—something like fire and ice raced up my arms and slipped beneath my flesh. I cried out at the same time that the guys grunted. They were obviously feeling the same effects of whatever that was.

"Something's not right," Sorrell finally conceded. Thank the Gods. Even if it was the ice cold asshole, at least someone had said it.

"We can't afford to stop," Roan replied.

"It's—" Just as Orion was about to offer his input a new wave of magic—one that I didn't recognize—wrapped around us. All three of them stiffened and dropped their arms, causing me to slow and do the same. I heard Roan curse as stones began to fall from the ceiling of the chamber. I looked up.

"It's crashing!" Orion yelled.

I didn't see him coming. One second, I heard the shout and the next I was being shoved down as a giant, boulder sized piece of the ceiling came crashing down right where I'd been standing. I gaped at the giant chunk of rock. *Dear Gods. That would've killed me!* I released a sigh of relief, turning towards Roan to thank him for saving me only to stop short when I realized it wasn't Roan's flaming red hair hovering over me. Instead, it was Sorrell's white-blue locks that slid across his forehead as he groaned and leveraged himself up and off me.

He laid on his back and I laid on mine, the two of us staying put as the castle finished shaking and trembling. Thankfully, no more stones or large pieces of ceiling fell overtop us as Orion and Roan rushed to our sides. Roan looked at me and when I waved him away, he nodded, going to Sorrell. Orion stopped at my side and reached for me, despite my attempt to wave him away as well.

My body felt like it'd been put through a beating. "Am I bruised?" I asked absently. "I feel bruised."

"You're not bruised," Orion answered. "But you are drained."

I groaned low in my throat as he lifted me from the ground, cradling me in his arms. I didn't even realize what I was doing until my arms were curling around his neck as I snuggled into his massive chest. Damn, he felt good against me. I pressed a kiss to his throat, earning a dry chuckle.

"What happened?" I asked. "Did we make it? Did we move the castle?"

Roan helped Sorrell to his feet just a few steps away and even as Sorrell clutched his side, he looked over at me with a scowl I didn't understand. I didn't warrant his ire so I had no idea why he was being such a butthead. "Something interfered," he growled. "You should've never tried to help. Now, we have absolutely no idea where we've fucking landed."

I arched away from Orion, nearly spilling out of his arms as I moved to smack the horse shit out of him. How dare he? "All I wanted to do was help!" I snapped as Orion dropped my legs, but wrapped his arms around my middle to keep me from reaching Sorrell.

"It's a miracle she survived," Roan said absently as he moved towards one of the small slitted windows that circled the room.

"You're a disaster waiting to happen," Sorrell accused.

"At least I'm not a bitter Fae with his head shoved up his ass!"

"Okay, that's enough," Orion said, wrestling me back as I tried to get out of his hold once more.

"No!" I snapped. "It's not enough. I don't know what your problem with me is, but I've never done anything to you."

"No?" Sorrell's cool blue eyes narrowed on me as he strode

straight up to me. Orion lowered his head and glared at his fellow prince over my shoulder.

"Sorrell," he said, his voice low and calm, but still resonating with warning.

Sorrell ignored him. "You, little Changeling—" he began, leaning into my space. I squirmed and wiggled and stood on my tiptoes on the tops of Orion's boots so I could be as close to eye level with him as possible. "—are nothing but a giant pain in my—"

"Guys!" Roan's sharp bark had the three of us turning our heads to him as he stumbled away from the window with a sick, pale look on his face, made worse by the fact that I was sure whatever power he'd fed to the Lanuaet had left him already feeling low.

Sorrell and Orion both immediately snapped to attention. "What is it?" Sorrell asked, striding over to him.

"I know where we are," he said. "We're in Alfheim."

Orion's arms grew slack around my middle and I stepped off of the tops of his boots, removing his limbs completely from me as I turned to look up at his face. "What is it?" I asked. "What's Alfheim?"

He didn't respond for a moment, staring across the room at Sorrell as he, too, looked out of the slit of a window and cursed. Finally, when I shook his arm and repeated the question, he met my gaze. "Alfheim is the realm of the Fae," he said, his voice so quiet it was nearly a whisper.

"Oh." I turned back to the other two. "Isn't that a good thing?" I asked. "We're in the country of the Fae." I'd never known what it was called—the nuns had taught us nothing of the Fae except that they were bad and evil and we were at war with them.

"We weren't targeting the Fae realm," Roan said, explaining as he and Sorrell headed back to us. He took my arm and steered me to look through one of the other nearby windows. I squinted and leaned into the frame. The window itself wasn't even as wide as my body. Over the castle walls beyond, I saw what looked to be another castle—this one coated in a layer of white.

"Then how'd we get here?" I asked absently as Orion looked out over my head.

No one answered for a moment and when curiosity got the best of me, I turned, pushing Orion back slightly as I brushed by him and flipped back around to eye the three of them. Each of them looked as though they were men about to face the gallows. A pit formed in my gut.

"What?" I asked. "What is it?"

"There's only one way we could've been pulled to Alfheim so soon—especially in the midst of a human assault," Roan answered me, his eyes darkening. "And that's if someone else pulled us here."

"Okay..." Still, I waited for someone to explain what the hell was going on. What did this all mean? I thought it was a good thing that we'd somehow landed in the Fae realm, but from the looks on their faces, it seemed more like we'd signed our death warrants. "Who could do that?" I finally asked.

This time, Sorrell didn't waste a moment before answering. He lifted his hands and ice began to form around his wrists, sinking deep beneath his flesh until drawings and artwork in blue began to rise up and mark his skin. I gaped, wide-eyed, as a crown of ice formed around his head.

He sighed before sending me a withering glare. "There's only one Court currently residing in Alfheim, Changeling. My Court—the Court of Frost."

I bit my lip and waited. When the three of them only stared at me like I was expected to know what that meant, I shrugged. "And that means...? What does that mean exactly?"

Sorrell glared at me. Nothing new there. It was Roan who spoke up. "Cress." I turned my gaze his way, noting that he too looked concerned, both dark red brows drawn down over his eyes and his lips pinched and frowning.

"What?" *What was so bad? If I was a Changeling, if I was Fae, then I had nothing to worry about being in the Court of Frost, right?* "Are they like … cannibals or something here? Because I draw the line at eating people."

"Cress, this is serious." Roan reached forward and grabbed my arms, startling me as he met my eyes and held them. "The Court of Frost isn't necessarily dangerous, they're just incredibly prejudiced. We're somewhat tolerant—"

I snorted, earning another scalding glare from Sorrell. Tolerant, my ass. But I didn't say anything and nodded to let Roan know he could continue.

"Cress, you brought your friend here. Your *human* friend," he said with emphasis. My mouth dropped open, but as my mind began clicking things together, he kept going. "There has never been a human in Alfheim before."

"At least, not any that lived to tell the tale," Sorrell commented.

My eyes darted from Roan to Orion. Orion frowned, appearing somewhat confused, and I realized that they hadn't known about Nellie. Only Roan had met her because he'd been the one to find us first when we'd managed to break back into the castle.

"I say let the human rot," Sorrell said after a beat of silence.

I ripped myself away from Roan and turned on Sorrell so fast my hair whipped into my face and slapped my cheek. "No!" I snapped, jabbing him in the chest with my finger. "No one touches her." The tip of my finger grew blue the longer I held it to Sorrell's chest. He narrowed his eyes on me.

"You shouldn't have brought her here," he stated.

Even if that was true… "Where else was she going to go?" I asked. "She saved me." I pressed my free hand to my chest. "A

Fae like you. If she'd gone back, she would have been as good as dead. A traitor to her own species."

Sorrell took a step forward, pressing me back as my finger fell away from his chest. Almost immediately, warmth refilled the digit and it throbbed in response. "Do you know what happens to humans in Alfheim, Changeling?" he asked. "Do you know what the Frost Queen will do to someone like your friend?"

I didn't know if he wanted an answer, but I gave him one anyway, shaking my head.

"Good," he said quietly, leaning closer as his icy breath washed over my face. "If you knew, there's no way you'd be able to go with us."

"G-go with you?" I stuttered.

"We cannot allow the Queens to come here," he said by way of answer, standing up straighter and backing away. He turned to Roan and Orion. "Get ready to ride," he said before turning and striding out.

I turned my head, feeling numb until I met Roan and Orion's gazes. "W-what happens to humans in Alfheim?" I asked hesitantly.

Roan looked down, but Orion met my gaze. His swirled with darkness, shadows, and something sinister. A shiver chased down my spine and even before he opened his mouth, I knew what he was going to say. His lips parted and he uttered the words, confirming my worst fear for Nellie.

"They die."

COURT OF FROST

Two Cruel Queens and the cold wrath of a Prince...

The truth is out.
But nothing can promise safety forever.

As the war between humanity and the Fae grows bloodier by
the day, the last of the Royal Fae Queens summon their
children back to Alfheim.

This time, only they know what the future may hold.

Only one person can play the game of Fae politics better than
anyone else. If I want to survive—and I definitely do—I'm
going to have to rely on the one prince I hate the most—the
Prince of Frost.

CHAPTER 1
CRESS

L ife wasn't fair to some people. Some people, meaning me. Life wasn't fair to me. "The Court of Frost?" I parroted, staring, open-mouthed at Sorrell as a cloak of ice finished forming over his entire body.

He sighed and cast a dark look my way as if this was all my fault. It wasn't, so I didn't know what the attitude was for, but I didn't comment. "Yes," he stated. "We've landed in Alfheim and a castle doesn't just appear out of thin air, you know."

"It doesn't?" That seemed questionable to me since that's exactly what that castle had done. At least, from my perspective, it had.

He glared my way. "No," he said. "It doesn't. It takes a lot of magical energy to transport a castle. There's no doubt we've been summoned by the Court of Frost."

"The ambassador will be here soon then," Orion said.

I turned my head his way. "Ambassador?"

"Whoever he is, he'll want to escort us to the Castle of Frost," Roan responded with a nod.

"And you," Sorrell snapped, his finger pointed straight at me, making me blink, "need to explain what happened. I want a damn good reason why I shouldn't throw you in the dungeon and—"

Before Sorrell could even finish his threat, Roan stepped in front of me. "It was Ariana," he said coldly.

I peeked around his massive frame, watching as Sorrell's eyes widened a fraction before narrowing with suspicion. He lowered his arms and crossed them over his chest. "What happened?"

Roan looked back at me and I sighed, scooting out from behind his protective form. "Ariana said she wanted to talk—to explain," I began. "She took me to one of the castle walls, the one near the garden, and when we were talking she pushed me over the side. I tried to get back in, but the castle wouldn't open the door like it had before."

"Only Fae can cross into the castle," Sorrell said meaningfully.

I cut a glare at him, tightening my lips. "Well, it let me in before and it let me in this last time, now, didn't it?"

He didn't say anything for several moments, his face just as impassive and cold as it always was. *Why the hell had he even saved me from that falling piece of ceiling?* I wondered absently. It was obvious he didn't like me or trust me.

"Go on, Cress," Orion said, moving closer and touching my arm lightly.

I inhaled sharply and blew out a quick breath. "When I couldn't get back in immediately, I didn't know what else to do, so I started heading back to the village—"

"So, you did lead the humans to us," Sorrell growled, his expression darkening.

"Not on purpose!" I snapped. "I didn't even make it there before I fell into a hunter's trap and hit my head. Some sheep found me, apparently, and they took me back to the convent I was in before."

"Convent?" Roan frowned as confusion twisted his features and lowered his brows.

"It's not important," I said, waving my hand his way. "The fact is, I woke up there. Ran into my friend—who helped me escape—and we made our way back. By then, though, the nuns had called the soldiers from the local village and they'd already—"

"Wait, a friend?" Sorrell repeated, swinging his gaze to Roan. "Tell me you didn't bring another human into our court," he demands.

"Well, technically..." I started.

"I wasn't asking you, Changeling," Sorrell snapped.

That was it. I was going to clobber him. I was halfway between the space that separated us before I even knew what I was doing, but that was just fine with me. I lifted my finger and jabbed it right in his chest, shivering when a wave of cold washed over me. Slowly—ever so slowly—Sorrell's cool white-blue eyes tilted down to meet my gaze as I resisted yet another shiver and continued to scowl threateningly at him.

"I've had about enough of your remarks," I said through tightly clenched teeth. "And yes. I brought a human here—one, not *another*, because I'm a Fae. I think I proved that enough by stepping in to help you transport your stupid castle. Humans don't have magic, but I seem to. I don't know what your problem with me is but you need to figure it out and resolve it on your own because my best friend—the one who helped me even though I'm Fae, the one that lost her parents to Fae—is staying. Had I left her, they would have killed her. I don't leave my friends. Ever."

With that, I dropped my arm and took a step back. Still, I felt like my whole body was vibrating with my anger. I wanted to scratch his eyes out, claw at him until he bled. The anger I was feeling made me forget about the chill that surrounded him. In fact, I didn't feel it any longer—I felt overheated instead. A warmth rose up beneath my skin, making it practically glow with a yellow light. All three pairs of eyes were on me, watching me with a mixture of fascination and wariness. I didn't like that either.

It wasn't until Roan pulled me back against his chest, and I could feel his steady heartbeat in my ear, that I finally started to calm down. "It's okay, Cress," he said, leaning down to say the words in my ear. This time, I shivered for a completely different reason. But now really wasn't the time for that. "Your friend will remain safe. We'll have to leave her with Groffet, but he's trustworthy. If possible, we'll see if he can come up with an illusion that will keep her humanity a secret."

I swallowed against a dry throat. "Thank you," I croaked, feeling all sorts of emotions fill me up and slide through my veins. Damn. Being over-emotional really sucked. I felt drained already. If I were a man, I could probably punch Sorrell and be done with it, but I couldn't fight my way out of a wet bag made of parchment, so I settled for glaring at him.

I nodded once to let Roan know I'd heard him and acknowledged his words. I didn't know if that was some sort of signal for Orion, but he stepped forward and put a hand on Sorrell's shoulder. "We need to prepare for the ambassador's arrival," he said lowly.

"What's going to happen?" I found myself asking.

Orion's eyes cut toward me, but it was Sorrell who answered. "If we've been summoned by the Court of Frost then that means we're being summoned by the Frost Queen and the Crimson Queen." I frowned, confused, but he continued in that cool as ice voice of his—emitting no emotions. "And if we have been summoned then it's because we've broken Fae law."

"We couldn't help the original landing," Roan said. "They expect us to be able to transport the castle without the proper amount of power."

"Other courts have managed," Sorrell replied, lifting his head.

Roan's hands tightened on my shoulders. "Other courts have four royals. We wouldn't have been able to move it again had it not been for Cress."

"Which is a miracle in itself," Sorrell snapped before turning his gaze back to me for a brief moment before looking between Orion and Roan once more. "She could have died. If you two care so much about your damn Changeling, then keep her on a tighter leash."

I bristled, but Roan pushed me back and released me. "We don't have time for this," he gritted out. "We need to prepare to travel to them when the ambassador arrives."

"Agreed." I watched from behind Roan as Sorrell took a step back, his ice crown melting away as well as the cloak—*why had it even appeared in the first place,* I wondered, *if he was just going to make it dissolve again?* "I will make the arrangements."

When neither Roan nor Orion said anything more, he turned and left—the chill that constantly surrounded him remained in his wake. As soon as he was gone from my sight, my body sagged as if it'd been on edge and prepared for a physical battle the entire time he'd been near. I glared at the doorway through which he'd departed. He may have been a handsome and powerful Fae prince, but he was still an asshole.

CHAPTER 2
CRESS

repare for travel. Those were the last words Roan and Orion had said to me before ushering me back down the hallway in the new outfit Roan had magicked up for me. I'd done as they'd asked and prepared to travel, the problem was I still didn't have a lot of clothing, or, well, anything really, so there wasn't exactly a lot to prepare. Therefore, when a gaggle of Fae clad in blue and white trousers and long fluffy cloaks came striding into the castle's main throne room, I was the only one waiting for them.

I froze on the spot, watching as three unfamiliar Fae paraded into the room. The Fae with their luminescent eyes and perfect features twisted their heads and gazed around, seeming to expect some kind of welcoming committee. When all they saw was me, mid bite of a roll in my hand as I sat on the steps of the throne dais—minus the actual throne—they stopped and stared expectantly.

Still, I waited to see which of them would be selected to approach. I was pretty sure when the guys had dumped me here and told me not to go anywhere, they'd meant to stay away from the incoming Fae. Had they not realized that this was the first place these people would probably look for them? I shook my head. Men—it didn't matter if they were human or Fae—they were all the same.

Finally, one of the Fae sighed and stepped forward, dipping his head as if he were unsure of whether or not he should bow. It was kind of funny. Who would bow to me?

"We have been sent ahead from the Court of Frost to prepare for Ambassador Solas' arrival. Where may we find the princes of the Court of Crimson or their Ambassador?" the young man asked.

What should I do? I thought to myself. On one hand, I could follow the prince's orders and keep my mouth shut and wait for them to arrive. *But that would be rude, wouldn't it?* My internal debate didn't last long. As much as I would've loved to keep myself out of it, the fact was they were here now and someone needed to give them *something*. Unfortunately, that someone had to be me. I looked down at the roll in my hand before standing with a sigh. "Pixies!" I called out.

The Fae before me blinked as several of the fluttering little creatures appeared from the rafters and hovered over my shoulders. I gestured to the man in front of me. "Can you help him get what he needs for the Ambassador? I promise there's at least two rolls in it for you."

A frightening smile formed on the lead Pixie's face as he shifted closer to me before turning and fluttering toward the Fae who'd requested assistance.

He stared at the Pixie before turning his gaze on me once more. "You bargain with your Pix?" he asked, shock clear in his tone.

I shrugged. "Sure, I do. Seems to work just fine."

"But…" He frowned. "Why?" He gestured to the Pixies. "You could simply command them to do your bidding. They are Pix. It is their role to serve us."

I pursed my lips and arched a brow. Even at my full height, I only came up to his chest. *Were all Fae this tall?*

"Because," I started, shaking off the wayward thoughts, "I respect all living creatures and believe they deserve to be rewarded for their work. Plus, there are plenty of rolls available and they love them, so why not?" I tossed one in the air to demonstrate and the Pixies had every crumb consumed before it could touch the ground. "Just tell them what you need."

I stepped away, moving further from the dais as the Fae turned toward the Pixies. As discreetly as possible, I motioned for one of the Pixies still hovering overhead to come down. As it flew closer, I peeked over my shoulder to make sure that the new arrivals were distracted before speaking to the Pixie.

"Go get the princes," I whispered to the little buzzing creature. "Tell them that their ambassador and his ... erm ... entourage is here and you might want to mention that I'm alone with them." That would definitely get their butts moving. I handed over a small morsel of food in payment and the Pixie was gone in a flash.

A few minutes later, the telltale sound of boots echoed up the walls as the princes arrived. Only then was I really able to breathe a sigh of relief.

"Darius, it's good to see you again," Sorrell called, striding to the forefront. He stopped and inclined his head ever so slightly to the man I had been speaking to.

Darius, on the other hand, dropped into a bow, the cape he wore flaring out all around him as he lowered his head.

"It's good to have you home, Your Highness; if only it were under better circumstances."

"Agreed. How were you able to get here so fast?"

Darius lifted his head slightly. "The Frost Queen sent us out a few days ago. She expected that you would land a decent trek from our home court and we were to wait until we could determine your location before we came to deliver you and your fellow throne brothers to the Court of Frost."

Sorrell hummed low in his throat. "And what of these circumstances you mentioned?" he asked. Before the man could comment, however, the doors to the throne room were thrown open once more. Who knew Fae could have such a flair for the dramatic? Silently, I reached for another roll and bit into it. This was better than the attempts at theater the children of the convent tried every so often. Those performances had been half hearted attempts at relieving boredom. This was a masterpiece. They were all so serious.

A man appeared in the doorway, leading the charge. *This must be the Ambassador,* I thought. He certainly dressed like someone who thought they were important. His coattails were decorated and his sleeves more puffed up than a chicken about to explode. Three of his minions tittered at his coattails while he strode boldly up to the princes and bowed at the waist, not showing nearly the same level of respect as Darius.

"Ambassador Solas, it's a pleasure as always," Sorrell said. I darted a glance at the Ice Prince. If his tone was anything to go by, there was no pleasure found in this new man's presence. I chewed on my roll and swallowed. Interesting.

"The pleasure is mine as always, Your Highnesses," Solas said. "I am here to inform you that the Frost Queen and the Crimson Queen have both requested your presence as well as the presence of your court brothers at their court."

"Why couldn't they bring the message themselves?" The question popped out of my mouth before I could stop it, and almost as soon as the words had left my lips, I wished desperately that I could take them back. *What was I thinking?* That was a dumb question. They were Queens. Of course they weren't going to ride across a country just to deliver a message.

Sorrell's eyes cut toward me and zeroed in. If looks could kill, I'd have been six feet under and honestly, I couldn't blame him for his irritation. While I kept my cool outwardly, inside, I was a rolling mass of nerves. Solas slowly turned and gave me an appreciative once over, his lips parting as he spoke. "Because the Queens do not travel, young one. You should know that ... unless you've been living under a rock?" The last bit was said with genuine curiosity, a question in his answer. His sapphire blue eyes held me in thrall as he spoke, and I didn't realize how close he had come until he finished speaking. I looked up.

I cleared my throat a few times before I managed to make my voice work properly. "I'm a Changeling," I said, hopefully— as in, hoping that he didn't try to kill me like the princes had the first time they had met me. I rushed to continue, just in case that was a thought running through his mind. "The princes only just found me and I'm still learning what it means to be a Fae and all that." I waved my hand nonchalantly. *There, that should do the trick,* I thought. I glanced toward the princes. *Or ... maybe not?* I mentally corrected. Both Orion and Roan were watching me with caution, their gazes flickering between me and Solas. Sorrell's expression, on the other hand, appeared to have grown colder. If that was even possible.

"A Changeling?" Solas' tone picked up, delight in every syllable. *Well, that was a change,* I thought. "Come out from that dark corner, let me see you in the light."

Solas offered his hand to me and I took it, albeit hesitantly. He clucked once at me, grasping my hand a bit harder before spinning me in a circle. Almost immediately, I felt the wash of magic suffuse over my form. The trousers remained but grew closer—clinging to my form as a new material shaped over my legs and thighs, crawling up to fit to my entire body like one perfectly sewn suit. The shirt covering morphed, falling away as fabric formed at my hips, swirling like a mass of skirts with one big split seam that opened to reveal the black tight pants beneath. I blinked as I came to a stop. The material molded to my breasts, and up around my shoulders, leaving my arms bare and more than a hint of cleavage that drew Solas' eyes.

He smiled and nodded, releasing my hand when I lightly tugged away from him. "Much better; now I can actually see you," he said. "This is just some simple illusion work, a small talent my family has." He grinned as he took a step back and his eyes descended, crawling over me with a light of interest flickering in his gaze. "Beautiful, just, beautiful."

I bit my lip to keep from saying anything. It seemed all Fae males had a habit of doing things without asking. I glanced over, jerking slightly when three pairs of very dark, angry glares slid past me to fixate on Solas. Though none of them said a word against the Ambassador's actions, it was clear that the princes were not happy.

"Darling girl, when we get to the castle, I should like to give you a tour, show you how the Court of Frost operates. Maybe I can even persuade the Queen to let me show you our winter veranda. It's quite stunning and a Changeling like yourself would be in awe of its beauty, just as I am in awe of yours," Solas said, snatching my hand back up in a startlingly fast movement, bending to drop a kiss on my knuckles.

"That would ... um ... be nice?" I chuckled uncomfortably and, as soon as he released my hand, I rubbed the back of it against my pants, giving him a stiff smile.

"Dear girl, it's far more than simply nice. It's a treat. But I find that I like your shyness. Yes, I expect you'll adore the Court of Frost," Solas said before adding, "I know this is not customary for humans but we also have pleasure gardens that I would be happy to show you, where I could take you to new heights of ecstasy. I've been told I am very skilled with my tongue."

Shock rolled through me. Dear Gods. Pleasure gardens? I didn't want to see any sort of thing—especially not with him.

He appeared to be preening like a peacock before me. Compared to this man, Sorrell was the epitome of humility.

A low growl rumbled in someone's chest. I couldn't be sure which of the princes was making the noise; all I knew was that I did not want Solas to find out that I was anything more than a simple minded Changeling. If he looked too closely at me—or my relationship with the princes—perhaps he'd find out other things ... such as the fact that I now had my *very human* best friend hiding out in the Court of Crimson. "Let's just see how the tour goes first, shall we?" I offered in a strangled voice.

"As my lady wishes, so shall it be," he said, nodding with a brilliant smile. He backed away.

As though he couldn't stand to watch Solas' attempt at seduction for a second longer, Sorrell cleared his throat and spoke up. "I believe we should hurry to gather our traveling entourage, Ambassador Solas, don't you think?"

Roan nodded. "Agreed. Cress, join me?"

Yes! I silently screamed. *Get me the fuck away from this guy!* But thankfully, my mouth hadn't yet caught up and the words didn't come out. I somehow managed to keep a calm expression as I nodded and took the hand he offered me. "Of course."

Sorrell shot me a glare, but considering how often he did that, I was growing immune. Orion moved ahead as Roan ushered me to the exit.

"Please excuse us, Ambassador Solas," Roan called back. "If you require anything, feel free to call for our Pix or for our Ambassador, Groffet."

"The Troll?"

"He's quite capable, sir, I assure you. We'll be preparing for our travels and expect to leave within the hour." The rest of the conversation faded as we turned the corner and I was pulled out of the room by Orion and Roan.

CHAPTER 3
CRESS

I was halfway down the next hallway and well away from prying ears and eyes when I pulled up short. "Wait," I said, tugging on Roan's arm to get him to stop.

Roan stopped and looked at me, which in turn caused Orion to do the same. He glanced back, his eyebrow raised. "I want to bring Nellie," I said. "I can't leave her here."

Roan's lips pinched down as he and Orion exchanged a look. Sorrell appeared, making me jump as he caught up with us and pushed Roan and me apart, striding right through the opening he'd made for himself until he was on the other side. *Rude.* I scowled at his back as he took several steps ahead and then halted, turning on his heels until he stood before the three of us, blocking our path. "Absolutely not," he snapped. "It's out of the question."

"She's my friend—" I started.

"She's *human*," he growled.

"What is she going to do?" I asked, ripping myself away from Roan to face off with Sorrell. "She's not going to hurt anyone and she needs to be protected. Nellie's—"

"It's not about any harm *she* might cause, Cress," Roan interrupted, his hand touching my shoulder gently.

"A human in our court is bad enough, but in the Court of Frost?" Sorrell shook his head. "She would be found out and executed before we even made it ten steps inside the court. Or is that your plan, little Changeling? To kill your friend before she can betray you?"

"She wouldn't," I said quickly, "and I wasn't—"

Sorrell raised his voice and spoke over me. "The human stays here," he said with a decisive nod. "As far from trouble as possible. Groffet will keep a firm eye on her. She is not to make herself known. If a whisper of the fact that she's even here gets back to the Crimson Queen or Gods forbid, the Frost Queen," Sorrell jabbed his forefinger in my direction, "then your little human friend won't be the only one losing her head, we *all* will." He lowered his arm and glared at Roan and me meaningfully before he turned and gave Orion a once over for good measure. He seemed to think that glaring at us was the way to get us to do what he wanted.

Sorrell pushed past Orion and strode off, his stomping steps reverberating up the stone corridor, each one a punch to my chest. I pressed my lips together and clenched my fists as a wave of frustration came over me. Fear for Nellie, fear for myself, and fear for all of them came to a head inside me. What had I been thinking, bringing Nellie with me? Fae and humans were enemies. She hadn't been able to stay in the village after helping me and she was in danger here. It seemed no matter what I did, I brought devastation wherever I went.

"Don't cry, Little Bird," Roan said quietly, pulling me into his chest. I hadn't even realized I had been crying until then. I sniffed hard and reached up to wipe the evidence away. "Sorrell's attitude isn't just about you," he assured me. "The Court of Frost is cold and barren of any emotions. He hates returning to his home court. He's afraid, and fear makes people say unkind things. It's not an excuse, but he's right—we need to be very careful while we're in Alfheim, especially in the Court of Frost. It would be better—safer—for your friend to stay here."

"I'm going to get her killed," I whispered, my true fear escaping on a heavy breath.

Roan sighed. "She matters to you, and so we'll try to keep her safe."

"The only reason I'm even somewhat safe," I replied, "is because I'm a Changeling. She's not. She's just a human. They'll kill her if they find out—Sorrell said as much. You practically said as much about me when you weren't sure if I was human or not." I pushed away from him and looked up, staring into the fiery darkness of his eyes.

"As much as I disagree with the way Sorrell said it, he's right," Roan admitted with a grimace. "Your human friend can't come with us. What we need is for her to stay here. Groffet is much older than any of us, and because of that, he'll have a better idea of what to do with her. He'll come up with a high level illusion that will prevent her from being discovered as a human."

"It was stupid of me to suggest bringing her," I agreed with a sigh.

"I've got to go catch up with Sorrell before he does something stupid, like bark at the wrong visiting Fae."

"Okay."

Roan nodded and took a step back, releasing me completely. When I expected him to turn and walk away, though, he surprised me by staying put. His lips thinned as he sucked in a heavy breath. *Oh no*, I thought. I knew that look. That was a bad news look. I hated bad news looks. I had seen far too many of those particular looks in the last several days.

Those looks always meant something like *Hey, Cress, I know you want to protect your best friend but you're actually putting her in certain danger and you could be the reason she ends up executed by one of the most powerful Fae in the Realm,* or even *Hey, Cress, maybe don't trust the super hot Fae princes that you're kind of in lust with because they might just end up killing you after all.*

Roan's lips parted and, through clenched teeth, he spoke. "As unfortunate as it is"—*Yup. Bad news was coming my way*— "Ariana has been temporarily released from the Crimson dungeons and she'll be coming with us." My mouth dropped open. He couldn't be serious. *She pushed me off of the roof of the Gods damned castle!* Roan held his hand up to silence my impending protests. "She's one of my mother's favorites. Her absence would bring more questions than we want to answer. Right now, we want to avoid any unnecessary attention. Plus, Mother should be able to tell if Ariana is lying, she's always been good at that. Ariana will behave around her, if only in public."

I hissed out a breath and crossed my arms over my chest. "Are you forgetting that she tried to kill me?" I asked testily.

"No, I'm not forgetting that at all," Roan replied. "I'll keep her as far from you as I can. Out of sight, if possible. But she will be expected at the Court of Frost."

What could I say? I wondered. A tantrum would get me nowhere. No matter how much I wanted to throw one. I fumed as I considered my very limited options. The next time I saw Ariana, I was going to punch her in the face … with a chair … and then I might do it again just to make a point. "Fine," I said through clenched teeth. Just as I was about to turn away from him, Roan leaned forward and gently cupped my cheeks. I paused. A warmth infused my face and burrowed down into my core. I found myself wanting to lean into the touch, to luxuriate in it. Was that normal? Was that right? I darted a look at Orion, but he didn't look particularly upset. His eyes practically glowed as he watched us.

"Careful who you trust in the Court of Frost, Little Bird," Roan whispered against my skin as he brought his lips to my cheek. "Solas may seem like a buffoon, but he was chosen as the Queens' ambassador for a reason. Some will just be curious because of your status as a Changeling—there hasn't been one in a few decades at least. But some..." He ran his lips down the length of my jawline. I shivered. "Some will mean you harm. Trust no one but us," he finished before pulling away. I was leaning toward him, my whole body gravitating toward the pleasure of his flesh against mine. We hadn't done nearly the same amount of sensual touching as I had with Orion—my eyes slid back to his at the reminder—but the promise of it made my mouth water. I bit my lip as Roan turned and walked away.

As soon as we were alone, Orion took a step toward me, his form towering over my smaller one. "I'm having the Pixies bring some of my warmer cloaks and blankets, so hopefully we can keep you warm enough on the road, but the temperature outside is nothing like what you're used to. I'm worried about how it's going to affect you."

"I'll survive," I said with a shrug. *Probably.*

He dropped his head and planted a kiss on my cheek, very close to my lips. I almost turned my head and captured his mouth, wanting to feel something—*anything*—deeper. I didn't, but I definitely thought about it, and I was pretty sure he could tell, if the smirk on his lips was anything to go by as he backed up.

"Do you mind if I go and let Nellie know that we're leaving for a while?" I asked.

"Of course." He nodded. "I need to speak with Groffet anyway." Orion took my hand and held it as we strode through the corridors of the castle. We made several twists and turns until we were back at a familiar doorway.

"You two look like you're up to something. Whatever it is, keep it out of my library," Groffet grumbled at us as we pushed the doors open and stepped inside.

"I need to talk to Nellie," I said in response.

Groffet huffed as he waddled through several stacks of books before he nodded toward a corner. I turned and spotted a familiar small frame nestled there. I released Orion's hand and approached slowly. She was tucked into the corner with a book in her face, her eyes scanning the page at an incredible speed.

"Nel?" Her head popped up. "Hey..." I hurried over and hovered for a moment before I sat down next to her.

"You're back!" She reached for me, flinging the book around my neck as she squeezed me. It'd only been a few hours since I'd left her and I hated that I'd have to leave her again, so I squeezed her back with just as much enthusiasm. "Where've you been?" she demanded, pulling away and sticking her finger in her book to hold the page as she closed the cover.

"Dealing with some ... things..." I hedged, glancing back at Orion, but he wasn't paying us any attention. Instead, Orion was speaking in low tones with Groffet, his head down as his lips moved. I expected that it had something to do with Nel, since he nodded our way once before continuing. I sighed, turning back to Nel and taking her hands. "Listen," I started, "I have to leave the castle and I need you to stay here with Groffet."

Her eyes widened and she glanced over my shoulder to the stout Troll several feet away before her gaze landed on me again. "Why?" she asked. "How long are you going to be gone? Am I coming, too?"

"We have to visit another court," I admitted. "I'm not really sure when we'll be back. It's a whole thing, but you know how the war is still going on in the kingdom?" She nodded. "Well, Fae in Alfheim hate humans even more than the ones from this court. I'm sorry, Nel, but you can't come with us."

Her brows drew down over her eyes as her lips pursed, but before she could say anything, Orion was there, invading my space as he reached down and gripped my shoulder. I stood abruptly and Nellie stood with me. "Do not worry, little human. It will be a good opportunity for Groffet to work on an illusion to disguise you."

"Are we sure she's not another Changeling?" Groffet asked. "Sex with a Fae would be able to at least hide her scent—"

"Nellie doesn't want that!" I said quickly, the words practically screaming out of my throat before I could stop them. All eyes turned to me. I took a breath and at a much more subtle volume, I continued, "She's too young for that. She knew her parents, too, and they were definitely human." I eyed her out of the corner of my vision, but thankfully, she didn't speak up or say anything to disagree. I didn't know what I would've said or done if she wanted to. She was five years younger than me, but still, I wasn't comfortable throwing her at a Fae and seeing what happened. I also didn't give a rat's ass if Groffet was older than the Abbess' entire family tree, it wasn't going to happen. Nel had been ready to take vows of celibacy until I'd brought her to the castle.

"Then all the better reason for her to remain here and for Groffet to work on his illusion. It needs to be stronger than the sense of power you gained from sex with me," Orion replied. Heat suffused my cheeks, but I didn't say anything as he continued, focusing on Groffet. "Make it as strong as you can. Finding another Changeling is highly unlikely at this point. So, we must assume that Cress is correct and her friend is fully human. Whatever spell you come up with needs to be long lasting. We'll be gone for a few days at least, a few weeks at most. I can't say for sure, but you're an intelligent master, Groffet. I'm sure you'll be able to come up with something within that time. Keep her under your watch. As for you—" Orion's arms came around me and he tugged me away from Nellie. "We need to get down to the stables and get ready to go."

Nellie snorted. "You're going to ride a horse?" she asked.

"I am. Why?" I demanded.

"Cress, I love you, but you're not exactly the most graceful of creatures," she replied. "Anything involving walking, riding, running, or well, any kind of coordination, just doesn't really suit you." Nellie laughed after ticking all the things I wasn't good at off on her fingers.

"Har har," I said dryly. "You're so amusing." I gestured between her and Groffet. "You two get to work on that illusion while we go face the music. Don't worry about my riding capabilities."

"Or lack thereof?" she added with a grin.

I slapped at the air. "Don't worry about it."

"She'll be riding with me anyway," Orion said, as he half lifted, half dragged me away from the two of them.

"Nooooooo," I whined. "I want my own horse," I said as we left the library.

"No, you'll freeze."

"I won't," I promised. *How cold could it be out there?*

"You will," he said, shaking his head as he lifted me into his arms to keep my feet from dragging. I circled my arms around his neck. A girl could get used to this. "You need to ride with myself or Roan so you don't freeze to death," Orion said.

"Fine, I'll ride with you," I said with a sigh. "But only because you're probably too scared to ride a horse on your own."

He snorted, the sound indelicate and rude. Yeah, it was a total lie. He'd probably been riding horses since before he could walk. I just didn't want to admit that Nel was right. Riding a horse by myself was a horrible idea. I was just being stubborn. I could probably ride a horse alone if I wanted to though. How hard could it be?

CHAPTER 4
CRESS

Hard, I realized hours later. *Very hard.* Every step the horse took made my ass ache.

Up. Why was it always up? Why did up have to be the way that we were going? Why couldn't it be down? Not that down was much easier, but it was a sight better than up. My ass hurt. My thighs hurt. Even though Roan was at my back, his warmth seeping through our clothes to keep me from freezing my toes off, I still ached. Up was evil. Up was the direction in which I wish someone would shove this whole trip.

Even though I'd promised Orion I'd ride with him, as we'd readied to mount up, Sorrell had called his attention elsewhere. I'd watched as they'd both spoken in low tones for several minutes before Orion had lifted his head and looked at me apologetically. He never gave me a reason why we couldn't ride together, but I guessed it had something to do with the Prince of Frost. Thankfully, though, Roan was left to pick up the slack. I knew him and was at least semi-comfortable with his presence and having my back plastered to his chest for hours.

We'd been riding for half a day—the sun was high in the sky and despite the chill in the air burning my cheeks and all other available surfaces of my skin, I felt sweaty and achy beneath my clothes. Horse riding was no joke. It was a serious workout. Roan's steed—the same black stallion that I'd seen before when Nellie and I had stumbled right through the castle's courtyard, escaping the hoard of villagers wanting to destroy the castle— shook his head and blew out a breath. I got it. I really did. I reached forward and patted the creature lightly. I knew that as soon as we stopped for the night and I slid off, I'd collapse. My legs would never be the same again.

I groaned low in my throat, eliciting a chuckle from the masculine figure behind me. Slowly, I tilted my head back and squinted at mister tall, dark, and flaming hair—a whole new meaning to hot head. He rubbed my back lightly through the layers separating us—Alfheim was apparently more than the home of the Court of Frost, it was a frozen tundra.

"Don't worry, Changeling," he said lowly, the baritone of his voice sliding over my half-frozen nerves like warm liquid. "We'll be stopping for the night soon and I'll warm you up." I could just imagine how he'd do that.

I harrumphed irritably, but that didn't stop me from leaning back and stealing more of his warmth. If we went much further than this, I'd be a frozen meatbag by the time we arrived at the Court of Frost. When the horse beneath me jolted as it side-stepped, narrowly missing a hole in the road we were traveling, I released another pained groan.

Orion glanced back from where he rode up ahead next to Sorrell. Sorrell didn't even bother to look back or acknowledge my agony in any way. Asshole. "Are you okay, Cress?" Orion's concerned question reached my ears as he pulled up on the reins of his own horse, slowing until he moved alongside Roan and me.

"I'm cold," I said.

His smile was full of sympathy. "We should be stopping soon," he offered by way of consolation.

"My nose is frozen," I stated. His eyes moved down to that particular feature.

"It's a cute frozen nose," he said, his eyes lighting up with an intensity that I hadn't seen in a while. A very … sexual intensity.

I blinked, feeling a warmth flooding my belly. I thought for a moment, considering my next words. "My hands are frozen too," I said, watching Orion for his response. I should've been watching the man at my back. Roan reached forward and took my hands in his, pulling them down and cupping them on the outside of his strong thighs. I shivered at just how close I was to his … other appendage—the one between said thighs.

"I will warm you up, little Changeling," Roan whispered against my ear, sending a rush of warm breath over my earlobe. I swallowed roughly as desire thickened my voice and made it difficult to speak. *Gods, these Fae were dangerous creatures.*

"Perhaps she needs more than one Fae for the job," Orion commented lightly.

I couldn't see Roan's expression, but I felt it when he turned his head to look Orion's way. They must have exchanged some sort of silent communication because Roan chuckled deep in his throat, his chest vibrating against my back with the sound. *Dangerous!* my mind reminded me. *Hot. Sexy. Dangerous—bad—makes your mind go blank because they were so fucking sexy princes.*

"Would you like that, little Changeling?" Roan asked.

I gulped and went for the stupid act—though the nuns claimed it was never an act. "Huh?"

"Would you like to lie between Orion and me?" he asked, pressing even closer to me so that I could feel the hardness of his cock at the small of my back. My eyes widened. Holy Gods! That had to be a weapon in his pants. There was no way it was a cock. It was just too big. My eyes darted to Orion who was watching the two of us with intense lightning flashing through his irises. "Would you like to feel our hands on your pretty flesh?" Roan continued, squeezing my hands against his outer thighs.

"I think I'm warm enough!" I said quickly, tugging them away even as my face flamed with heat. Warm enough was the understatement of the century. I was boiling hot.

Orion and Roan chuckled together this time. "I'll take that as a yes," Orion said as he retook the reins of his steed and pushed ahead a few steps. "Expect to find me in your tent this evening, Roan," he called back just before his feet kicked the horse and sent him galloping forward to catch up with Sorrell.

Roan's hands found my hips as I settled my hands in front of me, squeezing onto the front portion of the saddle, my nails digging into the worn leather. "So…" I started, unsure of what to say to start a new topic of conversation, but unwilling to sit in the awkward aftermath of our previous conversation. "Tell me about Alfheim?"

Roan grunted at my back. "What do you want to know?" he asked.

I shrugged, turning my cheek as I watched the passing hills dusted in snow. "I don't know," I said. "Anything? Everything? I know nothing about this place. Only that it's where the Fae are from. Is this where I'm from?" I asked.

There was a brief moment of silence and I wished I could turn to look at his face without giving away that I wanted into his thoughts. Finally, he spoke. "Not necessarily," he replied. "Not all Fae are born in Alfheim, it's simply where we originated. It's often known as the Realm of the Fae or in direct translation to human tongue—Fairyland."

"Human tongue?" I asked. "Isn't that … I mean, we're speaking it right now. Do Fae speak a different language?"

He grunted again, readjusting himself on the seat as he gripped onto me a bit tighter with one hand and held the reins in his other. "Once, long ago," he started, "the Fae spoke the language of the Gods. Our original ancestors—the first

Fae—were thought to be children of the Gods. There are many Fae spells and castings that still use the old language, but there are no remaining Fae who speak the language of the Gods."

I hummed in my throat and went for a new question. "How come no human has ever traveled to Alfheim before?" I asked. I didn't want to think about what might happen to Nellie if these new Fae knew of her existence in Alfheim. "I was always told that the Fae lived in a different realm."

"We do," Roan said. "Or rather, we used to. Alfheim isn't necessarily on the same plane as the human realm, but as you can see, it's not exactly livable." He gestured around the frozen tundra as we passed through, mounds of snow and ice on either side of the slender path we tread.

"The Court of Frost lives here, don't they?" I pointed out, looking back and meeting his gaze.

He stiffened and lifted his head, breaking the connection of our eyes as he stared straight ahead. "You'll find out soon enough that the Court of Frost isn't like our court. There's no court like that of the Frost Queen."

"But—"

"Enough," he said. "It looks like we're stopping for a break."

At that moment, my bladder let me know that the break had come at the perfect time. But as my insides screamed for release, I couldn't help but think it was a bit odd how Roan referred to the Court of Frost. The tone he used was stilted, careful, as if he were afraid of saying too much.

What, I wondered absently, *was it about the Court of Frost?* My eyes sought out the back of Sorrell's head as the horses slowed and several riders dismounted, pulling out the supplies for our stop.

"We'll eat here and then pick back up again for a few more hours before we find a new place to bed down for the night," Roan said as he too slowed our horse and then slipped over the side of the saddle, swinging his leg around the horse's backside and hopping off.

He reached up and helped me down. "So, I can take a break for now then?" I clarified.

He nodded. "Just don't go near Ariana."

That wouldn't be a problem. As much as I'd been trying to avoid thinking about the fact that I was traveling with someone who wanted to kill me and had already attempted as much, it was still there niggling at the back of my mind. "You don't need to worry about that," I said. I'd rather bury myself in snow than go near that vile creature.

Roan glanced at me with a peculiar look in his eyes that I couldn't quite decipher. Then before I realized what he was doing, he captured my face in both his hands, leaned down, and pressed his lips to mine. The kiss burned through me like wildfire—fast, out of control, unexpected. His mouth slid over mine possessively, consuming my thoughts in an inferno of heat. When he pulled back, I felt myself leaning toward him, wanting more. Instead of giving it to me, however, he simply released me, turned, and strode away.

I had no clue what to think of that.

CHAPTER 5
CRESS

I could feel Roan and Orion watching me as we stopped for lunch, their eyes boring holes into the back of my head. I kept my head down and my focus on my food. It was better than being stuck in the main group, discussing whatever it was that they were discussing. I had a feeling that I wouldn't like some of their topics of conversation, most especially since Sorrell was in the middle of it all and he kept throwing irritated glances back at me every once in a while as if my mere presence offended him.

If I found a snake, I decided with a glare of my own, *I was putting it in his tent.* That would just serve him right. Unfortunately, I doubted there were any snakes in this big pile of snow and ice that called itself a realm. But in any case, I was getting real sick of his dirty looks.

Movement caught my attention as the asshole in question lifted his arm and signaled that it was time to mount back up. Relief swept through me at the same time that a shiver wracked my form. I should've sucked up my pride and stayed with the group if only to steal Roan and Orion's warmth. After sitting by myself for so long, I was freezing. My cloak gave me barely any shield from the chill of the wind. I practically scrambled back toward the horses at the thought of being nestled up against Roan and all his warmth again. That man was like his own personal heater and I needed some of that heat in this Gods forsaken place. If I could bottle his heat, I'd do it.

"Ready, Changeling?" Roan asked quietly, seeming to appear out of nowhere behind me as I stood, waiting by his ginormous horse.

After taking a deep breath, sucking in ice cold air, I nodded. "Yep, let's do this thing." Another shiver stole down my spine. Ugh. Being cold sucked major horse balls. "How much longer do we have to go?" I'd meant for the question to come out with some casualness, but instead, it came out on a whine.

He chuckled, dropping a palm down on the top of my head. "We'll ride until nightfall and then make camp. You'll get some dinner—don't worry—and after that, we can bed down and I'll keep you nice and warm til morning." The slight growl in his voice made my skin tingle in the best way. I swallowed roughly as I stared back into his bright eyes. I'd keep the effect he had on me quiet for now. Roan's ego was big enough as it was.

"O-okay," I said, trying to sound nonchalant, but my voice came out breathy and needy, the exact opposite of what I was going for. It was like my body wanted him to know. *Bad body*, I snapped internally. *Do not let the incredibly attractive Fae prince know that we'd give our left tit to have him keep us warm ... all ... night ... long. Dear Coreliath. I was in such trouble.*

"Shall we?" Roan asked, gesturing to the horse. When I nodded, he took my hand and helped lift me so that I could latch onto the horse's reins and pull myself up. Then, in a much more refined movement, Roan put his foot into the stirrup and jumped, swinging his leg around behind me so that he, too, was sitting astride the animal. My back pressed against his front and his cloak wrapped around both of us, adding an extra layer of warmth to my shivering form. I'd always thought I was on the average side of sizing—not too tall, not too short, not too big, not too skinny. But this man—this Fae—made me feel petite.

The horses clomped forward in a long line and soon enough we were on our way once more. The wind began blowing harder the farther we went, the weather becoming even more unpleasant. I couldn't help but snuggle back into Roan and try to escape the frigid air that I could swear was swirling with minuscule icicles that stung my cheeks and any other exposed skin.

"Can I ask you something?" I blurted after a while, trying to take my mind off the slow numbing of my face.

"If you wish," Roan muttered.

"I don't ever remember a time when humans and Fae weren't at war. I don't even know why the war started. Do you?" My mind seemed awash with different ideas, different questions to ask now that I had Roan trapped for a while, but all I really wanted to know was why the Fae were living like this? Why was Alfheim, the place that was supposed to be their homeland—technically mine as well—like this? Maybe if I knew the answers to those questions, I'd be better equipped to understand why the Fae reacted to humans the way they did.

"There is..." Roan seemed to struggle with a response for a moment before a great big sigh left his chest. "It's a long story," he finally said.

I settled myself more firmly against him. "We've got nothing but time," I pointed out.

"It's just a very complex answer, Little Bird," he replied.

"Why don't—" I started only to be shushed as his eyes scanned the nearby vicinity. I had a feeling he was checking to see how far the others were from us. He hadn't been this cautious about interacting with me before and it made me wonder why now? I glanced over my shoulder and peered around Roan's solid form, my questions on the tip of my tongue. It wasn't until I saw a feminine rider several paces away that I realized why. Ariana was riding a lot closer to Roan than she had before and seemed to be edging even closer judging from the sound of her laughter and carrying on. I narrowed my eyes on her.

"The war started because the Brightling Court trusted humans too much," Roan said, surprising me, and as much as I wanted to jump in and pepper him with questions, I kept my mouth shut. "The Brightling Court was one of the oldest Fae courts; their lineage stemmed back from when the Gods first descended upon our realm, and they were human sympathizers. They believed that humans were equal to Fae and wanted our two species to coexist peacefully. They were the ones who participated the most in the Changeling exchange traditions. And they petitioned the other courts to bring humans to Alfheim."

He shifted at my back, one hand finding my waist and wrapping around to my front. His fingers pressed into my stomach, radiating with heat as he pulled me more firmly against his chest. My breath caught and something inside me flared to life once more. I closed my eyes for a brief moment, sucking in some much needed air. I let the icy cold burn of the air hitting my lungs cool some of the smoldering fire he'd lit within me as he continued.

"They were denied, of course, but once the humans knew of Alfheim's existence, they couldn't resist poking at it. Our portals between the human and Fae realms became compromised. Humans were not meant to be exposed to so much magic. There were complications. For many humans, it was like chasing a ghost—they became drunk on the possibilities. For others, it simply made them hungry for the power the Fae could provide. If one Fae with unlimited magical ability could change the tide of human disputes, what could an entire nation of Fae do?" He didn't pause, indicating it was a rhetorical question. "Soon they were siphoning off power in any way they could just from the portals and taking it back to their cities with them. Slowly, the portals began to grow weak. Many of them have been closed due to lack of magical energy.

"Alfheim could no longer pull magic from the human realm —from the very Earth itself, which is what it needed to do to keep our realm's climate. The spark of life in Alfheim's land was drained—leeched away by power hungry humans. Now, it is as you see it. Cold. Barren. A wasteland of ice and frost. The Court of Frost is the only court that remains here. They are the only ones that can stand it."

Sorrow grew rich in my chest, swelling in my stomach. The story wasn't even over and already I hated it. I felt guilty, despite the fact that I had nothing to do with the past actions of humans. Despite the fact that I was not really human myself, I felt responsible somehow.

"The courts began to fight amongst one another," Roan said, his voice quiet and somber. "There were some, only a few, though, that sided with the Brightling Court. They were convinced that the humans still had potential. That they did not understand the harm they were causing and if they knew, they would stop. Others, like my own Court of Crimson, as well as the Court of Frost, believed that the Brightling Court had endangered us all. Their lineage aside, the Brightling Court had brought the humans upon us and had allowed them to steal away our land's magic for themselves. There had once been a plethora of Fae courts, but now there are few. The more powerful courts began taking over the less powerful and soon it became a battle of wills and ideals, Brightling against most others."

"What exactly happened to the Brightling Court?" I asked, my voice just as quiet as his own, nearly swallowed up by the wind. I was grateful when he shifted and pressed against the top of my head, an acknowledgment that he'd heard me.

"The Brightling Court is no more," he said in a sad voice. "Centuries of magic, generations of Fae were lost to us. I can't be sure of how or why, but the rumor is that they were betrayed by their human allies, their magic stolen. A Fae without magic won't last long. Magic is our life force. That's why the loss of our land's magic was so devastating to us."

"Is that what really happened?" I bit my lip. Had the humans truly been the cause of the extinction of an entire Fae court? With all of their wisdom and magic?

He shook his head. "It is rumored that they were betrayed by their human friends, but I know that can't be the entire story," he admitted. "The main members—the Royals of the Brightling Court—were tried and executed by the Court of Crimson and the Court of Frost. The rest of their court dispersed—many killed in the ensuing war with humanity and many … well, there's no telling if there are any more of the Brightling Court left. It was enough for the rest of the Fae to have the Royals gone so there could be no other uprising, no more sympathy for humans after they had destroyed Alfheim and hurt the Fae people in ways that, although we didn't know it at the time, we would never recover from."

Silence echoed between us, punctuated by the constant clomping of horses' hooves beneath us as well as the soft laughter and talking that filtered to us from behind and in front. A chasm of sadness had opened inside me. It was several moments before Roan spoke again.

"After the dust settled from the wars between our own courts, the Queens of the Court of Crimson and the Court of Frost decided to launch their attack on the humans."

"Revenge?" I winced as I asked it. I wouldn't blame them, but I hated the thought that so many innocents were dying because of the crimes of the few. Innocents like Nellie's parents.

"Perhaps," Roan replied. "But I think it's more than that.

Fear. Humans have greater numbers than we Fae. Despite their lack of natural magical ability, they do pose a threat."

"Not all humans are bad," I pointed out. Nellie wasn't. She was good. She'd helped me despite her fear.

Roan's head turned down and I looked up, our eyes clashing. "Not all Fae are good," is all he said in response. It turned the sorrow in my chest into something else. Something cold and hard.

It turned the sadness into fear.

CHAPTER 6

CRESS

T he horse continued forward, it's svelte body flexing with the movements. The Frost Queen and the Crimson Queen waited ahead in the Court of Frost. My mind swirled with thoughts as the true understanding of why the Fae hated humans so much was brought to life. If they found out about Nellie, then everything Sorrell had said would be true. Nellie would die and it would be my fault for bringing her here.

I fell quiet for several minutes as I tried to absorb the information, tried to wrap my head around the idea that an entire court had been exterminated. *Was I ... was the Brightling Court where I'd come from?* I wondered absently. After what Roan had said about the Brightling Court—the fact that they were the court that had participated the most in the Changeling exchange—it made sense, didn't it?

Originally, we'd assumed that I was like Roan—a Crimson Fae. But that didn't appear to be true anymore. I didn't have the same powers he did. My hair didn't burn with my emotions the way his did. If the Brightling Court was where I'd come from and it was now extinct ... what did that mean for my future? What did that mean about my past? Had my parents sent me off to be exchanged because they'd known what was coming? Or had they even cared if I lived or died?

I'd never know because the fact was, they were gone.

A knot formed in my throat as the thought wormed its way into me and stoked the already burning embers of hatred for these two Queens into full flames. What made them so special that they got to decide who lived and who died? Or who got to experience Alfheim?

I cleared my throat. "You said the lack of magic from the portals made Alfheim like this?" I asked.

He hummed deep in his throat. "Well, yes. Initially. When the Court of Frost was the only court left in Alfheim, however, it got worse. The Frost Queen tends to have that effect on her surroundings when there are no other courts to balance out her magic. This is her base of power. Once she settled, she never left, and now I don't think she can. Her castle and her power are too tied to Alfheim or possibly even too weakened in general to leave." He paused and I could feel the quick intake of air as his chest shuddered against my back. "I would keep that to yourself while you are in her court," he said a moment later. "Sorrell's mother does not take kindly to any who would point out her possible weaknesses. Neither does my mother for that matter. Perhaps that is why they've remained such steadfast friends even in the wake of the Frost and Crimson Kings' demise."

He talked of his father's death and Sorrell's so casually. I wondered how long ago it happened. There was no emotion when he mentioned it. None that would reveal any great loss, anyway. When I spoke again, I decided to focus on something else.

"If your mother is in the Court of Frost then why doesn't she counterbalance the Frost Queen's power? She's the Queen of the Court of Crimson after all, isn't she?" I asked, questions making my head swim.

"She is, but much of her power comes from the court itself. I am now the controller of the Court of Crimson, along with Sorrell and Orion. It is our rite of passage to rule a court." Roan glanced over his shoulder in the direction we'd come from and I realized he was talking about the castle we had been in when we traveled here.

"Why don't the other courts come back then and help counteract the effects?"

"The other courts can only stand the cold for so long before they have to leave. No one can stand it for extended periods of time without being from the Court of Frost itself. Despite her hatred of humans, even my mother often visited the Court of Crimson in the human realm. She has slowly adapted though, stubborn woman that she is. Her power protects her, but it couldn't protect an entire Court from the Frost Queen's power. Maybe, if the Queens stepped down and gave their mantles of power to someone else, they could leave this realm and give it a chance to recover. I have my doubts that will ever happen though. They are of an older generation, set in their ways. They've also had the power they wield for too long. To step down would mean to give that up. And like humans, Fae, too, can become power drunk. So, Alfheim suffers."

If we hadn't been riding a horse at that moment, I would have hugged him tightly to take away the undercurrent of sorrow in his voice. If his tone was anything to go by then he didn't agree with what the Court of Frost and subsequently, his mother, was doing, but she was still a reigning monarch despite the fact that she'd given the court over to him and Sorrell and Orion. There wasn't much he could do. There wasn't much any of them—Sorrell included—could do. "Do you think it will die completely, eventually?" I whispered.

I felt him nod more than saw it. I couldn't help but wish I could see his face and the emotions at play within his eyes.

Before I could ask him anything more, a peal of laughter

that could have come from no one but Ariana sounded from right behind Roan. He pulled his cape tighter around me, almost completely hiding me from sight. I stiffened, but allowed it.

The faint slit of light that reached through the opening of his cloak felt like a spotlight on my face. With that light came a burst of cold air. I ducked my head, curling inward while trying to flatten my body against Roan to make myself as invisible as possible. I breathed shallow breaths that hopefully wouldn't be seen in the cold air as I heard another horse come up beside us.

"Roan, it's good to see you out and about after all that business with the Changeling," Ariana said, her voice sickly sweet. *She didn't know I was there*, I realized. So far she'd been sequestered in the back of the traveling caravan. I'd hardly seen her. Did she even know that I was traveling with them? Perhaps she didn't care. Whatever the case was, relief curled through me, along with a small amount of curiosity. *What would she say if she didn't think I was listening?* I didn't risk a glance up, but I did listen to the rumble of his voice as he spoke.

"I'm still not going to marry you, Ariana, so don't start that shit," he said with an irritated growl. My palm found his chest and I petted it encouragingly. The hand against my stomach reached up and snatched mine, squeezing it tightly. I frowned and tried to wrench it away, but he didn't let go. *What was his issue?* Something decidedly hot and hard poked at my ass. *Oh!* I blinked into the darkness of the cloak. *That* was his issue.

"Maybe not now, but we'll see what the Crimson Queen has to say about that, or the Frost Queen. I'd be fine with either of you, to be honest, plus I heard he's the better lover. It doesn't matter now, anyway. It will all get figured out once we get to the Court of Frost," Ariana replied before clicking her tongue and urging her horse on. Her words were spiteful, but I would be willing to bet she only said them because her feelings were hurt. She'd been rejected and women like Ariana did not take rejection well.

"Stay hidden, little Changeling. She's up to something," Roan muttered as I peeked out and watched her and her horse ride away. I swore even her horse's strut was sassy.

She quickly sidled up next to Sorrell, giggling and casting her flirtations his way. I sniggered when he barely even acknowledged her presence. For once, Sorrell's personality gave me some entertainment. The glance she shot over her shoulder at Roan was one of pure challenge, though. *Let her go after Sorrell*, I thought. She may have had her pride singed by Roan, but I'd bet money that she'd be frozen out by the Ice Man before we even got to the Court of Frost, and I would gleefully watch it all.

CHAPTER 7
CRESS

B y the time the sun had set over the horizon, I was sore all over. Our entourage slowed to a stop along the road, dismounting in a flurry of movement as everyone got to work setting up camp. Everything hurt. I released a loud and agonized groan as I slid over the side of Roan's horse, my feet landing on the ground and sending a vibrating shudder through my screaming muscles. My legs buckled and I nearly collapsed. I was saved from face planting into the cold ground by reaching out and snagging Orion's arm as he came up alongside me.

"Not used to riding, I take it?" he asked with a tilt of his head.

"Not usually and definitely not for this long," I replied with a wince.

Chuckling, Roan shook his head at me as he took the reins and led his horse toward a servant, dropping the lead into the younger man's waiting hands before returning for me. "This way, Little Bird," he said, his arm coming out to collect me as he moved past Orion.

I groaned again, shivering despite the warmth of his skin against mine. "I'm tired," I complained.

"I know," Roan said as Orion followed us.

"I'm cold."

"I know," he repeated.

"I'm hungry."

Roan sighed. "I'm well aware that you are in need, Changeling. I will take care of you."

"Let me take her," Orion said, his voice gruff as we stopped next to a spindly little tree barren of all leaves. It looked like every other tree in the vicinity, weak and old and no longer full of life.

Roan pulled me into his chest as Orion's hands landed on my shoulders. "I've got her," he snapped. "You haven't replenished your energy yet from moving the castle. Why don't you—"

Orion shot Roan a withering glare, but instead of continuing, Roan merely broke off with a chuckle. "Never mind, then."

"You're the same," Orion said stiffly. "You haven't—"

Dear Coreliath, I was not in the mood to deal with two warring males. I shoved away from Roan's chest, effectively stopping whatever Orion had been about to say. I glared up at them as they leveled twin expressions of concern on my smaller, shivering form. "Cress?" Orion's brow drew low over his dark eyes as he reached for me. "You're pale. You should sit down."

"I've been sitting," I said. "All day. On that damned beast. My ass hurts. My thighs hurt. My back hurts. I just want to lay down and go to sleep."

Roan sighed and his arms came around me once more as he gently nudged me toward Orion. "Fine, you take her. I'll lend a hand to get the tents set up. She sleeps with me though."

"I am capable of caring for the Changeling," Orion said darkly. "I will share her bed tonight."

My head rolled back on my shoulders at the same time that my eyes rolled into the back of my head. "I don't care who sleeps with me tonight," I said. "As long as I get some actual sleep!"

Tension spread through the air as Orion and Roan lifted their heads and gave each other another one of those enigmatic looks that they were always exchanging. How anyone could have an entire conversation with a mere look was beyond me. "Take her for now," Roan finally said with a grunt as he thrust me into Orion's arms so quickly, I released an *oomph!* as I landed against his masculine chest. "I'll set up camp." He turned his eyes down to me. "Stay," he ordered. "Behave."

I bristled. I wasn't some pet to order around, but before I could open my mouth and say as much, he was gone and Orion's hands landed on my back, his fingers digging into the skin as he massaged me. All thoughts of conking Roan over the head with a very heavy tree branch fled as pleasure suffused my system. I melted like warm butter as my limbs gave into the sensation of my sore muscles being relieved of their agony.

My eyes closed and I sank into his embrace. I became a liquid glob of goo, so incapable of standing that Orion had to catch me before I fell over. A low, quiet laugh echoed out of his throat as he lifted me against his chest and settled me more firmly against him as he took a seat on the ground. I curled into his warmth, and my lashes fluttered as I peeked my eyes open. I stared blearily across the space our entourage had taken as our temporary camp. People were milling about, tents swirling into a standing position as stakes floated into the appropriate places before they were driven into the ground. Fires in small pits burst to life. Magic seemed to make the whole ordeal faster. Yet, not fast enough, apparently, because even in the short time it took the others to set up camp, I found my eyes closing once more. I sank into Orion's body and before I knew it, I was dozing lightly—aware and yet also unaware of everything around me.

I felt the shift in the air a moment before my eyes blinked open. Sorrell stood over us, glaring down at me. I grumbled irritably, wondering why Orion wasn't saying anything, but when I peeked at him, I realized he, too, had fallen asleep. The poor man. I reached up and touched his cheek lightly. He didn't seem the type to fall asleep out in the open like this. He must've been exhausted.

"I don't know what you're trying to pull, Changeling," Sorrell spat in a low voice, reminding me of his presence, "but if you hurt my brothers, I will ensure you regret your very existence."

I turned my head back to him, letting my palm fall away from Orion's face. "I'm not trying to pull anything," I snapped back. "I don't know why you hate me so much."

Sorrell's gaze strayed to Orion before flitting back to me and growing colder. "I do not hate you," he said, enunciating each word carefully. "I simply don't trust you."

Could've fooled me, I thought. Instead of voicing that, I tried a different tactic. "If you don't trust me, why don't you convince them to drop me somewhere and leave me alone?"

His features tightened. "They are adults," he said. "They will make their own decisions and their own mistakes."

"And you think I'm one of those mistakes?" He didn't immediately reply, but he didn't have to. I knew the answer. It was there in his expression. I sighed. "I'm not trying to hurt anyone," I said quietly. "I'm just caught up in all of this. I'm just trying to figure out where I belong."

"And you think you belong with my court." His fists clenched.

I shrugged, trying not to shift too much. I didn't want to wake Orion. If he was tired enough to fall asleep right here then he needed the rest. "I don't know where I belong yet, but they're the only ones who seem willing to give me a place here, and I can't exactly go back to Amnestia."

Sorrell stared at me, his ice blue eyes losing a little of their coldness. "We'll see how you feel about them after you enter the Court of Frost," he said quietly. "I hope, for their sake, you can survive our next endeavor."

I didn't have anything to say to that, but even if I had, he didn't give me an opportunity to. Instead, he turned on his heel and stalked off. What a confusing man. I sighed again and tried to shift out of Orion's lap so I could stand and stretch my muscles. As I did, two hard hands found my hips and lifted me. I yelped in surprise, whirling as my feet hit the rough, uneven ground. Orion stared at me with eyes that were very much awake. *Had he heard that entire exchange?*

His eyes found mine as he stood to his full height, towering over me. He nodded over my shoulder. "Come, Changeling," he said, nudging me forward. Why hadn't he let Sorrell know that he was awake? "Let's find Roan." I guessed we weren't going to talk about it.

I STARED IN OPEN-MOUTHED AWE AS WE STRODE THROUGH THE camp that had been set up. The Fae had erected little tents, each separated by several feet. They looked as if only one or two Fae could sleep comfortably in them. How they would manage to house the entirety of our caravan, I had no idea. Orion led me toward one of the structures at the back of camp. He pulled the flap open and stepped back, giving me room to enter. I came to a stop just inside the tent and glanced around. Despite the fact that on the outside it appeared to be no wider than a small room, on the inside, it was a great cavern.

"Wha—how—it's bigger on the inside!"

Roan turned away from the table he'd been standing at and smirked at me. "Magic, Little Bird," he said. "Nothing more."

Nothing more! Nothing freaking more? There was a bed. A real one. It was covered in cushions and silken sheets. How had they managed to do all of this in such a short amount of time? There was no way this could all be an illusion. And because I couldn't help testing it, I took a running leap and landed against the circular platform bed that dominated the majority of the space. My face smacked into a pillow and I rolled. It didn't feel like an illusion. It was too soft. I groaned as I rolled over and stared up at the top of the tent. It was quiet. Too quiet. I narrowed my eyes and sat up, looking around.

Roan and Orion weren't there. What in the world? Where had they gone? Soft voices drifted in through the slightly open door flap. I got off the incredibly comfortable bed and made my way toward it.

"I'm not leaving," I heard Orion state.

"Neither am I. It's my tent. She's sleeping here," Roan replied.

"Then a compromise is in order. We've talked about sharing her, why not—"

"Someone has to keep a lookout," Roan argued.

"We're surrounded by other Fae. Sorrell will watch our backs. He always does. I think we can protect her quite well if we're both with her," I heard Orion say.

I pushed the flap the rest of the way open and strode between them expectantly. Both sets of eyes fell on me. "Whatcha talkin' about?" I asked. I knew exactly what they were talking about, but I didn't like being left out. Since it was obvious they were talking about me, I wanted to be included.

"Nothing, Little Bird. Go back into the tent and enjoy the bed," Roan said.

"No." I crossed my arms over my chest. "I don't want you two to fight over who gets to stay with me."

"We're not fighting," Orion said.

"Oh? Then what do you call it?"

"Discussion." His hand fell on my hip as he turned me back toward the doorway. "Do as Roan says."

I turned out of his grasp until I faced both of them. "Why don't you both sleep in the same tent with me?" I asked. "You want to keep an eye on me, right?" They exchanged a look. I growled. "Stop doing that!" Eyes widened as they both frowned at me. I pointed my finger, swinging it between their chests so they knew I was talking to both of them. "I know what you're doing," I said. "You're talking without actually talking. You're trying to *manage* me."

Roan cracked a smile. "Well, you must admit, you're a female that needs a lot of managing."

I threw my hands into the air. "You're just—you're … ugh!" I turned and stalked back into the tent. I strode back to the bed and flopped down on it.

In slow movements, both Orion and Roan came back into the tent, standing alongside each other. "We'll both stay with you," Roan said. "If that's what you really want, Little Bird."

I shrugged. "Why does it matter?"

Roan took a step forward, his body shifting. It was slow and graceful, the way he walked—like a calm predator approaching someone who might be his prey. My spine stiffened and my arms fell away from my chest as he hovered over me, coming down on top of me and pushing me until my back hit the bed.

"It matters," he whispered, his breath washing over my face, "because I am not yet sure if you're capable of handling two males in your bed."

My mind went blank as I tried to respond. "W-what?" He dipped his head, scrambling my thoughts even further as his lips touched my jawline. I sucked in a sharp breath. The bed dipped behind me and I tipped my head back to see that Orion had joined us, his big body crawling over the bed as he pushed me slightly up and then slid behind me. His strong fingers found my neck and slid upward, tilting my skull back as Roan descended, kissing a path down my throat.

"What do you think, Little Bird?" Roan's voice was gruff as he pulled back and met my eyes. Everything inside of me was on fire. My flesh felt singed by their hands as they touched me. "Can you handle us?"

"I-I…"

He leaned back. "That is why we need to decide who will stay with you tonight, because whoever you go to bed with will do more with you than sleep, Little Bird."

I blinked. *Gods. They were … very dangerous.*

I was suddenly very aware of Orion's chest against my back. Images of the last time we'd been together flickered through my mind. Of hands roaming against my skin. Of sweat slicked flesh. Of the way my entire body had clenched just before he'd given me my first orgasm. I breathed heavily as I let my eyes trail down to the front placket of Roan's trousers.

"I think I'm up for a challenge," I said, proud of how strong my voice sounded.

He blinked, surprise crossing his features. It was Orion who broke the tension with a bark of laughter. He yanked me into him, his whole body shaking with amusement. "Then that settles it," he said through chuckles. "It seems we'll both be sharing tonight."

From the frying pan and into the fucking fire.

CHAPTER 8
CRESS

I nto the fire was right. My body was burning, scorching hot, which was ironic considering how cold I'd been earlier. I couldn't focus with the way Roan was staring at me like I was his last meal, and the feel and scent of Orion surrounding me. Roan was right before me, his hands at his sides as his knees pressed into the end of the bed. Orion's fingers distracted me as he gently pulled my heavy blonde locks away from my neck and swept them to the side a moment before his mouth descended on the delicate skin of my collar bone, his tongue lashing out against my flesh and sending all thoughts of anything but him into a deep, dark void.

His hands guided me back, settling me so that I was resting directly against him, his chest to my back. His very naked chest, I realized. *When had he pulled off his tunic? Hadn't he just been dressed?* As if he could read my mind he chuckled, and pulled away, kissing my ear as he answered my question. "Magic, dear Changeling."

Oh, I thought, realizing I must've spoken those questions aloud. His chest rose and fell with his every breath, and his cock hardened against the small of my back, sending a thrill up my spine and straight to my core. Roan leaned forward and slid his hands up the outside of my arms.

I squirmed between them as their hands roved over me in unison. Roan's palms found the outside of my neck, his thumbs pressing inward gently. Sparks danced beneath my flesh, lighting me up inside. My need for them was steadily growing. I felt as though I were on a cliff, precariously close to tipping over the edge. When Orion nibbled on the same skin he'd been kissing just a moment ago. I gasped, letting out a moan. His hands found my breasts over my clothes, running his fingers down the sides and around—teasing me and making me squirm even harder against him.

"Well, now, Little Bird, how am I supposed to resist a call like that?" Roan's voice entered my head, but his words barely registered as I felt his fingers wrapping around my ankles. He tugged me down and spread my knees.

I slipped away from Orion, and his hands fell from my breasts. A reverberating growl sounded, vibrating against my back as they struggled slightly. Roan's head snapped up and his eyes narrowed. I huffed out a breath and snapped at them. "Either share or we're not doing this."

"Oh, we will, don't worry about that," Orion's voice rumbled like thunder in my ear.

Roan's eyes locked over my head and I watched as whatever expression on Orion's face must have convinced him. The tension in his shoulders lessened and his hands continued their ministrations. Roan's fingers skimmed between my thighs, making me quiver in anticipation. "As you wish," he whispered, leaning down and breathing against my knee. Who knew knees could be so erogenous? I shivered at the feeling.

Hands slowly worked together to divest me of my clothing until I was laid bare before the two of them, which was rather unfair since Roan was still fully clothed. I sent him a glare. "I'm not going to be the only naked one in this tent," I said.

"You're not," Orion reminded me with a light push of his cock against my back.

I rolled my eyes and refocused on Roan. "Clothes," I said. "Off."

"Commanding little thing, aren't you?" Roan commented with a quiet laugh. He clambered off the bed and I watched from within the circle of Orion's arms as he divested himself of first his tunic and then his trousers. When his cock sprang up, slapping lightly at his stomach, my eyes widened. Maybe it was time to rethink this whole 'share' thing. I knew how big Orion was and just staring at Roan told me he was either just as big or even bigger.

Wetness slicked against my inner thighs. Orion shifted me up once more so that he could climb off the bed as well, and together, the two of them came to stand at the end of the bed, their eyes meeting mine as they stared down at me. I gulped. I'd seen Orion naked before but I'd never had a chance to really look at Roan in this light. Having them both stripped bare before me was doing something to my insides. Seeing them, side by side, was like a study in shadow and color.

Orion's inky hair fell to his shoulders and the scars that littered his body only added to his beauty, highlighting the shadows and ridges of his skin. I wanted to run my fingers over them, trace the grooves, and kiss each and every mark. His cock was thick and long just as I remembered it and my core clenched in reminder of all the pleasure he'd brought me before.

Roan's fiery red hair was shorter and wilder in its style, as though the strands were made of flames. His muscles were covered in freckles, not scars, and my eyes couldn't help but follow the lines that curved over his body down toward the trail of red hair that led from the small indention of his belly button to a cock that was just as long, if not longer than, Orion's, though not as wide. I bit my bottom lip, trying—and failing—to stop myself from staring.

"I think she likes what she sees," Roan said as a wicked smile flashed across his face. I didn't have a chance to respond before he was on the bed, his hands finding my legs once again. This time, instead of a tug, he yanked hard. My back hit the silky sheets and he was on top of me, all around me. I breathed in his masculine scent. There wasn't a name for it, all I knew was that it was very much a singular spice that was only his.

I squeaked in surprise when he shoved my legs outward and settled between them. That squeak quickly turned into a moan when his mouth descended on mine. His skin was warm against me. Then, in one smooth move, he rolled us so I was straddling his lap and he was underneath me. His cock was like a bullseye between us, pulling all my attention to the hot skin pressed against my needy flesh. My hips rocked against it of their own accord and he groaned as I pressed against him, leaning away from his lips to gasp for breath.

Roan's hand reached up, fingers tangling in my short hair until they locked tight and pulled my mouth back to his, devouring me in a way that seemed to leave nothing behind except my want for more. A second set of hands lifted my hips from Roan's lap and pulled me back so that my knees were pressed against the mattress and there was no longer anything for me to rub against but the sheets. My pussy was exposed to the chilly night air that was creeping into the tent. I didn't know what to expect, but when Orion's breath swept over my wet flesh, I jerked, pulling my mouth from Roan's for a brief moment. Orion's hot tongue found my folds, and I cried out just before Roan slammed his mouth over mine once more, swallowing the sound with another scorching kiss. Everything in the world seemed to disappear in that moment except for the three of us.

Orion's tongue dove deep, swiping against the bundle of nerves there as one hand gripped the one side of my ass and parted my cheeks to make way for him to push two fingers into my channel. I whimpered into Roan's mouth, his tongue dueling with mine as I was pressed back to that cliff from earlier and sent careening over it. My body locked up tight as an orgasm stole over me. I quaked and twitched as I chased my release, but when my body began to tense and get ready to explode with pleasure a second time, Orion backed off, his panting breath still drifting over my pussy. I growled in frustration, fisting my hand in Roan's hair and pulling his lips from mine. Roan was smiling against my skin as he instead pulled me up so that I was practically sitting straight with Orion still beneath me. Roan began kissing and licking his way down to my breasts until he pulled my nipples into his mouth. I shuddered, my skin burning with a mass of sensations.

"If you don't let me finish soon, I'm going to scream," I gasped as Roan tugged on one of my nipples with his teeth.

"Oh, Little Bird, don't you know how much we like teasing you?" Roan asked. I looked at him, and for a moment, I was dumbstruck by his beauty, but he wasn't done talking. "This is just a taste, when we're settled and have this business with the Court of Frost taken care of, Orion and I will keep you in bed for days. We'll take you to levels of pleasure you've never even imagined." There was something in Roan's voice that wove under my skin and around my heart as though the pleasure he was talking about was more than merely physical.

Orion chose that moment to dive back in, his mouth returning to my pussy and his tongue spearing deep alongside his fingers. He had to be using magic. No one was that good with their mouth … were they? My body began to buck and writhe under their ministrations as Roan's hands found my nipples and rubbed them between his thumbs and forefingers.

They didn't stop. They didn't give me another second to breathe.

I flew into the blinding whiteness of my second orgasm of the night. My body was thrust away and everything blanked out as they overwhelmed me. Everything pulsed, and I lost myself to the release. After some time had passed, I blinked slowly, coming back to myself. With each slow lowering of my lashes and the subsequent lifting, the world came back into focus and I felt myself returning to my body. A chest was pressed against me. Roan's head turned as he laid beneath me and I caught him exchanging a look with the very large Fae at my back. I narrowed my eyes on Roan since he was the only one I could see. They were doing that silent communication thing again, and I had no clue what it meant.

Orion's warm breath touched my ear as he leaned down, distracting me in a beautiful fashion. "Welcome back."

I sighed and sank into them. It took me a moment to speak, but when I did, the truth blurted out. "That was incredible," I said. Orion slid to the side and Roan shifted so that I was between them.

"Glad you appreciate our talents," Roan said, propping his head up with his elbow against the bed. A yawn stretched his mouth and I squinted at him.

"Tell me that's not all you have planned," I said as I turned toward him, nuzzling into his throat.

"Told you she was a fast learner," Orion chuckled from behind me.

"Oh, you two have been talking about me, have you?" I asked, grinning as I looked up at the fiery Roan as I made my way down his chest. I licked and nipped at his skin, feeling my way along his broad form. My hand trailed down his side. He was still hard against me. His cock bumped my stomach, harder than steel as I reached up and palmed him. He sucked in a breath, his whole belly moving with the action.

I blinked down at him in my hand, well aware that Orion was watching over my shoulder. I could feel him too. The way his cock was rubbing against the globes of my ass. Nervousness had no place here, yet I wasn't exactly confident as I leaned down closer to Roan's manhood. I was going to do it, I realized. I was going to suck him. Yup. Like I'd done it a hundred times before. I could totally do this.

"If you stare at it any harder, it might catch flame," Roan said with a rumbling chuckle.

I shot him a look of indignation. I didn't exactly know what to say to that and I was sure no matter what I tried, it'd come out a jumbled mess. I wasn't exactly known for tact at the best of times and after having my brain scrambled by not only one, but two orgasms—suffice it to say, this was not the best of times.

Orion's hand slipped up my spine as I shimmied down. "You leave her be," he said, his voice deepening. *Did he like watching me touch Roan's cock?* I wondered. Was this a turn on for him? They'd been so belligerent and argumentative toward each other at first, but was watching a part of *their* fantasy? My hand tightened on Roan as I leaned closer. The shiny skin of the mushroom shaped tip was glistening with liquid.

"I'm merely teasing her, brother—*fuck!*" I didn't let Roan finish whatever he'd been about to say. I dipped my head forward and sucked him into my mouth.

In the next instant, Roan was speechless. I grinned around the cock between my lips as he moaned, his fingers coming up to cup the back of my head. Off to a good start. I swirled my tongue around the tip, tasting the slightly salty liquid, and began working my way further and further down the shaft until my head was bobbing up and down. I'd seen some of the female Fae in the Court of Crimson doing this in barely shadowed corners. I assumed this was what men liked. Roan certainly seemed to be beside himself with excitement. His cock practically leapt against my tongue as I hollowed out my mouth.

His fingers tangled in my hair, becoming more insistent the longer I went. I inhaled and exhaled slowly through my nose, not wanting to find a reason to pull away. I lost myself for a while in the movements, hypnotic as they were. His moans filled my ears. Orion's hands on my skin, stroking as I sucked, lulled me into a new sort of realm. This was a different kind of magic, one that I was falling prey to. I almost forgot that this wasn't how I wanted Roan to finish. I came back to myself when his body began to tense and his hips gyrated up. I reached up and gently tugged his hand from the back of my head and pulled myself away.

I pivoted, searching Orion out. His eyes met mine and he leaned forward—not caring what I'd just been doing with my mouth. His lips captured mine, his tongue sinking past my barriers and stealing away what little sanity I had left. Breathless, feeling like I was trapped between them, I fought my way up from the drugging kisses he was lavishing me with and pushed him away slightly.

Roan's eyes met mine when I turned my cheek. "I need you inside me," I said, panting. I shoved my hair back as the strands stuck to my face. Roan's muscles bunched as he got up on his knees. He looked like a wild predator ready to pounce. Without a word, Orion shuffled away, sitting up with his back against the headboard as he watched curiously.

"You want me, Little Bird?" Roan asked, his hand smoothing down his ripped abdomen until he took his cock, still wet with my saliva, in his fist.

I nodded sharply. I needed him—felt a fire burning inside me, wanting out. "Please." I watched his hand, the movement of his fingers squeezing his shaft, sliding up and down. The head of his cock disappeared in his fist, reappearing a moment later, looking even more purple than it had earlier. I flicked a glance back at Orion, but he had gotten comfortable, his hands folded behind his head as his eyes ate up the scene before him.

Roan prowled over me, pressing me into the smooth sheets of the bed. His hand left his cock and moved between my legs. I gasped as his fingers swiped between my folds, collecting the wetness there. My eyes widened when I watched as he spread it over the head of his cock before sticking his fingers in his mouth and sucking the rest off. "You taste even sweeter after your pleasure," he growled before I felt him push my thighs open and position his tip so that it rested against my opening. He breathed, his head dipping down, and I nearly whimpered in disappointment when he backed up at the last second.

His hands found my hips and he urged me over onto my stomach. I was shifted until my hands and knees pressed down into the bed, and I faced Orion, who gave me a dark smile. Roan's hands touched the backs of my thighs. Automatically, my legs opened, making way for him. I was ready—more than ready. *If he didn't fucking take me right now, I was going to strangle* —he surged forward, cutting that thought off. My eyes closed as the pleasure of being filled overwhelmed me, but when a hand gripped my chin and lifted my head, they snapped open once again. Orion hovered in front of me, a mask of lust covering his face. His own impressive cock stood at attention. Those glassy opaque eyes of his danced with an unspoken question, one I knew he wouldn't ask aloud. At least, not here and now, not in front of his friend, for fear of rejection. I wouldn't have rejected him anyway.

Without hesitation, I moved my hands so I could grip his cock. I tilted it toward my mouth, opening wide and keeping my gaze locked with his as I lowered my head. Thick, wide palms touched the back of my neck, curling around it as I swallowed him down just as I had Roan. And as I did, Roan pushed his cock deep. My hand fell away as his sudden thrust made me moan around Orion's cock. A shudder worked its way up the dark Fae as his head sank back on his shoulders and he released a low groan. Roan's hips slapped against mine, and I felt stretched in every direction. My pussy tightened against him and he grunted behind me, powering forward anyway.

A sliver of panic crept into me. Could I really handle this? It was a little late to be asking that, but he was so big. They both were. When I looked up at Orion, I saw that his eyes were back on me. He was stroking my hair, pushing it out of my face as I sucked him deep. He gave me an encouraging nod and I remembered how scared I'd been with him for my first time, and I knew this wouldn't be nearly as bad. One of my hands came up off the bed and held his cock at the base once more. I didn't know why, but it felt like the thing to do. It allowed me more control to move my head up and down his shaft. The faster and harder I sucked, the more Roan seemed to thrust. I was suspended between the two of them—the back and forth movement starting a new sensation in my belly that spread outward, lighting me up.

Magic, I realized. This is why Fae were such sensual creatures. Sex was magic. I could feel mine—newly awakened as it was—fill me up. It tingled along my nerves, crept into the corners of my vision in little sparkles. I didn't know if they were real or not. Orion and Roan didn't seem to notice, but maybe they were used to it. I felt like I was floating.

Soon enough, though, I couldn't focus on anything outside of the two of them. The sensations that Roan and Orion were providing as they touched me—Orion's fingers dipping below my chest and touching my breasts, finding my nipples and tweaking them until I clenched hard around Roan. I wasn't sure when but my eyes had drifted closed, and I couldn't force myself to reopen them. Roan's hand nudged under me as well. His fingers touched that bundle of nerves between my legs as if he knew exactly what I needed to go over the edge a third time. This one wasn't as strong as the first, which was good because if it had been I probably would have passed out.

While I cried out my pleasure and my pussy clamped down on and pulsed around Roan's cock, I felt his rhythm falter and he came a few moments later. Part of my brain could swear that I heard him growl my name, but I was already feeling Orion's cock throbbing in my mouth. My eyes popped open when he pulled out. I half collapsed on the bed as Roan rolled off me, his chest heaving as he lay next to us.

Orion continued to work himself with his hand. His eyes ate me up, wandering over my naked flesh, making me feel powerful under his stare. I held my hand out for him. "I want to feel you as well, if you want to?" I asked almost hesitantly.

"Cressida, there is never a time when I don't want you. Every moment I'm awake you batter at my thoughts like the sea against the shore. You're in every breath I take. Of course I want you," Orion said as his lips descended on mine.

He pushed me onto my back alongside Roan, and his legs moved between mine, gently nudging them apart as he positioned himself before pushing into me in one long, slow thrust. Roan may have been fast and furious, like fire itself, but Orion was slow and sensual like darkness, covering me with his body until he was all I could see, and I loved it. His movements were strong and sure, slowly working me to a different peak. We continued like that for what felt like forever, as though we existed in our own little universe, until suddenly neither of us could wait any longer.

Orion pushed his body up and off me slightly so he could reach between us and pressed on my swollen clit, pinching it gently and making my body jerk and shake as I erupted into another orgasm in his arms as he took me. I could feel my whole body pulling taut around him. I encircled him with my arms, holding him as close to me, and as deep into me, as possible. Just as my release subsided, his began. For the first time, I got to watch the pleasure wash over his face as he fought to look me in the eye.

I didn't know if he meant it to be as special as it felt, but I relished in the connection. We weren't just two bodies, just bed partners who'd tumbled into the act of sex. We were two souls coming together, clutching at one another as we tried to rip pleasure from our bodies. When he was done, I gently pulled his head down and claimed his mouth with mine, tangling my hands in his hair until we were so close together, I wasn't sure where I began and he ended.

Whatever private bubble we'd managed to lose ourselves in was soon popped as the storming of boots against hard ground sounded outside the tent. My head lifted just in time to watch as Sorrell pushed the front tent flap open and strode inside. Two steps in and he froze, his nose wrinkling in distaste as he swung his gaze toward the bed.

"It wreaks of sex in here," he snapped, eyeing us as his lip curled back in disgust.

Orion and Roan moved fast. One second they were languidly laying against the silken sheets and the next I was rolled and covered from head to toe by Roan's form as Orion launched himself off the bed.

"Sorrell, get out!" Orion roared, actually roared. I gasped as I tried to look over Roan's shoulder.

Sorrell's face was closed as Orion stood with his hands fisted at his sides. I didn't understand it. Sorrell was an asshole. He hated me—that much was clear—but he wasn't a threat. Roan reached down and snagged part of the sheet and drew it up over my naked frame. For that matter, why were they trying to hide me? Fae were sexual creatures. This wasn't—or shouldn't have been—out of the ordinary for them. Neither Roan nor Orion seemed too concerned with their nudity.

Once I was sufficiently covered, Roan backed up, sliding off the edge of the mattress as well.

Sorrell's gaze bounced between them, his eyes growing colder when they landed in the space between. Right where I was. I stiffened, holding the sheets up and staring back at him in confusion.

"When you're done fucking your plaything, come and find me so we can discuss the route for tomorrow." He turned abruptly as though he couldn't bear to look at me any longer. "And for fuck's sake, put some damn clothes on, unless, of course, she didn't satisfy you and you need to find more bed partners?"

Roan growled. "Fucking watch your tone, Sorrell. You may be my fucking brother in court, but don't think I can't put you on your ass."

Sorrell stopped just inside the entrance of the tent and glanced back, arching one white-blond brow. "Put me on *my* ass?" he repeated haughtily. "I think a few rounds with the near-human have you forgetting who is the better fighter."

Roan's entire body swelled. His muscles bulged and I watched in fascinated concern as sparks danced at the ends of his hair. Wrapping the sheet around my front, I moved to stand. Two steps was all it took for me to be at his back. I placed a calming hand against the center of his spine, feeling his start of surprise against my fingertips a moment before his arm moved toward me. His fingers wrapped around my wrist and tugged until I was flush against his side.

In a slower, much more mild tone, he replied to Sorrell. "We'll be there in a second. Just get out of the tent."

The flap of the tent fluttered, closing as Sorrell's icy blond hair disappeared behind it. "Orion, you stay with Cress, I'll see what Sorrell's so worked up about," Roan said, releasing me and pushing me gently toward the dark Fae. He quickly tugged on his trousers and shirt and turned to leave. He only managed a few steps before he was suddenly spinning back to the two of us as Orion urged me to sit on the bed. His feet ate up the distance between us and he ignored Orion as he leaned down, dropping a kiss on first my forehead and then my lips. I sighed into his mouth as his tongue met mine in a too short motion. *These Fae were so confusing.* I touched where his mouth had consumed mine as I watched him leave. *And addicting,* I added almost as an afterthought. *Way too damn addicting.*

CHAPTER 9
SORRELL

Those fucking fools. Wrapped up in a pretty face as they were, they had lost sight of the real trouble we were in. As I stormed back through the camp, I felt my body tighten, my groin reacting to the scent of sex and the image ingrained in my brain. A pretty face indeed. In the flash of time before Orion and Roan had covered her and shielded her from my gaze, I'd been subjected to a view of all that creamy flesh. Pinkened nipples peaked and hard in the cold air. Her hair had tumbled over her shoulders, blonde locks nearly as light as my own surrounding a heart shaped face that all but screamed to be fucked and protected.

The fact that they'd hidden her from view so quickly was another problem. Fae were open. Fae were carnal. As a species, hedonism was a trait we shared. It was only when a mating bond began to form that our protective instincts came out. The fact that both of them had reacted the way that they had told me that Cressida, the Changeling, had become a much bigger problem than I'd ever anticipated.

"Sorrell!" I paused at Roan's call, turning slightly and keeping the same facade of cool detachment I always did on my

275

face. He was flushed, his cheeks heated in his irritation as he stormed across the ground toward me. "What was that?" he demanded, stopping a foot or two away.

"That was you handing your balls over to a small Changeling with undetermined amounts of power," I replied coldly. "If you think I didn't notice the way you and Orion protected her, then you've lost your mind. Playing with the girl is one thing, but acting like that is absolutely ridiculous."

Roan's eyes widened and I cursed internally. He hadn't even noticed his own protective instincts. "Sorrell…"

"Dear Gods," I muttered, shaking my head. "You're in over your fucking head. Have you lost your mind?"

"She's—"

"A disaster waiting to happen," I reminded him. "And we're about to go into the Court of Frost, or have you forgotten?"

"I haven't forgotten anything," Roan snapped as his fists clenched at his sides. "Your distaste for the Changeling is starting to wear on my nerves though, *brother.*"

"She is more human than she is Fae," I pointed out. And humans were known to be conniving thieves. The Changeling may have been Fae by birth, but she was human by environment and rearing. I didn't trust her for a single second.

Roan scoffed. "Orion and I will handle her, don't worry about that. She's not a threat."

"So you say."

Roan's fiery gaze shot to my eyes, and for several long, tense seconds I wondered if he would hit me. He was tense enough to need the release of a good fight. I thought about saying something about him not getting what he needed from the Changeling, but sparks danced at the ends of his hair and I could practically scent the sex and magic on his skin. He'd gotten his release and a fulfillment of his own magic. Something I hadn't allowed myself in far too long. Suddenly, I was tense for a completely different reason.

I was an idiot. We were about to walk into the Court of Frost—a dangerous wasteland of dead emotions and predators —and I hadn't reupped my magic in far too long. After moving the castle not just once but twice. My cock leapt in my trousers as if the reminder had awoken his needs. Of course the fucking image that assaulted my mind then wasn't one of some name-less, faceless Fae meant only for relieving my stress and strengthening my magical reserves. No, it was of the Changeling. With her mouth open and her head tilted back, I pictured her under me, her soft flesh all mine for the taking.

I turned away, breaking the moment. "Just handle her," I gritted out. "I'm calling a gathering tonight. Make sure you and Orion are both there. We need to discuss more than just our route for tomorrow."

"We need to warn Cress about the Court of Frost," Roan replied with his nod of agreement.

I resisted an eye roll and strode off. The cackle of feminine laughter greeted my ears as I passed through a throng of servants and court members. "Sorrell! Darling, you must hear what Vincent was saying—" The scrape of Ariana's voice inside my ears made me pick up the pace.

"Another time," I called over my shoulder. As in never.

I hurried back to my tent, sure that Orion and Roan would be sharing and keeping the Changeling between them the entire night. I shoved aside the flap and turned, pressing my back against one of the poles holding the thing up as I reached for the placket of my trousers. My cock sprang into my hands the moment I had the ties undone.

I cupped myself, squeezing my fingers against my hardened flesh. Baring my teeth, I closed my eyes and sank into the fantasy that had started earlier. The Changeling—Cress—with those big luminous eyes, her peach toned skin, light blushing flesh. Dangerous as she was, I desired the girl. She must have been good if my court brothers were so obsessed with her. I wondered what it would feel like to have all of that innocence beneath me. I'd power into her, slide between her legs—shoving her limbs out of the way to get at what I truly wanted. Her magic. It would taste so delicious on my tongue as I sucked on her ripe pussy.

I grunted as I stroked my cock from base to tip. She may have been a virgin no longer, but by the Gods, there was a purity about her. A freshness. Perhaps it was her naiveté. Whatever the case, I wanted it with a fierceness I'd never felt before. I pictured her in all manner of positions. Not just beneath me, but on her knees before me. I bet she'd already sucked one if not both of the others. Would she swallow me down like the filthiest and most experienced of Fae females, or would she lick and suck with that same guilelessness as she stared up at me.

I came with that last image in my mind, of the girl, the Changeling—Cress—on her knees in front of my cock, her mouth hanging open, hands stretched beneath her tongue as she waited for what I had to give her. A grunt escaped my lips as I cupped a palm over the head of my cock and released into it.

Whether the others cared to admit it or not, the girl had pushed us all to a precarious edge that would either have us tumbling down into a darkness none of us were prepared for or rising to heights I didn't think were possible.

CHAPTER 10
ROAN

T he fire raged, sparks flying up, drifting into the night sky, and yet the only thing I could focus on was *her*. The way her white-blonde hair reflected the light. The way she took Orion's hand as he helped her perch on the end of one of the logs set in a circular pattern around the fire. Sorrell watched us all with his cold, impassive gaze. At least, I assumed it was cold and impassive. I couldn't be completely sure. There was something else there. Instead of focusing on Orion or me, his eyes strayed to Cress and stayed there—as if he couldn't pull himself away. I knew the feeling. She was like a light drawing us to her, moths to her flame.

"Alright," Sorrell announced, barking the word out as the soft murmurs of our traveling crew quieted down. "Tomorrow we'll be heading toward the Bavarian Pass. We need to plan accordingly. The path is narrow and through the jagged cliffs of the mountains. We have to go in a single file line. Groups of four or less are necessary."

The Bavarian Pass. The last major obstacle until we reached the Court of Frost. It wouldn't be an easy trek. If Cress thought that delicious ass of hers ached today, she'd be a sore little girl tomorrow. My mind drifted to other ways in which I could make that ass of hers sore. It was unnecessary and yet, I couldn't keep my mind from replaying what I'd witnessed in my tent. Her lips wrapped around Orion. The way her pussy had wept as I'd speared her with my cock. I'd fucked many a Fae female before her, but none had her spark. None had her innocence.

"We won't be able to stop for the night like we did tonight," Sorrell went on, drawing me from my inappropriate thoughts. The pass was one of the most difficult landmarks of Alfheim to cross. Magic would have made it easier had the land not been devoid of it. Even now, years later, it still didn't respond to our Fae magic the way it once had. There would be no getting through it easily. We would simply have to walk or ride the horses and deal with our barren magic. The Bavarian Pass was known to leech magic from whatever creature passed through and use it to fuel the coldness it emanated.

"As you know, the Bavarian Pass feeds on magical energy," Sorrell told the crowd that had gathered to listen to his short spiel on the dangers of our journey. "From tomorrow until we reach the Court of Frost, it is imperative that you do *not* use your magical energy. Save it for an emergency. We will decide on groupings in the morning."

Oh, there would be no deciding. Cress was with Orion and me. That was for damn sure. After tonight especially, I wouldn't want her more than a few arms' lengths away from me. I could still smell her fresh scent in my nose. I wanted to bury myself in that girl and inhale her light. I closed my eyes and forced the desires back, pressing them into the deepest, darkest parts of my mind so I could focus on what was needed in the here and now.

I moved up and took a seat next to her and almost immediately, I felt her lean into my side. I looked down and her face was tilted up, her eyes watching me. I couldn't help it. There was no way to delve into that mind of hers to know what she was thinking unless I asked. "What?" I kept my voice low, not wanting to interrupt Sorrell's tirade as he advised the rest of the members of our group. He was pissed off enough as it was.

"Why is there a pass that sucks up magical energy?" she asked, not bothering to show the same respect. I looked up and caught Sorrell glaring at her as he answered a question someone else had asked about teams and packing.

"It's a result of the loss of magic in the area." I whispered the words as I leaned closer to her. I inhaled her scent, wanting to bury my face in her hair at the same time that I wanted to bury my cock in her pussy. "It's also a protective measure for the Court of Frost. The Frost and Crimson Queens are a bit paranoid that they'll be assassinated." They had reason to be, but I didn't say as much. Sorrell's mother, as well as my own, were not well liked by other courts or even their subjects, but they were powerful and power, more so than personality, held far more appeal to Fae.

"Oh." She turned back to Sorrell as another member of the party asked a question and I lifted my head, scanning the area. Thankfully, it seemed that Ariana had chosen not to attend this particular meeting. I wanted to keep her as far from Cress as possible.

As Sorrell brought the meeting to a close, I lifted Cress by her waist, surprising her if the quick intake of breath was anything to go by. "Roan, we need to talk." I cursed when Sorrell called after me as I moved to lead her back to the tent. I wanted to get her back in bed and under me and see how she would scream when it was my mouth covering that delicious place between her legs.

I huffed out a breath and practically shoved her into Orion's arms. "Take her to the tent," I ordered. "I'll be along shortly."

He didn't hesitate. He nodded, and when a frowning Cress looked like she was two seconds away from arguing, he deftly lifted her into his arms and carried her off. I stared after them, wondering why it didn't bother me so much anymore that he was touching her—that he *had* touched her in other places and far more intimately. I'd shared plenty of women with my court brothers, but this one felt different. Cress was special, whether she realized it or not.

"What is it?" I asked once I was sure they were out of earshot. I knew I sounded rough, angry, but I couldn't help it. Surprisingly, he didn't rise to my tone.

"We'll be in the same group tomorrow," he said. "I assume the girl will be with you?"

"Yes," I answered. "I don't want her far and I certainly don't want her anywhere near Ariana."

"I agree. I've placed Ariana with the ambassador from the Court of Frost. I'm sure she'll be able to charm him and his entourage."

Tense, awkward silence settled between us. "Alright, well, if that's all…" I took a step away only to be stopped as he reached out and locked onto my shoulder. The movement startled me. Sorrell rarely touched me. Gods, the man hardly touched anyone, even the females he bedded.

"I know you're angry with me," Sorrell said. "You have to know that I'm not intentionally being cruel. I worry for both you and Orion. You've become very protective of the Changeling. When we get to the Court of Frost, you do realize that any special attention you lavish on her will be under close scrutiny."

"I'll deal with it."

"Will you?" He lifted his head and his eyes caught mine and held. "I can tell she's become important to you. If that's true, then at the very least while we're in the Court of Frost, you should keep her at a distance."

I didn't like that idea at all. If Cress was seen as an independent Fae—one without an escort—the other members would be all over her. She was quite an attractive little morsel and there was an air of innocence about her despite the fact that she was no longer a virgin. Innocence was so rare in a Fae court. I had already caught many members of the ambassador's group looking her over with lust in their eyes. If someone didn't lay claim to that girl, she'd be in danger.

Oh, no Fae would dare lay a hand on her without her consent. The Queens might've been power hungry, but they had made sure that anything so distasteful as rape wouldn't happen, and if it did … I shuddered to recall the punishments of such a crime. But Fae were also very persuasive and Cress seemed to enjoy pleasing—at least, she'd seemed quite adept and happy with pleasing me and Orion in bed. The idea of someone else seeing that side of her made me see red.

"Roan, your hair." I blinked and reached up, feeling for the heat along my scalp. Gods, I was losing control of my flames and it was all because of her. I took a deep breath and felt the heat die down as the fire along the ends of my hair dispersed.

"Don't worry," I said. "I'll take care of it. I'll make sure she's safe."

"Just make sure that she doesn't cause any problems," Sorrell replied. "It's bad enough that we're bringing her along at all. We should've left her with the fucking human."

"She's Fae," I said, narrowing my eyes on him. "She deserves to go as much as any of us."

"She was raised human," Sorrell snapped. "I don't trust her and I don't like the fact that you and Orion seem particularly obsessed with her."

"You can like it or not. I don't give a damn." My voice rumbled in my throat, deep, rough, and angry. I yanked my arm from his grasp and he let me. That heat I'd just put out was rising back up to the surface. "She stays."

"She's a threat," he argued.

"No, she's not. If you truly thought that then why the fuck

did you save her when the castle was crashing?" I volleyed back.

Sorrell paused, his face going carefully blank. "I don't know what you mean."

I glared at him. "When we were crashing she would've been crushed, but you dove for her. You saved her life. If you truly thought she was a threat, you wouldn't have bothered. I know you. You think ten steps ahead when everyone else is still learning the rules of the game."

Sorrell took a step back. "Watch the Changeling, Roan. She's your responsibility." With that parting statement, he turned and walked away.

Interesting. I watched him go, my mind working over the conversation. There was something more there. Something he didn't want me to see. Sorrell had always been secretive, had always kept his thoughts close. But in this—with Cress—he couldn't. It would endanger her, and I wasn't willing to let that happen.

CHAPTER 11

CRESS

Alfheim seemed to be designed just to torture anyone who might pass through. First, it was the cold temperatures, then the climb uphill, which I had only *thought* made my ass hurt. But now? Now this Batavia or Bavariat Pass or whatever it was they kept calling it was even worse. *Ugh.* I even sounded grumpy in my own head. *But Gods damn it! My legs felt like they were frozen solid.* Still, I waddled on with Orion at my side, holding onto me as if he feared I'd fall into one of the snowdrifts and be lost forever.

We'd been forced to abandon the horses at the edge of the pass once Sorrell got a look at the amount of snow and ice covering everything. Roan had petitioned heavily to keep them but Sorrell wouldn't budge, so now here we were walking through mounds of snow in a pass that ate magic. *Lovely*, I thought sarcastically. I glared at the back of Sorrell's head as we trudged through the snow and ice. If gazes had any physical heat, I'd be melting him under my impenetrable irritation right now. What. A. Dick.

"Wind's picking up," Roan shouted over his shoulder, which made Orion's grip on my cloak tighten.

He wasn't kidding either. As we rounded the corner of the ridge, the wind seemed to burst down the mountainside, almost pushing several of us over. I stumbled a bit and had it not been for Orion, I would've ended up on the cold, hard ground. Up ahead, I heard a shriek as Ariana did stumble and fall. Ironically, not one single person jumped to her aid. They were too busy trying to keep from falling over themselves. A wicked glimmer of satisfaction burst through me, but the evil feeling was quickly followed by a voice in my head that sounded strangely like Nellie. *Be kind to others, Cress. You never know what they're going through.* Except I did know what Ariana was going through—and it'd been a whole lot of power craving and jealousy that made her push me off the castle. Still, I didn't get to enjoy the pleasure of seeing Ariana being buried under snow as she struggled back to her feet and kept moving. It was like we were walking into the worst storm I'd experienced multiplied by ten because of all the snow and ice being whipped about.

I reached out and grabbed the back of Roan's cloak as I started to lose sight of him amidst the snow. White clouded over my vision until nothing but the few steps in front and on either side of me were visible. His hair lit up like fire for a split second before it sputtered out. When he turned toward me, he reached out a gloved hand and grabbed hold of my arm, tugging me closer until Roan, Orion, and I were doing a strange sideways shuffle so we didn't lose our hold on each other.

The ground dipped below us until there was nothing but air and a long drop. I looked up and saw that Roan was hugging the side of the mountain, his free hand touching the stone and gripping onto what looked like pre-gouged handles. I supposed people had come this way before. We weren't the first. The hairpin turn of the pass opened out in front of me, as though there was a crack running between the two mountains we were traversing. The other mountain alongside us was just out of reach by a few arm's lengths. It was a narrow split between the two mountains, but what frightened me the most—what sent my heart galloping in my chest—was the darkness below. There was nothing. No sound. No warmth. And certainly no light.

The moment we crossed it, a gust of wind slammed into us. The strength of it knocked me off balance. My feet slipped against the icy ground and I found myself falling into that crack, my mouth opening on a scream. As I started to fall, I couldn't help but think, *not this again.* As if being pushed off one of the castle's towers wasn't enough, now I was being blown down between two mountains, likely to be crushed the further down I went. Why did this stuff always happen to me? I couldn't even bring myself to scream properly. Instead, the sound caught in my throat and came out as a humiliating gurgle.

Two strong hands each grabbed a hold of my wrists and held. Unfortunately, though, the gloves I'd borrowed from someone else earlier that morning were caught up in their grasps as well. The momentum of my fall and the tightness of their fingers only managed to slip the gloves loose and I continued downward. One fucking disaster after another—it was the story of my life.

The princes exchanged a look as I slipped further into the trench. Then they shocked me by releasing their holds on the mountain. They dove after me at the same time. Mouth gaping. Eyes wide. A true scream found its way past my throat. *What were they thinking? Now all of us were going to die!*

The sharp sound of my surprise and terror echoed around the three of us long after I'd closed my lips again. My scream ricocheted up the trench's walls as we fell.

Down.

Down.

LUCINDA DARK & HELEN SCOTT

And down some more.

Of course, neither of the guys screamed. They moved like arrows through the air, diving like it was a competition to see who got to me first. They didn't peel their arms away from their sides until they managed to get within reach and then their limbs shot out, arms wrapping around me as the light dimmed around us and their bodies were all I could see or feel. And that was when we finally crashed into the top of a mass of trees.

Even as cushioned as I was by Roan and Orion's bodies, as a unit, the three of us slammed into branch after branch. Every instance jarred me and, at one point, I felt a branch slap me in the side of the head. I saw stars dancing before my eyes as we descended into the maddening, painful brush. Roan and Orion held me tighter as they grunted, taking their fair share of hits as we came to a crashing halt onto the icy ground below the trees.

When I was sure we were stopped for good and it appeared that we were all still alive—I could feel their harsh breathing above my head—I opened my eyes. It was dark. Inky blackness spread out in every direction. With only slivers of actual light from above there to outline the two men wrapped around me. I pulled my head back slightly and sighed when I realized that as close as they were, I could still make out their features.

Roan opened his mouth on a low groan. My body—when I tried to move it—agreed with him completely. Nothing felt severely damaged, but I was going to be sore for a long time following this for sure.

"Are you guys okay?" I asked. I pushed up between them into a sitting position so I could get a better look around.

Roan cursed and I felt hands on me. "I'll need a healing spell for this damnable pain in my back," Roan admitted. "I think I landed on a fucking ice mound. Let me check you over first."

I shoved his hands away and reached for him instead.

"What's wrong with your back?" I demanded, trying to roll him away from me so I could see. He winced as he sat up straighter. His eyes tracked my every movement as Orion did the same on my other side.

"I landed wrong. Are you hurt anywhere?" he asked.

I shook my head. "I'm sore," I replied, "but I don't think it's anything more than bruising."

He stared at me for a moment before he slowly got to his feet. Despite what he'd said about his back, I noticed that one hand was covering his side as well. I narrowed my gaze on that hand, wondering what he was hiding. "You're sure?" he demanded as his eyes ran over me with a desperation I wasn't used to, as though the simple thought of me being injured was more than he could bear.

"You cushioned my fall," I said carefully.

"Not really." Orion grunted as he shifted beside me and I turned immediately toward him to make sure he wasn't hurt. "If anything, the trees did that, but we should have been going much faster considering how far we fell. We should be a lot more hurt than we are."

"Speak for yourself," Roan muttered.

I pivoted my head back, but before I could say anything, Orion grasped me about my hips and lifted me onto his lap, his breath hissing through his teeth as he moved, letting me know that he was injured somehow too. "I am," he replied after a moment. "We should have broken bones."

"I didn't use magic, did you?" Roan asked.

Orion shook his head. "No. If I didn't do it and you didn't— that leaves Cress." His eyes focused on my face mere inches from his. "Did you feel any magic move through you? Any kind of energy?"

"No." I shook my head. I hadn't felt anything but the wind as it'd rushed around us and in the crevices of space between our entangled limbs. "Now, what's wrong with you?"

"Just a bruised rib, nothing to worry about. I'll be fine before we get to the Court of Frost, I promise," he replied, dropping a kiss on my forehead.

"Can't you heal it or something?" I kept my focus on him and when he blanched as I leaned too close, I decided to push off his lap. I got gingerly to my feet, testing out my legs and arms. Surprisingly, Orion was right—I truly didn't feel any worse for wear despite the fall. Banging through the trees should have left me with more wounds, shouldn't it have?

"I could," Orion replied, answering my question about healing. "But we're still in the pass, technically. Any magic I use will be at less than half the potency and it'll leave me dangerously low otherwise. We're not safe here."

I opened my mouth to tell him that I didn't care. He needed to be healed. I didn't like seeing him in pain. I didn't like seeing *either* of them in pain. Before I could get a word out, however, Roan reached out and grabbed my arm. "We need to move," he said, his voice dipping low as his head came up and he scanned the area. Orion got to his feet immediately, his eyes following the same path as Roan's. I tried looking around as well, but beyond the nearest trees, I saw nothing but darkness.

"What's wrong?" I asked. "I don't see anything."

"The forest has its own dangers," Orion warned quietly. His arm, too, came out and latched onto the arm opposite the one that Roan had. "He's right, we need to move."

"Won't the others notice that we've fallen?" I asked. "If we stay put, shouldn't it be easier to find us?" *If they wanted to find us,* a dark thought intruded. I was sure Ariana and Sorrell would be happy to be rid of me, but they would surely come for Roan and Orion, right?

Roan shook his head in response to my verbal question. "It's either freeze to death out here while we figure out where we are, or we can set up camp for the night and see where we are in the morning once this storm has passed. It shouldn't be too much further to the castle, but if we get turned around, we could be walking in the wrong direction, and in this weather, getting lost is not something you want to do."

Orion nodded. "We set watches," he said. "One at a time. There's no telling what else is down here."

"Easily done." Roan shifted away from me as he released my arm. Orion did the same.

I immediately missed his warmth as he moved ahead, reaching back and capturing my hand instead. He tugged me behind him, moving to a more open area, the snow crunching under our boots, the sound echoing up the dark tree trunks around us. I shivered. It was so quiet down here. None of the wind that'd been rushing through my ears before was present. It was nothing but yawning silence.

Orion followed behind us a moment later. As I trailed behind Roan, I tried to not think about the fact that the trees that we had fallen through suddenly looked even bigger and more imposing. The deeper we walked into the forest between the mountains, the colder the temperature seemed until I feared we'd be nothing but frozen Fae lost in the space between the mountains by morning.

CHAPTER 12

CRESS

We walked in silence for a while before it finally became too much for me. "Where are we?" I asked, clutching Roan's hand as we passed a tree I swore we'd already passed a couple of times before.

"The Bavarian Pass runs along the side of the mountain; this is the path we try to avoid at all costs because it's easy to get lost in," Roan replied, keeping his voice barely above a whisper. I wondered if there was a reason. Probably. He seemed to have a reason for everything he did. This time, I wasn't sure if I wanted to know the reason, though. He proved that a moment later by finishing his explanation. "There are creatures that live in these woods that have adapted to the cold and dark. They are vicious and ravenous, and exactly what we were trying to avoid. It's also much harder to get through the woods and over the crest of the mountain to the Court of Frost this way than on the pass since the visibility is so poor," he finished.

"Creatures?" I asked, fear winding its way through my chest as I audibly gulped and scooted a bit closer.

Roan looked back over his shoulder and something in my expression must have warned him. He paused and turned to face me, his hand coming up to cup my cheek. "Don't worry, Little Bird, I won't let them hurt you." He dropped a kiss on my forehead. "Orion and I would die before we let anything happen to you."

"Agreed," Orion said at my back. I wasn't sure if that made me feel better or worse. I didn't like the thought of them dying for me. The world would be a much more intolerable place without these two men in it. Sorrell, I could take or leave at the moment, he was kind of an asshole.

Roan pivoted back and continued on. It was only a few more moments before we came to a series of trees much larger than the ones we'd passed before. They towered over the rest of the forest, large and commanding. Their trunks were a veritable wall forming along the pathway. When Roan just stood in front of one, not saying a word as he stared up at the big behemoth thing, I began to worry that something was very wrong.

He inhaled and then released his breath with an irritated sigh. "Alright," he said, turning toward me and Orion. His eyes lifted over my head, zeroing in on Orion. "We're going up. Do you need a hand?"

To my utter surprise, Orion nodded. Admitting weakness was not common in the Fae courts from what I could tell, so to admit he needed help meant that my dark lover was in more pain than I initially thought. He stepped forward and Roan bent down, lacing his fingers together to offer his friend a boost to the closest branch, one that still seemed much too far away. Orion made it though, his hands gripping and pulling as he levered himself up onto the thick protrusion.

"You're next, love," Roan said.

I gulped, unsure that I would be able to make the same leap that Orion did, or have enough strength to pull myself up. It wasn't like I had a choice though, so I put my foot into Roan's clasped hands and pushed. I hadn't expected him to throw me, but throw me he did. When I landed, I scrambled hard—hands reaching out, trying to find purchase to keep from slipping off. My legs kicked at the trunk as I huffed and clung to the branch I'd landed on. My fingers were slipping and I squeaked as my upper body slid right off. If it weren't for Orion's hands reaching out and gripping around my wrists to yank me back up, I would've fallen back down. His gasp of pain was like an arrow straight to my heart though, and I hated that I was the cause. As soon as he released me, I flipped on him.

"Are you okay?" I demanded, wanting to touch him but afraid to hurt him.

His teeth flashed in the darkness. "Don't worry about it," he said tightly.

"Pulling me up a tree can't be good for your ribs," I said. "Maybe I should look at it."

"Got any medical skills you've been hiding, Sweetheart?" he asked.

"Um … well, no, not really—I mean, I tried to help one of the Sisters from the orphanage deliver a calf, but I kind of threw up at the first sight of the baby's head, so she sent me away."

Orion barked out a quiet laugh. "Then, no, don't worry about me. Just try not to fall off until Roan gets up here."

At the exact moment he said that, Roan called up from the ground. "I'm coming up." Seconds later, I heard him back up on the ground and take a running jump. The tree shuddered as he gripped onto the same branch I was half draped across and clambered up around me. Even as Roan shifted into position, he tensed and gritted his teeth.

"Are you sure you're okay?" I asked, worried.

He ignored me and instead, lifted me onto his lap, facing him. Orion settled in and cupped an arm around his side as if in pain. I shifted and eyed him with a sharp focus. He must have sensed it too because the second Roan stopped moving—

after having laid his back against the trunk of the tree with me leaning against his broad chest—he spoke.

"Stop worrying," Orion chastised. "I'm fine."

"I'll take first watch," Roan said, distracting me.

"Wake me when you want me to take over," Orion mumbled as he pulled his cloak around his shoulders and promptly fell asleep. How guys could just shut their eyes and fall into blissful slumber was a damn miracle to me. Even I had to lay there for several minutes just thinking before I finally tired my thoughts out enough that they would let me sleep.

Wait, I thought. *What did he mean by wake him?* "We're sleeping in a tree?" I asked, turning my head to look at Roan.

Roan just chuckled, his chest rumbling with the sound. "Yes, Little Bird. Now stop squirming."

"How are we not going to fall off?" I gasped as I looked down for the first time. We were much higher than I had initially thought. Even though I'd fallen off a mountain and been thrown off the roof of a castle and survived each time, the thought of falling out of a tree while I was asleep was somehow scarier. I mean, at least, I'd been awake all those other times. I'd seen it coming.

"Well, I'll be holding you, so you won't have to worry." Roan's voice was filled with barely suppressed laughter as his lips grazed the edge of my ear while he spoke.

"And what if you fall asleep?" I demanded, barely suppressing the shiver that stole up my spine from the minuscule movement.

"I won't."

"Oh, and it's just that simple?" I snorted. These two had to be out of their minds if they thought this wouldn't end with the three of us on the ground and in pain.

"It is. We've done this before, Little Bird. Trust me," he replied. It was those last two words that stilled my tongue. I knew if I argued he would take it as a lack of faith in him. The bond we'd formed was still new, fresh. I didn't want him to think I didn't trust him.

"Fine." I huffed out a breath. "But if you let me fall, I'll…" I trailed off vaguely, not really sure how to threaten a prince.

"You'll what?" Roan teased. I couldn't see so much as hear his grin in the dark. I'd bet my left tit that he was smiling at me —ridiculously amused. Okay, maybe not the left one. The left one was just slightly bigger than my right and if I was going to give up a tit, I'd probably want to give up the one that had less value. That's how it worked, right?

"Do you even realize when you drift off or does it just happen?" Roan asked suddenly.

I blinked. "Um … I guess it just happens," I answered.

He chuckled again and pulled me closer until there was literally no room separating him from me. And in this cold place, he was a warm breath of fresh air. I snuggled down into him and sighed.

"Go to sleep, Little Bird. I will keep you safe," he whispered into the darkness surrounding us. There was something about being in the dark, a certain dynamic feeling. I felt magnetized, drawn to him.

"Roan?" I said his name as quietly as I could.

"Yes?"

"Will you…" I bit my lip hesitantly. It was an odd request— the timing wasn't exactly appropriate, but I found that for some reason, I wanted him to kiss me. I wanted to feel his lips against mine in the shadows of night. I wanted to strain against him and feel him do the same. My heart raced in my breast, hungry for this. I felt my legs tighten around him. "Will you kiss me?" I shoved the question out as quickly as I could. And then, I waited.

The abrupt silence that fell between us felt like answer enough and my muscles tensed as I pulled away. "You don't have to if—" I started, but Roan's hands found my back and drew me back into his chest.

"No, I want to," he said. "I'm just surprised. What brought you to ask me for that? Especially right now?"

"Your dashing good looks?" I guessed.

He snorted, and his head bowed against me, his forehead pushing into my shoulder as he tried to hold back laughter. It took him several more moments to stop. "Not," he huffed out, still laughing, albeit quietly, "that I don't appreciate the compliment, but you can't even see me down here."

I shrugged. "I know what you look like. I know what I'll be kissing and you're prime kissing material, Roan."

"That I am," he agreed absently. "Lean toward me, Cress. I want to teach you how to really kiss."

"I know how to kiss," I said defensively, doing as he asked anyway. "I've already kissed you and Orion."

Roan's fingers trailed up into my hair, tugging on the strands and sending a thrill through me. His breath washed over my face, a warm reminder of other places his mouth had been. I felt myself tighten all over as he pushed against me, but his lips didn't land where I expected them to.

"Um ... Roan?" His lips touched my cheek and whispered down to my jawline. "That's not my mouth."

"No," he said. "It's not."

"When I asked you to kiss me, I meant my mouth."

"I know what you meant," he said, breath puffing against my skin. "But as I'm the one doing the kissing, love, I figured I should get some leeway."

My thoughts scattered like mice caught by the light as he dragged his mouth down the length of my jaw. His lips parted as his tongue touched my skin before he kissed the underside of my chin and pulled away. "Roan," I croaked out his name. "Please."

"Please what, Little Bird?"

"Please kiss me," I begged, unabashedly.

"With fucking pleasure." His mouth came down on mine hard. He parted my lips with his tongue and dove inside at the same time that his fingers clenched in my knotted hair. My nails locked onto his shoulders and dug into him, eliciting a grunt from him. Roan's hips tilted up, grinding into my core.

I panted, dizzy from his kiss as he dragged me away from him for a moment. I could hear his harsh breathing in the dark, as if he were trying to catch his breath. Then his head tilted down and his forehead touched mine. "You are so dangerous, Cress. Perhaps the most risky thing we've ever let into our court," he whispered.

"W-what?" I didn't understand. My mind was still caught up in that all-consuming, soul sucking kiss he'd just laid on me. One I'd asked for and one I wanted to experience again and again.

He lifted his head and his hair brushed my cheeks as he shook it. "Never mind. You got your kiss, love. It's time to sleep."

"I thought you said you weren't sleeping?" I replied.

He untangled his hand from my hair and pushed me down so that my cheek rested against his shoulder. Gods, it felt right to be in his arms. It felt the same as it had with Orion. It felt like home.

"I'm not. You are. Sleep."

A soft snore lifted into the branches around us and I glanced to Orion. In the dim light, I could see his head tilted back, and his mouth propped open ever so slightly. I watched his chest rise and fall in steady even breaths for a second before speaking. "How is he already asleep?" I asked.

"He's letting his body heal, sometimes that means the mind needs to stop and rest so the body can focus on what it needs to do," Roan answered. Then he shifted and wrapped both of us in his cloak, giving me an extra layer of warmth.

"He'll be okay though, right?" I asked.

"Of course he will. Believe me, Orion's been through much worse than this."

I wanted to ask what that meant. *What had Orion been through?* I considered asking, but a part of me wanted to hear it straight from Orion's mouth. I mean ... I wouldn't like it if someone was handing out my secrets like candy. So, I kept my mouth shut and let the thump of Roan's heart and his breathing relax me.

Then, despite his edict that I go to sleep, he spoke again. "I'm worried, Cress."

I didn't lift my head, my eyelids drooping even as I responded. "'Bout what?" I asked.

"I care for you," he admitted.

I smiled against his shoulder. "I like you, too."

He shook his head above me. "And I'm worried because the Court of Frost is a dangerous place," he continued. "I don't want you to get hurt."

"I'll survive," I said. "Apparently that's what I do." I tried to go for confidence, but it sounded hollow to my own ears; I just hoped it didn't to his.

"The Court of Frost is much different than the Court of Crimson. They are more ruthless and brutal than I can explain, but it's always in ways you won't expect. And there are conditions of going into a court that is not your own. We're not the ones in charge like we are in the Court of Crimson. We must bow to the Court of Frost's power heads."

"Your mother," I guessed. "And Sorrell's."

"Yes." Silence echoed after that one word and I could feel my sleepiness drifting away, making way for responding worry. I still hadn't thought of a thing to say when his chest moved as he sucked in a breath. "If you belonged to one of us, you'd be untouchable," he mused. The worry and longing in Roan's voice made my heart break for him.

"Then tell people I belong to you. I don't care so long as they leave us alone," I said. *That solved everything, didn't it?*

"Just like that?" he asked.

I yawned, my eyes sliding completely closed as I sighed and sank into him. "Just like that," I said. "I belong to you—see, it's not so hard to say." I could say it all day and night if it meant we'd get back to the Court of Crimson in one piece and I could see Nellie again. At the thought of my best friend, guilt crept into my heart. She must have been so scared without me. I missed her, but—and I'd never admit this out loud—the guys, including Sorrell, had probably been right to leave her behind. The only thing worse than being stuck in a dark crevice in the middle of an icy wasteland was doing it with my best friend. I'd already proven I could survive impossible situations, but I was sure she already regretted following after me and I didn't want to put her in any more danger.

Even as those thoughts lingered, sleep crept up on me. I wasn't sure whether it was from being snuggled against Roan or finally being away from all the tension of the camp and our traveling companions, but finally, I fell into blissful slumber.

No sooner than I felt like I'd fallen asleep something jerked me awake. I gasped, the sound hitting my ears loudly as I sat up abruptly. The body under me—Roan, my delayed mind recognized—shifted in discomfort and let out a sleepy grunt. Normally, I would've just tried to go right back to sleep, but something felt wrong. My senses were screaming at me. I strained to listen for what had woken me.

At first, I heard nothing, then a slow, low growl came from below us. I froze and then, half-terrified of what I would find, peered over the edge of the branch we were spread out on. A pair of red, luminous eyes stared back at me. My heart leapt into my throat when another pair appeared next to it, followed by another, and another.

I couldn't tell how many creatures there were, but their eyes lit up the floor of the forest. "Roan," I hissed, slapping at his chest. When he didn't respond, I groped around frantically. "Roan!" I said a little louder, snapping my hand out again.

"Ugh." He grunted. "Why are you hitting me?" his groggy voice asked.

"You said you weren't going to fall asleep," I accused in a panic, unable to look away from the eyes staring back at me. "There's something below us. A lot of them, I think."

I immediately felt the change in his body. Tension flowed through his muscles and when he leaned over and followed my gaze, a muttered curse left his lips.

"What are they?" I squeaked.

"What we were hoping to avoid by sleeping in a tree," he growled. His hands gripped my waist as he turned his face away. "Orion!"

I turned my head to where Orion was as he jerked up out of what appeared to be a fitful sleep. His hand snapped out and wrapped around the branch he was on, balancing himself as he came to full awareness in a matter of seconds. "What?" Orion's deep voice rumbled as he replied. "What is it?"

Roan didn't even get a chance to respond as a vicious snarl sounded from below. My gut clenched and I swung my gaze back to the ground, squealing as I saw one of the creatures—their shadows barely visible—lunge up into the branches.

"Roan!" I screamed.

He released me as he reached up and cupped both of his hands over my mouth. "No," he snapped quietly. "Don't scream. You'll only draw more."

More! I thought with alarm. It looked like a fucking army of creatures down there already. With dagger-like teeth and blood red eyes. Oh, I was going to have nightmares about this until the day I died. I just knew it.

"What do we do?" I couldn't breathe as I wheezed out the question. He pulled his fingers away from my face.

Another, even more feral, sounding growl erupted from below us, cutting him off as his mouth opened. "Shit!" he cursed. I tilted and the next thing I knew, something had snapped onto Roan's cloak and was pulling us both down.

I watched in horror as Roan's arm lifted and he caught himself with one hand, clinging to the branch we'd been sleeping on. But me ... I tumbled down behind him, literally being thrown to the wolves, or whatever these creatures were.

Despite Roan's urging not to scream, I couldn't help it. It was automatic. As I fell, my lips parted and I let loose the loudest scream I'd ever screamed in my life—and considering how many times someone had tried to off me as of late, that was definitely saying something. I saw the exact moment when Roan realized what was happening. I reached up as he lunged down, trying to catch me, but one of the creatures launched itself at me at the same time.

Teeth clamped down on my boot and I thumped to the ground with a jarring thud as red eyes hovered over me. Drool dripped onto my face as my scream cut off to make way for the rush of air that escaped at my landing. All I saw was way too many shiny white teeth and those creepy, pinpoints of red coming toward me as they began to circle. Without thought, I curled in on myself, bracing for impact, waiting for their sharp teeth to dig into me and rip me apart.

"Cress!" Orion's voice rose above the growls. "Run!"

There would be no running, I thought. *Only death.* My breath hitched as it finally came back to me. I curled tighter as the creatures crept closer, sniffing, drawing back—preparing for their attack.

No, I couldn't die like this. It wouldn't happen. I wasn't done yet.

What would happen to Nellie if I died? Would the guys keep her safe? Would they protect her even though she was human? I didn't know. I wasn't sure.

My panicked mind was racing so hard. I had to survive. At any cost. With that thought, I knew I couldn't just lay here curled on the floor of the forest waiting to be eaten. I had to … *they weren't pouncing*, I realized a bit belatedly. *Why weren't they pouncing?*

I lifted my head and looked around curiously, uncurling from my prone position. *They weren't attacking because they were … backing away?* Confusion filled me as I struggled to my feet, my legs feeling weak. I didn't understand.

Sweat coated my palms, drawing my attention, and it was then that I saw the light—a golden glow emanating from my fingertips, racing up my arms and down across my chest. I felt warm. More than that, I felt hot. Like I was boiling from the inside out. I couldn't breathe properly. My breath kept catching in my throat as if there wasn't enough air.

"No!" Roan shouted as he climbed down the tree. "Cress, stop! Your magic is being depleted! Stop using your magic!"

"She can't!" Orion shouted back as I looked up and saw them doing the same—both of them mirroring each other's movements as they scaled down the trunk of the tree. "It's the only thing keeping them at bay."

What was? my bleary mind asked. *Keeping … who … what … at bay?* I couldn't even think straight through the heat spreading inside my limbs. Couldn't remember why this was happening.

As if in answer to my unspoken question, a new growl filtered into the air as a large creature—like the rest—stepped forward. It was much bigger than the others gathered around with an ugly mug of a face and a scar that ran the length of its face on one side, splitting through an obviously blind eye. The alpha, I realized. There always was one. *Oh shit. Oh shit. Oh shit!*

Curses rained from above as the guys descended faster, but

it wasn't going to be fast enough. The alpha drew back, its hackles rising as it prepared to launch. Despite my glow, it wasn't going to go down without a fight. But it would find that neither would I.

The alpha lunged and at the same time, the glow from within me burst forward. It exploded out of me, illuminating the darkness surrounding us, taking over everything. Shoving back the alpha and its pack of creepy wolf-like creatures. I heard yelps of pain just as the light dimmed and disappeared and the smell of burnt fur reached my nostrils.

Just as quickly as it had come, my magic was gone again. My only thought before my mind fell away into the blackness was, *what the hell had I done?*

CHAPTER 13
SORRELL

I could feel sweat collected at the base of my spine as I strode down the corridors, my steps echoing up the cold stone walls of the castle—my mother and Roan's mother's court. When I'd gotten the news that Roan and Orion had come in nearly an hour before, my blood had raced in my veins. Something was obviously very wrong. Neither had tracked me down, and the rumor mill was already spreading.

Don't rush, I silently urged myself. *Remain calm. Remain cold. Do not let anyone see the emotion.* Emotion was a dangerous thing in this place.

"Your Highness?" One of my mother's ladies in waiting saw me and shuffled to the side, her eyes going downward in deference to my status as she curtsied and bowed her head. This was another thing I hated about the Court of Frost. The pomp, the circumstance, the fucking theatrics of it all.

I searched my mind for the girl's name. "Davina," I said shortly. "Have you seen Roan or Orion?"

She nodded. "I just saw them enter the infirmary, my Lord." It annoyed me that she kept her gaze down and her eyes averted. The Changeling would do no such thing. She'd lift her eyes and bat those lashes at me and spit vitriol my way in that reckless way of hers. When I'd turned back to see her slip into the Bavarian Pass's crack and my brothers dive in after her, my heart had damn near stopped in my chest. It had taken everything in me not to go after them. I knew Roan and Orion and knew that Roan, at least, had traversed the lower paths before. He would lead them out. They would keep her and each other safe. I'd believed that deep in my soul. And yet, I'd worked tirelessly to pick up the pace. We'd breached the pass and had arrived at the Court of Frost only to be informed that they hadn't yet arrived. I'd been on pins and needles ever since.

"Thank you, Davina. You may go."

"As you wish, Your Highness." She gracefully got back to her feet and strode away. I all but raced to the infirmary. I was within viewing distance of the double stone doors that led into the medical wing when they opened and Roan stepped out.

I stopped short, horror assailing me. At first, I thought it was just his powers coming back after being in the Bavarian Pass for so long, but the red I saw was too dark to be fire. It could have only been blood. It coated his hands and smudges littered his arms and face. There were deep gouges along his biceps and forearms.

I started forward again, walking slower this time as if I were approaching a wild animal. "What happened?" I asked, keeping my voice even.

Roan's head lifted and his eyes found mine. The fire I thought had been missing was suddenly found there. It raged incendiary in the depths of his gaze. He bared his teeth and hissed as he released a breath. "The Gods damned bortugals found us," he said.

Not by a flinch did I reveal just how emotional I was. Bortugals were bloodthirsty creatures—often starved for meat in the icy wilderness of Alfheim. They were on the decline, but only because they had begun eating their young when there was no other food to be had. And in this declining realm, there rarely was.

"How did you manage to fend them off?" I asked. "Did you turn them to ash?"

Roan's wild eyes met mine. "We didn't fend them off."

I could have heard a pin drop in the silence that followed that statement. "What do you mean you didn't fend them off?" I demanded. "You're here. Orion's—" My eyes widened and shot to the doors at his back. No. He couldn't. Orion had lasted years on the battlefields. He'd been squired at such a young age. He was brutal in war, cunning, decisive. But oh, I'd seen how he was around the Changeling. He was softer with her. He was gentle. As if he'd waited his whole life to show that other half of himself that I knew he'd kept buried in his years of bloody service to the war with the humans.

"He's fine," Roan said quickly once he realized where my thoughts had gone. "He's hurt, but it could have been much worse. He's being treated as we speak."

"Then what…" The doors opened and Orion stepped out, stopping what I'd been about to ask. There were new scars on his face. They'd been cleaned and bandaged and would likely heal by the end of the day now that we were no longer entrapped in the magic depleting vortex of the Bavarian Pass. The scars would remain though. They always did on him. It was hard to recall a time that he hadn't had many small markings on his person. He'd had them even as a child—a testament to what he'd faced in the Court of Midnight. If ever there were a place more dangerous than the Court of Frost, it was my friend's home court of darkness. Of pain. I shuddered to think of what might have happened if he hadn't been sent to us.

"She's resting," Orion said, speaking directly to Roan. The tension in Roan's shoulders seemed to ease as he released a breath.

"Good," he said with a nod. "That's good. Did the physician say there would be any lasting effects?"

"Lasting effects of what?" I asked, glancing from one to the other.

Logically, I recognized that they must be talking about the Changeling but they still had yet to tell me how they'd survived the lower paths. Orion lifted his head. "There was an incident in the crevice," he began.

"I saw the girl fall, and I saw the two of you dive in after her." I said the words with as much civility as I could muster, which wasn't much. I couldn't help but think that had the girl not slipped and fallen, we would not be here right now. Had the girl not even existed, we likely would not be faced with attending to the Court of Frost at all. We wouldn't have the knowledge that we were breaking about a dozen laws, committing the highest of treasons, by hiding a human refugee in our court, and potentially putting ourselves in a position to not only get our titles stripped, but to end our very lives. The Mother Queens of the Court of Frost were not known for their tolerance, nor were they known for their mercy, even against their own sons.

She was nothing. Nobody. Useless. Barely magical at all. Oh, she might have survived the tests and trials of her heritage, but there was no doubt that she was the least powerful Fae I'd ever met. She was trouble wrapped in a delicious package. A danger to me and to my brothers.

"Careful, Sorrell." Roan's voice deepened on a growl. "I'm protective of the Changeling, and I don't like your tone."

"I'm well aware of your feelings for the girl," I snapped back. "Don't let it slip your notice that despite your constant ignoring of my advice—the only voice of reason among us, I might add—I have kept to your deranged plans." I might have hated it, and I might have called them ridiculous imbeciles, but I would not leave them as they had never left me.

Orion put a restraining hand on Roan's shoulder when he would have moved forward at the cold tone in my voice. "We don't have time and this certainly isn't the fucking place," he said, his voice dangerously quiet.

I straightened. He was right. I glanced back down the corridor and was thankful that no one had come upon us. My emotions were edging toward precarious unruliness. I gripped the control I wore around me like a well loved cloak and pulled it back from the brink, letting a white mask of cold indifference fall back into place. There was no other way to be in the Court of Frost. And who knew when we'd be able to go back to our Court of Crimson, if we'd ever be able to go back at all.

"Alright," I said in a clear voice. "Tell me what happened."

And as they did, I could feel that control I'd hauled back and locked into place slipping just a bit more and more.

CHAPTER 14
CRESS

When my senses slowly began to filter back in, I couldn't focus on anything other than breathing and how much it hurt. I could no longer smell the cold. My nostrils didn't burn from it as they had while we were traveling; so did that mean I was dead? That would really suck if I was dead. Despite my avoidance of said action—dying, that is—I'd always pictured myself old and gray surrounded by heaping plates of food as I drifted off into a long, deep sleep. Yeah, that would've been a better way to go. Not being eaten by wild animals.

Then again, would I ache this much if I was dead? A moment later, a low male voice answered my question when a hand settled on my shoulder. "Easy, don't try to move too much. You're still healing."

I pried my eyes open and prayed to Coreliath or whoever was listening that I was inside and not having some weird sort of hallucination. Four walls. A ceiling. A bed. It was better than I could have hoped for.

The man appeared in my line of sight and I could tell, just from his clothing and the way that his hands glowed as they moved over my body, that we were in another Fae court—the

Court of Frost presumably. Never let it be said that Cressida of Amnestia was an idiot. I could totally figure stuff out on my own. I took a moment to examine the man hovering over me, his brows drawn down in deep concentration. He looked like he had been up all night, and the long white cloak that was wrapped around him was stained with blood. As I stared at those crimson drops, I was reminded that this man was new to me. Where were Roan and Orion? Whose blood was that? Mine or theirs?

I tried to think back. There was the tree and then ... the eyes. I shuddered, the motion making an ache spread throughout my limbs. Gods, I was sore. But despite the shudder, my mind replayed the memory again. Waking up to the eyes and the low growls and falling, oh falling, and then my scream as Roan reached for me, his hand barely grazing me—not quite fast enough. Then a white light and nothingness. It didn't quite make sense.

"You've sustained injuries from your encounter with the bortugals. You're lucky to have survived at all with how little magic you have. The princes are brave indeed for coming to your aid the way they did," the man said, as a movement out of the corner of my eye alerted me to a new figure. A woman with a severe looking face and white-blonde hair—similar to Sorrell's—stepped forward and began folding down the blankets that were covering me. Cold air assaulted my body, making me break out in goosebumps and shiver where I lay, which only made the ache in my skin that much worse.

"The princes," I began, swallowing around a dry throat. "Are they okay?"

"For the most part," the Fae doctor acknowledged. "A few new scars added maybe, but that's the price of taking the lower pass."

"We fell," I said defensively. I coughed as the air seemed to freeze my lungs.

"So I heard," the doctor replied, his tone sounding both bored and doubtful.

The nurse peeled back some kind of bandages they had put over my stomach and shoulder. Bandages I understood, but the sticky, foul smelling goo underneath? That was a new one. "What is that?"

"A healing balm. Do you not have these in the Court of Crimson?" he asked. His tone sounded bland but curious, and the way he was looking at me … it was like he was searching for any weaknesses he could find, other than the obvious injuries that his fingers were beginning to probe.

"Oh, um, I'm sure they do," I replied carefully. "But I've never needed them." That much was true because I hadn't been in the Court of Crimson long enough. No lies there. I honestly had no idea if the Court of Crimson had a healing balm, but I wasn't about to give him an opening by playing ignorant or admitting that I was a Changeling—at least, not until I talked to the guys. They probably had a plan they wanted me to go along with. They always had a plan. Or rather, Sorrell usually did and even if he was an ass, he was an intelligent ass and I would do what Prince Prick wanted me to so long as it kept me alive. I was a giver like that.

I hissed as the doctor touched the tender space around my ribs. "The area has begun to repair, another day with the bandages on and you should be healed," he said before turning to his nurse. "Her magic will replenish with time and exercise, but the pass seems to have taken most, if not all, of it for the moment. Make a note."

I winced when he pressed a tender spot once more. His eyes dipped to me for a moment before his probing fingers moved to my shoulder, with a much less gentle touch. I could have been a corpse and received more attention.

"The Queens have requested her presence," a new voice said from the door.

I leaned up as much as I could to see who spoke. Even doing that much sent shooting spikes of agony down my back and sides. Through the pain and some deep breathing I'd once seen a pregnant woman who'd come to the Abbey to give birth do when she was in the middle of her labor, I managed to focus on what was happening around me. A young man stood in the entrance, his hair cut short to his scalp. His cold eyes drifted across the room, settling first on the doctor and nurse and then me. There was fear in his eyes, hidden, but there. And that, combined with the fact that I saw neither Roan nor Orion—I would've even taken Sorrell at that moment; for all his grouchiness he was still familiar to me—gave my heart a kickstart. Was I in danger? Had they already found out about Nellie? Or me?

No, no, stop thinking like that, I urged myself. *They would've sent you straight to the dungeon if that were the case, or you wouldn't have woken up at all. You'd just be dead.*

"Thank you, Fredrick," the doctor replied before turning to the nurse and adding, "Apply more balm and get her dressed. Their Majesties have been waiting long enough. If her magic was stronger maybe we wouldn't have been in this situation, but for now, I will go and stall the Queens while you bring her along."

The way he spoke about me as though I wasn't there made me lift a brow. Now that I was past whatever panic attack I'd staved off, I was starting to get more and more irritated with him. What kind of doctor had his bedside manner?—even a Fae one. Maybe he and Sorrell were related. Gods knew they both acted like they couldn't care less what anyone else did so long as they followed their every command.

The doctor removed his blood stained cloak and picked up a clean one, donning it as he strode from the room. As soon as he was gone, I turned my head toward the nurse. "Could you help me sit up?"

She didn't blink or show any emotion as she moved to assist me. Her arms came around my back and together, we managed to get me halfway upright. *Never again,* I swore to myself, as I swallowed down bile. Nothing I had ever done in my life had hurt quite this bad. Not even being pushed off the damn castle. I continued breathing as though I were about to shove a squalling infant out of the place between my thighs—recalling how accidentally witnessing that birth at the Abbey had nearly made me pass out. Even without the whole giving birth thing, I was feeling the same. My head spun as I struggled to keep from vomiting all over the mute nurse as she helped me redress the wounds on my stomach and shoulder. I hadn't even had a chance to see them since I had been too afraid to move while I was on the table, but I could feel the new skin that was growing and the way it tugged against the old.

Once I was all bandaged up, she turned and reached for a swath of fabric laying at the end of the bed. The fabric turned out to be a flimsy dress made of the prettiest cerulean blue color I'd ever seen. It started at the top over the shoulders but quickly became darker as it trailed down to the end. I struggled to put it on, lifting my arms and tugging the opening for my head over and around my neck. The nurse stood by and watched with a passive expression and I realized she wouldn't help unless I asked for it. I groaned and cursed silently as I shimmied the dress the rest of the way down on my own. Finally, when it was situated right and I was panting up a storm, but feeling accomplished, I sent her a smug look of satisfaction.

Instead of responding to my expression, however, she lifted what looked like a leather layer meant to go on the outside of the dress. I whimpered as she leaned forward and wrapped the tight piece around my chest, clicking several buckles into place as it tightened against my frame. *Why?* I thought. *Why would it make any sense to shove the girl who's in pain into a torture contrap-*

tion? I narrowed my eyes on the nurse. *Was she actually trying to kill me?* Sorrell and the others *had* seemed to be pretty concerned with walking into the Court of Frost. They'd warned me of the dangers. *Was this one of them? Assassination by corset?*

Swirls of metal cupped my breasts before meeting in the middle and expanding over my waist in thick filigree. I was thankful for the leather that sat under the metal because it provided a shield against the cold material and also the possibility of being speared on something pointy. I kept a carefully suspicious eye on the mute nurse. She reached forward and attached a thick, wide black pendant that hooked into the collar of the top layer and looked like a necklace.

It was by far the fanciest thing I'd worn in a while—or ever if you excluded the dresses that Roan and Orion seemed to be constantly putting me in. They often acted like I was their doll. Their mothers must have not let them play as children. There could be no other explanation for why they relished dressing me up in ridiculous clothes that seemed less fabric and more sheer material. I wished I had a mirror to see myself, but there wasn't a single one around that I could see, and since the nurse was silently waiting for me at the door like a sheepdog, I didn't want to waste time looking. Dutifully, I followed her out and through the twists and turns of the pale stone hallways that seeped a chill that only seemed to grow more and more prevalent the further we went. It wasn't until we arrived outside two large double doors, one that was thankfully open, that I realized just how cold this place was. Nurse No Words, however, didn't even shiver as she directed me forward.

I frowned when I took in the crowd milling about what looked like a larger and icier replica of the Court of Crimson's throne room. I scanned the arched ceiling, looking for Pixies. I didn't see any, but that didn't mean there were none. Pixies, I'd come to learn, were quite good at hiding. When I pulled my gaze back, I noticed the nurse had disappeared into the crowd and left me out in the open with dozens of eyes on me and a sinking feeling that I had stepped between the jaws of a very sharp-toothed and dangerous creature.

I stood there, frozen for a moment, before I heard Orion's voice and relief slipped through me at the familiar timbre. I took several steps toward the sound only to slow to a stop once more. I hadn't noticed it at first, but Orion's voice sounded colder, meaner. I continued to follow it, but more cautiously. When I finally spotted him, I noticed he was talking to an older man with a graying beard. To be fair, the man that sounded like Orion was turned away from me, so theoretically it could have been anyone—but I'd know that ass anywhere. I stayed further away, waiting until I could catch Orion's attention when he turned around, but the longer I watched, the more uncomfortable I saw he was.

An increasing need to go to him rose within me. I didn't know what was being said—I could hear his voice, but not make out the words. Whatever was happening, though, was obviously making him uncomfortable if the set of his shoulders and the stiffness in his movements were anything to go by. The more I watched, the more I wanted to go to him. I was happy to see him still alive, but was I allowed to approach him here? I hesitated, unsure of my welcome. My gaze roamed over his wide frame, seeking a sign of something that would push me over the edge. He was a grown Fae, surely he could extract himself from a conversation he didn't want to have.

The longer I watched the more details I took in; the clenched fist at his side that he kept opening and closing as though he was reminding himself not to display his emotions. I also noticed that his clothing was not the normal black or gray he usually wore, but a deep purple, one that reminded me of his bedchamber and the garden he had first tasted me in. My body might have been injured, but it knew what it wanted, and in that moment, it was Orion.

He wasn't the only one, though. As Roan's voice reached my ears as well, I couldn't help but turn where I stood, my eyes searching for his fiery hair. When I found it and his eyes locked with mine, I almost fell to my knees with relief. It was so overwhelming that I had to reach out a hand and rest against the wall to steady myself.

I wasn't sure how I knew, since his expression remained blank, but the panic that rolled off him as he watched me lean against the wall was almost palpable. The men he was talking to didn't seem to notice in the slightest. It took only a few moments for him to excuse himself from his companions, but when he did, I watched him walk toward me, my relief turning to something else entirely as I stared at him. In the moments just before I'd passed out—when that bright, unrelenting light had overwhelmed me—I'd wondered if I might ever see him again. I had only been given a split second to mourn the loss of both him and Orion and yes, even the turdwad, Sorrell. For all his prickliness, I could tell he cared about Orion and Roan, and even if his honesty often had me wanting to punch his torturously handsome face, I liked his candor.

"Cressida, are you well?" Roan asked as he approached.

I balked at the use of my full name; it was something he never called me. It was always Little Bird or Changeling, sometimes even Cress, but never Cressida. "I'm recovering," I replied, unsure how to handle this different version of Roan. He didn't touch me and that in and of itself was the strangest thing. Roan always touched me. Any way he could brush his skin against mine and drive my libido absolutely insane, he would. When I reached for him, he took a step back—small and almost indiscernible, but I noticed. It hurt—that avoidance. I looked at him, frowning, and finally noticed the strain in his features. He—like Orion—was stiff, wooden in their movements as if someone had shoved sharp sticks up their asses. What was going on?

"I'm sorry, Cress," he said quietly. "Sorry, we weren't there when you woke. We couldn't—it's been..." He trailed off.

I shook my head. "You have another court to see to," I offered by way of answer, though it did assuage some wounded part of me that I hadn't even realized had been hurt by the fact that no one but strangers had been at my bedside when I'd come to.

Roan closed his eyes and hissed out a breath. "Come, the Queens requested your presence and will be eager to meet you." His words sounded kind, but there was something darker in his tone—sorrow, perhaps? Dread? Whatever it was, it remained present in his eyes as he took me by the elbow and led me forward. The deep crimson of his outfit kept drawing my eye as we walked, and I had to resist the urge to touch the metal that sat atop a leather doublet over his chest. Now was not the time or place for that, and he clearly wasn't in the mood even though just the slightest touch on my elbow from him made me want to move in closer.

As we approached the front of the room, I saw the two women sitting side by side. They were exact opposites, fire and ice. And that only made it clear who was who. Roan's mother was wearing a similar outfit to her son, only the metalwork over her chest was much more intricate. It was finely crafted and was studded with gems in all different shades of red which matched the crown that sat atop her head. She looked every bit the reigning monarch, as did the woman beside her. Sorrell's mother was the Crimson Queen's mirrored image, only instead of gems of all different shades of red, I noticed that the metalwork had a blue sheen to it and all the gems were white or clear, making it look like she was covered in frost. Of fire and ice, these were the two Fae Queens that still ruled Alfheim.

Roan stepped close but still didn't touch me as we cleared

the crowd and entered the space that remained empty in front of the Queens. Roan dipped his head in a show of respect and only then did he reach out and tug me forward by my elbow. I didn't know what to do, but these were Queens and when you were introduced to royalty you were supposed to curtsy or something ... right? Gods, I hoped that was right.

I dipped into an uneven curtsy, wavering as I dropped, barely managing to stay upright. When I started to stand up again, Roan's grip on my elbow tightened, and I realized that I needed to hold the position until the Queens deigned to notice us and release us from it. My legs shook, but I held, not wanting to disappoint him. In my mind, however, I was screaming at the two women up on their thrones to hurry it up. My knees were not meant to hold like this.

"Roan, my darling, who have you brought me?" his mother asked, finally acknowledging our presence. I sighed in relief as Roan's tug and subsequent release of my elbow let me stand back up.

I raised my eyes to meet the Queen's only to find a slight sneer covering her face and fire dancing in her eyes while Ariana, who I hadn't noticed before, stood to the side—just behind the woman's throne—glaring daggers at me. I felt the hairs on the back of my neck stand up as though they were urging me to run while I had the chance, and I knew that this wasn't going to go well at all.

"This is Cressida. We—" Roan began, but Ariana cut in.

"The Changeling." Her voice was loud and filled with what sounded like disgust, but I knew better, because I'd heard it a time or two before. It was hatred.

A gasp rose from the crowd behind us and the Queens both looked at me even more critically. Their expressions were almost identical, narrowed eyes and pursed lips that peeled back in disgust after a moment.

Mutters started up behind me while I endured the Queens'

equally terrifying stares and tried not to pass out since I was still recovering.

"Filthy humans..."

"Should have stayed with them..."

"Infections that need to be wiped out..."

"Some Fae she is..."

The words all rang in my ears. *Tough crowd*, I thought. I frowned as I glanced around. I had as much right to be here as any single one of them. I was just as much Fae as they were.

"Is Ariana correct? This is the Changeling you've been so worried about?" Roan's mother asked, her tone suggesting disapproval.

I saw him nod out of my periphery but never took my eyes away from the women on their thrones.

"And this … *Changeling* is the reason you haven't proposed to a Fae worthy of your court yet?" she replied, acting as though the very word that described my life was an insult while she gestured to Ariana, who was still standing next to the Queen.

The other woman's gown was similar to mine, only bejeweled to within an inch of its life. She glittered like some kind of expensive bauble, and while that might distract most people, I still saw the look of triumph on her face, the small smile that played about her lips as she watched Roan struggle with the trap she had led him into.

"I haven't proposed to Ariana because I don't care for her and I don't intend to spend the rest of my life tied to her." Roan's voice rang out as clear as day through the now silent throne room.

"She is the best match you could hope for," the Crimson Queen said with a wave of her hand. "She's perfectly suitable to be the next Crimson Princess."

"She may be suitable for you, Mother, but not for me."

Roan's words were quiet but strong, and anyone who could hear them knew that he wasn't going to back down easily.

The Crimson Queen's face darkened and she sat up straighter on her throne. Contrarily, though, the Frost Queen remained quiet, watching with icy eyes that held no emotion. I shivered when her gaze snapped to me. I blinked at the ferocity in her stare and turned away, refocusing on Roan and the Crimson Queen.

"I have waited long enough for a Crimson Princess to be crowned, Roan," the woman said.

"Is that why you have summoned me and my court brothers?" Roan asked. "Because you wish for me to marry."

"Yes!" Red skirts swished as the woman stood abruptly, pointing a finger down at Roan. "You have ignored my demands for the last time. You will propose and there will be a Red Wedding."

My stomach clenched as I turned and looked at the prince that stood at my side. No, I didn't like this. I didn't like this at all. The hesitation I saw on his face was like a punch to the gut. I turned back to the Queens and narrowed my gaze specifically on Ariana, who stood back, preening as if the decision had already been made. It wasn't, and if Roan even thought to propose to her, he was dead.

"You're right, Mother," Roan said, shocking me. I whipped about and gaped at him. *No!* my mind screamed. *No, she's not!*

The Crimson Queen's eyes narrowed, but her face softened and she lowered her hand. "Yes, I am, and I'm glad that you finally see it my way." She nodded approvingly. "Ariana will make—"

"Another male a very conniving wife someday, I'm sure," Roan interrupted. "But she will not be *my* wife and she will not be the Crimson Princess. I've chosen another to be my bride. As you've demanded, there will be a Red Wedding."

He'd already chosen a bride? I tried to pull my arm from his grasp, but his fingers tightened. He wasn't looking at me. I pulled again, harder this time. Still, he didn't release me. *Who was it?* I wondered. *Why would he kiss me? Why would he do those ... other things to me if he was already betrothed?*

Roan's mother's head went back. "Who would you select over Ariana?" she exclaimed.

"Cressida is to be my Crimson Princess," Roan announced, the sudden silence in the room making the words echo up into the top of the throne room.

My jaw dropped. The Crimson Queen's eyes swung my way as she paled. Even Ariana's face showed only shock. Then, somewhere in the room, someone began to clap. The sound of slow, steady applause grew louder as the people in the room shifted to the side, moving forward until a man clad in a dark cloak stepped into the empty space before the Queens' thrones.

"Ahhh, the Court of Frost never disappoints when it comes to entertainment, does it?" the man asked, turning to Roan and me. "Brother?"

CHAPTER 15
CRESS

There was an air of confusion and shock in the room, and this time, I wasn't the only one feeling it. I tried thinking back. *When had this happened? Had Roan proposed to me and I just hadn't known it?* My thoughts whirled. I was sure I would have recalled something like a proposal.

Regardless, he couldn't be serious. We hardly knew each other. But then again, weirder things had happened—I mean, I was standing in front of two eternal Fae Queens who were more or less the embodiments of fire and ice.

"Tyr." My head whipped around as Sorrell pushed through the crowd to stand next to Roan. "I wasn't aware you'd been summoned to the Court of Frost as well."

"I wasn't aware you'd respond to such a summons, brother," Orion said, coming to stand alongside me.

Tyr—the man who'd stepped forward and called Roan brother—smiled, and I found I didn't quite like it. Nope. Not at all actually. Especially when he turned that smile on me, strode forward, reached for my hand, and lifted it to his lips. My flesh crawled as he pressed a kiss to my knuckles.

"I'm so rarely summoned these days, and I'd heard about a

pretty Little Bird that had wandered into your court. I just had to come see for myself." He winked down at me, but as soon as he released my hand, I put it down and subtly wiped it on my skirts. It still didn't feel clean.

"You were not summoned to flirt with the Changeling, Tyr," a frigid voice spoke, the sound causing a ripple across the gathered crowd. Several heads dipped down in respect as the Frost Queen rose from her seat, her hands clasped in front of her as she looked down on those of us who'd gathered closer.

Unperturbed, Tyr turned toward the Queen. "Your Majesty." He dipped his head and bowed gracefully, pausing briefly and tipping his head back up when she nodded to him. "Why, pray tell, have you summoned us—I notice you have high ranking members of every Fae court here tonight. What have we all been brought here for?"

The Frost Queen lifted her chin and looked over our heads before speaking again. "You have been brought here because we have received word that the human kingdom's leader, King Felix, has obtained the usage of one of our magic orbs."

A gasp rose within the room, and I glanced around briefly— watching as the women paled, putting their hands to their chests as though they might faint. By contrast, most of the men kept their stoic expressions. Roan, Sorrell, and Orion's faces tightened at this announcement.

Sorrell was the first to speak. "How?" he demanded, stepping forward.

The Queen—his mother—didn't even spare him a glance as she turned toward Tyr. "Tyr," she continued, "you've been called to a meeting of the Fae Courts' Council. Two members of each of the ruling courts are required. It will be held in three days. You will remain until then."

"Why in three days?" I asked. "If it's important, wouldn't you want to do it sooner rather than later?"

Roan whipped his hand out and slapped his palm across my

mouth so quickly, I stumbled under the sharp movement, nearly tripping over my own feet. "What she means, Your Majesty," Roan said quickly as the Queen turned her icy eyes on us, "is would it not be more beneficial for your intentions to host the council meeting a little earlier?"

That wasn't exactly what I meant. It was—sort of—but why was he ... the Queen descended from the throne, disrupting my thoughts. My eyes flitted to her Crimson counterpart, but Roan's mother was silent as she watched it all with an examining glare as if she were waiting to see what would happen before she would erupt. Because I had no doubt that she was still furious—the anger simmered there, much like Roan's, just beneath the surface, waiting to be unleashed. The difference between her and Roan, though, was that I found his heated anger kind of sexy and I found hers disturbing.

"Remove your hand from the Changeling's mouth, Prince Roan," the Frost Queen commanded.

Roan hesitated and both Sorrell and Orion stepped closer as if preparing for an attack. Orion, I'd expected to come to my aid, but Sorrell? If he was concerned then I had a bad feeling about this. He hated me. So, if he was worried then we were in deep shit. Slowly, Roan eased his hand from my lips, but I kept my mouth shut as the Queen moved ever closer, a wave of chilled air following in her wake. I shivered under her gaze and scrutiny.

"I cannot expect you to understand the ways of the Fae when you, yourself, have no notion of our species," she said coolly, her words like ice chips falling from her lips. "We Fae have traditions—customs that must be adhered to—lest we fall into the barbaric ways of the humans." My eyes widened. Whoa. If that wasn't an obvious sign of species discrimination, I didn't know what was. "When the courts gather for a meeting of the councils, there must be a three day respite. It is the way it is done. It is the way it has *always* been done and we will not change our customs because of the opinion of some *Changeling*." She leaned closer, her eyes skimming down my form before returning to my face. It was clear by the dullness in her gaze that she found what she saw lacking. "Have I made myself clear?"

I released a breath and met her gaze. "As crystal."

She straightened and turned away, continuing to speak as she strode back up the steps to her throne. "Regardless of your supposed engagement to one of our Court Princes, your worth remains to be seen."

"She obviously has no worth, Adorra," the Crimson Queen commented dryly. "She's nothing more than a rebellion from my son."

"Nonetheless." Adorra—the Frost Queen—turned sharply and, in a movement far more graceful than anything I could've ever managed, sat back upon her throne. "He's claimed her publicly now. You know the law. Only either of them can renounce the claim once it's been made before a court."

I opened my mouth and then quietly shut it when Orion caught my attention and shook his head at me. Whether or not he knew what I'd intended to say, perhaps now wasn't the best time to argue about my engaged status. When Orion seemed satisfied that I'd keep my mouth shut, his eyes slid across the room. I followed his gaze, which was settled on the stranger who'd called him brother—Tyr.

"We will see," the Crimson Queen responded with a low hum in her throat.

The Frost Queen lifted her hand and waved it, lifting the volume of her voice as she addressed the room. "Hear me now. The Courts' Council has been called. The tradition of respite will continue. During such time, we will host the Feast of Beasts and, at the news of Prince Roan's engagement, we will also host the Run of the Gods."

I frowned—I'd heard of a Feast of Beasts before; it was

something the wealthy back in Amnestia had celebrated, usually reserved for grand welcomings. But I'd never heard of the Run of the Gods.

"As you wish, Your Majesty," Roan said, bowing. All around us, everyone bowed their heads, and when Orion lowered his, and I mimicked him. When we all lifted again, Orion shot me a look. I licked my dry lips and watched as his eyes zeroed in on the way my tongue moved from one side of my mouth to the other.

"With your permission, we'll adjourn to our chambers, Your Majesty," Sorrell said, drawing the Frost Queen's gaze.

My eyebrows rose as her lips curled down. She could've been looking at a great big pile of pig shit for all of the warmth she showed her own son. And instead of responding, she merely nodded her assent and, before I knew what was happening, I was lifted into Roan's arms and carted out of the room.

I glanced back, watching as Tyr stepped into the space left by our absence as people parted to let us leave the room. He folded his arms across his broad chest and the last thing I saw before we turned a corner was the wicked gleam of his smile and the wink he sent me.

How much trouble were we in? I wondered.

CHAPTER 16

CRESS

A s soon as the door to the suites closed behind us and I was set down, I spun and faced Roan. "What was that?" When he didn't immediately answer, I gestured between us. "You know, traditionally, for someone to be considered your *fiancée* you have to actually ask them to marry you!"

"Believe me. I didn't plan for this," Roan snapped back.

"Could have fooled me," Sorrell muttered as he pinched the bridge of his nose before dropping his arm and giving Roan a look that could have withered an entire mountain range.

While Sorrell and Roan glared at each other, I turned away. This wasn't happening. Or it was and I was fucked. Or perhaps this was a dream and I'd wake up any moment and find out that I'd actually been eaten by a pack of magical wolf creatures at the bottom of the Bavarian Pass. Either way, I was fucked.

Orion strode across the room and sat down hard on one of the many elegant chairs that had been placed in weird spots around the room. *Who would place a chair by a dresser and not in front of the vanity? Oh, no. There was one in front of the vanity too, I realized. Were they there just for decoration? Who thought, hey, you know what this room needs? Random fucking chairs.*

"And I did ask you," Roan snapped.

"Asked who?" I replied.

"You."

I frowned. "Asked me what?"

His face grew red. "Asked you to marry me!" Roan shouted.

"When?" I asked. "I have no memory of this."

"In the forest, below the pass," he replied. "That night—in the tree—when we were talking. You said that I could tell people that you belonged to me."

There was a brief moment of shock and silence. When no one said anything for several long minutes and Sorrell's and Orion's eyes remained on me expectantly, I realized it was going to be left up to me to break it. Blinking fast and inhaling through my nose, I tried to staunch the flow of annoyance.

"*That*," I said, eyeing Roan, "was your proposal?"

"Yes, it was," he replied sharply at the same time Sorrell apparently found his voice.

"You *proposed* to the Changeling?"

"You can't exactly propose to someone unless you ask the question '*will you marry me?*'" I pointed out.

They ignored me. "Yes, I did," Roan said, snapping back at Sorrell. "Why is that so hard to believe?"

"You didn't propose!" I shouted. "You insinuated a relationship—barely—and you talked about me belonging to one of you. But a relationship does not a proposal make."

"Because you're a Gods damned prince!" Sorrell yelled over me. "And she's—"

He stopped as his gaze strayed from Roan's face to look at me. I crossed my arms over my chest and narrowed my eyes, daring him to finish that sentence. Apparently, my daring face wasn't all that intimidating because he did. The asshole.

"She's barely Fae!" Sorrell continued with a shake of his head. "Much less a Court Fae. She's common—no education, no training, no anything. You've lost your mind."

"Cress is acceptable," Roan replied.

Acceptable! Acceptable? Oh, just what I've always wanted to be, I thought sarcastically. But of course, I didn't say anything. I honestly didn't know *what* to say. He continued.

"She's certainly preferable to Ariana. What's wrong with that?" *Dig dig dig—he was digging a hole so deep, I doubted he'd be able to reach the bottom when I would eventually shove him into it.*

Rage rocketed through me, heating me from the inside out despite the chill of the chamber and the castle itself. So far, Orion seemed to be the only one who had yet to piss me off. And it was mostly because he hadn't opened his mouth. I shot him a helpless look, seeking out comfort or something. *Anything* to make this all seem far less dire than it was.

"You've been obsessed with the Changeling ever since you first saw her. When she decided to let Orion deflower her, you looked like you'd just lost your favorite pet," Sorrell growled. "You're possessive and jealous, admit it!"

Orion didn't even seem to notice my stare. He was focused on Sorrell and Roan, his face dark with distress and concern. Roan paced away from Sorrell, his hands clenching and unclenching at his sides. After a beat, I watched as he ran them through the flames of his hair—literally. Small little tendrils of fire had ignited at the ends of the strands, some going out as he patted them away and some remaining behind, though never burning him.

"Okay," I said. It was definitely up to me to keep everyone calm. I was probably the worst person for the job, but alas, it was mine. "Can we just stop for a second and go back to when you announced me as your fiancée?" I turned to Roan. "Why?" I asked.

With a roll of his icy eyes, Sorrell scoffed and shook his head.

You are calm, I reminded myself. *You are serenity incarnate. You do not want to hurt, maim, punch, throttle, or ball kick anybody right now. Nope. Not even a little bit. Ball kicking wasn't even that fun. Even when the guy—Sorrell—was a fucking jerkwad of the highest order.*

Roan didn't respond immediately, but Sorrell, apparently, was ready for action. *Yippee.* "Yes, please, let's bring the attention back to the Changeling. As much as I am loathe to admit it, I believe she is a voice of reason here. Why did you do this? What could have possibly led you to believe that announcing that *she*—of all Fae—was an 'appropriate' choice"—I narrowed my eyes when he lifted his hands and pantomimed quoting Roan's own words against him— "for a fiancée? Or at the least, tell us why you would announce it *to the entire fucking realm!*"

Hello, my name is Sorrell and I hold the title of the most monumental asshole of the world. Was my eyeball twitching? I thought I could feel it twitching. That probably wasn't a good thing, was it?

Roan snarled in frustration, jerking his hands from his burning hair to gesture to the room at large. "Cress needed— no, she *needs*—protection," he said. "Not only from the Queens but from Tyr, and other members of the court like him. You saw it out there. You saw the way they looked at her. It was as though she's nothing more than a feast that they can't fucking wait to rip into. Without the announcement of our betrothal, she would have been taken by any number of high ranking court members. Damn the consequences."

Wait, what? "Taken?" I blurted. "Taken how?" *Hopefully to a nice tavern for a warm meal and good music?*

Sorrell groaned as Orion finally stood and moved closer.

"I was helping her," Roan said.

"No." Sorrell shook his head. "You've done nothing more than paint a target on her back! All you wanted to do was stake your claim. Well, here it is, Roan! You've Gods damned staked it. Are you happy now?" Sorrell exploded, his chest pumping up and down as he stomped back and forth, pacing in his fury.

"I didn't think you cared about her," Orion said, watching him.

Sorrell made a very un-Sorrell sound—a choked growl of some sort—and turned, pacing away from our little group. "You both care about her, and I care about you," he said. As he strode back and forth, I began to notice color filling his cheeks. He inhaled and exhaled in slow, steady waves as if trying to stave off the riled anger inside of him. Finally, when the color began to recede, he turned back to us and spoke again, in a much more smooth tone. "As much as I hate that she's even here in the Court of Frost with us, I cannot change it. Not now. The best thing to do is manage the damage her presence and Roan's announcement has and will cause because make no mistake, this can only mean catastrophe." The prince of the Court of Frost pointed an accusatory finger at me, and I felt like I'd just been caught eating vegetables by the nuns. "She is a walking disaster."

I eyed him with irritation before sighing and facing Orion and Roan. They, at least, might give me more answers. "What did you mean by 'taken'?" I asked again.

As soon as the question had left my mouth, an uncomfortable tension filled the room. Sorrell's shoulders stiffened and he stopped dead in his tracks. Orion's hand touched my arm, but it was Roan who answered.

"A high ranking member of the court could claim you as his consort," he said quietly. "And as a common Fae—one without land, title, money, or even much power—you would have no choice. You would be his to do with what he wanted, for all intents and purposes, until he released you."

Confused shock echoed throughout me. "How is that allowed?" I demanded.

"It's tradition. This is the first time in history that there have been more Queens in a court than Kings. Fae are governed by tradition more than anything else. Regardless of whether or not they would agree with the custom, they would be helpless to do anything, especially if the court member who did the claiming was of high status. If Tyr, for example, attempted to claim you … there would be absolutely nothing they could do. Tyr is heir to the Court of Midnight. He is a future King. And even though, right now, the Queens have more authority, especially in the Court of Frost, to anger a future King is unwise."

My mouth hung open. "But—"

Orion's hand tightened on my arm. "Despite what Sorrell believes," he said. "This is a good thing. You do not want Tyr or anyone else to claim you. Roan is trustworthy and honorable. You will be safe with him." I lifted my eyes and met the dark swirling pits of his gaze. They were deeper than normal, spinning with the shadows that pervaded his presence, the sense of secrets and horrors I hadn't yet uncovered from him tempting me. And also warning me.

Sorrell groaned, and I reluctantly peeled my eyes from Orion's. "Look, this all comes down to one thing, Roan. Your mother. You know what she wants. Not only that, but you lied to both her and my mother to ensure she doesn't get it. They are not merely our mothers. They are the power of the Court of Frost. They are our Queens."

Silence fell like a bomb in the room as the implications of what Sorrell said were realized.

Roan had lied not just to his mother, but to his Queen, not to mention Sorrell's mother. I had to admit that neither of them seemed like women that would be okay finding out they had been lied to.

"It's not a lie if I go through with it," Roan replied quietly. My heart stuttered to a stop in my chest and then, just as quickly, it restarted and began working overtime. It raced, sprinted, roared through my veins as if it meant to bound off and escape all of this tension.

Go through with it? I thought. *As in ... actually marry me?* I tried to picture it. Me, in a gown, walking up an aisle in a Temple of the Gods—*wait, did Fae get married in the Temples?*

Before I could ask, however, Sorrell shook his head. "You can't go through with it," he said. "We are princes, we do not always get to choose our brides." At first, I thought he was just being cruel—as he always was. But the last bit of his denial was said in a quieter tone, whispered with a small sliver of pain that belied his own reality. He'd said 'we,' I realized. It wasn't just Roan he was denying. It was himself as well.

Roan, too, was quiet for a bit, as if his thoughts consumed him. "She needs someone at her side," he finally said. "So, I can and I will go through with it, if that's what it takes to protect her."

My first thought: *That is sooooo sweet.* My second: *Um ... don't I get a choice?* I didn't have time to voice those thoughts, however. Roan's hair blazed as he looked at me, his eyes boring their way into my soul with a ferocity that made my pulse leap.

"Especially with the Feast of Beasts and the Run of the Gods," he said slowly. "She can't be entrusted to anyone else but the three of us."

Entrusted, he said. Like I was something special. Some*one* special. Was my heart melting? I think it was.

But still, as if he just absolutely had to be contrary, Sorrell spoke up. "All you've succeeded in doing is drawing more attention to her, making more eyes watch her, thereby putting her in more danger," he announced dismissively.

"What's done is done," Orion said. "You both need to let it go. What we need to do now is come up with a plan for the Feast of Beasts and Run of the Gods if we don't want her to get into any trouble."

"Fine, but I'm not going to apologize for protecting her," Roan said as he shot Sorrell a defiant look.

"Of course not," Sorrell bit back. Orion moved across the

room to a table amongst the many chairs. He took his place at the first chair and Roan and Sorrell followed. Roan took the next chair, but Sorrell paused as I came up alongside the table. We both stopped and stared. There was only one chair left. A deep inhale from him and he stepped back.

Before he could offer it to me, though—if that was, in fact, what he was planning on doing—Roan spoke up. "Come here, Little Bird." Roan held out a hand to me. I took it and he tugged me onto his lap. With stiff movements and a glare, Sorrell moved forward, taking the last chair. After a moment, Roan leaned his head close and whispered against my ear, "Forgive me?"

I lifted a brow as I turned to face him more fully. "I thought you said you wouldn't apologize."

"To them," he clarified, his lips quirking up. "You're a different matter altogether."

I sighed. "I understand why you did what you did, but if you were that concerned about it then you should have talked to me ahead of time."

A pained expression crossed his face as he said, "I tried to—"

"In the tree, I know," I said, cutting him off. "But you said that if I was in danger, I should act like I belonged to you. How is that a proposal?"

"Cress…" He sighed. "It's better for everyone to believe that we're engaged. Technically, making you my fiancée is staking a claim. As my fiancée, you belong to me—to the Court of Crimson."

I stared at him for a moment, but he appeared sincere. I huffed out a breath. "Fine. But just so you know, if that was your idea of a proposal, I'd hate to see what your idea of an actual wedding is. Maybe next time you propose, actually ask the question instead of staking a claim in front of your mother."

He chuckled. "It was for your own protection," he said, "but fair enough. Cress, I'm—"

"If you two are finished could we move this along?" Sorrell demanded, interrupting whatever he would've said next. The urge to slap Sorrell rose. Could I get away with it? Just a tiny slap. My hand would meet a chair and that chair would meet his face. Nothing more than a love tap, really. One that would knock him out and give me a little bit of peace.

Roan straightened and lifted his head. "Yes," he said. "Cress will need an attendant." His eyes slid to the darkest of them all. "Orion?"

"And leave Tyr to his own devices? As much as I would love to, trust me, my friend, I don't think it's wise. He's up to something. I didn't like the way he looked at her. I have no doubt that my brother will make a move for her—anything to drive chaos into the court. He feeds on it. I need to be available to follow and track him." He shook his head regretfully.

My curiosity rumbled through me. What kind of history was between them? Tyr had called them all—more specifically Orion—brothers. I didn't trust the man—not with how uncertain these three were about him. Orion was concerned and that, in turn, made me concerned.

"I can do it." All heads turned and settled on Sorrell. "What?" He frowned, folding his arms over his broad chest. "Do you have a better option?"

"No, I'm just surprised you would offer yourself," Roan replied, the rumble of his words vibrating through his chest as it pressed along my spine.

"I don't agree with your actions. I think both of you are mad for wanting the Changeling. She is dangerous. She is—"

"Sitting right here, Ice Man," I snapped. Was there really such a need to talk about me like I wasn't right there? It was rude.

Sorrell's white-blue gaze swung my way and I lifted my

head to match his glare with one of my own. There was a small bit of softening in his features as I did so. Perhaps ... no, could it be? Was that a modicum of respect? I mean it was tiny, for sure, but it was there. Damn, who knew the Frost Prince had it in him?

"As I was saying," he continued through clenched teeth. "I may disagree with everything you two are doing." His eyes flickered to Roan and Orion. "But my loyalty lies with you. You are my brothers—not by blood—but by Throne and Crown. We are stronger together than we are divided." He unfolded his arms, one hand falling, palm down on the table as he leaned back. "And though we argue in these chambers, I want to present a united front to the Court of Frost and the Council."

Roan released a breath that sounded relieved. "Agreed," he said.

"So, it's decided then?" Sorrell replied.

Everyone nodded—everyone but me, that is, because I was still wondering what need I would have for an attendant. The few times I'd acted as an attendant, it'd been to help one of the older nuns at the convent when she was too frail to do small things for herself. But this sounded like Sorrell would be attending to me. I could walk, run, and bathe on my own. So, what else did that leave for him to do?

Orion stood abruptly, disrupting my rambling thoughts. "I will go track down Tyr," he said. His face darkened. "I want to find out for myself what he's planning, if I can."

Sorrell and Roan nodded and I watched, silently, as he turned and left the room. "Cress?" Roan's voice was right by my head.

"Yes?" I replied as my gaze met Sorrell's. Those wintry eyes caught hold of some darker, base emotion, honing in like a predator on prey.

"Are you alright?" Roan asked.

I nodded. "Of course, but just one question." I held up a

finger. Both princes that remained in the room stiffened as they looked at me, expecting … well, I didn't exactly know what they were expecting. But one thing was for sure. I needed to know a lot more than I did and there was only one way to start. "Why do I need an attendant and why does it have to be Sorrell?"

Blue and brown eyes clashed as Sorrell and Roan looked at each other, and I had the distinct feeling it would be yet another complicated answer. *Great,* I thought sardonically. *Complications were soooo much fun.*

CHAPTER 17
ORION

R age echoed up through my limbs as I stormed through the corridor. The darkness of my power, an unadulterated aggression rising forth within me. I swung in front of the vile parasite that I hadn't seen in years and it brought him to an abrupt halt.

"What are you doing here, Tyr?" I demanded. My hands clenched into fists at my sides, balling in preparation to strike.

Tyr rocked back on his heels with a grin. "The same thing that you're doing here, dear brother," he replied. "I was summoned and I came."

"You never come—summons or not," I pointed out, "and *you* weren't summoned. Someone from the Court of Midnight was summoned. The Queens don't care who comes so long as it's someone from the Royal line. They never care who—just someone. Someone that would never have been you. I can be a representative."

"You're with the Court of Crimson now," Tyr replied with a shrug. "By your own choice. Someone else needed to come."

"It could've been someone else, anyone else. You don't trust Adorra or Yvienne."—Roan's mother—"So, let me repeat my-fucking-self, *brother,*" I spat the word back at him, loathing its truth with every fiber of my being. "What. Are. You. Doing. Here?"

Tyr's grin widened as the darkness that was my Midnight origins began to seep from my skin. It coated me, and if agony and hatred could have a scent, I would have smelled as if I were dipped in it. "Perhaps I am here on a familial errand," he said, never losing that far too annoying grin of his. "Perhaps I am here to gain some intel—intel which you seem chock full of. Tell me something," he said, sidling closer. He threw one arm over my shoulders, yet he was anything but brotherly as he leaned into my side and lowered his voice— whispering in my damn ear. "How many times have you fucked that Changeling of yours? Was it only once or have you had her on her back for weeks now? Is she any good? Care to share?"

My hand was around his throat and his back was against the stone wall before I'd even realized I'd moved. A feminine gasp at my back alerted me to the fact that we were not alone and had an audience. "You go near her, Tyr," I said, leaning closer than he had before, "and I will slit your fucking throat while you sleep. Do you understand?"

Tyr's eyes flashed red and this time, when he smiled, his teeth appeared razor sharp. That female gasp from a moment ago suddenly turned into a quick scurry as the maid or lady fled the scene of what would be a bloody crime of passionate rage if my brother kept it up.

"Do I smell a hint of possession in your tone, Little Ori?" Tyr's hands came up and knocked mine away far too easily. He spun, kicking my ankles together and the only thing that saved me from making a crashing fall to the floor were my hands on the wall. I growled and pivoted to face him again only to be slammed into the very position he had previously been in, except instead of his hand on my throat, it was his forearm. He pushed it in and upward, snarling at me as he laughed. "Oh, I think I do!" he cackled.

Magic swirled in the air, thickening with the tint of doom. As members of the Court of Midnight and all of its power—ours was a magic of something to be truly feared. All of the stories human mothers told their little children at night of the cruel Faeries coming to steal them away or slay them in their beds ... that had come from my home court. The very court that had sent me into battle at the tender age of twelve. No child should ever have to witness such death and destruction. No child should ever have to deal it out as I had—pillage and kill and plunder. My very soul—if there was anything left of it —was stained by those early years of my rearing. But unlike me, my brother—Tyr—had liked the pain he could deliver. He'd relished in the power of preying on people's hatred and fear.

I brought my hand up and grasped his wrist, twisting until his forearm was removed from my throat. I released him almost as quickly and we were left standing, two feet apart, with opposing expressions. Him, smug. Me, dangerously close to a dark side I hadn't unleashed in a long time.

"Cress is property of the Court of Crimson," I said slowly. "*My* court, Tyr. Mine and my brothers—"

"*I* am your brother," he interrupted.

"My throne brothers," I clarified. "The men who rule at my side. The men whose sides I rule by. We are one and the same. You are an outsider. You are of the Court of Midnight and, though we are not at war with other courts, we are also not friends, you and I. Stay away from the Changeling, Tyr. If you know what's good for you, you will stay far away from that girl. She is mine." *Ours*, a small voice in my head echoed. Mine and Roan's for sure ... Sorrell's ... well, on that, I wasn't all too sure. He stared at the Changeling as if he desired her as much as he hated her, but Sorrell was complex. Tyr wasn't.

Tyr's smug grin transformed into another cackling laugh. "You *have* fucked her!" he crowed. "My fucking Gods. She let you put your dick inside her. A girl like that—beautiful and—"

"Virginal," I spat. "She was a virgin and I was her first, do you understand what that means?" I took another step closer, our chests nearly brushing against one another. I seethed. "I claim all rights to the girl."

Tyr rolled his eyes. "Those are old, outdated traditions," he said in a bored tone. "Just as the Changeling tradition is old and highly unusual." He lifted a palm and scratched at the side of his jaw as his smile faded, and I realized how much I'd just fucked up. "How did you come across a Changeling?" he asked as I mentally cursed my anger and irrationality. "Her power pulses, but it's weak. Are you sure she's even all Fae? What if she's a halfbreed?"

Now, I was the one to roll my eyes. "Those don't exist," I scoffed.

But Tyr's expression remained serious. "Regardless of whether or not the Queens wish to admit or publicize the existence of halfbreeds, do you think the girl is one?"

"No," I gritted out, shoulders tensing. "She's Fae."

He hummed. "The Changeling tradition is also very specific to a court that…"

"We are aware," I barked, stopping him before he said the words.

Tyr dropped his hand with a smirk. "That makes her all the more intriguing, doesn't it, brother?"

"Not to you," I snapped.

"Oh, on the contrary," he said, taking a step back and circling me. I pivoted to keep him from pacing behind me. I couldn't and wouldn't trust this man at my back. Never again. Not since he'd left me on the battlefield, surrounded by angry human warriors, simply because he'd been bored by the exercise. "I find the girl fascinating. You don't want me to say it, I can see, but the Brightling Court was a strength to behold back in its day. Don't think the Queens aren't thinking it just because you don't say it."

Brightling. Cress. The threat to her grew by infinite leaps and bounds the longer he talked. "I will say this one last time," I said through clenched teeth as Tyr finally came to a stop. "The girl is mine—she is of the Court of Crimson—and you will not touch her."

"What if she asks me to?" he countered.

"She won't," I snapped. "Of that, you can be sure."

With that, I turned and strode off. *No,* I thought to myself. *Cress had been suitably warned.* She trusted us and, therefore, she would obey us. She would not allow Tyr near her. And if she dared to break that, she'd find herself in for the spanking of a lifetime.

CHAPTER 18

CRESS

I sighed as I stepped in front of one of the long mirrors that had been delivered to my room in the Court of Frost via the Pixie Express. Sorrell was going to be my attendant. *Heh*, I thought with amusement. *I bet he'd hate every second of it.* I stared at the frame of the mirror and then at the girl in its reflection. White-blonde hair swayed in uneven strands at my shoulders. My lips had been painted the darkest of blues in preparation for tonight. All I really wanted to do was return home.

I didn't know when I'd started thinking of the Court of Crimson as my home, but it was. And right now, all I wanted was to return to it. Perhaps I should've been overjoyed to have been brought into the secretive fold of the Fae. And I was. I'd learned of my heritage—found out where I'd come from.

As a child, a part of me had always been fascinated by the feared Fae, but now, I just wanted the game to stop. I wanted to spend time with Roan and Orion, Nellie, and Gods, even Groffet. I didn't want to suffer in silence while people criticized me for being something I wasn't or something I was—a Changeling. *Would I ever be truly a Fae in their eyes?* I hoped so because the Gods only knew I would no longer be human in the eyes of the people who had raised me. The only one who seemed to still love me was Nellie and she was separated from me now. Back at the Court of Crimson while I was here.

At the thought of my friend, I couldn't help but wonder how she was. Had she and Groffet become friends? Had he given her books? She used to love those. I hoped he'd found a way to disguise her from curious eyes too. While I was sure she was quite content in the library reading to her heart's desire with no one bothering her, I was still worried. I'd almost been slaughtered because the princes had originally assumed I was human—because *I* originally assumed I was human. What would happen to her if she were found out? The princes weren't there. I didn't even know who they'd left in charge. Groffet maybe?

Guilt and worry ate at me. I missed her. I worried about her. I wished I'd never left her behind. I wish I hadn't left at all. None of this would have happened. Not the pass fall. Not the engagement. I let my gaze fall away from the mirror as the door opened and a group of Pixies appeared, flying into the room and shutting the door behind them—several of their little bodies working to push the big plank of wood.

What did someone call a group of Pixies? A Herd? Pack? Gaggle? Swarm? Yes, there was definitely a swarm feeling about it.

"Hello," I said, waving with a smile, thankful to see creatures who didn't talk behind their hands as I roamed the hallways.

Their tiny faces contorted in horror as I opened my mouth to speak more, but then I abruptly snapped my mouth shut. Well then. Clearly, these weren't as friendly as the ones in the Court of Crimson, but maybe it was just because I hadn't fed them yet. I looked around for food to give them, but I'd eaten earlier and after I'd gotten ahold of that tray, there had been nothing left. What could I say? Growing girls needed their bread and cheese and crackers. I smiled to myself. Those had been delicious. The best crackers I'd ever had. I wondered if magic made things taste better.

The Pixies floated closer. They were different from the ones back at the Court of Crimson. There was something vicious about them. Their teeth appeared sharper and their dark eyes, beadier, if possible. The bulk of the swarm carried over a few containers and items, dropping them next to me unceremoniously.

Next, they opened the containers and as I stared somewhat absently and lost in my own thoughts, they withdrew shimmering fabrics. Finally, they held up a dress before me and I could see my reflection in the mirror through the gauzy material. The gown itself was a soft silver that made it appear translucent. Straps were held up by tiny arms as the Pixies flew back and forth, crisscrossing the strands to showcase how the garment was meant to be worn.

I sighed. Dresses were so confining. I'd love nothing more than to slip into a pair of breeches and a long shirt, but from the way things seemed in the Fae courts, women wore dresses —often skimpy dresses that left little to the imagination, but dresses nonetheless. And so, I was expected to wear them as well. Especially since Roan had announced our fake engagement. I slipped out of the simpler gown I'd been wearing and took the dress the Pixies held up, tugging the mass of skirts at the bottom over my head.

The fabric shimmied down the rest of my body and the Pixies picked up the straps, and I gasped as they molded into an icy blue tone that crossed over my front and wrapped around and under my breasts, holding them up. There were completely open slits in the sides of the skirt. I turned and glanced over my shoulder. This dress wasn't nearly as confining as the ones I'd worn before. My legs felt freer, too.

There were a few sections of the bodice that were cut out and the corset-like top made me feel like my ribs were about to crack as the Pixies tightened the back. I released an oomph as they wove the ties together. The neckline was studded with black jewels that glittered and sparkled in the light.

My arms remained sleeveless. I reached down, smoothing hands over my stomach. The material was so thin, I could feel the heat of my palms. The Pixies rose and fluttered around my head, their tiny fingers twisting the white blonde strands of my hair back into what felt like intricate knots and small braids around the top of my head. Kohl was smeared across my eyes and a mask was held in front of my face. I reached out and touched it, taking it in my hands.

The center of the mask, where the eye holes were, was smooth and black. The same jewels that decorated the top of my gown were scattered around the edges of the mask. I lifted it, fitted it over my face, and held out the silken strings as the Pixies took them and tied them to the back of my braided crown. A silver tiara was lifted and fitted at the top of my head.

I sucked in a breath as my eyes lifted and met my reflection. I didn't look like myself. I looked … ethereal. Different. Like a true Fae. It was then that I noticed the silvery hue of the dress wasn't just blue. The blue was most concentrated around the bodice, but the skirt shimmered with hints of red and purple. My heartbeat picked up. Never in a million years would I have thought that I'd be standing here. To be honest, I hadn't seen much of a future beyond the convent. I'd certainly never expected to stand in a castle made of ice and magic, dressed like a princess, preparing for a masquerade ball.

The Pixies dispersed, backing away as I turned and headed for the door. I stopped with my hand on the doorknob. Was I supposed to walk myself to the Feast of Beasts? No one had come for me and I could already hear the laughter and music coming from the great throne room. I'd never waited for anyone before, so I turned the knob and stepped out into the corridor.

As soon as I did, I nearly crashed into another woman. She stopped abruptly, the sapphire of her gown a brilliant color against the subdued gray stone walls around us. "My apologies," she said, dipping her head respectfully.

I looked behind me before flipping back around. Was she bowing … to me? My eyes bulged from my head. "Uhhh, no it was my fault," I said quickly.

She didn't say anything to that. Instead, she straightened and skirted around me, but I still wasn't sure if I was supposed to stay in my room or meet Sorrell at the party. "Wait," I called.

The woman froze, her dainty features scrunching as she turned back. "Yes?"

"I'm sorry, but I was hoping you could tell me…" I drifted off, gesturing to my cracked door. "Do you know if I'm supposed to wait for my attendant to come get me or am I allowed to go to the Feast of Beasts by myself?"

Her head tilted and her eyes roamed down my form. I straightened away from the door, letting it shut behind me. I was left standing in the corridor—no Pixies, no other Fae, just me and this girl.

"You don't know?" she asked.

Would I be asking if I knew? I thought a bit dryly, but I shook my head in answer instead of voicing it.

"You can reach the throne room on your own and descend the stairs—"

"Stairs?" I frowned. When I'd gone to the throne room before, there'd been no stairs.

The woman's lips tightened and she inhaled sharply. "Which court are you from?" she asked.

"Th-the Court of Crimson," I stuttered. My spine straightened. *Oh no. Oh no. The stutter had totally messed me up. She'd be able to tell I was lying. I mean, I wasn't technically lying, but she'd be able to tell something was wrong and then she'd tell the Queens—the ones who hated me—not that I had any other Queens who even knew of my existence or anything, but she'd say something to them and then they would order me tortured or killed or—*

"Well, I don't know how you do things in the Court of Crimson," she said, cutting off my internal panic. "But here, when there is an event such as the Feast of Beasts, the Queens widen and deepen the throne room. It's illusion magic, nothing more. Everything will look and feel different though. There will be a wide staircase when you enter. It's essentially for presentation. You can go to the top of it and descend. Your attendant should be waiting there."

"Oh." I blinked. "Thanks."

She shrugged. "Good luck. You're going to need it."

"What?" I reached for her and grabbed her arm as she turned to go a second time. Once more, she pivoted back and it was obvious from her expression that she was growing tired of me. *Well, too bad,* I thought. You couldn't just drop a vague comment like that and keep walking. "What did you mean by that?" I demanded.

Her brows rose. "Do you really not know?" she asked.

"Would I ask if I did?" I snapped.

She shook her head. "Ariana and the Crimson Queen don't like you," she said.

"Oh, that." I waved my hand. "I'm not worried about Ariana." I released her, only to be stopped as *she* grabbed onto *me.*

"You should be," she said, her tone urgent. "Ariana is and always has been the Crimson Queen's chosen favorite. She's warmed Prince Roan's bed ever since his last fiancée—" She stopped herself, gasping. Her hand released me to slap over her mouth.

"I know about his last fiancée," I said and, almost immediately, she sighed in relief.

The woman leaned closer, her hand dropping away. "After

that scandal, the Crimson Queen chose Ariana as his future bride. He never proposed, but they were all but engaged."

Irritated, I stepped away. "And now they're not," I pointed out. A feeling of possessiveness stole over me. It wasn't a natural feeling for me. In fact, it was confusing, but I couldn't stop it. The thought of Roan with anyone else—especially with Ariana—lit a fire in my blood.

"Yes, well," she coughed delicately, shooting me a sympathetic glance, "just a warning. The Crimson Queen usually gets what she wants. She does whatever she deems necessary to achieve her goals, and right now, you're a major obstacle. All I'm saying is that you should take care. Not everyone in this court is your friend."

"Why are you telling me this?" I asked. It seemed odd that she would tell me about having no friends and this is exactly what a friend would do—warn me.

She shrugged. "Just advice from one outsider to another."

"Outsider?" I repeated, more confusion filling me as my angry possessiveness faded.

She looked away. "I'm from a lesser court," she admitted quietly. "One that perished several years ago. I've never truly fit in."

I moved closer. "Can you tell me," I began, "does the Frost Queen have any say over the Crimson Queen's actions?"

"If it doesn't affect her, then the Frost Queen generally doesn't care. The second it does, however"—she cast me a hard look—"she'll act, and I promise you, you don't want that to happen." With that, she turned and left, and it was only moments later that I realized I never even got her name.

At least I'd gotten some information though, I thought as I waited another moment and then followed in the direction she'd gone. The laughter and chatter and music grew louder as I approached the throne room entryway. I paused just before I stepped through the doorway, wiping my hands down the sides of my dress.

I closed my eyes and stepped into the light, freezing as several eyes landed on me at once. I scanned the room, noting the differences. The woman had been right. The whole room had been changed. Columns circled the room, making it appear larger and more circular rather than the plain square it'd been earlier. Ivy dangled from the ceiling—a ceiling I couldn't see through a mass of fog that collected at it. More greenery was draped over every available surface, even twining around the columns, lending a more natural feel to the room. So this was illusion magic. Nice.

Reaching down, I fisted the front of my dress and dragged it up as I descended the staircase. *Don't fall. Don't fall. Don't you dare fucking fall.* I reiterated the words over and over in my head, hoping that if I thought them hard or loud enough that it would stop any clumsiness from happening. By some miracle of miracles, it worked! I reached the bottom of the staircase without tripping or falling or breaking my neck.

I found Sorrell several paces away and approached. He appeared distant, as if he were deep in thought. "Sorrell?" I said, calling attention to myself.

His gaze cleared and he jerked his head down, freezing as his lips parted. Nothing. He said absolutely nothing. Instead, he gaped at me. It was almost … cute, his shock. I smiled and his eyes widened even further. Well, I hadn't expected this reaction, but it was nice nonetheless. He spent so much time hating me and I spent so much time finding him to be a pompous asshole, that the silence from him was a bit of a reprieve.

Still, I found my eyes trailing down to take him in as he did the same to me. His muscular legs were wrapped in black trousers and knee high riding boots that made him look like he was going to go on a hunt rather than to a ball. A pale, icy blue doublet with black filigree was stretched over his broad chest.

The black leather that edged the bottom and the shoulders gleamed in the light. His mask was a pale silver, reminding me of a ray of moonlight cast across his face.

When my eyes lifted and met his once more, he cleared his throat. "Cress," he said gruffly. I shivered. He didn't ever say my name—well, rarely, anyway. It sounded different coming from him, especially in this setting. "Are you ready?" he asked.

Was I ready? Not even in the slightest. But when he held his hand out, I knew there was no way I could say no.

CHAPTER 19
SORRELL

Fae were fools for glittering things. Gems and jewels. Pretty feathers. Baubles of all shapes and sizes. Especially the females—they went head over heels for this kind of ridiculous spectacle. My head throbbed and pounded as I took in the scenery before me. There was more silk and lace and skin than practical wear. And here I was, standing at the edge of the room, waiting for my ... *companion.* I grimaced at the thought.

The Changeling had brought nothing but trouble. Yet, here I was. Awaiting *her* arrival. Because I was her fucking attendant. Why had I offered myself up for the position? That's right, because there was no one else who could do it. No one else who knew what we did—that she was as weak as a Fae could be and that we were secretly harboring her friend—*her human friend*—back home. Orion had to take care of his brother. Keeping Tyr as far from her as possible was necessary. Even I knew that. Tyr was partially the reason why Orion was so scarred. That Fae thought of no one but himself and would do anything in his plot to get whatever he desired. He was fickle and would sooner stab his own family in the back than pledge his loyalty to them. As her intended, Roan couldn't be near Cress in public without an attendant nearby until the wedding. I was the only logical option.

Are you sure it has nothing to do with how the girl makes you feel when you look at her? a secret voice in my head murmured.

I stiffened. No. Not in a million years. She made me feel nothing but irritation.

Irritation in your loins, perhaps, the voice replied.

I released a subtle growl of frustration. *One time,* I thought. *I'd only felt that way one time.* Even as I'd shoved those thoughts at the incessant inner voice of mine, I knew that it was a lie. I shifted from one foot to the other, a glass of Faerie wine clutched in my hand. Since that night at camp, I'd done nothing but think of her.

A clumsy oaf, yes, but at the same time … she was honest and blatant in a way other Fae females were not. Cress was not raised to be poised and proper at all times. When she got angry, she showed it. When she wanted something, she demanded it. It was something I was not used to. Something none of us were. Women were wicked creatures: slinking into beds, promising things and all the while they were planning, plotting. My very own mother was the Queen of them all. She'd seduced my father, had her heir, and then he was gone. A casualty in the early years of this war with humanity. A war that needed to end one way or another. We simply could not survive if it continued. Fae were a dying breed. Magic was leeching from the world faster than it was being reproduced. Humans could live without it—could flourish without it. We, on the other hand, could not. Soon enough, we would simply perish because of our own trials and traditions. As I looked around the room, I saw so much wealth and opulence. Expensive extravagance. Even as a people on the very brink of extinction. This would be our downfall—our vanity.

"Sorrell?" A familiar voice called me back from my darker thoughts and I turned, pausing as my mouth gaped open as I met her eyes. Her face was ivory and cream. Her pale blonde hair pinned back to show off her features, beautiful as they were. Her breasts were pushed up, presented as if they were two ripe frost melons ready to be plucked and devoured. I *wanted* to devour her, I realized at that moment. The annoying voice came back to snigger at my sudden discomfort.

I set my now empty glass down at a nearby table and smoothed my suddenly sweaty palms down the outside of my dark trousers. "Cress," I said gruffly. "Are you ready?" I held my hand out for her.

She took a step toward me, lifting her palm and resting it against mine. Lightning shards dug into my spine. The heated bolt of awareness of her skin on mine shot through me. I swallowed, my throat feeling parched despite the drink I'd just had.

"I'm a little nervous," she admitted quietly, her eyes lifting to dart around the room. *Was she looking for Roan?* I wondered with a scowl. She didn't need him. I was here. I would protect her. I tightened my hold on her hand when I realized the direction of my thoughts. "Sorrell?" Her luminous eyes lifted to meet mine again. "Are you okay? What is it? Is something wrong?"

"No," I replied, and then, before I could think better of it... "You look beautiful tonight."

Her lips parted as she blinked up at me. Silence. For several long seconds the only thing I could hear was the twitter of those around us, and then she seemed to collect herself. Of course, she had to be the first to do so because I was still too ... fucking dumbstruck just looking at her. Was this what Orion and Roan saw when they looked at this girl? If so, then I could see the reason for their obsession. I could understand it because I, too, suddenly had a great pang in my chest that warned me against leaving her side.

No matter how irritating, how uncouth, how wild she was —she was a gem. Rare and brilliant. And in a place such as the

Court of Frost, she would be left broken and shattered before she'd ever been given a chance if someone—if I—didn't look after her.

"Th-thank you," Cress stuttered, her cheeks flushing with a rosy hue.

"Dance with me?" I offered. *It was only proper*, I thought to myself. There was nothing wrong with asking her to dance. I didn't have to like her to dance with her. In fact, I still didn't like her. She may be beautiful, but she was dangerously impulsive. I debated on pulling my fingers away before she could accept. *This was a bad idea.*

"Why?" she blurted.

I blinked. "Why what?" I asked.

"Why would you want to dance with me?" she asked. "You don't like me."

Honesty. Openness. Transparency. All things that the Court of Frost worked to erase from any creature that passed through its corridors. But not her. Of course not. I could feel the corners of my mouth curl up, despite myself.

"I never said I didn't like you," I replied.

She eyed my still raised hand as if it might bite her and I lowered it. "Yes, you have," she replied. "Several times in fact."

Cheeky little brat. I huffed out a breath. "Okay, perhaps we were not always so cordial—"

"Are we now?" she interrupted, lifting a brow as her gaze rose to meet mine in challenge. The front of my trousers tightened at the serious fearlessness of that expression.

"We are," I said through clenched teeth, "and if you don't want to dance, all you had to say was—"

"It's not that I don't want to dance," she protested. I ground my teeth at the repeated interruptions, but she wasn't done. "I just don't want to dance with you."

Fury rippled through me, as well as astonishment. Every other female creature in attendance unrelated to me would kill to have me ask them to dance. It was not my pride that said so, it was the fact that I was a prince. I had a crown, a title, and royal blood that all equated immense power. I'd never been turned down before.

Before I could stop myself, I began to chuckle. The sound rumbled up through me and I laughed, drawing several shocked gazes, including *hers*.

"Uh … Sorrell?" She took a hesitant step away from me and that only served to make me laugh all the harder. "Is this one of those hysterical kinds of laughter?" she asked. "If so, can you tell me if it's one of the kinds that precurses death and destruction and my impending demise or just a really uncomfortable dance?" She winced when I reached for her, and in an effort to be kind—to be fucking gentle—I smoothed my hand over her knuckles before taking her arm and leading her onto the dancefloor.

"Nothing more than an uncomfortable dance," I assured her. For me and my increasingly tight trousers. Gods, this girl was like fire to my ice. "Besides," I said as I whirled her about and settled my other hand on the small of her back, drawing her as close as possible as the music switched its tune, "Roan and Orion would murder me if I let anything happen to you."

Her wide, wondrous eyes lifted as we began to dance. Her breasts pushed against my chest and the farther we spun, the more I lost track of the rest of the room. The little voice from earlier kept pestering me with questions. It wondered, *what could she smell like?* I leaned forward and closed my eyes as I caught the scent of fresh rose petals and snow. The scent of Faerie water. She must have bathed before tonight. Sometime, hours ago—the scent was faint now.

What could she feel like? She felt like fucking magic. More than magic. I'd held magic in my very palm. Magic could burn and sting and infiltrate your soul. It could smell like decayed corpses or fields of poppies. Magic had many feels. But she was all of the good it could ever be. Sunlight on my skin. Warmth in my veins. The quick racing of my heart just before a satisfying battle and even more satisfying victory.

What would she taste *like?* That, I wanted to know the most. I wanted to do more than just imagine. Damn it all to the Gods, but I wanted what Orion and Roan had with this girl. She irritated me beyond belief. She was rude and incompetent and weak in so many ways. Fragile and careless. But above all of that…

She didn't give a damn about *who* I was. *What* I was. Cressida did not see titles and royalty and crowns. She saw only men. Good men and bad men. And right now, she was looking at me like she wasn't sure which I was.

The music rose to its crescendo. The skirts of dresses spun all around. I felt my head dipping toward hers. Heat building. *Yes. So very close.* I wanted … Her eyelids lowered as she lifted her face. She was about to let me kiss her, I realized. Despite her worries about me. Despite my actions and words to her. Triumph had never felt so sweet.

Yes, I thought. *I would have her.*

Just as I closed my own eyes and felt the soft skin of her bottom lip stroke mine, the music stopped.

I jerked my head back and up. The other dancers had stopped and so had we. Cress blinked in confusion as I turned my head toward the front of the hall and saw that my mother, Adorra Chalcedony, Queen of Frost, stood at the base of the thrones, calling attention to herself.

It was time for the Feast of Beasts to begin.

CHAPTER 20

CRESS

My heart beat at an erratic, unnatural pace. It galloped through my ribcage even as Sorrell pulled away. *Did he ... like me?* No. It couldn't be possible. But then, why would he kiss me? Or, well, *almost* kiss me. Our lips had barely brushed and yet, that one small touch felt like lightning to my flesh.

Dazed and lost in thought, I let myself be led to the side of the dancefloor as everyone gathered around, waiting for the Queen to speak. My entire focus was on the man at my side. Sorrell's face was tilted up, his eyes locked on the front of the room. His white-blonde hair slicked back, revealing the fine bone structure of his face. The sharpness of his cheekbones, the square jawline. Even with our tenuous relationship, I had to admit he was handsome. For an asshole, that was.

His hand found my waist. Despite his coldness, his fingers were hot against the opening of my dress where his skin met mine. He was not emotionless, as I had once believed. Not callous. Even with all of the emotion that Orion and Roan showed—his was buried beneath a layer of ice. Tonight—just now—I felt a little bit of it melt. What would have happened if the music hadn't stopped?

Finally, I pulled my concentration back from examining him and faced the front of the room, refocusing my attention on the Frost Queen. She stood before her throne, which, despite the numerous changes to the room, hadn't been removed.

"Welcome," she called, "to the Feast of Beasts! Tonight, we celebrate our heritage as Fae with a tradition descended from the Gods of old. This event was gifted to us as a way to always remember who we are. Our lineage. Our magic." She turned her head and eyes the same color as Sorrell's found mine in the crowd. I shivered at the deadness in her gaze. "Our power," she continued. "The Court of Frost welcomes you all as guests and honors you as such by presenting all of the delicacies and treats our home has to offer. Each dish and drink holds a facet of life here in Alfheim as well as in the Court of Frost, and we are pleased to share them with you. In a few days' time, the Courts' Council will convene to discuss the future of Fae and this war with humanity. But for tonight—we drink, we dance, and we celebrate the Fae."

Applause rang through the hall and even Sorrell clapped, which I figured meant I should too.

The crowd dispersed as the Queen turned and sat upon her throne. I sighed and faced Sorrell once more. As soon as I did, I felt that heat slam back into me full force. Tension between us heightened, but before I could say anything, Ambassador Solas approached. "Prince Sorrell, how good to see you this evening. How is your homecoming?"

"It's well, Ambassador, thank you for asking," Sorrell replied stiffly.

I stepped back as Solas' gaze traveled to me. "My Lady," he said with a grin, "you look absolutely ravishing this evening. Congratulations on your engagement."

I forced a smile. "Thank you."

"We were just about to—" Sorrell began, his hand falling to

the small of my back, but before he could finish his sentence, Ambassador Solas spoke over him.

"Forgive me, Your Highness, but I've come to bid you to speak with Lord Telvakia."

"I'm acting as Cress's attendant tonight," Sorrell said as his hand fell away from my back. I looked up at him, frowning when I noticed the deep crevice between his eyes.

"Yes, I see that, and I am terribly sorry to ask, but you know he rarely makes appearances at court and he deeply desires to see you."

Sorrell pressed his lips together, and I could tell he was struggling. It was rude for him to turn down seeing a Fae lord, that much I could tell. Already, I could see the surprise in Ambassador Solas's expression—the way he watched Sorrell with confusion. His big brows were drawn down low, and his smile didn't quite reach his eyes. "You can go if you want," I offered. "I'll stay right here."

"I shouldn't leave you," he replied.

"Only for a moment," Solas suggested with a frown. "I'm sure Lady Cress can look after herself for just an introduction."

"I won't go anywhere," I said. "You can go over and say hello and come straight back."

"He should grab you a drink along the way," Solas agreed. "In fact, Lord Telvakia is just over there, you can likely see her from there as well. So, you'll be able to keep perfect track of your charge."

Sorrell sighed. "Will you give us a moment, Ambassador?" he asked politely. "I will be there momentarily."

Solas's smile blossomed. "Of course, Your Highness." He bowed and left.

Almost as soon as the man was out of earshot, Sorrell turned toward me and growled. "Damned court politics."

I offered a smile. "I promise I'll be okay," I assured him.

He eyed me. "I'll be right back," he said. "Don't go anywhere," he ordered. "Stay right here. Do not stray."

I held my hands up placatingly. "As you command, Ice Man."

His eyes narrowed. "Why do you call me that?" he asked.

I shrugged. "I don't know, you're the Prince of Frost and you're usually as cold as ice."

"Usually?" he repeated, his lips quirking.

My jaw dropped. "I … um … well, what I meant was—"

"Never mind." He shook his head, granting me a reprieve. I released a sigh of relief. "I'll be back. Stay here."

I nodded as he disappeared through a throng of chattering couples in masks and fine clothing. I turned to scan the rest of the crowd, curious to see if Orion or Roan had arrived yet. A flash of red appeared in my periphery. I pivoted, following it, and my eyes widened as I realized that the Crimson Queen was moving through the crowd with determination, heading straight toward me. I was rooted to the spot. Sorrell had told me not to leave. He would be right back. He'd said so. But I really didn't want to talk to Roan's mother. The unknown Fae woman from earlier and her warning still rang in my head. It also didn't help that she was not pleased that Roan had chosen me as his fiancée.

People bowed as she passed them, stopping mid-conversation to turn and give her the respect she, as a royal, appeared used to. She came to a stop in front of me, the corners of her lips turning up as a smile stretched across her face. It looked brittle and uncomfortable. Before I could say anything, she motioned behind her to the Frost Queen. "Adorra makes pretty speeches, doesn't she?"

I cleared my throat, shifting slightly as discomfort wove through me. "I guess," I said. "It was wonderful, yes." *That sounded pleasant, didn't it? Yeah. It definitely did. What did the guys know? I was definitely good at this court politics thing. I hadn't insulted anyone in the last several minutes. I was practically a professional.*

"Tell me," she said, turning to stand at my side so that it appeared as if we were watching the crowd together. *Oh, I thought. This wasn't a brief chat, she was staying. Great.* I grimaced. Cue awkwardness. Even the nuns hadn't been so cruel as to make me stand *with* them. No, they'd much preferred my presence when I was *away* from them. So had I. "How is court life treating you?"

"It's nice," I offered, unsure of what kind of answer she sought.

"Yes, nice…" She hummed softly in her throat. "You know, it could be a lot *nicer,* say … perhaps, here. For you, I mean."

"Here?" I coughed as the word squeaked out. "In the Court of Frost?"

"Yes, dear, that's exactly what I mean." She clasped her hands together and smiled with tight lips as others bowed to her when they passed on their way to the dancefloor. "I think you would find a good life here. I could introduce you to a Lord or two. Perhaps arrange a marriage."

I blinked. "A marriage?" I repeated. "But I'm already engaged."

Her fragile smile dropped into a scowl so fast, I wondered if it had been merely my imagination to begin with.

"That can be broken," she stated. "It *will* be broken." My eyebrows rose at the vehemence in her tone. Her eyes sought out the crowd, passing over the others, and I watched as her scowl evened out. Her smile never returned, as if the reminder of my engagement to Roan had upset her too much.

I frowned. "If you want to talk about broken engagements, maybe you should talk to Roan." I scooted a foot away and then another when it didn't appear she'd noticed. "In fact, perhaps, I should go find him for you…" Was I planning to disobey Sorrell's direct order? Yes, yes I was. This woman made me uncomfortable and even if that Fae woman from earlier hadn't warned me about the Crimson Queen, I would've already found her untrustworthy. There was something in her eyes when they slid toward me, stopping me in my retreating tracks. Something sinister.

"I don't think that's necessary," she said coolly. "I think this can be done between us, don't you? Woman to woman."

I resisted the urge to grumble or sigh, but now that her eyes were focused on me, I felt unable to move away. I prayed that Sorrell would return soon.

"You're obviously unaware of the massive responsibility heaped upon royals. As a ... *princess*," she choked the word out as if saying it—not just the word, but saying the word in regards to me—was distasteful to her. I arched a brow, waiting for her to continue. "As a princess, you would be expected to know all of the nuances of court life—which you do not. You're a Changeling. Wild. Untrained. And I've had a talk with the physician that oversaw your recovery from the experience you and my son had in the Bavarian Pass. Your magic is weak. Your bloodline is diluted. A royal is expected to be of the utmost breeding. To have power of their own. You're a weak Fae at best, an imposter at worst."

I stiffened at the word imposter. She was going for my obvious flaws and faults, but that word, I didn't like at all. Mostly because I felt like it. Standing in this illusioned throne room in a land I'd never heard of before meeting the princes, I felt like a big fake. The nice clothes that weren't mine. The engagement that wasn't even real. When I didn't say anything, however, the Crimson Queen took that as her cue to continue.

"I'm sure you think you've caught yourself quite the catch with my son," she said. "But it won't last. Roan likes whatever pretty thing appears before him. He's much like his father was in that way, but like his father—he will see reason. He cannot and will not marry you. Save yourself the disgrace and let me help you."

"What if I love him?" I blurted the question before I could think better of it.

Her head rotated, turning toward me in slow increments. It was creepy—like a puppet doll being forced to look a certain way by its master. "Love?" she repeated the word with a confused tone. "Fae don't love, dear. They lust." She reached out and patted my arm lightly. "Especially royal male Fae. I'm sure that's an assumption from your time in the human realm. But if you truly believe that you love him, then you shouldn't let him sacrifice his future to be with you when there are far more suitable candidates on the table."

"You mean like Ariana?" I asked.

The Crimson Queen narrowed her eyes on me. "Yes. Ariana is of good, noble blood. She has powers beyond your comprehension. She—"

"Tried to kill me," I said. "And she failed." Stunned silence followed my statement, and I took it as an opportunity. "Do you really trust a girl who couldn't even kill a naive Changeling to be a princess or even much of a mate to your son?"

Her chest rose as she inhaled sharply, her bosom jutting out from her low cut gown. "Ariana understands the needs of royals. She understands that you can't always keep your hands clean."

My jaw dropped. She had just admitted her approval of Ariana's deed. I took a step back openly this time. "You don't care about your son, do you?" I said. "You care about control." And a girl like Ariana could be controlled easily, even I understood that. Ariana liked fine things—jewels and power. Or at least the perception of power. I recalled the feeling of my blood heating beneath my skin just before I'd been attacked by those monstrous creatures in the dead forest. It returned, filling me with a sudden fury and righteous anger. I didn't understand how Roan had been raised by this woman, but what I did know was that she couldn't be trusted.

"I was right about you," she stated, her words cold. "You're an uncouth savage. Too *human* to be Fae, aren't you?" I bit my lip, hating that she saw calling me human as an insult. My best friend was human and she was the strongest person I'd ever met. "Be warned, child," she spat. "Even if Ariana could not finish the task, it will be accomplished one way or another. Cease this insane attempt to win over my son. End the engagement and I will let you live. I'll even find you another suitor."

A throat cleared to my left, alerting us of a new arrival. My head lifted with such hope, but it wasn't Sorrell who stood at my side. Instead, a pair of dark—almost opaque—eyes met mine and a cruel mouth grinned.

"Am I interrupting something?" the man named Tyr inquired. I knew it was him because his mask only covered one half of his face, leaving the side profile completely visible. I pressed my lips together, unsure of what to do or how to respond. Was I allowed to talk to him even if it meant making an excuse to leave or could I just walk off? Was that rude? Would that cause some sort of court slight that would end up with me in the dungeons or something? Who knew what these crazy Fae considered unreasonable.

Before I could say anything, though, the Crimson Queen raised her chin and scoffed at the man who was dressed as if the God of Death had arrived—all black leather other than the vest he wore, beaded with dark jewels. Tyr moved closer, reaching out and capturing my hand before I could pull it away. He lifted it to his lips. "Would you mind if I interrupted and stole the next dance, my dear?"

A dark chuckle escaped the Queen, and I frowned her way as she shook her head. "Of course the Court of Midnight would be interested in this abomination."

Abomination? I bristled at the insult. I was Fae, just as much as she was. *Maybe. Possibly. Definitely*, I argued with myself. I mean, there was no denying that I had some sort of powers now. After all, I hadn't died even when I'd been shoved off a castle wall. I'd managed to escape mostly unscathed from the Bavarian Pass and those wild creatures who'd tried to eat me. I didn't deserve her ire, no matter that she seemed more than willing to direct it toward me as if I were at fault for all of the things she disagreed with.

"I merely entertain the loveliest of ladies, my Queen," Tyr replied, winking my way. *Nope. I still didn't trust him.* But … I did wonder, *was this how Orion would look without all of the scars?* There was no denying that his brother was beautiful in a purely masculine way. Even if he did remind me of a slimy snake.

I opened my mouth to turn him down, nonetheless. The guys had ordered me to stay away from him and I wasn't about to use him as an escape from the Queen. I'd walk away before I did that. Unfortunately, my rejection never made it past my lips.

As if he could read my mind, Tyr's hand tightened on mine and he tugged me forward, his other arm winding around my waist as he spun me away. "Actually, I don't think I'll accept any other answer than 'yes,'" he said with a grin.

He turned me, lifting me off my feet into the group of moving dancers faster than my legs could carry me.

My eyes searched the crowd as it closed around us but found no familiar faces. The masks made it impossible. I clenched my teeth even as an unwelcome hand slithered down my spine and nearly to my ass. I was in deep trouble.

CHAPTER 21

ROAN

"Your Highness!" I cursed as a familiar voice called for me just as I was about to make my way across the room and away from the possessor of said voice. Unfortunately, now that she'd opened her Gods damned mouth, I couldn't ignore her. To do so would enrage my mother. So when Ariana approached, I turned and flashed her a tight smile.

"Ariana," I said, offering no more than that.

And as soon as I saw her Feast of Beasts gown, I realized why she'd approached me. Ariana was dressed for seduction. Her breasts were plumped up in a blood red bodice. It appeared to be several sizes too small, cinching her waist into impossibly tiny proportions and making her upper half appear that much larger. Gods ... could the woman breathe in that thing?

She stopped before me and bowed, her breasts nearly spilling over. Lord, I swore I could see a hint of a light pink nipple. I lifted my gaze and kept it on her face. A face with only a strip of matching red lace over her eyes as a mask. "What is it?" I said, hoping to escape her sooner rather than later.

"I was wondering if I might ask you for a dance, Prince Roan," she said, smiling brightly.

"No," I said. "Is that all? If so, I'll be going."

"But, Roan—" Her hand latched onto my arm and I sighed, frustrated beyond belief. I turned sharply, as a Lord Fae brushed by—his eyes eating up Ariana's expanse of flesh before he nearly slammed into an ivy covered column. I pushed Ariana into a darkened corner. She sighed in my grasp, going easily as I led her away. "Oh, Roan," she whispered, her hand reaching up to tangle in my hair as she lifted up to kiss me.

Without hesitation, I put a hand up, blocking her affections, and she stumbled back against a stone wall in surprise. "What are you—I thought you—"

"Thought I was bringing you over here to fuck you?" I supplied when she didn't appear able to finish a complete sentence. "No. I didn't."

She straightened, frowning. "Then why did you bring me over here?"

"To tell you to stop," I snapped. "We are over, Ariana." The words were spoken harshly, with as much venom as I could muster. She needed to understand. I was enraged by her actions. I didn't trust her. She was nothing more than my mother's spy, her pawn. And although I'd once found her beauty incomparable, that was no longer the case.

"You're only saying that," she said, her expression softening as she stepped closer to me. Once again her hands reached for me and once again, I caught them and held her away.

"I'm not," I said. "I'm engaged to Cress and you're *nothing* to me anymore. You're not welcome in my chambers, my heart, or my home. In fact, when I take Cress back to my court, I think it best that you stay here."

Shock wove through her features, tightening her lips, widening her eyes, and flaring her nostrils. "The Court of Frost is a dying court," she protested. "If you leave me here, I'll never be able to go back to the other realm—not without another court to take me."

"Then perhaps you should suck up to Tyr," I sneered. "Or just plain suck him, I'm sure he wouldn't mind your expertise. He's the only way you'll be leaving here because I can assure you that when the Court of Crimson returns, you will not be accompanying us. Whatever happens to you now, I don't care."

She cried out, tears filling her eyes. "You don't mean that," she said, shaking her head back and forth. "You can't!"

"I can and I do," I snapped, shoving forward and pressing her back against the stone. "I know what kind of woman you are—you tried to kill Cress, and as much as I want to kill you for your actions, I think leaving you here in this barren wasteland is as good a death as any. Remember, Ariana. *You* did this. Not me. If you'd simply accepted her, you'd still at least have your position in my court. Now you don't." I released her and she crumpled in on herself, her hands covering her face as she sobbed. "And if you try to win over my mother and get her to convince me to let you back into my court, or my bed..." I paused, letting the threat linger before I delivered the final blow. "I'll see to it that you'll never be able to betray me or anyone I claim again. Cress will be my bride. Accept it or die. Your choice."

With that, I spun on my heel and stormed away. Fury mounted within me, erupting in tiny flames at the ends of my hair. I sighed and patted them out as I approached Orion where he stood drinking next to a table, a dark half mask covering the majority of one cheek. I swiped the drink from his hand and downed it in one gulp.

The one brow I could see of his arched. "I wasn't finished with that," he said.

"Trust me, I needed it far more than you," I replied gruffly.

"Oh?"

I sighed and snatched two more as a servant passed through

with a tray full of the wine goblets. I handed him the new goblet, discarding the empty one, and drank from my own. "Ariana," I said, and it was all I needed to say.

He sighed, turning back to watch the mass of Fae gathered in the illusioned throne room. Music played from somewhere —the sound soft and lyrical. "Did you learn anything from Tyr?" I asked after a moment.

Orion's fingers clenched on his goblet and in one smooth movement, he lifted it and downed the contents just as I'd done. When he pulled the empty cup away, I took it from him and discarded it to another passing servant. "Tell me," I ordered.

Orion's eyes shot to mine and darkened. "He's up to something," he confessed, his tone ripe with irritation. "I don't know what yet."

"But…" I hedged. "You have an idea?"

His lips parted, revealing clenched teeth as he hissed out a breath. "He knows of my … interest and feelings for Cress," he said slowly.

"Fuck."

"I know."

Before I could say anything more, Sorrell appeared before us, slightly disheveled. I glanced to his side, expecting Cress to be near, but she wasn't. "Have you seen the Changeling?" he demanded quickly, sounding out of breath.

"What the fuck do you mean, 'Have we seen the Changeling?'" I barked. "You're supposed to be with her. *You're* her fucking attendant." My head jerked up as I scanned the surrounding area.

"I went to—" Sorrell began, but then stopped, shaking his head. "No, it doesn't matter. I was gone for a moment, just a moment."

"That bastard." Orion's low curse captured our attention. His eyes were locked on the sea of dancers several paces away and I followed his line of sight until I saw her—beauty that she was. It wasn't Cress, though, that had more flames igniting in my hair. It was the man holding her.

A haze of red descended over my vision. "I'm going to kill your brother." I stated the words clearly, wanting to be sure that there would be no confusion on this matter. My hands clenched into fists.

"I will help you," Orion replied.

And almost as if she sensed our gazes, Cress's head lifted and her eyes met ours. She looked a bit surprised, yet unafraid of the man she was dancing with, but she had no clue. Tyr was a dangerous Fae, and his hands were all over my fiancée.

"Roan." My eyes closed, cutting off the burn in my vision. Of course, the moment I needed to go to Cress most would be the moment my mother—the Crimson Queen—would appear. When I opened my eyes again, she stood before me. Blocking my path—if she realized it or not. Orion and Sorrell, however, were both gone and I could only pray to the Gods that they'd gone to save Cress from the man I planned to cut down very soon. Oh yes, anyone besides my court brothers who laid a hand on Cress would feel the steel of my blade across their throats or in their hearts. She was *mine,* no matter what anyone —Ariana, the Court of Frost, or even my own mother —thought.

Cress was mine.

And I protected what was mine.

CHAPTER 22
CRESS

"You look beautiful tonight, little Changeling." Tyr's grip never loosened as he whirled me about the dancefloor so fast it felt like we'd left my head somewhere far behind.

I nearly stumbled because of the speed at which we danced, but he merely picked me up and placed my feet on his boots and kept going. Smart. Sneaky. I lifted my head and kept my narrow-eyed stare on him.

"Thank you." The words came out stiffly, and he laughed.

"Don't like me much, do you?" he asked.

I huffed out a breath as we turned again, blending seamlessly into another circle of dancers. What was the use in trying to hide my distrust? "I'm not good at this," I said testily, ignoring his comment and question as I—once again—stumbled over my own two feet when they left the tops of his boots.

He laughed, strengthening his grip and re-lifted me so that I dangled in his arms. I squirmed uncomfortably. "Answer my question, and I'll set you back on my boots," he offered. "I want to know what you really think."

I snorted. "Really? You do? Fine," I said. "I think you're conniving and sneaky. You knew the Crimson Queen didn't like me, but you came over anyway. Most people want to avoid upsetting someone like her"—*so I'd been continuously informed*— "but that's not why I don't like you; I don't like you because my friends don't trust you, and neither do I."

"Those friends wouldn't happen to be the three princes, would they, dear?" he inquired, tilting his head to the side as he lowered me until my toes touched the tops of his shoes once more.

"Yes," I snapped.

"Well, I like you, Cress. I think you're quite fiery and honest. Honesty is rare in a Fae court, especially the Court of Frost."

"Thank y—"

"But it's also something that can get you killed," he interrupted, his voice deepening as his head dipped closer. "I wouldn't enrage the Crimson Queen any further if I were you. Women like her will do whatever they have to in order to stay in power, and Queen Yvienne's power comes not just from her position in the Court of Frost, but from the fact that her son is a powerhouse in his own court."

"Why would you tell me that?" I asked, frowning. *And how much of it was true?*

"Because, despite your dislike of me, sweetheart, I find you charming. You certainly bewitched my younger brother—"

"Orion?" I blurted.

He smiled. "Yes."

"How did I do that?" I asked. "He seemed perfectly normal the last time I talked to him. Is there a spell that I don't—"

"No." He stopped, laughing as he slowed his pace, our legs moving slower as the song changed. "No, not actual bewitchment—my, you're amusing. Do you take everything so literally?"

I shrugged. "Why say it if you don't mean it?"

"Because lies serve well in Fae court." Our steps slowed even further and I met dark eyes that seemed to swallow all color …

if there'd ever been any color in his eyes at all. All I saw was a blackness so opaque, the image of my face was reflected there. And I looked confused, dazed, almost as if *I* were the one under a spell. *Was I?* I wondered.

"Perhaps you don't realize it as of yet," he said quietly.

"Realize what?" I asked, my voice sounding far away, as if I were yelling from a great distance.

"That you've been lied to, as well, by the very men you call your friends," he replied. "They're not your friends, are they? They're more. Lovers, most certainly. But is there ... something else between you? Tell me, little Changeling, what are you to the Princes Roan, Orion, and Sorrell?"

"Sorrell hates me," I found myself admitting. The words, though, weren't my own—they were pulled unwillingly from my throat. I tried to stop them, call them back, but they were already out and then more followed. "Roan and Orion are my lovers, I-I've had—"

"Yes, you've fucked them, I understand that. Not Sorrell, though? Hmmm. That is surprising. He can't seem to take his eyes off you and he seems quite upset with me."

"What?"

Tyr's fingers left my hand and reached up, touching the edge of my chin to direct my face to the side. There, I saw them —Roan, Sorrell, and Orion—all standing together, their eyes piercing through the crowds of people and the illusion of the throne room. They were not happy.

"Did you know it was the Brightling Court that practiced the Changeling tradition the most?" Tyr asked suddenly, turning my face back to his.

Was my head always this fuzzy? I wondered. I felt muddled, even as I nodded and replied to his question. "I know," I said, "but we ... there was a test. I'm from the Court of Crimson. Not powerful, though. Not like them."

"Crimson? Really? I find that hard to believe," he cajoled.

"What about you?" I tried, fighting my way free of the fog that was clouding my head. "Orion said you don't come when summoned. They're not happy about you being here. Why is that?"

Tyr chuckled low in his throat. "Orion chose to be part of the Court of Crimson. Therefore, he can't represent the Court of Midnight. Since I'm the only other appropriate option at the moment, I thought it was best that I show up and not anger the Queens unnecessarily." I didn't believe that for even a second, but all I did was hum in response. He smiled at me. "What?" he asked. "Don't believe me?"

Was he reading my mind? Could Fae read minds? That would've been a much better power to get. That probably would've been far more useful. But then again, my greatest power at the moment was my ability to thwart death, and with so many Fae around me suddenly appearing like monsters in fine clothes, I should probably be more grateful.

"No," I answered honestly. "I don't. You don't seem like the kind of person to cater to the desires or whims of other people. You know that my friends—"

"Your lovers," he corrected.

I grunted in frustration even as he kept me pinned—my front to his—during this perpetually long dance. "What I'm saying is," I tried again. "That I'm naive, sure, but I'm not stupid. They don't like you and they don't want me around you. I think you know that. You're doing this to purposefully irritate them." *Kind of like a sulky child who wanted to play with someone else's toys,* I thought. "So, why are you really here? And why are you dancing with me?"

This time, he didn't laugh, just smiled slowly, and for the first time, I believed the princes when they said he was danger-ous. There was something dark and deadly behind his eyes. A cold and calculating emotion, as if he didn't care who he hurt so long as he achieved his goal. "Aren't you astute?" He asked the rhetorical question quietly, more to himself than to me. "You're much more intelligent than I would have expected a Changeling to be, and brave."

"Brave?" I frowned and shook my head. "I'm not brave."

"Perhaps I'm mistaken." He turned me and pressed onward as the music lifted higher into the room. "Perhaps I'm not. Alright then. Here it is. The humans may be planning a larger attack on The Court of Midnight's forward outpost. I'm here to report on it and gain the opinion of the Queens, as well as supplies, men if needed, and money. Also because a Courts' Council meeting has been called. Someone from each court must attend. I've come to hear them out and get what I want in the process. It's all very dull when it's not dramatic," he said, giving me a wink at the end, as though discussing the deaths of hundreds if not thousands of people could be amusing.

Very dull when it's not dramatic? I repeated his words in my head. *Really? He thought I was going to fall for that? If something wasn't dramatic, then it was obviously dull ... unless it was just ... I mean, what was something if it wasn't dramatic or dull? What was the in between stage of that? Average? Boring? No, boring meant dull. They were the same.*

"Have I lost you again, sweetheart?" Tyr's question drew me out of my internal debate.

"No," I said, "but that still doesn't explain everything. Are you planning to end the war then?"

He shrugged. "Humans have their place and their uses, just like everything else. Destroying them could upset the balance of the world and give more power to those who shouldn't have it," he replied solemnly. From what the guys had said this was the exact opposite of who he was. If anything, from their description he would relish a power imbalance so long as it favored him or gave him more power. He was lying, there was no other option. The princes couldn't be wrong ... could they?

Even Sorrell was honest with me, as brutal as he was sometimes.

"How noble minded of you," I replied dryly.

He chuckled. "You're quite different than what I'd imagined a Changeling to be."

I resisted an eye roll, though just barely. "So you've said." His lips parted, but there was no way in the realm of the Gods that I was going to stand here and listen to any more of his sinister intentions. A man didn't offer to dance with a woman, after all, out of the goodness of his heart. He always expected something—conversation, to make her feet ache, or sex. I worried that Orion's brother might be after all three. And he'd already accomplished at least two of those things—there would be none of the third.

"When is this dance going to end?" I blurted, cutting off whatever he'd been about to say. "We've been doing it for a while."

He laughed. "We've danced for at least three of the songs. What's one more?"

"My foot up your ass," I muttered.

"What was that?"

I blinked up at him innocently as he looked down at me. "What was what?" I inquired.

"What you just said."

"What did I say?" *Come on, Cress. Push the big innocent eyes. They may not have worked on the nuns, but those old maids had known you too well. This man knows nothing about you. For all he knows, you could be as pure as fresh snow. Yeah, that's what you are. Pure snow. Think it. Be it. Pure. Fucking. Snow.*

"Something about wanting to put your delicate toes some-where they likely would not be very comfortable," Tyr said with an amused grin.

"Did I?" I asked airily. "I don't recall."

Laughter erupted from him as he threw his head back and

let the sound out. His hand fell away from my waist, leaving the other in my palm. Several heads turned. My face heated with embarrassment, but I didn't say anything, just gripped his hand so hard that I hoped it hurt. He didn't even flinch as he slowly let his amusement die and his eyes returned to mine. I glared at him.

"I can see why my little brother is so taken with you, Cress the Changeling," he said.

"W-what?"

His free hand returned to my waist and we proceeded into the next dance. "I know that Orion was the one who took your virginity," he confessed. I stiffened immediately. A blush flew up my cheeks.

Orion told his brother he'd taken my virginity? When he'd given me a big long speech about how I couldn't say too much around Tyr because he would twist it to his advantage? I mean I'd already admitted that I'd slept with him, but I hadn't admitted the part about my inexperience. That was crossing a line, wasn't it? Man, there really should be a list of guidelines or something to follow for all this relationship business. There had to be some sort of book I could read that would tell me what the rules were. Something titled "The Rules to Bedding Multiple Princes." That sounded straightforward enough. If there was such a book, I had no doubt Nellie—or even Groffet—could find it for me. If there wasn't, well, by the Gods, I'd have to be the one to write it because this was far too confusing. Whatever the case, I shook my head and returned my attention to Tyr.

"It's nothing to be ashamed of," he said. "Nothing to even concern yourself with. It simply explains why he likes you so much—men do like the virginal ones and Fae so rarely are. You are a prize—or rather you were."

"What does that have to do with anything?" I snapped, growing more and more furious.

"Well, if Orion is so infatuated with you then it certainly

calls into question the validity of your engagement to Roan, doesn't it?" Tyr's words made my heart stutter in my chest.

"Roan and I are engaged," I said. "He was previously engaged and I can assure you, he wasn't a virgin before—"

"No, no, no." Tyr shook his head, cutting me off. "I'm not saying either of you has to be a virgin before your nuptials—if you ever get to that point." If we ever got to that point? This man was a bag of donkey dung. Worse than Sorrell by far. He might've been handsome in some ways, but the more time I spent in his presence, I realized the more I wanted to punch him in his long neck. His long rooster neck. Yes, that's what it was. I mean, sure, some women might see strength in the column, but I bet when he aged, his straight cut jawline would sink into unattractive jowls. Heavy ones. That looked like a man's testicles resting on his chin. Yeah. I could imagine that quite well. I snickered.

"What, may I ask, is so amusing, darling?" he asked, drawing me out of my reverie of insults.

"Nothing," I said sharply. "You were just explaining why you think there's a problem with me marrying Roan—which there isn't."

"Trying to," he agreed, "before you drifted off, that is."

"Oh that," I lifted my hand and waved it nonchalantly. "It happens when I'm bored. Ignore it."

"Hmmmm. I've never been called boring before."

I winced. I hadn't exactly meant to say it like that. "Your explanation?" I prompted instead of replying to his comment.

"I'm just curious, does Roan know, and is he okay with Orion—his throne brother—being your lover?"

"What happens between me and Roan is between me and Roan."

"What a polite way of telling me it's none of my business," he mused.

"Because it isn't," I huffed. "Who I have been in bed with has nothing to do with you or anyone else."

He shrugged. "That's just the human in you. Besides, I'm sure the whole court knows by now that my little brother was balls deep in virgin Changeling pussy." His words were designed to elicit a reaction and I couldn't stop myself from giving one. I jerked my hand from his grip and slapped him. Hard. And by the Gods, it felt fucking good. His head snapped to the side and when he turned back to me, I could see a grin on his lips.

Nervously, I took a step back and looked around, but no one seemed to have noticed. How had they not noticed? The dancers moved in a manner I hadn't noticed before. They weren't moving around me, they were moving right through me. As if my body were made of nothing more than mist. I gasped as a particularly fast couple spun through my side.

"W-what is…?"

"Word of advice, little Changeling," Tyr said, stepping into me, forcing me to back up. "Hitting a member of a royal family in public is cause for discipline."

"Why didn't they see that?" I asked. "Why are they—" I gasped as another couple moved through me, stopping my next question.

"You should be thanking me for casting this separation spell," Tyr said. "It allowed me to pull us into a detached pocket of existence just inside this court. We can see and hear everything around us, but they can't see us. A good thing, because if your little outburst had been witnessed by the Queens—or specifically, the Crimson Queen, since she most certainly doesn't like you—you could've lost your engagement to Prince Roan and possibly even your hand as well."

I frowned and glared at him all the while. "You deserved it," I hissed.

He shrugged and smiled. "Which is why I won't tell anyone if you don't."

I watched him with careful scrutiny. "Come here," he said, holding his hand out. "I'll drop the spell and we'll blend back in with the dancers."

"How can I trust you?" I demanded.

"You have no choice," he said simply. And I realized then how right he was. I didn't have a choice. I had to accept his help or I might be stuck in this separation spell of his forever.

I took a hesitant step toward him and as soon as I took his hand, he spun me back into the dancers and we blended into the mix. I lifted my head and watched as the spell dropped away. I hadn't even noticed the differences until they were right there in front of my eyes. The sounds were louder. I could feel the wind rushing across my skin as we danced. I could smell the food. I hadn't even realized those things were missing until it was too late. Orion and the others were right, Tyr was dangerous.

"I wanted to dance with you, Cress, because you're in a very precarious position. One I find interesting."

"How so?"

"You've taken the three princes right out from under all the crown seekers' noses. I wish I could have been there when Ariana realized she'd lost."

"I don't think she's realized it yet," I muttered grimly.

"Oh, I think it's been made very clear to her, or at least it will be soon. But now that you've got the attention of all three princes, you'll have the attention of the Court of Frost as well. I wouldn't be surprised if Ariana wasn't the only one trying to take you down a notch or two, maybe even steal a prince back for themselves. You'll need to watch for a blade in your back more than anything else." *A warning I'd already received, more or less.* "The politics of Fae Courts are interwoven, complicated things that have evolved over thousands upon thousands of years. Don't be too hard on yourself for not taking to it like a duck to water," he said gently. I wasn't sure if his words were meant to be kind or a warning, but either way, I knew he was telling the truth.

"I think I'm nearly done with this dance." I tugged my hand away, or at least, I tried. He held fast, fingers closing over mine and squeezing until I had to repress a wince.

"Take it from a man who understands Fae very well; you want powerful friends on your side, Cress." He slowly lifted my hand and pressed my knuckles to his lips. "I can be one of those friends."

I didn't have a response and it appeared he didn't need one as he didn't stay to hear one. Tyr nodded to me, bowing slightly before departing and leaving me—I realized a bit belatedly—at the edge of the dancefloor. I shook my head and turned to go in search of Sorrell, who would no doubt be furious with me as I'd seen him and the others not long ago standing and watching from the sidelines. I wasn't even allowed more than two steps from where I'd been left behind by Tyr before I was lifting my head and meeting the cold, furious gaze of the Prince of Frost.

Lucky me.

CHAPTER 23
SORRELL

"Keep her in the room." Roan's body practically vibrated with anger. Orion had disappeared nearly the moment Tyr had, likely to track the bastard down. It was clear that his earlier warning to the man hadn't taken hold. I wondered if one ever would. Tyr was not the kind of Fae to fear others. No. I'd be shocked if he'd ever known true fear. He was beyond sanity. He was madness dressed to appear logical. "And do not let her leave."

"I won't," I assured him.

"Stay with her," he repeated. "I mean it."

"I know you do, brother." I reached out and grasped his shoulder. "I will."

"I'm going to find Orion," he said, taking a step back, shrugging off my hand. He was on the edge, flames dancing at the ends of his hair. He wasn't in any mood to put them out either.

"I'll take care of the girl," I replied, shutting the door as Roan stalked away.

"I didn't invite him over," Cress said as soon as the door closed.

I turned and met her anxious gaze. "I know." After all, Roan and Orion and even I had warned her. "You're not to blame for tonight," I said. "It was my fault. I shouldn't have left you."

She stared at me, her brows drawn down low as her lips pursed. "You're not angry?"

I shook my head and sighed. "Not tonight."

She blinked before turning and striding across the room to the bed as if she didn't quite trust my mood. To be fair, I hadn't ever really given her a reason to trust me, but trust me, she had to. Because this was a place ripe with danger. The Court of Frost was a knife that everyone balanced on. One small slip could cut you and you'd lose your head. There were few alliances forged in this place that ever remained steady and unbreakable. The only one I knew of was mine with my throne brothers—and likely formed because the three of us were similar in that we understood the pain of betrayal. Fae with status' such as ours, with power such as ours, could not trust easily. But we trusted each other and from that, we had forged our own path in the Court of Crimson.

I grabbed a cushioned pillow from the mattress and tossed it to the floor. Every year more and more royals died and less were born. We were slowly dying out. I fisted the top layer of blankets, pulling it down and folding it into a makeshift sleeping pad alongside the four poster bed.

"You should get ready for bed," I said, turning and glancing at her over my shoulder.

She watched my work with an unreadable expression as she nodded her assent to my suggestion. Her eyes stayed on the floor where I'd put the blanket and pillow for a moment more before she spoke again. "Can you ... um ... turn your back or something?" she asked, hands fisting in front of her as if she were nervous.

"I won't look," I assured her. I moved away from my sleeping pad and picked up a carafe of wine from a nearby table and poured it into a goblet. I turned my back to her as I drank. It was odd to think of a prince, much less a Prince of Frost—the heir to the Court of Frost—sleeping on a cold hard floor just to give his bed to a girl with no status or royal name, but I was going to do it. The position I'd chosen was closer to the door anyway. And the discomfort would keep me on the edge of wakefulness. If someone came in, I'd know and I'd be up in time to protect her.

I'd seen the way Roan's mother had watched her tonight. I had no doubt, conniving woman that she was, the Crimson Queen had plans to get rid of her little problem. I wouldn't let it happen. Perhaps I'd been too harsh on her before. Maybe too untrusting, especially when she'd come back to us at great peril to herself. I fingered the rim of the now empty goblet. Behind me, I heard the dropping of cloth, the shifting of fabric as she undressed, and then her feet padded across the floor to the bed.

Cressida the Changeling. She was light and vibrant. A cheery ray of sunshine in the dreary world of war and intrigue. I didn't trust her before because I didn't believe she was genuine. But more and more, the unflagging conviction of Roan and Orion were beginning to wear me down. I only prayed to the Gods that she was real, that none of it was an act. Because I knew if she betrayed them—if she betrayed *us*—I would have to be the one to slay her. Roan was in too deep, it would kill him to hurt her. And Orion … he had a deeper attachment as well. He'd been the one to deflower her, after all.

My stomach tightened at that last thought. My fingers strangled the goblet. *What had she been like,* I wondered, *in the throes of passion between them?* Had she cried out in pleasure? Screamed her release? Or was she quieter, more reserved in bedroom activities?

With a wry smile, I set the goblet down on the table. For a girl like her, I highly doubted it. No. Orion and Roan were very much taken with her. Silence sounded behind me and I began to turn. She had to be—

My thoughts froze as I stopped and stared, my mouth gaping open. "What the fuck are you doing on the floor?" I demanded as her head of short blond strands poked out of the blanket pallet I'd made for myself.

She frowned at me. "I got ready for bed," she stated slowly, as if she were talking to someone who might have been partially deaf. "Now, I'm in bed. What's the problem?"

"You're in *my* bed," I said with a huff, storming toward her. "Get out!"

"W-what?" She sat up fully, the blanket falling away from her chest and ... *holy* ... *dear* ... *Gods*. Her nightdress was damn near translucent and her breasts were on full display. A fact she didn't appear to realize. Otherwise, she'd never have pushed the blanket away and stood up. "What do you mean I'm in your bed? I thought you made this pallet for me."

"No." The word came out of my throat as a croak. I coughed, clearing it, and tried to force my eyes away. But once they'd settled on her, it seemed they didn't want to leave. I took her in, soaked the image into my mind, and let it rest there. She was magnificent. Oh, I'd known it by the dress she'd worn earlier that evening, but it was different seeing her dressed up like all the other ladies of court, with a tight fitting bodice and beautiful jewels, to how she was now. Face scrubbed clean, hair unbound, body practically glowing—a brilliant beam of light beneath a nightdress that was no more than a thin layer of fabric. It concealed nothing. *What in the Gods was it even there for?*

It didn't have to be there at all, that voice from earlier—the small insane little creature—came back with a vengeance. *You could pull it off of her so easily. Lay her down upon the bed and spread her legs. I bet she tastes like honey. A sip ... all you'd need is a sip to know.*

"Sorrell?"

I shook my head and jerked my eyes back up to hers. She

still hadn't noticed my preoccupation, but by the look on her face—tight lips, hard frown, narrowed eyes—she was growing increasingly irritated by my silence. It was amusing, her anger. I almost wanted to see what she'd do if I didn't respond at all. Would she yell at me? No one ever raised their voice to me—no one who was not royal.

I cleared my throat and straightened. "I made the pallet for myself. To better protect you," I said. "You can take the bed."

She stared at me, and for several moments didn't say anything. Then she crossed her arms over her chest and her narrow-eyed look became sharp. "Why?" she demanded.

"Excuse me?" I rolled back my shoulders in surprise. I'd just offered her the bed while I would sleep on the stone floor and she asked me, 'W*hy*?'

"Why are you being nice to me?" she asked. "You're never nice to me. First, you don't get angry or yell at me or blame me for dancing with Tyr. Then you offer me the bed so you can sleep on the floor." She shook her head. "No. I don't believe it."

Before I could open my mouth, she gasped and whirled around, ripping the next layer of blankets and sheets from the bed, sliding her hands around—up and under the pillows and beneath the blankets. I moved closer until I stood at the bed by her side.

"May I ask what you're looking for or would that upset you as well?" I inquired.

"I'm looking for any spiders or snakes," she said.

That seemed like a random thing to suddenly search for. I mimicked her earlier tone. "Why?"

She turned to me and poked me in the chest with her finger. "Because I don't trust you," she said. "You hate me. You've made that clear. I don't know what kind of game you're playing, but I'm tired. I've had a long day and—"

I reached up and wrapped a hand around her finger and miracle of miracles, she stopped talking. "I'm not playing a game with you," I said. "There are no snakes or spiders waiting to bite you in the middle of the night. I just didn't think you'd be comfortable sharing a bed with me."

Slowly, she pulled her finger from my grasp. "Really?" She eyed me suspiciously.

I nodded. "Yes."

"Oh."

After a beat, I gestured to the bed. "Now, if you would be so kind as to get in. I'd like to turn in for the night as well. You're not the only one who's had a long day."

Surprisingly, she didn't say anything to that. Instead, she turned and after another brief review of the bed, she climbed in and snuggled under the sheets. With a sigh, I moved about the room and began putting out the candles until only one was left on the nightstand. After that, I toed off my boots and peeled my clothes away until all that was left were my trousers. Normally, I slept in the nude, but I left the trousers on out of civility. I glanced at the girl in the bed. Unlike how I'd allowed her privacy to undress, she'd watched me the entire time.

Turning, I approached the bed, and just as I bent to the pallet, she sat up again. "You don't really have to sleep on the floor," she said, her voice quiet. I glanced up. Twin pools of a miraculous blue and gray mix stared back at me. Her heart shaped face was pale in the soft glow of the candlelight. Hesitantly, as if she feared I'd reject her, she gestured to the bed. "It's big enough for both of us. We don't even have to touch."

Oh, but I wanted to touch. I wanted very much to feel what Roan and Orion had felt with her. It'd been some time since I'd taken a lover, and I could feel the depletion of my magic stores. I wanted to know what sex with Cress would be like. I doubted it would be gentle. No, with two people such as us—her so fiery and bright and me so controlled—I expected the sex would be explosive.

Even knowing that—knowing that choosing to crawl into

that bed with her would be like trying to walk a very fine line—
I bent and picked up the blanket and pillow anyway and moved
them to the mattress.

"Move over," I said, my voice nearly a whisper in the darkness of the room. "I'll take the side closest to the door."

She didn't argue and scrambled back to the other side,
pulling the blankets up to cover her as her big, luminous eyes
watched me. The mattress was cool and comfortable at my
back. The pillow was soft under my head. And my cock was
hard in my pants. Keeping them on had been a good idea. I
turned over, facing away from her and then reached out,
pinching my fingers over the candle's flame, letting a bit of ice
freeze the stem before I pulled back.

Darkness descended and I closed my eyes, praying sleep
would come soon.

CHAPTER 24
SORRELL

I knew it was a dream the moment it started. And yet, still, like a flaming ball of fire locked onto its target, I also knew that its course could not be directed elsewhere but at me. *A cursed dream?* I wondered. Sent by an enemy? Sent by my mother? Oh, how she used to torment me with them when I was a child. She thought it was tough love, but for a ten year old boy, the monsters she sent to spread nightmares over my sleeping mind had left behind scars. Though not visible, like Orion's, they were there all the same.

I appeared on the steps of a castle—one I knew quite well. It was Crimson Castle. My home. My body locked as my mind attempted to stop its forward movement, but I couldn't. My muscles clenched and unclenched, forcing my legs to move on their own. There was nothing else to do but let this blasted cursed dream take its course. Once it was over, I would waken and everything would be as it was. I would drink to clear away this nightmare. Gods, I would down barrels of Faerie wine if only to stop what I feared was going to happen here. I didn't know what it would be, but I could sense the presence of doom just around the corner as I strode up the steps and into the front hall of the castle.

Glowing bulbs of light were floating around the room, illuminating the space. Gone were the tables for feasts and banquets. Gone were the three identical thrones that would have graced the very front of it in reality. Everything had been emptied out. The stone tiles were cool underfoot, alerting me to the fact that my feet were bare. I rarely went bootless. Nowhere but my own chambers did I go without them, and even sometimes, I slept in them. An unprepared prince was a prince asking for assassination. That is what Adorra Chalcedony had always taught me. That and the idea that some women were just not meant for motherhood.

"Sorrell?" I stopped immediately at the sound of my name being called and when I turned to answer it—to see the speaker —I froze. It was Roan, but not as I knew him presently. It was a Roan from long ago. The child Roan. His flaming hair was pulled back into the loose ponytail that he'd worn until he'd reached maturity. Freckles danced across his cheeks. He was nearly two feet shorter as he smiled at me from the open doorway.

"Roan?" I looked around. "Is it just you in here?" I asked.

The young Roan smiled and bounded forward. "No, of course not!" he said. "Orion is here too. Won't you come play with us?" He reached for my hand and I nearly jerked it from his grasp, not sure if this was a trick. The pervading sense of that dark gloomy feeling hadn't dispersed. *What could this mean?* I wondered. To send me Roan's image in this way?

From what I knew of cursed dreams, the sender often steered it at first before the magic took on a life of its own and from there ... nothing could be done except to wait until the nightmare had been snuffed out. I reached for my waist as Roan frowned up at me.

"Damn it," I muttered, feeling the weightlessness at my side.

My sword was gone. I couldn't feel any well placed daggers on hand either. I was weaponless, something I hadn't been in a long time. I tried conjuring a light globe and released a sigh of relief when a small orb of white appeared at my side. I waved my hand and let it vanish. At least I still had the use of some magic in here.

"Are you coming to play with us or not?" Roan demanded, his frown turning into a soft childlike scowl of impatience.

I couldn't resist the small smile that curved my mouth. Time, it seemed, had not changed him much. "Are you going to take me to Orion?" I asked by way of answer. It would be much better if I could see them both. Then I could see for myself that this nightmare was not one that would see them dead. I'd had that before—walked straight into a blood bath with their lifeless bodies lying prone upon a glass floor. One of my greatest fears.

Already our courts were weakened. Courts meant to house families of royalty—four base members to each lending concentrated power to the Lanuaet. But with the dying royal lines, each court had taken severe losses. The Court of Frost, forever bound in Alfheim, only two Queens. And the Court of Crimson, three princes. What had become of the Court of Midnight, though, no one on the outside knew.

Child Roan rolled his eyes at me—very reminiscent of the current Roan. "Of course," he said, turning on his heel and running out.

I followed him at a much slower pace. Back out into the corridor and down it until we reached the library through many twists and turns that did not meet up with the true Court of Crimson's layout. Obviously, whoever was currently directing this dream had little knowledge of the actual Crimson Castle. That, at least, narrowed the list somewhat, albeit not by much.

"Here! Here! We're over here!" Roan called as soon as I

entered Groffet's library. The moment I saw them, I paused. Orion—as young as Roan was, children well before their maturity and yet well after their infancy—stood side by side with his friend, with *my* friend. It'd been so long since I'd seen him without the scars he'd acquired on the battlefield, I'd forgotten how he'd appeared before. Dark locks of hair curled over his forehead. Straight lips and an even straighter nose. His big eyes looked up at me as I approached.

"Why did you lead me here?" I asked, turning my attention back to Roan.

But Orion was the one to answer me. "We wanted to show you the princess," he said with a smile.

"Princess?" I frowned. There hadn't been a true Fae princess born in several decades. The last had been Roan's mother, nearly a century before, as Fae often lived ten times the lifespan of a human.

"Come, this way, before they burn her."

I froze. "Burn her?" Neither Roan nor Orion stopped at my startled question. They kept moving, racing to the back of the room where a secret door suddenly popped open. I followed after them, with no small amount of trepidation and confusion as they disappeared from my view.

"Roan?" I called. "Orion?" Their childlike giggles echoed back to me, but they didn't stop. My pace picked up. What princess? What did they mean by burn her?

I didn't have to wonder long, because a moment later I was flying out of the end of the long tunnel and stumbling into the courtyard where a pyre had been built. Except instead of a bed of sticks and wood, there was one giant stake in the center with a girl tied to it. Horror descended. My legs were once again my own. I raced forward, sprinted over stone and grass and land.

"Cress…" What should have been a shout was nothing more than a whisper as it escaped my lips. I watched a masked man smile as he lit the bottom of her pyre. Fire came to life, dancing at her feet. And when Roan and Orion reached the base of the fire, they turned, children no more.

"Come, brother," they said in unison, holding out their hands, "let us watch the princess who would have ripped us apart burn."

"No," I said, shaking my head in disbelief. Cress appeared to be dazed, as if she didn't realize what was going on around her. Bespelled, I realized. This was an old tradition, one that hadn't been seen in centuries. This was the execution of someone who had committed treasons against royalty. Her hands were bound by rope, though, instead of the metal that would have sucked away her powers, but no … here they didn't see any reason to bind her as a true Fae. In my eyes, I didn't know that she fully was. So weak was her magic, perhaps she was a half-breed. But should it even matter? What were they doing? How could they do this?

I was irritated by the girl, yes. Annoyed. Frustrated. Often wanting to throttle her pretty neck myself when she blurted out things in ignorance and challenged me with her glares and narrowed glances. But this was too far.

"Stop this!" I yelled, striding forward more urgently as I realized the flames licked ever closer to her bare feet. Mine were cut and bleeding as I hurried toward her … and them. "You can't do this," I said. "You don't want to do this. I know you. The two of you are besotted with her. Why would you have her burned?"

"She is dangerous," they said, once again united in their actions, words, and tone. "It's as you've warned us. She will only tear us apart."

"What do you mean?" I tried to step forward, lifting my hand to form ice alongside the wood to force the flames to die out. They didn't. I tried again and even as frost formed along the wood and Cress's lips turned blue with chill, the flames grew ever higher. Magic flames.

They would hate themselves if she died. I couldn't let it happen. But when I tried to climb upon the pyre myself, they stepped forward, stopping me. Roan and Orion both grabbed me, pulling me back, away from her. And I watched in horror as the fire finally reached her, first catching onto her skirts and then her legs. It traveled up and her trance was broken. Scream after scream tore from her lips, echoing into the air. Agonizing wails ripped from her throat as her flesh blackened and burned.

"No!" My scream matched hers. "Stop this!" I struggled against my friends, my brothers. "You can't do this!"

"It has to be this way," Roan said, his eyes devoid of emotion. "If the princess doesn't die then who would she have married?"

"You, you Gods damned bastard!" I shouted, throwing them off momentarily to punch him in the face.

Roan didn't even blink. He didn't try to hit back, but he did reclaim me as I once again went for the girl. "Even as Orion desires her?" he asked, tone steely. "Would he have her, too?"

Orion was silent as he held me with Roan, keeping me pinned as I watched the Changeling—no, not the Changeling. Cress. *Cress!* "You love her," I said as the fires reached her waist and she screamed anew. Her throat becoming hoarse, the shouts and cries weakened. It caught on the ends of her hair, lighting all the way up to her scalp. "Stop this," I pleaded.

"What would you have us do if we spared her, brother?" they asked. "Marry her to us all?"

"Yes!" I screamed. "Marry her to us all and save her!" Gods, anything to stop her horrifying shrieks of agony. I couldn't bear it. "Stop this," I begged. Something I hadn't done since I was a child. Not since … the nightmares, I realized.

I'd forgotten. None of this was real. It couldn't be. Roan and Orion would never do this to Cress. They loved her, whether or not they would admit to those words yet exactly. They definitely cared for her. This was nothing more than a cursed dream. Cress's screams faded as the scene wound down. It would keep going if I didn't stop it. The only way to stop a cursed dream was to snuff it out, I reminded myself. Snuff. It. Out.

And for this particular dream, there was only one way to do it. "Gods forgive me," I muttered just before a dagger of ice appeared in my hand—called forth by my magic. I turned, slamming the blade into Roan's throat. Blood spurted. Then I did the same to Orion with the same result.

Yet even as the dream faded, my fear did not.

CHAPTER 25
CRESS

Something hard jolted me from the bed, slamming into me with enough force to knock me off the mattress and send me sprawling to the floor. I landed with an audible *oomph*. "What the—" I started as I got to my feet, rubbing at my poor, bruised backside, only to stop as I saw what had woken me.

Sorrell was sprawled out on the bed, sweat coating his entire body—so visible that it'd soaked through his trousers. He'd kicked the blankets away enough for me to see that his pants were stuck to his body like a second skin, outlining everything, including his … erm … package. Which I noticed, despite attempting not to think about it, was just as large as Orion's and Roan's.

He was having a nightmare, I realized a moment later. Sympathy slid through me and without another thought, I leaned over and put my hand on his shoulder. "Sorrell?" I shook him roughly. "Wake up. You're dreaming."

Icy eyes shot open, startling me so badly that my hand dropped away and I jerked back. But it was too late. Sorrell's arms reached up and gripped me by my shoulders, yanking me down on top of him. I was only like that for a split second before he rolled and sank down. His palms trailed down, fingers circling my wrists as he brought them up and held them in one of his hands.

Sorrell didn't appear to realize what he was doing. His eyes, although open, were unfocused—dazed—as if he were looking to a faraway place. He was much heavier than I expected. I'd recognized his strength before, but he wasn't nearly as large as Orion or Roan. Still, he held me down with little effort. His muscles were tense and trembling. *With fear?* I wondered. *What had he dreamed to make him react this way?*

"Must stop ... you have to stop," he muttered.

"Stop what?" I asked. *Was he talking to me?* Unlikely. "Sorrell." I began to struggle, squirming under him as I tried to slip my hands from his grasp. He merely tightened his hold and lowered his chest to mine. I inhaled sharply as I felt his nakedness against me. The thin shift I wore wasn't much to keep the heat of his skin from seeping through. And whether or not he realized it, his body had hardened down below. His cock brushed against my belly. "Sorrell," I croaked out his name again, trying to get through to his groggy mind. "It's Cress. The Changeling. You have to wake up."

"Cress—yes, it's Cress," he said. "Don't hurt—you have to stop. Please. You don't want to do this."

"Do what?" I bucked my hips and squeezed my eyes shut when his cock jumped beneath his trousers. Holy dear Gods. He was thick. Was he ... he couldn't be thicker than Roan or Orion. It wasn't possible. Was it? They were both large enough as it was. *There was no way I could take—wait!* I stopped that thought. Was I really thinking about taking Sorrell's cock? No. I just wanted to wake him up. No matter how hot his skin was or how his tight grip made my insides tingle in a way I hadn't expected. Sorrell and I weren't going there. He was an asshole. An asshole that didn't even like me.

My eyes shot open. "Sorrell!" I shouted as loud as I dared,

not wanting to alarm others or make anyone come crashing into the room. Sorrell may not trust me, but I didn't want to embarrass him. Despite his feelings for me, he'd always put Roan and Orion first and since my loyalty was with them, I had to at least try to get through to him. "Wake up!"

Sorrell's head tilted and his white-blonde hair slid over one side of his face as he blinked, his gaze clearing. "Cress...?" His lower body brushed against mine, making me gasp. He jerked his hands away from my wrists in horror. "I'm so—"

I groaned, unable to help myself as he slid back and his cock lined up with my core and unintentionally rubbed. He froze, cutting himself off. Pink tinged his cheeks. His lips parted and sweat glistened on his brow. I panted, my body tightening and releasing as something crawled through me. A feeling I recognized from previous interactions with Orion and Roan as desire. But for Sorrell ... I'd never felt this way before.

"What did I...?" he trailed off, the question unfinished as his eyes heated.

I shook my head, locks of hair sticking to my cheek. "Nothing," I said breathlessly. "You didn't do anything bad. I just ... I tried to wake you and you were still asleep. Your eyes were open, but you were—"

"It was a cursed dream," he said. I didn't know what that meant. What I did know was that he still hadn't moved off of me and his eyes were focused on my chest. I looked down and realized that even though it was dark in the room, I could see because our skin was glowing. His, a subtle white glimmer and mine, a golden light. Unfortunately, with that glow, came reality. It made the cover of my shift pointless. He could see *everything*.

And I watched, as if caught in a trance, as his hand lifted and he cupped one breast. His thumb brushed over a nipple. Fire lit me from within and impulsively, I arched into his touch. His hands were large, warm, and calloused—surprising for a prince. I'd always assumed that royals were pampered and they didn't work like a common man. Then again, Sorrell—like the others —was Fae. They were not mere men. They were warriors. The swords they carried were not decoration. They'd likely wielded them and practiced with them regularly. Whatever the case, the rough feel of his hand on me made all rational thought flee.

I rose up, but his hand refused to fall away. I was going to do it, I realized. I was going to kiss him. I was going to finish what he'd started at the Feast of Beasts.

"Sorrell…" His name called on my lips had him raising his head. I leaned forward, as if pulled by some invisible force, and pressed a kiss to his mouth.

There was a pause as he absorbed the hesitant but sensual touch and his hand dropped from my breast. I pulled back. Had I read him wrong? Worry made me bite my lip. Before tears could threaten to burn my eyes, before I could apologize, before anything else could happen—Sorrell sank his fingers into my hair and yanked my head back.

This time when his head fell toward mine, it descended with a single-minded purpose. His tongue sank inside the cavern of my mouth. It sought refuge and I gave it. Relief poured through me as I kissed him back. My eyes slid shut and I leaned into him. Taking the kiss with as much fervor as he gave it. Heat sizzled in my veins. I shivered as I reached up and twined my hands around his neck, pressing my breasts against him, feeling the way my nipples scraped against his muscles through the fabric of my clothes.

Sorrell gripped me hard, directing where he wanted me to go. I felt contained and controlled. I was the instrument and he the musician. A moan bubbled up my throat as his body came down even harder over mine, pressing me back against the bed. He moved between my legs, his free hand sliding down and jerking up my shift. Without thinking, my thighs fell open and he moved to take his place between them.

Dizziness assailed me. Air. I needed air. I pulled away from his mouth, gasping, but he wasn't done. It was as though something had been let loose inside of him. Sorrell's head moved to my jaw, where he laid a series of open mouthed kisses. I couldn't draw enough air to fill my lungs.

Though his trousers remained fastened, I could feel his hardness rubbing against me. His hips rolled, pushing insistently in an age old rhythm. My hands fell to his shoulders. My nails sank into his flesh as I squeezed my eyes shut, a brilliant light roaring toward me. Pleasure infused my whole body as he hit a perfect spot against the bundle of nerves that the others had used to make me orgasm before.

I clutched him, whimpered, shook, as I lost myself in the haze of bliss. Sparks danced behind my closed lids.

"Sorrell…" His name came out on a whisper as I came back down from the high of pleasure only to realize he was no longer with me. At least, not as he had been. He was stiff all over, his muscles impossibly tight.

Sorrell pulled back and I relaxed, letting him go even though something inside me cried out for him. His face showed surprise and some horror as he stumbled from the bed. He couldn't seem to look at me and yet his eyes never left the bed. They trailed over my bare thighs, the tangled sheets, but he refused to look at my face.

"I'm sorry," he grunted, tripping and nearly falling as he backed toward the door. "I shouldn't have … forgive me for … I didn't realize what I was…" He couldn't even finish a sentence. I didn't know what to say. Suddenly, his head lifted and his eyes connected with mine. They flared and he jerked as if someone had branded him with a cattle prod. Sorrell whirled around. "I have to go." His words were stilted, formal, uncomfortable. Still, I didn't say anything. It was as if evil little Pixies had invaded my usually chatty self and sewn my lips shut. No words would emerge. "I'll be ... back." His eyes trailed over his shoulder for a brief moment, but when he caught me watching him—where else was I supposed to look?—he pivoted and strode to the door.

Just before his hand touched the knob, however, he froze. "Whatever you do, Cressida," he said, his voice serious and suspiciously clear of concern or embarrassment, "don't leave this room. I—*someone*—will come for you. But don't leave."

This time, I didn't even get the chance to reply before he was yanking the door open and storming out into the corridor. The door slammed shut behind him with enough force to echo against the stone walls of the room. And I had to sit there and wonder ... *what just happened?*

CHAPTER 26
CRESS

No one came. First, minutes went by. Then hours. Still, no one came, and I couldn't fall back asleep. Every time I tried to close my eyes, I pictured Sorrell. His white hair, ice-cold eyes, and his strong body against me. My stomach grumbled as I sat on the bed, waiting. I was hungry, but I also didn't know where or how to get food in this wretched place. It wasn't like this was the first time I'd gone without a meal; I'd just forgotten what it felt like.

I'd forgotten a lot of things, I realized. What the mountain air felt like on my skin. The sound of the bell that rang when the sisters went for their services in the chapel. I sighed and dropped my eyes down to my legs. I couldn't just sit here anymore, I decided, getting up. I searched the room and found some discarded trousers. They were not meant for someone my size, so I rummaged around some more and found a belt and a shirt to go with it. I pulled the trousers up my legs and cinched the belt tight around my waist until I was sure they'd stay before donning the shirt.

As I moved about the room, my mind kept drifting back to Sorrell and the conundrum that he presented. I was, for all intents and purposes, publicly engaged to Roan. He and Orion had come to an understanding, but what about Sorrell? He was their throne brother, as Tyr had so sardonically pointed out last night. Would they be angry about what happened between us? Did I want it to happen again?

I'd been the one to move first. I'd kissed him, but then I'd pulled away and that had broken something inside of him. The way Sorrell had taken control, even now, hours later with him mysteriously absent, I recalled it. He'd kissed me until I couldn't breathe, as if I was water and he was dying of thirst. *Why?* I wondered. *Why had I kissed him? Why had he kissed me back? What had he been dreaming of?*

The questions just kept looping around in my brain, along with the searing hot memory of Sorrell's hand on my breast, his lips claiming mine and demanding everything I had to give. Every time my mind flashed to the memory of those sensations and images my core tightened and ached. Shaking the internal thoughts away, I moved toward the door, debating on what I'd do next. Could I go out and find them? Would they be angry at me if I did?

Whatever the case, I knew I couldn't stay here. Not for much longer, anyway. I hesitated, though, with my hand on the knob. I didn't mind running into anyone—except perhaps the Queens—but there was someone even more disturbing to me than them. Tyr. A sinister sensation crept over my spine as I thought of Orion's brother. He was dark in many of the same ways as Orion, but whereas Orion's darkness called to me, Tyr's made me want to keep my distance.

He'd been caustic and unnerving during our dance the night before, but more than that, he'd been outwardly secretive at the same time that he'd professed to know all of my secrets. Yet he claimed he wanted to help me? Doubtful. He was the one person I did not want to see again. *Ever*, if it could be avoided.

My hand twisted the knob and I froze as a scrap of paper was pushed beneath the door. It hit my feet and there was a moment of pause as I looked from the floor to the door and back again. There'd been no sound to alert me that someone was on the other side. I'd been so close, and I hadn't known. My hand tightened on the knob and then, with a quick twist, I jerked it open to confront this secret note deliverer.

My breath released in a rush when I was confronted with nothing. Not just nothing, but nobody. There was no one in the corridor. I took a single step out of the room and glanced up and down the hall. The only thing that greeted me was the chill in the air that was constant in this place and the stone walls. I retreated back to the room, bending to pick up the curious note. I turned it over as I let the door shut behind me and pressed my back against it.

I unfolded it and glanced over the contents. I grimaced and shook my head. The handwriting was scratchy and barely legible; the nuns would have whipped whoever had written this for such poor penmanship. I struggled to decipher what the scrawl said, squinting at the page as I made out each word.

If you want to know what the Court of Frost's real intentions are toward you, meet me at the entrance to the garden.

YEAH, OKAY, I THOUGHT. *I'LL DEFINITELY FOLLOW THE instructions of an unsigned note that was creepily slipped under my door.*

That seemed completely reasonable.

Definitely safe, except not.

I mean, I knew I wasn't the most intelligent girl in the world, but even I wasn't that stupid. I fingered the thick parchment and bit my lip before shaking my head. Nope. Not even if I was curious. I mean ... I suppose it did take a special someone to leave something as secretive as this. *Who could it be?* I wondered. Tyr? The mysterious Fae woman who'd warned me to be careful? I narrowed my eyes . Perhaps it was Roan's mother or even Ariana—trying to trick me. *I should throw it in the fire,* I decided.

Yet, my feet remained right where they were.

What was it about the unknown that made it such a temptation? And why couldn't it leave me alone?

I groaned and strode across the room, slapping the note down on the table instead of tossing it into the fireplace where it'd burn among the crackling flames. The guys could look at it and decide what they wanted to do. I'd just leave it be—those were the wisest actions a girl like me could take. *Leave it be,* I warned again, even as my eyes strayed back to the table. *Nothing good can come from mystery. Except maybe death—but not mine. Or the guys. Preferably Ariana's. Yes, hers would do nicely. Something ironic, such as ... falling off a castle.*

I grinned at the amusing thought. Becoming Fae had certainly made me more bloodthirsty, that was for sure. Or perhaps it was just being around them that had done it. Whatever the case, something in me was definitely changing.

CHAPTER 27

ROAN

The afternoon following the Feast of Beasts, I walked into the council chambers and was relieved to see that nothing had changed. The large oval table that covered the middle of the room was surrounded by chairs, spaced out so that if someone got a Pixie up their ass about something then they couldn't just strangle the person next to them and start a war. Not that I'd been tempted to do such a thing nearly a dozen times or more. Except that I had and so had Orion and Sorrell. The space was necessary.

A few chairs were set up on a dais at the end of the room as well, next to a line of empty spaces where other chairs had been removed. Four thrones. Two larger, made for the Queens. And two slightly smaller, made for their heirs. It was where Sorrell and I would have normally sat. But as we were now the rulers of the Court of Crimson, we joined the other lords and ladies gathering around the council table.

As I took a look about the room, I noted that most of the chairs were already full. The majority of delegates had chosen to sit further away from the Queens, which left me, Sorrell, and Orion sitting at the head of the table on one side. Sorrell had been silent since he'd come to us early in the morning. Thankfully, he'd left Cress back in the room, where she'd stay until this damned council meeting was over.

When the door opened and Tyr walked in, I felt every single muscle in my body stiffen. Orion sat up straighter. Sorrell tracked his movements with an expressionless face. I couldn't be as cold as the two of them. Everything inside of me heated up at his presence. I wanted to drive my fist into his face and then keep doing it until he was bloody and broken or dead. Tyr's head turned, scanning the room, and I knew the moment he spotted the three of us because his smirk kicked up a notch and he made his way toward us. Pulling out the chair across from me, he sat and then leaned forward, watching us with his chin resting on his steepled fingers.

Outright murder—unlike hidden, secretive murder with plausible deniability—was frowned upon in Fae Courts. That was the only thing that kept me from lunging across the table at him. When I killed him, there'd be no denying it.

MOMENTS LATER ALL CHATTER STOPPED AS THE DOORS OPENED and the Queens in residence strode into the council chambers. Heads turned and eyes followed as the Frost and Crimson Queens made their way to their thrones.

"You have all been called to the Court of Frost because of a grave issue," my mother began. "Our informants within the human Kingdom of Amnestia have brought vital and dangerous rumors to light. Rumors we've recently found to be true. A human has stolen one of our sacred Lanuaets."

All around me, there were small murmurs of outrage and mutterings that I couldn't quite hear clearly. One thing was clear though, this was a serious matter.

The Crimson Queen nodded solemnly. "How a human could have managed to get their hands on one of our magic orbs is a curious thing," she said, narrow-eyed, as she examined the faces of the council. I kept mine placid as she roved over me and stopped. "It calls into question the strength of our soldiers, of our own courts. What we need to focus on is getting it back and ending this war once and for all."

"Our attack needs to be vicious, surprising, and most of all, crippling to the human race," Queen Adorra added, a savage glee coloring her usually calm and cool tone. Then again, her hatred for humanity was no secret. Of course, she'd be overjoyed by the prospect of a final wave of battle to wipe out their existence, if not force it into irrelevancy.

"Do we know which region the orb is in or how it was obtained?" one of the delegates, Oberstein of the Court of Fury, asked.

"It's in the Ostus Province in the southeast," Tyr said before either of the Queens deigned to answer.

"That's far from any of our normal crossing points," Oberstein murmured.

"We suspect this was the largest operation the humans have run this century. They are getting bolder and the Court of Midnight can only do so much to hold them off. Especially since our heirs are so few." Tyr paused, glancing to Orion. He kept his face cold, but small wisps of darkness began to coil from his flesh, drifting against his hair and face.

I focused on Orion, willing him to look at me, and when he did, I shook my head, letting him know to keep silent at the jab. His agreement to run the Court of Crimson with Sorrell and me had been highly controversial. No other member of the Court of Midnight royals had stepped outside of their reach so completely. But had he not, he'd likely be another body on the battlefield at this point.

Orion nodded in the most imperceptible motion, but it was enough to give me some relief. I turned my gaze back to Tyr and tried not to kill him as he sat back and grinned. Someone else chimed in, their voice low as they spoke. What they were saying was lost as Tyr and I locked gazes, neither of us willing to release the other. No matter what he had planned, I planned to keep Cress as far away from him as possible.

After the Run of the Gods, no one would be able to dispute that she was mine until the wedding itself. Once I caught and claimed her, she would belong to no one else. The wedding that would follow was nothing but a formality. Or at least it was for the older members of the court. The younger members definitely preferred the wedding. Despite the centuries of hatred and animosity, human culture had bled over into our own. It was as much of a tradition now as the Feast of Beasts or the Run of the Gods was.

"Once the orb is retrieved we will mount an assault from the north and join our brother and sister courts to squash the humans once and for all!" A voice from down at the other end of the table pulled me from myself. I glanced back to Orion. Thankfully, his attention was captured by the conversation around us. The same could not be said for Sorrell, however. I frowned as his gaze grew distant. He didn't speak up or respond as those around us began to talk in fast, demanding tones. Instead, it appeared as if he'd lost himself in thought, his fingers occasionally touching his lips.

The unusual movement made me frown. Was he concerned with the dangers Cress presented? If we were going to launch an all out attack on the human kingdom, we were agreeing with the majority that they needed to be eradicated. That wasn't exactly possible for us anymore. Cress's friend still remained behind, sequestered and protected in our court. If anyone found out now, we'd be arrested on the grounds of treason. Harboring a human was akin to plotting to murder our own mothers.

Sorrell was solid, though. I knew he'd never betray our trust or our confidence even if he disagreed with our actions or opinions. Then again, I wondered if his faraway look had anything to do with the rumors of him kissing her on the dancefloor at the feast. I was not one to judge considering I, myself, had entertained multiple lovers at once, but it was curious. Of all of us, he'd been the most opposed to her. *Had something changed?*

"What do you think, Prince Roan?" Tyr asked.

A curse hovered on my lips as I ripped my gaze away from examining Sorrell and returned it to the snake before me. The asshole knew I hadn't been paying attention. All eyes landed on me and I felt the weight of their expectations—just as heavy as the stares from the Queens. I sucked in a breath, releasing it as I lifted my head and met Tyr's amused expression with a glare.

"I think no one steals from the Fae and lives to tell about it," I said, my voice confident and strong.

A round of agreements went up from those around the table and when I turned my gaze to my mother, she nodded slightly—as approving as she'd ever been. Her approval, however, was something I'd stopped attempting to gain years before. The nod only did one thing; it affirmed that when we went back to the human realm, we'd be going back to a new level of war we hadn't known before.

CHAPTER 28
CRESS

"What the fuck is this?"

I blinked at the fury in Roan's tone as he and the others stared down at the note. "Well…" I started, "it looks like a note to me."

"Who did it come from?" Orion asked.

I shrugged. "I don't know."

"Where did it come from?" Roan demanded.

"It was slipped under the door," I answered, my eyes straying to Sorrell, who'd remained surprisingly quiet.

"Why are you wearing that?" Orion asked, frowning down at the loose trousers and large shirt that covered most of me. If it weren't for the gaping collar that was meant for a neck much thicker and a chest much broader than mine, it'd fit like a dress. As it was, the hem fell to my knees and swished there as I swayed back and forth, waiting impatiently for them to be done with the inquisition and tell me where they'd been.

"I didn't have any clothes," I pointed out.

Roan and Orion's heads swung to Sorrell. "You left her without clothes?" they said in unison, the confused shock in their tones pitched equally, as if they couldn't believe Ice Man had managed such an oversight.

Sorrell stiffened at their scrutiny. "She was clothed when I left her, I assure you," he said coolly.

"That was a nightdress," I pointed out. "You can't wear a nightdress in public."

"You can't wear that in public, Cress," Orion replied with a sigh, gesturing to my clothes.

"Why not?"

"Well, for one, the shirt is ... see through."

I looked down at the same time Roan and Sorrell's gazes jerked to my chest. Orion was right. My nipples were pretty clear to see through the thin white fabric. "Oh..." Heat rose to my face and I straightened, ever so subtly crossing my arms over my chest to cover myself. "Well, how was I supposed to know that? I didn't have anything else to wear."

Orion gave me a small smile. "I'll find you something, Sweetheart," he said gently before turning and leaving the room.

I looked to Roan and Sorrell sharply as the door shut behind him. Realizing that they were still staring, both princes yanked their attention back to the note in Roan's hand.

"It has to be Tyr," Sorrell said a moment later. "Who else would it be?"

"It could be anyone that works for my mother," Roan said, frowning.

"I mean, there is one way to find out who sent it," I offered. One pair of liquid fire and one pair of frosted ice eyes settled on me. "I meet whoever it is and you follow me."

"No," Roan growled.

Sorrell glared at me. "Absolutely not."

I shrugged, unconcerned. "It's the fastest and easiest way to find out who sent the note."

"You're not going, Cress," Roan snapped.

"Okayyyyyyyy..." I let the word drift off as I glanced away innocently.

"Cress."

I turned and looked back up at Roan with big eyes. "What?"

"You're not going."

"I heard you."

"Answer me."

"You didn't ask a question."

He growled. "You didn't agree," he pointed out.

"No*pe*." I popped the last syllable. "You're right. I didn't."

"Cressida—" Sorrell began, stopping as his face screwed up. I could see a parade of thoughts march through his head, spreading over his usually enigmatic expression. "You can't put yourself in danger," he finally settled on.

"Would I really be in that much danger if you were there?" I asked.

They both appeared at a loss for words. We stood there for several minutes in silence. Me, expectant. Them, horrified and distraught. They only seemed to reanimate when the door opened once more and Orion came in with a bundle in his arms.

"I managed to purchase a few things off of a nearby lady's maid, but we'll likely have to either create an illusion or purchase something far more elegant for the Run of the Gods later... What's wrong?" Orion froze when he realized the tension that had entered the room since his departure.

"Do you think I should go meet this mysterious person?" I asked.

Dark brows drew down low over his eyes. "No," he said simply.

I groaned and turned toward him, snatching the clothes from his arms before stomping to the bed. I spoke as I walked. "It makes perfect sense," I argued, stripping my shirt over my head and moving to undo the self-made belt I'd wrapped around my hips to keep the trousers up. "How else are we to catch this person or know if they mean me harm?"

"They obviously mean you harm!" Roan burst out. "Half of this fucking court means you harm. You're not going."

"You'd be right there with me," I continued, finally managing to undo the knot. I stripped the trousers down and reached for the bundle I'd tossed onto the bed, unfolding it to pick through and find what I wanted. I grabbed a pair of trouser-like stockings of pure darkness.

"Cressida." I paused in the process of bending over to pull the things on. That voice. It hadn't been Roan or Orion, but Sorrell. He sounded choked, as if all of the air in his chest had deserted him. I glanced over my shoulder and realized he wasn't the only one. All three of them stood there, eyes locked on my backside—on my *naked* backside.

With an internal scream of shocked horror that I'd undressed in front of them without even realizing it, I very quickly pulled the stockings on and reached for the first scrap of fabric to touch my hand as I fumbled around on the bed. I ripped a dress over my head and covered myself as quickly as possible before turning around fully. Had the sun suddenly taken up residence in my face, I wouldn't have been surprised. I felt as though I could cook a nice meal from the heat currently burning my cheeks.

Ignore it, Cress, I silently urged. *Pretend it never happened and maybe they will too. It wasn't like they hadn't seen it all before. All of them. Besides, people got naked all of the time. If they hadn't, there'd be no babies, right?*

Roan was the first to speak. "With the number of people in the Court of Frost, especially those under my mother's purview, that wish you harm, being without one of us at your side is dangerous," Roan said slowly, with forced composure. "I wish that wasn't the case,' but we have to accept how it is. Thankfully, it's not for much longer. We've completed the Feast of Beasts, and the Courts' Council meeting. Now, once we complete the Run of the Gods, we'll be released to go back to our home courts."

"We can finally go back?" I repeated, hope flaring brightly in my chest. I'd finally get to see Nellie again!

"Yes," Sorrell said. "And we'll be going back to the human kingdom."

"There's been a development in the war," Orion said. "We have to prepare for that—"

"What development?" I asked. When they exchanged glances but remained silent, I huffed a breath and glared at them. "What are you planning?" I demanded.

"It's not us, specifically, Sweetheart," Orion said, taking a step closer. I frowned at him. "Humans are dangerous to us all. It appears they've found some way to steal one of our Lanuaets."

When I stared at them in confusion, Sorrell sighed and answered my unspoken question. "It's the magic relic that allows us to use our magic to transport our courts," he said.

"Yes, I know what that is," I said, waving my hand. "But I'm confused as to how someone could steal one. Why is that bad? Humans don't have magic, and I thought it could only be powered by royal Fae?"

"It has magic of its own. To move a castle, of course, it requires more power. Yes, specifically from royal Fae. However, the orb itself usually still contains power after use— remnants of royal power—and that is enough to be cause for concern."

"But, what—"

"The incoming battle is unavoidable, Cress," Roan said, cutting me off. "And we will deal with it when it comes. For now, we must do whatever we can to simply get home. The Court of Crimson is the safest place for you."

"What about Ariana?" I asked.

Roan's expression darkened considerably. "She'll be staying here. You won't need to concern yourself with her anymore. She won't be a problem." Somehow, I doubted that.

"What we need to focus on now is getting ready for the Run of the Gods tonight," Orion said, gesturing to the new dress I now wore. "Like I said earlier, I could only gather so much from the ladies…"

"That's not going to do for tonight," Sorrell said. "You know what is expected."

Roan examined me from head to toe. "The Pixies—"

"I don't trust these Pixies," Sorrell interrupted. "They answer to my mother and yours."

Roan pondered that for a moment. "I have an idea." He stepped forward and took my shoulders in his hands, running his fingers lightly down the sleeves of the gown. "*Est aurum de pulvis. Fabricae tuum fingunt. Et tu iubes.*"

I gasped as a warmth burst from his palms where they touched me and smoothed over the rest of my body. The dress I wore molded to my form, altering right before my very eyes. It cupped my breasts and traveled down to my thighs where the fabric wrapped more loosely. The skirts split on either side of my legs, affording me more room for movement. My neck and arms were left bare.

I blinked down at the new creation. It was no longer the bronzy color it'd been before, but a shimmering gold that complimented the warm hues of my skin. I twirled around, pulling myself from his grasp as I tucked my chin against my shoulder, trying to look behind me as I spun. It was a whole new creation.

"You're going to have to teach me that kind of magic," I said when I stopped spinning.

"I'm afraid it's a special skill of mine," he said with a grin.

"How so?" I asked curiously.

"He can change the shape and physical appearance of a

material at will," Sorrell answered from behind him. "But that still leaves her without shoes," he said to Roan.

"Sandals would be best," Orion said, coming forward as he, too, looked me over. He turned his head to Roan with a scowl after a moment. "If you were just going to show her this, you might've told me that before I ran to grab more clothes."

Roan shrugged noncommittally. I stared down at the shimmering color of the dress. The pale blonde seemed designed to match my hair and I felt like my skin was glowing beneath it. Not just warm from heat, but … something else.

"Get the sandals then," Sorrell ordered. "I think it's time for us to head out."

"Now?" I asked. "But it's not even nighttime yet. I thought the run wasn't until after dark." As I said the words, I realized I didn't know much about the run at all. It had the word 'run' in it so I assumed that I'd be doing some sort of physical movement. I grimaced inwardly. Ew. To be honest, I'd much rather lie in bed and eat cheese and bread than go running through anything.

"The Run of the Gods is a bit farther out than the throne room," he said. "We better get the horses ready or we'll be late. The run begins at twilight."

I groaned as they bundled me up and whisked me out of the room. For once, I'd just really like a night in. It also didn't escape my notice that they'd somehow led me away from the topic of meeting the note-leaver. Sneaky Fae.

CHAPTER 29

CRESS

The guys had bundled me up and onto a horse before we rode out into what felt like the middle of nowhere. I glanced around from where I was perched, my back to Roan's front as we gathered, along with a significant number of others —all dressed similarly as I was—before a massive field of ice plains.

The women wore provocative dresses that left little to be desired. If the fabric wasn't drawn tight over their chests, then it was loose flowing and obvious that they wore nothing beneath. There was no in between. The men, on the other hand, were dressed like warriors. Before we'd ridden here, the guys had stopped to change into their own strange attire. For them, that meant vests made of leather and metal, and tight leather pants laced up over their sides and their crotches, molding to their frames like a second skin.

I shivered as I waited atop the horse, pressing closer to Roan as I turned and burrowed into his chest. He chuckled, the sound reverberating through me. "Cold?" he asked, amused.

"*Freezing!*" I said with emphasis.

"It'll start soon, Little Bird," he said.

"When?" I whined.

"When the illusion reveals itself," he replied.

"The what?"

Just then, the horizon shimmered, catching my attention. I sat up as the field of ice transformed as the sun sank beyond its backdrop. "Mother of the Gods..." I whispered, enthralled as a giant maze appeared. Dark brush blacker than night. Silver spikes protruding from the top of the entrance.

Roan kicked at his horse's flanks and the creature began to clomp forward. "Roan..." I said hesitantly.

"Yes?"

"Do I really have to run from you in a dress and sandals?"

Orion chuckled as he approached us on one side. "The Run of the Gods is an ancient tradition from when the old Gods first came to this realm. You've heard the stories of them coming down and ravishing maidens, yes?" I nodded, wide eyed as we passed through the maze's gates and then I saw that it wasn't a maze at all—or rather, it was more forest than maze. "The Gods were insatiable creatures when they first came down. They would hunt the surrounding lands day and night for their prey."

"Their prey?" I squeaked.

Sorrell approached on the other side and took up the explanation. "This is a tradition rarely enjoyed," he said. "For it engages a male's primitive side."

"P-primitive side?" I repeated.

He nodded, keeping his head forward, though I saw the twitch of his lips at the concern in my tone. "A female will enter the garden and her chosen will enter after her," he explained. "Her chosen will attempt to catch her. All males will have a choice of their own to make. Hunt their prey or let her go."

"You, we won't be letting go," Roan warned quietly. I sighed as the heat of his breath touched my throat. He nuzzled inward, pressing a kiss against my pulse, making it leap at the attention. My thighs clamped down harder in the saddle. His hardness pressed against my backside—hot and heavy. Inside, I melted. My teeth bit down on my lower lip and I tried to steady my breathing.

I blinked, clearing my vision as I realized I'd lost all sense of reality as he'd rocked against me. My head turned and I caught Sorrell's gaze. My throat closed up at the heat I saw reflected there. Far from icy, he looked ready to leap off his horse and drag me from mine. A stormy sort of darkness echoed from within the depths of his eyes, making me shiver.

"Sorrell and I will be there as well," Orion said. "We're going to keep an eye on the Queens if they bother to show up. Oftentimes, matrons of the Court don't come because it's an event specifically designed for the younger generations. But if they do, we'll watch out for them."

"I doubt they'll cause much trouble if they do," Roan said with a nod.

Sorrell mumbled a quiet agreement.

I cast him another curious look, but instead of looking back at me, he averted his eyes.

"All you have to do is run for a little while," Orion continued. "Not even very far if you don't want to. Roan will chase and catch you. All females are given a head start, to make things interesting. Once caught, Roan can ravish you on the spot, like the old Gods would have upon their chosen prey, or bring you back to the castle and claim you there. Once you're claimed, the run is just for sport. The rest of the couples and groups participating will be left to do what they wish. You can just sit back and by this time tomorrow we'll be on our way back to the Court of Crimson."

My eyes flicked over my shoulder to Roan, who looked very smug about the whole thing. "Do not *ravish* me in front of everyone," I said with a narrow-eyed glare as we came to a stop and dismounted. "It's bad enough I'm expected to run around in the cold mostly naked, let alone the fact that I don't have any decent shoes." I gestured to the strappy leather sandals they'd given me upon our departure. "How am I supposed to run in these? They are ridiculous."

"Tradition," Roan said with a shrug and a grin as he reached up and helped me down off the horse. "Just like the ravishment."

I groaned and slapped lightly at his chest before bending down to retie the annoyingly long laces on the sandals. They reached all the way up my calves. How was that necessary? Shoes were meant to be worn to keep one's feet clean and unharmed. Not … whatever these were meant for. Which I couldn't tell because they appeared far too dainty for anything other than garden walks.

"What if I want to?" Roan challenged.

"Want to what?" I asked, distractedly.

"Want to ravish you in front of everyone? Show off that you are mine in every way that matters," he replied, pressing against me from behind. His hips met my ass and I stood up straighter as once again that hard cock between his legs made its presence known.

"Th-then I'll know you don't respect my wishes," I stuttered. At the same time, though, I pictured it. What would it be like? To allow him to take me here. With others watching. Orion would be turned on, that was for sure. He'd enjoyed our time together—him, Roan, and me. Would Sorrell? As if pulled by some invisible force, my gaze strayed back to him, but he'd turned away and walked over to speak with some of the nobles that had come to the event.

At my back, Roan gave a mock sigh and then wrapped his arms around me. "What if I ravish you now?" he inquired in a whisper.

"What if we both do?" Orion agreed, moving to cover my

front. Their heat surrounded me, their cocks prodding at me with expectation. It'd been several nights since I'd had them and even though I'd been a virgin nearly a month or two ago, I found that once that barrier had been breached, I wanted it done again and again. With these two, they made me as insatiable as any lustful God.

I leaned into them and opened my mouth to reply, but before I could say a word, Sorrell was back and frowning at the three of us. "We don't have time. We need to escort Cress to the waiting area for the females. It's starting soon."

Roan and Orion both huffed in frustration. The sentiment, I completely understood. Both men took a step away from me and then stripped their vests off one after the other. I turned and gaped. Then when Sorrell did the same, my eyes nearly fell out of my skull.

"What are you doing?" I hissed, jerking my gaze around to see if anyone had noticed that they were stripping their clothes off right in the middle of everyone.

"We're preparing for the run. This is to be our attire," Sorrell said. *Was that ... no, it couldn't be. Was he preening?* I couldn't be completely sure, but the corner of his mouth curled up as he watched me rake my eyes over him, as if he knew my thoughts. His chest wasn't nearly as defined as Roan's but it was tight and compact. His abdomen was taut and stacked, ridges of muscle clearly visible beneath the skin. And the scars that littered Orion's chest made him no less desirable. Roan, however, turned away as he shoved his vest into his saddlebag, presenting me with the golden hued skin of his back.

Fuckkkkkkkkk.

After a moment more of ogling, I swallowed against a tight throat and spoke. "Yeah, right. Your attire." I breathed slowly through my mouth. "Where's the rest of it?"

"This is it," Roan said with a grin as he turned back around.

The three of them bent and removed their boots. No shoes, no shirts, just the pants, if they could even be called that.

"Why do I get sandals and you don't even get shoes?" I asked.

He shrugged. "To make it easier for you to run, I suppose."

Apprehension attacked my nerves. "What if I don't want to?" I asked suddenly. "What if we just went back to the castle and waited until morning. We could still leave, right?"

"You have to run, Little Bird, or the engagement won't be considered legitimate," Roan said, his hand coming up to cup my face. "I'll catch you, though, don't worry."

My heart fluttered at his words.

He leaned over and rested his forehead against mine. "I'll always catch you."

My breath hitched and I blinked rapidly as I felt a curious burning behind my eyes.

"*We* always will," Orion said emphatically as he approached my other side.

I waited, but when I lifted my head, I saw that Sorrell was placing his vest and boots into his saddlebags as well. He didn't turn or meet my gaze, though by the stiffening of his back—the ripple of muscle across the blades of his shoulders—I sensed that he could feel it. I don't know why it hurt that he hadn't said anything. After the kiss, I'd thought … well, I supposed it didn't matter what I thought. It was clear he didn't want to have anything to do with me. I wondered briefly if he'd told the others, but one glance at their faces—and the lack of attention they paid him—I doubted it.

After a moment more, Sorrell spun and his focus lifted over my head. "Time to go," he called. Roan and Orion each settled a kiss upon my lips before backing away. As I took their hands, though, I couldn't help but stare at Sorrell as he began to stalk toward the other Fae who'd gathered in clearly distinct groups at the mouth of the wide forest that had magically appeared.

His voice hadn't been cold, but there was a distinct sadness to it that I couldn't understand. It made me want to throw my arms around him and force him to tell me what was wrong. I had to admit, that like Roan and Orion, even through all of the rudeness and hostility, I'd come to care for the Ice Man after all.

CHAPTER 30
CRESS

I stared into the opening set between two tall ebony trees, my heart thumping in my chest as the other women gathered around. As the bride to be, I was going first. Of course, I was always either first or last, there was no in between. For once in my life, I wished I could just blend into the middle somewhere and pretend I was just like everyone else. I hated the feeling of all eyes centered on me. I wiggled a little bit where I stood. It felt like tiny insects were crawling over my skin.

I took a deep breath and looked over my shoulder at where the men had gathered several paces behind us. Some of their eyes glinted in the near darkness as the sun finally set below the horizon. The three of them stood back there—Roan, Orion, and Sorrell. They stared at me with quiet expectation as I faced the entrance once again as a horn blew. It echoed up toward the sky, sounding from all angles and all sides, loud and sharp to my ears.

I blinked and looked around. *Where the hell was it coming from?* Someone nudged my side. I jerked my head down.

"You're supposed to go," a woman hissed behind me. "You're the bride, you must take the first step."

"I—"

She gestured wildly and then put her hands to my back, pushing me forward. As soon as I took a single step the rest of the women around me, all growing antsy, finally took that as their cue to go and dashed forward. Giggles rose into the atmosphere as they disappeared into the woods.

With a jolt, I followed them. I dashed into the dark woods. As soon as I entered the illusioned forest, I realized that there was something different about it. The golden hue of after twilight was gone. Instead, the entire matted undergrowth was covered in shadow with slitted rays of silver shining down as if a moon hovered close overhead.

My feet pounded on the ground as I ran. The girl who'd pushed me disappeared as she ran alongside me. One second, we were running together and I could hear her excited pants coming quickly between spurts of outrageous laughter. The next, she'd vanished and all I heard was nothingness.

Just run, they had said. *They'd find me. But what if I ran too far? What if they didn't catch me? What if someone else...* I stopped cold as I realized I was surrounded by darkness. I turned and tried to seek out the entrance, but that too was gone. Somewhere far behind. A shiver stole over my back, alerting me to the fact that I wasn't alone.

"Hello?" I called out. "Roan?" No response.

I stumbled forward, hands outstretched, searching.

"Pretty little Changeling like you should be captured and ravished right away, you know."

I squealed at the new voice and whirled in a circle, hunting for it in the darkness. Thin beams of moonlight cut through the forest. The palms of my hands grew damp. My breath choked in my throat as I backed up, slamming into a nearby tree. Something overhead twittered and the sound of little animal legs scratched at the tree. *There were* animals *in this forest? It wasn't even real. Were they real?*

A face appeared before me, pale with dark eyes and a familiar grin. I gasped and pressed myself even more firmly against the trunk of the tree. "What are you doing here?" I snapped. "I didn't see you waiting with the others."

Tyr came fully into the silver beam of light directly in front of me. "I came for you," he said. "You didn't meet me where you should've."

I gasped. "It *was* you!" I said, pointing at him accusingly. "Why would you—"

He reached forward and snagged me, lifting me as though I weighed no more than a sack of grain, and threw me over his shoulder. *What was it with men and carting me around like food? Was it some sort of subconscious masculine desire to see me as something to eat? I mean, that could be attractive ... were I in the right frame of mind or with the right man. If it were the guys, I could be convinced—they were good at convincing. But even they seemed to pick me up and put me down wherever they pleased. It was damn rude.*

"Now, I don't have time to wait for you. It's time to go," Tyr said.

"Go?" I pressed my hands to his back and lifted my head, searching the surrounding area. "Where are we going?"

I could hear the amusement in his voice. "You'll see." I couldn't see, but I could feel him lift his arm and then a gust of air rushed over my backside, nearly flipping my skirt up. I shrieked and squirmed in his grip, trying to get down. "Stop moving," he ordered.

"Put me down!" I countered.

"Cress!"

My head snapped to the side at the familiar call of my name. It was Roan, several paces away, his face coming clear through the darkness as he passed beneath another ray of moonlight.

He disappeared just as quickly as he kept moving forward, but I could still hear the movement of his legs as he tramped through the forest toward me.

"I'm over here!" I called, fighting against Tyr once more. "Put me down, asshole!"

Tyr heaved a great sigh, all amusement gone from his voice as he spoke. "You're quite irritating when you want to be, do you know that?"

It didn't sound like he was really looking for an answer, but I gave him one anyway. "Really?" I replied. "'Cause I'm not even trying right now." I pounded his back with my fists, threw my body side to side, and still, he held tight. "Let." *Punch.* "Me." *Kick.* "DOWN!" I screamed in frustration when nothing I did was good enough. "Why are you doing this?" I demanded to know. "What is it about me? I just don't understand."

Seriously, I thought with annoyance. This was the question I'd been asking myself ever since I'd heard that horrible noise and found the Court of Crimson. *What was it about me that drew random Fae to kidnap, imprison, chase, and want me? I wasn't special! Or, if I was, then why couldn't someone else be more special. There had to be someone out there.*

"Cress!" Orion's voice shouted through the darkness and then Sorrell's.

"Cressida!"

"Here!" I yelled back. I could hear them getting closer and as they did, the wind picked up. There was a strange buzzing noise in my ears. A dizziness assailed me as I tried to shout again, and my words were swallowed up.

Tyr grunted, though I wasn't sure if it was under my weight or because of whatever he was doing. "You'll soon learn, little Changeling, that there is much you don't understand," he said.

I leveraged up and over, turning my head back to peer at whatever it was he was doing. My lips parted in shock as I saw a circular portal open, a haze of leaves and twigs spinning around it. He took a step toward it even as I tried to throw myself one last time from his grip.

A crash sounded to my right and I glanced over just as Orion spilled into the opening he'd created in the underbrush. Sorrell appeared at his side, and then Roan. They took one look at Tyr and me and dove for us just as Tyr stepped through the portal and we were swallowed up.

CHAPTER 31

ORION

As we ushered Cress to the waiting point for all of the females, I scanned the area for Tyr. So far, there had been no sign of him. It was a good thing … if it lasted. A sharp tingling sensation on the back of my neck pervaded me though, warning me of some impending doom. I reached up and rubbed my fingers against it, trying to will it away. Always in the midst of battle, that sensation had warned me of an attack and I'd never ignored it. I didn't ignore it now, but I couldn't shake the feeling that, this time, no matter what I did, there would be no avoiding what was coming.

My eyes slid to Roan. The flush of excitement was on his face. Embers sparked at the ends of his hair, but fires hadn't yet erupted. I didn't want to spoil this for him—the Run of the Gods was a stimulating event. So, I kept my mouth shut. I bypassed him in favor of looking to Sorrell, who stood on his other side.

Something had changed in my Frost brother lately. His eyes were focused on the mass of Fae women gathering before the entrance to the illusioned forest. I wondered if he was beginning to feel the same way Roan and I did about Cress. She was light in the world of darkness we'd known for so long. To me, more than most.

When the trumpets blared, I turned and watched as Cress looked around frantically—confusion clear on her face. Another female pushed her forward and the mass of women dove for the trees. She followed soon after, her shorter legs working twice as hard to catch up as the rest of them disappeared into the woods.

One minute. I could feel the anticipation racketing up. *Two minutes.* Several of the men shifted forward, toeing an invisible line we all knew not to cross until it was time. *Three minutes.* Logically, I understood that it was tradition to give the females time to race forward. However, that didn't stop the craving to release—to spring forward and chase down our prey. *Four minutes.* One more. *Five minutes.* The sound of the booming signal to release us echoed around us. We took off.

It was an explosion of action as different groups went in search of their chosen females. Cress's trail wasn't hard to find and for a moment I worried she was going to make it too easy for us. Broken twigs. Footprints. I shook my head. She wasn't even trying.

"We did tell her that we'd catch her, but does she think that we're too dumb to find her trail?" Roan asked aloud, sounding more amused than offended.

"I don't think she's *trying* to do anything," Sorrell said, several paces back and to my left. I agreed. She wasn't trying to evade us. She wasn't trying to make it difficult to find her as other Fae females would have. She was just running. Trying to find the path that made the most sense to her and taking it.

Ironically, I'd always imagined that the Run of the Gods was more metaphoric than literal. Yes, the Gods had tracked their prey in this realm when they'd first established themselves. They'd hunted the women they wanted and taken them. Many of the women had been more than happy to succumb to a

God's advances but many more hadn't. It was a dark reality often glossed over. But now, as we trailed through the illusioned woods, I began to wonder if there wasn't a deeper meaning.

While other females made their paths as difficult as possible —some even setting traps to evade their hopeful suitors— others made it too easy. Cress was neither. She seemed to pay no mind to the fact that the three of us were trailing her, intent on finding her and at the very least, *one* of us ravishing her. Instead, she just forged ahead, trying to make her own path to wherever that led her.

I glanced at Sorrell, whose face showed no emotion. He didn't appear particularly happy about this endeavor, nor did he seem irritated by it. Surprised noises as females were caught sounded from some distance away. I slowed my pace.

"She's not making it hard," I said as I stopped completely. Roan and Sorrell came to a stop as well, peering at me through the darkness and beams of moonlight as they shone through the canopy above.

"No?" Roan said. "So, why have we stopped?"

"We should've caught her by now," I said.

Roan and Sorrell's bodies stiffened and their gazes swung out to the surrounding areas, scanning fast. That tingling wave of unease came back full force. This time, they could feel it too.

The illusion of the forest was always immaculate, the Queens prided themselves on it. There was nothing for us to find but what they wanted us to find. Cress's scent was there, in my nostrils. It was right there. We were nearby.

"This way." Roan and Sorrell fell into step behind me as I forged ahead. I paid no mind to the noise I made and neither did they. We weren't trying to be subtle or sneaky, we were trying to be fast.

A feminine scream of outrage reached us and I nearly stumbled over a fallen tree limb when I recognized it as Cress's.

"Hurry," I snapped to the others, even as my mind rolled with dread. What in the name of the old Gods was going on? Who would be brazen enough to steal the Prince of Crimson's intended bride?

I knew the answer.

Tyr.

A dark scowl curled my lips back as I rushed forward, swatting leaves and branches out of my way and stomping through the underbrush. We were impossibly close.

"Cress!" Roan yelled.

Then, in the darkness, I heard her reply. "I'm over here!" she yelled, sounding far closer than I'd expected. Then to someone else, she snapped, "Put me down, asshole!"

I lifted my head and tracked her through the brush. "*Visus nocte*," I muttered, casting a spell over my eyes to enhance my sight in the darkness. It was illegal to cast such a spell during the Run of the Gods, but this was an emergency. As soon as my vision cleared, I saw her through a wall of trees. She struggled in another man's grip as he held her over his shoulder. Tyr. A low growl started in my chest and struggled up my throat.

Roan lifted his hand and summoned a fireball, throwing it toward the wall of trees. When it flew through and was absorbed easily, the three of us froze. More magic. The trees in the illusion would feel real to anyone who touched them. It should've burned. Realizing that this portion of the forest wasn't illusioned like the rest of it, I sprinted forward, bracing slightly for an impact that never came.

I came out on the other side drenched in the scent of magic from my home court. The snarl I'd barely repressed was released. The trees were made of smoke and shadow.

"Cress!" I yelled her name as I saw her across a short distance, far more clear than she had been with just my spelled sight.

"Cressida!" Sorrell roared next to me.

"Here!" Her voice rang with panic.

I could feel the buzz of magic over my skin like the smallest of insects with fiery venom gnawing on my flesh. We spilled into a small clearing that was besieged by strange winds. No, I realized, not strange winds, but the magic of a portal being opened. One that shouldn't have been possible.

Branches and twigs and leaves hovered in a circle as lightning flashed within the center. I got a good look at Tyr as we raced toward him. Sweat shimmered on his forehead, concentration drawing his brows into a hard V. He could sense through our blood how near I was. How angry I was.

For the first time in my life, I understood my capability. Never before had I wanted to harm him. Not when he'd left me in battle. Not when he'd abandoned or betrayed me numerous times before. Now … I wanted to do more than harm him. I wanted to kill him.

Cress's head came up and she turned, meeting our gazes for a split second. I reached out. Almost there. And just before I could grasp onto her, Tyr stepped forward and disappeared into the portal.

My knees hit the ground. The wind immediately ceased. The branches and twigs and leaves dropped to the ground. A loud crack boomed and suddenly the trees before us began to wither away, sinking into the underbrush as that too dried up and ice formed beneath our feet.

The illusion had been broken.

The bright icy cold of Alfheim's icefields spread over us as everyone in attendance was revealed in their various placements. There were dozens of Fae scattered around. Many were naked. Many were halfway through ravishment and claiming. Shouts of alarm sounded as people realized that something had gone terribly wrong. Male and female Fae alike rushed to put clothes on as the warmth of the illusion dispersed as well. My gaze stayed fixed on where the portal had been. The three of us stood there, horror and fear in our hearts. I didn't have to look at them to know that was true.

Roan roared. I didn't even have the strength to look back. I knew what I'd see. His head engulfed in flames. Fire dancing at the ends of his fingers. Fury mixed with shock and panic. And for Sorrell ... the exact opposite. He would be frozen. If he felt even a quarter for Cress as we did, he would likely feel the slow creep of ice forming over his skin—magic unbound as it overtook him.

Cress was gone. Kidnapped. Stolen from right under our noses. My fingertips had barely even grazed her before she vanished.

Darkness wrapped around me like a blanket as I collapsed in on myself. It was a sensation I hadn't felt since I was a child, abandoned on the battlefield. Fire, ice, and darkness; the three of us were forces on our own and together we were all consumingly powerful. We should've been. And yet, we'd failed.

EPILOGUE
CRESS

Something was wrong with me. Seriously wrong. I repressed the urge to vomit, clutching my hands over my stomach as we stepped through the portal. Only when the urge to upchuck the contents of my insides had receded was I finally able to look up and cast what I really hoped was a withering glare at the man who'd kidnapped me. I should've taken lessons in withering glares though—the nuns should've taught them because they had that skill perfected—I decided when it appeared that Tyr was unaffected by my obvious irritation.

"How did you—"

A sly grin twisted his lips and stopped my words in their tracks. "There are a great many things you still don't know, little Changeling, and I believe now is the time to change that," he said. "You should've joined me when I first asked."

I frowned. "What are you—"

He cut me off. "Now, I think I have a better use for you."

The sound of metal clanking and booted feet echoed around us, drawing my attention to the fact that we were no longer in the dark forest that had been created for the Run of the Gods. We were in some sort of large stone room with fires lit down each side, revealing tall and disturbing paintings of men on horseback riding through crowds of strangely beautiful people—Fae, I realized, with their otherworldly allure depicted as a certain pale glow in their skin, and large eyes.

I slowly got to my feet, gaping at the images even as the sounds of that metallic clanking grew nearer. It was both stunning and horrific to bear witness to the images around us. The crowds were of Fae people—but not the Fae people I knew. These Fae had fangs and eyes of fire and smoke. These Fae had large wings outstretched behind them as they rushed toward the men on horseback with hands drenched in fire—magic, I presumed. While the men sitting astride their horses carried big heavy swords, swinging them at each other. Decapitated heads rolled at the bottom of the paintings where the horses trampled over broken, still bleeding bodies.

"What is this place?" I managed to whisper.

A great boom erupted and I whirled around as a giant set of twin doors was shoved inward and a horde of men clad in armor came rushing in, swords drawn. I snapped my gaze to Tyr, but he merely stood by, casually eyeing them and then turning to me as he grinned.

"Welcome back to Amnestia," he said coolly, "to the Capital and to the King's throne room."

My mouth gaped and no sooner had the words left his lips than a man larger than the rest came barreling through the mass of men that had gathered just inside the room, facing us with their weapons. He removed a helmet that looked as if it were made from pure gold, revealing an older, haggard face with a twisted beard and cold, cruel eyes. I shrank away from him as he approached, but before I could run, Tyr reached out and snagged my arm, locking me firmly in his grip.

"Let go!" I snapped as I tried digging my free hand between his palm and my arm. "You stupid, bird-brained asshole!"

Tyr didn't even blink at the insults I hurled. "Rotten, dumb, bastard"—he shot me a look of amusement—"backstabbing, conceited,"—he laughed outright, causing my face to heat with fury—"fuckface!" *What even was a fuckface?* I didn't know, but it sounded good and insulting. *What was worse than a fuckface?* I contemplated during my struggles as the man with the golden helmet came nearer. I couldn't help but feel a sense of foreboding, as if this man was someone to fear.

"What have you brought to me this time, Tyr?" he inquired.

Tyr arched a brow at me and then hauled me forward and shoved me to my knees before the man. "A Fae spy in your midst, your Majesty," he announced.

My whole body froze in shock as Tyr bowed to the man that I now understood must have been the King of Amnestia. The King of Amnestia … who was human and whose exploits I'd only known as heroic in the eyes of the nuns I'd been raised by, but who I suddenly realized was a greater threat to me now than when I'd been growing up. Because now it was more than clear what I was—Fae—and this man's hatred for Fae was the greatest that had ever existed.

So … that begged the question, what was he doing with a Fae like Tyr?

I stared up at the man who curled his lip down at me with contempt and summoned the only word I could seem to muster. The only word that perfectly encapsulated this painstakingly horrible moment.

"Fuck."

COURT OF MIDNIGHT

A King blinded by hate and the last Changeling...

War knows only loss and agony and this one is coming to a
final end.

A wicked plan.
A king's wrath.
A girl with a secret in her blood.

If any of us want redemption then we must be willing to
sacrifice what no one has before.

Our loyalty lies with the bonds we've created.
Through fire. Through frost. Through darkness.

We will prevail ... or perish trying.

CHAPTER 1
CRESS

I paced from one end of my tower cell to the next. I'd never felt this trapped before. I didn't like it. I couldn't see the sky. I couldn't feel fresh air on my skin. I felt like I was suffocating and in the dark no less since I'd been given no light. There wasn't even a damn window. Tyr—Orion's rotten bastard of a brother—was the cause.

As if my thoughts had summoned the creature straight from Death's realm, the door to my prison rattled and opened and he stepped into the entrance, framed by the firelight behind him. Oh, how I wanted to run him through with one of the Princes' swords. I wanted to claw his eyes out. Punch him in the throat. Kick him in the balls.

I took several steps towards him, intending to do just that when he held up a hand and invisible manacles encircled my arms and legs, stopping me from moving any further.

"I can understand your reasonable anger, Cress," Tyr said as he stepped into the room. He lifted a hand, the movement a shadow across the floor at my feet. Within seconds, fires erupted around the room—clinging to lanterns that had been hung there previously but had gone unlit. "But you won't harm me—or rather, I won't allow you to."

I narrowed my eyes on him. "What?" I snapped in challenge. "Are you scared of a little girl?"

He chuckled as the door behind him closed. "Of course not. Give me just a moment," he replied calmly.

Fuck his calm! I wasn't calm. I was angry. Angrier than I'd ever been. I listened to the sound of keys jingling in the lock as the door was relocked. Only then did Tyr lower his arm and the invisible bindings disappeared. I didn't even hesitate. I continued my forward momentum, brought my foot back, and nailed him right between the legs.

"Fuck!" He went down on his knees, throwing a hand out at me. A wave of power hit me and propelled me backwards. My spine hit the stone wall, and I winced as I slid down. That was going to bruise. I didn't care. It'd been worth it to kick him right where the sun didn't shine. So fucking worth it.

"You are a feisty one, I'll give you that," he wheezed. "Seems my brother chose well for his mate ... and his friends' mate."

I clenched my teeth against the pain in my back as I got on my knees and leveraged myself up. I stood and held my ground, my hands balling into fists at my side. Already I could feel the soreness in my back. It was going to make sleeping really painful, I knew. "Why would you do this?" I demanded, ignoring his comment. "Why would you take me? What could I possibly have to help you gain anything? It's clear you're in this for power. Right?"

"Right." He nodded and I took some pleasure in the fact that he still looked pale. When he stood, he did so slightly hunched as he moved further from me and back towards the door to lean against the wall alongside it.

It didn't matter. I'd done what I wanted. I knew there was no way I'd get much more than one hit in. I was effectively trapped here. And even if I did manage to escape, I knew nothing about the King's truth. Sure, I'd grown up in Annaea, but I hadn't ever left the small abbey I'd been raised in until I'd met the Princes.

"It's more than that, little Changeling," he said gruffly.

I narrowed my gaze on him and waited. Slowly, ever so slowly, Tyr straightened his back and looked at me. "I admit," he said, "originally, I was bored."

My mouth dropped open. That couldn't be right. He couldn't possibly be telling me that he did all of this—betrayed his race and his *brother* because he was bored. As if sensing my thoughts, he grinned ruefully.

"I'm sure my little brother has told you very little, if anything, about his home Court. The Court of Midnight is as secretive as it is powerful," he said. "We are taught from birth to play the game and play it well."

"What game?" I demanded. "Life and death? That's no game."

Tyr tilted his head and slowly lowered his eyes until they had passed over the rest of me. "There is a reason we keep to ourselves, a reason why ours is the Court called upon for action and war, little Changeling." I snarled, hating it when he called me that. *They*—my Princes—could call me that, but he couldn't. He ignored the sound and continued. "The Court of Midnight possesses old magic, ancient and dangerous magic. We were the ones called upon when Courts of old needed to be taught a lesson."

When Courts of old needed to be taught a lesson ... My lips parted and shock rocketed through me. He couldn't mean what I thought he meant. Did that mean ... was his Court—Orion's Court—responsible for the loss of the Brightling Court?

A cruel, twisted sneer lit his face. "I can see you understand," he said. "Midnight is the power that steals all other magic. We are not life. We are death incarnate. With such power comes a great deal of tediousness. What does one do when you have all of the power of the world, hmmm?"

My muscles jumped and shook. Anger poured through me, and yet, I couldn't move. I simply stood there and watched him, cautious, confused, and yes, even a little scared. It wasn't a Fae that stood before me but a monster.

"Orion, of course, was always a little different. When heirs are young, they are sent away to other Courts to begin their training. He met Sorrell and Roan at the Court of Frost and Court of Crimson and when The Crimson Queen decided to step down from her Court to give her son some ruling experience, well, it came as no shock to me when Orion leapt at the chance to join him. He always was a weakling."

"He's not weak!" I snapped. My skin heated. My face flamed. Something deep within me burned with the agonizing heat of the sun and it made me want to melt his smug face off. "Orion is one of the strongest, bravest men I know. If anything—you're the weak one."

Tyr's eyes widened for merely a fraction of a moment before he burst out laughing. "Truly amusing," he barked. "I almost believed you there for a moment myself."

"You should believe me," I said through gritted teeth. My hands clenched into fists. I wanted so badly to hit him, but I didn't trust that it wouldn't come back to bite me in the ass. "I'm serious."

"I'm sure you are," he replied, sounding arrogant in his sarcasm, "but you keep interrupting me. Don't you want to know why I did this?" He waved his hand to the stone prison.

I clamped my lips shut.

He grinned. "There, now, that's better. Keep your pretty mouth shut and you might just make it out of this alive," he offered. *I'd show him a pretty face.* I bet his face would look a whole lot prettier with a couple of bruises. My previous anger towards Ariana held no candle to the fury I felt for this man.

"Now," he continued, "as I was saying. Yes, I began this endeavor out of boredom—the whole betrayal thing really adds some spice to life, don't you think? Humans are so easy to manipulate. They ignore magic that's right before their eyes." He lifted his hand and a flame so dark it was blue danced at his fingertips, illuminating his face in a grotesque mass of shadows and dancing light before it disappeared. "They'll believe what they want to believe and if you use it against them, they aren't even smart enough to realize."

Tyr pushed away from the wall and took a few steps into the room. I didn't move. In fact, I felt my body lock up as I pushed back against the wall, wanting to stay as far from him as possible. "Then a grand idea appeared before me," Tyr said, throwing his arms out wide. When he smiled this time it was too tight with a maniacal gleam in his eyes. "Why control only humans? Fae are just as easy to control? What if I could control the world? Everything!"

I frowned. My brows drew down low and I shook my head back and forth. I didn't understand. "What?" I blurted.

Tyr lowered his arms. "It's simple," he explained. "All I have to do is let them kill each other. I won't even have to lift a finger or dirty my hands. I am the player and they are my pawns. All I need to do is push them into place and let them finish the work. Afterwards, I'll be able to rule over the remains with no opposition. And you—" He stopped and turned to me. "You came along at the most perfect opportunity."

A sick feeling of dread curled in my stomach and I swallowed reflexively.

"My brother has no idea the power he wields," he confessed. "And I made sure to keep it that way."

"The scars..." I whispered. "You did that." His tone was too smug, too proud for it not to be true.

He shrugged. "If he wasn't strong enough to beat me once, what made him think he could do it again?"

"He can beat you now, though, can't he?" I asked. That was why he'd tortured him as a child, I realized. Because he knew the kind of power Orion would grow into. I'd never seen it myself, but I'd felt it. And Orion was backed by Sorrell and Roan. They were each powerful on their own, but together .. they were unstoppable. And that's why he'd needed me.

"All I needed to do, once I'd understood the kind of power you held over them, was incite them."

I felt so foolish. So stupid. *But how could I have known?* I lifted my arms and curled my fingers into my hair. *No no no. This couldn't be happening. Was I the reason that they would be hurt?* I knew that was true in the deepest parts of my soul.

"I lied before," Tyr admitted. *Shocker*, I thought as I released my hair and glanced up. Except it wasn't. It really wasn't. "You won't make it out of this alive. Your death will instigate the next part of this war. The final part. And from the ashes, I will rise."

I was disgusted. Horrified. And utterly at a loss. My lips parted but no words emerged. What could I say? What could I do? Nothing. I could do and say nothing that would stop the course that he'd set.

Tyr grinned again, recognizing the emotions on my face. "Be overjoyed, little Changeling." This time, when he said that name, I didn't flinch. "You'll be the reason I finally get my wish. You'll be the very pawn used to decide the next God among humans and Fae. Me. Fitting, don't you think? All those years ago, I was ordered to kill the entirety of you and your brood. Yet here you stand before me and finally, my task will be carried out."

"What?" I gaped at him. "What do you mean you were ordered to kill me?"

He arched a brow. "You still haven't figured it out?" He laughed, sounding more than amused. He sounded crazy. Deranged. Completely cut off from sanity. He stopped abruptly, turning and striding towards the door that led to freedom. He knocked once, twice, three times before turning back to me. "You are the last heir to the Brightling Court, Cressida," he said. "You are the Brightling Princess and it was my duty to slay you. You escaped once. You won't escape again. Instead, you'll be used to hand the world over to me. Who knows?" He chuckled again as the door was unlocked and pulled open. "Maybe you're technically a Brightling Queen now since your mother is long dead. At my hands, too."

"Wait!" I jerked forward as he stepped out and the door closed behind him. I slammed into the wood, feeling the hit shake me to my core. I wanted to know more. No, I *needed* to know more.

"Don't worry, Cressida." Tyr's voice drifted through the wood. "Like I said, you'll be leaving here soon and you'll be joining your true family in the afterlife."

I sank against the door, turning and pressing my back to it as my bones trembled. My knees hit the cold, dirty ground and I curled into myself as his words echoed in my mind over and over again. I closed my eyes and let darkness take me into oblivion.

CHAPTER 2

ROAN

S*he was gone.*
The thought beat at me like the heat of the sun, unrelenting in its force. Wave after wave of heated anger pulsed through me. We had fucked up. We'd missed it. And Tyr was a fucking traitor. Perhaps he didn't know yet that we knew where he'd taken her, but just before the portal had closed, I'd glimpsed a hint of where they'd landed. The human Kingdom, and not just any place, but the Royal human palace.

When I get my hands on him, I'm going to burn him to ash, I swore silently.

The urge to track her down, to save her from whatever Tyr was planning, was almost uncontrollable. My bones and muscles vibrated with the desire—it swelled up even beyond the initial shock.

I looked to Sorrell and Orion. Silence echoed between us as we made our way back to the Court of Frost's castle. A darkness had overtaken Orion. For all of his Midnight powers, he'd never truly appeared as though he was a part of their Court. He'd been too compassionate, too sane, too gentle. He was anything but that now. Even in his silence, I could sense the dark force within him. There was no denying it, no hiding it.

And surprisingly, Sorrell wasn't much better. No matter how much he preached against Cress, his anger was nearly as potent as mine. His very skin was whiter than ice, nearly blue as frost crept up over the side of his neck, inching forward. Every step he took left a path of ice in his wake. None of us could control it—the emotions swirling within our bodies demanding restitution.

"We need to get back," I said, stopping in the corridor just outside of the Court of Frost's throne room. "We have to go after her."

Neither of them said a word, but their strides did slow and stop alongside mine. I closed my eyes and forced my anger back. I grabbed each of their arms and yanked them along with me. Shoving until they both slammed into the wall.

"Wake *the fuck* up!" I yelled. "We are in no position for this. We need to figure out what we're going to do. We have to form a plan of attack." Cress was depending on me, she was depending on *us*.

Sorrell blinked at me, a light seeming to reenter his eyes, though not fast enough for my liking. Orion remained expressionless.

"It's time to fucking go," I gritted out. When, once again, neither of them said a word, my Royal fire burned out of control, and for the first time since I was a child incapable of controlling my powers, I lost it. I roared as fire licked against my scalp, and turning, I slammed my fist into a nearby stone wall. So many turbulent emotions were pent up.

I didn't think. I just reacted to all of it. I pivoted, grabbed onto Orion, and yanked him towards me, shoving my face into his.

"You think this is going to help Cress?" I demanded. "It's not. We need to go out, find her, and get her back. And I swear to you, Orion—throne brother of mine or not—I will kill your blood brother if it's the last thing I do. I will not settle for less. He took what is mine."

Orion blinked and I could feel something seeping from his pores as a darkness wafted over my skin. "Ours," he rasped.

For a moment, relief poured through me. "Yes," I agreed. "She's ours, and we need to get her back." I took a deep breath and fixed him with a look. "Don't make me do it alone. I need you." I knew he cared for her as I did. There was no one else I would want at my back than my throne brothers.

"You are not going alone," Sorrel said as he stepped up alongside Orion and me. His cool, icy gaze traveled over us both. "I'm coming as well."

Orion didn't look at him, not even when I took my hands back and released him from the wall. The three of us stood in a semi circle and there was a jagged piece of us missing—a piece I hadn't realized was so important until that moment. Her. She was everything. And perhaps I'd just been claiming her as my fiancée and future Crimson Princess to protect her in the hostile frozen Court of Sorrell's ancestors, but the truth was, I expected to marry her. I wanted her. *They* wanted her.

And there was nothing that would stop us from taking her back.

I dragged in a lungful of air. "We must speak to the Queens," I said.

Sorrell and Orion both nodded, and together we turned and moved towards the throne room.

We stopped just inside the entryway and my eyes widened at what I saw. The Frost and Crimson Queens sat, side by side, entertaining their guests from their thrones, seemingly unconcerned, or perhaps unaware, of what had occurred at the Run of the Gods. It didn't take long, however, for them to notice our presence.

"Roan," my mother bid me, lifting her hand towards me as she beckoned me to her side. "Is the Run over already?" Her lips tilted up into a half smirk and already, I sensed her thoughts. She likely believed that our early arrival must have meant that I'd called off the engagement. That assumption was far from the truth.

"There has been a breach in our security," I stated, not moving from my spot. Orion and Sorrell remained vigil at my sides. "Cress has been taken by Tyr into the human realm. He's working with the humans."

Gasps echoed up from those present in the room. Sorrell's mother jerked her head towards me, her cold blue eyes narrowing. "What is the meaning of this?" she demanded.

"It's exactly as he said," Sorrell answered. "Cress has been kidnapped. We are leaving at once for our Court and we will be going after her."

"All three of you?" my mother demanded.

"Yes," Orion replied.

There was a moment of silent shock from both of them and before either could think to order us to stay, we turned as one and left. Orion went one way and Sorrell another. We didn't have to speak to know our plans. Each of us would pack our belongings and leave by horse within the hour. There would be no sleep or stops along the way. We had to make it back to our Court with all haste.

I arrived at my chambers and was already beginning to pack when the door was unceremoniously flung open and the Crimson Queen came storming in.

"This is an absolute outrage," she snarled as she approached. "How dare you come into my throne room and disrespect me by leaving without my leave—"

I turned and pinned her with a look. "It is not your throne," I reminded her, my voice sharp with cruelty. "You chose to remain in Alfheim, and therefore, you hold a seat in that throne room, but make no mistake. This is not your Court, mother," I said. "You no longer have one."

She gasps. "I am your mother," she said, shocked. "How dare you treat me this way? I demand that you stay here and apologize."

I snorted, shoving another item of clothing into the bag in my hand. "You cannot stop my leaving," I replied. "I will find my fiancée, and as soon as I have her in my arms once more, I will make sure that she is protected."

The woman before me rolled her eyes. "That child does not deserve this level of loyalty, Son," she replied. "If anything, this only proves that you should marry Ariana. It's clear that your Changeling was likely having an affair with Tyr. You know how humans are, easily seduced by—"

A snarl worked its way up my throat and I dropped the bag in my hand, turning on her so abruptly that she stumbled back a step. "She is *not* a human!" I yelled. "We are leaving. We will find her. And when I do, I will marry her and make her the next Crimson Queen once I have come of age. I may be a Prince now, but make no mistake—unless you plan to kill me— there will come a time when my power far outweighs your own."

"You would defy your mother, your Queen?"

"Without hesitation. No one takes what is mine and lives to tell about it. I will have her back and have Tyr's head on a spike."

"You wish to start a war between the Court of Crimson and the Court of Midnight? Fine. But do not expect any assistance from me or Adorra."

"I never have," I snapped, returning to my task.

"The Court of Midnight is dangerous," she continued as though I hadn't spoken. Try as I might to ignore her words, they pierced into my mind as she hurled them at me. "They will tear you apart as they do their own young!" she exclaimed.

"And you would go willingly into the battle for a girl with no wealth or status or talent. You have lost your mind."

The door to my chambers opened and Sorrell and Orion both stood there. Their packs rested against their shoulders as they looked into the room and spotted us. They must have heard her proclamations because, without hesitation, Orion stepped inside and fixed her with a look.

"We will tear my brother apart," Orion said, a dark sinister aura coating his skin like smoke as it twined around his hands and up his arms. His eyes practically glittered with the Midnight danger my mother spoke of.

In typical fashion, my mother ignored him and addressed me instead. "Is she really worth all of this? What is she other than the byproduct of a forgotten line? There is nothing special about her, no good breeding, no family to speak of, no money, no power. She's just a momentary entertainment. Now she's gone, probably run away with Tyr, and you should let her go. Please, for the love of the Gods, marry Ariana; she has everything that your Changeling lacked, plus she is an excellent example of how Fae women should behave, unlike that child you brought before us who talked back to her queens."

"She is not a child, that I can guarantee," I said coldly, lifting my bag and slinging it over my shoulder. "And while she may not be the typical Fae noble, to us she's better, she's honest, and not trying to use us for her own gain. She's stronger and more special than you think, and that's exactly why we are going to get her back. Ariana has no place in the Court of Crimson. As of this day, she has been exiled. She will remain here in the Court of Frost and if you refuse to house her, you may cast her out, but she will never be welcome in my Court again."

Sparks lit the ends of my mother's hair as she scowled at me. "You are a fool," she snapped. "You would leave The Court of Crimson open to a human attack if you leave to follow that girl."

"That is no longer any of your concern," I said, shouldering past her as I made my way to my brothers. "We can handle our Court ourselves."

I didn't look back as I left the room, feeling Orion and Sorrell following as we made our way to the stables. As Orion disappeared to find stable hands to assist in readying our mounts, I sucked in a lungful of icy air and pushed it out in a rush. Seconds later, I felt the niggling of eyes on me. Turning slightly, I caught a glimpse of the very bitch I'd exiled.

"What do you want?" I asked, calling Ariana from her hiding place.

After a moment, she gave up pretending and slowly slid around the corner, her eyes turned towards the ground.

"Spit it out," Sorrell snapped, just as through with her as I was. "We don't have all day."

"Is it really true?" she asked. "That I won't be allowed back into the Court of Crimson?"

"You put my betrothed at risk, you attempted to kill her, and only by her mercy are you even alive," I growled. "Yes, it is true. If ever you show your face in our Court again, I will have you shackled in silver and then burned at the stake."

Her head jerked up and she took a step forward, her hand reaching out blindly. "Roan—"

Without stopping to think, I took the few steps to reach her, raised my palm, and backhanded her across the face. Ariana fell to the ground, her hand coming up to cover her face as tears tracked down her cheeks. A hollowness filled me. Something twisted and dark. Cress would have been so angry had she seen my actions, and yet, I didn't care.

"Do not speak to me so disrespectfully, peasant," I snapped. "I am a Royal and you are nothing. I am a future King of the Crimson Court and you will address me as such. If I ever see your face again, I can promise you nothing but pain and misery. Your home is now the Court of Frost. You are not welcome anywhere else."

I turned my back on her and walked over to my horse as Orion and two stable hands came around the opposite corner, each with a mount in hand. There wasn't a single feeling of remorse, I noted, as her quiet sobs followed me. Sorrell didn't say a word as we each took our steeds and headed out. A sick sinister feeling coated my every movement and I blinked, turning my nose down and sniffing at myself. But no, I had to be imagining it. Every ounce of hatred I had for Ariana, every modicum of disgust, had finally seeped out of me. It was only my anger that had caused my actions.

Still, my eyes slid towards Orion as he mounted his horse and took the reins. Regardless of my behavior, we had more important things to attend to. Our focus needed to be on getting back to the Court of Crimson and then to the human realm. Cress was waiting.

CHAPTER 3

SORRELL

The Court of Crimson appeared over the hill and, as if the others felt the same renewed sense of urgency at the sight of it, our pace increased. With just the three of us, we'd managed to keep our mounts through the Pass and were now so very close to our Court and our way back to the human realm. Sweat slicked the back of my neck as my mind rolled with thoughts, possibilities, and plans.

How long had Tyr been preparing for this betrayal? His treachery didn't come as a surprise, but ... my gaze slid to Orion on the other side of Roan. Cold fury burned hot inside my core. He would regret his deception, that much I would make sure of.

The front gates of the Court of Crimson opened and I slowed as Roan passed through first, then Orion, and I brought up the back. Roan rode towards the stables and we followed. I slipped from the saddle, handing the reins over to a stable hand without a second thought.

"The Lanuaet," I said as I turned towards the castle's front entrance. Orion and Roan followed behind as we made our way into the front corridor.

"Your majesties!" a familiar voice called out.

"Groffet." Roan stepped forward as the short dwarf hobbled towards us.

"How—" The old man stopped and adjusted the spectacles at the end of his bulbous nose, glancing behind us. "Where is the Changeling?"

"She has been stolen," Orion stated, his voice lowering. I cut a look towards him as the scent of ash and doom intensified in the immediate area.

Groffet's eyes widened and he glanced back over his shoulder as if waiting for something to appear. "Should I tell the..." He let his sentence trail off, but we knew who he meant. Cressida's human friend.

I gritted my teeth. "No," I said with a shake of my head. "We will be moving the castle today. Make sure she remains with you. Do not let the girl out of your sight."

Groffet nodded but remained right where he was. "Do you have the energy to move the castle?" he asked a moment later.

I saw Roan's back stiffen before I felt mine do the same. My jaw clenched. The answer was not an easy one. Truth be told, I wasn't sure if we could or if we did, what the results of the strain on our bodies would be. It didn't matter. We had to get back. We had to find her. Though we'd cut our trip short by traveling with just the three of us on horseback—it had still taken us nearly a day and a half to return. Added to the fact that none of us had slept or eaten much since the Changeling had been taken ... we were not at our most powerful.

"It will happen," Roan stated before pushing past the dwarf. "We will find a way."

With that, he took off. Orion didn't hesitate to follow him, and I was left standing between their retreating backs and Groffet's knowing look. I leveled him with a glare when still he hadn't said anything. "Speak your piece," I commanded. "And then be gone."

He sighed, shaking his head. "If you overexert your strengths—even between the three of you—it may damage your magic abilities," he stated. "You're all still young. You are powerful, but none of you have yet come into your full potential. If you damage your bodies now, you may never reach it."

I knew he was right, loathe as I was to admit it, but it no longer mattered. I would push my body to the brink of death if it meant saving that damn Changeling. She had weaseled her way into our Court, into my throne brothers' beds, and into our lives. When I didn't respond, he heaved another great sigh and turned around to waddle away.

My feet carried me to the Lanuaet chamber where Orion and Roan were already waiting. As soon as I stepped inside, their heads lifted and their eyes met mine.

"We will need replenishment when we get there," I stated as we gathered around the orb above us. It buzzed with barely repressed magical energy. The feel of it was like lightning grazing my skin as I moved closer.

"You may take a lover," Roan grunted as he lifted his arms, "but I will not."

"*No.*" The word barked out of my mouth, harsh and violent. Roan's arms paused and his head turned towards me. He arched one singular brow. "I will take matters into my own hands as I suspect you will as well."

"It will not be enough," Orion said.

No, it wouldn't. Masturbation only did so much for the healing of sexual energy, but then again, I had waited long enough—repressed my attraction to the Changeling long enough—that nothing else would do now. There wasn't a single body within the walls of our Court that I wanted but hers, and I'd finally decided that I would have it or no other.

Orion took a step closer to the Lanuaet. I closed my eyes and lifted my arms. Already, I could feel the orb's need to devour. "To the human realm," I said, reopening them and fixing my gaze on the clouded magical element hovering just out of physical reach. It had all started with this sacred piece of Fae energy. The Lanuaet had landed us in the middle of Amnestia and we'd found who was likely the last of her line. This time, it would bring us back to her or her back to us. Either way, it didn't matter so long as she was within our reach once more.

"To the human realm," they repeated back.

At once, the orb began to glow and spin. The floor beneath our feet trembled and swayed as the castle reacted to the Lanuaet's power. I stood my ground as the world grew fuzzy, my vision blurring into obscurity. Sweat beads slid down my back until the droplets became rivers, soaking through my shirt, making the fabric cling to my skin. My muscles strained and my hearing disappeared completely as my magic was sucked from my every pore.

Pain rocketed up my spine, daggers in my temples. None of it mattered.

None of it but *her*.

CHAPTER 4

CRESS

I heard the footsteps before the keys in the lock. My head jerked up from its resting place upon my knees as the door to my prison swung open. Unfamiliar guards strode inside. I glanced behind them, but there was no Tyr. On shaky legs, I tried to stand. My heart thumped in my chest.

"What's going on?" I demanded. "Why are you here?"

"Turn around," one of them commanded.

"No!" I took a wary step back and glared at them. "Not a chance."

One of them removed a sword and brandished it at me. "We were told to bring you before his Royal Highness. King Felix has commanded that you be presented. He did not say you had to be unharmed. Come with us willingly or else."

I hesitated. "W-why do you want me to turn around?"

"You must be restrained," the second one said, producing a pair of thick metal cuffs.

I swallowed nervously. "Is that silver?"

He nodded. "Of course."

Shit. Shit. Shit. My mind whirled with thoughts. What to do? My eyes darted to the half open door. There was no way I'd

462

be able to make it past them and out the door before they caught me, was there? And even if I did, what could I do? Never in my life had I been inside the King of Amnestia's palace. I didn't know where I was. There were no escape routes in my mind. Only this ever increasing need to flee.

My throat burned as I slowly turned and presented the guards with my back. The sound of scuffed boots thudding against the ground as they approached ratcheted up my fear. For a split second, a thought crossed my mind.

If only Roan or Orion were here. Dear Coreliath, I'd take even Sorrell's grumpy self. A single tear escaped and slid down my cheek as I felt my hands being pulled behind my back and locked into the restraints. Before turning back around, I sniffed hard and turned my face against my shoulder, wiping the evidence of it away. This was not the time for crying.

The guards led me out of the cell I'd been locked in for the last few days. To the right, there was a long, steep staircase. One went ahead and the other lingered at my back. I kept my head facing forward, but took the opportunity to examine my surroundings. Every several feet there was a slit window barely wide enough to fit an arm through, and certainly not a body. They would offer no escape, but they did at least give me a glimpse of the outside world.

Dark gray storm clouds hovered above us. The scent of ash and smoke was on the wind. *What was happening out there?* I wondered. I wasn't given the chance to think about it too long because as we reached the bottom of the stairs, I was pushed towards the right and down an even longer but straight corridor.

My bare feet scraped against the cold ground and I shivered as a chill stole over me. We stopped before twin arching doors made of a deep red wood. I tilted my head at the front of it. Unlike doors I'd seen in both the Court of Crimson and Court of Frost, these had been horribly burned. Yet, it looked like it had been ... purposeful? Because within the burn marks, I could see a scene taking place before me. Like a tapestry or painting but in wood.

A great human King with a sword in one hand and the head of a Fae in the other. The image made me gasp and step back. A heavy hand fell on my shoulder and pushed me forward as the doors were opened and I stumbled under the urging until I fell onto my knees, wincing as the stone beneath cut a gash across one.

The scent of blood lifted to my nostrils and I lifted my head a moment later, meeting the cool, calculating gaze of my kidnapper. Tyr stood to the side with a smirk on his face and his arms crossed. He leaned against the side of the King's throne while the King himself glared down at me as if I were nothing more than a bug who'd made its unfortunate way into his food.

"So," he began. "This is one of the Fae responsible for the chaos in my Kingdom."

I blinked, but before I could respond, Tyr answered. "She is, Your Majesty," he said politely before throwing a wink my way.

Narrowing my gaze on him, I wanted nothing more than to throw him my middle finger or perhaps introduce his balls to my kneecap. Bloodied or not, I bet it would hurt. I turned my face to the King.

"That man is a Fae, too," I stated, nodding towards Tyr. "I'm not bad. I've never hurt anyone. You have no reason to keep me captive."

There was a moment of silence before the King lifted one large bushy eyebrow. "You claim that a member of my Court is a Fae?" he inquired, his voice a low rumble.

I straightened my back, not turning my gaze away. "I do."

He scowled. "How dare you, you vile piece of trash," he snarled.

"It's the truth!" I snapped. "He brought me here through a

portal he created!"

"This man is one of my most trusted advisors. He has been with me for years. I would know if he were a despicable Fae," the King snapped.

"Well, that's obviously not true," I deadpanned. "I mean, he *is* a Fae and yet, you don't believe it. Why would I lie about that?"

"To try and save your own skin of course," he replied.

"What? My own skin? What have I done?" I yelled. "Nothing! I haven't done anything!"

"You are guilty of treason."

I shook my head violently. "You're making a mistake. Sure, okay, yeah, maybe I'm Fae—technically, I'm a Changeling. I was raised with humans—"

"In a convent, yes?" he interrupted me.

My head tipped back as I eyed him with confusion. "Yes," I said. "How did you—"

The King waved his meaty fist and an unfamiliar man clad in armor—like the guards had been—stepped forward, handing him a scroll. "The orphan Cressida," he stated, opening the scroll and reading from its contents. "Over a month ago, I received reports that the village that protected the convent in the hills of my Kingdom had been attacked by a female Fae and she had been chased away, but not after stealing a human child."

Nellie wasn't really a child. Then again, I didn't believe arguing that point would do me any good, but still, I shook my head. "I was raised there!" I insisted. "I didn't even know I was a Fae until the castle appeared!"

"You masqueraded as a human, deceived the people of my Kingdom, and will be sentenced to death." The King's cold eyes lifted and met mine as he snapped the scroll shut. My lips parted in shock.

Death? No. Nononono. Death was not in the plans. "You're making a mistake," I insisted. "I'm not a bad Fae, I'm good—"

"Bah!" He handed the scroll back to his soldier. "There is no such thing as a good Fae."

I frowned. "That's not true!" My hands tightened into fists within my cuffs. My skin grew heated. My breath came in ragged pants as panic began to set in. I strained against them and felt an unfamiliar burning sensation. A fog swirled in my mind and my energy suddenly left me in a rush. So quickly that had it not been for one of the guards reaching forward and clasping my shoulder, I would've fallen over. Turning my cheek, I glanced over my shoulder.

What was happening to me? Why couldn't I think straight?

"I see the silver cuffs are coming in handy," Tyr said with a small chuckle.

I whipped my head back around and stared at him. He'd done this? He knew what silver did to Fae. Wait? This was silver and it was weakening me. Had it happened? Had my powers finally come to the forefront? The physician at the Court of Frost had said my Fae powers were weak, practically nonexistent. Could I ... I considered what to do, but no matter how heated my skin grew, as soon as I felt a tingle of magical energy pour into it, it was quickly washed away by the effect of the silver.

"I'm innocent," I mumbled. "I haven't done anything wrong."

"You are Fae and you are no innocent." The King strode down the steps of his throne until he stood right before me. My head fell back onto my shoulders and I looked up into his older, scarred face. *What had he done to receive those scars?* I wondered. *How many had he killed in his effort to rid the world of Fae?*

It was wrong. Why couldn't he see that? Fae were part of nature. They were neither bad nor good. Just as humans were neither bad nor good.

"You destroyed a large portion of the countryside of my Kingdom, little treacherous Fae girl," he said coldly.

I had? It was growing harder and harder to think.

"In one week's time, you will be presented to the public and at dawn on the seventh day, you will be executed. Your death will mark the final battle between humans and Fae. With the help of my advisor"—my head sank forward and turned until I could see Tyr, who watched me with sinister amusement—"we will finally be rid of your dangerous race and, with your extinction, we will usher in the Age of Mankind."

Genocide. That's what he was talking about. The extinction of an entire race of creatures. The only ones who might escape would be those in Alfheim. Actually … with Tyr on the side of humans, perhaps even they weren't safe. What did he have planned? I had to find out.

"What—" I began, but the King waved his hand, cutting me off.

"Take her away," he ordered.

Hands gripped my arms and jerked me up. I bent over, breathing hard as sweat slid down my temples. An aching started at the top of my spine and ricocheted up through my skull.

"With one of your magical orbs, we will destroy you and your kind," the King called after me as I was pulled from the throne room. "Enjoy your last days on this Earth."

Despite my weakness, I struggled against the guards' grip. My vision blurred. "No!" I yelled. "You can't! He's not human! It's all a trap!"

I argued. I fought. I struggled. But the throne doors closed behind me as I was hauled up and over a man's shoulder and, just before the black creeping at the edges of my vision overtook me completely, I saw the image of a human King with the head of a Fae. My mind replaced the burned portrait of a generic head with that of first Roan's then Orion's and finally Sorrell's.

No matter what, I had to stop this.

CHAPTER 5
ORION

By the time we got back to the Crimson Court, I was ready to throttle anyone who got in my way. We needed to move the castle, so that was what we did, just the three of us, dragging it back to Amnestia. I couldn't lie, it was harder without Cress there.

Well, if I was being honest, everything was harder without her.

Moving the castle seemed to drain us all more than usual, and since we weren't about to go to bed with any of the other Court ladies it meant that it was going to take us a while to recover our power after such a taxing task. We each sat there for a while after we'd landed just trying to gather ourselves together.

"We should check on the human girl," Roan said quietly.

The three of us pushed to our feet and began to make our way to the library. I wasn't sure if it was just me, but the hallways felt so much longer and darker. Even though we were back in Amnestia, we didn't have a plan on how to find Cress, and every time I even thought about it my mind went on the fritz, panic and darkness clouding it.

Finally, the large wooden doors of the library loomed in front of us and my legs almost gave out in relief. The trek from the Lanuaet to the library had never felt so long before. As I looked at my throne brothers, I knew I wasn't the only one feeling the effects of getting the castle out of the Fae realm and back to Amnestia.

When we pushed the doors open my heart stopped as I saw Nellie, in all her human glory, sitting there chatting with a young Fae male. The three of us froze as we each took in the scene before us. Nellie and her Fae companion looked up at us as we entered, the blood draining from the male's face.

"What is he doing here? And with her?" Sorrell said, stabbing a finger in the direction of Nellie and her companion as Groffet came around the desk area.

"I-I-I've helped Groffet in the past, my Lord," the Fae male said, speaking up unexpectedly. From the looks of him, pale and rather scrawny looking, I'd expected him to cower, especially in the face of Sorrell's anger, but he didn't. He may have been a lesser male, but he was brave and stood his ground, something I found impressive.

"Ash is trustworthy. He has helped me on many occasions, and I know he wouldn't betray us or Ms. Nellie over there. He'll keep his mouth shut if he knows what's good for him," Groffet said as he crossed his arms over his chest, daring Sorrell to disagree with him.

Of course none of us did. We were all smarter than that. Disagreeing with Groffet when he felt strongly about something was like yelling into the wind. It might be heard, but it didn't stick around. Nor did it change a damn thing.

"Fine," I growled before either of the others could say anything more.

Roan stepped in and leveled both Groffet and the male Fae, Ash, with a dark look. "We need to speak with the…" He flicked a glance between them and surprisingly, instead of saying "human" he spoke the girl's name. "We must speak with Nellie."

"What's wrong?" she asked, and then she seemed to realize something. Her eyes roamed between us, scanning for something—Cress—and when her search came up empty, a worried frown turned her lips down. "Where's Cress?" she asked.

A dark, sinister feeling stabbed me in the gut, and having felt this particular emotion many times before, I could easily place it. Guilt. The vile creature clawed at my insides, laughing as it reminded me that this girl's friend, someone we had—*someone I had*—sworn to protect had not returned with us. Nellie's gaze pleaded with us, as if she could sense the onslaught of bad news and still hoped that her instincts were wrong.

It shredded something inside me to confirm her obvious fears. Except, I didn't get the chance. My answer was interrupted by another.

"She was taken." Sorrell's voice was icy as the temperature of the room dropped. A wave of cold air washed outwardly from his figure, visible only in the way Nellie shivered and stepped closer to her newfound friend. His anger was palpable.

"What do you mean t-taken?" Nellie stuttered, eyes round, luminous. Lost. I gritted my teeth when she shook her head and seemed to suck all of that fear back inside herself as she took a step towards us, a brighter fury coming forth. "Where is she?" she demanded. "What's happened to her?" Were she Fae, I suspect, the fire in her eyes might rival even Roan's. Unfortunately for her, however, she was not. The girl possessed no magic, and in our Court, she was nothing but a guest—the guest of a lost Changeling who had been stolen from us—and she was precariously close to the edge of both of my throne brothers' tolerance for humans.

"The fault is mine," I said quietly. "It was my brother that took her." My blood brother. The wicked soul that he was.

Cruel. Senseless. And soon to be very, very dead. I sucked in a breath before continuing. "Tyr is using Cress to get to me, *to us*," I corrected, "and because of my inability to predict his behavior, she's now paying the price." Nellie's eyelashes flickered as she stared at me in cold shock. "We will figure out how to find her," I assured the human girl. "Of that, you can be sure. I will find Cress and I will bring her back." I turned to Groffet and swelled with breath as I spoke to him directly. "And I have come to request your assistance with this matter."

"It's *not* your fault," Roan snapped before Groffet could reply.

Blinking, I glanced in his direction only to find him glaring at me with a burning rage. Of course he would not want to blame me. Roan, for all his faults and arrogance, would not blame me for what was so clearly the result of my failures. Cress's abduction, however, *was* my fault. Tyr was *my* brother. Everything he did was to get to me, or to get around me, or to torture me somehow. Why? I didn't know. All I knew was that it had been this way since I was young. Perhaps it was simply how Midnight Fae were, and I was the peculiar one for not falling in line. I never should have let him see how much Cress meant to me.

When I returned my gaze to the human, Nellie was watching me, her eyes glistening in the low light of the library as silent tears streamed down her face. "What's he going to do to her?" she asked shakily.

I opened my mouth to respond, but nothing came out. There were so many cruel things Tyr was capable of. Things I, myself, had experienced, but for some reason when I tried to think of them—it only made me sick. I didn't want to tell this girl the horrors I'd known at the hand of my brother, and the possible torment Cress could be going through even as we spoke.

Roan saved me. "He enjoys mental games," he said. "But

Cress is strong. She knows we would never leave her with him. We're going to get her back before anything can happen to her, so don't worry about it."

"Something bad has already happened," Nellie replied. "Cress is gone!" Fat tears began to slide from the girl's eyes as she inhaled trembling breaths, looking like one strong push would break her into a million pieces. I couldn't say I blamed her. I didn't. The mere sight of her, so distressed and horrified over her friend's disappearance made the sick feeling in my gut even more painful. I closed my eyes and relished in that pain. I deserved it.

When I opened my eyes again, anger and despair warred on the human's face. Her words, however, had pushed Roan too far. The icy chill of the room faded as Roan's rage grew hotter.

"We will get her back," he insisted. "She will be fine. Cress will return and when she does, she will become my bride. I will ensure that nothing and no one ever thinks to take her from my side again."

"Our side," Sorrell muttered a beat later. No one agreed, but neither did any of us deny the statement. The fact remained that Cress had become our center in a short amount of time. She was wild and reckless. A breath of fresh air that we so desperately craved and needed after having been locked in our Courts for too long. Perhaps … a thought occurred to me. Perhaps the hatred between humans and Faekind had finally reached its peak. Gods knew we were tired of the war. It could not go on forever.

But before we could focus on that, we needed to get her back. Cress was our utmost priority.

"Bride?" Nellie stared at Roan in shock, her mouth agape. "You're going to marry her?" She didn't even comment on Sorrell's quiet statement. Perhaps she hadn't heard.

Roan nodded once. "Yes. Cress is Fae whether or not she

was raised by your people, she is ours now, and ours she will remain."

The Fae male, Ash, rushed forward and took Nellie's hands in his before he turned her to face him. "The Princes will figure it out. I'm sure they are just as upset as you are. Trust them to get your friend back," he said quickly, his gaze flicking up to us as if to sense whether or not his words were accepted. When his eyes landed on mine, I nodded once to assure him.

Nellie looked up into his face, her tears falling harder, and then, with a surprising amount of strength, she crushed herself against the male's front and openly sobbed. Without a second thought, Ash scooped her up so she was cradled in his arms, her own tangled around his neck as she buried her face in his chest and cried. After a beat, he lifted his gaze from her head to the rest of us. "May I please take her back to her chambers?" he asked gently. "I promise to stay with her and ensure she rests, if it's permitted."

Groffet was the one that answered. "I think that's a sane idea," he said with a huff. "Take the girl back and watch over her, Ash." The male nodded and hurried from the room, bowing slightly to the rest of us as he passed by. "Now then." Groffet lifted his head and narrowed his eyes at the three of us. "Come, let us propose a strategy to retrieve the Changeling."

The three of us—Sorrell, Roan, and I—followed him as we moved towards the library's main open area. Roan immediately plopped down next to the fire. Sorrell wandered over to the open window, and I took my place in one of the three nook seats set within the walls surrounding the space. With the wall at my back and the open space in front of me, I felt marginally enclosed, as if I were sitting within the wall, itself, watching the scene before me even as I channeled my inner thoughts to calm and focus.

"The Changeling was taken," Groffet said the words, but they were not a question.

Regardless, Roan answered. "Yes."

Groffet nodded and hobbled over to a table stacked high with tomes and volumes. He grunted and muttered beneath his breath as he searched, pulling book after book and checking their contents. If he found one satisfying, he set it on the ground and if it wasn't, he tossed it.

"Let's see," he began. "You could try and track her? Scry for her?"

"Already tried that." Sorrell's tone was biting as though he was insulted that Groffet would suggest something so simple.

"And what about the Midnight Heir?" Groffet asked, one bushy brow rising as he glared back at the Prince of Frost. "Did you attempt to track him?" Silence. Groffet huffed out a breath before selecting a particularly hefty looking volume and moving over to the three of us. "If he's the one that took her maybe tracking him will lead you to her?"

"Tyr has protections around him at all times to prevent that from happening," I said. "It always drove our mother insane…" That is, before she actually *had* gone insane.

Groffet harrumphed at that statement, slamming the book he carried on the ground in the center of the space and flipping it open. He paged through the contents. More muttering emanated from the small, old man, but none of it was sensical. Finally, he grunted and stopped flipping the pages. His head turned from side to side and after a moment, he lifted it.

"What about a dream spell?" I didn't have to look at the others to know that they had perked up some. Groffet noticed our captured attentions and nodded. "Yes, I think that might be good."

Sorrell took a step into the center, his arms falling away from his chest. "Someone cast one on me while we were at the Court of Frost," he announced.

Roan growled. "Why didn't you say something?" he demanded.

Sorrell didn't look at him as he replied. "I assumed it was my mother. She used to do things like that when I was a child," he explained. "It was her way of … teaching me a lesson. To say she was unhappy about Cress's presence in our Court would be an understatement. Though she didn't show her irritation as well as the Crimson Queen, my mother is not our ally."

"Do you think she could've helped Tyr?" I asked, curious. I doubted it, but I wanted to hear his response.

Sorrell's eyes found mine and he shook his head. "No. She doesn't approve of Cressida, but she has never once trusted a member of the Midnight Court. She wouldn't be working with Tyr. I suspect he's working on his own."

I nodded.

"Regardless," Roan said, bringing us back to the main point, "what would a dream spell do? We can get into contact with her, but what if she doesn't understand what's happening? Dream spells aren't always easy to perform."

"It still has potential," Groffet replied. "And whoever goes will need to be very careful with her. She is still unused to Fae magic. Treat her as though her magic is still in its infantile stage."

The only issue that remained was that none of us were particularly skilled with dream magic. Dream magic wasn't forbidden, but it also wasn't encouraged, for a reason. It was dangerous. Dreamscapes were fickle and confusing places. One wrong turn down a dark memory or a mind that was too clouded, and the caster might end up trapped in the other person's mind.

Forever.

The decision, though, was easy. If there was a chance we could get into contact with Cress, an opportunity to save her, then there was no real question as to if we would do it or not. I lifted my gaze and met each one of my brothers' before centering my attention on Groffet. "I'll do it," I announced. "And you're going to teach me, old man."

CHAPTER 6

CRESS

The feeling of arms holding me awoke my senses. Fast. Running. Trees blurred past. The arms that held me, however, were warm and I felt ... safe.

Why did I feel safe? *I wondered.* Who was holding me? Was it one of the guys? No. It didn't feel like one of them. The arms encircling my frame were much more slender than any of them. They felt almost feminine. And whoever it was that held me, did so against a soft chest. I tried to open my eyes but found that when I did everything appeared in dark and light tones of blacks, whites, and grays. Like the whole world had been leached of color.

"How much farther?" a soft, female voice asked, her tone shaky and ... scared? It was hard to hear. The scent of something pungent and something sweet permeated the air around me and there was a sudden rush of air as if a small wind tunnel had opened up and sucked me and the woman holding me through it.

"Not much farther," a male voice answered. He was close by, the sound of his voice soothing, but there was no disguising that he, too, was uncertain of something. His tone, although strong, was tight—as if pulled taut from some sort of strong emotion.

"Henri," the woman called. "Henri!"

"*Keep going, Marcella. We have to. They're tracking us.*"

"*We can't keep running,*" the woman said, her fear much stronger now as she slowed to a walk and then stopped altogether. "*Not with her.*"

Who was 'her?' I wanted to ask. The woman above me sniffled and something wet hit my forehead and slid down the side of my face. Why was she crying? For some reason, I didn't like hearing this woman's pain. It made something in my chest tighten. I wanted to tell her everything would be okay even if I didn't know exactly what was going on.

"*Marci.*" The man's voice grew closer and then the warmth I felt being cuddled into the woman's breast was increased as he wrapped his arms around both her and me. "*It's going to be okay, but we have to keep moving.*"

The woman continued to cry and other than a few breathy gasps, she kept her pain and sorrow and fear to a quiet murmur. When she finally regained the ability to speak, she pushed back against the man with one arm. My eyes flickered between the two of them. I could make out their heads, bent over mine, but not their features. It was as if someone had blurred out what they looked like and left only the vaguest of outlines for me to draw information from. What I could tell, though, was that they were both looking down at me.

"*We have to leave her behind,*" the woman said.

Silence. Then, "*Are you sure?*" The man sounded strained as if it cost him to even say the words, to even consider the woman's claim.

The woman shook her head. "*No. I'm not sure of anything anymore,*" she whispered in the darkness of the forest. "*I thought we could trust the Courts. I thought our friends would survive. I've thought so many things, Henri. I don't trust my instincts anymore. But I think ... this time, maybe ... her best chance is away from us. With the humans.*"

That's when it hit me. Who these people really were. What this was. It wasn't a dream. It was a memory. Why had I recalled this now? What was the point of this memory surfacing after so long? I *couldn't make sense of the reason, but the truth of it could be felt in the fires of my veins. I knew these two people. These were my parents. My real parents. It all became too much for me. I opened my mouth— to say what, I didn't know—but before I could say anything, a horrifying squalling noise erupted from my throat.*

"Oh, no, my dear." Marci—the woman, my mother—shushed me, rocking me in her arms back and forth. "Oh, you poor thing. I know, my darling. It's scary, but trust me—trust us—we love you. We only want what's best for you."

"We want her to live," Henri, my father, said. "And if we're going to do that, we need to find a place to leave her, now, before they catch up with us."

"The humans," she said. "They'll take her in."

"We can't say what she is," Henri replied.

My mother's head shook. "No, we won't even see them." She started moving again. "There's an abbey not far from here. We can leave her there. On their doorstep. The nuns of Coreliath will take her in."

"Hold on." The sound of heavy footsteps stomping back to the two of us sounded in my ears. "If we're going to do this, my love, we have to protect her from them as well. The humans will take her in, but she'll start showing signs of her magic soon. We have to..." He trailed off, the hoarseness of his voice becoming too much for him.

"Yes," my mother finished for him. "You're right." Another tear fell onto my face. "Alright then." She reached out and took his hand, drawing him closer, once more, to the two of us. "Then let us cast it."

A wide, masculine palm landed gently on my cheek. My father's thumb stroked down my smooth skin. "Our little Princess," he murmured. "How I wish things had been different for you. How difficult your life will be. I hope one day, you can forgive us for this."

Forgive them? What were they going to ... I screamed as I felt something moving in me as they began to speak. Their words were hard to understand. I didn't hear them with my ears but in my mind as something wove into my body, beneath my skin. Far beyond the recesses of my mind, I heard a door slam. Was that real or was it my imagination?

Everything grew heavy. My limbs. My eyelids. Darkness encroached. A weight landed on my chest, and suddenly my mother's arms fell away and I descended into a dark oblivion.

"Cress?" a voice called out to me in the darkness. "Cress, are you there, sweetheart?" I recognized the sound. It was someone I knew. Someone I cared for. Who? Where was I?

Two strong arms came around me, lifting me back out of the shadows, and I gasped as my eyes popped open. Orion's face appeared over me and as I sat up and looked around, I realized my memory had faded. No longer was I in the forest with the man and woman. I was sitting in a stone room, not unlike my cell except there was no furniture and no door. None of that mattered right then because Orion was there!

"Orion!" I launched myself into his arms, clinging tightly. He returned my embrace without reserve, his arms banding around me as he squeezed me right back. "Oh, I'm so glad you're here," I whispered thickly against his chest.

"Of course I'm here," he said after a moment. "I'll always come for you when you need me."

I let myself have a few more moments with him, but when I realized that this wasn't exactly reality either and it wasn't possible for Orion to be locked in a stone room with no entrance with me, I pulled back. "What's going on?" I asked. "What are you—"

"Cress." He stopped me, his dark eyes looking down at me through even darker lashes.

I didn't need to say it, but I did nonetheless. "This isn't real," I whispered. "Is it?"

He shook his head. "This is merely a dream. I'm here because we're searching for you, Sorrell, Roan, and I. I need you to give me some information about where you are. Anything can help. Do you remember—"

"I know where I am," I interrupted him quickly.

His brows rose in surprise as if he hadn't expected that. "You do?"

I nodded. "I'm in Amnestia," I said, and then with a sharp inhale, I told him the next part. "I'm in the King's prison tower," I admitted. "Tyr's working with King Felix. The King has no idea that he's a Fae. Orion, it's bad. Tyr's planning to let the humans and Fae destroy each other. I don't know how long he's been planning this, but there's going to be a battle—"

"Shhhh." Orion's heavy hand stroked down the side of my face as he quieted me. "It's going to be okay." His eyes were sharp when they connected with mine. "Go slow. Tell me everything, and then when you wake, know that we are coming for you."

"He's going to execute me," I said, my lips trembling. I hadn't wanted to admit it before, but sitting here, in Orion's lap, my fear was impossible to disguise. I couldn't deny it or hide it any longer. "On the seventh day of my imprisonment," I continued. "At dawn. Orion ... it's coming soon."

"No," he growled the word, palming the back of my head and bringing me closer until his forehead pressed to mine. "We will not let that happen."

"But—" He didn't let me finish. Orion's lips crashed down hard on mine and he swallowed my words, draining my fear with his mouth. His tongue moved against mine and I felt myself caving to his ministrations. My whole body rocked into his and before I knew it, my fingers were sinking into the silky dark strands of his hair. I clambered onto his lap, sliding my legs around his waist until the familiar feel of his cock pressed against my core.

Orion pulled away long enough to emit another growl as he pushed his hips up into me, as if he couldn't even help himself. "I'm sorry, Cress," he said, his voice trembling. "So fucking sorry. I will find you. I will save you. Believe me, sweetheart. I will—"

"I do," I said, cutting him off.

Orion tilted his head down, closed his eyes, and kept going as though I hadn't spoken. "When we free you," he said. "I'll leave." Ice washed through my veins and I reared back, shocked. "I'll make sure you're safe and then I'll make sure I'm never the cause for something like this again."

Anger and pain sliced into my chest. I pressed my lips together and fought back the sting of tears as water filled my eyes. "Orion." I cupped his face. "Orion, look at me."

His eyes opened.

Sucking in a deep breath, I pressed my lips to his in a soft, feather-light touch. And that's where I held them as I spoke in a soft whisper. "Your brother's actions are not yours," I urged. "You are not your brother. This is not your fault."

"I—"

"No," I snapped, cutting him off. I wouldn't let him say it again. I couldn't bear to hear it. "Stop it. Don't pity yourself. Don't act the martyr. Just get off your ass and come get me because, Orion, I'm scared. I'm scared and I fucking need you. Please don't leave me."

His hands clenched against my sides as if he wanted to pull away, but something—hopefully words— was preventing him from doing so. "I love you." The words were so quiet, I almost didn't hear them. They were like the sound of a bird's wings beating against the wind. There with each breath he took, but so natural, a person could forget its existence.

"I..." A tear broke through the surface and slid down the outside of my cheek. "I love you, too." I pushed him back. "Now hurry up and come get me."

He nodded, his eyes meeting mine. "I will," he said "We will. We're coming, Cress. Just hang on."

Another tear slid down my opposite cheek and Orion's eyes tracked it. "Okay," I whispered. "I'll wait."

I leaned forward, just wanting one last kiss. One more to hold me until I could feel his arms around me—for real.

The kiss never came.

CHAPTER 7

ORION

Lips untaken were the most delicious of fruit, and that last kiss would have been the sweetest, had I not been ripped away. Dream magic was fickle like that. It was dangerous and never quite as easy as it sounded once one was encompassed in another's mind. The user never knew how long they had or when they'd be snapped back to their own reality.

My heart seized as I came back to myself in the present. Sweat dripped from my pores and slid against my temples. The urge to go to her was beyond anything I'd ever felt before. I counted each breath I took as I fought against those instincts.

I hadn't gotten the chance to kiss her, but even if I had, one single kiss wouldn't have been enough. I needed more—the weight of her in my hands, the warmth of her body pressed against mine, the scent of her filling my nose. I craved it all. Despite coming back to the world of awareness, without her, all of my senses felt dulled. But my objective had been fulfilled. We now knew where she was. The darkness that had been haunting the edges of my vision receded slightly.

Breathing in and out through my nose, air flowed into my lungs and left without leaving me feeling like I was breathing in jagged pieces of glass. The dream magic dispersed and the darkness was pushed back as I recalled the way she'd looked when she'd seen me. The beauty of her sunshine colored hair and those wide eyes. *How was it that in the course of only a few short months, I'd fallen for her as hard as I had?*

When I finally opened my eyes, the library was dark, but I was not alone. Roan and Sorrell waited just a few paces away, watching me with their brows lowered and a deeply rooted concern in their expressions. Unlike them, I could see in the darkness—it was where I'd been born and it was where I belonged. Fires flared to life, illuminating the room, as Groffet lit a few candles. I forced myself into a sitting position, reaching up and wiping the sweat from my brow.

Groffet's little body waddled to another part of the room as he continued to light the rest of the candles along the walls. Roan grunted. "Enough," he snapped, and suddenly all of the candles in the room flared to life.

The old man shot him a look that—had anyone else attempted to deliver the same harsh glare, they'd find themselves in iron chains in the dungeons. Groffet, though, was far too valuable and he knew it. Roan drew all eyes to him as he pushed away from the wall. "Well?" he demanded. "How did it go?"

Three pairs of eyes settled on me expectantly. I opened my mouth to speak and coughed. Dry and hoarse, my throat felt as though I'd not drunk water in ages. Groffet hurried over and picked up a pitcher, pouring me a glass before handing it over and stepping back. I drained the liquid, gasping in relief. Dream magic had so many irritating side effects, but I should count my blessings that I hadn't gotten lost and ended up sleeping for months, years, or worse. I should count myself lucky that I hadn't ended up dead.

"Orion," Roan said. "Did you find her?" His leg bounced up and down in front of him as though he was struggling to restrain himself. He ran his hand through his hair and pushed it back, away from his face, squashing some of the smaller flames that had flickered to life as he spoke.

"I found her, but we have a problem," I said. The hoarseness was not yet gone and I had to stop and swallow around the crusty feeling in the back of my mouth. *Problem* was an underestimation of what we faced. We had a fucking catastrophe on our hands.

"But she's alive?" Roan asked.

"Yes." I coughed again and again, had to take water from Groffet, before the feeling of being suffocated by sand and dust finally receded.

"Get on with it," Sorrel snapped. "Where is she?"

"She's being held prisoner." How could I explain the rest? The words stuck in my mind, right on the tip of my tongue. I turned my gaze down as I clutched the sides of the small settee I'd laid upon before passing into the spell. Wood creaked under my fingers as I clenched hard. "Tyr is with the human King. She's being kept in a tower within the castle." Had Tyr not considered that we would find her? I wondered. Or was he planning on it? I couldn't say. I didn't know what he was thinking at all.

"She's alive, though. We can save her as long as she's still breathing."

I hated to destroy the relief in Roan's voice, but it was necessary. I lifted my head and met his gaze, letting him feel the weight of my stare. "Tyr is antagonizing relations between Fae and the humans. The King's planning a battle of some kind."

"Like the Queens…" Sorrel said, his gaze straying away as he considered my words.

The worst part had yet to be spoken. "They're not just holding her," I said. "They're planning to execute her on the seventh day of her imprisonment."

A brief echo of silence descended and then all of their wrath broke loose. Fires erupted across Roan's scalp at the same time Sorrell's head snapped to the side and the roaring heat of my Crimson brother's fire was doused by the icy chill of his anger.

"He's going to execute her?" Sorrell roared. He stormed forward, grabbing me by the front of my shirt. His fingers clenched into the fabric and I could feel icicles forming in my lungs as he breathed in my face. "Next time," he hissed, "lead with that."

"What the fuck are we going to do?" Roan panted, his fires burning bright and fizzling out as the icy coat that was taking over the room lingered in the air above us.

"We don't have much time," I said as Sorrell released me and allowed me to stand.

"We have to move the Court again. We need to get to her. We cannot fail."

I agreed. Cress needed us, all of us.

Roan gritted his teeth and turned his back on us. His long legs ate up the distance as he paced back and forth. Sweat collected on the back of my neck and spilled down my spine with every pass he made near me. I could feel the burning fire of his emotions—untamed, uncontrolled. Wild—like him and the depth of his feeling for a unique little Changeling.

"That's the problem, though, isn't it? How are we going to move the Court again to be close enough to the King's castle to rescue her if we're all drained? Gods, how are we going to keep it hidden from the humans?" Sorrell argued. "The very second we land in Amnestia, they'll be on us like flies on cow shit." He shook his head. "We need to strategize."

He was right, we did need to strategize, but I couldn't, not when my mind was filled not just with Cress's smile, but with my own fear. I closed my eyes and recalled the image of her just before it had slipped away. In my mind's eye, I saw her before me once more. Her face was hardly illuminated, most of it cast in shadow but I could still see the way her lips trembled as she told me of her impending execution. It wouldn't happen. I would not let it.

My eyes opened. "I will return," I said abruptly.

"Orion, wait! What about—" I didn't stay to hear anymore. The doors slammed against the stone wall as I pushed out into the corridor. I couldn't take the chance that they wouldn't allow me this time—time that I very much needed. My footsteps sped up until I was well out of range.

She had been in my arms, and though I knew it had just been a fantasy, it had still felt real, and it had felt like a piercing blade through my chest to be ripped away from her again. My brothers only had to suffer through that once. It was so much worse the second time. I hadn't realized it would be like reopening an old wound and infecting it with poison. That poison slowly seeped into my mind—telling me all sorts of horrible thoughts.

Would we get to her in time? What if we were too late? What if? What if? What if?

My legs moved faster and faster, as if I could outrun those questions. I wove through the halls and up and down stairs as I headed for the one place that was mine—not part of the Castle that I shared with the others, not a public area or somewhere that anyone could simply intrude—but my own safe haven. And the first place where I had taken Cress.

The door loomed in front of me and I reached out, shoving the wood as I slammed into my chambers, turned, and locked the door. Breath was released from my chest like a cork being pulled from a wine bottle. Relief—if only for a brief moment—touched me. And then there was nothing but anger.

I took two steps into the chamber, turned, and slammed my fist into the door. My knuckles split and pain radiated up my arm, but nothing could compare. Nothing could dampen my rage at this whole situation. Cress's abduction. The impending execution. Tyr.

Never before had I felt the same darkness that I knew was in him make itself known in me. My brother was a monster, but for years, I'd simply let it lie. He was my brother—my blood. A part of me thought that perhaps if I never admitted it, I wouldn't have to claim that piece of myself. Because as true as it was, his blood and mine were the same. His powers and mine were connected.

If he wanted to destroy the Fae and the humans then he would. And perhaps I wouldn't have cared as much as I did had it not been for his involving Cress. Whatever he had planned, it was no good, I knew that. His anger at me for forsaking the Midnight Court had caused this and therefore, I had caused this. But Tyr was smart enough to know that in taking Cress, he had earned himself no reprieve. There would be repercussions. We would come for her.

Pulling my hand away from the door, I stared down at my bruised and bleeding knuckles even as my magic worked to heal the minor damage. A heavy breath left me and I headed for the stairs, tipping my head back as my garden came into view. The very garden where I'd first lain her down and made love to her. Halfway into the garden area, my legs gave out and I crashed to the floor. Exhaustion hit me, seeping into my bones. When my hand came out to steady my weary frame, I realized that as much as my magic was trying to close the wounds—I was depleted.

I needed to replenish my magic's source. I needed to *fuck*.

But there were no women to have. No other could make me even hard enough to get the job done save for one and she was far from my grasp. My fingers clenched and scraped against the floor as I turned and laid back. No, this was a solo job. Was it as good as sharing my magical energy with another? Of course not. But it was better than nothing.

I brought up the memory of the two of us together, on that first night. My lips twitched as I recalled her nervousness. The shimmer of her sunshine hair around her shoulders as she had looked up at me with such fascination. Such a funny little creature, our Changeling. Who would have known she would come to mean so much to each of us?

My hands slipped to the waistband of my pants. I pushed them down and out of the way, raising my hips to aid the process along. I remembered the feel of Cress's soft skin against mine as she had sat astride me, grinding her pussy against my cock.

I palmed myself, gripping my shaft and slowly working my hand up and down as I let my memories and imagination run free.

My hands touched her thighs, slowly tracing upward as I held her in place for my cock to push against her folds. I could feel her heat through her clothing, and I wanted more. The soft fabric of her dress bunched in my hands and I pulled, tearing it away from her form, revealing her to me.

"You ruined another dress! This is why I wear pants. Less likely to get them torn off," she said with a huff. The smile at the end let me know she didn't really mind though.

"Maybe I'll have to start tearing your pants off you, as well, then." I grinned as the top of the dress fell away. Roan and Sorrell were there with us. Their mouths descended on each side of her neck and her head fell back in pleasure as a groan escaped her perfect lips.

I pushed up onto my elbows and sucked one of her nipples into my mouth, flicking it with my tongue and grazing it with my teeth until it was as hard as stone under my lips, then I did the same thing to the other. Her hips began to buck and grind against me and her breathing sped until I knew she was already on the edge of her first orgasm.

When I pulled away she whimpered at the loss of my touch which only made my cock throb harder. I slid my hands under her hips and lifted her slightly until the head of my cock pressed against the wet heat of her folds. I eased myself into her inch by inch and relished the hot, vice-like grip her pussy had on my cock.

Her moan as I filled her almost made me lose it right then and there, like it always did. I had to sit still for a moment, even with her squirming on top of me, as my throne brothers teased her. Finally, the tight sensation I felt right before I came passed and I ground my hips up against her, making her release a throaty moan.

I began to move against her, thrusting up into her heated core with ever increasing speed until the sound of skin smacking against skin was the only thing that filled my ears. My body ached as I filled her over and over again, needing release.

Roan's hand slid down her stomach and dipped between us, and parted her folds so he could circle her clit. His mouth dropped from her neck to the nipple that was closest to him. The pink, rosy bud disappeared into his mouth as Sorrell mimicked his action on the other side.

Cress's brows drew together and I felt the inner walls of her body tightening around my cock as we all pushed her over the edge. She screamed and her body clenched around my own, triggering my orgasm, my seed spilling into her heated core.

Except it wasn't her core at all, it was just my hand. I felt a faint buzz of magic in my veins and knew that this would only be the beginning if we wanted to move the castle again. I'd give myself a brief respite before round two, knowing that I'd do whatever I had to for us to get Cress back safely.

CHAPTER 8
CRESS

My eyes cracked open, but for several long moments, all I saw was gray and blurs. My head felt like a weight had been pressing down on me for ages. My limbs felt the same. A groan bubbled up past my lips as I forced my body to the side, turning and leaning over the threadbare cot and dry heaving onto the ground. Nothing escaped my lips but spittle and gagging noises.

I closed my eyes and breathed through my nose, trying to repress the urge to heave again. There was nothing in my stomach. The only thing that came up was bile and I didn't feel like going through the burn of that. Keeping my eyes shut, I crawled off of the cot and pressed my cheek against the cool stone floor.

Sweat collected against my skin and dried there. I couldn't say how long I remained like that. It could've been minutes or hours. The sound of keys jangling in the locks of my prison roused me some time later and I peeked my eyes open, sitting up and leaning my back against the cot as an unfamiliar soldier walked in carrying a tray.

I eyed it with trepidation. *Were they really feeding a prisoner meant to die? Or were they trying to advance the process by poisoning me?* My stomach rumbled with hunger nonetheless. I looked up to the guard. He was clad in leather armor and cautious as he moved towards me with the tray.

"Here." He tossed the tray to the ground in front of me and I winced when the edge smacked into my toes. The bowl that'd been sitting on the top of it, trembled and tipped over, whatever gruel that they'd slopped into it spilling out onto the ground. I didn't care. My eyes weren't on the bowl. They were on the hunk of bread to the side. It looked a little stale, but there were no mold spots.

The guard, however, didn't turn around and walk out like I expected him to. I lifted my eyes back to his and only then did he speak. "You should be grateful," he spat at me. "His Majesty shouldn't even be feeding a vile creature such as you."

"Vile creature?" I repeated the words, confused, before I realized he meant a Fae. "I'm not a vile creature," I snapped. "I'm a person and I have a name. It's Cress."

He scoffed, his head rearing back, but his eyes stayed on me. It took a second for me to put together why he was still in the room. Despite his harsh words, he was curious. Growing up in the convent, I'd always been told similar things about Fae—that they were faithless, disloyal, and dangerous. I'd never really paid attention, but that was mostly because I'd seen, firsthand, how some of the nuns had gone against their very own teachings to display the same accusations they hurled at others.

"What makes me so bad?" I asked the man, reaching for the tipped bowl on the tray and setting it upright.

"You're Fae," he replied.

I waited a beat and when he didn't say anything more, I tipped my head at him. "And that makes me intrinsically bad?" I asked.

His eyes flashed with anger. "I know how the Faekind are," he gritted out, hanging over me with a malevolent appearance.

"Oh? If you're so knowledgeable about them," I snapped back, "then tell me what you know. What kind of Fae am I? I've never really been told—there's a lot of speculation, but no answers."

The guard crossed his arms over his chest. "I will not stand for your trickery."

"Trickery?" I shook my head. "I just asked you a question." I reached for the bread as my stomach rumbled again, the feeling of not having eaten in a long while finally clawing at my insides. "Don't blame me if you can't answer it."

"I will not fall for your spells!"

I rolled my eyes as I tore off a bite of the bread and sniffed it before popping it into my mouth. It wasn't nearly as good as the delicious rolls the pixies brought me. "If I was capable of casting a spell, don't you think I'd use it to get myself out of here?" I asked, chewing loudly as I leveled him with one of my 'are you serious?' looks. "What's your name, anyway?" I couldn't really talk to this guy without knowing his name. I'd already introduced myself. It was a little rude that he hadn't reciprocated.

"I'm called Geoffrey."

"Well, Geoffrey," I tore off another piece as I finished swallowing the lump of soggy bread in my mouth. "Sorry to break it to you, but I'm innocent."

His arms unfolded to his sides and he stepped forward until his booted foot kicked at the edge of my tray. "Liar!" he exclaimed. "You are Fae. The King's advisor—"

"Whoa, whoa, whoa!" I said quickly. I reached back and heaved myself up onto the cot, but something about my legs felt funny—was I still weak from that dream I had of Orion? —I shook my head. I needed to worry about what was in front of me right now. Orion would inform the others of my predicament. They'd do something. Soon. I returned my attention to the man in front of me. "I never said I wasn't

Fae." He stopped moving, and I continued. "I said I was innocent."

Geoffrey's eyes followed my movements as I finished eating the bread. "No Fae is truly innocent," he finally replied.

I frowned. I had yet to see them, but I had to assume there were Fae children. I'd been a child once, myself. "Of course there are innocent Fae," I told him. "Just like you, Fae have babies. There are those who hate this war just as much as we do."

"Fae hate war?" The sound that he made was decisively not amused. "Fae live for war." This time when he looked at me, it was less of a stare and more like he was seeing through me. Into another place. Into another time. And the expression on his face made my chest hurt.

"Have you ever seen a Fae spew fire?" he asked, but before I could answer, he continued talking. "I have seen the beasts that they are. They can turn an entire battlefield into ash in a second if they're so inclined. The only reason they even put up with this war is because it amuses them. They love it. They crave it."

"That's not true!" I burst out. "They hate war just as much as we do!" How could I make him understand? It's not humans or Fae. It's Tyr! "Your King has no idea what's happening!" I confessed in a rush of breath. "His advisor is a Fae. Tyr is—"

I didn't see the slap coming until it was too late, but I certainly felt it as the back of his gloved knuckles smacked into my cheek and sent me sprawling. My foot tripped over the wooden bowl still sitting upon the tray on the ground and the rest of the gruel went flying, chunks of it hitting my leg as I fell. Heat radiated from my cheek and for several long beats of silence, all I could do was sit there. Shocked … confused … angry.

A heat built within me, sliding through my limbs. It infused my very soul.

"You are nothing but a disgusting liar!" Geoffrey spat at me. A bit of his spittle landed on my cheek, and a sizzling sound reached my ears. I blinked and lifted my palm to my cheek— the same cheek he'd backhanded. My hand was glowing—it was dim, barely there, but visible. As if a light had been turned on beneath my skin. "Our King is great! He is going to be the one to save us! You and your kind should never have been brought into existence. I curse the Gods who created you for they are not the same who created man!"

Geoffrey's words flew out at a great speed. So loud that they echoed in my mind. I heard them but didn't comprehend each word until several seconds after it was spoken. I was still too shocked. I'd been raised by humans my whole life. Up until a few short months ago, I'd thought I was human, but never had I suffered this kind of hatred in another creature as he so obviously did.

Not even the nuns. Some had been cruel. Downright uncaring to an orphan with nowhere else to go, but never before had I hated another person. Ariana was the first—I hated her—but not in the same way this man hated Fae.

As I raised my head and slowly got off the floor, I listened to him spew his anger and all I saw in him was sadness. *Why was there so much sorrow emanating from him? Why did it pierce me so?*

The louder he screamed, the more I felt it. Until it was as if a thousand knives were stabbing into my skin. *Stop!* I wanted to cry out. *Please! It hurts!*

I didn't know what led me to reach for him, but it was intrinsic knowing—I had to touch him. Or else something bad would happen. He didn't even see it coming. One moment he was there, screaming his lungs out, and then my fingers had barely brushed the side of his arm.

Geoffrey froze, his lips parted, but no words came out. His eyes dropped down to where I touched him and they widened when he realized that my skin was illuminated. It wasn't enough. My arm rose, further and further, until I felt flesh against the inside of my palm. The side of his neck and then his cheek as I pulled it in my hand. All of the pain I felt in him was magnified at the very moment of contact. Tears sprang to my eyes as a vision appeared in my mind's eye.

A beautiful woman with a happy, smiling face. Long dark hair. Running away from me … no, not me. Him. These were *his* memories I was seeing. And something awful was about to happen.

The memory changed, morphing into something darker. Clouds rolled into the sky of the image I was seeing. Lightning and fire. Brimstone and death. I could smell it as if it were actually there. That same woman's face appeared once more, only this time, she wasn't smiling. She was crying. Silent tears ran down her face, clearing it from the sudden grime and blood that appeared on her skin.

"Amelie…" Geoffrey's croak broke the spell that had woven itself over the two of us. He blinked and then I did as well. The memory was gone, but the sorrow remained. "How did you…?"

"I-I don't know," I answered him honestly.

He stumbled back, trembling even as I tried to reach for him again. I didn't know why I wanted to comfort him so, not when he was just saying such horrible things about Fae—about creatures like Orion and Roan and Sorrell. Perhaps it was a deeper part of my being, the part that understood loss and pain the same that he had experienced.

"Keep away from me!" he said as he hurried towards the door. He banged on it once and it opened.

There was no chance to go after him. And even if I'd managed to, what would I have done? The door banged shut behind him as he disappeared. I lowered my arm and sank back down onto the floor, drawing my dirty legs up and wrapping my arms around them as I let myself cry.

She must have been someone very important to him, I realized. And even if she'd died because of the war, that didn't mean that others hadn't suffered a similar loss.

A new memory arose in the back of my mind—both a recent and old one. My parents in the forest. Was it real? I wondered. Had they really left me to save my life?

I sniffed hard and pressed my forehead to the tops of my knees. Hopefully, their sacrifice hadn't been in vain because even if I wanted to save the Kingdom and the Fae from their own deep rooted hatred of each other, there was no way I could do it from a prison cell, and there was even less of a way for me to do it once I was dead.

CHAPTER 9

CRESS

I stared at the gray stone of my cell wall. A bug crawled out of the cracks, skittered up the brick and into another one. My head thumped back against the wall at my back. How long had I been here? How much longer did I have to go?

Geoffrey hadn't returned, but I wasn't left alone. Other guards must've been assigned to me because they came in random intervals I could never time. Some dropped off buckets of water, and some had chucked crusts of bread at me. Others had just slid the metal covering over the window at the top of the door, far higher than I could reach, and spat at me before walking away. Time was growing shorter and shorter.

Even as my stomach grumbled and growled for food, I found myself curling in against it—cradling it and wondering … had my mother been this afraid before she died? Had she known that I was safe when she was taken into the realm of the Gods? Had my father?

My hands tingled as I lifted my head and stared at the black marks against the stone. My fingers twitched, little sparks coming to life, but a split second later they dispersed. Magic wasn't as easy as I had expected it to be. Roan had made it seem so simple. When he got mad, flames had just erupted without any actual effort on his part. These last few days, I'd tried repeatedly to conjure the feeling of magic I'd experienced before. The only time I managed to make anything tangible was when I thought of Tyr. The anger pressed forward and shot out of my fingertips, leaving scorch marks on the walls of my cell, puny though they were. That, too, left me feeling exhausted, and I had to conserve my energy if I was going to try and escape this place. I was sure the guys had a plan, but unfortunately, with them out there and me in here, there was no real way for us to communicate or for them to let me know what it was that they were planning. As each day passed, my panic and fear only grew.

Each time I tried to summon my magic on purpose, it felt like I was simply trying to move something with my mind. *Could Fae do that?* I wondered. If they could, I hadn't figured out how to do that either.

There was no doubt that I had magic—Groffet's exercise had proven that weeks ago. But useable magic? Whatever magic I did have, wasn't enough to aid in any kind of escape attempt. My frustration mounted. What good was it being Fae if I couldn't *do* anything? I couldn't rescue myself. I couldn't protect myself from Tyr. I couldn't even get Roan's mother to like me and I was going to be her daughter-in-law—that is if I found a way out of my current situation. I wondered if I could, if that would impress her. Probably not.

I closed my eyes and resolved to try conjuring another bright orb of light and fire. Just as I decided that I was ready to try it once more, the lock on my cell door clanged as a key was inserted. I jerked my head to the side and shoved my hand under my butt to stifle any lingering brightness as the door opened.

A guard appeared, followed by two more. My heart pounded as they looked down on me. The first stepped forward and gestured for me to stand. "You're being allowed to bathe before your execution tomorrow as a courtesy to the executioner. If you fight or try to escape, we are authorized to beat you into submission and bathe you ourselves." He gave me a dark look. "You will not like our method of bathing."

I had no doubt he was right. I nodded even as my stomach twisted into a knot and his words hit me a second time. *Tomorrow? I was going to be executed tomorrow?* Shock and horror wrapped around my heart, squeezing the organ in my chest so tightly that I feared it would burst.

A second guard strode forward, slipping a keyring from the belt at his hip. "Up," he commanded as he approached.

I stood and locked my knees to prevent myself from falling over as painful prickles assaulted my limbs. I'd been lying down for too long and my legs had gone numb.

The third guard remained silent, but I could feel his beady eyes watching my every movement. I wondered if they would try to fabricate an escape attempt on my part simply to be given the pleasure of beating me. "Follow me," the first guard ordered, turning back towards the door.

The second guard who had unlocked my shackles prodded me in the side roughly to get me moving. My knees felt like they would give way at any moment, but I took a wobbly step forward and then another and another. As soon as I got close enough to the wall to use it as a crutch, I did. My hands fell on the stone and then slipped alongside the rough surface as I followed behind the first guard, out of my cell.

My original hope when they had told me I'd be leaving my cell was that the bathing chambers would be somewhere else. Despite their threat to beat me if I attempted an escape, I was planning to try, but as soon as I realized that they weren't taking me out of the tower, my hopes plummeted. No, wherever they were taking me, it was clear that it was in the same tower—likely just a different room made for bathing.

I was led to a small chamber barely bigger than the cell I'd been in for the last week. The door slid open and I was shoved inside. There was nothing in it save for one barrel in the middle filled to the brim with water. I sighed. It was still better than nothing, I supposed. The fact was, being cooped up in the tower's cell for a week, I was starting to smell like the backside of a horse. My nose wrinkled as I leaned down and sniffed my shirt to confirm. Yup. Definitely needed this.

"Soap." One of the guards tapped a bar of soap on my shoulder, and I took it. "That's your tub, beast."

"Thanks," I said. Beast, indeed. I shook my head and reached a finger into the barrel. The water was cold. I shivered just as it reached up to my second knuckle. This would not be a long bath, that was for damn sure.

I waited for the sound of the door to close as they left, but when it never came, I turned back and my eyes widened. The three guards stood there, blocking the exit with their bodies as they glared at me. "Um ... are you going to leave?" I prompted. "I can't get undressed and bathe with you in here."

"You cannot be trusted," the first and tallest one snapped. "Get on with it."

Horror sank into me. They were serious. "Can you at least turn around?" I replied. The Princes were one thing, but there was no way I'd feel comfortable letting just anyone see me naked!

The head guard narrowed his dark eyes on me before slowly turning to face the door. He then nudged the other two and they did the same. It wasn't much, but it was better than having their eyes watching me as I undressed. I reached up to my shoulders and grasped the fabric around my chest and began to tug upward until I stripped the dress off. After I was finished undressing, I realized that the chamber itself was just as cold as the water. Goosebumps broke out over my skin, and I couldn't stop shivers from stealing over my body.

"Hurry it up," one of the guards snapped.

I hooked my foot around the stool next to the barrel and dragged it forward, then using it as a step ladder, I climbed up and into the barrel. Water sloshed out over the sides and I gasped as the cold water sank into my skin. The guard on the farthest right turned and looked back.

I squeaked and sank into the barrel up to my shoulders until the majority of my body was covered. "Turn around!" I huffed.

He glared at me but turned back. There was no getting used to the cold water. It just wasn't possible, but just dipping myself into the barrel made me feel ten times better than I had the hour before. I turned my body so that even if they looked back at me, all they would see was my spine. With care, I lathered up the hard cake of soap and used it to try and scrub the worst of the grime and dirt off my skin.

The soap they'd given me wasn't great. It scraped across my skin, leaving light pink marks. Once I'd done my best with my body, I moved the lather up to my hair. My hair was normally a golden blonde but now was a dirty light brown. I stroked the soap down my scalp, trying to wash the strands from the roots to the ends.

Once I was done, I dropped the soap out of the side of the barrel, covered my mouth and nose, and dunked my whole head underwater, scratching furiously at my scalp until I was sure I'd done my best to get clean. I popped up out of the top of the barrel with a loud gasp and slicked my hair back over my shoulders.

My teeth were chattering as I began finger combing the tangles from my hair. I was so focused on my business that I didn't even notice when the door to the bathing chamber opened once more. I dunked a second time, and when I reemerged, a new—and unfortunately familiar—voice stood out among the rest.

Tyr. I looked down. Of course, he would come when I was most vulnerable. Naked and cold.

"You can wait outside," he said as I scrambled to think of a way to get out and get dressed without being seen. It was impossible with how small and barren this room actually was. Me and the three guards were far too many people inside of it as it was.

"Sir, we're supposed to keep the prisoner under guard at all times," the head guard replied.

"You think I can't handle a small Fae woman who doesn't even have any power to speak of?" Tyr demanded.

"Of course not, sir."

There was a moment of silence where I prayed to the Gods that the guards wouldn't leave, but then, "We'll be right outside, sir." I could have cried or thrown something at the head of the guard who'd answered. Number three. The dickbag.

"Of course," Tyr replied lightly.

I peeked over my shoulder and watched as he stepped aside and the guards moved into a single file line as they exited the room. The door closed behind them and I jumped when the sound of a key in the lock turned, leaving me alone. With a fucking monster.

Tyr pivoted and met my gaze. A smile came to his face. "I wanted to come and make sure you weren't planning any last minute escape attempts," he said as he rounded the barrel, moving steadily closer and closer as his footsteps echoed up the walls. I sank deep into the water and crossed my arms over my chest even as I glared at him. "Your execution is currently set for tomorrow morning, just as the sun rises over the mountains. It's quite kind of His Majesty, don't you think?" he asked. "You'll be able to feel the sun on your face one last time before you die."

"How would I even begin to escape?" I asked. "I'm just one person. And as you so kindly said yourself, I'm not even powerful." His eyes dipped down to where my arms crossed over my front and I wanted to let go for just a moment—not caring if I flashed him everything—if only I could hit him. Give him a nice, clean throat punch right to his stupid neck. You know, now that I was close to him—he wasn't nearly as handsome as Orion. His neck was too long. His face too angular. His eyes too evil.

Slowly, as if he relished in making me feel uncomfortable, his eyes traveled up from my naked chest to my neck to my face. His smile was smug. "I also came because I heard you've been telling stories, Cressida." He tsked at me. "Naughty. Naughty. Telling all of those fine guards out there that I'm a disgusting Fae."

"How can you say that?" I demanded. "You are. I told them the truth. You don't truly believe that Fae are disgusting—you're just using them. The truth is that you're a monster and when I get out of here, I'm going to make sure everyone knows it."

He shrugged. "Silly girl. The truth is whatever I say it is," he replied. He stepped right in front of my barrel and leaned close. "And darling..." Tyr bent closer until I could see the darkness in his eyes, the way his pupils had all but swallowed the color of his irises, "the only way you're getting out of here is when you're being led to your death. That, I can assure you, is a kinder fate than any I would've given you. You should be grateful, really. I don't hate you—I just find you a nuisance. You're in my way. Nothing more. If I truly despised you, little Changeling, you would have no barrel to hide behind."

My eyes darted to the side as a chill went down my spine. He had a point. We were alone—the two of us. He could do unimaginable things to me if he so chose. No one would stop him—no one *could* stop him. As small as it was, this barrel was the only barrier I had from him right now. He could dump me out of it if he wanted. Kick me to the floor and beat me. He had magic—magic that was far more powerful than mine. I shivered as he stared at me, his eyes somehow seeming even darker in the dim light of the bathing chambers. The singular torch on the wall flickered, growing weaker as if he willed it to do so. I shrank down even more as his hand cupped the top of the barrel. If I let him, he could snuff out all of the hope I had placed in the guys. I swallowed roughly.

"Someone will figure out what you've done and you'll be punished for it," I said. I wanted to sound strong and intimidating, but even to my own ears, my voice didn't hold the same strength his had.

"That day will never come," he said as he finally released the top of the barrel and stepped back. "For now, I'm the King's advisor. He listens to me above all others. As for the Fae, I am untouchable. The first heir to the Court of Midnight. I will have my war, little Changeling, and when it is over—the ruins of this world will be mine. I intend to build my people up from the graves I save them from. This ridiculous charade won't be needed much longer, especially after your death tomorrow. Roan and Orion will be devastated. The Crimson Prince will lose himself and my brother, my dear, sweet, weak brother will go mad—it's in the family, after all. Everything is going perfectly." Tyr circled the barrel and moved back towards the door and as he did, I turned, following him with my gaze.

"You're wrong," I said. "They will stop you—even if I die." Though I knew they wouldn't let that happen.

Tyr paused and glanced back. "Oh darling, they won't even have a chance. You are simply the match that will light the flame that will set fire to this world. Without you, those two will fall apart."

"What about Sorrell?" I demanded.

Tyr shook his head. "You should know by now," he said. "All I need to do to ruin the Prince of Frost is tear apart his friends.

Your death will kill them and killing them will kill him. Now, be a good girl and die prettily tomorrow."

He banged on the door and it opened a second later, allowing for his graceful exit, but even as he stepped from the room a dark laugh echoed back to me. After his departure, I didn't even care if the guards saw me anymore. It was far too damn cold. As they stepped inside, I hurried to scramble out of the barrel. One of the guards tossed something my way—a threadbare towel. I snatched it up from the ground where it had landed and used it to quickly dry myself off.

No sooner had I yanked my dirty dress up from the floor and slipped it over my head, and one of the guards stepped forward and grasped my upper arm. "Time to go back to your cell," he said.

I didn't make another sound; I didn't even ask another question as they led me back to my original cell and shoved me inside. They shackled me back the same way I had been and as soon as the door locked behind me, I collapsed onto my cot. I clasped my hands together and prayed that the guys wouldn't be too late. I'd given Orion all the information I could. They had to be on their way by now.

The light in the room waned over the next few hours and as it did, night fell. Each minute, I realized was yet another closer to my potential death. I trusted the Princes of the Crimson Court. That was all I could do now—give them my trust and hope that they would come through.

Death wasn't something I'd ever spent much time thinking about before now. I always assumed that I could survive what-ever life threw at me. I had survived the nuns. I'd survived nearly dying after Ariana had shoved me off of a wall. I'd even survived the Court of Frost. I needed to believe I would survive this as well, so I closed my eyes and conjured the happiest memories I could. It wasn't any surprise to me that they all revolved around three stubborn Fae—one masked in darkness, one in fire, and one in ice.

Yes, even Sorrell. My cold hands reached up and touched my lips—recalling the kiss we'd shared in my bed in the Court of Frost. I knew what I wanted the rest of my life to look like, and it didn't involve me dying or us fighting a never ending war because Tyr wanted to burn it all down.

I had to believe that there was more to my existence than being used for another's gain. I would not let myself be a pawn. Be that as it may, though, the second I saw the guys again, they were going to know the meaning of pain. I was going to kick the absolute shit out of their shins. Just because I trusted those assholes didn't mean they had to leave my rescue to the last minute like this.

I settled into my cot and curled my knees up against my chest. Even with my irritation making me grumble to myself about stupid Princes and their need for perfection and leaving me in a crummy tower like this, I hoped ... more than anything that even if I did die tomorrow, I'd at least be able to see them one last time.

CHAPTER 10
ROAN

The darkness of night encroached. Muted sounds echoed from the forest at my back as I stared up at the massive structure that was the capital castle of Amnestia. Cress was there just beyond our reach. After tomorrow, though, she would be back where she belonged. With me—with *us*.

"Roan." Sorrell's quiet voice called to me from the campfire side.

I didn't respond for a moment, choosing instead to let my eyes rest upon the outside of the castle a moment longer. My eyes slid shut and an image of Cress's face came to mind. Her beautiful smile—dangerously deceptive. If she never opened her mouth, she could've masqueraded as a high born lady of any Court. It was her personality that separated her from the others. Her laughter—loud and boisterous. She was so unapologetic in her excitement and adventurous nature. Knowing she was locked away in the darkness left a pang in my heart. Her kind of light should never have to suffer this kind of atrocity, and after tomorrow, I would ensure she never would again.

"Roan." Sorrell's voice grew nearer until I could sense him

standing alongside me. I opened my eyes. "Come. You need to eat and then sleep. I'll take the first watch."

I nodded and as the two of us turned back to the fires, Orion stepped out of the darkness of the trees and into our little clearing. We lifted our heads to look at him. "The Court is secured," he announced before striding forward and lowering himself into a cross-legged position next to the fire.

Fatigue pulled at my bones. I knew they could feel it too. It had been exhausting to move the castle, not only from Alfheim to the human realm but to do so once more. The three of us were drained and I knew the only surefire way to increase our energy and replenish our magic was to fuck. Too bad none of us seemed all that interested in doing so unless it was with one golden-haired, smart-mouthed Changeling.

Orion withdrew a flint stone and one of his blades, then began sharpening the end. A battle was coming and on the break of morning, it would arrive. I could feel the clinging vines of bloodshed already weaving through my body. My blood boiled. My senses—though drained—were still as sharp as ever. We were so close to her. I wanted to feel her in my arms. I wanted to press her beneath me and pound my cock into her.

"Do you think the illusion will hold?" Sorrell inquired, directing his question to Orion.

Orion's hands paused their consistent up and down movements against the blade. "Groffet has everything under control," he said. "Ash will be helping, and for our purposes, the illusion will hold for as long as it needs to."

I knew what that meant. There was no way humans wouldn't see a Fae castle so close to the human King's and not attack it. We'd had to leave it several miles behind, but that also had been far too close for comfort. The spell that Groffet had concocted to shroud our Court in a repellant illusion would do its job, though. It'd make anyone who approached it confused and lost and the closer to the castle they got, the more their minds would weave shadows and disorientation over their memories. It would, however, likely only last for the next day or so.

That wouldn't be a problem since by this time tomorrow I expected Cress to be back in our arms or the human race would go up in flames. If she were hurt in this process, I would ensure it. Their lives meant nothing in the way of my devotion to her.

"Shall we go over the plan once more?" Sorrell asked. I grunted in response, which he took as an affirmative. Lifting a slender branch in his grip, he began drawing images in the dirt. "The execution is scheduled to happen at daybreak," he began, "when the sun reaches the horizon. As soon as the sky begins to lighten on the morrow, Roan and I will head into the crowd drawn by the announcements of a Fae execution."

I scowled at that. *Yes, we had heard.* King Felix had not made the news of the capture and soon to be murder of Cress secret. Tomorrow, amidst the upheaval, there would be onlookers ready and willing to watch her die.

And none of us would let them get their wish.

"As we wait for the King to arrive and oversee the proceedings," Sorrell continued, striking a line from two x's to a circle, "Orion—you'll enter the castle while everyone is preoccupied with the execution set up."

He had to find her before she was taken to the public, I thought, feeling my muscles tense. If he didn't … I didn't want to think of what might happen if we messed this up. We couldn't. There was too much at stake. I took a deep breath and reminded myself—that was the very reason Sorrell and I would be in the crowd. We hoped to get in and get out without a huge battle, but if things were to go awry, we would be prepared to do anything—sacrifice anyone—to get to her.

"I should be able to sense her presence with the lingering

effects of the dream magic," Orion said. "I will ensure that I am not seen."

Sorrell nodded and turned his eyes back to the drawings he'd sketched out. I could only imagine what he was thinking. Considering every angle of the strategy was his specialty. Orion's was stealth. But mine ... mine was fire. Mine was only necessary if all else went wrong and for both their sake and Cress's, I hoped tomorrow would go as planned.

"Sleep, Brothers," Orion muttered a moment later. "I will take the first watch."

"I've already told Roan that I would," Sorrell replied.

Orion shook his head. "No need."

"Yes, there is," he argued. "You need sleep as much as any of us."

I snorted. "We don't need sleep," I said. "We need *her*."

Silence echoed around me in the wake of that statement. Neither of them denied the claim. I groaned and rolled to my feet. "But if you two want to argue over who'll watch first, then I suppose I'll just take the first shift of sleeping. Better make up your mind sooner or later. Wake me when it's my time."

They nodded in unison and watched me with knowing eyes as I slipped behind the next copse of trees. I strode into the forest, unconcerned by the sounds of small wild creatures skittering around in the underbrush or the little insects that crawled across my boots. They were a part of nature and no threat to me.

When I guessed I'd gone far enough, I turned my back to a large oak and sank down until my ass touched the ground. I had a violent need inside of me and as I closed my eyes and returned to the image of Cress, it surged forth.

At the camp, she'd been so soft and smooth beneath Orion and me. Her little hands had touched with an innocence but a curiosity that was natural to all Fae. Though I had once doubted her heritage, there was none now. My cock practically pulsed behind the placket of my trousers and without thought, I reached down, undoing the laces as I freed myself to the cool night air.

I gripped my stalk and pictured Cress—my Crimson Princess—on her knees before me. Her plump pink lips circling the head of my cock as she bobbed over me. The creaminess of her skin sliding against the roughness of mine. Magic power rose within me as I pumped my cock. I trembled as I squeezed and fisted myself.

It wasn't good enough. Nothing would be until she was with me again. Under me. All over me.

And it wasn't just me, I knew. No. Orion and I would have her again together. I'd come to accept that. She'd enjoyed his touch as much as she'd enjoyed mine and it was all I wanted in this world: to see her happy. Sorrell—the provoking bastard that he was—would fall as well if he hadn't already. That, most of all, was the ultimate fantasy.

Cress between not just Orion and me, but the three of us. Her mouth stretched around my cock as Orion pushed into her lower depths and Sorrell … a grin formed across my face. The icy prick would likely want the one place she'd be most hesitant to give. Even experienced female Fae had shied away from *that* particular act, no matter how desirable their partner.

My balls pulled tight against my inner thighs as my release grew closer and closer. My fantasies shifted and suddenly, it wasn't Sorrell laying across her back and spreading those hind cheeks of her hide. It was me. Oh, what it would feel like to press into that small, forbidden little chamber of hers. I'd press my cock head to her pussy first, circle it in her juices. There would be no denying her there. I'd have to fuck her if only to keep my sanity before I pulled back and ran the hot, wet, head up to her dark place.

The sound of her gasp filled my ears. It wasn't real, but Gods, I could practically fucking taste her anticipation. She would be so needy for me, so ready. Perhaps she wouldn't even deny me that place. I would be gentle with her, of course. At first, anyway. I would slip my cock into her backside and push until all of the breath had escaped her lungs. Then, once she'd gotten used to me filling her hole, I'd show her the true meaning of magic and release.

The muscles in my legs jumped as I tightened my grip around my shaft and pounded my fist in quick movements. One knee came up as I bent slightly towards the ground. I squeezed the palm of my hand over the head of my cock and groaned as spurt after spurt of cum came rushing up and out.

After several moments, I dropped my leg and leaned back. I'd have to clean myself eventually, but for the moment—despite the rush of euphoria and magic energy that had suffused my system—I was depleted. I looked up through the clear patches between the treetops and stared at the glittering night sky.

Tomorrow.

Tomorrow, we would find and rescue Cress. Only then could my fantasies finally come true.

CHAPTER 11
CRESS

Footsteps sounded on the stone floor outside my cell and my stomach dropped. *It couldn't be time yet, could it?* The Princes hadn't come for me yet. There had to be a mistake right?

The keys clanked in the lock on my door and I knew that whatever time I had was up. A guard walked in and sneered at me, and as though that wasn't enough, Tyr appeared right behind him. The man was like a fly, just when I thought I'd gotten rid of him, there he was again, buzzing around and annoying the hell out of me.

"Ah, isn't it a glorious day, little Changeling? Just smell the fresh air. The weather is taking a turn for the better I believe and I'm sure your life ending will only please the Gods even more. What do you think? Should we get on with it? Or maybe we should sit and chat a while more, let you hang in suspense." He laughed.

Was that a hint? I wondered. *Hanging? Was that how I was going to die today if I didn't get out of here?*

The guard cleared his throat.

Tyr nodded. "Yes, you have a point, Samson," he said, taking a step further into the room.

I watched him, feeling my heart start to beat faster. I felt stalked—like prey cornered by a much bigger predator. When it came down to it, that was exactly what I was. Prey to his predator.

"We should get this over with," Tyr continued. "After all, we don't want to keep the crowd that's come to watch the festivities waiting." Tyr grinned at me as I stared back at him. "Your death will be our entertainment for the day," he said. "It will be only one of many to befall Faekind and soon, all that will be left is a memory of what you once were."

His words were merely for the benefit of the guards surrounding us. There was no possible way he could want his own race to be killed. That was … genocide. As Tyr approached and bent down, and I gazed up into his eyes, I had to wonder … maybe he really didn't give a fuck who won this war after all. Because in the end—no matter who was left to claim victory—both sides would lose. That was how war went.

Clamping my lips shut, I glared up at him. It was difficult not to show my fear.

"So quiet now," Tyr commented. "What's wrong, little Changeling? Cat got your tongue?" He grinned as he reached for my wrist and yanked me up to my feet.

My lips parted, but before I could utter a word in response, he reached out and grabbed my face, pinching my chin in his tight grip and squishing my cheeks. "You're very pretty for one, you know," he commented. "A Changeling, that is. What a pity."

I gasped as quick and sharp as a whip, he tilted my head to the side and then dragged his tongue up my cheek, from the bottom of my jaw straight to my temple. A shudder of disgust ran through me.

"I expected salt," he said, "from last night's tears. Did you not cry, little Changeling? Attempting to be brave?" He used his grasp on my face to shake me back and forth. "You taste delicious, nonetheless. There's something to be said about the fear of a young woman about to die. I can never quite get enough of it," he whispered just as he flipped my head to the other side and licked my other cheek in the same manner.

My muscles tensed as he chuckled against my temple. More disgust whipped through me. I shuddered with revulsion even as my gaze darted to the guard standing by, silently pleading with him to stop this. When our eyes clashed, however, he merely curled his upper lip back and looked away.

Why? I thought. *Even if I was a prisoner, why in the world would anyone treat another person like this? Why would he just stand there and let it happen?*

"Keys," Tyr said abruptly, holding out the hand that wasn't clamped onto my face to the guard. I heard the jangle of metal as the keys landed in his palm, and he finally released me so he could undo the chains that had been anchoring me to the wall. The second the weight of the fetters was gone I wanted to sigh in relief, even if they were just replaced with a set of new manacles that would lead me out of this hole and into something far worse—death.

The metal was cold on my wrists. Tyr's hands found my shoulders and turned me around, shoving me forward until I stumbled towards the door and I took solace in the fact that he hadn't chained my feet. "Let's get moving," the guard said, turning and allowing me out into the corridor.

I shuffled along, darting my eyes from one side to the next. There was no opportunity in sight, though. No spare moment where I wasn't surrounded by human guards with swords and dark looks. They would no doubt be more than willing to kill me before I even got to wherever it was this execution would take place.

They led me down a winding staircase and out of the prison tower—past silent cells where eyes gleamed in the quiet darkness. The silence was far more insidious knowing what was to come. Then finally, I was led out into the morning light. I halted just as fresh air—and the sunlight—hit my face. After being locked up for so long, the brightness of the sun was overwhelming and my vision was overcome with intense pain as I squinted to try and see my surroundings.

Slowly but surely, my eyes began to adjust. The guards, however, paid no heed as they shoved me along. I stumbled, nearly falling several times, as I was marched out into what seemed to be a courtyard. When I spotted the stage they had set for my execution my feet froze and refused to move again no matter how many times the guard behind me pushed against my back. My knees almost gave way several times, but all I could do was stand there and stare up into the unrelenting sun at the wooden stage—a beacon of my doom.

Finally, the guard huffed out a breath and picked me up, lifting me off my bare feet, and half carried, half dragged me towards the instrument of my demise. As he marched me up the stairs, I turned and looked out and realized that Tyr hadn't been lying; there was, in fact, a crowd. My stomach sank as I stared back at the onlookers who had all come to watch me die. My lashes flickered.

Where the fuck were the guys? Even as I tried to tell myself not to panic, panic was all I could feel. That was normal, I guessed, considering I was about to be horrifically murdered in front of so many witnesses. Oh, they could call it execution and justice all they wanted—the fact remained, I was innocent and they were going to kill me. It was murder in my book.

How could so many people want to watch someone else die? I asked myself. *Did the hatred between our people really run that deep?* Who was I kidding? I knew it did. Even if they'd taught me nothing else, the nuns had taught me that.

My fingers flexed inside my manacles. The desire to use my powers—the ones I'd been so desperately working on this entire week—rose, but I was unpredictable. My powers came and went. Even if my death was the end, I couldn't bring myself to unleash an unknown violence on people who didn't know any better. I needed another option, but as I tried to think of one, I was positioned into place and the King took to the stage, stepping in front of me to command everyone's attention. As soon as he was in my sights, all thoughts except rage vanished from my mind.

King Felix stepped before me and raised his hands to his audience. "Ladies and gentlemen," he announced. "You have come here to bear witness to a most auspicious event. This," he exclaimed, "is a traitorous Fae!" He turned and pointed my way just as one of my old guards stepped up and placed a noose around my neck before tightening it. I gasped, fear overtaking my anger for a brief moment.

There were several jeers from the crowd. Slurs. Curses. Blind hatred. I didn't understand it, and yet at the same time, how could I not? They were afraid. They were seeking out someone to blame for all they had lost in this Gods forsaken war that had gone on for too long.

"She infiltrated our country," the King went on, "learned of our ways and weaknesses, and then she went back to her Fae Kings and Queens and gave them the information."

"That's not true!" I cried.

"Silence!" he shouted back.

I tried to shake my head, but as I did, the rope dug into my throat, making it hard to breathe, and they hadn't even done anything yet. One of the guards stepped forward and lifted me off my feet as another placed a stool beneath me.

No! my mind screamed in rebellion. *No! Where were they?* They had to be here. The guys would never let me die like this, not even Sorrell, despite the fact that I irritated him. My eyes sought out the crowd once more, but instead of looking at the people who had chosen to come to this horrible event, I looked for a familiar head of red hair, of ice white hair, of hair so black it resembled a raven's wing.

Tears began to prick at my eyes, and my throat tightened as I fought not to cry. Especially when the crowd began to steadily agree with the horrible things the King was saying. They began yelling at me, spitting terrible words that the nuns would have lashed me for even whispering. I gritted my teeth and bore it.

Yes, I was terrified, but the longer it went on, the less fear I felt and the more my anger grew. I refused to turn my gaze away. Not after everything I'd been through. I raised my head and looked out at the crowd.

"The Fae are dying in droves. Their poor weakling soldiers are unable to stand up to our men. Mark my words, before the year is over we will have a victory over the Fae and they will be eradicated from our lands. It will be the greatest victory our people have ever seen," The King shouted.

"That is not the truth," I said defiantly. "The truth is that *you* are the one killing innocents and you're killing Fae for simply existing. Whether it's Fae killing human or human killing Fae, it's wrong. You're wrong and the Fae are wrong. But you won't see that." I turned and glared at where Tyr stood by, smiling at me. "Not so long as you have a traitor in your Court."

There was a moment of silence that drifted over the crowd at my words, and a few even hesitantly looked at each other as if they weren't sure how to react. Finally, the King stepped forward and brought his hand down in a sweeping gesture. "Enough!" he called. "It's time."

Hands landed on my shoulders and I was forced to my knees. It wasn't going to be a hanging after all, I realized as my eyes widened when a man stopped before me and set a stained block of wood before me. It was to be a beheading. My gaze jerked up and met Tyr's. His smile widened and he waved.

Then, as if he didn't even care to stay, he turned and walked away.

Orion, Roan, and Sorrell's faces all danced in front of my eyes as the hands pushed me over the block of wood, my chin resting in the notch that had been carved out.

Just as the King raised his hand once more to signal the executioner, the ground rumbled beneath us. My chin was jarred as it smacked into the side of the block of wood. I lifted my head and when no one forced me back down, I realized something much larger had happened. The Earth was shaking. It went on for several long minutes and I felt the collective shock and breath that everyone in the crowd held. They were waiting for it to stop, I realized.

Instead, the shaking got worse. There were several gasps and before I understood what was happening, screams split the air. Several members of the crowd moved back, falling as they tried to get away. I turned, noting that my guards were all fixated on the tower above us as long tendrils of cracks began to form from the ground up.

This was my chance! I pushed to my feet, the manacles around my wrists clanging, and then just as black smoke began to pour out of the tower and a great explosion wracked its frame, I leapt to my hopeful freedom—off the platform and into the crowd.

CHAPTER 12
ORION

The capital of Amnestia was a bustling place, and in the early morning hours, when children should have been just waking and marketplaces should have been preparing to open for the day, there was, instead, a lingering sense of excitement. A curiousness to the crowd as they ambled over the cobblestoned streets to the opened doors of the castle courtyard.

My brothers and I mingled in with the humans, casting magic over ourselves to keep our slightly otherworldly looks hidden. The slightly pointed ears. The vibrant hair colors. The sense of strangeness we exuded to these people. As much as we could disguise our looks, we could not hide our dispositions.

Anger. Concern. Fear. It hovered over each of us—that heavy sense of dread.

"Alright," Roan said, quietly turning away from me as he and Sorrell slipped further into the amassing crowd as more and more people came from the city to witness the event that would take place this sunrise.

An execution.

"It's time," Roan continued. "Go."

I nodded and, without another word, I called upon my magic—the very same I had been born with. The darkness of midnight. The ability to seep into the shadows and find the isolating darkness that dwelled within the corners. It was everywhere at all times because without darkness—*without me* —there could be no light.

Shooting forward between people gliding through the open gates, I wove through the lines—bypassing the guards. There was a reason we had waited so long to do this. Not only would the defenses of the castle be down as they prepared for the execution this morning, but it was an old human custom to invite onlookers to watch as the King killed a criminal. Only this time, it wasn't a criminal. It was Cress, my Cress.

When I glanced at small children, some barely old enough to toddle next to their parents as they entered through the gates, I felt a sickness pour into my stomach. Fae could be cruel, that much was true, but where, I asked myself, were there differences between our species? Humans, too, it seemed, could be bloodthirsty.

Shaking my head and dismissing that thought, I hurried to do my duty. Halfway into the main courtyard that all onlookers were led to, I separated myself and found an open alcove. Dipping into it, I hunted through the open corridors until I found a door leading inside.

The castle was well underway in preparation for the morning's activities. Deeper I sank, into the shadows, avoiding all detection as servants bustled about and guards patrolled.

Closing my eyes, I sought out a hint of Cress. It was there, in the recesses of my mind, a lingering effect of the dream magic I had used mere nights ago. A vibrant glow of her energy. I grabbed onto it and followed the feeling of it, letting the trail of her power lead me. It was faint, muddled, and faded. Lack of sleep and high levels of stress would do that to a spirit. I only hoped that that was all that she had suffered. I didn't want to consider what the King might have done to what he thought was a traitorous Fae in his Kingdom. He was executing her now, but he'd had her for a week. In that time...

No! I couldn't stop to think of it. I needed to focus. Stopping inside an empty stairwell, I rasped out a breath, shaking my head and shoving my concerns back. It was my duty to find her, here and now, and retrieve her before anything more happened.

When I reopened my eyes, however, I froze. Dark wisps of power drifted towards me, rolling over the stairs before me, and these were not mine. The curling tendrils snapped at my ankles, wrapping quickly and jerking until my whole body was yanked into the air and held suspended.

Years of training—years of war—were finally found to be good for some things. It took no thought at all for me to retaliate. A knife flew from my grasp, yanked from my boot, and sliced through the shadows. A shrieking wail of agony pierced my skull and I was abruptly dropped. I lifted my arm and captured the knife before it fell.

"That's no normal blade, Brother."

Violence seeped into my bones as I lifted my head and caught sight of the man responsible for my presence in the human King's castle today. He came around the corner slowly, grinning as he clapped his hands.

"Iron," I stated solemnly as I stood and met his amused gaze with a wrathful glare.

His eyebrows rose. "And yet you wield it with no pain."

Of course I did—I'd wrapped the Iron blade, one of the few things that could cut through a Fae's manifestation of magic, in a protective handle covering. The blade, itself, was free, and it was what I would use to gut him where he stood. I took a step forward and Tyr lifted his hand, stopping me with a wall of black fire that erupted between us. I debated my chances of stabbing my way through it, but even with an Iron blade, I would still receive wounds from such a large mani-festation.

The walls and stairs, however, remained unscorched. "Tut. Tut. Dear Brother," Tyr said. "You come to me with a look of such hatred in your eyes."

"You've taken something that belongs to me," I snapped. "And we are no longer brothers!"

Tyr's hand touched his breastbone. "That hurts, you know," he said mournfully. "Especially when I went through all of this trouble to find you. After all, as soon as you stepped foot within the castle, I knew you were here. I'm surprised it took you this long to come for your Changeling."

"Where is she?" I demanded.

A sigh left his mouth. "Gods, look at you. So consumed with lust for the poor thing. She's rather scrawny, if I may say so, especially after her days in here. The guards didn't much care to feed the thing."

I didn't even think. I simply let the second blade in my hand fly. Tyr stumbled as it slammed into his shoulder and just as quickly, the fire he'd conjured dispersed as his concentration was broken. My booted feet flew up the short steps between us and I slammed my hand into his throat, gripping and lifting him until his back crashed against the stone wall. Little bits of rock and dust floated down as I crushed his throat in my grip and leaned in close.

"Where. Is. She?" I demanded once more.

The fading light of her magic in my mind was growing fainter and fainter. It was more difficult than before to summon it back. Soon it would be gone. It would be far easier to get the information I needed from Tyr and then slay him here and now.

A hoarse, rough laugh left Tyr's lips. "You think killing me will save her?" he asked. "No, join me, Brother."

My mouth parted in shock. *Join him?* I reared back and

simply stared at him—at the face of the man I'd grown up alongside, but also at the face of a brother who'd time and time again left me in battle to fend for myself. Simply out of boredom or amusement.

"Blood brothers should remain together, Orion," Tyr continued. "Though you may not like it, though you may hide from the truth, the fact remains, you and I"—he grins and leans into my grip—"we are Midnight Fae and the Midnight Court is the most powerful of all."

I could feel a fire of rage welling up inside of me. "I may be a Midnight Fae." I said the words slowly, carefully as I watched every detail of his expression. "But I will never be one with you." With that, I reached up with my other hand and ripped the iron blade out of his shoulder.

Tyr grunted as it left his body. "More is the pity," he whispered.

My hand flew down, the blade in my grasp aiming directly for his heart. Murder, even among Fae, was blasphemous, but in this, I knew I was right. Tyr was a monster. He had betrayed not only me but the entirety of Faekind. He could not be allowed to live.

Yet, even as my dagger flashed, pain shot through me, starting in my stomach and spreading. My arm grew weak and dots flickered in front of my vision. *Wait ...* My eyes shot downward. No. How had I not…

Another blade, almost exactly like my own, stuck out of my abdomen. My head lifted and my eyes met Tyr's. My hand fell away from his throat as I stumbled back, reaching down to rip the thing free.

"You're not the only one who learned a few things in war, Orion." Tyr's words reached me just as I yanked the new blade from my skin. Blood soaked across my shirt. "You should've poisoned your first blade." The tone of his voice was smooth, unbothered, as if he was merely talking to me about the weather rather than the fact that he'd poisoned the blade that he used to kill me—because I was dying. I knew it. I could feel it in my veins.

My vision wavered again and the next step I took, a last ditch effort to strike at him, fell short. Both daggers fell from my grasp and my head smacked into the wall as my body tumbled to the ground and then further, rolling down the stairs until I hit the bottom. Breath wheezed out of my chest, aching and sharp, and bringing me absolute agony.

In my ears, the ringing clomps of Tyr's steps grew ever closer until a shadow passed over my face. I opened my eyes, not realizing that I'd closed them, and stared up as he bent low over me, brushing my hair back away from my face as he smiled.

"I'll let you in on a little secret, Brother," he spoke slowly— or perhaps it was merely my mind slowing everything down. It felt like each second lasted an eternity. The pumping of my poison drenched blood through my veins made everything seem so painfully never ending. Tyr reached into his shirt and produced something.

My eyes widened as a globe illuminated in his palm. Barely the size of a small animal's head, I knew what it was right away. Though it was an impossible feat—though it shouldn't have existed—there, in his palm, was a Lanuaet. A miniature version. The Midnight Court's version.

"This is going to bring me everything I've ever wanted," he explained.

Lifting up as much as my body would allow, I tried to reach for it. Something inside of me told me to rip it away and destroy it before it was too late. Tyr pulled it back with a laugh. "Ah, ah, ah. Can't have you messing this up for me," he chuckled before putting it back into his shirt.

"What ... do ... you ... want?" I asked, panting through the anguish—both the mental fear and the physical suffering.

Tyr looked down at me as he rose back to his full height, and this time, when he answered, there was no amusement in his expression. No laughter in his eyes. This was the true him. The cruel brother I had known. The monster underneath the veneer of pseudo-friendliness he always put off.

"Power," he said. Tyr took a step back and lifted his arms, pointing them both to the ceiling.

An explosion rocked through the building and with wide, horrified eyes, I realized the truth. The ceiling cracked— spiderweb like fissures crawling across the surface before me. Finally, when it became too much, the whole thing buckled inward and came crashing down upon me and the world became nothing more than a gaping hole of true pain as flames burned across my chest.

Just before I descended into that darkness, the sound of Tyr's voice filtered back. "Until next time, dear Brother."

CHAPTER 13
CRESS

Screams filled the air as the crowd realized what was happening. I dove off the platform, wincing as I prepared to hit the ground with jarring pain. The second my legs flew off the dais, however, warm arms closed around me. I flailed, panic taking over my mind. I didn't know how the guards had realized what I was planning, but I couldn't let myself give this chance up. I needed to escape.

My captor fell against the ground with a grunt and as I scrambled away, kicking up dirt in my haste—his hands fell on my waist and yanked me back. "Cressida!" Sorrell's deep, irritated tone reached me a split second later and I froze, only then realizing that it wasn't a guard but he who held me in his arms. "Stop fighting me," he ordered. "I need to conceal you."

The moment I stopped moving, something cold washed over my skin, making me shiver. The bindings holding my wrists together broke and fell away, and finally, I was able to move my arms. My head tilted back and met the cool, icy gaze of Sorrell. Never in my life had I been so overwhelmed and relieved to see such an expression of utter irritation.

"Are you harmed?" he asked.

I shook my head and then proceeded to throw my arms around him. I burrowed into his chest, tears pricking at my eyelids. They'd come. I knew they would, but they had sure let the clock tick down to the last fucking second. Recalling that, I pulled away and punched him.

"What took you so long!" I snapped.

Sorrell's gaze was an arrested one. He blinked down at me, his lips twisted into a grimace of shock. Then with slow deliberate movements, he took me by the shoulders and moved me back. "Don't ever do that again," he ordered.

Cue the eye roll. I snorted and would've said something had it not been for a screaming woman in a large peasant dress who ran between us, not paying any mind to the escaped prisoner—the one who'd almost been executed as well as the giant frost Fae at her side.

"What's going on?" I asked, turning my attention to the crumbling remains of the King's tower. "Was that part of the plan?" Small flames flickered in the near distance, but more worrisome than that were the plumes of black smoke that rose into the sky.

"No," Sorrell said haltingly. "It was not." My gaze returned to him and I noticed the deep set of his brow as he, too, tilted his head back and stared up at the tower. He appeared to shake himself out of whatever dark thoughts consumed him a moment later as he returned his attention to me. "We must go," he said, taking my arm and dragging me after him.

The urgency of his movements had me following after him. My feet stumbled along as we tried to avoid the leftovers from the crowd, many of whom were scrambling over one another trying to escape the falling debris.

"Where are we going?" I tried to ask above the noise, but it was either swallowed by it all or Sorrell simply ignored it in favor of yanking me further and further away from the castle. My money would be on the 'ignore Cress' option, and I wouldn't have minded so much, especially since he was here—rescuing me—except after several more steps something brought me to a sharp halt.

"What are you doing?" Sorrell snapped, whirling around as he tried to pull me forward again.

Against my will, my head turned back the way we'd come. "Something's wrong," I said. My chest felt tight, a darkness creeping into my soul. The trees were within sight, our escape right there, but a small voice inside was telling me to turn back. The wind pushed against my face, whipping my hair in tangles around my face. The effect of whatever force was driving me rippled out through the rest of my body.

"Cressida," he growled, nearly yanking me off my feet with his next tug. "We have to go. *Now*."

"No." I turned and stared at him. Something was really wrong. My limbs felt like they weighed hundreds of pounds as I took a single step towards him—away from the castle. "Something's happened."

Sorrell stared down at me as though I were crazy. Maybe I was. Maybe this was a trick—magic put on me by Tyr—but I couldn't deny that every single drop of blood in my body was vibrating with anxiety. My hands tingled with awareness, sparks dancing at the edges of my fingers, my magic making itself known.

"What are you—"

"I think we have to go back," I said, cutting him off.

"Are you insane?" He gaped at me.

"I'm sorry, Sorrell..." No matter what he thought, I was. I truly was. He had come all this way to rescue me, but I couldn't leave. Not just yet. I had to follow whatever this feeling was. I didn't want to think of what would happen if I didn't.

His brows crashed down over his eyes and he reached for me intending, I suspected, to simply lift me up and toss me over his shoulders to force me along, but I couldn't let that happen. I didn't let him get the chance. Without a second thought, I turned and dove back into the crowd—fighting against the stream as I moved through people running in the opposite direction. Whatever spell he had put on me appeared to still be working because as I made my way back across the courtyard, towards the burning tower, and into the first entrance I could see, no one stopped me or even seemed to notice my presence.

I hadn't made it up a handful of stairs before a large body crashed into me, slamming me into the stone wall. With a gasp, I fought back, bringing my elbow back and smashing it into the sternum of the man behind me.

"Gods damn it," Sorrell's deep curse stopped me. "I will knock you the fuck out and toss you over my shoulder, Changeling."

"No, you can't," I insisted. "There's something really wrong. Please." I turned and looked up at him, beseeching him with my eyes. "*Please*."

He regarded me with a scowl for several seemingly eternal seconds before he pushed me forward with a curse. "Be swift," he ordered.

Thank the Gods, I thought as I pivoted back the way I'd been going and raced up the stairs, taking them two at a time. There was a string in my chest—a beacon that I followed, letting it lead me to whatever was waiting for me. The stairs grew more and more difficult to climb as the destruction of the tower was revealed. Several parts were completely covered by pieces of wall and roof and I had to crawl my way over them as Sorrell stomped behind me.

I didn't notice it until I nearly stumbled over the body in my path. My ankles slammed into something and I went down, falling hard and slamming my knees into the stairs. "What—" My words fell to silence as I realized who I was looking at. "Orion!"

He was half covered in rubble, several large chunks of the wall and wooden beams over his legs. I turned back, ready to beg Sorrell for assistance, but he was already there, his face sallow with horror as he lifted and tossed the beams to the side. I blinked when he took a large chunk of stone and threw it and, as it crashed into the wall opposite of us, it broke into several pieces, leaving a rain of dust and gravel falling from the crater-like hole he left behind.

"Orion?" He hefted Orion's completely limp body into his arms. I reached forward, running my fingers over his dirt streaked face, but as I wiped the worst of it away, I finally saw the truth. "Gods..." Sorrell's voice was horrified.

Dark, black lines were drawn across his body. Up his neck and over his arms—they covered every inch of his skin. My eyes rose to Sorrell's. "What does this mean?" I asked, shakily.

Sorrell's expression was pale and concerned. "Nothing good," he replied as he tapped Orion's cheek. "It's poison," he cursed a moment later.

Fear swelled in my chest. "What do we do?" I demanded. "We have to do something."

Sorrell cursed again as he stared down at Orion's slack face. Through clenched teeth, he took the front of Orion's shirt and ripped it open to reveal his chest. More black spiderweb veins traced down and collected over where his heart was.

"See how his veins are black?" Sorrell asked. I nodded. "There are only a few things that can do that to Fae, and humans don't know about them, which can only mean this was done by another Fae."

"Tyr," I breathed.

The dark look that crossed his expression would have fucking terrified me had it been turned my way. As it was, I knew the cause was the name I'd just uttered. "Yes," he said through gritted teeth. "That would be my guess."

"So, what do we do?" I asked. "How do we help him?"

He bared his teeth as his eyes settled on Orion's chest, glaring down at the lines in his skin. The longer he went without saying anything the faster my heart raced. "Sorrell?" I tried again. "We have to try."

Finally, he hissed out a breath and shut his eyes, shaking his head. "We can try to boost his magical energy so that his body can fight off the poison on its own," he said.

"Okay, how do we do that?"

"It's dangerous," he replied. "That's the issue. For a poison this concentrated, it'll take an enormous amount of magical energy. More than either of us have. And even if we're successful, I can't very well carry both of you out of here."

"Then let me do it," I suggested. "Just to get him up and moving."

"It won't get him up and moving," Sorrell replied. "It would take both of our energies and some just to wake him, much less get him on his feet."

"Well, we have to try!" I snapped. "Just tell me how to do it. If we just leave him like this ... he'll die, won't he?"

After a brief, tense moment Sorrell cursed again and nodded. "Fine. Fuck. Okay. It's—difficult to explain. It's usually something a Fae learns as they grow up and master their magic, but you haven't."

As if I needed another reason to feel sorry for myself. I shook that thought off and pressed my hands down on Orion's chest. "Just tell me what to do," I ordered.

"Keep your hands there," he said, watching me. His gaze flickered from where my fingers rested, pushing harder into the black veins spreading over Orion's body to his face. "Close your eyes and reach for the power you have inside—every Fae in existence has a well of it. It's inside. For me, it's like a long dark lake of water and ice. To pull power from it, I need to focus on moving it with my mind. Lifting it and breaking the glaciers over it as they sink further and push my power back up with it. For each Fae, though, it's different. It may bring to your mind a different image, but start there."

I closed my eyes and tried to picture what he was describing. Try as I might, though, the image of a lake of ice and water never came. Instead, I found a glowing sun, burning bright and hot in the center of my core. I waved my imaginary fingers over it and though it felt warm to the touch, it didn't hurt me. The darkness around it pressed against the sun, making it smaller and smaller—pulling it away from me. I knew I couldn't let that happen. If I did, my magic would never come and Orion would die here in this crumbling stairwell of a prison tower.

Shoving myself forward, in my mind, I fought my way back towards the sun, and just as my fingers reached out and grasped it—the darkness gave way to a blinding light. "Yes." I heard Sorrell's voice in the back of my mind. "Just like that."

I felt my whole body grow warm as I brought the sun closer and cradled it to my breast. "Now, will it into Orion's body," he said. "Let it fill you and then push it outward, through your palms."

I did as he said, letting the warmth of the sunlight fill my body—letting it overpower me and grow even stronger until it became too much. Then I began to push it. I shoved it forward, feeling the tingle of awareness move down my limbs—down my arms—as I let it release from my palms and fingertips. More and more, I pulled the light from my sun and pushed it outward.

Sweat collected at my temples. Pain began to radiate up my spine. I ignored it and kept going. "Cress..." Sorrell's voice was far away. "Roan's on his way—I sent out—"

Whatever he was saying was cut off as I shook my head and forced myself to concentrate on the task at hand. More light poured from me. My head began to ache. The warmth was dying down. It wasn't enough. Tears pricked behind my closed eyes. No, I had to give him more.

"Cressida," Sorrell's voice came from miles away. As if he were yelling over a vast amount of space. "You have to stop."

Stop? I thought. No I couldn't do that. Not until Orion was safe.

"Now, Cress!" Sorrell sounded angry. Had he ever called me Cress before instead of Changeling or Cressida? It seemed like such a stupid thought to have in the moment, but I couldn't help the wandering of my mind as I felt my body sag.

My eyes opened, but it felt as though I was lifting rocks off of them just to crack them. Beneath me, I saw that the black lines marring Orion's flesh had receded. Sorrell's ice cold gaze stared at me. "Stop," he ordered.

My head swam, and I had to put my hands on the stone floor to prevent myself from falling over. I was so dizzy that I didn't even notice that Sorrell had already stood and picked up Orion, slinging him over one shoulder like a sack of potatoes.

"Roan's coming," he stated. "He'll be here soon."

I would never know, I thought in the next instant because, as I tried to stand back up, the whole world grew distant and I felt myself falling back into oblivion.

CHAPTER 14

CRESS

The first thing I heard when the world slowly came back to me was someone talking—a female. Whoever she was, she was really close. Practically right next to me, and she was nervous. Was she crying? The sound of sniffles reached my ears and I couldn't keep my eyes shut anymore.

Before I could seek out the girl, my eyes settled on my surroundings. Familiar stone walls that didn't have bugs crawling out of the cracks. No cobwebs either. But what told me that I was truly, finally back in the Court of Crimson was the little buzzing noise and then a flit of wings above my head as a pixie carried a big, fat, delicious looking bread roll. My mouth watered. My stomach rumbled.

"Cress?" The sound of my name being called in that familiar voice had my eyes seeking the girl out.

"Nellie." Her name came out on a croak. Gods, my throat was parched, but I'd never been happier to see my best friend in my life.

Nellie flung herself at me, her arms going around my neck as I placed my elbows on the bed and tried to leverage myself up. The pixie above me jumped and the roll slipped from his tiny little hands and dropped on my head before rolling onto the mattress beneath me.

"I'm so glad you're awake," Nellie said. "We didn't know what to think. You collapsed on the way back and—"

"I'm fine," I assured her as the fingers of my free hand sought out the roll the pixie had dropped. I hoped he hadn't been carrying it anywhere to go to anyone else because I was famished. I shoved the whole thing into my mouth until my cheeks bulged and then quickly hugged my best friend back. Sweet, delicious yeast—my Gods this was the best thing I'd ever eaten in my life.

Even as dry as my throat was, it went down easily and already I wanted more. Maybe being cooped up in a tower and fed mystery soup and moldy bread for days on end would do that to a girl, but right then, I could've eaten a whole mountain of these things.

I coughed and sat up even more as Nellie pulled back and wiped quickly beneath her eyes. "You have no idea how worried I've been," she said, reaching for something on the table alongside the bed. I sighed in relief as she lifted a mug of water towards me.

Without even hesitating, I took it from her and downed what was in the cup. "I think I have some idea," I told her as I finished the drink and handed the empty mug back to her.

She set it on the table and turned back towards me, but before she could get another word out, the door opened and in walked Roan. He came to an abrupt halt when he saw me and then he jerked as someone behind him slammed straight into his back.

"Roan, what is—" Sorrell's irritated voice cut off as Roan stepped to the side and he realized the reason for Roan's sudden stop. "Cressida..." My full name sounded so strange to my ears, but sweet at the same time. It didn't matter that he was kind of an asshole. I was just so happy to be home that I didn't even think; I flung back the covers and dove out of the bed and straight into his arms.

Nellie squeaked as she, too, was thrown from the bed and onto the floor. Sorrell caught me readily enough and I looked down. "Sorry," I said quickly.

With an exasperated look, Nellie got up from the floor and rubbed her rear. "Well, good to know you're still the same as ever after being captured and almost killed," she said sardonically.

"Did you really think it would change me?" I shot back.

Her lips parted, but once again, before she could give out a reply, she was interrupted. "Nellie, could you give Cress and us a few minutes alone?" Roan asked.

Her lips pressed together and I could tell she wanted to argue. Instead of doing so, however, she sighed and nodded. Her hand gently touched my arm as she headed out the door. "I missed you, Cress," she said quietly. "I'm glad you're back. There's so much I have to tell you."

I reached out and snagged her fingers with my own before she could let go. "And I want to hear it all," I replied. "Soon." Nellie looked up at me, her pale face tilting up as she smiled, and then she pulled her hand away and was gone, letting the door close behind her on the way out.

Sorrell released me and let my legs slide to the floor. Yet, when I moved to pull back, his arms encircled me, halting the movement. "Do you know how dangerous that stunt you pulled was?" he demanded, shaking me slightly.

My head jerked back as I looked up into cool, ice blue eyes full of such fury and something else … that wasn't. No. It couldn't be. "Were you … afraid for me?" I asked cautiously.

"Was I—" Sorrell's hands disappeared from my sides as he yanked himself away, turning as he stomped several paces away before turning back just as quickly and pointing a finger my way. "You are a menace!" he accused.

I blinked. "Yes? And?" *Did he think I would be shocked by that little proclamation?* The nuns had called me that more than once or twice. Coming from him, I wasn't surprised.

Sorrell's face registered an expression of shock and then more fury and then...

"Are you turning purple?" I asked before looking at Roan. "Roan, I think he's turning purple. Is he breathing? Make sure he's breathing."

"I'm breathing just fine!" Sorrell snapped, dropping his arm. "You, on the other hand, are lucky to be breathing at all! You could have died."

I knew that and perhaps it said something about me as a person that upon waking that wasn't my first concern. "Where's Orion?" I asked.

Sorrell frowned. "He's resting in his chambers," he said.

"What happened to the poison?" I took a step towards him. "Is it all out? Is he okay? Is he recovering? Can I see him?" With every question I asked, I took another step in his direction until I was right before him.

Roan huffed out a breath. "He's out of the initial danger," he answered, drawing my attention. "But he is severely depleted of his magic reserves. Groffet made a potion that will keep the poison at bay, but we need to get his magic back at full strength —Gods, we all do." At that last statement, he put a hand to his neck and cracked it. "It's been a few days since we rescued you from the Amnestia capital. There's more at play here and we don't know how much time we have left before we can expect another onslaught. Whatever happened at the King's castle—"

"Tyr," I said suddenly, cutting him off. "Tyr is planning something horrible. We have to stop him."

Sorrell and Roan exchanged a look. "What do you know, Cressida?" Sorrell demanded.

"Tyr is using King Felix for his own gain. He plans to have the races wipe each other out and when the King is killed and the leaders of the Fae are gone, he plans to take over and rule over what's left." My hands found the front of his shirt and clutched it for dear life. "We can't let that happen," I beseeched him. "So many people will die."

Sorrell's hand curved over mine and gently—much more gently than I expected from him—pulled them away. "We will stop him," he said. "Make no mistake—Tyr will pay for his crimes against Faekind."

"And the humans," I reminded him.

"For now," Roan said, stepping forward as he tugged me away from Sorrell and wrapped me up in his arms, "we need to recuperate." His fingers sank into my hair as he dragged me close. His nose touched my scalp and he inhaled. "Gods, how we have missed you, Little Bird. The very thought of your life being snuffed out before it was time—even if it was your time … I couldn't allow it. I can hardly believe that you're here now, in my arms."

The tremble of his voice reached deep within me and I found my arms lifting to encircle him, to drag him even closer. "I'm here," I whispered back. "I'm alive."

"You almost weren't," he choked out. "Cress, Little Bird, you cannot do that again. Ever."

"I tried to fight him," I said. "I didn't go willingly."

Hot breath touched my neck and then my head was ripped back and Roan's mouth descended over mine, devouring me and scorching me all the way to my core. My pussy pulsed with a fiery need I hadn't felt in days. I moaned into his lips.

Fingers against my scalp. Heat beneath my skin. I pushed up against Roan's chest, practically climbing him and, when his hands went from my head to my ass as he lifted me ever closer, I completely forgot that someone else was in the room until a cool hand touched my arm and Sorrell's voice intruded. "Roan, that's enough," Sorrell snapped. "If anyone could use the replenishing, it's Orion."

My head pulled back and I blinked as the lust Roan had created in me died down once more. "Replenishing?" I repeated, dazed.

Roan's hands gripped me firmly and a growl rumbled up from his chest. Then his grasp softened and slowly but surely my feet made their way back to the floor. My thighs were shaking with need, though. Just because he'd stopped didn't make the feelings go away. I felt as though I were on the edge of a crash—as if I'd stayed awake for far too long and exhaustion was about to pull me under, and yet I needed something. Something far greater than anything I'd ever experienced before. Needed it—whatever it was—like I needed to breathe.

Roan cursed. "Sorrell's right. Orion needs you far more than I do right now," he said through gritted teeth.

"He needs me?" I asked. "Then why are we just standing here? Take me to him!" I wanted to see him, to assure myself he was all right. The image of those black veins working their way beneath his skin rose to the forefront of my mind. It made me sick with worry. I could feel sweat beads pop up along my skin. "Please, Roan. I have to see him."

"He's in bad shape, but he's going to be fine," he assured me. "We'll take you to see him, but Cress … you need to understand what he needs."

"What does he need?" I demanded the answer from him. Whatever it was, I would fight tooth and nail to get it for him. I would go to the ends of the Kingdom. I needed him to be okay.

"You, Cress," he said. "He needs you."

ROAN AND SORRELL LED ME TO THE SAME CHAMBERS THAT I'D spent my first night in when I'd initially stumbled upon their magical castle. What I knew had only been a few short months ago felt like a lifetime. My hand hovered over the door's latch and I glanced back as they both stepped back.

"We'll let you have some alone time," Roan said. "We have to shore up the castle's defenses."

I gulped. "What about you two?" I asked. "Don't you need to replenish your magic as well?"

Sorrell's jaw hardened, but it was once again Roan who answered. "We will be fine for the time being." He nudged me with a small smile. "Take care of him and then you can take care of us."

My eyes flitted to Sorrell, waiting for a denial from him. I half expected him to tell me that he wouldn't require my help in that snotty, aristocratic tone of his, but when he looked back at me, all I could see was melting ice and the promise of something dark. I shuddered in response, quickly turning back to the door and lifting the latch as I pushed my way in and let it close behind me.

Inside of Orion's chambers, the room was dark, but I followed what I could remember. The stairs were to the side, and my hand curved around the banister as I climbed into the garden. The smell of flowers and wet leaves assaulted my nose and the glass that let in the light from the sun and moon— however fake it was since the windows didn't always ascertain the true time on the outside—illuminated the immediate area.

A dark shadow was cushioned on a mattress on the floor. "Orion!" I cried, hurrying towards him. My knees hit the ground at his side and my hands roved over his body. He'd been stripped from the abdomen up and there were still some fine gray markings under his skin. Tears assaulted my eyes. "Oh, Orion..." I sniffed as I closed my eyes. "I'm so sorry."

"Cress?" Orion's voice was quiet and his hand rose to touch my cheek. My eyes popped open and I jerked my gaze up to meet his. His eyes were cracked, though just barely, but his face was pale and his lips were practically as gray as his veins.

"What has this done to you?" I asked him.

"Nothing you can't help me with," he said. Orion's hand caressed my cheek, his thumb stroking slowly over my skin. I raked my teeth over my bottom lip and leaned into that touch.

"They told me what you need," I said. Sex, I thought. Fae needed touch to survive—they needed it to replenish their magic. And all three of them had refused to take a lover since I'd been gone. My heart was both full and broken at the same time. *What must that have cost them?*

"We don't have to do it now, sweetheart." His words drew me out of my haze of guilt.

"What?" I jerked back. "Of course, we have to do it now. Look at you! We're doing this."

I reached for the blanket over his lower half and pulled it down, stopping when I realized he wasn't naked from the waist up, but completely and utterly naked all the way down. My eyes bulged. "Uhhh..."

"I'm surprised you didn't notice before," he chuckled as I stared at the hardened shaft jerking against his belly.

"I was a little distracted," I muttered as I pulled back and reached for the fabric of the gown I'd woken up in. Lifting it, I tossed a leg over both of his and lowered myself down until I was straddling him. "But it's good, I can work with this. You're going to be fine."

"Cress—" His hands moved up my arms as he struggled to sit up.

"No!" I pushed my palms against his chest and tried to shove him back down. "I got this!"

"Cress, you don't have to—"

"Yes, I do," I snapped, pushing harder. *Damn it, why was he so much stronger than me even when he was ill? It just wasn't fair!*

"Cress, I will be fine. Groffet has a potion—"

I let my head thump against his chest even as his cock pressed against my slit. "I want to," I whispered, stopping him.

"Please, Orion. I want to." I needed to assure myself that he was truly here, alive and well. I didn't need anything else but that.

A large palm landed on the back of my head and I felt his lips press against my scalp. "You know that I cannot resist you when you're like this," he whispered.

"Does that mean you're going to give me what I want?" I asked, gently lifting my hips and rubbing against him.

A groan left his chest and that was all the answer he gave before his other hand went beneath the folds of my gown to grasp his shaft and guide it towards my opening. A soft gasp escaped my lips as he sank inside. It'd been so long—forever, it felt—since we'd done this. My hands arched up to wrap around his back and in movements as old as time, I began to ride him.

Up and down, up and down, I lifted myself and fell back over his shaft. His clenched teeth did nothing to hide his grunts of pleasure. My vision swam as I held onto him. Heat poured from me into him and then from him into me. *Magic*, I realized. *Fae magic.*

Orion's fingers stole beneath my gown and found the little bundle of nerves above where we were connected. I gasped and arched up as his hips lifted and pounded against me with more force even as his fingers pinched and rolled that bundle. Stars danced before my eyes—little flashes of light. My air sawed in and out of my throat as my nails sank into the skin of his back and dragged downward.

He groaned and fucked into me even harder. Our heads tilted and our lips connected. Tongues tangled. Breaths mixed. And on the next shift of his cock into me, he pinched my clit again and I exploded. Fire raced through my mind, burning away all clear or logical thought until there was nothing but him. Nothing but us. Nothing but the magic.

CHAPTER 15
SORRELL

"What do you think you're doing?" Roan's quiet but firm question made me turn back towards him as the door to the library closed behind us. Across the room, Groffet bustled between rows and stacks of books, seeking an answer to all of our problems—as if it could be found in a mere dusty volume.

"What do you mean?" I inquired absently, wiping a bit of dust from my shirt as I brushed against one of the towers of books Groffet refused to find a new place for. The crazy, old man.

"Cress," Roan stated, catching me off guard.

I paused and looked back. "I will repeat," I said slowly. "What do you mean?"

His fiery gaze locked onto my face. Then he shook his head. "I've seen the way you look at her, Sorrell," he said. "You pretend like you don't feel it, like you don't see how you feel— but it's obvious."

With careful movements, I pivoted my body so that instead of looking at him from over my shoulder, I was facing him fully. "I don't know what you're talking about," I stated.

"That," he snapped, gesturing towards me. "It's that right there—you're refusal to admit it. Willful ignorance. You know, but you don't want to know. You feel it, but you don't want to feel it. You're drawn to her."

"I am not drawn to the Changeling," I sneered, working to put a little disgust into my tone.

Roan's gaze, however, remained steady—unimpressed and no doubt, unconvinced. "Why do you fight it?" he asked.

"There's nothing to fight." I sniffed and turned away, moving across the room until I reached the platform that held Groffet's workspace. I sought him out, but the damn troll had disappeared on us. I growled in irritation. "Where is that old man?" I snapped.

"You can't walk away from this." Roan's voice lifted and floated to me from across the room.

I sighed and spun to face him once more as he approached at a much slower pace. "I'm not walking away from anything," I said. "I do not feel the same way that you feel towards your little Changeling."

"You were worried for her," he pointed out.

I gritted my teeth and cursed my powers as ice began to form along my fingertips. Anger always came out as cold—always cold. Whereas she was anything but. The Changeling—Cressida—she was like a ray of sunshine, warm, life giving, beautiful. I shook my head, warding away those unwelcome thoughts.

"What do you want from me?" I asked, fixing Roan with a dark glare. "What is it that you hope to get from me by trying to convince me that I care for the Changeling the same way you and Orion do? I'll allow that the two of you care for her. I'll even step back and let the two of you keep her. You still plan to marry her; I'm no idiot. You meant every word you said at the Court of Frost. You intend to make her your Crimson Princess."

"She could be yours as well."

Shock ricocheted through me. *Was he ... offering the girl to me?* A deep yearning awoke within me. The desire to feel her golden locks across my chest, stroking down my abdomen. Her mouth around my cock. Her body in my bed.

With a croak, I responded. "She wouldn't want me." I meant it. She was smart enough to realize that I was no good for her. I had been nothing but cruel to her since the moment she'd fallen into our laps and there was nothing in me that wanted to stop now. She responded so beautifully to my icy rage. She didn't shrink away in fear. Wasn't deterred by it. She rose to my challenges and made me want to pin her down and show her just what I could do to her to make her submit to my will.

"Sorrell," Roan barked.

I blinked and realized the ice had reached up to my forearms and small dustings of snow were falling from the edges of my hair. With a jerk, I reached up and shoved my fingers through the strands, stripping away the snow and letting the ice fall to the floor and melt beneath my boots.

"You want her," Roan said. "Admit it."

I stiffened. "Why is this so Gods damned important to you?" I growled.

"Because hiding from your feelings will only serve to destroy you later," he answered. "Of anyone in this world, the three of us should know that best, don't you think?"

Words escaped me. I could not tell him he was wrong. It would be a lie, and yet, I wasn't ready to admit to anything that had to do with the Changeling. The longer Roan waited, the more frustrated he became until small little tendrils of smoke began to seep from his hair. He huffed out a breath and turned away just as a small flame erupted.

He didn't appear to even be aware of his movements as he reached up and patted it out. "You'll regret your obstinance, Brother," he snapped. "Gods help you, but I hope you cave soon.

Don't think I haven't noticed how you haven't touched another Fae female since she arrived. We need to be restored and if the only one you're willing to let help you is her, then I truly hope you pull your head out of your ass soon and realize what she means to you, or risk her hatred. The choice is yours." With that, he stormed for the exit, opened the door, and left.

I sank into a nearby chair as the library doors clanged shut behind him. My head sank back and I found myself staring up into the ceiling. *Was he right?* I wondered. *Of course, he was.* The Changeling had altered everything. She'd fallen into our world and had wrecked all of our well laid plans to master each of our magics, end the war, and take our places as Kings.

Maybe it appeared that I hated her now, but my feelings were as far from hatred as they could possibly be. Anger—yes, I felt anger. At myself. For wanting her. For desiring her. And then I felt it towards them. That was what made me feel the deepest guilt. I was angry at my friends, my throne brothers— the only men who had ever gained my trust and kept it— because they wanted her, they felt no need to hide it or fight it, and because of that, they had her.

Right now, I had no doubt that Orion was fucking the Changeling. Bringing her to orgasm over and over again. Giving her the very same pleasure I wanted to pull from that fragile looking body of hers. I was in trouble. She had wormed her little self between the three of us, but I wondered … briefly … if maybe it wasn't to pull us apart, but to seal us even closer together. With her between the three of us, there would be no power in the world that could separate us.

An idea popped into my head, and as I sat there, my mind gave it life. We Fae were weakened when separated. In our individual Courts meant to give power to no one great entity, but what if the Courts were brought together? What if all of Faekind could be ruled under one entity. Not a King, but perhaps a Court of Kings?

I sighed and I shifted back, my hand falling over the side of the chair to bang into something beneath the table at my side. I jerked and looked down, finding a familiar instrument. With a frown, I reached beneath the table and sought out what I'd seen, and when I pulled my hand free, in it was an old violin I hadn't seen in ages.

"What the—"

"I see you've finally found it." Groffet's words made me jump from my chair and whirl around.

"Groffet," I gritted his name out through clenched teeth. "Do not sneak up on me, you insolent troll!"

He stared back at me over the wide bridge of his nose and huffed. "Do not be angry at me, young Prince, for your own absence of mind."

"I wasn't—" The denial died on my lips. I had been absentminded, too focused on her. I shook my head and turned away, only belatedly realizing the instrument I clutched in my hand until it banged loudly against the table. "Shit!" I cursed, pulling the violin up and inspecting it to see if it was damaged.

Groffet tsked, the sound an irritating judgment in an otherwise silent room. I lifted my gaze and offered him a dark look. "If you have something to say, old man, say it."

Groffet waddled across the floor until he stood just on the other side of the table and then shuffled around it until he was at my side. His fat troll fingers reached for the violin, and though I narrowed my eyes, I released it to his grip.

"You have not played her in a long time," he said quietly, as he moved his hand down her neck and over her body. Several strings were missing, as was the bow. "But I believe you have found her again for a reason."

"There's no time for music lessons, Groffet," I said. "What have you found?"

Groffet didn't answer me right away, but as much as I hated it, I'd grown accustomed to his impertinence. He would speak when he was ready to and no sooner. "There is something in the works," he finally said after several long moments. He handed the violin back to me and took a step back. "But it will not be ready for a night or two. I must make the necessary preparations. I recommend you and the other majesties take this opportunity to heal. You will need it for what is coming."

Although his words were serious, my mind stuck on the word majesties. I snorted. "Since when do you refer to us by our titles?" I asked with a shake of my head.

Groffet smiled, revealing crooked, yellowed teeth and a small dimple set into the side of his face that I'd never seen nor noticed before. "The time is coming where all will know you only by those titles," he said cryptically, but before I could ask what he meant, he shuffled away and left me standing there holding an old violin.

I sighed. I would need something to keep my mind off of Cress and the others, something, perhaps that could distract me long enough for me to finally make a decision.

About her. About our Court. And about Faekind as we knew it.

CHAPTER 16

CRESS

My body ached in the most delicious way when I awoke the next morning. The warmth of a masculine body was pressed to my back. Real sunlight—at least, I was pretty sure it was real—streamed in overhead.

It was by far the most peaceful way I'd woken up since being captured. So, instead of ruining it by turning and waking up my bed partner, I exhaled and snuggled back into Orion's embrace. His arms tightened around me, pulling me back against him even more. A low growly noise sounded behind my ear as he released a breath.

"Cress." My name was a sigh on his lips and it made me smile even as my chest tightened.

We stayed like that for a long moment. His hands clenched and unclenched around my stomach and his heart beat faster against my back, letting me know that he was awake. As my sleepiness faded, too, I wriggled around until I was facing him, earning a deep, throaty chuckle from his lips. His dark eyes gazed intently into mine while his hand came up and brushed a lock of hair from my face. While his expression started off amused and pleased, it slowly morphed. His brows drew down low over his eyes and his lips pinched

"Cress, I—" he began

"What's wrong?" I cut him off, reaching for him. My hands moved over his naked chest and abdomen. "Is it the poison?"

"No, Cress." His hands captured mine, stilling their frantic movements. "It's nothing to do with that. The poison is receding. I'll be completely healed before the end of the day." His dark eyes met mine. "Thanks to you."

"Are you sure?" I pressed.

"Yes." He nodded and then lifted his hand to slowly stroke a knuckle lightly down the side of my face.

"Then what's wrong?" I asked insistently, worry creasing my brow.

His pinched lips curled down into a deep grimace. "I…" Orion sucked in a breath and only when it shuddered back out did he continue. "You were taken because of me," he said. "For that, I'm sorry. If Tyr hadn't known of my interest in you then you wouldn't have been in danger. I put you in that position."

"Orion." I reached up between us and touched his face, securing my gaze to his and staring into his eyes for a second longer before I continued—just to make sure he was paying attention. "You are *not* responsible for your brother's actions. You are not Tyr." His lips parted and before he could get out another word to oppose what I was saying, I reached up and silenced him by holding one of my hands over his mouth. "In fact," I said, glaring at him meaningfully. "I'd say you're about as opposite from your brother as you could get. You care about others, you care about me, you care about how this war is affecting Fae kind. The only thing Tyr cares about is power. Nothing else."

I took a breath, trying to calm the riotous anger that was blisteringly hot inside of me. "Do not equate yourself to him," I ordered, "because you are so far above him, there's no competition. You are brave and amazing and you mean more to me than you could possibly understand..." My words trailed off, and as they did, he reached up and gently tugged my hand away from his mouth before turning to place a kiss against my palm.

"Do you understand?" I wondered aloud.

He frowned but didn't say anything for a long moment. Then, still holding my hand, he reached forward and pulled me onto his lap. "Understand what, Cress?" he whispered as I settled over him.

"How much I love you?" I asked. His brows shot up and his lips parted in surprise. I hadn't exactly intended to blurt out the question, but there was no taking it back. So, I shored up my courage and sucked in a breath. I straightened my spine and met his gaze head on. "I do," I stated. "I love you—and Roan." When he didn't immediately respond, I harrumphed and glared at him. "Well?" I pressed. "Are you going to say anything?"

He coughed out a laugh, shaking his head—the dark locks of his hair swiping back and forth with the movement. When Orion lifted his head once more to look at me, though, and I saw the blossoming smile spread across his face, my nerves settled. I breathed out a sigh of relief and loosened my hold that had dropped to his shoulders. I hadn't even realized I'd been squeezing so tight.

"I love you, too," he said. "More than life itself—I would die for you."

My heart felt like it could soar right out of my chest. I swallowed roughly, blinking back tears. *Why in the name of Coreliath was I on the verge of crying? What was wrong with me?* I sniffed hard and forced them away. Happy. I was happy. This feeling was so incredibly intense that it swept through me and I found that my lips were twitching, a smile forming that could have rivaled Orion's.

Orion's hands moved down and around my body until he pressed them against my spine, pulling me closer so that my breasts were smashed against his hard chest. His head came down and mine lifted. I knew what he wanted. His lips met mine and I shuddered as he consumed me. It wasn't the starving ravenous hunger we had for one another last night, but a reassurance that the bond between us was solid and unshakable. This kiss was a slow, leisurely exploration of each other, but at its core was a new tenderness, one that came from the depth of our bond.

The door down on the lower floor of Orion's chambers rattled and was thrown open and Orion and I broke off the kiss. "Good morning!" Roan's voice sounded from down below, followed by the thumping of his footsteps as he ascended the stairs and his head popped up over the garden's railing before the rest of him followed. "Good to see you're both still alive. I brought breakfast."

He waved his hand as a contingent of pixies floated forward, carrying a couple of trays laden down with fruits and breads and cheese. "How's the patient?" Roan asked, nodding between us as he swiped up a fruit and pulled a knife from his pocket, slicing it into chunks that he popped between his lips.

"Much better," Orion grunted as he gently settled me off of his lap and to the side. I reached across him and grabbed what looked like a shirt that had been tossed aside. He'd been naked when I'd come in last night, but this area was a mess of clothes strewn about. It was sort of amusing—all these plants surrounding a dark, messy figure. I pulled the fabric over my head and reached for one of the trays, snatching up a bun and shoving it into my mouth.

The warm and yeasty goodness practically melted on my tongue.

"You look well, Brother," Roan said, moving over as he watched the two of us.

"Cress worked her magic on me," Orion said as a wicked grin curved his lips.

The back of my hand slapped his chest before I'd even realized I'd moved. "I—uh…" I stuttered as they both shot me knowing looks. "Can you pass me more bread?" I asked.

As Orion did, he turned and faced Roan. "Where are we with a strategy?" he asked.

Roan popped another piece of fruit into his mouth and swallowed before responding. "I've got a meeting scheduled with the guards. Before we came back, I sent a few men to scout the area and follow the King's supply chain."

I shoved another one of the delicious rolls into my mouth and groaned as I chewed it slowly before a thought occurred to me. "Where's Sorrell?" I asked, tilting my head so that I could see around Roan's form against the railing, but there was no sign of anyone else but the three of us in the room.

Roan pursed his lips and tossed the core of his fruit at the pixie flitting above his head. The pixie snatched it out of thin air and my eyes widened as I watched the little creature unhinge its jaw to a disproportionate size compared to its small body. It bit into the dead core and swallowed the thing into two bites. It was kind of gross, but when the pixie finished its impromptu meal, it sighed and its wings fluttered as if it were happy.

"Sorrell is concerned," he said.

I eyed him. "Regular stick up the ass concerned…" I prompted. "Or…"

Roan didn't even crack a smile at that and instead, merely shook his head. Shit. That meant it was a serious type of concerned—one he likely agreed with. "The human King—"

"King Felix," I said, cutting him off briefly.

He shot me a look that made me suspect he didn't appreciate the interruption. I merely shoved another roll into my mouth and tilted my head back, batting my eyelashes—the picture of complete and utter innocence ... because, you know, that's totally what I was. Innocent.

"King Felix," Roan restated, narrowing his gaze on my upturned face as he did so, "has gotten far too brave. His colluding with Tyr is evidence of that."

"He doesn't know that Tyr's a Fae, though," I said, swallowing my mouthful quickly.

"Regardless," Roan said as Orion put a hand on my arm when I moved to get up, "the fact that he even considered kidnapping a Fae and executing her—never mind that we were able to stop it—proves that this war is far from over. I have no doubt that he's gearing up for an attack on our countrymen."

"And Sorrell?" Orion questioned.

Roan sighed. "He's overthinking our options. We have Cress back, and we know at least some of what Tyr is planning, but we don't have any definite steps forward and Sorrell seems to think that something big is on the horizon. I, unfortunately, can't disagree with him. If King Felix is willing to go to such lengths just to kill one Fae." He paused and gestured to me before continuing. "There's no telling what else he's willing to do or already planning. And Sorrell..."

I frowned, leaning forward, across Orion's chest as I waited, impatiently, for Roan to finish his last thought. When he didn't, I raised my brows. "Sorrell *what?*" I demanded.

"He's lacking in magical energy," Roan replied with a glance to his boots. He closed the pocket knife he'd been holding, shoving it along with his hands into the pockets of his dark trousers as he leaned against the railing. His brows furrowed in concentrated thought. "He hasn't replenished in well over a month, and I worry that he's going to insist on risking his life for the cause—No." Roan shook his head, the red locks of his hair sliding across his forehead as he did so. "I *know* he will.

"So, we can talk to him," I said, looking to Orion. "Right?"

"It's not going to be that simple, Little Bird," Roan answered and when Orion shook his head at my hopeful expression, I feared they were both right.

"It's not just him, it's also about the coming battle," Roan said thoughtfully. "We need to figure out what to do with the humans. We can shepherd our own people, but if we want to have any chance of peace, we need the humans to stop fighting us, and they don't seem likely to do so, especially after years of the King's propaganda against us."

I sank against Orion's chest, my own squeezing tight. The odds were stacked against us. What could we do? They were Royals, yes, but to face the facts—they only had so many men and King Felix had an entire Kingdom.

"Can Groffet do anything?" I asked, an idea popping into my mind. He was old, wise, and had hundreds of books in that library of his. He was the only one I knew of that the Princes looked to for guidance. "Couldn't he help us come up with a plan?"

Roan and Orion each looked at me with sad frowns. I hated it—that expression on their faces. It was as if they were thinking that the war was already lost. It wasn't.

"We have to do *something*," I insisted.

Orion calmed me as he stroked my arm and pressed a chaste kiss against my forehead. "We will," he assured me.

Roan gestured absently to the room. "This is what it's like, Cress," he said, his voice growing grave. "This is what it means to be a Royal. We have to make the decisions that will affect the entirety of our people—and if we choose wrong…"

He let the statement hang, but I only shook my head. "Then we won't choose wrong," I said. "We *will* figure this out."

They were both quiet for a long moment, Orion's fingers smoothing up and down the outside of my arm. "There will be panic," he finally said. "We have to keep things under wraps for now. Only people we can be sure to trust must know of everything that's happened."

Roan nodded and so did I. I was fine with that. I even agreed with it, as long as they didn't give up hope. Because in the darkness of war and all that we were bound to lose, hope was the one thing that, if taken from us, would truly result in the loss of everything we held dear. When I took Orion's hand in mine and looked at Roan as he met my eyes from across the room, I realized I had finally found where I belonged, and I wasn't giving that up, not without a fight.

CHAPTER 17
CRESS

After Roan's less than ideal news and the conversation we'd had over breakfast, I'd left Orion to recover in his chambers and had gone in search of Sorrell myself. While Roan was at a strategy meeting, I planned on finding Sorrell and finding out if there was something he knew that the rest of us didn't.

My search, however, had reached a dead end halfway through the day. He was nowhere to be found. Not outside where new guards were patrolling the wall. Not in his chambers—which had been difficult enough to find on my own, even with a few pixies along to guide me. Not even in the library—and that had been my most hopeful place to find him. Wherever he was, it was apparent that he didn't want to be found. It almost made me want to find him just to spite him and his annoying ability to hide from me.

I moved along the corridors slowly, thinking, trying to figure out any of the other places that I knew he could be. Every so often, I'd see one of the other Fae nobles who lived in the Court. Some would pause when they saw me, seeming insure of what to do. A few bowed. A few ignored my presence and kept walking as if they didn't see me. It didn't bother me much; if I was going to sneak up on Sorrell, I'd need all the invisibility I could get. He probably knew I was hunting for him and had hidden away on purpose. The asshole.

After several more hours of searching, I finally gave up and headed for the throne room where I knew Roan would be. I paused on the threshold of the room. The doors had been closed, but it appeared that whoever had come in or left last had accidentally left one of them cracked. I peeked in, listening to the sound of Roan's commanding and authoritative voice as I did.

Set in the middle of the room was a long wooden table. From where I stood, I could only make out papers and small figurines on top of it. Around it though, there were plenty of massive Fae—all clothed in the same leather coverings I knew soldiers wore beneath their armor.

I stepped closer to the door, placing my palm against the surface and leaning my ear into it. The second I did so, however, the door creaked open and several heads lifted and turned my way. Heat rose to my face as Roan turned and caught me standing there.

Whelp, I'd never been much for stealth anyway, I thought, deciding to push forward. I crept into the room, shifting the door open even further to allow me access. I lifted a hand and waved.

The corner of Roan's lips twitched and he shook his head at me before waving me forward and continuing on with his speech to the soldiers. As I moved forward, heading for the outstretched hand he offered me, my mind was catapulted back to a time not that long ago, when I'd snuck in here and been caught just like I had moments before. Though I knew it wasn't, it felt as if that event that had happened so long ago. As if it had been a different life, like it had happened to a different person.

"I want three on this wall, two on this one, and at least one lookout," Roan was saying when I finally made it to his side. "Are you okay? What's wrong?" Roan asked as soon as I was close enough for us to have a private conversation and not have to shout over the soldiers.

"It will be done, Your Highness," an older Fae with a silvery beard said.

"See to it," Roan said before glancing down to me. "And give me a moment. I'll be back."

"You don't have to stop for me," I protested as Roan's hand touched my side, rounding it as he led me several paces away from the table.

"It's fine," he said. "The men needed the mental break anyway. Is everything okay?"

"I'm fine, just taking a walk," I reassured him. "I was trying to find Sorrell, but he's—"

"Don't worry about Sorrell right now, Cress," Roan said, cutting me off. "You need to rest and recover from what happened to you."

I frowned up at him. "What happened to me?" I repeated, confused.

Roan's eyes darkened. "What you experienced at the hands of the human King—"

"King Felix," I corrected him again.

He glared at me, and I shrugged. "I'm fine," I assured him. "Really. Now that I'm back, I feel better than ever. I'm golden, really."

"You're sure you don't need anything?" Roan pressed, his hand tightening on my side.

I liked the hot pulse of his palm against me even if it was over fabric, and if he'd meant in any other way, I would've said I needed him to take me to his chambers and fuck me until I couldn't see straight. But I knew his intentions and they had nothing to do with anything other than my wellbeing. "No,

Roan," I said on a sigh. "I don't need anything. I was just searching for Sorrell"—I eyed him with a glare, wondering if he knew where he could be and was keeping it from me—"and I got curious as to what you were strategizing in here."

He sighed, sounding exhausted. "I'm just concerned," he said, finally. "Word of your almost execution has reached the other Courts and we've received communications from them indicating their concern."

I arched a brow. "Really?" I deadpanned. "Your mother is concerned for me?" If that wasn't a bald faced lie, I'd eat my left shoe—and though I could pack in the rolls, shoes ... not so much.

Roan's lips twitched for a brief moment. "Fair," he said. "Perhaps she doesn't much care for you, but she and the Frost Queen are concerned. You may not have been my mother's choice for me, but you will be the future Crimson Princess and eventual Crimson Queen. You were abducted and almost executed by the human—"

I eyed him and he sighed.

"By King Felix," he said, correcting himself before he even finished. "Our race was betrayed by one of our own. This showcases that it's no longer our guards or our soldiers that are very much in danger; we all are. King Felix is no longer happy to just sit back and murder our brethren on the field of battle, where we might expect. He no longer seems to care about honor or dignity. He and Tyr have threatened you, which means they have threatened us all—including royalty."

"What do you mean?" I couldn't quite wrap my head around his words. If royalty was threatened then that meant both he and Orion—even Sorrell—were in more danger than I'd originally believed. "You're not planning on going out to the battlefield are you?" I demanded.

Roan frowned. "Of course we are," he said.

"You can't!"

"Cress." When I would have moved away from him, Roan's hands found my upper arms and held me still in front of him as his head dipped and his eyes met mine, colliding with what I was sure was a show of fear and panic in my own expression. "We are used to this. Sorrell, Orion, and I—we've all been on the battlefield before. We can handle ourselves."

"That was before I knew you," I said. It was before I had come to care for them, to love them.

Roan's hands tightened on my arms, squeezing roughly. "Our race was betrayed by one of our own," he stated. "You, as my fiancée, are by extension considered part of the Royal Court families. Tyr went after you. It's only a matter of time before they come after all of us. We have to hit them before they hit us." I gulped at his words, but I didn't say anything. His hold loosened until finally he released me and took a step back. The second his skin left mine, I felt bereft, but I couldn't make myself reach out to touch him. I was in too much shock, trying to process his words, and think of something—*anything*—that I could do to fix it. "The Court of Frost is talking about coming to Amnestia. They want to provide more soldiers and support to us when we retaliate for your abduction."

"What? I didn't think they had that kind of power anymore. I thought they remained in Alfheim because they couldn't move to the human realm?"

Roan blew out a breath. "The Queens are determined. They know that if we were to attack the King on our own, we'd be weak. They are also very angry over Tyr's deception and betrayal. They've contacted the Court of Midnight to determine whether or not Tyr was acting on his own, but the Midnight Royals aren't responding to the messengers."

"What have the messengers said?" I asked. Surely, whoever had gone had gotten the information about the Court of Midnight would know something we didn't. "I'm pretty sure that Tyr is working alone," I said. "He didn't speak as if he had partners—at least any that knew of his plan."

"The Queens have sent messengers, but when I say there's been no response," Roan replied, "I mean that there's been absolutely nothing. The messengers haven't returned. If what you told us is true and Tyr is expecting to rule what's left after this war—the Queens would rather die in battle than live to see that happen."

I bit my lip in frustration, but before I could say anything, the older guard from before stepped around the table and called out. "Your Highness?"

Roan huffed out a breath, turning towards him. "One moment, I'll be right there," he called out before pivoting back to me. "I have to go, Cress."

I crossed my arms over my chest and stared up at him.

"Don't be upset," he said.

"I'm not upset," I said. Upset was far too tame a word for what I was feeling. "I'm scared. I'm worried. I'm frustrated."

Roan lifted a hand and cupped the back of my head, bringing me towards him as he leaned closer. "I know," he whispered. "But I promise you, this will all be over soon."

I shook my head. I couldn't see how that was possible. Though I knew the war had been going on for decades now, it felt as if recent events had made it all new again. It felt as if it had just begun. "I'm going to head to the library to see Groffet and Nellie," I tell him.

"Okay, have fun. Don't harass Groffet too much," Roan said. His fingers slipped out of my hair and he sighed, turning away. I watched him take several steps back towards the table and just as I was about to leave, he jerked to a halt, flipping back around and moving faster than before until he reached me.

My eyes widened as Roan grabbed me around my waist. My hands lifted and flattened against his chest as he crushed me against him and his head descended. I moaned involuntarily as his lips took mine in a bruising kiss.

Desire whipped through my body like a sudden wildfire. His tongue delved into my mouth as one hand splayed against my back and the other rose to cup the nape of my neck, positioning me just where he wanted me. His lips were hard and demanding against mine.

By the time he was done, my lips felt swollen and I was light-headed. He pulled away, just far enough that we could make eye contact, and whispered, "Tonight, you're mine."

His lips landed on mine once more, but only for a brief second, and then he was gone. When I opened my eyes, I saw him moving back to his soldiers, his head held high and his shoulders pushed back. He appeared every single inch the Royal Fae Prince. The commander and the protector.

I stumbled away, my hand grasping at the wall the second I grew close. Once I was out of the throne room, I leaned against the cool stone wall of the empty corridor for a moment, letting my heart calm itself.

Nellie, I reminded myself. I had to go and see Nellie. She'd said we needed to talk the last time I'd seen her. Hopefully she would be enough of a distraction to keep me from turning back and dragging Roan back to his chambers when I knew he had work to do.

CHAPTER 18
ROAN

Cress's departure brought me back to where I needed to be—strategy and planning. War. Even though humans and Fae had been at war for two decades, in the last several months, things had changed. A Changeling had been found—the last of her kind. I wondered if Cress even realized how special she was.

Changelings were creatures born of Fae and yet raised among humans. A tradition that had been popular when the coexistence of each race had been symbiotic. Now, all I could see lying in wait for us was extinction. This war would end, but the cost … the cost, I worried, might be too great.

I didn't enjoy the idea of killing off the humans. There was something intrinsically wrong about eradicating an entire species. And if it came down to it, I knew Cress would fight against it. My head lifted and I stared through the entryway where she'd gone. Then there was the matter of her little human friend. A dull pounding ache began in my head.

"Your Highness?" the sound of one of my soldier's voices brought me back to the present.

I gave him my full attention. "Where were we?" I demanded

He straightened at my tone and then gestured to the table before us. "We were discussing entry points into Norune Castle."

"How many are there?" I asked, looking down.

The map before me was hand drawn—but applied with magic, bringing the etchings to life. The mountains and castle stood upright as well as the little village that surrounded our target. We were given a bird's eye view of the place that would be our next objective.

"Three main gates, Your Highness," the man stated, pointing to each of them in turn as he continued talking. "The main entrance at the front between the village and the main road. A side entrance to receive supplies for the main hub, and a back entrance that appears to be sealed to make people think it's unusable."

"Is it?" I inquired, narrowing my eyes on the placement of that entrance—with its main wall facing a forest that would be easy to conceal ourselves in.

"No sir. We believe it's fully functional and merely 'sealed off' to present the idea of inoperational. From what our scout managed to gather, the entrance is an emergency one to be used in the event of crisis. It was likely built for the Duke and his family to escape if they were under siege."

I shook my head. They would be under siege soon, but there would be no using that entrance. That entrance was about to be one of our operating bases. I pointed to it on the map. "I want two men stationed inside the forest," I ordered. "We're not going to let anyone leave with the supplies they have in there." I lifted my head and looked across the table to the Fae who'd brought me this information—Xantho. "You're sure they have a hidden cache of supplies in here for the King?"

This information needed to be good. The war had slowly descended into mere tensions, but after Cress's abduction and Tyr's betrayal, a new phase of this long suffering conflict had finally hit. Now it was our turn to hit the human King where it hurt—his supply train.

"Yes, sir." Xantho nodded. "I seduced a young human who works within the castle and made some inquiries. She said that the Duke Everett is a close personal friend of the King's; he's been storing the King's extra supplies there for years."

If we did this—no, I shook my head, *when* we did this—an entire castle would be out of food. It was distasteful but such was the product of war. Hard choices that harmed innocents in the effort to stamp out the evil of hatred. I closed my eyes and reached up, pinching the bridge of my nose.

"Your Highness," Xantho said, leaning forward. I opened my eyes and fixed him with a look. "This is the right decision," he said. "Once the human King has no extra supplies, nor anywhere to store them, we'll be able to lay siege to his castle. If he decides to retreat and block us off—he'll receive no aid, no food, and no medicines until he surrenders."

"He won't surrender," I replied. That much I knew for sure. I'd seen his conviction at Cress's intended execution. The rage in his voice, the hatred he had spewed into the crowd of onlookers had been melodramatic and over staged. Yet, I had seen the honesty in his face. With each and every word, he truly believed in his right to kill as many Fae as he could until we were all wiped out. As it was, our race was not thriving. We couldn't in Alfheim now. It was a barren wasteland just waiting to perish. It was ruthless and dangerous. Soon enough, even the Frost Queen and my mother would have to come to grips with the fact that they resided in a dying world. I sighed. "King Felix would rather die than surrender to us," I finished.

The first guard slammed his fist on the table. "Then he dies," he said harshly. "That man has taken numerous lives of our loved ones. Even if he does surrender, we will show no mercy." The others surrounding the table shifted and grew restless. A few even voiced their agreement.

No. I wouldn't ask them to show mercy to a man such as him. My upper lip curled back. "He will be tried and executed for the crimes he's committed in this war," I assured my men. "But the villagers..." I gesture to the surrounding area of Norune Castle. "Like this one, the King's palace is surrounded by a capital city. There are people who live there—women and children. We kill the fighters," I stated. "The soldiers and the men, but we leave the innocents aside."

"Children grow into adults," an older guard, Leif, with a long scar torn down the side of his face spoke up. "We leave the seeds to grow and they will plant more destruction in the end."

No. This was where I drew the line. I let anger darken my voice. Fire erupted at my scalp and I did nothing to tamp it down. "We leave the children," I repeated. "Regardless of your convictions or beliefs, I am your Prince and you will follow my commands." I took a moment to glare around the table as silence descended. Several of my men frowned. They were confused by my statement—they agreed with Leif that to let the children of the soldiers who had killed their friends and family live made no sense.

I had to make it make sense, I realized. I pointed to the map and conjured magic, slowly—one by one—little figures began to draw themselves and then lift off of the parchment. Small figures. Pregnant figures and little ones who ran around the larger, slender frames of the others like darting little animals.

"If we eradicate the possibility of another generation of humans," I began, "we become the very monsters they believe us to be."

"Who cares what the humans think?" one brave soldier erupted. "We know the truth."

I lifted my gaze to the man and stared him down until he grew uncomfortable, shuffling back away from the table a few steps before lowering his eyes. Only then did I continue. "If we do this," I said. "Kill the children—the seeds—we will no longer simply be suspected evil, but we will be true evil." I shake my head. "No. Our main objective is the King and the former heir of Midnight, Tyr Evenfall. You may not like it, but you will obey. Any man seen killing unjustly will be reported to me and tried for the same war crimes as our counterparts." I searched the room, meeting the eyes of every Fae brave enough to raise his head. "We are not monsters," I told them. "We are Fae. We are warriors."

Silence echoed in the wake of my announcement and one by one, each Fae stood back and brought their right fist up, clenching and slamming it against their chest as a sign of respect. I nodded to them, an acknowledgment of their brav-ery, of their sacrifice thus far and future sacrifice if our war should need it, though I prayed to the Gods, we wouldn't.

"Go," I ordered. "Replenish your magic. Train and rest. We will leave for Norune Castle within the next two days. You have until then to prepare."

The men dispersed and I sighed, already feeling as if I were another hundred years older. "You spoke well," a familiar and welcomed voice said.

Turning, I offered Orion a small smile as he approached. "How is your recovery?" I asked.

He nodded. "I'll be well enough to travel with you when you go to this castle," he stated, stepping up to the table alongside me. He remained quiet for a moment and then he spoke again. "This is the beginning of the end," he said. "When the King is dead, and my brother, we will have won the war that has plagued us for decades."

"We should feel celebratory, shouldn't we?" I asked sardonically.

Orion's dark eyes rise to meet mine. "No," he replied. "It's understandable why you wouldn't. In war, there are no true winners. Only victors. We'll attain our victory."

I watched him curiously and sympathetically. Of all of us,

he had given the most in this war. Few people truly knew of the horrors he had endured on the battlefields. The scars that coated his body were messages—remembrances of what he had suffered. Lifting a palm, I grasped the shoulder closest to me.

"When Tyr is executed," I let the words linger on the edge of a whisper as I spoke them. He and I both knew that there would be no other outcome. When Tyr was captured, regardless of whether or not the Queens would demand a trial, he would die. We couldn't allow any other conclusion, not after all Tyr had done. "We will be here for you—Sorrell and I—as we have always been."

Orion stiffened under my hand and moved so that he shifted out from beneath it. "I will kill him myself," he said suddenly.

"No, Orion." I began to shake my head, but before I could utter another word, a blast of darkness rushed out from beneath the cuffs of his shirt, startling me back. I reared away as smoke darker than the inky blackness of night seeped from beneath his clothing. His neckline, his pants legs. Soon enough, he was shrouded in it. Covered completely as the smoky darkness clung to his frame, wrapping it's disturbingly lifelike tendrils around his body until he appeared to be drenched in a cloak of his own making.

Darkness.

Shadow.

Cold, quiet, fury.

"I will end this," Orion announced. "Once and for all."

My lips parted, but no words emerged. It was all I could do to stare back at him, watching as the magic he usually kept contained was unleashed. A lesser man might have run. Perhaps it made me the same as a lesser man to admit that, in that moment, I feared him. I feared the ferocity in his tone, the wildness in his eyes that I hadn't seen since he'd first arrived at the Court of Crimson—silent, cold, and seemingly unfeeling.

He'd been nothing more than a boy, afraid to love, afraid to care for anything, and far too broken.

He didn't need me to fear him now. He needed me to be with him. To help him. To center him. Mindful of the pain the shadows could cause, I stepped closer rather than away. I reached into it, grasping at his shoulders and shaking him slightly to get him to look at me.

"Together," I rasped as the skin over my knuckles and hands began to prickle. It was as though a thousand tiny needles were being driven into my flesh over and over again. I gritted my teeth and bore the pain. He had endured far worse. "We will get him and the King," I said. "And we will do it together."

CHAPTER 19

CRESS

When the library doors were finally in front of me, I hesitated. It wasn't that I didn't want to see my best friend, but so much had happened in such a short time that I wasn't sure what she would want to know and what I could divulge. The guys hadn't said anything about keeping what happened a secret, but wasn't it illegal to tell humans certain things about Fae Court? I sucked in a breath and decided that it didn't really matter. Nellie was my best friend. She was exempt from such laws ...hopefully.

I pushed open the heavy wood door and saw Groffet sitting at his workstation. He gave me a nod of greeting and said, "Your human friend is in the back stacks on the left."

"Thank you," I said, flashing him a quick smile.

I wound my way through the aisles of books and other items, most of which looked like scrolls and leather bound volumes of ancient texts, but other items didn't look like anything I'd seen before—jars of weird looking animal body parts, herbs-like branches that looked more humanoid than tree-like. My steps slowed as I passed them, but I kept walking until finally, I saw Nellie sitting in the furthest corner, surrounded by cushions and books, with a heavy tome open on her lap. Despite the open book, however, her eyes were closed. I got closer, only realizing when I was a step or two away that she'd fallen asleep. Soft snores were emitting from her half open mouth.

"Nellie," I whispered, trying not to laugh as I sat down on the cushion next to her.

When nothing happened, I shook my head and reached out —patting her arm and then pushing it gently until her lashes fluttered. Nellie jerked up and blinked, looking around. It only took her a moment to realize I was the reason for her sudden awakening. As soon as she saw me, her face broke out into a wide smile. She shoved her book aside and flung herself forward, her arms wrapping around me. "You came," she said as she pulled away. "I was worried you'd get sidetracked again."

"Well, better late than never, right?" I said with a wince. I wasn't surprised by her assumption. The Princes had taken up pretty much all of my thoughts recently. A result, I assumed, of all that we'd been through together, and okay, maybe the fact that I was, kind of, stupidly falling for them.

"I know, but those Princes keep you pretty occupied," Nellie replied with pursed lips as if she'd been reading my mind.

I narrowed my gaze on her. "You haven't picked anything magical up since you've been here, have you?" I asked suspiciously.

She smacked my arm. "I am not the one who goes running into any castle they find," she replied tersely.

There was a brief moment where I widened my eyes at her innocence and she stared at me with a reproachful look that I knew so well. Then, all at once, the two of us burst out laughing. I doubled over, clutching my stomach as my laughter ricocheted up to the rafters of the library and Nellie shook her head at me.

When the giggles died down, she sighed and then touched

my arm, reaching down to take my hand and pulling it into her lap. "I want to know everything that's happened," she said seriously. "I was so worried for you, especially when they came back from that other Court without you."

I took a breath. "It's a lot," I admitted. "I don't even know where to start."

"At the beginning," Nel suggested, her fingers tightening on mine.

"Just the trip to the Court of Frost was intense," I told her. "Then when we got there—I met the Fae Queens."

Her eyes widened. "What were they like?" she asked, her voice dipping to a whisper as if they were watching. It wouldn't surprise me, though, if those two rotten, old hags were spying on me—especially the Crimson Queen.

"They were perfectly horrid," I snapped. "They hated me— that much was clear. And Roan..." I stopped and groaned. "He didn't help matters when he just suddenly announced me as his fiancée."

"He did what?" Her jaw dropped, her mouth gaping open.

I nodded and pulled one of my hands out to pat the top of hers gently in understanding. "Oh yeah," I said. "Didn't ask, just announced it. To be fair, he did it thinking that it would act as a protection against anyone who tried to hurt me."

Her expression turned worrisome—her brows drawing together and forming a little wrinkled V in the middle of her forehead. "That obviously didn't work," she said quietly.

I winced. "No," I said. "But I can understand the attempt. Do you know exactly what happened?" I inquired.

She shook her head. "Just that you'd been kidnapped and taken to the King's castle. No one would tell me anything, but I had a feeling it was bad. After you were back, that's when I found out about the execution." Her hands began to tremble against mine. "I was so scared."

Yeah, I understood that. Had our roles been reversed, I

would have been terrified out of my mind. "I'm okay now," I assure her quickly, squeezing her fingers roughly. I bit down on my lip, considering what to tell her. "There were courtship events," I said. "Special ceremonies that happen when a Royal gets engaged. In the middle of the last one, it was Tyr—Orion's brother—who disrupted it. He kidnapped me and opened some portal to the Kingdom of Amnestia." I swallowed against a dry throat as I recalled the Run of the Gods and how it had started so differently than how it had ended.

"Why?" Nel frowned at me. "Why would he do such a thing?"

"Because he's helping the human Kingdom," I confessed. "His plan is to force the Fae and humans into a battle that will wipe out all of the major players."

"Even his own brother?" Her lips parted in shock. "How could he do that?"

"Because he's evil," I said. "Because he doesn't care who gets hurt as long as, in the end, he's the one left with power. He wants to rule over the ruins of what's left after the war and he doesn't care what he has to do to make that happen. When the Princes came to rescue me, he even…" I trailed off, remembering how Sorrell and I had found Orion with his veins turning black with poison. "He tried to kill his own brother," I finished.

Nellie and I sat in silence for a moment. Neither of us spoke and yet so much connection filtered between us. The fear. The relief. The worry over what the future would bring.

Finally, she spoke. "So, what happens now?"

I shrugged. "We come up with a plan and we take him down, I suppose," I said.

The corner of her mouth curled up in a rueful grin. "You make it sound so easy."

"Psh." I lifted one of my hands away from hers and waved it through the air. "We can do it. We've faced much worse.

Remember that one time when Sister Madeline tried to cook the Winter's feast?"

Nellie's face blanched and she shuddered. "Cook was furious," she said. "She burned the whole hog."

I wrinkled my nose. "It smelled horrible," I agreed.

"Not that you would've eaten it," she replied, eyeing me. "I've noticed, though, that you seem to eat well here."

"The food here tastes good," I said.

"Do you think it has anything to do with it being Fae food?" she inquired, leaning forward as she reached for the book she'd laid aside. "I think I figured out why you had such a hard time eating at the convent. Fae are supposed to eat only things that come from nature. Wheat and fruits and nuts and—"

"Well, I do eat a lot of bread," I supplied, cutting her off. "Does that count?"

She rolled her eyes, snapping the book shut once more. "Yes," she huffed. "It counts." The two of us lapsed into another moment of quiet, and then, she grinned at me. "So…" she began. "You and the Crimson Prince?"

My eyes shifted away as I reached up and gently scratched the underside of my jaw. "He was just trying to protect me," I said.

"But … you're engaged?"

I winced. We hadn't really talked about it since I'd been back. "Sort of?"

"Either you are or you aren't," Nellie said with a raised brow.

"We are?"

"Are you telling me or asking?"

I blew out a breath and dropped my hand back to my lap. "Oh, I don't know." I released a groan. "When he did it, it was because of the Court of Frost and his mother—it was like a vow of protection. Not really an engagement."

"That's not how he acted when he returned without you," she replied with a mischievous grin.

I narrowed my eyes on her face. "What do you know?"

"Clearly he still doesn't realize how much trouble you attract."

"I do not attract trouble!" I reached over and smacked her arm. Both of her brows rose as she pursed her lips at me. "Not much," I amended in a quieter tone.

A bubble of laughter left her, bringing a smile to my face. It was nice to see her laugh again after all we'd been through in the last few weeks. "Okay. I'll stop pressuring you," she said, then after a beat, she added, "about him—you will, however, have to tell me about the dark Fae. What was his name?"

"Orion?" I guessed.

"Yes." She nodded. "He seems quite taken with you as well. How does that work?"

"We … uh … share?" I said, feeling my cheeks heat. Nellie and I had never had the opportunity or a reason to talk about things like this before. We'd been raised around mostly women and young boys our whole lives. The only boys we'd ever known had come from the village and they'd been nothing like the Fae I knew now. Roan, Orion, and even Sorrell were warriors. Their shoulders were twice the width of an average boy's. They were men—Royals—and far more than I'd ever anticipated.

Nellie's mouth had dropped open and she just stared at me in shock for a moment before asking, "Does that make you a Princess then?"

I snorted in response to that. "I'm being called the Crimson Princess, but that doesn't make me a real Princess," I told her.

"You're a Gods damned Princess," Nellie suddenly burst out.

I blinked, staring at her in shock. "Did you just curse?"

"Hey, I have the right to be shocked by everything that's happened," she said, pointing a finger in my face. "It's not every day that I find out my best friend is a Fae Changeling and then, a Princess!" Nel shook her head again. "No wonder that cold one was concerned—he was a bit frightening when they returned without you." Her eyes turned to her lap and she shivered as if recalling something particularly unwelcome. "You're royalty."

"Wait." My mind wasn't catching up as fast as I thought it was. I pushed a finger into my ear and wiggled it around before turning my head and leaning closer. "Can you repeat that? Who was worried?"

"The cold one," Nel repeated. "You know the one with the longer pale hair?"

"*Sorrell* was worried?" My brows shot up towards my hairline. "Are you sure?"

She nodded, looking at me as if I was acting odd. I couldn't be acting any more odd than the Frost Prince of assholes actually giving a horse's ass about me. Then again ... he had been there to rescue me with the others. I thought that had just been because of the others, but what if it was more?

"I know you know that Roan and Orion both care about you, but he does as well. It's pretty clear that they all feel something for you," Nellie said with a sigh.

I was quiet for a moment before I replied. "I care about each of them as well," I admitted quietly. "I never expected this ... any of it really. I think that night I came here, it was the castle calling me. The horrible noise." I shuddered at the memory of how it had pierced my skull and rendered me unconscious. "I think ... maybe it was fate. That we were meant to meet. I'm grateful to the Gods—because without what happened, without finding this castle and meeting the Princes, I would have never known what I was. It's bizarre to think about, but they each..." I sighed. "They each complete me in a way I never expected. I didn't even think something like this was possible, let alone with multiple people."

"It's certainly different from the abbey," Nellie said, sounding slightly wistful.

A thought occurred to me. Nellie hadn't asked for this. I'd uprooted her from her life and forced her into this world with me. Guilt blossomed sharp and ugly in my stomach. "Would you want to go back there?" I asked quietly, curious

"No, not at all," she replied. "Even though I was terrified out of my mind to begin with, you're my best friend." Her eyes met mine and a smile formed. "Wherever you go, I want to be there for you. It's just ... I do sometimes wonder what's happened to them, you know?"

"I know what you mean." I scooted over and slung my arm around her shoulders. "I bet Sister Madeline is dancing with joy that neither of us have returned to corrupt any of the younger children."

"Sister Ermine is probably feeding them something foul to help cleanse the evil from their souls," Nellie added with a chuckle.

"Sometimes I wonder how I survived that place at all," I said. "But then I think about everything I've gone through since and wonder if the sisters being the way they were really did prepare me for what the world was like."

Nellie was quiet for a long moment before she leaned her head against my shoulder and said, "Maybe. It wasn't like they knew what you were, though. Both of our lives have changed. In fact, they both changed the night the castle showed up. Yours may have changed faster, but I think I'm catching up." I squeezed her shoulder. "Both of our lives have morphed into something terrifying and dangerous, but it's an adventure I don't think either of us would change. What the nuns did for us was prepare us for change. Each day is something new, something that tests us and who we are at the core of our beings. Something that helps shape us into who we are going to be. We can let it grind us down or we can rise up and fight against it.

"It doesn't matter if it's something to do with the Fae or with the humans, we have to treat it all the same so we can show them that they are equals. You and I might understand how similar Fae and humans are, but from their perspectives, they are polar opposites. If we lead by example then maybe they will catch on. It means we can't let any of it break us, though. We have to be strong for each other and for the people we represent."

"That was quite the speech, young lady," I said, nudging her with my elbow. "Sister Eleanor would be proud. She always knew you were smarter than me, which is completely unfair, I might add," I teased. "I'm the older one here. I should be the wise one."

Nellie pulled away from me and turned to face me. "It's not just you and me, Cress."

"What do you mean?"

"There's … someone I've come to care for." Her words were quiet but said with conviction. There's a sharpness, a force in her tone I've never really heard before. "He's been my rock through everything. As much as the Princes care for you, they don't really think about me, and when they told me that you'd been taken, I fell apart. If Ash hadn't been there, I don't know what would have happened. As much as I wanted to believe them, to have faith that they would get you back, the three of them against the King and his army seemed impossible.

"I've never been so scared, but Ash was there through all of it. He helped me stay strong. He's so sweet and caring and smart. Not to mention he has a wicked sense of humor. The best part, though?" She sighed and seemed to prepare herself for something. "Cress, he knows I'm human, but he doesn't care."

"Wait, he's Fae?" Of course he was Fae, I already knew exactly who she was talking about. I recalled seeing him in Groffet's library. I shook my head.

Nellie licked her bottom lip before continuing. "He's kind and understanding and strong, Cress. I thought he would be like all of the humans are towards Fae—angry and scared and hateful, but he's not. I think … I think I love him and that he returns my feelings."

My heart squeezed tight inside my chest. "Wow." It was all I could manage. The only word that I was able to slip out because I was still frozen in a state of pure surprise.

"Are you upset?" she asked hesitantly.

"What? No!" I jumped forward and snatched her hands up once more. "No, of course not, I'm glad you've found someone. I'm happy for you, really. I'm—okay, truthfully. I'm a little jealous that this has been going on, but I've been so mixed up with the Princes and the Court of Frost and then the near execution—"

"It's not your fault," she said, stopping me with a laugh. "I understand why you haven't been around."

"What I'm trying to say," I began again, feeling a burn at the back of my eyes, "is that if you love him then I'm happy and he's stupid if he doesn't love you back."

"Are you tearing up?" she asked.

"Me? No," I lied. I cleared my throat. "You'll have to officially introduce me to him so I can give him the appropriate warnings and whatnot."

"Warnings?" Nellie's eyebrows rose.

"You know, just the general 'hurt my best friend, and I'll break your kneecaps' or 'if you don't treat her right, I'll have Roan set you on fire'—nothing too horrifying," I said with a grin.

"Threatening to break someone's knees or burn them alive should not make you so happy." Nellie frowned as she pulled her hands back and crossed her arms over her chest.

"It's not the threat that makes me happy but the fact that it's needed. You have someone for me to threaten. That's a fabulous thing."

"You don't need to threaten him. He won't tell anyone anything, he's very discreet, and he's promised to protect me for the rest of my life should I need it." A blush rose to her face, staining her cheeks bright pink.

"It's going to happen, so you may as well get used to it. He needs to know where I stand on the matter. Besides, if I can scare him that easily I'll be surprised. Roan and Orion certainly don't find my threats very menacing." I sighed and had to stop myself from pouting. Just once it would be nice to threaten them and have them take it seriously.

"You're a Princess now though, that in itself might scare him," Nellie reminded me.

"Meh, not really a Princess. Roan and I are engaged, but we're not married yet—if we ever will be." I grew somber. "The war needs to end before anything else happens."

Nellie's gaze softened. "It will," she said. "I truly believe that people—of all races—don't want to live in such fear and hatred."

I forced a smile as I leaned forward and hugged her to me. I hoped she was right. I prayed to the Gods she was. Tyr was my biggest concern, though. Something told me he would not be defeated easily. The future was unclear and it was that more than anything else that scared me.

CHAPTER 20

CRESS

Roan's chambers were well warmed. Someone had stopped by several hours before to light a fire in the hearth, for which I was grateful. It seemed as though eons had passed since we were in the Court of Frost, but honestly, I was glad to be back here. Where there was warmth in more ways than just the temperature.

The door creaked open well after night had fallen and dinner had been brought and taken away. Roan appeared in the doorway, his head down. In his hands, he carried something I couldn't quite see. He stepped into the room and let the chamber doors shut behind him before he looked up and noticed my presence.

"Cress..." He seemed surprised to see me there.

I floundered for a moment. Hadn't he said that he would see me later tonight? Was I mistaken? I didn't think so. Maybe he'd forgotten. I shuffled forward, pausing several feet away before I reached him, unsure if my presence was welcome.

"Hey," I said. "I thought—do you want me to go?" I asked, gesturing to the door at his back.

"What?" He blinked. "No. Of course not." Roan's head jerked

down to the satchel I now saw he was carrying and then back to me. He sighed and tossed it on a lounge nearby before striding forward. "I'm sorry," he said as he approached me. "I didn't expect to see you here."

"But you said..." I didn't get a moment to finish reminding him about his earlier words before his hands were on my shoulders and his mouth was on mine.

I sighed and sank into him. My arms came up to wrap around his neck as I arched up onto my tippy toes and kissed him back. He tasted of fire and ash and heat. When Roan finally pulled back, I was gasping for air.

"I forgot that I'd asked you to come to me tonight," he whispered, panting. "Forgive me?" I was happy to know I wasn't the only one left affected by the burn of that kiss.

My chest felt tight as I dragged more air in. I felt lightheaded. "There's nothing to forgive," I replied.

He smiled and brushed his full, masculine lips over my mouth once more before leaning away. "Give me a moment," he said. "I've been in the war room all fucking day. I'm tired and I would really like a bath before we do anything else."

Feeling brave and more than a little unwilling to let him go, when Roan released me, I reached up and snagged his arm— holding him by the wrist with both of my hands. His eyebrows rose.

"Maybe I could join you?" I offered.

There was a brief moment of silence and then a beaming smile overtook his face—he looked so boyish like that. Almost nothing like the hardened, mistrustful Fae he'd been when I first met him. But then again, I had seen that Fae again in a smaller way when I'd spied on him during his strategy meeting.

Unlike me, who'd grown up in isolation far from the majority of the war, I had to remember that Roan and the others ... they'd grown up in the middle of it all. They had seen battle and bloodshed and the front lines. My hand tightened on his wrist.

Roan stepped forward and brushed my cheek as he grinned down at me. "I would love that," he admitted. "Give me a few moments to get ready?" he asked. "You go ahead to the bathing chambers, I'll make sure no one disturbs us."

"Don't be long," I said, firming up my voice even as the corners of my mouth twitched.

He chuckled. "I wouldn't dream of keeping you waiting," he replied.

I released his wrist and stepped back. "You better not," I warned him playfully before I turned and headed for the door.

The corridors were quiet as I headed towards the bathing chamber, recalling how—not so long ago—I'd been over-whelmed by this castle. Now, it seemed like the only home I'd ever known. The convent hadn't been a home; just a roof over my head with lots of strings attached. My mind wandered as I roamed the hallways. Every once in a while, I'd run into another Fae. Some of them turned their noses up at me still and kept walking, but a few—far more than I expected—paused and nodded their heads in greeting.

By the time I made it to the bathing chambers, there were fewer people. No one hovered outside the bathing chambers and when I peeked inside, there was no one present either. Stepping into the warmed room, I spotted a pale skinned little pixie fixing a pile of bottles and vials along one of the large bath's shelves. Its little oblong shaped head popped up and its beady black eyes widened upon seeing me.

One moment, the creature was focused on its task, and the next, it was flying at me. Chirping and waving its hands around as if it was trying to communicate. I grimaced and shook my head before putting my hands up.

"It's okay," I said, thinking the pixie was trying to get me to leave. "Prince Roan sent me."

That seemed to calm the pixie. It stopped waving its arms and stared at me for a long moment before huffing out a breath and flitting away—back to its duties. I'd guessed right, I assumed. It had been trying to get me to leave, obviously preparing for Roan's bath. I turned away from the creature and began to undress. I removed my dress and underclothes, laying them across a nearby half wall. Despite the steam wafting up from the waters in the bath, once I was naked, a chill swept over me.

I decided I wouldn't be waiting for Roan after all. Without a second thought, I rushed into the bath, diving into the heated, swirling milky white liquid and sighing as warmth began to seep back into my skin. Leaning back, I dunked my head and ignored the high pitched chirping of the pixie as I accidentally flicked water his way.

This is so much better than that stupid barrel, I thought as I swam halfway across the bathing pool. The water rippled around me as I spun in a circle before squeezing my eyes shut and taking a huge breath and sinking deep into the center of the bath.

I hovered like that for so long, so focused on just feeling the clean and heated water around me, that at first, I didn't notice new ripples moving within the bath until a wide male arm wrapped around my waist and pulled me up to the surface.

I gasped as Roan pressed his mouth to my ear. "What are you doing, Little Bird?" he asked, the deep timbre of his vibrato sliding through me, heading straight to my core. "Hiding from me?"

My chest squeezed tight as I tried to capture my breath. "No," I said, but with the way my voice came out all breathy and airless, I didn't sound too confident.

Roan chuckled, the sound of his amusement vibrating against my back, making me close my eyes as I rested against him. He was naked. So was I. I could feel the hard length of him at my back, his cock pressing against my ass. When I felt his other arm lift, I opened my eyes and saw that the pixie had stopped its work and was staring at us expectantly—as if waiting for a command.

"Go," Roan ordered, swiping a hand through the air.

The pixie nodded once and then flitted up and away, disappearing as it slipped from the room, and then I was left alone with a mountain of a Fae at my back—hot, horny, and feeling very playful. I liked that, too, I admitted to myself. We hadn't had much time to play. There hadn't been a true moment of leisure in a long while.

As soon as the pixie was gone, Roan spun me around and I found myself chest to chest with him—my breasts brushing against the top of his abdomen as I stared up into his fiery gaze. "Now that we're alone..." he said, his eyes trailing over my face and lowering until his attention landed on my breasts. A low groan left him. "By the Gods," he whispered. "Little Bird..."

Roan's head dipped down as the arm encircling my waist lifted me up against him just enough that he could kiss the top of one breast and then move even lower until his mouth closed over one stiffened nipple. I gasped as my hands shot into his hair. Fire licked against my fingertips, hot and dangerous, but I didn't care.

Desire flamed my belly, opened me up as I arched into his mouth. Roan's tongue flicked over the hardened bud before he switched and lavished attention on the other one. All the while, my thighs began to rub together. Wetness sticking to my skin that had nothing to do with the waters surrounding us.

When he lifted his head once more, his lips rising to take mine in a fast movement, I jumped, wrapping my legs around his waist and clinging to his frame with all the strength left in my thighs. He chuckled against my mouth, reaching beneath me to capture my buttocks in his grip and heft me further against his chest. I shivered as air rushed over my wet skin, but I couldn't help myself.

I kissed him violently, passionately—eminently aware that I had nearly died a handful of days ago. I needed this. I needed him.

"Roan." His name was a rasp pulled from my throat when we broke off to take a breath of air. He strode forward, wading through the pool of water until we were at the shelves alongside the bathing chamber's center. He settled me there, freeing his hands to rove over the rest of me. Despite the low station of the shelves, my lower half was still surrounded by water and the higher shelves with the bottles and vials the pixie had been fussing with earlier clanged as Roan pushed against me even harder.

I could feel him, the hot, hard length of him pushing against me. "Cress," he whispered back. "Cress, Little Bird, I need you."

My back arched as he reached between us, down into the water, and stroked his fingers down my entrance. He slipped back up and circled the bundle of nerves there and my head went back, the ceiling taking over the entirety of my vision as I shook against him. It was there—the peak of my pleasure—just out of my reach.

"Roan," I croaked, reaching up and grasping his shoulders. I stared up into his eyes, seeking, begging silently. "Please."

It was all I needed to do. Roan reared back, his palms going to my inner thighs as he shoved them apart to make room for his wide hips. He pushed forward, sinking into the water as he pushed the head of his cock into my entrance. Then as his fingers circled around, gripping into my asscheeks, he pulled me forward and straight onto his shaft until he'd plunged in to the hilt.

A shocked gasp left my lips just as a low groan left his. I could feel my skin tingling. My heart racing. Everything in the room narrowed to him and me. Magic sizzled along my nerve endings, heating me from the inside out. Roan's head lifted and his eyes met mine as he pulled out and then in a slow, torturous move, sank back into my pussy.

Pleasure filled me as my nails sank into the skin on his upper arms. I moaned as he began to pound me, his hips pulling out and thrusting back in until my ass scraped the shelf he'd set me on and my head grew faint from the movement and steam. I held onto him for dear life, and I could feel it when he grew close to his own release—knew it was upon him when he reached between us and stroked that bundle of nerves once more. I started shaking before it even came, but the second he pinched me, I lost it.

I opened my mouth on a silent scream that was swallowed by him as his lips descended and he shoved himself forward into my pussy one last time, holding me tight as he came apart under my hands and lips.

This, I realized, was everything. This was what I was fighting for.

Roan pulled his mouth away and dropped so that his forehead was pressed against mine. "You fucking wreck me, Little Bird," he admitted through panting breaths.

I stroked my fingers up and down along his spine as I turned my head and pressed my cheek to his chest. "The feeling," I admitted into the quiet of the bathing chamber, "is entirely mutual."

CHAPER 21

CRESS

I stared at the closed throne room doors and counted down the number of seconds that ticked by. I'd lost count ten times, and each time I restarted, I always hesitated—hoping the doors would open and I'd be allowed entry. As it stood, however, the Princes had been locked inside with some of their top soldiers for a while now. Days, it felt like—but hours was probably more accurate.

Finally, after what felt like forever, my eleventh countdown was cut short as the doors were thrown open. I scrambled back and jerked to the side, out of the way, as Sorrell stormed into the corridor, a layer of ice trailing beneath his booted feet as he moved. The second he saw me, his eyes sparked and snow began to fall from the ends of his hair.

Instead of unleashing whatever fury he was so obviously feeling—a strange occurrence for sure since I was accustomed to seeing him act stoic and unreadable—he whipped around and pointed a finger back towards the entryway. I peeked around and saw that Orion and Roan stood there, both of their arms crossed and severe expressions on their face.

"I am not staying behind!" Sorrel shouted, the echo of his

deep voice making one of the chandeliers within the throne room shudder in the background.

My eyes widened. Several soldiers stood around a table towards the center of the room, but each one of them was turned away.

"Calm yourself, Sorrell," Orion said as he and Roan stepped further into the corridor. The doors closed behind them, leaving the four of us in relative privacy, though I had a feeling Sorrell hadn't expected me to be out here, waiting for them. And now I was privy to whatever was going on and my presence only seemed to irritate him further.

"This is ridiculous," Sorrell hissed. "I'm perfectly capable of riding and fighting." A wave of cold air slapped me in the face and I shivered involuntarily. Roan noticed and moved closer, unhooking the cloak at his back and wrapping it around my shoulders.

"We're not questioning your ability to ride and fight," Roan said as he stroked a warm finger down my cheek before returning his attention to his throne brother.

"Then you'll be taking me with you," Sorrell commanded, his tone leaving no room for argument. But an argument there still was because neither Roan nor Orion appeared to be caving in to him.

"You're wasting the precious little magic you do have by throwing a tantrum!" Roan turned and shouted back.

"When was the last time you replenished your magic supply?" Orion's voice was calmer but no less intense. His dark eyes fixated on Sorrell and refused to deviate.

"I have plenty," Sorrell replied.

"That wasn't an answer," Roan pointed out with a dark huff. "Just tell us the truth."

"I am the Prince of Frost and one of the rulers of this Court," Sorrell's voice lowered and ice began to form along the wall around us. I drew Roan's cloak even closer.

"Cut the Gods damned theatrics, Sorrell," Roan snapped, his voice lowering. "You're exhausted and it's starting to show. Orion isn't even shivering—" He paused and gestured to where Orion stood, completely unfazed by Sorrel's magic ice.

In the blink of an eye, the cold air receded. The frost that had been spreading over the door and floors and walls thawed, leaving behind nothing but the residual moisture. "We're doing this because we are concerned," Orion said. "We understand you're frustrated, but until you replenish your magic, you need to rest."

"Yes," Roan agreed with a nod. "And even if that wasn't the case, one of us would have had to stay back anyway. What if something were to happen to the two of us out there? You would need to remain behind to lead."

"We have our seconds," Sorrell said. "You know I do not *need* to be here. I should be out there—fighting for our people."

"Not until you're rested," Orion repeated.

"And what, pray tell," Sorrell bit out, glaring at the two of them and completely ignoring my presence, "am I supposed to do *here*?"

Both Orion and Roan exchanged a look. "Have you considered training Cress?" Roan asked. "You were quite adept at it in the field."

"As I can attest," Orion agreed.

Sorrell's face went slack and then, slowly, he pivoted and stared at me. I blinked at the ferocity in his glare. I put my hands up. "I didn't suggest it!" I said quickly.

He shook his head, but instead of responding, he turned and faced Roan and Orion once more. His hands curled into fists at his sides and it looked as if he wanted to slam one of them into their faces. Finally, his fingers relaxed and he stepped away, turning and pushing out a deep, unsatisfied breath.

"Do not get yourselves killed," he said quietly, so quietly that

I wasn't even sure if he had meant for the three of us to hear. Roan and Orion's stern faces softened, and then together, they stepped forward, and each of them clapped a hand on an opposite shoulder.

"We wouldn't dare," Roan said. "Only you have the right to kill us."

"You're Gods damned right I do," Sorrell replied, sounding mulish.

Orion said something I couldn't hear and Sorrell turned, glancing over his shoulder at my wide-eyed expression. He scowled but nodded at whatever his friend had said. Roan let his hand slide off his shoulder and he, too, turned and faced me.

I glanced down quickly at the cloak he'd draped over my shoulders, wondering if he was about to request it back now that it appeared that Sorrell's anger had calmed enough that I didn't feel as though we were back in Alfheim. He stepped closer, completely eclipsing my vision of Sorrell and Orion as his hands fell on me. He gripped my waist and hoisted me against him.

"You're leaving," I said, realizing what was happening. "When?"

Roan buried his face into my neck as I wrapped my arms around him. "Soon," he said. "Sorrell will be remaining behind."

Yeah, I wasn't the brightest, but I'd caught that much. I sighed, scraping my teeth over my bottom lip. When I pulled back I barely had a chance to look at him before his lips were on mine, hot and demanding. He kissed me like I was the sun and he'd been in the dark his whole life. He devoured me, his tongue sinking into my mouth and twining with my own. The kiss continued until I was left panting and weak at the knees as he unwrapped the legs that he'd urged around his sides not moments before and set me back down on the ground.

"You'll be safe," Orion promised, startling me as he appeared at our sides.

I jumped slightly, but before I could say anything Orion was pulling me into his embrace as well. His head dipped and his lips were on mine just as fast as Roan's had been. While Roan's kiss had been all fiery passion, Orion's was a slow, sensual seduction that had me aching for more than just a kiss by the time he was done.

"We'll be back soon, Little Bird," Roan said, dropping another kiss—a much more chaste one—on my forehead before touching my cheek with his fingertips and then turning to look at where Sorrell stood with his arms crossed over his chest.

"We'll be back as soon as we can," Orion said, mirroring Roan's actions.

"You both better come back safe and sound or Coreliath help me..." I rasped.

I heard them both chuckle just before the doors to the throne room opened. It was as if their soldiers had been eavesdropping or perhaps had known to wait a specific amount of time before exiting. Roan and Orion nodded to them and as a unit, the men all headed off, leaving me staring after them with dread forming a pit in my gut.

Sorrell's head pivoted back from where he'd watched them go until his cool, blue eyes settled on me.

"They'll be okay, right?" I asked, needing the reassurance.

"They are warriors, Changeling. Each of us has fought in the war for years. This is not an excessively dangerous mission. The likelihood of them not returning is low. I have no doubt they will return to us unharmed."

I nodded, but inside, I couldn't help the worry that had yet to disperse and it became too much for me to hold inside. My gaze trailed back the way they'd gone. "It doesn't matter," I found myself saying, "if they've been warriors since the beginning of time. I don't care if they've never fallen in battle. Until I see them again, I won't be able to think of anything but them." I curled my hands into fists, feeling Roan's cloak warm against my sides. "I hate that I can't go—that I have nothing to give them on the battlefield. No skills of my own. That I can't protect them."

Sorrell sighed out a long breath. "Then I suppose I will be training you," he said. "For a Fae, the first step in entering the battlefield is learning how to control your magic."

"I'm not much of a fighter," I said with a wince. "But I hate seeing them go alone. Not knowing whether or not they are okay, or even alive—it's worse when I can't see them. It makes me feel sick." My fingers clenched against the outside of my stomach.

"They aren't alone," Sorrell replied, though I noticed that his gaze had returned to where they'd gone as he spoke. "They have each other as well as our soldiers."

"And what if the King expected us to attack his pantry? What if there is a whole battalion waiting there for them?" I shot back.

"What if the sky turns purple?" he countered.

"Don't," I warned as I knew the logical lesson he was preparing to give me.

"You can't focus on the what ifs, Cressida. It does nothing for you. Focus on the now, on what you can do in this moment to make it better, to prevent yourself from feeling this way again."

"You don't get it, do you? The only thing my mind will focus on is them, on how my heart feels like it's out there with them." I threw my hand up toward the window. "Riding around with them, getting ready to fight. It doesn't feel like it's in my chest anymore. It's like I can almost see them in my mind, but I don't know what's happening. The mere thought of them dying without someone there—without me there—it breaks me. It scares me."

Silence descended between the two of us and I knew I'd probably insulted him. I couldn't find it in myself to care, though. Everything I'd said was true. When I looked up, I found Sorrell's eyes on me. We stared at each other for a long moment as I waited for him to say something, until I couldn't stand it anymore. "What?" I blurted.

He stared for another moment before shaking his head and turning away. "Nothing," he said.

He began to walk away, only to stop and turn back. He moved with such strength and purpose. Had Roan said he looked exhausted? I couldn't see it in him now. Only intensity. I backed up as he towered over me, his icy gaze glaring into the depths of my soul. "If that's how you really feel—like you want to join them on the battlefield—then I will train you," he said. "Some Fae are more powerful than they appear and, with the right training, you might, *might*, be able to ride with them someday."

"Really?" I asked. "You think so?"

"I never say anything I don't mean," he replied coolly.

"Thank you, Sorrell. Truly."

When he turned and started to walk away again, he looked over his shoulder and arched a brow. "Are you coming?"

I blinked. "Oh, you mean now?"

"Yes. Now," he growled at me as his gaze dipped to the cloak around my shoulders. "And get rid of that thing. It'll get in the way."

With that, the Prince of Frost stormed off and I slipped Roan's cloak off my shoulders as I trailed after him, preparing to figure out if he was right and maybe I was one of those Fae who was more powerful than I appeared. I prayed to the Gods he was right.

CHAPER 22

CRESS

Sorrell's anger was visible—actually tangible. A layer of ice coated the ground beneath his feet as he led me out into what appeared to be a courtyard made for training. There were no bushes or shrubbery, just an empty space with bales of hay and blocks of wood

He didn't even seem to be aware that he was oozing frost. I bit my lip and considered telling him, but when he stopped suddenly and whirled around, nearly causing me to collide into his back, I decided against it. I wanted to live and he looked mad enough to cut me down without batting an eye.

"Training," he spat the word as if it were vile and offensive. To him, I supposed it was. He'd been ordered to stand down by Roan and Orion and even as little as I knew about Sorrell, I knew that orders were not something he took easily. "Here is where we'll train until they get back," he stated.

"Okay," I said easily.

"You managed to do well enough in the heat of the moment," he continued. "But healing and sharing energy to restore life is not the same as being able to actively use your magic defensively."

"What about offensive?" I inquired. "Won't I need to know that?"

His anger melted a bit, but his facial expression remained cold. "No."

I frowned. "Why not?"

"You simply won't need to use your magic offensively," he said.

I huffed out a breath and crossed my arms over my chest. "I'm not stupid," I snapped.

One light colored brow rose. "I never said you were," he replied.

"We're in the middle of a war," I said. "Of course I'll have to use my magic offensively. Hell, I could've used it in that damned tower. I tried—" My voice cut out as I recalled my absolute failure. In the face of my capture, imprisonment, and escape, I had been utterly useless. I'd had to rely on others for assistance and things were only going to get worse. "I practiced in my cell," I admitted to Sorrell. "But even with a week of practice, all I managed to conjure were a few orbs of light and heat."

I waited a beat after those words left my lips. I half expected that Sorrell would scoff at me and tell me he wasn't surprised that a Changeling like me was incompetent. Even the physicians at the Court of Frost had said that my magic was weak, but any magic was better than none, right? When he still hadn't said anything after a long moment, I glanced up.

Sorrell was looking at me with a peculiar expression. One I hadn't seen on his face before. As if he were stunned by my mere presence and then also, at the same time, trying to dissect what I was.

"Do you believe yourself to be ... weak?" he asked hesitantly.

I shrugged. "Well, yeah." Wasn't that obvious? Ever since I'd found out I was, in fact, a Changeling and ever since my magic had first formed, I'd wondered why it came so much harder for me than it seemed to for everyone else.

"Why?" Sorrell commanded, his brows drawing down low over his eyes as he continued to stare at me.

"I can't *do* anything," I confessed, and despite my best efforts, I could tell my feelings of frustration and shame were heard as well. "I was trapped in a small room in the dark for a week with nothing else to do but practice and all I managed to do was shoot off a few sparks. My magic is worthless."

"No magic is worthless," he said sharply, stepping up to me so fast that I nearly stumbled as I tried to back away—so used to him trying to keep from touching me rather than seeking me out—but he captured me and held me with his hands on my elbows and his eyes on mine. "Say it," he ordered.

"W-what?" I stuttered. My mind had gone blank. The only thing I could see or think of was the swirling mass of blue in his eyes.

"Repeat after me," he said. "No magic is worthless."

I frowned at him. "Mine is," I argued. "It doesn't do anything. I think I'm magic-incompetent."

"That is unacceptable," Sorrell said, shaking his head. He squeezed my elbows until I winced. "Say it."

I pressed my lips together out of rebellion for several long seconds, but Sorrell's gaze remained on mine, fixated on my face as if he was ready and willing to hold me in place until I caved to his demands. I shifted on my feet, and still, he kept his hold.

Huffing out a breath, I finally surrendered. "No magic is worthless," I grumbled under my breath, just loud enough for him to hear.

His cold, icy eyes narrowed on me for a moment and then he released me, nodding. "Good," he stated. "That's the first step in your training."

I gaped at him. "A sentence?" I blurted. "You've got to be joking."

"I do not joke," he replied.

That much was obvious, asshole, I thought, but once again I kept my mouth clamped shut so the words wouldn't accidentally slip out. That had earned me many nights of no food with the nuns.

Sorrell turned away from me and strode across the courtyard until he stopped several paces away from a large block of wood. He lifted his arm and pointed a finger. Immediately, the temperature in the area dropped and long spikes of ice formed in mid-air, hovering just behind where his finger was aimed. Then, with a flick of his wrist, he sent the spikes shooting through the air and straight into the block of wood.

"Offensive magic can kill," he began, and I realized that this was part of my first lesson. I hurried to stand closer to see better. Sorrell didn't appear to realize until he moved to face me and found me right there. He froze for a split second and then continued, his body moving stiffly as he stomped past me to the hay bales, his words flying off his tongue.

"Defensive magic is meant to protect," he said. "While offensive magic is meant to attack. Neither of these is the core of what the purpose of magic truly is."

"Then what is it?" I piped up.

Sorrell paused as he hefted a hay bale off of its pile and dropped it in the middle of an open space. "Magic comes from the Gods," he stated, slamming the hay down. "And therefore, it comes from nature. Nature is neither defensive nor offensive— nature does not fight, it simply is."

I wrinkled my nose. "And that means..." I hedged, waiting for him to finish his explanation.

He rolled his eyes as he rounded the bale of hay and crossed his arms over his chest. "It means that magic is a part of nature. It is in how you use it that determines what it becomes."

"Yeah?" I crossed my arms over my chest as well, mirroring him. "Well, I'm terrible at using it."

Sorrell inhaled as if he were trying to contain a violent emotion. His chest expanded and his eyes closed briefly and when they reopened, they centered on me. "If you say something like that again, you will regret it," he warned me.

I snorted. "What are you going to do?" I asked. "Spank me?" He arched a brow, but neither confirmed nor denied it. I frowned. "You can't."

"Oh?" He tilted his head to the side, a sinister grin appearing on his lips. I was so used to him frowning that seeing anything close to a smile on his face made my whole body respond. I stepped back and let my arms drop to my sides. "Try it," he offered.

And give him permission? I thought. *No, thank you.* Then again … I remembered what it had felt like having him over me on the bed back in the Court of Frost. In that moment between sleep and wakefulness, he'd been all over me—hotter than I'd ever seen him. His mouth had devoured mine.

Instinctually, my thighs tightened and I bit down on my lower lip. Sorrell's gaze moved down to that lip, focusing on it for a long, silent moment, and then he straightened and turned away, the muscles in his shoulders pulled taut as he strode back to his place in front of the hay bale.

"Enough delaying," he snapped sharply. "I want you to practice on this." He kicked the bale.

I stepped forward, looking from him to the hay, "Practice on that?" I repeated. "What exactly am I supposed to do with it?"

"You're going to light it on fire," he stated.

I blinked. "I think I heard you wrong," I said. "It sounded like you said I was going to light it on fire."

"You did not hear me wrong," he replied. "You are."

"I can't!" I hissed at him. *How many times was I going to have to tell him before he got it through his thick skull? I couldn't use my magic like that!*

"Yes, you can," he said. "And you will." I shook my head. He was crazy. "At least give it a try, Cressida," he ordered. "How am I to train you if you don't even try?"

I grunted and grumbled under my breath. "You're going to regret this," I muttered as I turned and stomped a few feet away before whirling back.

This time, I mimicked what I'd seen him do earlier. I lifted my arm as he stepped to the side and watched. I inhaled and focused on the hay bale, concentrating all of my energy into the tips of my fingers. The heat began to build under my skin, all of it sliding forward as I worked to push it towards my hand.

"Come on," I hissed under my breath. "Do *something.*" I shook my hand as if that would make the magic come.

A spark formed and then fizzled out. I stared at my hand in half horror and half humiliation before my gaze jumped to Sorrell. He didn't even blink as he said, "Again."

"But—"

"Again," he ordered.

I turned back and started all over again. The energy built. The heat built. I pushed it forward. It rushed beneath my skin, all of it sliding through until it reached the tips of my fingers. I closed my eyes and let out a breath.

Just let it go, I thought. Just release it. Let it out.

Almost as soon as those words had entered my mind and flitted back out, I felt something rush out of me. All of the heat and energy, and as my mind connected the dots, my eyes shot back open in time to see a puny little glowing orb slam into the bale of hay. Except instead of setting the thing on fire as we both expected, it merely sank into the hay and glowed for a moment as rays of golden light emitted from it. The thin ropes that bound the bale together snapped and the hay collapsed in a heap. I frowned down at the mess my magic had made.

"Interesting..." Sorrell said, sounding both confused and curious.

"Interesting?" I squawked, looking to him in horror before pointing to the hay. "Did you see that? It didn't do anything!"

"That's not exactly true," Sorrel said with a shake of his head.

"Well, snapping a few measly little ropes doesn't mean that my magic works," I huffed.

"Your magic works just fine, but I believe there's something we need to ask Groffet about it."

I scrubbed my hands down my face, hating the tears burning in the backs of my eyes. Sparks and light and no fire. That was it. I was the worst freaking Fae in the history of Fae.

"Cressida?" I barely heard Sorrell's voice as he approached. I was too caught up in my own self loathing.

Why was I even here? I wondered. *What was the point of my existence if I wasn't even good at anything? The nuns had been right. I was clumsy. Stupid. Too stubborn for my own good. I was absolutely unimpressive. A problem everywhere I went.* I sniffed hard.

"Cressida!" Sorrell's shout finally caught my attention, but I just couldn't deal with his scolding right now. It was too much.

I spun to face him. "What!" I shouted back.

"Look," he snapped, pointing down at me.

I followed his gesture with my gaze and gasped at what I saw. My skin was glowing. It was as if every pore of my body was filled with a dull light. I was illuminated. Golden sparks danced along my skin. Across the courtyard, the protective magic vines that covered the stone wall began to slither against one another, vibrating as if they felt a strange presence.

"W-what...?" My gaze found Sorrell's again. "What does this mean?" I asked.

He shook his head as he stepped closer and then carefully,

very carefully, he reached up and grasped my wrist. Together, the two of us watched as my skin very slowly, returned to its previous state. The glow faded until it was gone completely.

"Sorrell?" I prompted.

He shook his head, staring at me once more with that peculiar look. "I don't know, Cressida," he admitted. "I don't know."

My heart sank. If Sorrell didn't know, then this was definitely not a good thing.

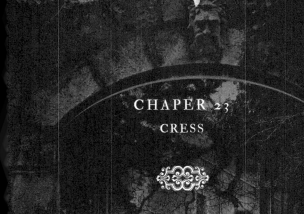

CHAPER 23
CRESS

S weat slicked down my back. It soaked through my clothes and made the fabric stick to me. My skin felt overly warm, as if I was very close to a fire. I opened my eyes and looked down to see that it wasn't just warm, it was glowing. *I was glowing.* I gasped as the light emanating from beneath my skin grew brighter and hotter. I wasn't near a fire. I *was* the fire. Blazing hot light was pouring out of me. My sweat sizzled on my skin. I scrambled back, trying to get away, but there was no getting away. Whatever was making me feel this way was *inside* of me.

My body fell into the darkness and the second I hit something, my eyes slammed open and a scream lodged in my throat. It took me several seconds to realize that I wasn't burning alive. I was in Roan's chambers and I'd fallen right off his bed. My breath came in short eclipsed pants.

What in the name of Coreliath was that? A dream, I knew, was the answer, but it had been so real and so strange. There'd been no one there with me. It had all just been … me. I shook my head and slowly worked my way up the side of Roan's bed until my trembling feet were beneath me once more. There would be no more sleep after that nightmare.

A deep sigh left me as I looked up and scanned the room. No doubt the horrible illusion had been the result of all of my hard training. Sorrell had worked me over good and my limbs felt their exhaustion. Still, I wasn't able to do so much as light a bale of hay on fire. I was a terrible Fae. Useless.

The darkness of the room made me squint as I wavered forward, moving slowly through the rest of the room with my hands outstretched. My head pounded and my stomach rumbled. I stopped as I reached the chair next to the door. My feet paused there, and I wondered if it would even matter if I left the room now as I was. It wasn't like I was naked. Did I really need to change out of my nightgown to go grab a bite to eat in the middle of the night?

My hand fell to the door latch and I pulled it open with the decision—no, it didn't matter. I wasn't likely to run into anyone anyway. I meandered down the stone hallways and passed closed doors—likely chambers of the other Fae who lived here.

Down the corridor, several dull beams of moonlight poured in through open non-glassed windows. A soft melody caught my ear. Something soft, growing louder and louder. The closer I got, the more I realized it was coming from outside.

Someone was playing music.

I hadn't heard music like this before. It was enchanting. I stopped halfway down the corridor and simply closed my eyes for a moment, taking it in. Each note felt like a caress. It was sad —so sad. A wailing of a violin, singing into the night of things lost and never found. Of souls ripped apart and hearts broken. Then the tone lifted and it was as if the sun was rising to a new day. A beginning was forming and I realized it was the same melody played over and over again. It sounded like a whole life being lived and then the death of a loved one only to be reborn.

Finally, my curiosity got the better of me. My eyes opened and I continued forward. I felt compelled—dragged—towards whoever was playing this song. Heart in my chest, I moved towards the open windows, where I found a garden. Three small steps led into a grassy area very unlike the training court-yard from earlier. This garden had miniature stone statues and trees and rose bushes and the smell of night blooms that scented the air around me.

I kept my footsteps light as I strode through the small garden until I saw it—the stone table and alongside that, the musician. My eyes widened at who it was.

In the silver gleam of the moon's light, Sorrell held a black violin tucked beneath his chin. The melody he played captured my heart. It was one of lost loves. Of sorrow and an agony so great that I couldn't help but feel it deep down. He played without tears, though every note lingered—clinging ever desperately to the air surrounding him.

Somewhere in the back of my mind, I realized what I was doing. I was intruding on a very private moment. I shouldn't have been there. Yet, like the small beady pixie eyes I caught every so often as I glanced about the garden—hiding in the shrubbery as they, too, listened to the lonely Prince's song—I couldn't pull myself away.

The night air was fresh and chilly against my skin, but I paid it no mind. It was hard to notice anything but the man with the violin. His eyes were closed as he played. Mine couldn't help but follow him as he swayed to the music. It was odd seeing him like this—so unreserved, so open, so … soft. Gone was the usual bitter expression he usually wore. It almost appeared as if he was sleeping as he played. He was so relaxed, his fingers easing along the bow and neck of the instrument.

It was mesmerizing to watch.

Glints of silver moonlight touched the violin every so often as his bow drew across the strings and his fingers danced on the neck of the instrument. It didn't hold a candle to the beauty of his face though. As he worked towards the crescendo the earlier relaxation of his features turned pinched. The sharp planes began to contort with emotion and his pale skin and icy hair glowed in the moonlight as though that was where this ethereal being belonged.

Each sweep of the bow seemed to pull at my heart, the melancholy sounds only reaching further into my soul now that I was closer. The sorrow and pain that was being expressed through his music was unlike anything I'd heard before and it made me ache for him. It made me want to march forward into the garden, stop him, and pull him close. I wanted to hug him, hold him, to promise him that whatever made him play this heartbreaking music … would be okay. That he would be okay.

It was too much. *I shouldn't be here!* My mind finally screamed at me. I'd known it, but it had been too exhilarating watching him as long as I had. Now, it was time to go.

When I turned to leave, my foot caught on the edge of one of the larger statue platforms—only instead of a statue sitting upon it, a potted plant was. A grunt flew out of my lips as I fell forward. My hands smacked outward, grabbing onto the platform. I tried to wrap my fingers around the pot, but the thing slipped away from me at the last moment—crashing to the ground and bringing the haunting music to a sudden halt.

I froze. My heartbeat froze. The breath in my lungs froze. Then, slowly, I lifted my head to meet Sorrell's gaze.

His eyes were sharp fragments of ice, shining wickedly without emotion. Though he was far slimmer than many men I'd come into contact with, there was still a strength in his gait. There was a calm, cool confidence in his usual demeanor that was gone now—no, not truly gone, just less prevalent. It was because he was open. His expression, usually so guarded, was vulnerable.

His gaze clashed with my own, and that vulnerability faded. "What are you doing here, Cressida?" he demanded.

CHAPTER 24
SORRELL

There were very few things in life that had surprised me as much as one little Changeling woman. Cressida was becoming far more than surprising though. She was a mystery. And the one question we should have been asking continuously until we'd gotten a satisfying answer repeated itself over and over in my mind:

Where had she come from?

Not the convent, obviously, but before she'd been dropped there. Who was she? Who were her parents? What Court would practice the Changeling tradition amid the beginning of a war with the very creatures they would be giving their child to? Were they still alive?

When we had first come upon the Changeling—Cressida—Groffet had devised the test. He was the one who had told us that she was of the Court of Crimson, but now I wasn't so sure. *Could it be?* I wondered absently as I strode through the empty and quiet corridors of the castle. Was she ... from *that* Court?

I almost dreaded the concept. The Court in question had been eradicated on what I suspected were my own mother's orders—hers and the Crimson Queen's. I had been too young to know much about the fourth Court of our lineage. The Brightling Court.

It was a sad story—the Brightling Court. I hoped I was wrong. The only way to know would be to ask Groffet. Something I would have to do later when the others had returned. An insidious feeling rose at the reminder that they were out there—Roan and Orion—doing what I, too, should be doing. Fighting alongside our soldiers. Infiltrating the castle of the King's ally. Destroying supplies. Weakening him. Wounding him as he had wounded us when he had taken Cressida and nearly killed her.

Anger rose up, fast and furious, inside me. My fists clenched at my side. The hard thumps of my booted feet sounded against stone as I stormed through the castle back to the library. I was in desperate need of a distraction. Moonlight streamed in through the windows—real moonlight. I slowed to a stop as I neared one of our inner gardens. There, resting against a stone table beneath the sky, was my violin.

With a frown, I stepped out into the night and moved toward it until I was standing in front of the table. I stared down at the instrument in confusion. I could have sworn that last I saw this piece, I'd left it in the ... *Groffet,* I realized. That meddling, old man. He was planning something. Teasing me as he always did—leaving out reminders, little mementos to tempt me.

My fingers moved to the neck of the instrument and slowly, I stroked my hand over its frame. I couldn't help but feel tempted by this old thing. It was certainly one of humanity's greatest accomplishments—the violin. Unlike its creators, the instrument was completely and wholly gentle. *Fragile, in a way,* I thought absently as I lifted it from the table's surface.

My eyes caught on the bow, just to the side. Groffet was smart. He knew I'd be up roaming the corridors—I could never sleep when Roan and Orion were out there. Not so long as they were not near me. Perhaps it was the pain each of us had suffered as children—the loneliness of being Royals that had driven us together, made us into what we were. True brothers of the throne. Whatever the reason, I was as bound to them as they were to me. I did not like the feeling of not seeing them, of not being there to fight alongside them.

But maybe this ... this old memory could distract me, if only for a moment.

I lifted the violin and reached for the bow, lining up the instrument under my chin as I pressed down and then slowly dragged the bow across the strings. In the light of the moon, the music came to me. I needed no sheets, no instructor—only muscle memory. The music that rose from the strings was a pure cadence. It lifted into the air, a melody that I knew from the heart simply because that was where it came from.

It was no true song, not one with a name, only a collection of notes strung together that I had long thought of. I was its creator. Its master and slave as I played it until it was done and then started it all over again.

I couldn't say how many times I played it only to replay it, when the sound of something breaking startled me out of my reverie. My fingers froze along the bow and I quickly set it down, turning towards the noise, when I realized that the focus of my thoughts before I'd found the violin once more had appeared.

Cressida stood there, eyes wide, golden curls hanging around her face as she stood over a broken potted plant that had obviously been knocked over by her attempted exit.

I scowled. "What are you doing here, Cressida?"

"I-I-I ... uh..." she stuttered, her gaze jerking from the plant to me and back again. "I'm sorry?"

I sighed, stepping away from the nostalgic instrument and towards her. "An apology does not answer my question," I stated.

She blushed, her eyes lowering to the floor as a delicate pink hue rose to her cheeks. I paused, frowning at her. *Why would she be blushing?* I wondered silently.

"I heard the music," she confessed quietly. "And I ... I came to see who was playing it."

I stiffened. Shit. I hadn't even been thinking. Of course, I shouldn't have played that damned thing here. In the center of the castle. Anyone could have walked by—someone did walk by, I amended my thoughts, returning my attention to the Changeling.

"I apologize for disturbing you," I said.

"Oh no." Her head whipped up and she shook it vehemently like an animal shaking off water—*how in the world could I find that so adorable*? I wondered. *No,* I mentally corrected myself. *I didn't. It was annoying. She was annoying. She was a danger.*

"I thought it was beautiful," she said. "You didn't disturb me."

Discomfort sidled beneath my skin. I coughed as I turned away. "It was nothing," I said, and then, "let me walk you back to your chambers."

Cressida tipped her head back and stared at me. "Why won't you let me compliment you?" she asked suddenly.

I froze, my lips parting in surprise. "What do you mean?"

"You don't let me compliment you," she repeated. "Do you let anyone?"

It took me a moment to gather an answer to such an absurd question. "Compliments are unnecessary," I told her, leading her back towards the inner corridor and away from the garden.

"No they're not," she replied. "They're very necessary."

"No, they're not," I corrected her.

She shot me a dark look. "Just because you don't see a point in them doesn't mean they're unnecessary."

"Then what, pray tell," I challenged her as we walked, "is the point in complimenting a person other than to gain their favor?"

Her pretty blue eyes rolled. *No, not pretty, damn it.* "True compliments are given without the expectation of anything—not even favors or good standing," she said. "Complimenting someone with sincerity makes the other person feel good. It expresses a person's kind opinions. Like just now." She gestured between us. "I told you that I thought your music was beautiful, but you called it nothing. I'd think it was just because you didn't like me if I didn't know any better."

"Oh?" What a curious and obstinate little thing she was. "Then do you?"

"Do I what?" Her head tipped back once more as she looked up into my face. I was captured by her and for the first time, I realized that she and I were well and truly alone. Earlier, we had been alone in the courtyard for her training—but this was something entirely different.

We were in the dark—no Roan, no Orion. Just her and me. It was a unique thing, something I'd never expected to happen, and that was an error of my own design. I should've realized that there would come a time like this. She was here to stay. Cressida—Cress—was intertwined with Roan and Orion and … for the first time, I thought to myself how I might not quite hate the idea of her being the same way with me.

"Sorrell?" she called my name, recapturing my attention and pulling me from my thoughts as we moved through the darkened hallways.

"Hmmm?" I hummed back.

"Do I what?" she repeated.

Ah, yes, her question, I thought. "Do you know better?" I finished.

Her full lips split into a wide grin. "Normally, I'd say absolutely not, but with you, I'm starting to understand."

"And what is it that you think you understand?" I questioned.

"You," she replied. "You're so cold and bossy, and you

alienate yourself from nearly everything and everyone—save for two others. Roan and Orion." Her gaze fell away from my face as she turned back towards the corridor, walking forward. "You don't deny my compliment because you hate me—though..." She trailed off for a moment before looking back at me. "There was a time that I thought you truly did hate me."

"There was a time in which you were correct," I said. The words were out of my mouth before I could recall that they would be offensive, but to my utter shock, she didn't act insulted or even surprised. She simply nodded at me as if she had expected that answer.

"But you care about *them*," she continued as if I hadn't said a word. "I think if anyone else were to compliment you but those two, you would still say the same thing you said to me—that it was nothing."

I sighed. She was looking far too closely at something that didn't matter. "Roan and Orion are my brothers," I told her. "They do not compliment me. They give me their opinions."

"And if they gave you the opinion that your music was beautiful, what would you say?" she asked.

I gritted my teeth. "It's just music," I told her.

That brought forth a laugh, and Cressida laughed like she lived—fully and with no reserve. Her hair shook at the sides of her head as she tipped her chin up and released her laughter. It brightened her face and I was transfixed. My feet slowed to a stop.

She stopped, too, pulled to a halt by my inability to keep going. "What's wrong?" she asked, tilting her head curiously.

What was wrong? I repeated the question to myself. All of it was wrong—I had been wrong. About her. About myself. As I stood there in a corridor filled with shadows, she glowed like the only source of light. Brighter than any flame. More brilliant even than the Goddesses of old.

"Sorrell?" she frowned at me, stepping closer as her hands

drifted up to my arms—as if touching me could ease the turmoil I didn't think she even realized was causing to riot inside of me. But as soon as her fingertips grazed my flesh, I was unleashed.

Grabbing her, I turned and slammed her back against the wall. A sharp gasp left her lips just before I dipped my head down and devoured them. It took a moment for the shock of the suddenness of my movements to reach her, but once they did—I half expected her to push me away or to fight me. She did neither.

Instead, Cressida's arms lifted even further, wrapping around my neck and pulling me against her body. I crushed her into the wall—her soft, small frame delicate and oh so breakable beneath me. I had always wondered how smaller people—humans and delicate females—could face the world as if they were not constantly on the verge of shattering. Cressida was one such female.

She took my fucking breath away. She feared very little and what she did fear, she still faced. It was time that I admitted that my so-called hatred for her had been born out of a place of fear—of what she could do to me. Of what she could do to my brothers. This little woman—although infinitely delicate in stature—had the heart of a warrior. And whether she realized it or not, she had completely overtaken the three of us.

Yes, the three of us. Not just Roan and Orion, but me as well. I was enraptured by her. I hated that fact, was terrified of it. *But what if,* I wondered idly, *what if I stopped pushing her away and just accepted it?* Accepted that she was undeniable to me now.

My mouth parted from hers as we both gasped for air, panting, our chests pushed tight against one another. "W-why would you..." Her words came with no small amount of confusion. "Sorrell ... do you ... want me?"

"Cressida," I whispered her name as I reached up and held

her head in my hand. "Want is a pathetic word for what I feel for you." *Desire. Craving. Need.* Even those were not enough.

She shook her head as if trying to clear away her thoughts and yet, when she returned her gaze to mine, there was still clear bewilderment. "I-I thought you hated me," she said.

"Hate," I replied, "is a powerful emotion to cover up another powerful emotion."

"What—" I didn't let her finish asking the question. I couldn't. I wasn't ready to admit it yet. All I knew was that right here, right now, I needed her. My lips pushed hers apart and I let my tongue sneak forward. She rose to my bait, moaning into my mouth as I reached down and hefted her into my arms. The skirts of her nightgown pushed up her thighs all the way as her legs spread and she wrapped them around me.

"Cressida," I said, releasing her once more. "Tell me yes. Say yes."

Even after all that I had put her through—all that I didn't deserve, but would take anyway—she didn't hesitate. And in that darkened hallway, with her legs wrapped around my hips and my hand in her hair, she tipped her beautiful face back and gave me everything with one word.

"Yes, Sorrell. I'm saying yes."

CHAPTER 25

CRESS

My back slammed into the wooden frame of the door, but I didn't offer anything more than a light grunt as Sorrell's mouth came down on mine—*hard*. Everything about him was hard. He was massive and all over me. Inside of my mind, and soon, he'd be inside of my body too.

He fumbled for the door—it was almost cute how rushed he seemed. Almost as if he were afraid I would rescind my consent. I wouldn't dare, not now. The fact was, I wanted this as much as he did. Perhaps more. This, it seemed, was something we'd been slowly moving towards since we first met. Since the first time he'd looked at me with those cold, angry eyes.

There was nothing cold in his look now. He was all molten heat and sinful promise even as he pulled back and, instead of unlocking the door as a normal man might, he reared back and kicked it in. I gasped as my whole body jerked against him.

"Sorrell!" I snapped. "Don't destroy the castle."

"It's my castle," he replied. "I'll do whatever I damn well please."

I didn't have a response to that, not that he gave me time to think of one. As soon as the door was opened, he strode through and turned, slamming it shut—only this time, it didn't close all the way. Probably had something to do with the gaping broken side. Sorrell groaned and I knew it had nothing to do with how he was still carrying me.

I smirked down at him. "I told you so," I said.

His eyes flashed. "You enjoy testing me, don't you, Changeling?" Somehow, in the time between when we'd first met and now, that name had become more than an insult. He didn't say it with anger or disgust, but with a heated promise of something pleasurable that would soon come my way.

Sorrell turned and strode across the room, stopping before a large bed. He unwrapped my legs from around his waist and deposited me there. "Do not move," he warned.

"Or what?" I asked. "Are you going to punish me?"

One finger came up and curled under my chin to tip my head back. "Yes," he said. His head tilted down and then the tip of his nose touched my jawline. "I'm going to spend the rest of the night punishing you for all that you have put me through."

I shivered. Whatever punishment he wanted to exact, I had a feeling I was going to like it. "Now stay," he ordered.

Sorrell stepped back, leaving me bereft of his presence—of his burning intensity. I was left to watch him stride back across the room to right the door. He shut it properly and then put his hand to the frame. Slowly, a blanket of ice began to form over the broken lock. It crept up and around the entirety of the door until the whole thing was sealed shut with a layer of frost. Only then did Sorrell pivot back and face me.

"Now you're mine," he said. "And no one will be disturbing us for the night."

I watched him as he moved back across the room, inching towards me. He paused halfway to me and my pulse began thumping faster as he reached for the hem of his shirt and ripped it over his head. The white, filmy fabric dropped to the floor, forgotten. My lips parted and my mouth watered. I'd always known that beneath the clothes, Sorrell was hiding the body of a warrior.

Strong lines were etched into either side of his abdomen and across. His shoulders were broad, but his eyes—they were the most formidable. He continued his path to me even as my eyes dipped to the pale blond happy trail that led from his belly button into the top of his black trousers.

When Sorrell once again stood before me, he stared into my eyes. His hand reached up and cupped my head, fingers sifting through my curls as he pushed lightly. "Get on your knees, Cressida."

Between my legs, my core throbbed. I was transfixed, completely at his mercy. It was heady, my desire for him. Unable to control my limbs—my knees bent and in small increments, I slid to the floor until I was on my knees before him, looking up at his massive frame. His hand remained in my hair, a comfort as he continued to stroke me—running his fingers through my blonde locks.

"You know what I want?" he asked.

"Yes," I whispered back.

He nodded to the front of his trousers and immediately, my hands lifted. I touched the front, feeling the ridge of his cock beneath the fabric. Within seconds, I had him freed from his pants. I gasped as I saw his cock for the first time. Long, thick, and pale, it made my mouth water.

"Cressida," he urged, grasping it by the base with his free hand. "Suck it."

My lips parted, my mouth opened, and I let him guide the head of his shaft between my lips. The pressure on the back of my head was warm, but the feeling of taking him into my mouth was hotter. I sucked him down, swallowing around his hardness—following the velvet covered vein with my tongue as I lapped at him.

A low moan escaped from above, sounding in my ears as I attended to him. I squeezed my thighs together—pressing them into one another as hard as I could. The sound of his pleasure in my head as I sucked his cock was pure ambrosia. A trickle of thrill shot up my spine. This was happening. I was really doing it.

Sorrell's cock pulsed in my mouth, against my tongue. Slowly, we began to work together in a rhythmic movement. I'd pull back, pushing against the hand holding my head, and then he'd push me forward once more—thrusting his dick to the back of my throat. My hands came up, clenching against his rock hard thighs.

He thrust into my mouth again and again, sometimes moving slow and sometimes moving fast. I relished in it all, feeling both submissive and powerful all at once. Until finally, he'd had enough. Sorrell's hand contracted at the back of my skull, his fingers sinking into my hair and then curling as he ripped me away.

"That's enough," he said through gritted teeth. A moment later, I found myself being lifted into his strong arms and thrown back onto the mattress. "Spread your legs," he ordered as he shucked his pants the rest of the way off and then toed off his boots.

I moved further up the bed, feeling the leaking wetness of my arousal on the inside of my thighs. I grinned back at him, feeling dangerous and playful.

"What if I don't?" I shot back.

Sorrell's eyes flashed—glowing in the dark room—a brilliant blue that was so light it was almost white. "You will regret not following my commands, Changeling." His voice lowered and that, too, left me feeling mischievous.

I walked backwards on my hands and feet until I reached the headboard.

"Spread your legs, Cressida," he repeated as he crawled onto the end of the bed. "Or I'll make you."

I grinned. "Then make me," I challenged.

No sooner had the words left my lips than a shriek followed it as Sorrell dove on top of me. His hands found my wrists and brought them together, pinning them in one of his palms. With his free hand, he reached down, finding the hem of my night-gown, and ripped it up my thighs.

"Tell me something, Changeling," he panted as he leaned close. I closed my eyes and arched into his touch as I felt his fingers slipping up my thighs. "Do you like pain?"

It took me a moment to fully comprehend his question. My eyes opened once more. "Pain?" I asked.

Sorrell released my hands and reached for the neckline of my nightgown, grabbing it and ripping it straight down the middle. The sound of tearing fabric reached me just before the feeling of the material pulling taut over my skin only to be released once more did. He quickly divested me and began tearing it even more—ripping it into strips.

"Yes," he said. "Pain. Specifically, the erotic kind."

I was too consumed by his actions—confused and also a little curious—as he used the torn strips of fabric to quickly bring my hands together and tie them. He then anchored them to the headboard, fitting my hands inside slots I hadn't seen before and then tying me there as well.

"I've never really experienced it, I guess..." I said absently.

"Would you like to?" he asked, trailing his hands down my now naked sides. I trembled beneath him as air washed over my skin.

"I-I don't know," I confessed.

Sorrell moved over me, his hands pushing between my knees as he forced my legs up and out. "Do you trust me?" he asked, leaning close. His warm breath feathered over the skin of my stomach.

"Y-yes?"

"Are you asking or stating?" he clarified.

"Stating?"

"You don't sound sure," he said.

I huffed out a breath. "I'm not sure," I admitted testily. Here we were, naked and pressed against one another in his bed—not something I'd ever really seen happening—and I felt my pussy pulse, but all he was doing was asking me questions. Questions I didn't understand. "I don't know how pain can feel good," I told him.

Sorrell pressed down on top of me, his shaft lining up with my core, but instead of slipping it inside, he merely let the underside rub against me—between my folds and over my clit. I clenched, tightening, and felt empty inside. When he chuckled, the sound vibrated against my nipples, making me moan in humiliating wanton desire.

What the hell was he thinking? I wondered even as I shifted my hips to rub against him more insistently.

"Patience, Cressida," he said, kissing the tip of my nose. "If you say yes, I promise you won't regret it. Now, answer me correctly this time, *do you trust me?*"

I stared up into his ice blue eyes for a moment, biting down on my lower lip before I jerked my head in a nod. "Yes," I breathed.

He smiled, a radiant and also disturbingly evil look crossing his face. "Good," he said, slipping back until he was almost completely off of me. With his wide, strong hands, he grabbed me around my hips, lifted, and flipped me as if I were no more than a sack of laundry.

The bindings around my hands grew tight, but there was still enough elasticity that, even though my wrists jerked and remained bound, it didn't hurt. I felt Sorrell move in close, arranging me how he liked. I should've known it would be like this with him. With Roan and Orion, sex had always been out of control—fire, burning in the moment. Even in the tent in Alfheim, there'd been a point where we'd thrown all attempts to make it last out of the window.

But Sorrell—I really should have expected that he would be far too controlling to let that happen. Especially in this. His hands moved over my skin, touching my spine, trailing down it until his fingers sank down between my buttocks and even further until he touched my pussy. His thumb flicked over the bundle of nerves above it and I jerked, gasping as my bound hands smacked into the headboard.

I didn't feel it. I couldn't feel anything but what he was doing to me. All I could focus on was him. "I'm going to make you scream, Cressida," he whispered against my spine even as his fingers worked down below.

I believed. Gods, I was halfway to screaming right now and he hadn't even entered me.

"I want you to count them for me," he said.

"What?" I looked back just in time to see his free hand arch up and come down hard across my ass.

I gasped out, jerking forward once more. The burn of pain spread across my butt. He waited a beat and then repeated himself. "Count, Cressida, or it will quickly turn less pleasurable."

Thoughtless. Confused. And embarrassingly ... still very, very wet ... I obeyed. "O-one," I stuttered out.

His hand came down again.

"Two."

Again.

"Three."

He spanked me with his palm, never hitting the exact place more than once. He peppered my ass with the smacks. I shuffled around on my knees, feeling uncomfortable. He said to trust him, but I didn't understand. *Why this? Why a spanking?*

The teasing, I realized a bit belatedly. I'd teased him. This was the punishment he'd been talking about.

Only, the more he continued, the less like a punishment it felt like. The pain spread and grew heated until I rested my head against my hands, mumbling the counts that my mind was somehow able to keep up with even though I didn't even hear the numbers as they slipped out of my mouth. I was so focused on how *good* it all felt and trying to figure out *why.*

Every spank sent tingles up my spine. My ass was growing sore, and when he paused to cup it, his hand felt cool against my heated skin. I moaned as he moved down to my thighs. Slapping each one in turn and then covering them in the same burning treatment as my butt. I couldn't stop myself even if I'd tried. I couldn't help it. I was growing restless with one hand spanking me and the other gently moving over my folds. I wanted more—I needed more.

"Want something, Changeling?" I'd never heard him sound so amused before. I might have appreciated it if I hadn't been so desperate.

"You know I do," I shot back, earning myself another harsh spank right in the crease between my ass and the back of my thigh that made me bite down hard on my lip to keep from crying out.

"Then maybe you should try being polite, Cressida, and ask for it," he suggested.

"Please," I hissed out.

"Please what?"

"Please fuck me," I begged.

"That'll do, Cressida," he said, pulling his hand from my pussy. Sorrell's hands found my hips and he knocked my knees apart, guiding the head of his cock to my core. As soon as he pushed inside, I moaned. My hips moved back on their own, wanting more.

He shushed me as I hissed and struggled to get more. I tried to shift backwards with my knees pressed to the bed, but he held me still. "Let me," he said. "Just stay still."

He thrust, stretching me inside as his cock powered forward. I whimpered. Fuck, he was big. Just as large as Orion and Roan, but perhaps longer. It felt like his thrust would never end and I was surprised when I finally felt his hips pressed against my thighs.

"There." Sorrell's voice was rough as he spoke. He reached up and stroked his fingers through my hair before grabbing hold of it and leaning in to my ear. "Now, comes the fun part," he said.

That hadn't been the fun part? I thought a split second before he pulled out and slammed the full length of his shaft back into me.

"Oh, fuck..." I breathed.

Sorrell chuckled but didn't say a word as he began his ride. He fucked into me, thrusting his cock back and forth into my pussy. Sometimes, he would move slowly, dragging it out and then inching it back into me in what felt like long increments. And then, he would fuck faster—driving my body forward until he was fucking me against the headboard with my breasts against my bound hands and his hands gripping my hips, using them as holds by which he could push me away and pull me back onto his cock.

He felt hot, almost as if he were on fire. His skin seemed to radiate the heat. *Magic?* I wondered. That was right—he needed this. The sex. The intimacy. He'd been denying himself, but now I could feel the surge of my magical energy replenishing itself. I wondered if he, too, could feel his.

I moaned and whimpered. Animal like sounds left my lips and I had no control. No. None of it was mine. All of the control belonged to him and he used it to drive me up and over the edge. When my orgasm hit me, I threw my head back and screamed as the pleasure slammed into me.

In the distance of my mind, I recognized that I wasn't the only one that had reached the peak. Sorrell's hands grew rougher against my sides. His head dipped down to kiss the space between my throat and shoulder and he groaned into my flesh as he released himself inside of me.

When the two of us came down from the high, I found myself clinging to the headboard for dear life. Panting. Soaked. Shaking.

"Let me help you," Sorrell rasped, reaching around me to quickly untie my bindings. I slumped over onto the mattress, exhausted and completely spent.

"I think you killed me," I said. "Roan and Orion are going to be pissed."

Sorrell paused as he got off of the bed, holding the remains of my nightgown and ties in his grasp. After a moment, he kept moving. "You think so?" he inquired. I could tell that he was forcing himself to appear unconcerned. His tone was light, but the stiffness of his shoulders suggested otherwise—especially after what we'd just experienced.

"Yeah, I'm pretty sure they wouldn't like it if I died," I replied.

Sorrell moved to a bowl in the corner of the chamber and filled it with water. Using the scraps of fabric torn from my dress he dipped it into the water and cleaned himself before using another to come over to me and do the same for me. My face flamed and grew heated as he spread my thighs and wiped along my core.

"You're not dead." He sighed.

"You tried though," I said. "You tried to kill me with sex."

The look he gave me when he straightened and tossed the rags to the side and climbed into bed with me was unamused. I pushed against his chest and smiled up at him. "What's wrong?" I demanded.

He looked down at me for a moment before rolling to the

side. Sorrell, for all of his intelligence, was a warrior in body. He weighed a ton, and as such, the mattress sank under his superior weight and I was unintentionally rolled towards him. Once I was against his side though, he didn't seem inclined to push me away. Instead, an arm came around me and I was cuddled up to him in less than a heartbeat.

I liked this new version of Sorrell. Oh, he was still commanding. Constantly in control. This was the lover in him. The man who felt emotion and stopped hiding behind it but only in front of people he truly trusted. I was now one of those people and I'd never felt more honored.

My fingertips stroked against his chest. "Sorrell?" I prompted.

"Hmmmm?" He hummed in the back of his throat, sounding distracted.

"You're thinking of something," I said. "What is it?"

His jaw tightened and then slowly released after a moment. "Roan and Orion—they will return soon," he said.

"Are you worried they won't like this?" I asked, meaning us —what had happened between us tonight.

His lips pursed. "I'm not sure." His brows drew down low over his eyes as he seemed to contemplate something. "Roan said something not too long ago..."

"About me?" I asked.

"Yes, about you," he answered before looking at me. "I don't think they'll be upset."

"Then what's the problem?" I asked.

"I don't know why they wouldn't be," he said. "We have shared everything since the three of us embarked on our journey as future Kings. We saw our counterparts—the other Royals—all drowning beneath expectation and pressure from the old generation. Some perished in war and the three of us ... we decided that we would not be like them. We separated. Roan managed to convince his mother to give up the Court of

Crimson to him—a feat she regretted later on, especially after she learned that he planned to share leadership with Orion and I."

"They're not going to blame you," I assured him.

"I know," he said. "That's just it, though. Roan ... he spoke as if he expected this to happen, and at the time, I still denied it."

"Denied what?" My nose twitched and I forced back a yawn.

He shot me a rueful grin, one of the first of its kind I'd ever seen from him. "My attraction to a stubborn little Changeling," he answered.

"I kind of like you, too, even if you act like a horse's ass sometimes," I said.

He shook his head and then curled his arm, pulling me so close that I felt as though I were half on top of him. I couldn't find the energy in myself to care. He was warm and so was this bed. My eyelids flickered and that yawn I'd forced back burst free.

"You should sleep," he suggested. "You're tired."

"But I want to make sure you're okay," I protested even as my eyelids drifted down.

A wide, masculine palm slid down my back, stroking slowly and lulling me deeper into oblivion as exhaustion overcame me. I felt a press of lips against my forehead and then Sorrell's voice rumbling beneath my ear. "Sleep, Cressida. I will wake you in the morning."

And as much as I wanted to stay awake, my body had other plans. Even as I drifted, falling deeper and deeper into the oblivion of sleep, I wondered if maybe he hadn't taught me in other ways tonight. Because when he commanded that I sleep, my body instinctually settled in against him and I found no will to fight against him or his orders. Like Roan and Orion, Sorrell had me completely captured now and I didn't want to ever get away.

CHAPTER 26
ORION

Norune Castle stood before us like a mountain in the night. The weak illumination of moonlight cast the entirety of the structure in shadow, making it appear more ominous than I believed it would have seemed had the sun been shining down on it.

Roan motioned toward the first squad of soldiers and at his silent order, they separated from us and moved ahead and to the right of the wall that surrounded the castle. If we needed it, they would be our distraction. Our footsteps were silent as we made our way through the castle's outside grounds, an easy spell that muted any sounds we made. Added to the cloaking spell we were using, even the few guards stationed along the walls of the castle, marching slowly back and forth under the moonlight, wouldn't be able to detect us until it was too late.

"Go," Roan said to his second commander. "Quickly. Be swift. Be silent. No casualties. This is not a killing mission."

"Understood, Your Highness," the commander replied with a nod.

I turned my attention back to the wall for a moment, scanning as Roan and I waited for the others to slip around to the door we had seen on the map. Only two lookouts would remain, but I still felt better knowing that there would be several guards missing from tonight's shift—all out on the town, drinking and whoring. Whores that a few of my men had assured would be well compensated for distracting the Duke's soldiers.

The map had made this door seem like an unusable entrance, but unusable it was not. It was overgrown and nailed shut with planks of wood crisscrossing over the surface of the entrance. Easy obstacles that we had quickly overcome.

"What are you thinking?" Roan inquired. "You're quiet. Are you sure you're up for this?"

"I'm fine," I replied. "Just being cautious."

He and I waited several moments, listening to the night and sounds of nature deep in the forest. "Come on," he said after a beat. "We're next."

Together, Roan and I slipped inside the 'unusable entrance' and found the darkened corridor that lay beyond. I could hear the sounds of our men several yards ahead, moving swiftly towards our target. As we moved towards the men, a soft noise had the two of us halting our footsteps. Conjuring a ball of fire, Roan turned back and froze, his eyes widening. I followed his gaze until my own landed on the small upturned face of a pale human child. Her hair hung in flat strands around her rounded cheeks, and in her left fist she held the paw of a stuffed animal creature—sewn together with what looked to be different colors of patchwork cloth.

Her little nightgown was at least a size or two too large for her tiny frame. Big blue eyes blinked up at us and she lifted her free hand to rub at her eyes as if trying to understand what she was seeing. A servant's child. That was the only thing that made sense. As far down in the castle as we were, the servants' quarters were likely not far from the storage chambers we were after.

Roan and I exchanged a look. "What are you doing?" the small child inquired, sounding both sleepy and confused.

"Orion," Roan hissed. I knew what he wanted, an illusion, but human children were far less susceptible to our powers than their elders—a fact I doubted any human realized.

I ground my teeth together. No, an illusion may not work, but there was no way we would kill this innocent child. It was the one sin none of us were willing to commit. Soldiers and adults were fair game, but children knew not of their parents' and elders' hatred. Children still had the opportunity to overcome that tainted bile.

It appeared that both of us were hesitating far too long for the child's attention because after a moment more, she toddled forward, eyes wide as she reached for the leather encasing the boots that reached up to my knees.

"Whoa," she muttered. "I can see myself." She turned her face upward—so trusting it made my chest ache. The child's golden hair reminded me of Cress and all at once, I wondered if this was how our Changeling had seemed as a child. Youthful. Vibrant. Innocent. Loving. I tried to picture it and the image that came to my mind was so very easy to form. "Who are you, sir?" the small girl inquired again.

Her little chin twitched and just before I was set to answer her, she reared back and sneezed. Roan grimaced, but I didn't mind. It was cute. I reached down and with gentle hands, I lifted the child into my arms. As she slipped her slender, frail hands around my neck, she released her grip on her stuffed toy. Without being asked, Roan dipped down and retrieved it, handing it back to the girl.

"Take care of her," he ordered quietly. "And meet us at the room."

I nodded my understanding and was relieved when he marched off, though he left a hovering orb of fire nearby so that the child and I weren't in complete darkness. "Where'd he go?" the girl asked.

"Never mind him, darling," I said. "You're lost, aren't you?"

Her blue eyes lifted and met mine and I stilled as I felt one of her tiny hands touch my chin, her soft fingers smoothing against the unshaven bits of my jawline. "You're prickly," she said with a high pitched giggle.

Holding her in my arms lit a craving within me. To see Cress as a girl, or perhaps to see her hold her own child in her arms—*our child.*

"Are you lost, sweetheart?" I asked again.

The girl tilted her face up and nodded. "I had to go potty," she confessed quietly, her cheeks turning pink with embarrassment. Even as young as this child was, I understood. Such things were private, especially for little girls.

"That's alright," I told her. "I'm here to lead you back. If I take you to the main part of the castle, can you find your way back to your chambers on your own?" She considered my request for a moment before nodding. "Good, then let us be on our way. Can you tell me which way you came from?"

She pointed into the darkness and I began walking. As I strode down the corridor, I kept the cloaking spell up and lifted a palm to cup the back of her head. Though it would be far more difficult for a child to believe a full fledged illusion, it wouldn't be that hard to settle her into a light sleep and put the thought into her head that our meeting had been nothing but a strange dream.

The girl's head dipped and rested against my shoulder, her skin warm against my own as she nuzzled into my neck like a curious animal. Soon, the soft little snores began to drift up from her mouth. I shook my head.

"I'm sorry, little one," I whispered to her, though I knew she couldn't hear me. It felt only right to apologize for what I was going to do. "When you wake, all will be well, but for now, I must corrupt your dreams," I said quietly as I sent a tendril of my darkness into her through where my hand was connected to the back of her head. It delved into the sides of her head and in through her open nose and mouth.

Not once did she stir, and once I was satisfied, I quickly found my way up to the main hub of the Duke's castle. There, beneath a large open window, I found a small sitting area and laid the small child upon it, turning her face away from the light, hoping that soon, when she woke, she would only remember wandering the halls and falling asleep here with no one else the wiser.

I pulled myself away from her little by little, finding it far more difficult than I expected it to be. Any child, even human, was precious. It went against my instincts to leave her so out in the open even knowing she would be safer here—away from me and the other Fae that were hunting for our targets down below.

When I made it back to the tunnels, I saw Roan waiting out in the corridor for me. He lifted a hand and extinguished the flame that had followed me before turning towards the open door at his side.

"There's something you should see," he said.

I nodded, allowing him to lead me further into the room—a large open storage space filled to the brim with barrels and bags of food and wooden boxes that had been pried open to reveal weapons. Beyond the main room there appeared to be a much larger door, thicker than the others, and by looking at the vault like security it held—the extra bolts of metal and the strange mechanism over its locking device—there was no doubt that it held important information.

The locking device, too, was built and coated with iron. I narrowed my eyes on it and shook my head. As though an amount that small would deter us. Perhaps had I been from another Court, a more merciful one, it would have. It certainly had Roan and the others standing out of reach. Not me, though. I marched forward, assessing the lock.

In the Court of Midnight, iron had often been used to "strengthen" children, to develop a tolerance for pain. Nothing could be seen as a weakness. To be weak was to be easily killed. I recalled that all too well. Even the old scars along my back and against my chest seemed to tighten as I sucked in a breath. I had trained with shackles of iron on my ankles and wrists. I had tested myself for endurance, been weakened down to even less than a human and yet, I survived. In the Court of Midnight, only the strongest ever did.

Reaching forward, I clenched my hand around the lock. Several soldiers winced as they heard the sizzle as the metal touched my skin. I paid it no heed. Instead, I gripped tighter and then ripped the thing free. The door swung open outward and banged against the wall as I stepped back.

Almost immediately, I realized what we had found. Roan and I stepped inside and the others came in after us, moving gingerly as if fearing they might trigger a trap. But no, the humans—Amnestia's King and his Duke—had not planned on us coming here. They did not expect that, were we to infiltrate them without their knowledge, we would ever make it this far. Because had they done so, they might have realized just how dangerous it was for them to leave so much behind.

Maps covered the walls and notes were scattered over the large table that was the centerpiece of the room. They had been tracking our movements, that much was clear. Someone had been feeding them information. *Tyr.* A familiar anger rose within me and before I could stop it, small plumes of smoke began to fall from my arms and collect around my feet. Several soldiers noticed and were smart enough to avoid it.

I turned my attention to the maps along the walls. I recognized where the Court of Crimson had been and had a vague notion of where my home Court—the Court of Midnight—was last. There were several markings, though, and no way to tell where it actually was presently.

I looked over at Roan who was scanning the notes. He lifted one for me to see. Letters with the Royal seal, I realized. Sketches and diagrams and all one might need to plan another attack. What was more terrifying were the blueprints to build a castle—one like the Courts—and at the center of it, a Lanuaet.

Humans with the same abilities as Fae. The thought was preposterous and yet, with Tyr's help, possible. And all it would result in would be death and destruction. There were no limits to the humans' hatred whereas Fae were bound to protect the Earth as much as possible. We could not destroy without having to give back. Not like the humans.

Fury danced in Roan's gaze and it matched my own. He raised an eyebrow at me in question and I nodded. I knew what he wanted. "Torch the supplies," Roan ordered. "Keep it contained, and when everything is destroyed make sure you put it out. We don't want this moving to the rest of the grounds."

As he and I stepped out the room, holding the documents we deemed most important, we turned back as a unit and watched as two Crimson Fae stepped up, lifting their arms and sending blast after blast of silent fire raging into the secret chamber we'd found. I felt the heat of flames warm my face.

"What are we going to do now?" Roan muttered.

"We go back," I said. "And show Groffet what we found. If anyone will know what all this means, it's him."

"This is too far," Roan replied. "Tyr needs to be taken care of."

"Yes," I agreed. He may have once been my blood brother, my past, but he'd lost all connection to me the moment he'd taken my future. Cress was my future and so was our race and I knew, beyond a shadow of doubt, that I would do what needed to be done to see Cress and our people safe. Even kill him.

CHAPTER 27
ROAN

Anxiety slithered across my nerve endings as I stalked the halls of the Court of Crimson. I could feel the tension in my shoulders. The mission had gone well—aside from the human child mishap, but I trusted Orion to have taken care of that issue.

No, there was a new issue at hand. Something far more devious, a new threat that now hung over our Court, our people, and our lives. Tyr was helping the human King build a fortress. The very moment we'd returned, Orion and I had headed for Groffet before anyone else. Before our people and men. Before Sorrell. Even before Cress.

Groffet was ancient. He had served my father and my grandfather during their reins as Crimson Kings, but something told me that my time as a King would be quite different from theirs. The past was receding. Traditions as we knew them were changing. The Fae, despite having the advantage in this war, were dying. Our magic was depleted and our people were fewer in numbers than they had been twenty years before when it had all started. Unlike humans, we did not breed so often for heirs and even more than that, no one in their right mind wanted to bring children into this world simply to fight a war.

I was brought out of my thoughts as the scent of smoke tickled my nose and drew my curiosity. *A fire within the walls?*

I followed the scent until I came to the training courtyard and beyond the entrance, as I stepped down the stairs and into the mini arena, I saw two familiar heads—one blonde and one a pale silver. Cress and Sorrell. My lips parted as I noted how close they were to one another, standing over a bale of hay that had been set aflame.

"I did it!" Cress shrieked and leapt at Sorrell, her arms encircling him. I half expected him to growl at her to release him, but he merely pulled her closer and leaned down, taking her mouth in a shocking kiss.

Sorrell, the ice King, himself, was kissing Cress. The Changeling, as he called her. Often refusing to even utter her name. And it was a true kiss, one filled with passion that I had not seen from him in many years. I stared in absolute stunned silence as he wrapped his arms around her, lifting her off her feet as he devoured her mouth with his own. Then, as if realizing they were no longer alone, he deposited her on the ground once more and lifted his head. His eyes clashed with mine and he froze.

"Sorrell?" Cress's trembling voice indicated she was oblivious to my entrance. Her cheeks were flushed and her smile confused until she turned and spotted me as well. "Roan!" she shouted. "You're back!"

And just like that, the spell of surprise I'd been under was broken. Cress raced from his arms straight into mine, slamming into my chest as her arms came around me and she practically climbed my body. "You're safe!" she said excitedly. "Oh, I'm so glad you're back. Look!" She turned and pointed to the still burning hay hale. "I did it! I blasted it!"

"I see ... well done, Little Bird." I glanced from her face to Sorrell's as he approached at a much slower pace. "I see the two of you are getting along as well."

Cress's eyes widened and though her smile remained, a hint of pink tinged her cheeks. Before she could say anything, however, Sorrell spoke first. "When did you return?" he asked.

"A few hours ago," I admitted.

He frowned.

"Orion and I went to speak with Groffet first," I told him, sliding my hand beneath Cress's body to hold her up.

His eyes followed the movement, lingering for a moment on where her ass was pressed beneath my forearms. I wondered, briefly, just how much closer they'd become in our absence. It didn't anger me. On the contrary, I was glad to see that he'd finally broken his abstinence. Without a moment to lose, as well, because with mine and Orion's return—there were only more problems waiting for us. My relief at seeing the two of them would be short lived, no fucking doubt.

"What did you find at the Duke's castle?" he demanded, lifting his gaze to meet mine once more.

"Nothing good," I replied. "Nothing good at all."

Cress pushed back away from me and wiggled. "What's going on?" she asked. I set her down between Sorrell and me, the two of us towering over her much smaller frame. She flicked a glance back to him before resettling her gaze on me. "Roan?"

"Orion is in the library awaiting us," I said.

"Then we must not keep him waiting much longer," Sorrell replied with a nod. "Cress?" She blinked as she turned to him, the flush rising curiously back to her cheeks. "Lead the way?" he suggested. I half expected her to snort and walk off—I'd become so accustomed to their apparent dislike of each other, especially his, it was odd to watch his gaze soften and hers to heat as she nodded.

Just as she strode past me and I moved to follow, Sorrell's hand came out and captured my arm. "A moment," he said. "We'll catch up."

She paused on the threshold of the corridor, narrowing her eyes at him before sighing and striding off. "Very interesting," I commented once I was sure she was out of hearing range. "When I last saw you two, I was beginning to doubt my assumption that you had any feelings for her at all."

He leveled me with an icy look and I lifted my hands in a placating gesture. "She is..." He trailed off, as if he didn't have the words to describe one single Changeling Fae woman.

"Yes," I said with a nod. "I know." She was sunshine and moonlight. Fire and Earth. Warmth that could melt even the coldest heart—now so much more obviously proven. "You finally gave in."

He nodded. "She makes it impossible not to." That comment I understood all too well. Cress was becoming more than just a Changeling. "Now." Sorrell's face shifted back to his serious expression. "Tell me what we're walking into."

"Like I said," I told him. "It's not good. Tyr has been feeding the humans information—on the Courts' whereabouts, ours and Midnight."

"That's treason," he growled.

"Yes, well..." I sucked in a breath. "I don't really think he gives a fuck anymore. He and the King are planning to build a castle—much like the Courts—with ... can you guess? A fucking Lanuaet at the center."

Sorrell's eyes widened and his face went from pale to dead white. "No..." It wasn't a denial, but a hope. A hope that what I said wasn't true. It shouldn't be, but it was.

"We have to end this war," I said, "and soon. We cannot let that thing be built. It'll spell nothing but disaster for all involved."

His eyes met mine and the weight of this knowledge settled over both of us. We were rulers, future Kings. The lives of our people were in our hands. It was a lot to bear—the weight of it could be stifling and almost murderous as time wore on. That was why the three of us had formed this outcast Court. Yes, it was necessary for more than one Royal to move the Court, but only one needed to truly rule it. Royals had been in such short supply since the war that having more than two at a time was a feat and a distinction of strength. But the three of us—Sorrell, Orion, and I—we were bound by more than our race or our Royal lineage. We were bound by more than blood because none of us were truly related.

The three of us were bound by honor. By trust. By hope. That one day this war would end and the dark clouds that hovered over us day in and day out would finally fade and the sun would rise once more.

I put a hand on his shoulder and squeezed. "I am truly glad to see you happy, to see you and Cress happy together," I said. "In the coming battle, I think you'll need her."

"She's not a fighter," he said. "Though she's been doing better, she is far from ready to take to the fields."

"I don't mean as a fighter, my friend," I replied. "I mean as a lover."

His brows lowered. "She's to be your Queen," he said slowly. "And yet you knew what would happen between us."

I shrugged. "Orion had her first, I second, and somehow, I just figured—we've shared everything since we were adolescents." I grinned at him. "Why not her so long as she agrees to it?"

He shook his head. "Sometimes, I forget just how truly hotheaded and insane you are."

"I think the bond between all of us makes us stronger," I argued. "Not just because we are all more connected, but I feel like my magic is stronger as well. Now"—I stopped and slapped him on the back as I pivoted and headed for the courtyard's exit—"let's head to the library and pray to the Gods that Groffet will help us find a way to win this thing before it's too late."

CHAPTER 28
CRESS

Sorrell and Roan arrived at the library alongside each other. Though they noticed Nellie and Ash's presence with raised brows, neither of them said anything. Instead, Roan simply turned and closed the library doors behind him.

For a long moment, silence echoed throughout the chamber, and then Orion spoke. "Last night, Roan and I executed an incognito mission to destroy the King's supply storage at Norune Castle. While there, we uncovered some concerning information," he said.

"What kind of information?" I asked.

"The King has been tracking our Courts and is planning to build a moveable fortress much like ours," Roan stated.

"Movable?" Nellie shook her head. "That's not possible. Humans can't use magic."

"Humans don't *have* magic," Sorrell corrected her. "They can, however, use magical items—this castle and the magic orb that controls it, for example."

Nel's eyes swung my way and I knew she was trying to determine if this was real, but this was the first I'd ever heard of such a thing.

"What does that mean?" I asked, focusing on Orion.

"It means," he said, "that our timetables must be moved forward. We can't allow King Felix to complete that castle."

Roan stepped forward and then leveled each of us with a look. The last person he landed on was Nellie, and I realized, now, why they hadn't immediately kicked her out of this meeting. They wanted to see what she would do, and how she would react to this information. I glared at him and stepped in front of her.

"Don't," I warned him.

"I'm sorry, Little Bird," he said. "We have to be sure."

"She's loyal," I snapped. "Whatever you have to say, she's not going to go blabbing it to another human. You keep her locked in here—there are no other humans in the Court of Crimson."

"Cress, it's okay." Nellie's words were soft, but my anger was still sharp. It wasn't until her hand landed on my arm and she forced me to turn and meet her gaze. "They're wise to be cautious—keep your friends close and your enemies closer and all that. I'm perfectly fine with anything they have to say."

"Brave words," Sorrell commented before I could respond.

I swung my gaze his way and stared him down.

"There is only one way out of this," Orion said, drawing my attention.

"Say it," Nellie offered. "I can take it."

"We must kill the King of Amnestia."

I watched as Nel's face paled, but she kept her lips shut. She was the daughter of doctors—of healers. Murder and war and bloodshed was not something she cared for. To be honest, the statement wasn't a shock for me. I wasn't even against it. Not after what I'd seen in the capital castle, but there was still a larger problem at play.

"Without a King, what will happen to Amnestia?" I asked.

Orion, Roan, and Sorrell exchanged a look. "We can't say," Roan finally replied.

"Then we can't do it," I said.

It was as simple as that. The King was corrupt and rotten, but without him, all I could see were the aftereffects. The people of Amnestia knew nothing but the monarchy. Dear Coreliath, if there was no ruler in place, chaos would take its place. Chaos was even worse than war.

"Cress, remember what he did to you—" Roan started, his face darkening. "Remember how you were held and almost—"

"I remember," I said, cutting him off. "I'm not defending him. I'm thinking of the people. What happens after he's dead?" I demanded. "Who will take his place?"

The three of them fell silent and I wasn't surprised that neither Nellie nor her Fae 'friend,' Ash, had anything to say. It was an impossible position. The King was the villain in our storybook, and yet, killing him would make us villains. It would destroy the country not to have someone in place to lead them back into the light, into a prosperous world without war and pain as the driving forces of their lives. I sensed the tension in the room, felt it rise as flames erupted at Roan's scalp. He turned and marched one way before swiftly pivoting and starting back.

No matter what, though, none of us had a clear answer.

We couldn't just kill the King and leave the Kingdom of Amnestia to rot. There would be nothing but chaos—the exact opposite of what we were trying to accomplish. We needed peace, not pandemonium. We needed to end this.

"There is another option," Groffet said suddenly. All eyes turned to him.

"Well, we're all ears, Groffet," Roan snapped. "Please, by all means..." He gestured to the rest of the group. "What other option do we have?"

Groffet eyed the red haired Prince and even though he was barely half Roan's size, he still somehow managed to look down his nose at him. "Humans—like Fae—believe in the line of succession," he began. "Therefore, if we can find a Royal of Amnestia who is willing to take over the crown and not the mantle of war, we may yet still have a chance for ending this bloodshed."

"The King never had any children," Nellie piped up. The Fae at her back, Ash, stepped closer as the Princes' gazes all turned to her. She shrank back slightly, but I watched as he lifted his hand and gently pressed it to her back. My eyebrows shot up when she appeared to sigh and lean into him.

"How do you know this?" Sorrell asked. "Is it common knowledge among your people? Do King's of the human realm not hide their offspring in case of an attack?

"It's common knowledge," Nellie said. "If the King had had a child, there would have been a celebration. Plus..." She paused as if unsure whether or not she should speak the next part, but one look from Ash and she lifted her gaze to meet Sorrell's head on. "The Queen was killed during a Fae raid many years ago. It's the reason why he's so hateful towards them now."

"Fae raids..." Orion's brows pinched as repeated those words. "Those haven't happened since the very beginning of the war."

"Then it's likely another reason why the war was started," Sorrell surmised.

Groffet grunted. "I did not say a child of the current King," he clarified. "I said a Royal of Amnestia—someone from his line. It doesn't necessarily have to be a child."

"The King had no children or siblings," Nellie argued. "There are no more Royals of Amnestia. He is the last of his line."

I stepped forward. "Shouldn't we try to find out anyway?" I asked. "Just to be sure? What could it hurt?"

For a moment, there was nothing but silence. Then, one by one, everyone agreed. Even Ash, though he looked more interested in Nellie than he did in the subject at hand, no matter its importance to our survival. Our eyes found Groffet's once more.

"What do we do?" Roan asked.

Groffet turned and waddled away, calling back over his shoulder as he moved. "There is a spell," he said, "that will determine if a person exists. We will use it and it will find them —wherever they may be."

"What if they're not even in Amnestia?" Ash asked.

Groffet went to a stack of books and pulled the top half off, using the stack as a step stool to reach the table. "*Wherever* they may be," he repeated.

My foot tapped with nervousness and I found myself wanting to pace—move—*something*. Anything but stand still. A cool hand fell on my arm and I nearly leapt out of my skin until I realized it was Sorrell. I looked up into his icy gaze and felt my whole body soften. "It will be alright," he whispered. "We will find a way for this blasted war to end with peace—even if we have to rule Amnestia ourselves."

"A Fae can't be the one to do it," I said with a shake of my head. "A Fae can't take over Amnestia." It might work for a time, but never for the long run. I could see the disastrous effects in my head. "Even if you have good intentions, they won't see it like that. The country's people would grow resentful, and eventually, even if you have peace at first, they'll rebel." There would be another war, and I could say with certainty that I was freaking tired of war. Exhausted by it and everything else.

"She's right," Roan said. Sorrell turned his gaze back to him and so did I. Roan's eyes found mine and he nodded. "Think of it like this," he continued. "What would our people do if Fae were to be ruled by humankind?"

Sorrell scowled. "That's preposterous," he replied. "We wouldn't allow such a thing to happen. Fae are superior."

"No, we're not," I snapped. "And it's that kind of thinking that created this Gods forsaken war in the first place."

Sorrell's head whipped back to me and he narrowed his eyes. "Fae have magic that humans cannot even conceive of, much less use. They are born magicless. We are closer to the Gods."

"Yet the Gods abandoned us as they did the humans," Orion pointed out.

Sorrell gritted his teeth. "I am not the villain here. Tyr and that blasted King are!"

"No, you're not," I said, "but your thoughts are villainous, nonetheless. Thinking the way you do—that there are those who are superior and inferior is exactly what causes hate like this to build. It's wrong. How can you not see that?" When he didn't say anything more, I grabbed onto the lapel of his shirt and held it tightly in my grasp. "What do you see when you look at me?" I asked.

"I see a woman who is insane," he replied. When Sorrell shifted and tried to remove my arm, I held on.

"What else?" I pressed.

"Ugh." He tried again and again, but I refused to release him. "Fine! I see a woman who is far too stubborn for her own good. I see a woman who has time and time again gotten herself into trouble—who has refused to back down even when she knows she should. Who..." I stared up into those cold eyes of his and for a brief moment, they softened.

"What?" I asked.

For a long moment, Sorrell didn't speak. Then he lifted his hand and touched the side of my face, his palm curving to my cheek. "Who is far more brilliant than I ever gave her credit for."

I took a breath. "And am I any different from that girl you first met?" I asked.

A snort left him. "You're a little better at not almost dying," he conceded.

"Anything else?" I insisted.

He sighed. "No."

"You thought I was human when you first met me," I pointed out.

He frowned. "We weren't sure."

"No, but you thought I was human, and nothing else has changed about me since then except for the fact that—according to you"—And I wasn't sure that I liked this being the only thing—"I've gotten better at not almost dying. Nothing else has changed," I repeated, trying and hoping against hope that I was getting my point across. "I'm still the same. I'm still me. I was no different than when you thought I was human."

Sorrell's brows drew down low over his eyes. "That's a pointless argument," he said. "You are Fae. We know that now."

"But you didn't know it then," I huffed. "Please, at least try to understand." I shuffled to the side and gestured to where Nellie stood. "Nellie is my friend," I said. "And she is, absolutely, without a doubt, human. Do you hate her?"

He lifted his eyes and looked at her across the room. His lips curled down, but he shook his head. "I don't particularly care for her either way," he stated, "but no, I don't hate her."

"Then it's just a race you hate," I said. "And I can promise you, they have been hurt just as much as you have by this war. Hating someone without reason simply for being something that they cannot change is worthless. Hate does nothing but perpetuate itself, but love ... understanding ... care. Those things can do so much more." I rested my hand against his chest and pushed myself against him. "You're a Prince of Frost." I lowered my voice so that only he and I could hear. "You will be a King someday. Don't be a King that perpetuates something so evil. Be the King I *know* you can be."

LUCINDA DARK & HELEN SCOTT

Sorrell looked at me, his icy gaze holding such uncertainty. I bit my lip and waited. "I don't trust humans," he admitted.

"I'm not asking you to trust them," I said. "I'm asking you to trust me—to trust Roan and Orion. You trust them, right?"

His gaze lifted and over the top of my head, he looked to them. Without looking back to me, he sighed. "Yes," he agreed, "I do."

"Then give this a try," I urged. "Don't let your hatred for humans color your view of what's right. They deserve to rule themselves just as Fae deserve the same."

This time, when Sorrell looked back at me, it was with a peculiar expression. Not exactly one I could pinpoint. It was as if he were looking at something new, something he didn't quite recognize, and yet he was trying to understand how it worked.

"You sound like a Royal," he said.

"A Royal?" I frowned.

Nellie was the one that answered. She stepped up alongside us and reached for my hand. "He means you sound wise," she clarified. Her eyes rose to meet his, but instead of hatred or disgust in Sorrell's eyes when he looked back to her, all I saw was begrudging respect.

The moment was disrupted, however, when Groffet waddled forward and slammed a book down on a nearby table. "Found it!" he called.

CHAPER 29
CRESS

"What do we have to do?" Roan demanded. He stepped up to look over Groffet's shoulder, towering over the small troll.

"A spell," Groffet explained. "One that will identify the closest lineal Royal heir to the Kingdom of Amnestia."

"Okay," I said as the rest of us gathered closer. "What do we need to do to pull it off and how are we going to get to them when we do locate them?"

"One thing at a time," Orion said gently as he came to stand at my side. With him against one arm and Sorrell against the other, I felt pinned, yet safe. I inhaled sharply and forced my attention back to the spell.

The words on the page were all a jumbled mess to me. Try as I might to read over Groffet's shoulder like everyone else, it was Fae language—something the nuns definitely *hadn't* taught us in school. "What does it say?" I asked.

"We will need a mirror," Groffet said, flicking his hand out.

Ash rushed to the other side of the library and came back a moment later, lugging a large covered object. With a grunt he set it down several feet to the side of the table and then pulled the sheet that had shielded it away, revealing a tall, ornately carved mirror. Groffet nodded in thanks and then went back to reading the book.

He grumbled something to himself, turned, and when he found the majority of his audience less than a foot from him, he huffed and pushed his way through.

"It'll require magic, correct?" Sorrell inquired.

"Yes."

"Will it need the three of us?" Roan asked.

"No."

"What do we need to do?" Nellie asked.

"Nothing."

It was clear Groffet was growing agitated by all the questions. I watched as he flitted about the room, shoving books off of their carefully placed-though haphazard looking-stacks. A wooden bowl was scrounged from beneath another table. Dusty papers were procured. A vial of something that disturbingly resembled blood, and a bag that was as big as it was shapeless also appeared.

"Uh..." I lifted a hand as Groffet set the bowl down and leaned over the book, grumbling and reading as he crumbled the papers and tossed them in the bottom of the bowl. "Is that"—he uncorked the vial and upended what was definitely a red goopy liquid of some sort—"blood?"

"Yes," he grunted.

I grimaced. "Please tell me it's from an animal," I said, looking at Orion.

He cracked a smile, but it was not reassuring. "It's best not to ask," he replied.

Definitely not an animal then, I surmised. He was right. It was best not to ask. I didn't want to know whose blood it was, where it came from, or how they came to possess it ... scattered about like knick knacks in their Court's library. Nope. Definitely didn't want to know.

A split second later, I gasped. "Are those *bones?*" I hissed, as Groffet opened his bag and withdrew a handful of what looked like the bones of a small animal.

"Like he said," Sorrell answered. My eyes jerked to him. "Don't ask if you don't want to know."

"Roan," Groffet snapped. Roan stepped up and lifted his hand, curling each of his fingers down. All but one, and as soon as he did, a flame appeared at the end of his nail. Roan dipped his finger into the bowl, setting fire to the edge of the now soaked papers until it began to burn and ashes lifted upward. Setting fire to something in a wooden bowl seemed dangerous, but as I took a glance around ... maybe it was best not to ask? Or point it out?

The seven of us—the Princes, me, Nellie, Ash, and Groffet— stood back and watched as the contents of the bowl were incinerated by Roan's fire until there was nothing left but a black mixture. Whatever kind of blood it was that Groffet had poured into the bowl—it wasn't flammable apparently. It was the only thing left and it mixed with the ashes of the bones and papers.

Orion leaned down. "Roan's flame burns much hotter than the average fire," he whispered.

"Then why didn't the blood burn up?" I whispered back.

Orion's dark, midnight gaze locked on mine. "Because it's magic."

I absorbed that as Groffet lifted the bowl and turned toward the mirror. Without concern for whatever heat remained behind, he dipped two fingers into the bowl, stirring them around until his fingertips were coated in the mixture. Only then did he use them to paint markings in a line up the mirror's surface.

Halfway up, he had to stop, and Roan kicked over a stool for him to use. We watched as he clambered up onto the stool and finished the markings. They resembled some of the ones

I'd seen in the book, but once more they were nothing legible. I shook my head, unable to make sense of it.

"What does that mean?" I asked, tugging on Orion's sleeve.

"They're glyphs," he answered. "The old written language of the Fae is close enough to the language of the Gods that the writing itself contains magic. The words are the spell, the question, the mirror is the conduit of the answer. Whoever appears within it is who we're going to be looking for."

I swallowed roughly and shivered as the mirror began to glow. Groffet backed up, tossing the bowl to the side without a second thought. We crowded closer, curiosity lingering in each of us. Whoever this person was, they would be the next King. We would need to find them as soon as possible, convince them to work with us, and then … a coup d'état.

It wouldn't be easy. That much was for damn sure. They would be risking a lot to help us. They could have a family. A life. Children. What were we about to ask of a total stranger? I looked around the room, my eyes leaving the mirror's surface to survey the faces in the room. I was so focused on my guilt and worry, that when Nellie gasped, I didn't immediately understand what had happened.

"By the Gods," she whispered, stumbling back.

My gaze shot to her and then to the mirror. *What was it? What had I missed?* When I saw the image in the mirror, my lips parted and my jaw dropped.

It was her. It was Nellie, but as a little girl. Playing alongside a tall dark haired man and a light haired woman. It was her running through a battlefield with gauze in her arms and tears on her face and blood in her hair. It was Nellie a few years later, solemn and quiet, as she washed dishes at the convent. The Nellie in the mirror paused, having heard something. Her head lifted and her eyes went to the window before her. A small smile appeared and then she shook her head. A moment later, I came in, covered in chicken feathers. I remembered that day. I'd been running from Sister Madeline through the chicken coop and had disturbed a very angry mother hen who'd nearly pecked my toes off.

"I don't understand," Nellie said, shaking her head. "It's broken. It has to be. My parents were doctors!"

Roan shot a look to Groffet. "Could there have been a mistake?" he asked.

Groffet shook his head. "No mistake," he replied. "She is the closest heir."

Silence descended and then, "Well," I said, drawing everyone's attention, "at least this saves us the trip."

Nel growled my way. "No, it doesn't," she argued. "Because it's not true. How can it be?"

Groffet waddled her way, his bulbous body swaying back and forth as he maneuvered around Roan and Ash to stand before her. "Doesn't matter what you say is true, girly," he snapped, his hands landing on his hips as he glared up at her. "The magic does not lie."

"Then you did the spell wrong!" she exclaimed. "You have to do it again. It didn't work."

"Nel." Ash reached out and grasped her hand, holding her as she began to shake.

"Ash," she said. "You have to know it's not true. I'm not related to the King. I can't be. I wouldn't have been in a convent orphanage if that were true." She looked at me. "You know me, Cress! You know I'm not some Royal Princess in disguise."

"Groffet is never wrong," Ash said.

I stepped forward, moving until I was right next to her. I took her other hand and held it in mine, squeezing as she had done for me so many times before. Then I turned to Groffet. "Is there a way to prove it?" I asked. "To make sure."

He sniffed as if the very idea was insulting, but when I didn't take back my request and I met his beady little eyes with a glare of my own, he huffed. "I can do another spell, but it will only prove the inevitable; she is of the King's bloodline."

I looked at Nellie. "Do you want him to do the second spell?" I asked. Her face was pale, her eyes wide with shock, and she kept biting down on her lower lip, chewing it until I was sure she would bruise herself. "Nellie," I repeated her name when she didn't seem to hear me. Her hand jerked in mine and her eyes lifted to meet my gaze "Do you want him to do the second spell?" I asked once more.

She nodded. "He has to, Cress." Her words were whispered. "Because I'm not the King's daughter. There's no way. My father was a doctor."

"We'll figure it out," I reassured her. I turned back to Groffet. "What do we need to do?"

He eyed me for a moment but then he stepped back. "You don't need to do anything," Roan said as he moved forward and Groffet shuffled over to where Orion and Sorrell now stood, watching the proceedings. Groffet flipped through another book and uttered a few garbled words that sounded foreign and hypnotic all at once.

The language of the Gods? I wondered. As he did Roan lifted a knife from the nearby table and sliced his arm, running his fingers through the blood before painting glyphs around the outside of the mirror. Groffet then waddled forward and lifted Nellie's arm, eyeing her as if asking for permission. He gently took the blade from Roan and then did the same to her arm and used her blood to run over the markings.

"Why—" I began, confused.

"Roan's Fae blood will act as an accelerant," Orion said, answering my unfinished question. "While Nellie's blood will be used to trace her bloodline. It'll go fast, so pay attention."

She and I nodded and then, taking her hand once more, together, we watched the mirror shift and new scenes arise. Nellie's parents, each of them unique in their own way, but it was easy to see that Nellie took after each of them. Her father's large oval eyes. Her mother's petite nose and rosebud mouth. The strength of her father's chin and his coloring with her mother's hair. Nellie's hand squeezed mine as she stared at them. I could only imagine the mixture of love and pain she was feeling and a part of me wondered if I would recognize my parents if I were to see what they looked like.

The image in the mirror moved, slipping backwards from their deaths to their marriage to their meeting to their childhood. And then as they separated, the scenes focused on the father—so he was the true heir, I thought as we stared in quiet curiosity as his life ran down. From adulthood to adolescence to childhood to infancy. Until...

Nel's gasp sounded and rebounded around the room as she watched her father's mother—her grandmother—tossed from the capital castle. Hitting the mud as the King stood above her and guards threw her to the ground. Words were said, but we could not hear. All we could do was watch as she cried and begged, grabbing at the young King Felix's robes with pleas in her eyes. And it came as no shock to anyone to watch him turn away and walk back into the castle—leaving Nellie's grandmother in the streets.

"What does that mean?" Nellie's lips trembled as she asked the question and the images in the mirror went dark.

"She was likely his mistress," Roan said quietly and though he was normally so commanding in his tone, now his voice was soft and quiet, sympathetic. "And when he found out about the baby, he threw her out. Bastard children of Royals—whether human or Fae—are rarely looked upon with anything but disdain."

"He just threw her out like garbage," Nel whispered. "How could he do that?"

Because he was cruel, I thought, though I didn't voice it. When she turned into me and clutched my sides, I had no choice but to hold her and let her tears soak the front of my dress. I didn't care if she needed to soak a hundred of them. Her pain was my pain. When I lifted my head, I noticed that while Orion spoke quietly with Groffet, both Roan and Sorrell appeared to be watching Nellie and me. Of the two of them, Sorrell appeared contemplative. He now stared at Nellie with an open curiosity that I knew we all felt.

Nellie as the King's heir? It seemed too good to be true. Too unpredictable and yet ... perfectly aligned with everything we needed. For a brief moment, I wondered ... but no, the Gods had long ago stopped meddling in the lives of humans and Fae. There was no way they had set this up, was there?

CHAPTER 30

ORION

My brother had once thought me broken, and perhaps, at one point, I might have agreed. The things I survived in the Court of Midnight—the most detestable of Courts—were not for children to understand. Yet, as a child, I had more than understood it. I had lived it, breathed it, and now, as an adult, I would vanquish it.

Hatred. Fear. Sorrow. Pain. The darkest parts of nature were in our blood—Tyr's and mine. These were also the very reasons I had left. Had I stayed, there was no doubt that I would have risen to my brother's side. I would have been a Prince of Midnight as wicked as he was, but in that dark hole where I'd been born and raised, two creatures had looked in and they had reached their hands down to help me out.

Roan and Sorrell. Each of us had our own pains. Our own lives had been fraught with nothing but Court politics, commanding orders from our parents, and control that we had only just managed to scrape back to ourselves before our fourth and final piece—a bright little Changeling—had fallen right into place.

As I gathered my weapons and strapped them to my body,

preparing for the battle that was coming, I wondered what might have happened had Roan and Sorrell not come into my life. What might I have been had they simply acted as every other Crimson and Frost Fae before them—turning away in fear from a Prince of a Court known only for its darkness?

I would not be here, I decided, and I would not even consider helping the human King's heir take her place on the throne.

No, I may have been born as part of the Court of Midnight, but as far as I was concerned, I was no longer theirs. I was *hers*. My little Changeling. Sweet. Fiery. Unbreakable.

Even as my thoughts veered away from the darkness in my mind, I couldn't help but consider the other questions we had yet to answer. No messenger that had been sent to the Court of Midnight had yet to return. We could not expect their assistance in this war—if they were even alive.

There was no proof to lend to my gut instinct. No solid evidence. Nothing tangible that I could use to pinpoint why I had the thought that it—the Court of Midnight—was no more. Only something deep inside of me said that it was true. Something horrible had happened to my home Court. And worse, a part of me did not mourn them. My guilt for that seeped into my soul and reminded me that no matter how I gave myself over to my friends—to my new family—I wouldn't ever have their light.

Once all of my smaller weapons—daggers and the like— were attached to my body, my hand fell to my sword. Nothing prepared me more than the task of lifting this weapon. The weight of it never felt light, but today I lifted it and turned it against the light pouring in from my chambers above, letting the sun glint over its shimmering surface. In the surface of the blade was a reflection of a familiar and welcome face. I turned and met Cress's look. Her eyes fell on the sword in my grasp.

"You're preparing," she said.

It was not a question, but I answered it nonetheless. "I am."

Her lips pressed together. "I'm going with you."

My head began to shake, but before I could open my mouth and utter an argument, she was storming towards me. "Don't tell me no, Orion," she ordered. "I'm going. I've already talked to Roan and I'll be riding with him."

"It's not safe on the battlefield and you are not a soldier," I said.

"My best friend is going out there," she replied. "Nellie's human and she's going."

"She needs to be in the castle when the King is killed," I argued. "We have gone over this. The plan does not work without her presence."

"Which I understand." Her small, heart shaped face tipped up and those bright shining blue eyes met mine. "But I'm going to be there whether you like it or not."

I frowned, feeling the tingle of anxiety creep up my spine. My powers didn't just feed off of others' negative emotions. It fed off my own, and presently, the thought of Cress in the middle of a bloody battlefield with no way to defend herself made me swell and smoke began to lift from my form and curl around me. "I don't."

Cress laid a gentle hand on my chest and as if she had some will to dissipate the disturbing possibilities running through my mind, I felt my whole self soften. My shoulders came down and I moved closer, running a hand along her side as I tugged her to my chest.

"I'll be fine," she said, looking up at me.

I recalled thinking, the first time I met her, that females were such curious creatures and that she was no different. How wrong I had been. She was by far the most infuriating and contrary female I had ever come across.

"I would go into the depths of the Divine for you," I whispered. "Do not cross that threshold."

"I won't." Her promise was soft on her lips, and it was far

too enticing for me to turn away. My head dipped and my mouth captured hers. A soft sigh escaped her as she burrowed closer to me. Her little hands wrapped around my body as I pushed my quickly hardening cock against her belly. The things I wanted to do to her. I wanted to pin her to my bed and make her scream as I licked her sweet little pussy. Then, when she would push my head away, claiming it was too much, that she had reached her peak too many times—I would merely grab her hands and hold them in mine as I devoured her core even more. Until she was so languid with pleasure and tender from all that I had done, she would never think of putting herself in harm's way again.

"Cress..." I said her name as our lips parted. Dark lashes fluttered against her skin. Despite the lightness of her hair, they were a stark contrast to her pale face. Those and the dark brows above her eyes. A wonder ... a curiosity ... I reached up and pushed a lock of her curls back.

Groffet had come up with the notion that she was of the Crimson Fae bloodline, but I had a suspicion he was only partially right. And if it was true—if our Cress was part of that long erased Court, the Brightling Court, then that meant she was the last one. Where the source of the Crimson Fae abilities came from blood and fire, Brightling Fae pulled their powers from light. Light could burn. Could set things aflame. But light could also drive out the darkness. And if it was true, then it was no wonder I was so drawn to her.

My little ray of sunshine. A blessing from the Gods of old. I didn't know how she had survived the purge, if I was right, but I was grateful. The only thing that made me hesitate, however, in sharing my theory, was the thought of her response. If she knew she was the last of her kind, that there were no others like her, that all of her family and potential friends had perished because of the Queens' and Court council's fears and animosity ... it would break her spirit. And that, I couldn't let happen.

"Is there something else you're worrying about?" Cress asked, leaning away.

She was perceptive. I shook my head. "No, just your safety," I lied.

Her pretty eyes narrowed on me and then cleared. "It's about Tyr, isn't it?" she guessed.

"What?" I looked at her in surprise, but even as she said it, I realized it was true. Tyr's involvement and betrayal had been weighing heavily on my mind. So, too, was the knowledge that there was a likelihood I would face him again. That I would kill him. "I'll do what needs to be done," I finally said.

Cress watched me with thoughtful eyes for a long moment before she spoke. "It's okay to be sad about it," she said.

"Sad?" I shook my head. "There's no need. He betrayed not just me, but our people. He deserves his fate."

"That's true," she agreed with a nod. "But you can still mourn his loss. It's not a crime."

"Mourn the loss of a criminal and traitor?" I stared at her. "Why would I do that?"

"Because he's your brother," she said. Then she waved a hand through the air, sighing and turning away as she moved towards the center of the room. "You won't hear me say he was a great person or anything—I'm a realist like that—but he *was* your brother and you feel a connection to him. That's not wrong. Even if you don't mourn the person he was, you can mourn the person he might have been—should have been—a brother, a friend, and an ally.

"What I'm trying to say is that whatever you're feeling is allowed. If you're sad, it's okay. If you're angry, that's okay too." Her eyes settled on me with meaning. "No one has to live with the actions you take but you. No one can tell you what's right or wrong to feel, just you, and you have to trust that whatever you're feeling is valid. You can't punish yourself for someone else's actions."

My heart froze at her words, and at some point during her speech, I'd stopped breathing. She was a queen, or at least she had all the makings of one. It was stunning to see in action. Breathtaking. When I still hadn't responded, Cress raised her eyebrows at me expectantly.

All I could scrape out of my raw throat in that moment was, "Thank you."

Her eyes softened. "Always," she replied. It was both a response and an oath. Come what may, she would remain on my side even if I truly did have to play my own brother's executioner.

CHAPER 31
CRESS

T he sun rose in the East, sending a kaleidoscope of colors washing over the sky. Dark blues turned to light and then oranges and reds and yellows as it slowly peeked above the horizon. Today was the day.

Roan's chest was warm against my back. I drew in a deep breath and looked up at him. "When does it start?" I asked.

Roan's eyes were on the castle in the nearby distance. The clomp of horse hooves beneath us rattled me as we continued forward in silence for a long moment more until...

"We will try our best to keep the casualties to a minimum," he began, his hand tightening on the reins. "But you should know, it will not be entirely possible."

I knew that much. My hand reached for the dagger Sorrell had given me. Strapped against the leather trousers beneath my purple skirts. It felt like a small weapon in light of all that was about to happen. A battle—a true one with swords and magic and fire and blood and death. I shuddered just thinking about it. As much as I knew this was necessary to end the war, it seemed a little counterproductive to fight to end the fighting, but there had to be one clear victor. This hatred had to come to an end.

"When the morning bells ring," Roan continued, "we will ride down to the castle's entrance."

"They won't let us in though," I said.

Roan shook his head. "They won't need to. We've already sent our scouts ahead and we have magic on our side. The humans can shore up their defenses all they like, but there's no way to truly deflect something they have no control over."

I pressed my lips together, looking up and spotting Nellie's head several paces away, her face tipped up as she talked with the man at her back. Her own rider, Ash. I watched the two of them together for a long moment, noting the gentle way he held her to him and how his eyes flickered down to meet hers as he both rode and listened to whatever she was saying.

"It may work, you know," Roan commented a moment later.

"What?" I asked. "The plan? I should hope so. Otherwise, this will be all for nothing."

"No," he replied. "Your friend and Ash."

A sigh escaped my lips. "I don't know how," I said honestly.

He chuckled, the sound vibrating against my back and sending a warmth through me that I didn't feel on the outside. "What happened to all that bravado and talk about not judging someone based upon their race?"

"It's not about his race," I replied. "It's about how long he'll live compared to her."

"I see." Roan straightened and our horse continued forward. "I understand your worries, but they're both in charge of their own hearts."

"I just don't want her to get hurt."

"Life is about getting hurt," Roan replied. "It is what makes living so exciting. You love and you lose. You fight and win. Without any dark, there cannot be light. Without death, there is no life. Without love, there is..." His words trailed off and I bit my lip.

"I get what you're saying," I said, "but Fae live far longer than humans. He'll outlive her by hundreds of years. How can he go into something with her, knowing that she'll pass long before he will?" My chest clenched at that thought. For the last several weeks, I'd lived with the knowledge of what I was, but it was just then that the reality of it hit me. I was Fae and my best friend was human. It wasn't just Ash who would suffer the loss when she died. I would, too. Tears pricked at my eyes and I squeezed them shut to ward off the pain.

Roan's heat moved closer as he leaned down and pressed his lips close to my ear. "Would you give her up now, knowing that?" he asked.

My eyes popped open. "Of course not." Every moment with her was even more precious because I knew that.

He nodded. "Then you understand how he feels," he said with a smug note in his tone.

I turned my head up and glared at him. He was smirking, the small curling of his lips making him appear even more handsome in the early morning light. I couldn't be too angry, though, because he was right. I sighed and turned back to face forward, adjusting myself in the saddle.

My eyes scanned the area. There were three main battalions of Fae soldiers on our side—with the Queens' soldiers coming in from the North. Each of them clad in chainmail and plated armor. Even the Princes. I looked down at the leather and metal plates that covered my upper chest. I felt woefully under-dressed for a battlefield, but at the same time, I wouldn't be fighting. Though I was sure Roan was unhappy about not taking part in the battle himself, he, Nellie, Ash, and I would ride through the fighting into the main hub of the castle. It was our job to get to King Felix.

Sorrell would stay behind and lead both his and the rest of

Roan's men. Orion would fight and search for Tyr. And ... Gods be with us, by the time this day ended, it would all be over.

"Get ready," Roan said a moment later, making me tense. I felt my back stiffen and my hands clench against the hump in front of me. My nails sank into the brown leather of the saddle as we picked up the pace. Our horse trotted to the front, rounding a line of Fae soldiers.

At first, there was nothing but silence. Not even the birds were chirping. As if nature, itself, sensed the violence that was about to happen. Then ... the bells. They rang once, twice, and then a few more times and by the time the last had faded into the morning quiet, we heard a battle cry and Fae were swarming forward. Hooves beating fast against the ground, dirt flying up in every direction.

Roan snapped his legs against his steed's sides and we galloped forward. Wind whipped at my face and I leaned forward unconsciously willing us to move faster, to get there before the blood began to spill. By the time we reached the wide open front gates of the village, the wood split and seared and smoking by some sort of fire magic, it was too late.

There were already Fae and human soldiers fighting and slashing. Fire was conjured. Water. Ice. Every element one could think of was being used during the battle. Dark smoke poured around the cobblestones street and I turned, looking back. as I realized that Orion had entered the fray. His face was expressionless as he rode through the streets, the dark clouds pouring from his body as he swiftly dove through a ring of soldiers swinging their swords.

I whimpered as he nearly got clipped. Roan urged me to face forward once more. "Don't worry about him," he ordered. "He knows what he's doing."

"But what if—" I tried, but Roan merely shook his head and forced the horse to move faster. We were flying over the streets now, dodging swords and screaming soldiers. Something occurred to me as we raced ever closer to the main castle. "Where are the people?" I asked, glancing around. "There are women and children that live here." *Even if they knew what was going on and decided to hide, wouldn't we have seen some of them?* I wondered silently.

Roan looked down at me and frowned. "Did you think we would risk innocents in our fight?" he asked, shaking his head.

"Then what did you do?"

"They're asleep," he stated.

I blinked and gaped up at him. "All of them?"

He nodded, steering the horse around another group of soldiers as they raced towards us. "Why didn't you just put everyone to sleep then?" I asked curiously. It would've been so much easier to just ride through the sleeping village and into the castle without all of this bloodshed.

Roan's head dipped and he grunted as the horse leapt over a fallen man, jarring the two of us. "This type of magic consumes a lot of energy, Little Bird," he replied. "You requested as little bloodshed as possible, and we agreed to spare the innocent. This was our compromise. Trying to keep a whole village asleep—especially one as big as this—would render us useless by the time we reach the castle. As it stands, the spell will only last for an hour or so. We must hurry."

Just as we were passing another group of village soldiers, he withdrew his sword and leaned over, swiping it across several men at once as they attempted to spear us. I winced when the end of one of their weapons struck at my leg, tearing into the leather and leaving me with a long cut.

Roan cursed and gripped the reins tight, pulling us to a stop. "No!" I shouted. "Don't worry about it. Keep going."

He growled and glared backwards, but his legs kicked up and the horse stopped its deceleration and continued on. I released a relieved breath. Though my leg stung, it was nothing compared to what he would have unleashed against those men, and the best way to end it all was to just get to the castle.

"Yes," he gritted out. "They're all asleep. They remain unaware of what is happening and all of our men have been instructed to harm only those who wish them harm. The women and children will be safe. The sleep spells they remain under were cast over the village and it will ensure they're protected from all untoward harm—magical or otherwise. How's your leg?"

"It's fine," I said. "We have to keep going."

His eyes dropped down to meet mine and his lips pressed together, but instead of saying anything more, he merely spurred our horse even faster, catching up with Nellie and Ash. We made it into the castle's secondary main gates and beyond, stopping once we reached the entrance to dismount. As I listened to the sounds of the raging battle down in the village— the clashing of swords, masculine shouts, and the clomping of horse hooves—I stopped and glanced around at the empty courtyard.

The platform that had once been there was gone, apparently dismantled and taken away, but something more than the fact that this was where I'd nearly died made this place feel off to me. I shivered and rubbed my arms with my hands as Nellie and Ash stepped up to Roan and me.

"Where's the throne room?" Ash asked.

Roan and Nellie both looked to me and I realized that I was the only one who'd ever been there. Despite my circumstances of having been there, I could still recall the general layout of the castle when I'd been dragged before the King. I sighed and moved across the stones towards the entrance.

"This way," I called.

Roan moved ahead of me, his sword at the ready. He paused at the entrance, looking inside before conjuring a globe of fire and sending it down the first corridor. This ball of flame wasn't so much destructive as it just hovered in mid-air, giving off enough of a glow for us to see ahead and behind us. It fluttered along the hallway, illuminating the dark path and the drawn drapes on all of the windows that would have let in light had they been open. Nellie fell behind me, walking with unsure footsteps that faltered every once in a while. Ash was to the back.

"I'm not so sure about this," Nellie said quietly.

I glanced back at her. "About killing the King or about taking the throne?" I asked.

"Both," she said. "I'm not a fighter, Cress. I'm not a ruler."

I sighed and took her hand. I didn't know what to say to reassure her. To be fair, there was nothing I could say that would leave her with no doubts. She would always have them. Even if—Gods willing—this whole plan worked out and she was placed on the throne and the Kingdom of Amnestia finally ended the war with the Fae, she would still have them.

So, I said the only thing I could think of. "You care," I whispered in the shadows of the corridor. "You love. You believe. All of these things make you a great person, Nellie, and they will make you a wonderful Queen."

Even in the dark, I could hear the swish of her hair as she shook her head. "I'm not brave like you, Cress."

I wanted to stop and turn around and stare at her. The urge was there, fast and so very consuming, but I forced my feet to keep moving. We didn't have time. Instead, I just pushed as much of my emotions into my tone as possible. *How could she think she wasn't brave?*

"You are one of the bravest souls I know," I whispered harshly. "You gave up your life at the convent for me. Entered a Fae castle, even knowing what happened to your parents. You didn't reject me when you found out what I was. You still loved me."

She huffed out a breath. "Because it doesn't change who you are," she snapped.

I laughed, a low, quiet breathy sound. "Exactly," I replied. "And you realize that. You won't hold someone's abilities against them. You're not the type to see only what lies on the surface, but you hold what's underneath to the light. Someone's character, their actions, their intelligence." I shook my head. "Being willing to admit mistakes and working to correct them makes you brave. Not just holding a sword and cutting down enemies. Besides, I can't even do that."

"But you have magic," she said.

"A little," I admitted, "but I'm still weak by Fae standards. I'm not this great and powerful being, Nellie. I'm just me. Cress the orphan. Cress the Changeling. I'm stubborn"—I didn't have to see her to know she was grinning at that—"a little insane at times—"

"A little?" she countered.

"Hush when I'm complimenting you and telling you how amazing you are," I said.

"You're right, please continue."

"No," Roan said, stopping. I bumped into him and brought the three of us at his back to a halt. "There's no time."

He was right. We were here. The flickering of yellow candlelight beyond the throne room was visible in the darkened hallway. It was time to face King Felix. My hand squeezed Nellie's tightly. It was time to bring this Gods forsaken war to an end.

CHAPTER 32

CRESS

The doors of the throne room swung slowly open as we pushed against them. The room was just as I remembered it, stone floors and walls with a dais directly across from the entrance upon which were two thrones, one slightly smaller than the other. Fires lit each side of the room in a series of fireplaces and braziers.

Just as we entered, the King looked up. It was early in the morning, but it was clear he had not slept. There were deep, jagging shadows beneath his eyes and a scowl on his face that I was all too familiar with. Beneath him were a series of men—his Royal guard. None of this was shocking. What was shocking was seeing Tyr there alongside King Felix. He had to have known we would come here and that he would be outnumbered. Tyr seemed the kind of man who'd flee a fight he knew he couldn't win. So, why then, was he still here? The second he laid his eyes on me, just behind Roan, a sinister grin formed over his lips.

An uneasy feeling surfaced in my gut. I pressed it down as I flicked a look first to Roan—he held his sword at the ready as he strode forward—and then behind me to Nellie, whose wide eyes took in everything within the throne room with both awe and fear.

"So, the traitorous Fae bitch has returned," King Felix said as he rose from his throne and took a step towards the edge of his dais. Tyr hung back, content, it appeared, to watch the proceedings. I didn't like that. I didn't trust it.

"Roan..." His name was a warning on my lips but it was interrupted as Ash rounded Nel and me to come to his side.

"I am Prince Roan of the Fae Court of Crimson," Roan announced, his gaze scanning the Royal guard as they withdrew their weapons. They held back, though, waiting for the King's signal. "And you, King Felix of Amnestia, have been defeated. As we speak, my soldiers and those of the other Courts are laying siege on this very castle. The war is over, Your Majesty. You have lost."

For every beat of silence that reigned after Roan's words, I felt the tension in my body grow tighter and tighter. Then, with a bellow, King Felix began to laugh. His body shook with it. It was startling to see a man so much older be so capable of such a loud laugh. As his amusement waned, however, he lifted his head and fixed his gaze on the four of us.

"I agree," he said, sounding far too smug for my peace of mind. "The war is over—for you. Guards! Kill them."

As he brought his arm up and swept it downward, announcing his will to his soldiers, King Felix's voice was cold, devoid of any emotion other than fury and disgust. All at once, the Royal guard sprang forward—their weapons at the ready as they attacked. Nellie's gasp had me moving quickly to the side. With her wrist in my grasp, I yanked her behind me and backed her towards the side of the room just as Roan and Ash entered the fray.

Bodies went down under the slash of their metal. Fire erupted and in one fell swoop, Roan cleared half of the guard. Still, my eyes couldn't help but drift back to the King and Tyr.

There was almost a child-like excitement on the King's face. A desire for bloodshed. It was disturbing.

Nellie's free hand sank into my arm, making me jerk my attention back to the battle before us. Ash was bleeding from his shoulder as he fended off two of the guards who were still on their feet after Roan's initial blast. I looked down at my hand. I had to help them somehow. But even as I willed my magic to spark to life, all that came forth was a puny ball of light.

Still, I thought, it was better than nothing. Without a second thought, I sent it hurling into the battle, straight at another guard as they crept up behind Ash, sword over their head, ready to cut him down.

The enemy guard took the hit and was flung across the room, slamming into the wall across from us. Nellie's nails softened and she breathed a sigh of relief. "It's okay," I assured her. "They know what they're doing." Yet, my gaze remained rooted on the scene.

It wasn't until the last guard fell and a panting and bloody Roan stepped from the bodies of the fallen guard to stand before King Felix that I felt any kind of relief. Unfortunately, it was short lived as I watched the King withdraw his sword and throw off his cloak.

"Do you think that frightens me, boy?" he demanded, staring down his long aristocratic nose as Roan's fiery head tilted back. Sparks and embers danced at the ends of both his and Ash's hair as Nellie's friend moved forward to take his place at Roan's side. "I will go down in history known as the King who defeated the Fae. I will drive you from our land and wipe you from existence. You are a scourge upon this Kingdom."

"*Your* land?" Roan inquired. My back straightened at the deep, strange tone that overtook him. He moved forward a step. "You think that this land belongs to you? No." He shook his head, sending a rain of sparks flying around him. "This land was a gift from the Gods. It is *their* land, and a creature such as you has no claim on it. You may live on it and work it and rule it, but make no mistake, you cannot own it."

The King brought his sword up and darted forward—far faster than I'd expected from a man of his age. Roan and Ash spun out of the way, moving as if in sync with one another.

"You cannot kill me!" the King yelled, spinning to face them once more. "I am this country's heart and soul! My people will never respect you, they will never live under your wishes— they would rather die!"

"They won't need to!" I shouted. As if he'd forgotten my presence, the King jerked and spun towards me as I pulled Nellie forward. "The Fae aren't planning to rule Amnestia," I told him. "Unlike you, they just want this Gods forsaken war to end. They want the violence to cease as it should have years ago."

He laughed, the sound sharp and quick but not nearly as smug as he had been earlier, I noticed. "Foolish girl," he snapped. "If they do not plan to rule my Kingdom, then who will?"

I stepped to the side, revealing Nellie. "She will," I said. "Nelemente of Amnestia. Your granddaughter."

There was nothing but silence for a long moment, but as the King's eyes fell on Nellie's face, he paled. "I-I do not have a granddaughter," he spat back.

Nellie inhaled a breath as if realizing this was a crucial moment and, in true fashion of her character, she quietly moved until she was standing between me and the King. "We've never met," she said. "But you are my father's father. Perhaps you remember a young woman who you threw from this very castle several decades ago?"

"Eleanor..." The King stared at Nellie as if in shock. Yes, we'd seen the features of her parents and how she'd reflected them each, but what I hadn't noticed was how she, too, had looked so much like her grandmother. Her father's mother. "No..." He shook his head as if trying to ward off unwanted memories. "She was to get rid of her child."

"Your child," Nellie snapped, standing straighter. I blinked as she moved forward. "My father was your child too. He was brave and strong and kind and intelligent. He became a doctor for your war and he died for it—treating both Fae and humans alike."

The King's gaze jerked to the side as he glared up at Tyr, who had moved forward and now sat upon the King's throne as if he were enjoying a dramatic theater play. "You said the child would lead to my death!" he yelled. "You said it would be a girl."

Tyr shrugged. "And I have been proven right," he said.

My lips parted. "He told you?"

The King ignored my question and turned fully to face Tyr, gritting his teeth as his hand clenched upon his sword. "You lied! I cast my own son out because of your prophecy!"

"Prophecy?" For a moment, all I knew was confusion. Prophecy. Corruption. Power. Then it hit me, Tyr had been plotting this for far longer than any of us had suspected. I strode towards the King. "Don't you see?" I snapped, capturing his attention. "He's lied to you. You thought he was some prophet? He's a Fae! He betrayed us and he plans to betray you."

"He's my advisor," the King said, though he sounded far less confident.

Roan and Ash watched the two of us carefully and I stopped when Roan stepped forward. That was the line, I realized. The second I got too close to the King, he would move. Already I could tell that he was angry with me. His eyes were sparkling and glittering with retribution. I could only hope that he would spare my ass because I knew Sorrell wouldn't if he found out. Neither would Orion.

"Then why isn't he advising you now?" I challenged, gesturing up to the throne. "Look at him. He doesn't care about you or his people. All he cares about is power."

The King looked at Tyr. "But I..."

"Haven't you wondered why he hasn't aged?" I snapped. Seriously, just how far was this man willing to overlook. "Was he the same all those years ago?"

"She's right," Ash said gingerly, circling us. His eyes lingered on Nellie and her proximity to the King. In the distance, I could hear the clash of swords. The others had made their way to the castle, I realized, as Ash continued to speak. "Fae live for centuries longer than humans. We age at a much slower rate."

The King considered this and then he lifted his sword to point it at Tyr. "Explain yourself," he commanded.

All eyes turned to our enemy as Tyr sat and watched the five of us with a bored expression. "I do see the future," Tyr said after a beat. "Sometimes. It's part of my unique powers. Not many in my Court possessed it. I did see a girl usurper. Never did I imagine though that it would be your granddaughter!" Tyr's head went back and he laughed. No one appeared to notice the sounds of fighting growing closer and closer out in the corridor.

"You..." Shock coated the King's face and for a moment—a brief one—I felt sorry for him. Lied to. Betrayed. I knew that pain all too well. It lit a fire in my blood and made me feel a rage I'd never felt before. "You vile, loathsome creature!"

The King's outcry was followed by a jerk forward as he raced towards Tyr, his sword pointed and poised to strike the death blow. I stumbled back as Ash darted forward and grabbed Nellie, yanking her to the side. Roan's eyes followed the movement with horror and as I turned my cheek, I could see why.

Time seemed to slow and though I believed King Felix deserving of death for his crimes against Fae, in the moment, as

I watched Tyr lift his hand, and with no weapon at all, send his head rolling with no more than a slash of darkness through the air, I wanted to take it back. I wanted to rewind time and figure out a less horrifying death. The only kind thing I could say was that it came quickly at least.

Nellie gasped right before Ash shoved her face against his chest, keeping her from seeing the King's—her grandfather's—head being severed from his body. It thunked upon the stone floor alongside his lifeless body and was consumed by Tyr's shadows for several moments. When the shadows receded, all that was left was a faceless and fleshless skeleton.

The doors to the throne room creaked and I spun as Orion and Sorrell both entered, their faces etched with war. Their bodies were covered in blood and gore, the red smeared on their skin. My heart seized with hope as I saw their soldiers coming forward just before the doors slammed shut at their backs.

My eyes, along with everyone else's, moved to Tyr. "Now that we're all here," Tyr said with a smile. "The real fun can begin."

CHAPTER 33

CRESS

Horror struck me. Tyr had planned this. Somehow, he'd known our plans. He'd watched us and he'd waited. He ...med that Nellie's presence was a shock to him, but in a way, ...asn't. *How could he have known?* I wondered. *When we had no* ...?

I edged backwards, fear making my heart pound even faster ...n it already was. I could feel it, a wild thing in my chest. My ...ath came in pants. Ash seemed to feel it too as with each ...p that Tyr descended towards the main floor of the throne ...om, he backed away, taking Nellie with him. I'd never been ...re grateful for him in my life. We didn't know each other ...yond a few passing words, but his actions—the protective ...y he held my friend and guarded her against whatever Tyr ...s about to unleash—told me all I needed to know. He did ...re for her. He did love her. And I could trust her to him if I ...dn't make it through this. Gods, I hoped I made it through ...is.

Tyr's feet made it to the main floor and as casually as if he ...ere showing us a mere trinket, he withdrew a small dark ...obe from his pocket. Roan, Sorrell, and Orion each took a collective breath. I knew what it was. A Lanuaet—one of the very magical items that powered the Fae Courts. This was the thing that allowed them to move the castles and remain both a safe distance from the war and right upon their enemies.

Perhaps he wasn't intending to build a fortress around the Lanuaet, but to use it on the capital castle we were standing in. My body tensed as if preparing for such a possibility.

Instead, though, Tyr lifted it above the King's skeleton and the bodies of the fallen Royal guard and began to recite a language not all unfamiliar to us. These words were similar to the ones Groffet had uttered to show us who the Royal heir was and to show us how Nellie had come to be it. They were spoken in an ancient tongue, the words similar, though we couldn't translate them.

My lips parted on a gasp as I watched, transfixed by the sight before me. The King's bones crumpled under the weight of whatever spell Tyr was casting. He became nothing but dust that lifted and circled the miniature Lanuaet before being sucked into its core. The fallen Royal guard's bodies did the same. Their skin melted to nothing, their blood dried and the bones that remained were all pulled to the globe in Tyr's hand. With each set it consumed, the glowing item grew in size.

"What are you doing?" Roan's horrified tone boomed throughout the room, making me jump at the suddenness of it.

As soon as the last of the bodies were retrieved, Tyr held it high and laughed. "I'm doing what I should have done years ago," he replied. "I'm claiming what is rightfully mine."

His gaze turned to his brother as Orion shuffled past me, striding towards Tyr without a single ounce of hesitation clear in his confident step. "No!" I reached for him, only to be pulled back as Sorrell's arms closed around me.

"Don't," he warned quietly. "He must do this for himself."

"He's going to get himself killed!" I argued, struggling, but all of my fighting was in vain. Sorrell was much stronger than I was and as his arms banded around me, they grew tighter and tighter with each attempt to break free until I could scarcely breathe. "Please, Sorrell," I begged. "Don't let him do this."

Tyr's grin widened as Orion moved towards him. "What is your plan, little Brother?" he taunted. "Do you truly think you can take me one on one? What an unimaginative approach. I'm disappointed in you."

"Tyrian Evenfall, first Prince of the Court of Midnight. You have been found guilty of treason against your people." The deep well of sorrow and rage combined in the sound of Orion's voice had my struggles against Sorrell's chest slowly fading until I stopped altogether. Everyone was spellbound as he stood before Tyr, sword in hand, dripping with the blood of those he had killed to get here. His face stoic and unfeeling. His appearance dispassionate—a direct contrast to the agony in his words as he spoke them.

"There's been no trial," Tyr replied haughtily.

"And there won't be," Orion said just before bringing his sword up and swinging it downward, straight towards the center of Tyr's head.

My limbs tensed as I watched with disbelief. It couldn't be that easy, could it? No, it wasn't. Tyr's arm moved far faster than I expected as he brought the Lanuaet in his grasp up and, the second Orion's blade hit it, a resounding boom echoed around the chambers. Orion's body was flung backwards—he flew past Roan and then Sorrell and me and then Ash and Nellie at the very back of our group until his back slammed into the closed throne room doors.

"Orion!" Sorrell released me to run to him as Orion's sword clattered to the ground. Blood poured out of his mouth as he leaned over and vomited.

Just as I reached him, the sound of Tyr's laugh rose and commanded the entire room. I went to my knees, my hands hovering over Orion, wondering if I shouldn't try to heal him by pouring more of my own energy into him. He was awake and though in obvious pain, he glared across the room at his brother.

"Did you think you would be fast enough to kill me, little Brother?" Tyr asked. With my hands finally settling on Orion's shoulders—needing to touch him in some way to assure myself that he was okay—I turned my gaze back to the man who had us all trapped. Tyr shook his head and lifted the Lanuaet. "Do you even know what this is?"

"Of course we know," Roan snarled through gritted teeth. He, too, glared at Tyr as he clenched his fist on the handle of his sword.

"Oh, you know that it's a container of magic, an item so powerful it can move entire Courts," Tyr agreed. "But do you know how it's made?" No one answered his question. I suppose no one did know—I know I didn't. Tyr's face split into a cruel smile. "Blood and bones," he said. "The Queens have been keeping so much from you, little Princes, things that would give you night terrors. Things that would make you cry tears of blood if you were to witness them firsthand."

His laugh chilled me to the bone. Orion shifted, pressing back against the doors as he slowly worked himself back to his feet, and my hands fell to my sides as my eyes remained on Tyr.

"It takes many sacrifices to make even a single Lanuaet," Tyr continued. "It's essentially, though, the perfect power source. They just didn't have the stomach to use it for what it could really do—not after what they'd done."

"What they'd done?" I repeated. "What are you talking about?" Out of the corner of my eye, I saw both Roan and Sorrell's faces blanch as they glanced quickly back at me— almost in unison—before refocusing their gazes on Tyr.

"You—" Sorrell began.

"Oh, you haven't told her?" Tyr asked, cutting him off. Orion's hand touched my arm, distracting me for a moment. I didn't see it when Roan decided to rush him, but just as my gaze was lifting to meet Orion's, Roan's cry of outrage and subsequent grunt of pain jerked my eyes back to the rest of the room and I saw Tyr arch out a palm—sending Roan crashing into one of the side pillars. The post cracked under the brunt force of Roan's body slamming into it and he slid down and crumpled at the bottom. Strong, fearless, fiery Roan—knocked unconscious with one hit.

What kind of fucking monster were we really dealing with?

"Let me enlighten you, little Changeling," Tyr said as he glided forward. "Twenty odd years ago, there was a fourth Fae Court. The Court of Brightling. It was headed by a powerful, if not far too empathetic Royal family."

I remembered this. The guys had told me of a separate Court, but why did that matter here? What did that have to do with what was happening now?

"The Brightling Court adored humans, you see," Tyr went on. With every step in my direction, I could feel Orion tense further at my side. "And with the war starting, Fae grew mistrustful of them. The Queens sent out an order to have them exterminated, and thus, the Lanuaets that we now depend on today were born."

Realization dawned on me. The Queens had used the deaths and bodies of the entire Brightling Court to create their power source items. Sorrell chose his moment carefully. I hadn't even noticed that he had been preparing, but just as Tyr stepped past him on his way to me, he turned and lifted his hands. Bolts of ice shot up from the ground, crisscrossing over Tyr's legs and trapping him. Sorrell wasted no time, withdrawing his blade and slicing it through the space Tyr's body stood. Only...

The second the blade struck, Tyr was gone and the only thing that remained behind were the severed ice tips that Sorrell's sword had cut through in his stead. Tyr reappeared just behind him.

"Tsk. Tsk. I expected better of you, Sorrell. I expected you to learn from Roan's mistakes."

Before Sorrell could so much as turn towards him, he, too, was sent flying across the room. His sword clattered to the stone floor as Sorrell's body went crashing into the double throne chairs atop the dais. Once he was down, he did not get back up again.

"You need to get out of here, Cress," Orion said quietly. "I'll distract him when he gets close, but you need to get through those doors."

"Oh, I don't think that will be happening, dear Brother," Tyr said and, in a split second, he was right before us—wicked smile in place and a bloodlust in his eyes that made my chest clench with panic. "I'm not done with my story yet."

Tyr blinked in and out of existence for only a second—the Lanuaet, I realized. He was using it to move at will, far faster than he ever had before. When he was back, he held Orion's sword in his hand and I watched in horror as he slammed it right into his brother's chest.

"No!" I screamed as Orion's stunned shout of surprise was disrupted by yet more blood choking up from his mouth.

Ash chose that moment to attack, moving up from behind to strike. Tyr chuckled, the sound twisted and grating in my ears. "I think we've had enough distractions, don't you?" he asked, looking at me even as he held the Lanuaet out. Power poured from the small globe and darkness began to creep up from the ground, encircling both Ash and Nellie. They struggled and fought as it wrapped its tentacles around their limbs, holding them secure until it consumed their entire bodies and they were left frozen in what looked like no ice I'd seen before. It was pitch black save for where their bodies were, pressed to the inside of the crystal—their faces awash in fear.

Tyr twisted the blade in Orion's stomach. "Stop it!" I screamed. "You're killing him."

"That's the point," Tyr said. "To get this Lanuaet to the power level I need it, it requires more sacrifices."

"Why didn't you just take the one from the Court of Midnight?" Orion asked as he gripped the blade, slicing his palms as he stopped the twisting motion Tyr continued to use.

Tyr's expression grew thunderous. "Our parents, it seemed, were well aware of my plans—I've been leading that damn human King on my leash for as long as I can remember. They knew, and they let it happen. The war only brought them more power, you see, but the second I turned my sights on them, of course, they destroyed their Lanuaet. The selfish cunts."

"Please," I begged, reaching for the blade. "Take it out."

Orion chuckled, though his slight amusement was only tinged with pain and more blood. "They finally saw you for what you were, eh?" he said.

Tyr shrugged. "I had to kill them for their betrayal, of course," he replied. "And then the rest of the Court—it was the only way to kickstart this new Lanuaet."

"But there weren't enough," Orion spat. "The Court of Midnight has been dying for decades."

Tyr ripped the blade free and Orion slid back down to the ground. I went with him, tears I hadn't even realized I'd started crying pouring from my face as I tried to clutch my hands over his seeping wound. "The Court of Brightling had been massive," Tyr said, glaring down at his brother, flicking his gaze to me. "And their power far stronger than Midnight's—the Queens hadn't needed so many bodies to create the three Lanuaet's they needed for the Courts left to live."

"Cress, run," Orion rasped.

"What?" I shook my head, pressing my fingers more firmly into his stomach. Was he insane? I couldn't run now. If I did, he'd die for sure.

"Go!" he barked. Before I could even get another word out, Tyr released the sword in his grasp and reached for me. His hand sank into my hair, ripping out several strands as he jerked me up from the ground. "No!" Orion's pain filled cry was followed by several dark tendrils wisping around both my body and Tyr's. Tyr glanced down at the powerful shadows and shook his head right before he lifted his boot and stomped their ends out of existence.

"At your level, Brother," he said, turning a sneer to Orion as I fought to free myself from his grasp to no avail, "you couldn't even defeat a pixie."

"Not ... her," Orion panted.

"Oh, yes, her," Tyr said with a laugh. When he turned his attention back to where I was trying to kick and punch at his side, he moved his face closer. "Do you know why I've told you all of this?" Tyr asked.

Shivers danced up my spine. I had a sinking feeling. One that I didn't want to admit to.

"I knew it as soon as I saw you," Tyr continued. "You look just like the Brightling King and Queen. Their daughter. Their precious little Princess. Oh, how I thought you'd died with your clan, but to see you in the Court of Frost. To see how you'd ensnared my brother and his friends with your beauty and your bumbling ineptitude. It was hilarious. And I finally knew what I needed. It was simple really. One single Brightling Royal can bring this Lanuaet to complete and utter God level power."

I gasped as he released my hair, his hand going instead to my throat before I could drop from his grip. My air was cut off and I struggled, growing weaker and weaker as I fought back. I kicked. I punched. None of it had an effect.

"But..." I tried to gasp, "the execution?"

He laughed again. "I was serious when I said I could foresee parts of the future. I knew those men would come for you and that you would be rescued—all of that talk of watching you dangle and die in front of a crowd? I just wanted to play with you. This was the path that guaranteed me the highest chance of success. Now, here we are, and you will die to serve my purposes." My lips parted, but no more words came. I was out of time and air. "So, thank you, dear little Changeling," Tyr whispered as he leaned down and pressed his lips to my ear. "I know it's been a long journey to get here. All I need now is for you to die."

His hand crushed my throat and the darkness crept in on either side of my vision. Soon, my struggles waned and then stopped altogether. It was no use. He had won and I was about to do exactly as he said.

I was going to die.

CHAPTER 34
CRESS

L ife. Death. Sex. Love. All of the things you would expect to cross a girl's mind right on the verge of death crossed mine. So did all of the self deprecating questions:

Are you really going to let this happen?

What kind of wuss gets choked out by an evil Fae intent on taking over the world?

Wait, I'm a fucking Princess? Like a real one?

Okay, so that last one didn't really have much to do with the death part so much as it had to do with the life part. I couldn't help but be shocked, though. I mean, who would've thought that I'd be a Princess? Kind of had me wondering why I always imagined Princesses to be these elegant, fragile little flowers who couldn't lift a spoon to their lips if it wasn't pure silver.

The only spoon I'd ever eaten off of was wooden. The only thing flowery about me was my winning personality. And elegance? Definitely not my style. But fragile? Until this moment, I'd never considered myself fragile. I'd nearly died half a dozen times since I'd been led to the Court of Crimson and the Fae. I'd been almost murdered, shoved off a castle wall, chased by an angry mob, attacked by unknown shadow creatures in Alfheim, and glared down by the Queens who had—apparently—ordered the slaughter of my entire Court.

It all sounded like a bedtime story gone horribly wrong.

And yet, Tyr thought that there was some hidden power inside of me that would complete his magical murder orb? No. I could hardly toss a fireball at a bale of hay. There was no hidden talent, no power reserves deep within me. If there was, I would know it … wouldn't I?

It's not inside, a voice suddenly said, *but on the outside...*

I froze. The voice was familiar and feminine. It sounded like a dream I'd had long ago. No, more recent. It sounded like the woman from my dream in the prison tower. The one who'd been running from something with a man...my mother?

Power is all around you, the voice continued. *It's steeped in your skin. In the air you breathe. In the flowers that grow. Call for it and it will come. All you need to do is trust in the Gods and give over to them. They will guide you.*

Kind of difficult to take power from breath when I had none, I thought sardonically, but at this point, what was there left to lose? Nothing.

Roan and Sorrell had been knocked out cold. Ash and Nellie frozen in some strange black ice-like crystal. Orion... if I didn't at least try, he would die right along with me. And that, more than anything, made me focus.

All around me, I thought. All around me. I … just … needed … to … breathe …

I cried out as air rushed into me and my eyes shot open. Tyr stood above my prone body, the Lanuaet in his fist raised above me. All around us, black powder swirled. When he noticed that I was awake, a dark scowl overtook his face.

"I should've known that wouldn't be enough to kill you," he snarled. Once more, he disappeared and then reappeared, this time with a dagger in hand as he held it over me.

"Not this time," I shot back. The second his arm descended,

the dagger aiming straight for my heart, I lifted my arm. The blade pierced my forearm, making me scream at the pain it sent—but pain was better than death. It was better than not breathing.

The Lanuaet was glowing, hovering between us. "It won't matter!" Tyr screamed at me. "It will take your life force anyway!"

An idea formed. I didn't know if it would work and there was no time to figure out a second plan of action. If the Lanuaet wanted power, then I would give it power. All of it. My skin glowed as I reached up and yanked the dagger out of my forearm. Blood oozed from the wound before being lifted and sucked right into the glowing orb's spinning sphere.

I panted as I closed my eyes and focused on the space around me. Power was everywhere, the voice had claimed. In the air. In the stone. In the breath we breathed. I conjured it, calling it forward. Focusing as Sorrell had taught me. Only instead of flames, I was pulling *everything*.

My body felt hot—sweat beaded on my brow and that, too, was taken into the Lanuaet's dark globe of magic. I pushed more and more out. Like I was trying to heal Orion all over again. I pictured the sun within me and let it burn outward. I would give until there was nothing left. I would make Tyr regret this.

"What are you doing?" Tyr demanded as the Lanuaet began to vibrate in his palm. He screamed and the sound of burning flesh reached my nostrils. I didn't care. I had to focus.

More and more power was thrust into the orb Tyr tried to keep hold of until finally, it became too much for him. He released the sphere with a shout, holding his shaking burned hands out in front of him as he gaped at the thing he'd created, hovering all on its own.

"Stop!" he screamed.

A white light blinded me as a fissure cracked across the

surface of the orb, emitting the power that it had consumed. Tyr jumped towards it and, just before his hands touched it, another crack formed and the power that slipped out slammed into him. Blood spurted out across my body, raining down over my chest. I turned my face to the side only to watch as Tyr's severed body fell to the stone and his unblinking dead eyes met mine.

In the next instant, the Lanuaet shattered and a brilliant white light crashed into me, sending me straight back into the same oblivion that I had almost let myself die in. *At least this time,* I thought just before my mind winked out, *the others would survive.*

⚜

I WOKE TO SOMEONE RATTLING METAL NOT VERY FAR FROM where I laid. My thoughts were murky and my head felt as though someone had slammed it into a stone wall more times than I could count. A groan left my lips seconds before my eyelashes fluttered open.

"Miss?" A round faced woman with large eyes and wearing a white apron stood alongside the bed I lay in holding what looked like a fireplace poker. "You're awake?"

I looked from the poker in her hand to the look of shock on her face and back again. "If you're planning to kill me with that, can you wait until I have the energy to defend myself?" I asked around a groan.

"I must tell the Queen!" she half screamed. I winced as the high pitched sound of her voice ricocheted into my skull, but before I could say another word the maid was gone, leaving the door on the bedroom chamber hanging open as her fast footsteps faded down the hall.

I doubted she'd even heard a word I said. Slowly, as gingerly as possible, I rose from the bed and stared down at the gown I now wore as well as the growth in my hair. The dress was a silk nightgown with puffy sleeves and lace on the cuffs. Though I couldn't remember getting into it, even stranger than that was the fact that my hair was no longer cut short. It was far lower than it had been the last time I'd been awake. Instead, it now reached almost to my collarbone. I tried to recall something— anything that might have led to the dress or the hair change— but I could hardly remember anything at all aside from the last image I'd seen right before I'd passed out. Tyr's cold, dead eyes staring me in the face. A brilliant white light. The Lanuaet exploding over my body.

What in the name of Coreliath had happened?

More footsteps sounded outside of the chamber and I groaned again, not ready to face another contingent of confused, screamy maids. "Please, just—" I stopped as I turned towards the doorway. It wasn't a maid. It was Nellie.

She looked ... different. Her face was smoother, her hair pulled up into an elegant chignon that made her appear older. Her shabby peasant girl dresses that she normally wore were replaced with a fabric that was such a deep burgundy that it resembled expensive wine.

"Cress?" Her voice shook as she entered the room. "It's really ... I mean, you're really awake. You're here. You're alive."

"Yeah?" I arched a brow even as I wavered on my feet. "Why wouldn't I be?"

"Y-you've been asleep for weeks," she confessed. Tears formed in her eyes. "I didn't know if you'd ever wake up again. None of us did."

"I was?" I blinked at her for a moment before scanning the room. "Where are the guys?" I asked.

"They're being informed," she replied. "I just needed..." She sniffed as the tears came crashing down and suddenly she was in front of me. Nellie's arms wrapped around me and she clutched onto me as she sobbed. "Oh, Cress, I thought we'd lost you."

I didn't know what to say, but when your best friend held you like she was afraid you'd disappear, crying her eyes out, there was only one thing to do—you hugged her back.

"I'm okay," I whispered as I wrapped my arms around her slightly shorter frame. "I'm alive. I'm here."

"You stupid," she sniffed. "Arrogant. Dumb. Selfish." Nellie pulled back and punched me in the arm. "Don't ever do something that stupid!" she screamed.

"Ow!" I rubbed the place she had hit. "What'd I do?"

"You almost got yourself killed!" she yelled. "Just because I was trapped inside that ice thingy doesn't mean I wasn't aware of what was going on! I saw what you did. You almost—" She broke off and for a brief moment, I was honestly worried that I'd survived Tyr's murder attempt only to be killed by my very own best friend. She looked ready to strangle me. "You almost died, Cress. You scared the Gods damned shit out of me."

My eyes widened. "You don't curse," I blurted.

She shot me a glare. "I do when my best friend is being stupid," she snapped back.

"Hey," I replied, "be nice to me, I saved your butt."

There was a brief moment of silence and then she sniffed again. "You did, Cress. You really did."

"So, that's it then?" I asked. "Tyr's dead. The King's dead. The war is over?"

"The war is over," she agreed with a nod.

I remembered what the maid had said just before bolting out of the chamber. "And you're the Queen now?" I asked.

A light flush touched her cheeks. "Not yet," she confessed. "They call me that—it was ... there was a lot that happened after your men woke up—the dark one, Orion, had to be healed, and they helped me explain things and convince the rest of Amnestia's army and nobles. I wanted to wait, though, to be crowned until ... well, until you woke up."

I sagged back onto the bed, my butt hitting the mattress and sinking down. "It's over." I said the words more for my own ears than hers. I just couldn't believe it. Exactly what we wanted. The war was over. Nellie was now the Queen—or would be very soon. It had worked. It was finally...

Tears pricked at my eyes and I lifted my gaze to Nellie's. Before I could say a word, however, there was a loud bang at the doorway and three men crashed into the room. Their eyes wild. Their bodies tense. And then they saw me.

Alive. Awake. And crying my eyes out like a blubbering baby. Nel smiled at me. "I'll give you some time," she said. "But now that you're awake, I hope you'll come to my ceremony. I wouldn't be here if it weren't for you. None of us would."

I didn't respond—she already knew my answer.

As soon as the door shut, though, I turned to the three men waiting on me. "Well?" I asked, sniffling as I wiped away the snot dripping from my nose with the lacy cuff of my sleeve—which was not as easy as it sounded. "What now?"

Three pairs of eyes landed on me. One cold as ice. One hot as fire. And one as dark as midnight. And one by one, they moved closer.

"Now, Little Bird," Roan said as he leaned down and took one of my hands before lifting it to his lips, "we get married and we live."

"All of us?" I asked, looking between the three of them.

Both Orion and Sorrell nodded. "All of us," they agreed.

EPILOGUE
CRESS

I t was over. Well and truly over. After all of the fighting, the years of war, of loss, of hatred, it was almost … impossible to imagine, but here it was. The end of the war that had ripped apart the lives of so many.

Months ago, when I'd been nothing more than an orphan, preparing to age out of the convent's good graces, I'd known so little about the rest of the world. Back then, even though it was such a short while ago, the idea of war had been a distant one. Sure, I'd known it was happening. I'd been aware of it, but because it had never affected me—never caused me loss or grief—it'd been almost like a fairytale. Told in whispers before bed. Holding a wealth of warnings and lessons to learn. Do not go too far from the convent. Do not trust the creatures who would use magic to hurt you. Now, here I stood on the balcony of Amnestia's Royal castle overlooking the large courtyard where mere weeks ago, I'd nearly died.

So much had changed.

I had changed.

The world had changed.

And Nellie, too, had changed.

My body turned towards the sound of footsteps on the stone floor as they approached and my best friend rounded the corner, dressed far differently than I'd ever seen her. She looked up and spotted me.

"There you are!" Nellie rushed forward, nearly tripping over the red and gold skirts that appeared massive on her petite frame. As the end of the dress's train came into view so did the two lady's maids who were attempting to hold it up off the dirty floor. Nellie turned back to them as soon as she realized they were there. "You don't have to do that," she said quickly.

"Your Grace," the older of the two women began, "your gown—it will be—"

"Fine," Nellie insisted. "Please." She gestured to me. "Would you give us a moment?"

The older women frowned, obviously very displeased, but what could they say? Nellie was about to be crowned a Queen. Another thing that I hadn't predicted would ever happen.

As soon as the lady's maids were out of earshot, Nellie whirled back towards me. "Do you believe this thing?" she said with horror as she waved a hand down to the dress she wore.

I bit back a grin. "It's beautiful," I said.

"It's heavy," she complained.

"It's fit for a Queen."

She grimaced and then gestured to my attire. "I'd rather wear what you're wearing," she said.

I glanced down to the mass of dark purple skirts beneath which I wore tight fitting leather trousers that molded to my frame. I shrugged. "Next time find out that you're a Fae rather than a would be Queen," I told her.

"You better be careful," she said. "Or I'll command my new guards to cut off your head."

I lifted a palm and conjured a ball of heated light. It sparked and danced between my fingertips. "Just try it," I challenged with a smile.

There was a beat and then both of us burst out laughing. By the time we managed to calm down, my light had faded and I was wiping the tears from beneath my eyes. For a moment, the two of us just remained silent after catching our breaths. And as I stared into her eyes, I could see the trail of emotions as they collided into one another. I understood it. I was feeling them too.

Nellie's eyes softened and gently—as gently as she'd always been and likely always would be—she reached for my hands and took them in her own. "I want to say something," she said. I waited, but when it appeared she wasn't yet ready for whatever it was that she wished to say, I decided it was an opportunity for me to say what I was thinking.

"You're my sister, you know," I told her. She lifted her eyes away from our hands and met my gaze. I smiled softly. "You've always been. Ever since we met at that stupid convent."

She rolled her eyes. "It was not stupid," she retorted. "You just have an issue with authority."

I laughed. "Now that you're Queen are you going to hold it over my head?" I asked.

She smirked. "Perhaps I will."

"Ha." I shook my head. "Good luck with that. I've got three Princes to contend with and they've got magic."

"Yeah, but they also have the poor intelligence to be in love with you, too," she shot back.

"Yes," I said, unable to stop the ridiculously wonderful smile from overtaking my face. "They do."

"What I wanted to say," Nellie began again a moment later, "was thank you."

I blinked and frowned at her. "For what?" I inquired.

A sigh left her lips and she shook her head lightly. "For … it's hard to say what it is, it's more than one thing," she confessed. Her hands squeezed mine tightly as she beseeched me with her gaze. "Thank you for being my friend," she said.

"You don't have to thank me for that—" I started, only to be cut off as she kept going.

"Thank you for being my sister. Thank you for believing in me. Thank you for coming back for me, and Cress..." She paused and then dragged me forward—with far more strength than I expected in her small body—into a hug. As her arms wrapped around me, Nellie turned her cheek and pressed it to my shoulder before whispering the last of her thank yous. "Thank you for being you."

Tears assaulted my eyes. My tongue swelled and stuck to the roof of my mouth. There was nothing more I could do but accept her hug. I tightened my hold around her and reached up to cup the back of her head, stroking my fingers lightly through the curls her new lady's maids had no doubt spent all morning trying to perfect. I was sure she wouldn't mind if I messed them up a smidge—this was an emotional moment after all.

I sniffed hard as one of the tears escaped to cascade down the side of my face. When we pulled away from each other once more, I realized I wasn't the only one affected. I touched her face, grinning as her tears overlapped my fingers. Her face, even splotchy and red, was lovely.

"You are going to make the best Queen Amnestia has ever seen," I promised her.

Nellie's hands reached up and slipped over mine. "Will you be with me?" she asked.

It was an impossible question with a bittersweet answer. Because after what had happened on the battlefield ... after the full breadth of my powers had been awakened, Roan, Orion, and Sorrell had explained what that would mean for me. An average Fae often outlived the lifespan of several humans. I wasn't an average Fae. I was the last of the Royal line of the Court of Brightling. Nellie was wholly and completely human.

My lips parted and I uttered an oath to her that I would

take into her grave and then my own. No matter what else happened to this world, I would keep this vow unto my dying breath.

"I will be with you for as long as you need me," I said to her. "And when you no longer have that need, I will pass it on to your children and your children's children. For as long as your blood remains in this world, I will honor and protect it."

More tears came, pouring down both of our cheeks and, when the last of the words of my oath—sealed with an unspoken magic, a promise to a friend—Nellie pushed forward and hugged me again. We stayed there like that, for several long moments—clinging to one another until the lady's maids came back and the sound of their outrage and horror over Nellie's ruined hair and makeup forced the two of us to part with laughs.

"You're still coming to the coronation, right?" Nellie asked quickly, her eyes seeking reassurance as she was gently prodded back towards the corridor.

"I wouldn't miss it for the world," I said. She paused on the threshold with each of her arms engulfed by one of her maids and then with a brilliant smile, she nodded back to me and disappeared to ready herself for one of the biggest days of her life.

The coronation of the new Queen of Amnestia.

I remained behind on the balcony for a long time after that, watching the proceedings down below as people flitted back and forth in preparation for the after coronation celebrations. It wasn't until I felt a chill down my back that I realized I was no longer alone. Turning back to the entrance to the balcony, I spotted Sorrell leaning against the stone wall there.

"Thought I might find you here," he commented, pushing away from the wall.

"Oh?" I asked lightly.

He approached quickly, not stopping until my hips were

pressed right up against the stone railing and his arms were on either side of me, caging me into his embrace. "You've been gone for quite a while," he said.

"I've been thinking," I replied.

Cold, blue eyes no longer devoid of emotion met mine. "About your friend?" he guessed.

"Yes and no," I answered. "About what the three of you told me."

"You knew that Fae lived a long time, my love," he said.

"Yes," I replied. "I guess I just hadn't given it much thought." My hands slipped up the black and blue coat he wore. It gaped open revealing a snow white shirt underneath. I gripped the lapels and used my hold to drag him closer. "I've been a little preoccupied," I admitted.

"Yes, you have," he agreed.

"Everything's changing." My words dropped to a whisper as his head dipped and he drew dangerously close.

"You won't be alone, my love," he said.

No, I wouldn't. I'd always believed that I would be just fine on my own. I'd always been an independent soul. Now, though, it was nice to think that I'd always have someone. Someone to live with me, laugh with me, love me as I loved them in return.

As if he sensed the direction of my thoughts, Sorrell pressed forward and kissed me. My eyes slid shut and my arms lifted, winding around the back of his neck as I let myself sink into the great passion that I'd learned he'd been hiding from everyone—including himself, I suspected.

However long our kiss lasted, when we parted, I was left shivering and laughing as I flicked frost off of my shoulder. He grinned ruefully—so unlike him and yet becoming more and more the norm that it made my heart swell.

"We should hurry," I suggested. "It'll start soon."

Together, Sorrell and I headed away from the balcony towards the center of the castle—a giant throne room in which

I'd once been paraded before the previous King Felix in the hopes that he'd kill me. All of that was behind us now. The King was gone and so was Tyr.

My head lifted as soon as we entered and I found Roan and Orion waiting for us near the dais where the castle's highest ranking officials—those that had survived the war and not been charged with war crimes—and the priest of the Gods waited.

"You made it," Roan said as we approached. "We were worried we'd have to go looking for you."

I scoffed and rolled my eyes. "I wouldn't miss this," I told him, the same words I'd said to Nellie. "If I did, I have a feeling the new Queen of Amnestia would try to kill me. Can't have her starting another war, can we?"

"That's not funny," Roan said dryly.

"Get ready," Orion announced. "Here she comes."

I hurried to move to the side, facing the front as the doors to the throne room opened and music began to play. In the time that we'd been separated, Nellie's makeup and hair had been perfectly restored. She lifted her head and held it high as a parade of people lined up behind her. The long gold and red train of her gown drifted across the stone surface. I could tell that Nellie had ordered her lady's maids to let it because as they followed behind her, they stared down at it with pinched, broken looks.

I smiled and lifted my fingers, flicking them towards my friend as she strode by. The skirts lifted and hovered over the ground, trailing behind her as if she were gliding on air rather than walking. The maids' eyes widened and I heard the gasps before they jerked their heads up and to the side. I met their stunned looks with a wink as Nellie proceeded to the front of the throne and knelt before the Priest.

As I stood there, staring at the delicate shoulders of my best friend as she was blessed with the water of the Gods and an

ornate golden crown was placed upon her head, I realized …
this was more than just the end, this was a new beginning.

For Nellie and her Kingdom

For me and my Princes.

For all of Fae and humankind.

ABOUT THE AUTHOR

Lucinda Dark, also known as USA Today Bestselling Author, Lucy Smoke, for her contemporary novels, has a master's degree in English and is a self-proclaimed creative chihuahua. She enjoys feeding her wanderlust, cover addiction, as well as her face. When she's not on a never-ending quest to find the perfect milkshake, she lives and works in the southern United States with her beloved fur-baby, Hiro, and her family and friends.

Want to be kept up to date? Think about joining the author's group or signing up for their newsletter below.

Facebook Group (Reader Mafia)
Newsletter (www.lucysmoke.com)

ALSO BY LUCINDA DARK

Fantasy Series:

Awakened Fates Series
Crown of Blood and Glass
Dawn of Fate and Fury
TBD

Twisted Fae Series (completed)
Court of Crimson
Court of Frost
Court of Midnight

Barbie: The Vampire Hunter Series (completed)
Rest in Pieces
Dead Girl Walking
Ashes to Ashes

Dark Maji Series (completed)
Fortune Favors the Cruel
Blessed Be the Wicked
Twisted is the Crown
For King and Corruption
Long Live the Soulless

Sky Cities Series (Dystopian)
Heart of Tartarus

Shadow of Deception

Sword of Damage

Dogs of War (Coming Soon)

Contemporary Series:

Gods of Hazelwood: Icarus Duet

Burn With Me

Fall With Me

Sick Boys Series (completed)

Forbidden Deviant Games (prequel)

Pretty Little Savage

Stone Cold Queen

Natural Born Killers

Wicked Dark Heathens

Bloody Cruel Psycho

Bloody Cruel Monster

Vengeful Rotten Casualties

Iris Boys Series (completed)

Now or Never

Power & Choice

Leap of Faith

Cross my Heart

Forever & Always

Iris Boys Series Boxset

The *Break* Series (completed)

Break Volume 1

Break Volume 2

Break Series Collection

Contemporary Standalones:

Poisoned Paradise

Expressionate

Wild Hearts

Criminal Underground Series (Shared Universe Standalones)

Sweet Possession

Scarlett Thief

ABOUT THE AUTHOR

Helen Scott is a USA Today Bestselling Author of paranormal romance and reverse harem romance who lives in the Chicago area with her wonderful husband and furry, four-legged kids. She spends way too much time with her nose in a book and isn't sorry about it. When not reading or writing, Helen can be found absorbed in one video game or another or crocheting her heart out.

Website
Facebook Group
Newsletter

ALSO BY HELEN SCOTT

Legends Unleashed

(Cowritten with Lacey Carter Anderson)

Don't Say My Name – Coming Soon

The Wild Hunt

Daughter of the Hunt

Challenger of the Hunt – Coming Soon

The Hollow

(Cowritten with Ellabee Andrews)

Survival

Seduction

Surrender – Coming Soon

Salsang Chronicles

(cowritten with Serena Akeroyd)

Stained Egos

Stained Hearts

Stained Minds

Stained Bonds

Stained Souls

Salsang Chronicles Box Set

Cerberus

Daughter of Persephone

Daughter of Hades

Printed in Great Britain
by Amazon

42777703R00411